FIRST EDITION

THE READER'S DIGEST ASSOCIATION LIMITED
25 Berkeley Square, London W1X 6AB

THE READER'S DIGEST ASSOCIATION
SOUTH AFRICA (PTY) LTD
Nedbank Centre, Strand Street, Cape Town

Printed in Great Britain by Petty & Sons Ltd, Leeds

Original cover design by Jeffery Matthews M.S.I.A.

For information as to ownership
of copyright in the material in this book see last page

ISBN 0 340 25790 3

Reader's Digest
CONDENSED BOOKS

SHARPE'S EAGLE
Bernard Cornwell

MAN, WOMAN AND CHILD
Erich Segal

THE CITADEL
A. J. Cronin

HELL AND HIGH WATER
Thomas Thompson

COLLECTOR'S LIBRARY
EDITION

In this Volume:

by Bernard Cornwell ***(p.9)***

The year was 1809 and the British army, under the future Duke of Wellington, was in Spain, fighting the French. And a brilliant young rifleman, Lieutenant Sharpe, was with them.

But Sharpe, for all his brilliance, was under threat of court martial and ignominious discharge. Only an act of surpassing courage could save him.

It was a time of stirring pageantry, of pomp and military splendour. It was also a time when, at the head of his troops, one brave and ingenious man could still turn the tide of battle.

MAN, WOMAN and CHILD

by Erich Segal ***(p.155)***

Marriages, it is said, are made in heaven. But the trust that sustains them must be earned anew each day . . . . The best-selling author of *Love Story* recounts movingly what happens when suddenly that trust fails. When the secret past catches up with the present. When a structure of happiness crumbles.

Jean-Claude was ten. Totally innocent. He should not be made the victim of adult clumsiness. But it seemed a situation in which no matter what, Jean-Claude must suffer.

The Citadel

by A.J. Cronin *(p.247)*

Times were hard in the Depression years. When young Dr. Manson first graduated he could have taken a research position in his university. But Manson had ideals and a powerful sense of vocation and he chose instead a far humbler, but decently-paid, post as doctor's assistant in a small Welsh mining village.

In this fine, classic medical novel all the early struggles of a dedicated young doctor and his wife are vividly portrayed. Shown too are the subtle dangers of success, as Manson comes near to forgetting his true vocation amid the material and social temptations of a fashionable London practice.

Hell and High Water

by Thomas Thompson *(p.421)*

Three young people, two men and a woman, lost, adrift on their upturned trimaran in the frightening immensity of the Pacific Ocean. No radio, little food and drinking water, their situation clearly desperate. And even more desperate when, inexplicably, even those few supplies they possessed started disappearing. . . .

This is a true, and absolutely amazing survival story: survival against terrible odds and in the face not only of sun and wind and water, but also of human behaviour at its most bizarre.

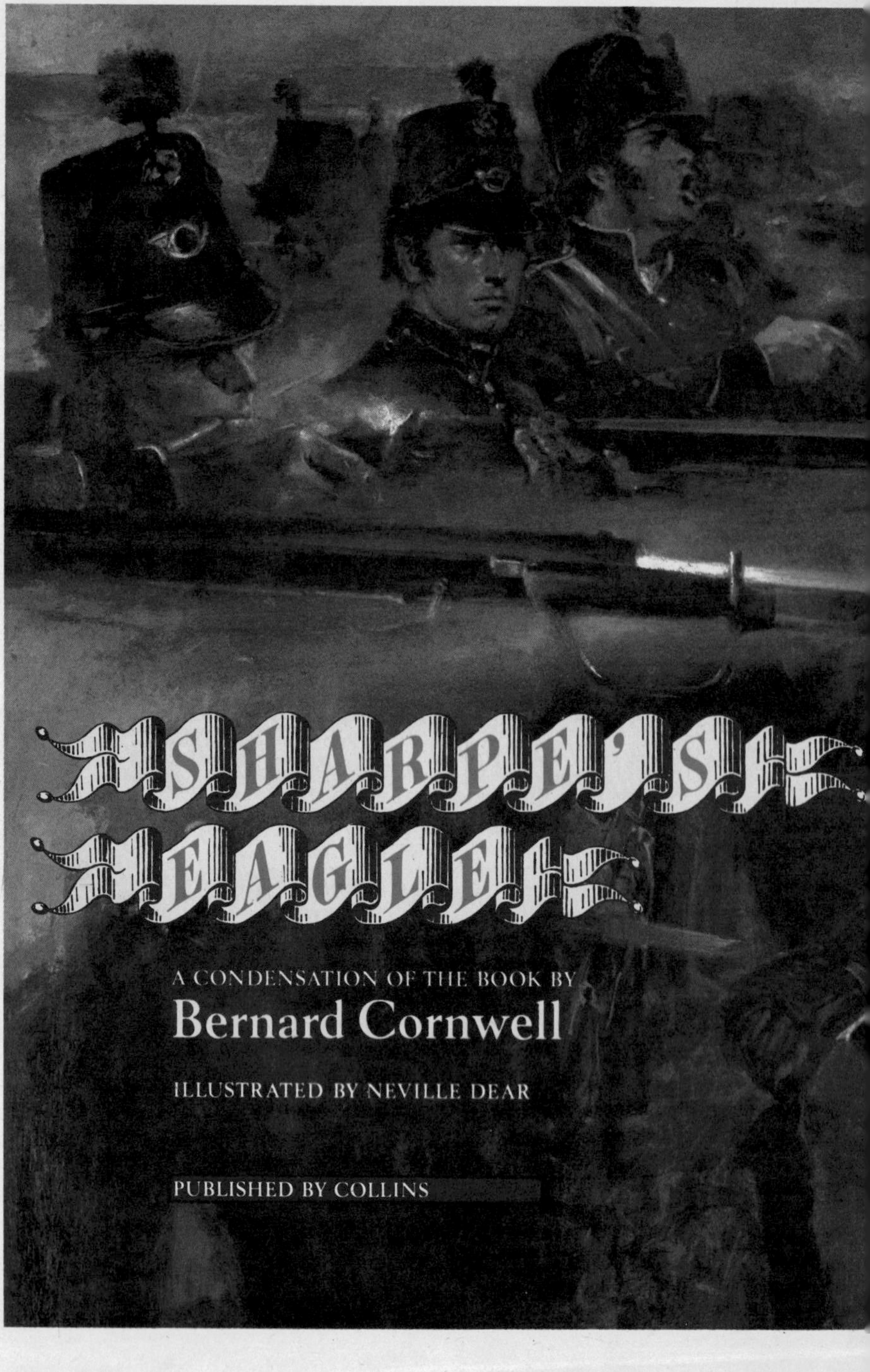

SHARPE'S EAGLE

A CONDENSATION OF THE BOOK BY

Bernard Cornwell

ILLUSTRATED BY NEVILLE DEAR

PUBLISHED BY COLLINS

When Napoleon's armies marched out to battle they carried with them ornately gilded Eagles, proud symbols of France's power. And it was one of these that Lieutenant Richard Sharpe, serving in Spain in the army of the future Duke of Wellington, was grimly determined to capture.

He was not driven simply by regimental pride, nor by his promise to a dying comrade, nor even by his love for the beautiful Josefina. It was in fact his entire future career, threatened by the bigotry of a superior officer, that depended on the success or failure of his desperate enterprise. . . .

One brave man, his hopes and fears, are here set against a vivid back-cloth: the magnificent squalor of mighty armies on the move, the blood, and the chivalry, of battle, the heart-warming comradeship of soldiers for whom war was still a game—all this, and much more, brilliantly evoked in a powerful first novel by an exciting new author.

CHAPTER 1

The guns could be heard long before they came into sight. The hooves of the great horses mixed with the jangling of traces and chains, the hollow rumbling of the blurring wheels, and above it all the crashes as tons of brass, iron and timber bounced on the broken paving of Abrantes's streets and squares. Children clung to their mothers' skirts and wondered what dreadful thing made such noises. Then the guns were in view with their limbers, horses and outriders, the gunners looking as tough as the squat, blackened barrels. The mothers pointed at the guns, boasted that these British would make Napoleon wish he had stayed in Corsica.

And the cavalry! The Portuguese civilians applauded the gorgeous uniforms, the curved, polished sabres unsheathed for display. The fine dust from the horses' hooves was a small price to pay for the sight of the splendid regiments who, the townspeople of Abrantes said, would chase the French clean over the Pyrenees and back into the sewers of Paris itself. Who could resist this army? From north and south, from the ports on the western coast, they were coming together and marching east on the road that led to the Spanish frontier and to the enemy. Portugal would be free, Spain liberated from the unpopular rule of Napoleon's brother Joseph, and these British soldiers could go back to their own wine-shops and inns, leaving Portugal in peace.

The soldiers themselves were not so confident. True, they had beaten Soult's northern army, but they wondered what lay beyond Castelo Branco, the next town, the last before the frontier. Soon they would face again the blue-coated veterans of Jena and Austerlitz, the masters of Europe's battlefields, the French regiments that had turned the finest armies of the world so much into mincemeat.

Lieutenant Richard Sharpe, waiting for orders in his billet on the outskirts of town, watched the cavalry sheathe their sabres as the last spectators were left behind. Then he turned back to the job of unwinding the dirty bandage that was round his thigh. As the last few inches peeled away, maggots dropped to the floor. Sergeant Harper knelt to pick them up and place them in a tin box before looking at the wound.

"Healed, sir. Beautiful."

Sharpe grunted. The sabre cut had become nine inches of puckered scar tissue, clean and pink against the darker skin. Another memento of thirteen years in the British army. He picked off a last fat maggot and gave it to Harper to put safely away.

The sergeant closed the box and looked up at Sharpe. "You were lucky, sir."

That was true, thought Sharpe. The French hussar had nearly ended him, the man's blade halfway through a massive downstroke when Harper's rifle bullet had lifted him from the saddle. Sharpe had twisted desperately away and the sabre, aimed at his neck, had sliced into his thigh. It had not been a deep wound but Sharpe had watched too many men die from smaller cuts, the blood poisoned, the flesh discoloured and the man left to rot to his death in the charnel houses they called hospitals. A handful of Sergeant Harper's maggots did more than any army doctor, eating away the diseased tissue to let the healthy flesh close naturally. He stood up and tested the leg. "Thank you, Sergeant. Good as new."

"Pleasure's all mine, sir."

Sharpe pulled on the French cavalry overalls he wore instead of the regulation green trousers of the 95th Rifles. He was proud of the green overalls with their black leather reinforced panels, stripped from the corpse of a Chasseur colonel of Napoleon's Imperial Guard last winter. The outside of each leg had been decorated with more than twenty silver buttons, and the metal had paid for food and drink as his small band of refugee riflemen had escaped south through the Galician snows. The colonel had been a lucky kill; there were not many men in either army as tall as Sharpe, but the overalls and the Frenchman's soft, rich, black leather boots fitted him perfectly. Sergeant Harper had not been so fortunate. Tall as Sharpe was, the sergeant topped him by a full four inches and had yet to find any trousers to replace his faded and tattered pair. And, as long as their parent battalion was home in England, the huge Irishman could find no commissary officer willing to complicate his account books by issuing him with new ones.

Sergeant Harper handed Sharpe his uniform jacket. It was as worn as those of the rest of his company, but nothing, not the best-tailored corpse in the world, would have persuaded Sharpe to throw it away. It was the dark green jacket of the 95th Rifles, and it was the badge of an elite regiment. British infantry wore red, but riflemen wore green. Sharpe took pleasure in the distinction of his uniform: it was all he had, his uniform and what he could carry on his back. Richard Sharpe knew no home other than the regiment, no family except for his company, and no belongings except what fitted into his pack and pouches.

Round his waist he tied his red officer's sash and covered it with the black leather belt with its silver snake buckle. After a year in the Peninsula only the sash and his sword remained to denote his rank as officer, and even his sword, like the overalls, broke regulations. Officers of the Rifles, like all Light Infantry officers, were supposed to carry a curved cavalry sabre, but Sharpe hated the weapon. In its place he wore the long, straight sword of the Heavy Cavalry: it was an ill-balanced brute of a weapon, but he liked a savage blade that could beat down the slim swords of French officers and crush aside a musket and bayonet.

For ten years Richard Sharpe had marched in the ranks, first a private, then a sergeant, carrying the smooth-bore musket across the plains of India. Now the Baker rifle was his mark, and he still carried it, as well as a sword, into battle. It set him aside from other officers, and sixteen-year-old ensigns looked warily at the tall, black-haired lieutenant with the slung rifle and the scarred cheek which, except when he smiled, gave his face a grim look. Few new officers stopped to think of what the rifle really represented: the fiercest struggle Sharpe had ever fought, the climb from the ranks into the officers' mess.

Sergeant Harper looked out of the window into the square soaked in afternoon sunlight. "Here comes Happy, sir."

"Captain Hogan."

Harper ignored the reproof. He and Sharpe had been together

too long, shared too many dangers, and the sergeant knew precisely what liberties he could take with his officer. "He's looking more cheerful than ever, sir. He must have another job for us."

"I wish to God they'd send us home."

Harper, his huge hands gently stripping the lock of his rifle, pretended not to hear the remark. He knew what it meant but the subject was a dangerous one. Sharpe commanded the remnants of a company of riflemen who had been cut off from the rearguard of Sir John Moore's army during its retreat to Corunna in northern Spain the winter before. It had been a terrible campaign in bitter weather. Men had died in their sleep, their hair frozen to the ground, while others dropped exhausted from the march and let death overtake them. The morale of the army had crumbled and the rabble was saved from disaster only by the few regiments, like the 95th, which kept their discipline. As 1808 turned into 1809, still the nightmarish battle went on, a battle fought with damp powder by freezing men peering through the snow for a glimpse of the cloaked French dragoons. Then, on a day when the blizzard bellied in the wind like a malevolent monster, the company had been cut off by the horsemen. The captain and the other lieutenant were killed, the rifles wouldn't fire and the enemy sabres rose and fell. The damp snow muffled all sounds except for the grunts of the dragoons and the terrible chopping of the blades cutting wounds that steamed in the freezing air. Lieutenant Sharpe and a few survivors fought clear and scrambled into high rocks where horsemen could not follow, but when the storm blew out there was no hope of rejoining the army. The second battalion of the 95th Rifles had sailed home while Sharpe and his thirty men, lost and forgotten, had headed south away from the French to join the small British garrison in Lisbon.

Since then Sharpe had asked a dozen times to be sent home. But riflemen were scarce, and the army's new commander, Sir Arthur Wellesley, was unwilling to lose even thirty-one. So they had stayed and fought for whichever battalion needed its Light Company strengthened. Harper knew his lieutenant harboured a sullen anger at his predicament. Richard Sharpe was dog poor, and would never have the money to purchase his next promotion. To buy a captaincy would cost him fifteen hundred pounds and he might as well hope to be made King of France as raise that money. He had only one hope of promotion and that was by seniority, to step into the shoes of men in his own regiment. But as long as he was in Portugal and the regiment was in England he was being forgotten and passed over.

The door of the billet banged open and Captain Hogan stepped into the room. In blue coat and white trousers, he was one of the tiny number of military engineers in Portugal, and he claimed his uniform had been mistaken for a Frenchman's so often that he had been fired on more by his own side than by the enemy. Now he grinned as he took off his cocked hat and nodded at Sharpe's leg. "The warrior restored? How's the leg?"

"Perfect, sir."

"Sergeant Harper's maggots, eh? Well, we Irish are clever devils. God knows where you English would be without us." Hogan took out his snuff box and inhaled a vast pinch. As Sharpe waited for the inevitable sneeze he eyed the small, middle-aged captain fondly. For a month his riflemen had been Hogan's escort as the engineer had mapped the roads across the high passes that led to Spain. It was no secret that any day now Wellesley would take the army across and along the River Tagus to Madrid; and Hogan, as well as sketching endless maps, had strengthened the culverts and bridges which would have to carry the field artillery as it rolled towards the enemy. It had been a job well done—and in agreeable company until the crazy-eyed French hussar had nearly made a name for himself by his mad solo charge at the rifleman. Sharpe still shivered when he thought of what might have happened if Harper's rifle had not fired.

The sergeant collected the pieces of his rifle lock as if he was about to leave but Hogan held up his hand. "Stay on, Patrick. I have a treat for you; one that even a heathen from Donegal might like." He took a dark bottle out of his haversack and raised an eyebrow to Sharpe. "You don't mind?"

Sharpe shook his head. Harper was a good man, good at everything he did, and in their three years' acquaintanceship Sharpe and Harper had become as friendly as an officer and a sergeant could be. Sharpe could not imagine fighting without the huge Irishman beside him, and together they were a formidable pair. Captain Hogan set the bottle on the table and pulled the cork. "French brandy captured at Oporto. With the compliments of General Wellesley himself. He asked after you, Sharpe."

Sharpe said nothing. Hogan paused in his careful pouring of the liquid. "Don't be unfair, Sharpe! He's fond of you. Do you think he's forgotten Assaye?"

Assaye. Sharpe remembered all right. The field of dead outside the Indian village where he had been commissioned lieutenant on the battlefield.

Hogan pushed a tin cup of brandy across the table to him. "You know he can't make you into a captain of the 95th. He doesn't have the power!"

"I know." Sharpe raised the cup to his lips. But Wellesley did have the power to send him home where promotion might be had. He pushed the thought away, and leaned forward to Hogan. "So? Any news? Are we still with you?"

"You are. And we have a job." Hogan's eyes twinkled. "And a wonderful job it is, too."

Harper grinned. "That means a powerful big bang."

Hogan nodded. "A big bridge to be blown." He took a map out of his pocket, unfolded it onto the table, and traced the river Tagus from the sea, past Abrantes where they now sat, and on into Spain, where it made a huge southwards loop. "Valdelacasa," Hogan said. "There's an old bridge there, a Roman one. The general doesn't like it."

Sharpe could see why. The army would march on the north bank of the Tagus towards Madrid and the river would guard their right flank. There were few bridges where the French might cross and harass their supply lines, and those bridges were in towns where the Spanish kept garrisons to protect the crossings. Valdelacasa was not even marked. If there was no town there would be no garrison and a French force could cross and play havoc in the British rear. Hogan stabbed his finger down onto the map. "The bridge is in bad repair. We're told you can hardly put a cart across, let alone a gun, but it could be repaired and we could have the French up our backsides in no time." He lowered his voice conspiratorially. "It's a strange place, I'm told, just a ruined convent and the bridge. They call it *El Puente de los Malditos.*" He nodded as if he had made his point.

Sharpe waited a few seconds and sighed. "All right. What does it mean?"

"'The Bridge of the Accursed' . . . . It seems that, years ago, all the nuns were taken out of the convent and massacred by the Moors. It's haunted, Sharpe, stalked by the spirits of the dead!"

Sharpe leaned forward to peer more closely at the map. The bridge must be sixty miles beyond the border and they were that distance from Spain. "When do we leave?"

"Now there's a problem." Hogan folded the map carefully. "We can start for the frontier tomorrow but we can't cross until we're formally invited by the Spanish. And they will only let us blow up their bridge if a Spanish regiment goes along with us. It's a question of pride, apparently."

"Pride!" Sharpe's anger was obvious. "If you have a whole regiment of Spaniards, then why the hell do you need us?"

Hogan smiled placatingly. "Oh, I need you. There's more, you see." He was interrupted by Harper. The sergeant was standing at the window, staring into the small square.

"That is nice. Oh, sir, that can clean my rifle any day of the week."

Sharpe looked through the window. Outside, on a black mare, sat a girl dressed in black; black breeches, black jacket and a wide-brimmed hat that shadowed her face but in no way obscured her startling beauty. Sharpe saw a wide mouth, dark eyes and hair, and then she became aware of their scrutiny. She half smiled at them and turned away, snapping an order at a servant holding the halter of a mule. Hogan made a small contented noise. "That is special. No wedding ring, I see. I wonder who she is?"

The army was collecting its customary tail of women and children who followed it to war. Each battalion was allowed to take sixty soldiers' wives to an overseas war but no one could stop other women joining the "official" wives—prostitutes, seamstresses and washerwomen, all making their living from the army. This girl looked different. There was the smell of privilege about her. Sharpe presumed she was the lover of a rich officer, as much a part of his equipment as his thoroughbred horses. There were plenty of girls like her, girls who cost a lot of money. Sharpe felt the old envy rise in him.

"My God." It was Harper again, still staring out of the window.

"What is it?" Sharpe leaned forward and, like his sergeant, he could hardly believe his eyes. A battalion of British infantry was marching steadily into the square—but a battalion the like of which Sharpe had not seen for more than twelve months. After a year in Portugal, Wellesley's soldiers' uniforms had faded and been patched with the brown cloth of the Portuguese peasants, their hair had grown long, the polish had long disappeared from buttons and badges. Sir Arthur Wellesley did not mind; he only cared that a soldier had sixty rounds of ammunition and a clear head. But this battalion was fresh from England. Their coats were a brilliant scarlet, their crossbelts pipeclayed white, their boots a mirror-surfaced black. Each man wore tightly-buttoned gaiters and, even more surprising, they still wore the infamous stocks; four inches of stiffly varnished black leather that constricted the neck and was supposed to keep a man's chin high and back straight. With them went running sores where the rigid leather dug into the soft flesh beneath the jawbone.

"They've taken the wrong turning for Windsor Castle," Harper said.

Sharpe shook his head. Whoever commanded this battalion must have made the men's lives hell to keep them looking so immaculate despite the voyage from England and the long march from Lisbon. Their weapons shone, their equipment was pristine, while their faces bulged red from the constricting stocks and the unaccustomed sun.

"Who are they?" Sharpe was trying to think of the regiments who had yellow facings on their uniforms.

"The South Essex," Hogan said. "They're new. Just raised by Lieutenant-Colonel Sir Henry Simmerson, a cousin of General Sir Banestre Tarleton."

Sharpe whistled softly. Tarleton had fought in the American war and now sat in Parliament as Wellesley's bitterest military opponent. Sharpe knew enough about the politics of high command to realize that the presence of Tarleton's cousin in the army would not be welcomed by Wellesley.

"Is that him?" He pointed to a portly man riding a grey horse in the centre of the battalion.

Hogan nodded. "It is. Sir Henry Simmerson, whom God preserve or preferably not."

Lieutenant-Colonel Sir Henry Simmerson had a purple-veined face and pendulous jowls, on either side of which sprung two prominent ears like the protruding trunnions of a cannon barrel. He looked, Sharpe thought, like a pig on horseback. "I've not heard of the man."

"That's not surprising. He's done nothing." Hogan was scornful. "Landed money, in Parliament for Paglesham, justice of the peace and, God help us, a Militia colonel." Hogan seemed surprised by his own lack of charity. "He means well. He won't be content till those lads are the best damned battalion in the army, but I think the man has a terrible shock coming when he finds out the difference between us and the Militia."

Like other regular officers, Hogan had little time for the Militia. Britain's second army was used exclusively within Britain itself, never had to fight, never went hungry, never slept in an open field, yet it paraded with a glorious pomp and self-importance. Hogan laughed. "Mustn't complain. We're lucky to have him."

"Lucky?" Sharpe looked at the engineer.

"Oh, yes. Sir Henry only arrived in Abrantes yesterday but he tells us he's a great expert on war. The man's not yet seen a Frenchman but he's lectured the general on how to beat them!" Hogan laughed and shook his head. "Maybe he'll learn. One battle could take the starch out of him."

"I suppose he's a flogger?"

Hogan grimaced. "Floggings, punishment parades, extra drills. Sir Henry will have, he says, only the best. And there they are. What do you think of them?"

Sharpe laughed grimly. He loved the army: it was his home, the refuge that an orphan had needed sixteen years before, but most of all it gave him, in its clumsy way, the opportunity to prove that he was valued. He had been lucky that in those sixteen years he had rarely stopped fighting. The battles in Flanders, India and Portugal had called for men like himself who reacted to danger the way a gambler reacted to a deck of cards. He suspected he would hate a peacetime army, with its petty jealousies and endless polish, and in the South Essex he saw just that.

"God keep me from Sir Henry Simmerson," he said. "That's not too much to ask, is it?"

Hogan smiled. "I'm afraid it is. I told you there was more. If a Spanish regiment marches to Valdelacasa then Sir Arthur feels, for the sake of diplomacy, that a British one should go as well." He glanced at the polished ranks and back to Sharpe. "Sir Henry Simmerson and his fine men are going with us."

Sharpe groaned. "You mean we have to take orders from him?"

Hogan pursed his lips. "Not exactly. Strictly speaking you will take your orders from me." Sharpe glanced at him curiously. The only reason why Wellesley had subordinated Sharpe and his riflemen to him must be because the general did not trust Simmerson.

"Does the general expect there to be a fight?"

Hogan shrugged. "The Spanish say that the French have a whole regiment of cavalry on the south bank of the Tagus, with horse artillery. He thinks they may try to stop us blowing the bridge."

"I still don't understand why you need us."

Hogan smiled. "Perhaps I don't, but I want someone with me I can trust. Perhaps I just want you along as a favour?"

Sharpe smiled. "For you, sir, it will be a pleasure."

Hogan smiled back. "Who knows? It might be. *She's* going along."

Sharpe followed Hogan's gaze out of the window and saw the girl raise a hand to an officer of the South Essex. Sharpe had an impression of a blond man, immaculately uniformed, mounted on a black horse. The girl spurred her mare forward and, followed by the servant and his mule, joined the rear of the battalion that was marching down the road to Castelo Branco and the Spanish border.

Sharpe leaned back and began to laugh. But the sergeant's face stayed gloomy. "God save Ireland."

Hogan raised his cup. "Amen to that."

CHAPTER 2

The drumbeats were muffled, sometimes blending with the other sounds of the city, but insistent and sinister, and Sharpe was glad when the sound stopped. He was also glad they had reached Castelo Branco, after a tiresome journey that had meant forcing Hogan's mules along a sixty-mile road cut with deep, jagged ruts. Now the mules, laden with powder kegs and all the equipment Hogan needed for Valdelacasa, followed behind the riflemen as they pushed their way through the crowded streets towards the main square.

As they spilled into the bright sunlight Sharpe's suspicions about the drumbeats were confirmed. Someone had been flogged. Soldiers were taking down four wooden triangles that were propped against the far wall of the square. It was over now, and the victims had been led away. Sharpe, watching the hollow square formation of the South Essex, thought: Four men flogged. Dear God.

Hogan reined in his horse as Sir Henry rode delicately out to the centre of the square. "This doesn't seem to be the best moment to talk to the good colonel," he murmured.

His men collapsed at the foot of the wall, their packs and rifles discarded. Sir Henry's voice carried clearly to them.

"I have flogged four men because four men deserted." Sharpe was startled. Deserters already? He wondered how many others were tempted to escape from Simmerson's ranks. "Some of you helped these men plan their crime, so I have flogged four men to remind you of your duty." His voice was curiously high pitched; it would have been funny had the man's presence not been so big. He had spoken in a controlled manner, but suddenly he waved an arm as if to point at every man in his command. "You will be the best!" The loudness was so sudden that pigeons burst startled from the ledges of the houses. The colonel turned his horse and rode away, leaving the cry lingering behind like a threat.

As the companies marched from the plaza, Sharpe saw resentment in their expressions. He, too, believed in discipline. But he kept the rules simple. He asked three things of his men. That they fought, as he did, with a ruthless professionalism. That they stole only from the enemy and the dead, unless they were starving. And that they never got drunk without his permission. It was a simple code, and it was backed by punishment because Sharpe knew, for all that his men liked him and followed him willingly, that they must fear his anger when they broke his trust.

He crossed the square towards an alleyway, looking for a water fountain, and noticed a lieutenant of the South Essex Light Company riding his horse towards the same dark-shadowed gap between the buildings. It was the man who had waved to the black-dressed girl. The lieutenant's uniform was elegantly tailored, the curved sabre was expensive, and the horse he rode was probably worth a lieutenant's commission by itself. Sharpe resented the man's wealth and easy superiority, and his resentment annoyed him because he knew it was based on envy. He squeezed into the side of the alley to let the horseman pass, looked up and nodded affably, and had an impression of a thin, handsome face.

The lieutenant stopped and stared down. "Don't they teach you to salute in the Rifles?" The lieutenant's voice was as smooth and

as rich as his uniform. Sharpe realized that the lieutenant had mistaken him for a private. It was hardly surprising. The deeply shadowed alleyway, Sharpe's slung rifle and unorthodox uniform all helped to explain the mistake. He glanced up and was about to explain when the lieutenant flicked his whip. It slapped Sharpe's face.

"Damn you, man, answer me!"

Sharpe felt the anger rise in him, but stayed still. The lieutenant drew the whip back. "What battalion? What company?"

"Second battalion, fourth company." Sharpe spoke with deliberate insolence, remembering the days when he had had no protection against officers like this.

"You will call me 'sir'. Who's your officer?"

"Lieutenant Sharpe."

"Ah!" The lieutenant kept his whip raised. "Lieutenant Sharpe who we've all been told about. Came up from the ranks, didn't he?"

Sharpe nodded and the lieutenant drew the whip back farther.

"Is that why you don't say 'sir'? Has Mr. Sharpe strange ideas on discipline? Well, I will have to see him, won't I, and arrange to have you punished for insolence." He brought the whip slashing down towards Sharpe's head. There was no room for Sharpe to step back; instead he put both hands under the man's stirrup and heaved upwards. The man cried out, and the next instant he was flat on his back on the far side of his horse.

Sharpe smiled. "You'll have to wash your uniform, Lieutenant."

The furious lieutenant struggled to his feet and put his hand to the hilt of his sabre.

"Hello there!" Hogan was peering into the alley. "I thought I'd lost you!" He rode his horse up to the strange lieutenant. "Afternoon. Don't think we've met. My name's Hogan."

"Lieutenant Christian Gibbons, sir."

Hogan grinned. "I see you've already met Sharpe. Lieutenant Richard Sharpe of the 95th Rifles."

Gibbons looked at Sharpe and his eyes widened. Hogan went cheerfully on. "You've heard of Sharpe, of course. He's the laddie who killed the Sultan Tippoo. Then, let me see, there was that ghastly affair at Assaye. No one knows how many Sharpe killed there. Terrible fellow, equally fatal with a sword or a gun."

Gibbons could hardly mistake Hogan's message. The captain had seen the scuffle and was warning Gibbons about the likely consequence of a formal duel. The lieutenant took the proffered escape. He picked up his shako, then nodded to Sharpe.

"My mistake, Sharpe."

"My pleasure, Lieutenant."

Hogan watched Gibbons retrieve his horse and disappear from the alleyway. "You're not very gracious at receiving an apology."

"It wasn't very graciously given. Anyway, the bastard hit me with his whip. Why do you think I dumped him?"

Hogan shook his head. "There's nothing so satisfying as a friendly relationship with your fellow officers, my dear Sharpe. What did he want?"

"Wanted me to salute him. Thought I was a private."

Hogan laughed again. "God knows what Simmerson will think of you. Let's go and find out."

They were ushered into Simmerson's room to find the colonel sitting on his bed wearing nothing but a pair of trousers. A doctor knelt beside his forearm holding a towel and a metal box with a trigger mounted on the top, trying to find a patch of skin that was not already scarred with strangely regular marks.

Sir Henry barked to Hogan. "Do you bleed, Captain?"

"No, sir."

"You should. Keeps a man healthy." He turned back to the doctor who was still hesitating. "Come on, you idiot!"

In his nervousness the doctor pressed the trigger by mistake and from the bottom of the box Sharpe saw a group of wicked little blades leap out like steel tongues. He realized it was a bleeding machine, the modern scarifier that was supposed to be faster and more effective than the old-fashioned lancet. The doctor forced the blades back, placed the box on the colonel's arm, glanced nervously at his patient, then pressed the trigger again.

"Ah! That's better!" Sir Henry closed his eyes and smiled momentarily. "Always too much spleen after a flogging."

"That's very understandable, sir," Hogan said in his Irish brogue.

Simmerson eyed him suspiciously. "You must be Captain Hogan?"

"Yes, sir." Hogan nodded amiably.

Simmerson turned to Sharpe. "And who the devil are you?"

"Lieutenant Sharpe, sir. 95th Rifles."

"No, you're not. You're a damned disgrace, that's what you are!"

Sharpe said nothing. He stared through the window at the far blue hills where the French were gathering their strength.

"Forrest!" Simmerson pulled on his shirt. "Forrest!"

The door opened and a major came in. "Colonel?"

"This officer will need a new uniform. Provide it, please, and arrange to have the money deducted from his pay."

"No." Sharpe spoke flatly. For a moment Sir Henry said nothing, he was not used to being contradicted, and Sharpe kept going. "I am an officer of the 95th Rifles and—"

"Damn you, Sharpe! You're a disgrace!" Simmerson began to go red. "You're not a soldier, you're a crossing sweeper! You're under my orders now and I'm ordering you . . . ."

"No, sir." This time Hogan had spoken. "You see, Sir Henry, Sharpe is under my orders. The general was quite specific."

"But . . ."

Hogan raised a hand to Simmerson's protest, unleashing all his Irish charm. "You are so right, sir, so right. But I think the general had it in his mind, sir, that you would be so burdened with the problems of our Spanish allies and then, sir," he leaned forward conspiratorially, "there are the exigencies of engineering that Lieutenant Sharpe understands."

Simmerson gave a bray of a laugh. Hogan had taken him off the hook. He pointed at Sharpe. "He dresses like a common labourer, eh Forrest?" The major smiled dutifully. Simmerson pulled on his vast scarlet and yellow jacket. He turned back to Sharpe. "Done much soldiering then, Sharpe?"

"A little, sir."

Simmerson chuckled. "How old are you?"

"Thirty-two, sir." Sharpe stared rigidly ahead.

"Thirty-two, eh? And still only a lieutenant? What's the matter, Sharpe? Incompetence?"

"I joined in the ranks, sir."

The colonel's mouth dropped open. Those who made the jump from sergeant to ensign were few and could rarely be accused of incompetence. There were only three qualifications that a common soldier needed to be given a commission. First, he must be able to read and write, and Sharpe had learned his letters from a fellow prisoner in an Indian gaol. Second, the man had to perform some act of suicidal bravery. The third was extraordinary luck.

Simmerson snorted. "You're not a gentleman then, Sharpe?"

"No, sir."

"Who commissioned you?"

"Sir Arthur Wellesley, sir."

Sir Henry gave a neigh of triumph. "I knew it! No standards at all! I've seen this army, its appearance is a disgrace! You can't say that of my men, eh?" He looked at Sharpe. "What makes a good soldier, Sharpe?"

"The ability to fire three rounds a minute in wet weather, sir." Sharpe invested his answer with a tinge of insolence. He knew the reply would annoy Simmerson. The South Essex was a new battalion and he doubted whether its musketry was up to the standard of older battalions. It took time for a soldier to learn the fast, complicated drill of loading and firing a musket.

Sir Henry stared at him thoughtfully. "Three rounds a minute?"

"Yes, sir."

"And how do you teach men to fire three rounds a minute?"

Sharpe shrugged. "Patience, sir. Practice. One battle does a world of good."

Simmerson scoffed at him. "Patience! Practice! They aren't children, Sharpe. They're drunkards and thieves!" His voice was rising again. "Flog it into them, Sharpe, flog! It's the only way! Give them a lesson they won't forget. Isn't that right?"

"It's the last resort, sir."

"The last resort, sir." Simmerson mimicked Sharpe. "You're soft, Sharpe. Could you teach men to fire three rounds a minute?"

Sharpe could feel the challenge in the air, but there was no going back. "Yes, sir."

"Right!" Simmerson rubbed his hands together. "This afternoon. Forrest? Give Mr. Sharpe a company. The Light will do. Mr. Sharpe will improve their shooting!"

Sharpe looked out of the window. It was a hot, dry day and there was no reason why a good man should not fire five shots a minute in this weather. It depended, of course, how bad the Light Company were. He looked back to Simmerson. "I'll try, sir."

"Oh you will, Mr. Sharpe, you will. And you can tell them from me that if they fail then I'll flog one out of every ten of them."

Sharpe realized he had been tricked into what was probably an impossible job and the outcome would be that the colonel would have his orgy of flogging and he, Sharpe, would be blamed. And if he succeeded? Then Simmerson could claim it was the threat of the flogging that had done the trick. He saw the triumph in Simmerson's small red eyes and he smiled at the colonel. "I won't tell them about the flogging, Colonel. You wouldn't want them distracted, would you?"

"You use your own methods, Mr. Sharpe. But I'll leave the triangles where they are; I think I'm going to need them."

Sharpe clapped his misshapen shako onto his head and gave the colonel a salute of bone-cracking precision. "Don't bother, sir. You won't need them. Good day, sir."

Now make it happen, he thought.

"I DON'T BELIEVE IT, SIR. Tell me it's not true." Sergeant Patrick Harper shook his head as he stood with Sharpe and watched the South Essex Light Company fire two volleys. It was not that the men did not know how to load and fire their muskets; it was simply that they did it with painful slowness. There were officially twenty drill movements for the loading and firing of a musket, and the battalion's insistence on doing it by the drill book meant that Sharpe had timed their two demonstration shots at more than thirty seconds each. He had three hours, at the most, to speed them up to twenty seconds a shot. Harper was openly scornful.

"God help us if we ever have to skirmish alongside this lot! The French will eat them for breakfast!" He was right. But Sharpe hushed him as a mounted captain trotted across to them. It was Lennox, Captain of the Light Company, and he grinned at them.

"Terrifying, isn't it?"

Sharpe gave a non-committal answer and Lennox swung himself out of the saddle to stand beside him. "Don't worry, Sharpe. I know how bad they are, but His Eminence insists on doing it this way. If he left it to me I'd have the men doing it properly, but if we break one little regulation then it's three hours' punishment drill with full packs." He looked quizzically at Sharpe. "You were at Assaye?" Sharpe nodded. "Aye, I remember you. You made a name for yourself that day. I was with the 78th."

"They made a name for themselves, too."

Lennox was pleased with the compliment. "I know what you're thinking, Sharpe. What the devil am I doing here with this lot?" He did not wait for an answer. "I'm an old man, I was retired, the half pay wasn't stretching and they needed officers for Sir Henry bloody Simmerson. So here I am. Do you know Leroy?"

"Leroy?"

"Thomas Leroy. He's a captain here, too. He's good. Forrest is a decent fellow. But the rest! Just because they put on a fancy uniform they think they're warriors. Look at that one!" He pointed to Christian Gibbons who was riding his black horse across the field. "He's Simmerson's nephew, he's interested in nothing but women, and he's an arrogant little bastard. Can't do any wrong—apple of the colonel's bloodshot eye."

So that, Sharpe thought, is Simmerson's nephew. Lennox pointed at the company. "I'll leave you Lieutenant Knowles and Ensign Denny, they're both good lads. And good luck to you. You'll need it!"

Sharpe was left with the company, ranks of faces that bulged over the stocks and stared at him as though fearful of some new torment. He walked to the front of the company, and faced them. His own jacket was unbuttoned, shirt open, and he wore no hat. To the men of the South Essex he was like a visitor from another continent. He said, "You're in a war now. When you meet the French a lot of you are going to die. Most of you." They were appalled by his words. "I'll tell you why."

He pointed over the eastern horizon. "The French are over there, waiting for you." Some of the men looked that way as though they expected to see Bonaparte himself coming through the olive trees. "They've all got muskets and they can all fire three or four shots a minute. Aimed at you. And they're going to kill you because you're so damned slow. You." He pointed to a man in the front rank. "Bring me your musket!"

At least he had their attention and some of them would understand the simple fact that the side which pumped out the most bullets stood the best chance of winning. He took the man's musket, a handful of ammunition, and discarded his own rifle. He held the musket over his head.

"Look at it! One India Pattern musket. It fires a ball three quarters of an inch wide, nearly as wide as your thumb, and it kills Frenchmen!" There was a nervous laugh but they were listening. "But you won't kill any Frenchmen with it. You're too slow! So, this afternoon, you will learn to fire three shots in a minute. In time you'll fire four shots every minute and if you're really good you should manage five!"

The company watched as he loaded the musket. It had been

years since he had fired one but compared to the Baker rifle it was ridiculously easy. There were no grooves in the barrel to grip the bullet and no need to force the ramrod with brute force. A musket was fast to load which was why most of the army used it instead of the much more accurate rifle. He checked the flint, found it new and well-seated in its jaws, so he primed and cocked the gun. "Lieutenant Knowles?"

A young lieutenant snapped to attention. "Sir!"

"Do you have a watch that can time one minute?"

Knowles dragged out a huge gold hunter. "Yes, sir."

"After I start firing you will tell me when one minute has passed. Understand?"

"Yes, sir."

He turned away from the company and pointed the musket down the field towards a stone wall. The swan neck with its gripped flint snapped forward, the powder in the pan flashed, the main charge exploded, and he felt the heavy kick as the lead ball was punched out of the barrel in a gout of thick, white smoke.

Now it was all instinct. Right hand away from the trigger, let the gun fall in the left hand, and as the butt hits the ground the right hand already has the next cartridge. Bite the bullet. Pour the powder down the barrel but remember to keep a pinch for the priming. Spit in the ball. Ramrod out of its socket, up, and down the barrel. A quick push and then it's out again, the gun is up, the cock back, priming in the pan, and fire again.

And again and again and again and memories of standing in the line with your sweating comrades and going through the motions as if in a nightmare. Ignoring the billows of smoke, the screams, edging sideways to fill up the gaps left by the dead, loading and firing, letting the flames spit out into the fog of powder smoke, hoping the unseen enemy is falling back. Then the command to cease fire and you stop. Your face is black and stinging from the explosions of the powder in the pan just inches from your right cheek, your eyes smarting from the smoke, and the cloud drifts away leaving the dead and wounded in front and you lean on the musket and pray that the next time the gun would not hang fire, snap a flint, or simply refuse to fire at all.

He pulled the trigger for the fifth time, the ball hammered away down the field, and the musket was down and the powder in the barrel before Knowles called "Time's up!"

The men cheered. Harper was grinning broadly. He at least knew how difficult it was to make five shots in a minute and he had noticed how Sharpe had cunningly loaded the first shot before the timed minute began.

Sharpe stopped the noise. "That is how you will use a musket. Fast! Now you're going to do it."

There was silence. Sharpe felt devilment in him; had not Simmerson told him to use his own methods? "Take off your stocks!" The men stared at him. "Come on! Take your stocks off!"

Puzzled, the men gripped their muskets between their knees and used both hands to wrench apart the stiff leather collars.

"Sergeants! Collect the stocks. Bring them here."

The battalion had been brutalized too much. There was no way he could teach them to be fast-shooting soldiers unless he offered them an opportunity to take their revenge on the system. The sergeants came to him, their arms piled with the hated stocks. "Put them down there." Sharpe made them heap the stocks about forty paces in front of the company. "That is your target! Each of you will be given just three rounds. And you will have one minute in which to fire them! Those who succeed, twice in a row, will drop out and have a lazy afternoon. The rest will go on trying until they succeed."

The men were grinning and there was a buzz of conversation that he did not try to check. When all was ready he gave the word and bullets began smashing into the leather. To the men the collars represented Simmerson and his tyranny. After the first two sessions only twenty men had succeeded, but an hour and three quarters later the last man fired his final successful shot into the fragments of leather that littered the grass.

Sharpe looked at the lane that led from the town. Simmerson was coming to claim his victims for the triangle.

"For what we are about to receive," Harper said softly.

"Quiet! Make them load. We'll give the man a demonstration." Sharpe watched Simmerson's eyes as the significance of his men's unbuttoned collars and the leather shreds on the grass dawned on him. As the colonel took a deep breath, Sharpe ordered, "Now!"

"Fire!" Harper's command unleashed a full volley that echoed like thunder in the valley. The colonel could only watch as his men worked their muskets like veterans.

The last volley rattled onto the stone wall and Lieutenant

Knowles tucked his watch back into a pocket. "Two seconds under a minute, Sir Henry, and four shots."

"I can count, Knowles." Four shots. Secretly Simmerson was impressed. But a whole company's stocks? At two and threepence apiece? "God damn your eyes, Sharpe!"

"Yes, sir."

Sharpe knew that he had made a fool of the colonel in front of his own men and that it had been a mistake; he had made an enemy who had both power and influence. The colonel edged his horse closer to Sharpe and his voice was surprisingly quiet. "This is my battalion, Mr. Sharpe. Remember that." He looked for a moment as if his anger would erupt but he controlled it and shouted at Knowles to follow him instead. Harper was grinning, the men looked pleased, and only Sharpe felt a foreboding of menace. He shook it off. There were muskets to clean, rations to issue and, beyond the setting sun, enemies enough for anyone.

CHAPTER 3

Patrick Harper marched with a long easy stride, happy they had at last crossed the frontier and were going somewhere. Sharpe had started the day's march at the Rifle Regiment's fast pace, three steps walking, three running, and now Essex were some way behind them. Harper grinned as he remembered the stocks. There was a sobering rumour that the colonel had ordered Sharpe to pay for every one of the seventy-nine ruined collars.

Harper enjoyed being a soldier, even in the army of the nation that had taken his family's land and trampled on their religion. Like so many of his countrymen he had found a refuge from poverty and persecution in the ranks of the enemy. But it was hard now to think of the English as enemies. Familiarity had bred too many friendships. The army was one place where strong men could do well and Harper liked the responsibility he had earned, and the respect of other tough men, like Sharpe. He was content for the moment to be a soldier and took his pleasure where it could be found. Yesterday, for instance, he had seen a peregrine falcon, high over the road, and his soul had soared to meet it. Harper loved birds, and never tired of watching them.

At midday they found Major Forrest with his small, mounted advance party waving to them from a stand of trees that grew between the road and a stream. The major led the company to the spot he had chosen to bivouac. "I thought, Sharpe," he murmured, "that it might be best if you were some way from the colonel."

Sharpe grinned at him. "I think that's an excellent idea, sir."

An hour later the battalion arrived. The men threw themselves onto the ground and rested their heads on their packs. Some went to the stream and sat with their swollen feet in the cool water. Sentries were posted, weapons stacked, the smell of tobacco drifted through the trees, and a desultory game of football started. Last to arrive were the wives and children, Hogan and his mules, and the herd of cattle that would provide the evening meals until the last beast was killed.

In the somnolent afternoon Sharpe felt restless. He got up from the grass, took his rifle, and strolled towards the near picquet line and beyond. It was a beautiful day. No cloud disturbed the sky, the water in the stream flowed clear, a whisper of a breeze flickered the pale leaves of the olive trees. He walked back between the stream and a field of growing corn, and into a rock-strewn field of stunted olives. Nothing moved. Insects buzzed and clicked, a horse whinnied from the camp site. He sat beside a gnarled tree trunk, rifle across his knees, and stared into the heat haze. He felt comfortable and lazy, at peace with the world.

Then there was a noise. There were horses on the road, only two from the sound of their hooves, moving slowly and uncertainly. He curled his right hand round the narrow part of the rifle's stock. He doubted that the French would have cavalry patrols in this part of Spain but he still got to his feet and moved silently through the grove, instinctively choosing a path that kept his green uniform hidden and shadowed until he stood in the bright sunlight and surprised the travellers.

It was the girl and her servant. She was still dressed in black trousers and boots, with the same wide-brimmed hat. She was walking, or rather limping like her horse, and at the sight of Sharpe she stopped. The servant, a slight, dark man leading the heavily loaded mule, stopped ten paces behind and stared mutely at the tall, scarred rifleman. The mare swished its tail at the flies, and stood patiently with one hind leg lifted off the ground. The shoe was hanging loose, held by a single nail, and the animal must have suffered agonies on the hot stony road. Sharpe nodded at the hind foot. "Why don't you take the shoe off?"

Her voice was surprisingly soft. "Can you do it?" She smiled at him. Sharpe guessed she was in her early twenties and she carried her looks with the assurance of someone who knew that beauty could be a better inheritance than money or land.

Sharpe nodded and moved to the horse's rear. He pulled the hoof towards him, holding the pastern firmly, and the mare trembled but stayed still. He tugged the shoe clear and let the leg go. He held the shoe out to the girl. "You're lucky. It can probably be put back on." He felt clumsy in her presence, aware of her beauty, suddenly tongue-tied. She made no move to take the shoe so he pushed it under the strap of a bulging saddlebag. "Someone will know how to shoe a horse up there." He nodded up the road.

"Is the South Essex camped up there?" Her English was good, tinged with a Portuguese accent.

"Yes."

"Good. I was following them when the shoe came off." She looked scathingly at the servant. "That fool is frightened of horses."

Sharpe expected her to go but instead she stayed still and stared at him with an expression of amused tolerance. He wondered if she expected him to lead her horse for her and he felt his anger rise in his usual reaction to the assumption of arrogance. She looked him up and down, as Gibbons would have looked at a horse, then deflected his anger by smiling again.

"You are an officer?"

"Lieutenant Sharpe, Ma'am."

"Thank you, Lieutenant, I expect we will meet again. I'm going with you to Madrid." She clicked her tongue at the horse and led it on towards the stand of trees and the first drifts of blue smoke where the cooking fires were being blown into life. Sharpe watched her go, let his eyes see the slim figure beneath the man's clothes, and felt the heaviness of his desire. Damn Gibbons and his money, damn all officers who could pay for beauties who rode thoroughbred mares behind the army.

From the battalion there came the sound of musket fire and he knew that bullocks were being slaughtered for the evening meal. There would be wine with the stew, and stories from Hogan about old friends and forgotten campaigns. He had been looking forward to the meal, to the evening, but suddenly everything was changed. The girl was in the camp, her laughter would invade his peace.

THE SOUTH ESSEX marched hard for four days to reach the rendezvous with the Spaniards at Plasencia, but the town was empty of Spanish troops. Storks flapped lazily from their nests among the steep roofs that climbed to the ancient cathedral, but of the Regimienta de la Santa Maria there was no sign. The battalion waited.

Finally, two days late, the Spanish regiment arrived and next morning the South Essex mustered at five to begin their march south to Valdelacasa. There was a chill in the air as five thirty, the hour set for departure, came and went and there was still no sign of the Santa Maria, and the men stamped their feet and rubbed their hands to ward off the cold.

At six, Sharpe looked up at the rising sun and tried to pin down his apprehensions about the operation at Valdelacasa. It sounded simple. A day's march to the bridge there, a day for Hogan to destroy the already crumbling arches, and a day's march back to Plasencia where Wellesley was gathering his forces for the next stage of the advance into Spain. But there was some instinct that told him it would not be that easy. It was not the Spanish that worried him. If they proved as useless as their reputation suggested, the South Essex should still be strong enough to cope. But Sharpe had little faith in Colonel Simmerson. If there really were French on the south bank of the Tagus, and if the South Essex had to repel an attack on the bridge while Hogan laid his charges, then Sharpe would have preferred an old soldier to be making the decisions and not this colonel of Militia whose head was stuffed with theories learned on the safe fields of Essex.

Seven chimed and a group of horsemen appeared from the houses and spurred towards the waiting battalion. But they were British. All of them were in uniform save one, who wore blue trousers under a grey cloak and on his head a plain bicorne hat. Sixteen-year-old Ensign Denny was standing near the riflemen and Sharpe asked him if he knew who the apparent civilian was.

"No, sir."

"Sergeant Harper! Tell Mr. Denny who the gentleman in the grey cloak is."

"That's the general, Mr. Denny. Sir Arthur Wellesley himself. Born in Ireland like all the best soldiers!"

A ripple of laughter went through the ranks. Then they all straightened up and stared at the hawk-nosed man who would lead them towards Madrid. They saw him take out a watch but there was still no sign of the Regimienta even though the sun was well over the horizon and the dew fading fast from the grass.

One of the staff officers with Wellesley broke away from the group and trotted his horse towards Sharpe.

"Lieutenant Sharpe!" The voice was familiar. He saw the staff officer, a lieutenant-colonel, waving to him but the face was hidden beneath the ornate cocked hat. "Richard! You've forgotten me!"

Lawford! Sharpe's face broke into a smile. "Sir! I didn't even know you were here!"

Sharpe remembered when the Honourable William Lawford was a frightened lieutenant and a sergeant called Sharpe had guided him through the heat of India. Then Lawford had repaid the debt. In a prison cell in Seringapatam the aristocrat had taught the sergeant to read and write; the exercise had stopped them both going mad in the dank hell of the Sultan Tippoo's dungeons.

Lawford swung easily out of the saddle and took off his hat. "You look dreadful! You must really buy yourself a uniform one of these days." He shook Sharpe's hand. "It's good to see you."

"And to see you, sir. A lieutenant-colonel? You're doing well!"

"It cost me three thousand five hundred pounds, Richard, and well you know it. Thank God for money. How are you?"

Sharpe grinned. "As you see me."

Lawford was the same age as Sharpe but there the resemblance stopped. Lawford was a dandy, dressed always in the finest cloth and lace. He spread his hands expansively. "You can stop worrying, Richard, Lawford is here. The French will probably surrender when they hear. God! It's taken me months to get this job! I pulled a hundred strings to get onto Wellesley's staff."

The words tumbled out. Sharpe was delighted to see him. He liked Lawford, and could feel no resentment against him. He supposed that it was because, for all the assurance of his birth and for all his finery, Lawford was a fighting soldier. Sharpe held up a hand to stop the flow of news.

"What's happening, sir? Where are the Spanish?"

Lawford shook his head. "Still in bed. At least they were, but we're told they're coming now." He leaned closer to Sharpe and dropped his voice. "How do you get on with Simmerson?"

"I don't have to get on with him. I work to Hogan."

Lawford appeared not to hear the answer. "He's an extraordinary man. Did you know he paid to raise this regiment?" Sharpe nodded. "Do you know what that cost him, Richard? Unimaginable!"

"So he's a rich man. But it doesn't make him a soldier." Sharpe sounded sour.

Lawford shrugged. "He wants to be the best. I sailed out on the same boat and all he did, every day, was sit there reading the Rules and Regulations for His Majesty's Forces!" He turned to look at Wellesley. "Well, I can't stay all day. Listen. You must dine with me when you're back from this job. Will you do that?"

"With pleasure."

"Good!" Lawford swung up into the saddle. "You've got a scrap ahead of you. We sent the Light Dragoons down south and they tell us there's a sizeable bunch of Frenchies down there with some horse artillery, so good luck!" He raised his hat and rode away.

Hogan joined Sharpe. "Friends in high places?"

"Old friend. We were in India."

Hogan said nothing. He was staring away across the field now, his jaw sagging in astonishment. "My God!"

The Regimienta had arrived. Two trumpeters in powdered wigs led the procession. They were mounted on glossy black horses, bedecked in uniforms that were a riot of gold and silver, their trumpets festooned with ribbons, tassels, and banners.

"Hell's teeth." The voice came from the ranks. "The fairies are on our side."

The Colours came next, two flags covered in armorial bearings and threaded with gold, carried by horsemen whose mounts stepped delicately high as though the earth was scarcely fit to carry them. They were followed by the officers. Everything that could be polished had been burnished to an eye-hurting intensity; epaulettes of twisted golden strands were encrusted with semi-precious stones; coats were piped with silver threads, frogged and plumed, sashed and shining. It was a dazzling display.

The men came next, a shambling mess, rattled onto the field by erratic drummers. Sharpe was appalled. All he had heard of the Spanish army seemed to be true in the Regimienta; their weapons looked dull and uncared for, there was no spirit in their bearing. Madrid seemed suddenly a long way off if this was the quality of the allies who would help clear the road. Now, the two trumpeters challenged the sky with a resounding fanfare. Then silence.

"Now what?" Hogan muttered.

Speeches. Wellesley, wise in the ways of diplomacy, escaped as the Spanish colonel came forward to harangue the South Essex. Hogan, who spoke passable Spanish, told Sharpe the colonel was offering the British a chance, a small chance, to share in the glorious triumph of the Spanish over their enemy. The Spanish cheered the speech while the South Essex, prompted by Simmerson, did the same. Salutes were exchanged, arms presented, there were more fanfares, more drums, all climaxing in the appearance of a priest who, riding a small grey donkey, blessed the Santa Maria with the help of small, white-surpliced boys. Pointedly, the pagan British were not included in the pleas to the Almighty.

Hogan took out his snuff box. "Do you think they'll fight?"

"God knows." The year before, Sharpe knew, a Spanish army had forced the surrender of twenty thousand Frenchmen, so there was no doubt that, with leadership, the Spaniards could fight.

At half past ten, five hours late, the battalion finally shrugged on its packs and followed the Santa Maria out of Plasencia. By midday the column had covered a mere five miles and had come to a complete stop. Trumpets sounded at the head of the Regimienta, officers galloped in urgent clouds of dust up and down the ranks, and the soldiers simply dropped their weapons and packs and sat down in the road. There were still fifteen miles to Valdelacasa.

Simmerson and Major Forrest arrived with a clatter of hooves. "What the devil's happening?"

"I don't know, sir," Hogan told him. "The Spanish have sat down."

Simmerson licked his lips. "Don't they know we're in a hurry?" No one spoke. The colonel looked round the officers as though one of them might suggest an answer. "Come on, then. We'll see what it's about. Hogan, will you translate?"

The mounted officers rode up the column and the riflemen sat by the road with their packs beside them. The Spanish appeared to be asleep. The sun was high and the road surface reflected a searing heat. Sharpe touched the muzzle of his rifle and flinched from the hot metal. Sweat trickled down his neck; the glare of the sun, reflected from the metal ornaments of the Spanish infantry, was dazzling.

A quarter of an hour passed before Simmerson, Forrest and Hogan pounded back from their meeting with the Spanish colonel. Sir Henry was not pleased. "Damn them! They've stopped for the day!" He pounded his saddle pommel. "What are we to do?"

The officers glanced at each other but none of them answered his question. Simmerson was the man who had to make the decision.

Sharpe looked at Harper. "Form up, Sergeant."

Harper bellowed orders. The Spanish muleteers, their rest disturbed, watched curiously as the riflemen pulled on their packs and formed ranks.

Simmerson looked nervously. "What the devil are you doing, Sharpe?"

"Only one thing to do, sir."

Simmerson looked at Forrest and Hogan, but they offered him no help. "Are you proposing we should simply carry on, Sharpe?"

It's what you should have proposed, thought Sharpe, but instead he nodded. "Isn't that what you intended, sir?"

Simmerson was not sure. Wellesley had impressed on him the need for speed but there was also the duty not to offend a touchy ally. But what if the bridge should already be occupied by the French? He looked at the riflemen, grim in their dark green uniforms, and then at the Spanish who lolled in the roadway. "Very well."

"Sir." Sharpe turned away to Harper. "Four ranks, Sergeant."

Harper took a deep breath. "Company! Double files to the right!"

There were times when Sharpe's men, for all their tattered uniforms, knew how to startle a Militia colonel. With a snap and a precision that would have done credit to the Guards, the even-numbered files stepped backwards; the whole company, without another word of command, turned to the right and instead of two ranks there were now four facing towards Valdelacasa. Harper had paused while the movement was carried out. "Quick march!"

They marched, scattering mules and muleteers before them. They pushed their tempo up to the Light Infantry quick march and the dust flew up. Behind them the South Essex were forming up, before them the Regimienta split apart into the fields. The Spanish colonel, a vision of golden lace, appeared at an inn doorway. He was without his boots and in his hand he held a glass of wine. As they drew level with the inn, Sharpe turned to his men.

"Company! To the right! Salute!"

He drew the long blade, held it in the ceremonial salute, and his men grinned as they presented their arms towards the Spanish colonel. He was in a quandary. In one hand, the wine, and in the other a long cigar. Sharpe watched the debate on the colonel's face as he looked from one hand to the other, trying to decide which to abandon, but in the end he stood to attention in his stockings and held the wineglass and cigar at a dutifully ceremonious angle.

"Eyes front!"

Hogan laughed out loud. "Well done, Sharpe!" He looked at his watch. "We'll make the bridge before nightfall."

Let's hope the French don't, thought Sharpe. Defeating an ally was one thing, but his doubts about the ability of the South Essex to face the French were as real as ever. He looked at the dusty road stretching over the featureless plain and for a fleeting moment wondered whether he would return. He pushed the thought away and gripped the stock of his rifle. With his other hand he unconsciously felt the lump under his shirt. Harper saw the gesture. Sharpe thought it was a secret that round his neck he had a leather bag in which he kept his worldly wealth, but all his men knew it was there. Sergeant Harper also knew that when Sharpe touched the bag with its few gold coins looted from old battlefields then the lieutenant was worried. And if Sharpe was worried? Harper turned to the riflemen. "Come on, this isn't a funeral! Faster!"

CHAPTER 4

Valdelacasa did not exist as a place where human beings lived; it was simply a ruined nunnery and a great crumbling stone bridge. And from the bridge, the land spread outwards in a vast, shallow bowl bisected by the River Tagus in one direction and the road which led to and from the bridge in the other.

The battalion had marched down the almost imperceptible incline as the shadows of dusk began to creep across the pale grasslands. There were no signs of life; just the ancient ruin, the bridge, and the water slipping silently towards the far-off sea.

"I don't like it, sir." Harper's face was genuinely worried.

"Why not?"

"No birds, sir. Not even a vulture."

Sharpe had to admit it was true. It was like a place forgotten. "There's no sign of the French." He could see no movement in the darkening landscape.

"It's not the French that worry me." Harper seemed infected by some ancient gloom. "It's this place, sir. It's not good."

"You're being Irish, Sergeant." Sharpe tried to ignore Harper's concern but he began to feel that Valdelacasa really did have a sinister air about it. And Hogan did not help.

"That's the *Puente de los Malditos;* the Bridge of the Accursed." Hogan walked his horse beside them and nodded at the building. "That must have been the convent. The Moors beheaded every single nun. The story goes that their heads were thrown into the water but the bodies left to rot. They say no one lives here because the spirits walk the bridge at night looking for their heads."

Darkness fell. The riflemen were guarding the far, southern end of the bridge, the bank on which the French were loose, and it was a nervous night as shadows played tricks and the chill sentries were not certain whether they imagined noises that could be either headless nuns or patrolling Frenchmen.

But the new day, even if it did not bring the Regimienta, brought a brilliant blue sky with only a scattering of high, passing clouds. Harsh ringing blows came from the bridge where Hogan's artificers hammered down the parapet at the spot chosen for the explosion, and the apprehensions of the night seemed no more than a bad dream. The riflemen were relieved by Lennox's Light Company and, with nothing else to do, Harper stripped naked and waded into the river.

"That's better. I haven't washed in a month." He looked up at Sharpe. "Is anything happening, sir?"

"No sign of them." Sharpe must have stared at the horizon, a mile to the south, fifty times since dawn, but there had been no sign of the French.

Harper came dripping wet out of the river and shook himself. "Perhaps they're not here, sir."

Sharpe shook his head. "I don't know, Sergeant. I've a feeling they're not far away."

Lennox, who had joined them, looked at him seriously. "You think so? I thought it was us Scots who had the second sight."

Sharpe walked onto the bridge. There was no sign of the Spanish either, and it occurred to him that possibly the whole job would be done before the Regimienta arrived. . . . Hogan was up to his neck in a hole in the bridge. Sharpe peered down and saw, in the rubble, the curving stonework of two arches. "How much powder will you use?"

"All there is!" Hogan was happy, a man enjoying his work. "Those Romans built well. You see those blocks?" He pointed to the exposed stones of the arches. "They're all shaped and hammered into place. I'm going to have to go down into the pier and blow the damn thing out sideways. If it works, Sharpe, it'll bring down two arches, and make one hell of a bang."

"How much longer?"

"I'll be finished in a couple of hours." Hogan heaved himself out of the hole and stood beside Sharpe. "Let's get the powder up here." He turned towards the convent, cupped his hands to his mouth, and froze. The Spanish were in sight, their trumpeters in front, their Colours flying, the blue-coated infantry straggling behind.

"Glory be," Hogan said. "Now I can sleep safe at nights."

The Regimienta marched to the convent, past the South Essex who were being drilled in the field, and kept on marching. Sharpe waited for the orders which would halt the Spaniards but they were never given. Instead the trumpeters paced their horses onto the bridge, the Colours followed, then the gloriously uniformed officers and finally the infantry itself.

"What the hell do they think they're doing?" Hogan stepped to the side of the bridge.

The Regimienta picked its way past the hole Hogan had dug. The engineer waved his arms at them. "I'm going to blow it up! Bang! Bang!" They ignored him. Hogan tried it in Spanish but the tide of men flowed on past. Hogan shook his head wearily. "I'm tempted to blow it up with that lot on the wrong side."

"They're our allies, remember."

The kegs of powder arrived and Sharpe left Hogan to pack the gunpowder deep in the base of the arches. He walked back to the south bank where the riflemen waited, and watched as the Santa Maria paraded in a long line across the road that led to the distant skyline. Lennox grinned down at Sharpe from his horse.

"What do you think of this?" He waved at the Spaniards.

"What are they doing?"

"They told the colonel that it was their duty to cross the bridge! It's something to do with Spanish pride. We got here first so they have to go farther. You know what Simmerson's thinking of doing? Bringing the whole battalion over. If they cross, we cross." Lennox laughed. "Mad, that's what he is."

There were shouts from Sharpe's riflemen and he followed their pointing arms to look at the horizon. "Do you see anything?"

Lennox stared up the track. "Not a thing."

A flash of light. "There!" Sharpe climbed onto the parapet and dug into his pack for his only possession of value, a telescope made by Matthew Berge of London. He suspected it had cost at least thirty guineas. There was a brass plate inset into the walnut tube and engraved on the plate was an inscription. "In gratitude. AW. September 23, 1803." He recalled Wellesley's piercing blue eyes looking at him when the telescope had been presented. "Remember, Mr. Sharpe, an officer's eyes are more valuable than his sword!"

He snapped the tube open and slid apart the brass shutters that protected the lens. The image danced in the glass, he held his breath to steady his arms. Damn the tube! It would not stay still.

"Pendleton!"

The young rifleman came running to the bridge and, on Sharpe's instructions, jumped onto the parapet and crouched so that Sharpe could rest the telescope on his shoulder. The skyline leaped towards him; he moved the glass gently to the right. Nothing but grass and stunted bushes. The heat shimmered the air above the gentle slope.

He moved the glass back, concentrating on the spot where the white, dusty road merged with the sky. Then, with the suddenness of an actor coming through a stage trapdoor, the crest was lined with horsemen. Pendleton gasped, the image wavered, but Sharpe steadied it. Green uniforms, a single white crossbelt.

"French chasseurs."

There was a murmur from the Regimienta, the men nudged each other and pointed. Sharpe mentally split the line in half, then in half again, and counted the distant silhouettes in groups of five.

Lennox rode over. "Two hundred, Sharpe?"

"That's what I make it."

A second line of horsemen appeared. The French were making a dramatic appearance; two lines of cavalry, two hundred men in each, walking slowly towards the bridge. Through the lens Sharpe could see the carbines slung on their shoulders and, on each horse, behind the stirrup, a netful of forage was strapped. He straightened up and told Pendleton he could jump down.

"Are they going to fight, sir?" The young boy was eager for a brush with the French. Sharpe shook his head.

"They're just having a look at us. They won't come near. They've nothing to gain by attacking."

When Sharpe had been locked in the dungeon with Lawford, the lieutenant had tried to teach him to play chess. It had been a hopeless task. They could never remember which chip of stone was supposed to represent which piece, and their gaolers had thought the scratched grid on the floor was an attempt at magic. They had been beaten and the chessboard scratched out. But Sharpe remembered the word "stalemate". That was the position now. The French could not harm the infantry and the infantry could not harm the French. The cavalry were too quick for the foot soldiers to get near them, and if the cavalry chose to attack they would be annihilated by the dreadful close-range volleys. Any horse that survived the bullets would swerve away or pull up rather than gallop into the close-packed, steel-tipped ranks. There would be no fight today.

And meanwhile, Sharpe thought, the job was done. They'd mined the bridge and it would take a good hour to get this lot back over.

Simmerson thought otherwise. He rode up, waving his drawn sword cheerfully. "We've got them, Lennox! We've got them!" The colonel was in his element. "Form your company on the left! Mr. Sterritt's company will guard the bridge and, if you please, I'll borrow Mr. Gibbons from you as my aide-de-camp!"

"Your gain is my loss, sir." Lennox grinned at Sharpe. "Aide-de-camp! He thinks he's fighting the battle of Blenheim! What will you do, Sharpe?"

Sharpe grinned back. "I'm not invited. I'll watch your gallant efforts. Enjoy yourself!"

The Regimienta, too, was preparing to advance. Simmerson assembled his company commanders and Sharpe listened as he gave his orders. The South Essex were to cross the bridge, form line in four ranks like the Spanish, and advance behind them. "We'll wait and see what the enemy does, gentlemen. Unfurl the Colours!"

Lennox winked at Sharpe, who wondered what Simmerson would do when it finally dawned on him that the French would not attack. Probably the colonel would claim that he had scared the enemy away.

The ensigns pulled the leather covers from the South Essex Colours, unfurled them, and hoisted them into their sockets. They made a brave sight and Sharpe felt the familiar pang of loyalty. The first raised was the King's Colour, a great Union Jack with the regiment's number in the centre, and next the South Essex's own standard, a yellow flag emblazoned with the regimental crest and with the Union flag stitched in the upper corner. It was impossible to see the flags and not be moved. They were the regiment; should only a handful of men be left on a battlefield, the rest slaughtered, the regiment still existed if the Colours flew. They were a rallying point in the chaos of battle, but more than that; there were men who would hardly fight for England's King and Country but would fight for their regiment's honour, for the gaudy flags that were carried in the centre of the line by the youngest ensigns and guarded by veteran sergeants armed with long wicked-bladed pikes. Sharpe had known as many as ten men in turn carry the Colours in battle, replacing the dead. Honour was all. The flags of the South Essex were new and gleaming, the regimental Colour devoid of battle honours; neither was torn by bullet or roundshot, but seeing them filled Sharpe with emotion.

The South Essex followed the Regimienta towards the horsemen. Like the Spanish the British line was a hundred and fifty yards wide, its four ranks tipped with bayonets, the company officers riding or walking with drawn swords. The Spanish halted, some four hundred yards up the road, and Simmerson had no choice but to stop his battalion also, to find out what the Regimienta intended.

Hogan joined Sharpe. "Not joining in the battle?"

"I think it's a private party. Captain Sterritt and I are guarding the bridge."

Sterritt, a mild man, smiled nervously. Hogan was wiping his hands on a piece of rag and Sharpe asked him if the job was finished.

"Aye. It's all done. Ten kegs of powder snuggled down, fuses laid, and the hole filled in. As soon as these gallant soldiers get the hell out of my way I can find out whether it works or not. Now what's happening?"

The Spanish were forming square. A good battalion could march from line into square in thirty seconds but the Spanish took four times as long. It was the proper formation when faced by attacking cavalry, but as the French showed no lunatic inclination to charge four times their own number the Spanish convolutions were hardly necessary. Sharpe watched as the officers and sergeants chivvied their men into a slightly lopsided square on the right of the track.

"It's a good job the French don't have guns," he said.

There was no more fatal combination than cavalry and artillery for men on foot. Infantry in square were totally safe from cavalry; all the horsemen could do was ride round the formation hacking uselessly at the bayonets. But if the cavalry were supported by cannons the square became a deathtrap. Grapeshot would blast holes in the ranks, the cavalry could ride into the gaps and slice down with their sabres.

Simmerson had watched the Regimienta form their square. So he gave his orders and with a marvellous precision the South Essex demonstrated, on the left of the road, how a battalion *should* form a square. Even at half a mile Sharpe could see the French horsemen clapping ironically.

Now there were two squares, the Spanish nearer the French, and still the horsemen made no move. Time passed. The sun climbed higher in the sky, the French horses lowered their necks and cropped at the thin pasture. Captain Sterritt, guarding the bridge with his company, became plaintive.

"Why don't they attack?"

"Would you?" Sharpe asked.

Simmerson was looking increasingly foolish as the enemy refused to fight. Now he was stranded, like a beached whale, in a defensive square. It was virtually impossible to make an ordered march while in a square formation; it was easy enough for the leading edge, but the sides had to step sideways, and the rear edge walk backwards. Simmerson wanted to move but he did not want his neat, ordered square to be torn out of alignment as he advanced. He could have resumed the line formation but then he would look even more foolish for having formed a square at all. So he stayed where he was.

"Someone's got to do something!" Captain Sterritt frowned in bewilderment. War was not supposed to be like this!

"Someone's doing something." Hogan nodded at the South Essex. A horseman had been released from the square and was galloping towards the bridge.

"It's Lieutenant Gibbons." Sterritt raised a hand to his colonel's nephew who pulled his horse to a violent stop. He looked down on Sharpe, his face filled with the seriousness of the moment.

"You're to report to the colonel."

Hogan coughed. "Lieutenant Sharpe is under my orders. Why does the colonel want him?"

Gibbons flung an arm towards the immobile French. "We need a skirmish line, Sharpe, something to sting the French into action."

Sharpe nodded. "How far ahead of the square am I supposed to take my men?" He spoke in sweet reasonableness.

Gibbons shrugged. "Near enough to move the cavalry. Hurry!"

"I'm not moving. It would be madness!"

Gibbons stared down at Sharpe. "I beg your pardon?"

"I will not kill my men. I go more than fifty yards from that square and the French will ride us down like hares. Don't you know that skirmishers fall back from cavalry?"

"Are you coming, Sharpe?" Gibbons made it sound like an ultimatum.

"No."

Gibbons turned to Hogan. "Sir? Will you order Lieutenant Sharpe to obey?"

"Listen, laddie." Sharpe noticed that Hogan had broadened his Irish accent. "Tell your colonel from me that the sooner he gets back over the bridge the sooner we can put a hole in it, and the sooner we get home. And, no, I will not instruct Lieutenant Sharpe to commit suicide. Good day, sir."

Gibbons wrenched his horse round, clapped his spurs into its side, shouted something unintelligible, and galloped back towards the impotent square. Sterritt turned to them, appalled.

"You can't refuse an order!"

Hogan's patience snapped. Sharpe had never before heard the Irishman lose his temper. "Don't you bloody understand? Do you know what a skirmish line is? It's a line of men scattered in front of the enemy. They'll be ridden down! What does he think he's doing?"

Sterritt blanched in front of Hogan's anger. He tried to placate the engineer. "But someone's got to do something."

"You're quite right. They've got to get back over the bridge and stop wasting our time!"

Some of Sterritt's company began tittering. Sharpe felt his own patience snap. He did not care if it was his job or not.

"Quiet!"

The French must have been as bored as anyone else. Sharpe heard the notes of a bugle and watched as they formed into four squadrons. They still faced the bridge, their leading squadron about three hundred yards beyond the Spanish square. Instead of the two long lines they efficiently made ranks of ten men, their commander ironically saluted the squares with his sword, and gave the order to move. The horsemen went into a trot, they circled towards the Spanish, kept on circling, turning to ride away, back up the hill and off to rejoin Marshal Victor's army in the east.

Then disaster happened. When the French were at the closest point their wide turn would take them to the Regimienta, a distance of about two hundred yards, the Spanish colonel in frustration, gave the order to fire. Every musket that could be brought to bear exploded in flame and smoke. A musket was optimistically effective at fifty yards, but at two hundred the volley was simply thrown away.

"Oh God!" Sharpe had spoken out loud.

There was a simple arithmetic to what happened next. The Spanish had shot their volley and would take at least twenty seconds to reload. A galloping horse could cover two hundred yards in much less time. The French colonel had no hesitation. His column was sideways to the Spanish, he gave his orders, the bugle sounded, and with a marvellous precision the French turned from a column of forty ranks of ten men each into ten lines of forty men. The first two spurred straight into the gallop, their sabres drawn, the others trotted or walked behind. There was still no reason for them to succeed. All the Spanish soldiers had to do was stay still, keep the bayonets firm and the horses would sheer away.

Sharpe ran a few paces forward. With a dreadful certainty he knew what would happen. The Spanish soldiers were ill led, frightened. They had fired a terrifying volley but the enemy was suddenly on them, horses baring their teeth through the veils of musket smoke, riders tall in their stirrups, galloping straight for them. Like beads off a snapped string the Spanish broke. The French launched another two lines of cavalry as the first crashed into the panicked mass. The sabres fell, rose bloodied, and fell again. The chasseurs were literally hacking their way into the packed square, the crush of screaming men. The third line of Frenchmen swerved away, and launched themselves against the Spaniards who had broken clear and were running for their lives towards the South Essex.

The French were instantly among them, hacking down expertly on the heads and shoulders of the fugitives. Behind them more lines of cavalry were trotting knee to knee into the attack. The French sabres came down right and left, the Spanish Colours went down. The South Essex could not see what was happening, only the Spanish running towards them and the odd horseman in the swirling dust.

"Fire!" Sharpe repeated the word. "Fire, you idiot."

Simmerson had one hope for survival. He had to blast the Spanish out of his way, otherwise the fugitives would break into his own square and let the horsemen through after them. He did nothing. With a groan Sharpe watched the Spanish reach the red ranks and scramble to safety. The South Essex gave ground, they split to let the desperate men into the hollow centre, the first Frenchman reached the ranks, cut down with his sabre and was blasted from the saddle by musket fire. Sharpe watched the horse stagger from bullet wounds, it crashed sideways into the face of the square dragging down all four ranks. Another horseman came to the gap, he hacked left and right, then he too was plucked from his horse by a volley. Then it was over. The French poured into the gap, the square broke, the men mixed with the Spanish and ran. This time there was only one place to go. The bridge. Sharpe turned to Sterritt.

"Get your company out of the way! Come on, man, move!"

"What?" Sterritt gaped at Sharpe, stunned by the tragedy before him. Sharpe turned to the men. If the company stayed at the bridge it would be swamped by fugitives.

"This way! At the double!"

Harper was there. Dependable Harper. Sharpe led, the men followed, Harper drove them. Off the road and across the dusty earth. Sharpe saw Hogan alongside. "Get back, sir!"

"I'm coming with you!"

"You're not. Who'll blow the bridge?"

Hogan disappeared. Sharpe ignored the chaos to his right; he ran on, counting his steps. At seventy paces he judged they had gone far enough. Sterritt had disappeared. He whirled on them.

"Halt! Three ranks!"

His riflemen had needed no orders. Behind him he could hear screams, the occasional cough of a musket, but above all the sound of hooves and of blades falling. He did not look. The men of Mr. Sterritt's company stared past him.

"Look at me!" They looked at him. Tall and calm. "You're in no danger. Just do as I say. Sergeant!"

"Sir!"

"Check the flints."

Harper grinned at him. The men of the South Essex had to be calmed down, their hysteria soothed by the familiar, and the big Irishman went down the ranks forcing the men to take their eyes off the shambles ahead and look at their muskets instead. One of the men, white with fear, looked up at the huge sergeant. "What's going to happen, Sarge?"

"Happen? You're going to fight." He tugged at the man's flint. "Loose as a good woman, lad, screw it up!"

The sergeant looked down the ranks and laughed. Sharpe had saved eighty muskets and thirty rifles from the rout. The French, God bless them, were about to have a fight.

CHAPTER 5

It was a shambles. Four minutes ago sixteen hundred British and Spanish infantry had been ranked on the field, now most of them were running for the bridge; they threw away muskets, packs, anything that might slow them

down. The French colonel was good. He concentrated some of his men on the fugitives, driving the panicked mass to the killing ground at the bridge's entrance. Other horsemen had been ordered against the remnants of the British square, a huddle of men fighting desperately round the Colours, but Sharpe could see more cavalry, standing motionless, the French reserve which could be thrown in to sustain the attack.

There was no point in defending the bridge. It was well enough protected from the French by the turbulent mass of men struggling for its dubious safety. Sharpe guessed that perhaps a thousand

men were trying to thread themselves onto a roadway just wide enough for an ox-cart. The French had no chance of cutting their way through such an immense barrier of bone and flesh. Instead they kept the panic boiling so that the men had no chance to reform and turn on their pursuers. Sharpe saw one Frenchman cheerfully urging the fugitives on with the flat of his sword, but the veteran chasseurs waited until they were level with their targets and then cut backwards at the unprotected face. Sharpe turned to his front.

Here there was proper fighting. The Colours of the South Essex were still flying, though the men surrounding them had been forced into a crude ring, and fought off the sabres and hooves with sword and bayonet. It was a desperate fight. The French had thrown most of their men against the small band; they may have stood no chance of capturing the bridge but inside the terrified ring was a greater prize. The Colours. For the French to ride off the field with captured Colours was to ride into glory, and the chasseurs tried to break the British resistance with a savage fury. The South Essex were fighting back desperately, their efforts fired by the fanatical determination that their flags should not fall. To lose the Colours was the ultimate disgrace.

It had taken Sharpe only a few seconds to comprehend the utter chaos in front of him; there were no choices to be made, he would go forward towards the Colours hoping the ring of survivors could hold out against the horsemen long enough for his company to bring their muskets and bayonets into range. He turned to the men. Harper had done his work well. Riflemen were scattered through the ranks to bolster the frayed nerves of the men from Sterritt's company. The men in green jackets grinned at Sharpe. The men in red stood appalled. Sharpe noted that Harper had put a file of riflemen at each end of the company, the vulnerable flanks where only steady nerves and rigid bayonets would deter the swooping horsemen.

"We're going forward. To the Colours." Some of the faces turned to Sharpe were white with fear. "There's nothing to be frightened about. As long as you stay in ranks. Understand? You *must* stay in ranks." He spoke simply and forcibly. "If anyone breaks ranks they will be shot. And no one fires without my orders. No one." They understood. He unslung his rifle, threw it to Pendleton and drew his great killing blade. "Forward!"

He walked a few paces in front listening to Harper call out the dressing and rhythm of the advance. He hurried. There was little time, and the difficult stretch would be the final hundred paces when the company must keep in ranks while they stepped over the dead and wounded and when the French would realize the danger and challenge them. He wondered how much time had elapsed since the fatal Spanish volley. It could only be minutes, yet suddenly he was feeling again the familiar detachment of battle. He noticed irrelevant details; it seemed as if the ground were moving beneath him rather than he walking on the dusty, cracked soil. He saw each sparse blade of pale grass; there were ants scurrying round white specks in the dirt. The fight round the Colours seemed far away, the sounds tiny, and he wanted to close the gap. There were the beginnings of excitement, elation even, at the nearness of battle. Sharpe had been a soldier half his life, he knew the discomforts, the injustices, he knew the half-pitying glances of men whose business let them sleep safe at night, but they did not know this elation.

The French were being held. Someone had organized the survivors of the British square and there was a kneeling front rank, its muskets jammed into the turf, bayonets reaching up at the chests of the horses. The sabres cut ineffectively at the angled muskets, there were shouts, screams of men and horses, a veil of powder smoke in which flashes of flame and steel ringed the Colours. As he walked, the great sword held low in his hand, he could see riderless horses trotting round the melée where chasseurs had been shot or dragged from the saddles.

A bugle call. He looked right and saw the French reserve trot forward deliberately towards the carnage round the Colours. They held no sabres and Sharpe knew what was in the mind of the French colonel. The British ring had held and the light cavalry sabres could not break it. But chasseurs, unlike most cavalry, carried carbines as well as sabres, and they planned to pour a volley from close range into the red-coated ranks that would tear them apart and let the swordsmen into the gap. He increased his pace but knew they could not reach the Colours before the fresh cavalry and he watched, sickened, as with meticulous discipline some of the hacking swordsmen wheeled their mounts away to give the carbines a field of fire. He saw the British feverishly loading muskets, but they were too late. The French stopped, fired, wheeled to let a second rank stop and hurl their volley at the South Essex. A few muskets replied, one chasseur toppled to the ground, a ramrod wheeled wickedly through the air as some terrified soldier shot it from his half-loaded musket. But the French volleys tore the front ranks apart; a great wound opened in the red formation and the enemy poured in towards the greatest prize a man could win on the battlefield.

Sharpe's men were among the bodies now. He stepped over a British private whose head had been virtually severed by a sabre cut. Behind him someone retched. He remembered that most of the men of the South Essex had never seen a battle, had no idea what weapons did to a man's flesh. The survivors in the square were falling back. He saw the Colours dip and rise again, caught a glimpse of an officer screaming at the men, urging them to fight back at the hooves and the terrible sabres. He saw a French officer tugging at his men; Sharpe's company had been spotted and the Frenchman knew what a hundred loaded muskets could do to the packed horsemen who were concentrated round the flags. He pulled a dozen men out of the fight, aligned them hurriedly, and launched them against the new danger. Sharpe turned.

"Halt!"

He kept his back to the French horsemen. In his head he knew how many seconds he had, and the frightened men of the South Essex desperately needed a demonstration of what well-fought infantry could do to cavalry.

"Rear rank! About turn!" He needed to guard the rear in case any horsemen circled round. Harper was there. "Front rank, kneel!" He walked towards them, calmly, and climbed over the kneeling front rank so that he was in the safety of the formation. The horses were fifty yards away.

"Only the middle rank will fire! Riflemen, hold your fire! Only the middle rank! Wait for it! Aim at the stomach! We're going to let them come close! Wait! Wait! Wait!"

The swords of the French were bloodied to the hilt, their horses were lathered, the riders' faces set in the rictus of men who have fought and killed desperately. Yet their victory over four times their number had been so easily gained that these horsemen thought themselves capable of anything.

The dozen Frenchmen rode at Sharpe's company, oblivious of their danger, confident that these British would collapse as easily as the two squares. Sharpe watched them come at a reckless gallop, saw the clods of turf thrown up by the hooves, the bared teeth and flying manes of the horses. He waited, kept talking in a measured, loud voice.

"Wait for them! Wait! Wait!" Forty yards, thirty. At the last moment the French officer realized what he had done. Sharpe watched him saw at his horse's bit but it was too late.

"Fire!"

The chasseurs disintegrated. It was a small volley, only a couple of dozen muskets, but it was fired murderously close. The horses fell, a couple skidded almost to the front rank, riders were hurled onto the ground in a maelstrom of hooves and sabres. Not one chasseur was left mounted.

"On your feet! Forward!"

He stepped in front again and led them past the bloody remains of their attackers. One Frenchman, his leg broken by his falling horse, slashed upwards at Sharpe with his sabre. Sharpe did not bother to cut back. He kicked the wounded man's wrist so that the blade fell from his hand. The company stepped round the dead men and horses; they began to hurry, the fight round the Colours was being lost, the British being forced back, the French inching forward. Sharpe saw the long pikes of the sergeants who guarded the Colours being used; one of them crashed onto a horse's head so that it reared up, throwing its rider, blood streaming from its forehead. The discipline of the square had vanished with the French carbine fire. Now the French were close to the Colours and men from the shattered square were running towards Sharpe and the safety of his levelled bayonets. He screamed at them to go to the side, but he had to halt, unable to make headway against the fugitives, and he swung the flat of his blade at them. Harper joined him and the Irishman's huge bulk forced the running men to the flanks where they could safely join Sharpe's company. Then it was clear and he went on, the blade still swinging. The Colours swayed, a Frenchman's hand on a staff was cut down by an officer's sword, and then the Colours collapsed.

Sharpe screamed unintelligible words, he was running, the men behind him stumbling on bodies and slipping on blood. A dismounted chasseur came for him, the sabre cutting at him. He put up his blade, the Frenchman's sword shattered, he cut at his neck, felt the man fall and stumbled on. He caught a glimpse of Harper bodily pulling a chasseur off his horse, the sergeant's face a terrible mask of rage and strength. There was still a group of redcoats by the fallen Colours, and Sharpe saw two Frenchmen dismount to pull at the last defenders with their bare hands.

Then the red jackets seemed to disappear; there were only chasseurs and French shouts of triumph as the dead were heaved from the staffs and the Colours snatched up. Sharpe turned and held his blood-covered blade high over his head.

"Halt! Present!" He was directly in their line of fire and he threw himself flat, pulling Harper down, as he screamed the order to fire. The volley smashed overhead and then they were up and running. The musket balls had plucked the Frenchmen from the Colours, the flags had fallen again, but this time surrounded by enemy as well as British dead.

There were only a few yards to go but there were more horsemen spurring in. Sharpe threw himself over the bodies, reached for a staff and pulled it towards him. It was the regimental Colour, its bright yellow field torn. The King's Colour was too far away. Harper was going for it but a horse cannoned into the sergeant and threw him back. Another horse reared and swerved from the great billow of yellow silk in Sharpe's hand, a sword struck the staff and Sharpe saw splinters fly from the new wood, then he was hit by the net of forage strapped to the saddle and thrown over. He could smell the horses, see the hooves in the air over him, the face of a Frenchman framed by his silver shako chain, bending towards him to pluck the Colour from his hands. He held on, saw Harper swinging a great pike. He hit the rider in the spine with its blade and the man slid gently on top of Sharpe, his last breath sighing softly in the rifleman's ear.

Sharpe pulled himself from beneath the body. He left the Colour there, it was as safe as in his hands. Where was the company? Sharpe looked round and saw them running towards the fight. They were so slow! The horsemen still came, trying desperately to force their unwilling horses onto the mounds of dead. Sharpe screamed again, Harper was bellowing, but there was no enemy within sword's length. He went forward towards the King's Colour, lying beneath two bodies some five yards away. He slipped on blood, stood again, but there were three dismounted Frenchmen coming for him with drawn sabres. Harper was beside him; one chasseur went down with the pike blade in his stomach, the other sank beneath Sharpe's blade. But the third had got the Union Jack and was holding it out to the mounted men behind. Sharpe and Harper lunged forward, the pike thunked into the chasseur's back but he had done his job. A horseman had snatched the fringe of the flag and was spurring away. There were more Frenchmen coming, clawing at the two riflemen for the second Colour, too many!

"Hold them, Patrick! Hold them!"

Harper whirled the pike, screamed at them, stood with his

legs apart, his huge height dominating the fight, begging the Frenchmen to come and be killed. Sharpe scrambled back to the regimental Colour, pulled it from the body, and threw it like a javelin at his advancing company. He watched it fall into their ranks. It was safe. Harper was still there, defying the enemy, but there was no more fight. Sharpe stood beside him, sword in hand, and the Frenchmen turned, found horses, and mounted to ride away. One of them turned and faced the two riflemen, lifted a bloodied sabre in grave salute, and Sharpe raised his own red sword in reply.

Someone slapped his back, men shouted as though he had won a victory when all he had done was halve the victory of the French. The company watched the chasseurs trot away with the King's Colour. There was no hope of retrieving it; it was already three hundred yards away, surrounded by triumphant horsemen.

Sharpe felt sickened and ashamed. The Spanish Colours were there too, but they were not his concern. His own honour was tied up with the captured flag, his reputation as a soldier.

He touched Harper on the elbow. "Are you all right?"

"Yes, sir." The sergeant was panting, still holding the pike which was bloodied for half its length. "Yourself?"

"I'm fine. Well done. And thank you."

Harper shook off the compliment but grinned at his lieutenant. "It was a rare one, sir. At least we got one back."

Sharpe turned to look at the Colour. It hung above the company, tattered and bloodstained, lost and regained. Below it Sharpe recognized Captain Leroy, whom Lennox had described as the only other decent soldier in the battalion, his face masked in blood.

Sharpe pushed through the ranks towards him. "Sir?"

"Well done, Sharpe. This is a miserable shambles." His accent was unusual, and Sharpe remembered he came from America; one of the small band of loyalists who still fought for the mother country.

Sharpe indicated Leroy's head. "Are you hurt badly?"

"That's just a scratch. I've a shot in the leg though."

Sharpe looked down. Leroy's thigh was smothered in blood. "What happened?"

"I was at the Colours. Thank God you came."

Sharpe turned towards the bridge. The field between was still full of French horsemen, but they were no longer fighting. Bugles called them from the slaughter, back up the road to where they formed ranks round their trophies. They should feel proud of themselves, thought Sharpe, four hundred light cavalry had broken two regiments, captured three Colours, and all because of the stupidity and pride of Simmerson and the Spanish colonel.

He turned to Leroy. "Have you seen Lennox?"

"No. He was in the square."

Sharpe looked round the field. It was an appalling sight. The spot where they stood was ringed with bodies. There were wounded men, stirring and crying, horses that lay on their sides, coughed blood, and beat the soil in a frantic tattoo. Sharpe found a sergeant.

"Get those horses shot, Sergeant. Hurry!"

He turned to count his riflemen.

"They're all safe, sir." Harper had counted already.

"Thanks." They had been in little danger as long as they stayed in ranks and kept the bayonets steady. He remembered thinking the same thing as the South Essex proudly marched up the field, banners waving. He tried to estimate the butcher's bill. There were no more than thirty or forty dead Frenchmen on the field, a high enough price, but they had gained glory for their regiment and had inflicted appalling losses. It was impossible to guess the number of the British and Spanish dead. It would be high, and there would be far more wounded, men whose faces had been laid open by the horsemen, blinded men who would be shipped home and abandoned to cold charity. He shivered.

But it was not just the dead and injured. In its first fight Simmerson's battalion had lost its pride. For sixteen years Sharpe had fought for the army, and this was the first time he had seen a British flag taken on the field and he knew how his enemies would celebrate when the trophy reached Marshal Victor's army. Soon Wellesley's army would have to fight a real battle, in which the killing machines of the artillery made survival a game of chance. Their enemies would now go into that battle with their spirits raised because they had already humiliated the British. He felt the beginnings of an idea, an idea so outrageous that he smiled.

"We did it, sir! We did it!" It was young Pendleton, waiting to return his rifle.

"Did what?" Sharpe wanted to savour his idea but there was too much to do.

"Saved the flag, sir. Didn't we?"

Sharpe looked at the boy's face. His eyes were shining. Sharpe smiled. "We did it."

"I know we lost the other one, sir, but that wasn't our fault, was it, sir?"

"No. Without us they'd have lost them both. Well done!"

The boy beamed. "And you and Sergeant Harper, sir." The boy's words tumbled out in his urgent need to share the excitement. "They was terrified of you, sir!"

Sharpe took his rifle and laughed. "I was fairly frightened, too."

Pendleton laughed. "You're just saying that, sir!"

Sharpe smiled and walked away. There was so much to do, the dead to be buried, the wounded to be patched up. He looked towards the bridge again. It was emptying now, the fugitives crossing to the far bank. The French were half a mile away, in ordered ranks, except for a lone horseman who was trotting towards Sharpe. He supposed it was an officer coming to discuss a truce while they sorted out their wounded. Sharpe felt a great weariness. He looked back at the bridge, saw Simmerson on the far side, surrounded by officers, and wondered why he was not sending any men across to start the gravedigging, the bandaging, the stripping of the dead. It would take a whole day to clear up this mess. Sharpe slung his rifle and started walking towards the chasseur officer. He raised a hand in salute.

And at that moment the bridge exploded.

CHAPTER 6

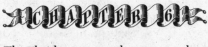

The bridge was reluctant to be destroyed. The central pier gave a deep shudder that was felt as far away as Sharpe and his company, and for a second it seemed as if the bridge might hold. Then the road on the bridge rose into the air, hung suspended for a fraction, and slowly collapsed into the water. A huge, dirty plume of smoke, boiling with ancient dust, rose over the ruined spans; only slowly did silence follow the thunder, the river rearrange itself to the new pattern of stones on its bed, the black smoke drift slowly westwards. Forty feet had been ripped from the bridge, Wellesley was safe from marauding cavalry to his south, and Sharpe and his men were now marooned on the wrong side of the Tagus.

Captain Leroy collapsed on the grass. He nodded towards the bridge. "Why the hell did they do that?"

Sharpe wished he knew. Hogan surely would have waited for Sharpe and his swollen company of two hundred men to reach the safety of the other bank before lighting the fuses?

"Sir, sir." A rifleman was calling him. The French chasseur officer had arrived, a captain with a suntanned face split by a large black moustache. Sharpe walked to him and saluted. The Frenchman returned the salute and looked round at the carnage.

"Congratulations on your fight, monsieur." He spoke perfect English.

Sharpe acknowledged the compliment. "You have our congratulations, too. You have won a notable victory, sir." The words felt stilted. It was extraordinary how men could fight each other like demented fiends, yet in a few moments become polite, generous even, about the damage an enemy had inflicted. The French captain smiled briefly.

"Thank you, m'sieu." He paused a moment, looked at the bodies lying near the bridge, and when he turned back to Sharpe his expression had changed; it had become less formal and more curious. "Why did you come across the river?"

Sharpe shrugged. "I don't know."

The Frenchman dismounted and looped his reins on his wrist. "You were unlucky." He smiled. "But you and your men fought well." He nodded at the bridge. "And now this?"

Sharpe shrugged again. The chasseur captain looked at him for a moment. "I think perhaps you are most unlucky in your colonel, yes?" He spoke quietly so that the men should not hear. Sharpe did not react but the Frenchman spread his hands. "We have them, too. My regrets, m'sieu."

It was all getting too polite. Sharpe looked at the bodies lying untended in the field. "You wish to discuss the wounded?"

"I did, m'sieu, I did. Not that I think we have many but we need your permission to search this piece of the field. As for the rest, we are the masters of it." He waved a hand at the destroyed bridge. "I think you will have problems on reaching the other side?" Sharpe nodded; it was undeniable. "I think, m'sieu, my colonel will want to renew the fight after a suitable period."

Sharpe laughed. "When you are ready, sir."

The Frenchman laughed too and pulled out a watch. "Shall we say that we have one hour in which to look after our wounded? After that we shall talk again."

He was giving Sharpe no choice. An hour was not nearly enough for his two hundred men to carry the wounded to the entrance of the bridge and devise a way of getting them to safety. On the other hand, an hour was far more than the French needed.

The captain unlooped his reins and prepared to mount. "My congratulations again. And my sincere regrets. *Bonne chance!*" He mounted and cantered back towards the skyline.

Sharpe took stock of his new company. The survivors from the square had added some seventy men to his small command. Leroy was the senior officer, of course, but his wounded leg forced him to leave the decisions to Sharpe. And there was Lieutenant Knowles from the Light Company.

The working parties took jackets from the dead, threaded the sleeves onto abandoned muskets, and made crude stretchers on which wounded men were carried to the bridge. The French were swiftly finished and started rummaging through the blue-coated bodies of the Spanish. The British did the same, there was no stopping them, the spoils of a fight were the one reward of the survivors. The riflemen, on Sharpe's orders, collected abandoned muskets, and ammunition pouches, dozens of them. If the French should attack, then Sharpe planned to arm each man with three or four loaded guns and meet the horsemen with a continuous volley that would destroy them. But he doubted if the French really meant to attack again. The losses they would incur would hardly be worth the effort; perhaps they were hoping for his surrender.

He helped Leroy to the bridge, propped him against the parapet, and cut away the white breeches. There was a bullet wound in the American's thigh, dark and oozing, but the carbine ball had gone clean through and Sharpe summoned Harper to put maggots from his tin into the wound before binding it with a strip torn from the shirt of a dead man. Forrest was alive, stunned and bleeding, found where the Colours had fallen with his sword still gripped in his hand. Sharpe seated him next to Leroy. He put the Colour with the two wounded officers, propping its great yellow flag over the parapet as a symbol of defiance to the French. Then he walked gingerly to the edge of the broken roadway and hailed the far bank.

"Hello!" There could only be thirty minutes of the hour left. "Hello!"

Hogan appeared, and came across the other part of the broken bridge. It was reassuring to see the engineer's blue coat and cocked hat but there was something different about the uniform. Sharpe could not place the oddity.

"What happened?"

Hogan spread his hands. "Not my doing. Simmerson lit the fuse. He got frightened. Thought the French would swarm all over him. I tried to stop him but I'm under arrest." That was it! Hogan wore no sword. The Irishman grinned happily. "So are you, by the way."

Sharpe swore viciously and at length. Hogan let him finish. "I know, Richard, I know. It's all because we refused to let your riflemen form a skirmish line, remember?"

"He thinks that would have saved him?"

"He has to blame someone. You and I are the scapegoats." Hogan took off his hat and scratched his balding pate. "I couldn't give a damn, Richard. It'll just mean enduring the man's spleen till we get back to the army. After that we'll hear no more about it. The general will tear him apart!"

It seemed ridiculous to be discussing their mutual arrest in shouts across the gap where the water broke white on the shattered stonework. Sharpe waved his hand at the wounded.

"What about this lot? We've got dozens of wounded and the French are coming back soon. We need help. What's he doing?"

"Doing?" Hogan shook his head. "He's like a chicken with its head chopped off. I've told him he's got to get timber and ropes." He pointed at the forty-foot gap. "I can't hope to bridge this but we can make rafts and float them across. But there's no timber here. He'll have to send back for it!"

"Has he done it?"

"No." Hogan said no more. For a moment they discussed who was dead, who was wounded. Hogan asked after Lennox but Sharpe had no news. Then there was the clatter of hooves and Gibbons rode onto the bridge behind Hogan. He stared down at the engineer.

"I thought you were under arrest, Captain, and confined?"

Hogan looked up at the arrogant lieutenant. "I needed a piss."

Sharpe laughed. Hogan waved, wished him luck, and turned back to the ruined convent, leaving Sharpe facing Gibbons across the water.

"You're under arrest, Sharpe, and I am ordered to tell you that Sir Henry will request a general court martial. You must surrender your sword to me, and return the regimental Colour."

Sharpe could scarcely believe his ears. Behind him were rows of wounded men whose cries could clearly be heard yet Simmerson had sent his nephew to demand that Sharpe surrender his sword and hand over the Colour.

"Why was the bridge blown up?"

"It is not your business, Sharpe."

"It damn well is, Gibbons, I'm on the wrong bloody side of it." He looked at the elegant lieutenant whose uniform was quite unstained by any blood or earth. He suspected Simmerson's uniform would be the same. "Were you going to abandon the wounded, Gibbons? Was that it?"

The lieutenant looked at Sharpe with distaste. "Will you please fetch the Colour, Sharpe, and throw it over to this side of the bridge?"

"Go away, Gibbons." Sharpe spoke with an equal disdain. "Get your precious uncle to talk with me, not his lapdog. As for the Colour, it stays here. You deserted it and I and my men fought for it. It stays with us till you get us back across the river. Do you understand?" His voice was rising with anger. "So tell that to your fat windbag! And tell him the French are coming back for another attack. They want that Colour and that's why I'm keeping my sword, Gibbons, so that I can fight for it!" He drew the thirty-five inches of steel. There had been no time to clean the blade and Gibbons could scarce take his eyes off the crusted blood. Sharpe turned back to the wounded and dead.

Harper was waiting with a distressed face. "We found Captain Lennox, sir. He's bad."

Sharpe followed Harper through the rows of wounded. There was so little he could do! He could bind up wounds but there was no way to dull the pain. And now Lennox.

The Scotsman was white, his face drawn with pain, but he nodded and grinned when Sharpe squatted beside him.

"I told you he was mad, Richard. Now this. I'm dying." He spoke matter of factly.

Sharpe shook his head. "You're not. You'll be all right. They're making rafts. We'll get you to a doctor."

It was Lennox's turn to shake his head. It moved with agonizing slowness and he bit his lip as a fresh stab of pain shot through him. The lower half of his body was soaked in blood and Sharpe did not dare pull at the torn uniform for fear of making the wound worse. Lennox breathed a long sigh.

"Don't cheat me, Sharpe. I'm dying and I know it." His Scottish accent was thicker. "The fool tried to make me form a skirmish line."

"Me too."

Lennox frowned. "What happened?"

Sharpe told him. When he spoke of the King's Colour, Lennox flinched. The disgrace of it hurt more than the ripped-open body that was killing him.

"Sir! Sir!" A private was calling Sharpe but he waved him away. Lennox was trying to say something but the private insisted. "Sir!"

Sharpe turned and saw three chasseurs trotting towards him. The hour must be up.

Lennox's hand gripped Sharpe's. "Listen. I have something I want to ask you. Will you come back? Promise?"

Sharpe nodded. "I promise." He stood up, surprised that he had to wipe his vision clear, and walked to the waiting chasseurs. The captain who had come before was there and with him two troopers. Sharpe saluted.

"M'sieu, the hour is up."

"We have still not collected all our wounded."

The Frenchman looked round the field. There was another hour's work and that was before Sharpe could hope to begin dealing with the dead. He turned back and spoke gently.

"I think, m'sieu, you must consider yourselves our prisoners."

Sharpe thought of the muskets he had collected, each one loaded, each checked. They would destroy the French if they were foolish enough to attack. He bowed slightly to the chasseur.

"You will see sir, I am not from the regiment whose standard you captured. I am a rifleman. I do not surrender." A little bravado, he decided, was not out of place. After all, the French captain had to be bluffing; he was experienced enough to know that his men would not break a properly led formation and he had proof enough that the tall rifleman could provide that leadership. Sharpe looked pointedly at the rows of wounded. "I must get on, sir. If you wish to attack again, that is your affair." He turned away but the Frenchman demanded his attention.

"You do not understand, Lieutenant."

He pointed up the hill to the far skyline where there was a sudden movement. Sharpe saw riderless horses, and knew what they meant. A gun. The French had brought up a field gun that could pound his small force into oblivion. He looked back to the captain who shrugged.

"Now you understand, Lieutenant?"

Sharpe stared at the horizon. Only one gun? It was probably a small four-pounder so why only one? Presumably the chasseurs, faced with two regiments, had sent a message back to their main force. But if they were short of horses then it was possible that the others were still miles behind. There was an idea far back in his head. He looked at the captain.

"It makes no difference, m'sieu." He held up his sword. "Today you are the second person who has demanded my sword. I give you the same answer. You must come and take it for yourself."

The Frenchman smiled, raised his own sword, and bowed. "It will be my pleasure, m'sieu. I trust you will survive the encounter and do me the honour of dining with me afterwards."

The captain rattled orders in French and the three men turned their horses back up the slope. Sharpe hurried back to Lennox and Harper, all the time trying to pin the thought in his head. There was so much to be done and so little time to do it, but he had promised Lennox he would return. He glanced back. The gun, with its limber, was coming slowly down the hill. He had half an hour yet.

Lennox was still alive. He spoke softly and quickly to Sharpe and Harper, who looked at each other, but promised the Scotsman his last request. Sharpe squeezed his hand.

"I had already promised that to myself."

Lennox smiled. "You'll not let me down, I know. And Harper and you can do it."

They had to leave him to die alone, there was no choice. The Scotsman's only other request was that he should die with a sword in his hand. They walked reluctantly away.

The big sergeant said, "Can we do it, sir?"

"We promised, didn't we?"

"Aye, but it's never been done."

"Then we'll be the first!" Sharpe spoke fiercely. "Now come on, we've got work to do!" Keeping the promise must wait: first there was this day's business to complete. He stared at the gun. He knew now that his idea could work. There were unanswered questions, and he put himself in the place of his enemies and tracked the answers down, measuring distances, angles, lines of fire. He was excited, there was hope despite the field gun. He summoned the lieutenants, the sergeants.

"Listen . . . ."

FORREST MARCHED beside Sharpe, the two of them a few paces in front of the solitary Colour that waved over the small formation of one hundred and seventy men who had paraded in three ranks across the road.

Forrest had insisted on coming along rather than stay with the wounded by the bridge. He was still a little dazed by the blow on his head, and he had refused Sharpe's offer to command the survivors in the face of the new French onslaught.

"Will it work, Sharpe?" he asked.

His companion grinned. "So far it has, Major. They think we're mad."

Sharpe was grateful that Forrest had given his blessing to what seemed to be an act of utter folly, yet Sharpe's instincts told him the plan would work. To the watching and waiting chasseurs it looked as if the small British force was intent on committing suicide by a hopeless death-and-glory charge. Forrest had asked, almost plaintively, why the enemy were continuing the fight, had they not already won a big enough victory? But the French must know how pitifully small was Wellesley's army, just a little over twenty thousand men. If they could utterly destroy this Light Company, the French were giving themselves that much more certainty of annihilating Wellesley when the real battle came. Besides that, Sharpe was now offering them the chance to capture a second British Colour.

"Is it time, Sharpe?" Forrest was anxious.

"No, sir. A minute yet."

They marched straight up the track towards the gun, which was now three hundred yards away. Sharpe's plan had depended on two things, and the enemy had obliged by doing both. First they had brought the small four-pounder as close to the British as safety allowed. They would not want to use solid roundshot against the infantry. Sharpe knew they would load the gun with canister instead: the deadly metal container of musket balls and scrap iron that shattered as soon as it left the barrel and sprayed its lethal mixture like bent nails fired from a coachman's blunderbuss. And now the British were marching straight for the gun, like sheep walking into a slaughterhouse, so that the French gunners no doubt imagined they would probably need no more than three rounds to tear them apart and could then let the cavalry finish the dazed survivors off.

Sharpe's second guess had been about the cavalry. The ground to the right was thinly strewn with bodies, unlike the left which was an obstacle course of dead men and horses, and Sharpe had guessed that the French colonel, charging obliquely to the fire of his cannon, would want an unobstructed path for the horsemen. Nevertheless, he felt an enormous relief when they did indeed parade to the right. If they had gone to the left the plan could never have worked and the British would have had no option but to die by the bridge.

He watched the French gunners. They were unhurried, and they glanced constantly at the British force which marched conveniently towards their gun. It was pointing directly at Sharpe. He could see the dirty green-painted carriage, the dulled brass barrel, and the blackened muzzle. Now a blue-coated gunner was putting the serge bag with its one and a half pounds of black powder into the cannon. A second man rammed it down and Sharpe saw a third man lean over the touch-hole and thrust down with a spike so that the serge bag was pierced and the powder could be set off by the fuse. Another gunner was walking forward with the metal canister. It was only seconds now before the gun would be ready to fire. He lifted his rifle into the air and pulled the trigger.

"Now!"

His one hundred and seventy men began to run. Each soldier carried three loaded muskets, two slung on their shoulders, one carried in their hands. They kept roughly aligned, so that if the cavalry moved they could close ranks in seconds, form an impenetrable wall of bayonets. The French gunners heard the rifle shot, paused to watch their enemy break into their cumbrous run, and grinned at the futility of the men who thought they could charge a field gun. Then everything changed.

In the twenty minutes after the visit of the chasseur captain the British had continued to collect their wounded. Sharpe was certain the French had noticed nothing odd about the stream of men who went to and from the bodies that lay thickly around the spot just a hundred paces away to the left where he and Harper had saved the regimental Colour. In those twenty minutes Sharpe had hidden thirty men among the dead, ten riflemen who lay crumpled in borrowed red jackets, and twenty men of the South Essex. Each rifleman carried two rifles, one borrowed from a comrade, and every redcoat lay with three loaded muskets.

Harper lay among them, sweating in his borrowed jacket. It was much too small for him and he had ripped the seams in both armpits. But the red jackets were essential. The French would have been certain to notice if suddenly ten bodies in green uniforms had appeared among the corpses. Harper watched Sharpe march towards him, still two hundred and fifty yards away, and heard Lieutenant Knowles sigh with relief as the sound of Sharpe's rifle shot came flatly up the field. Harper stretched his cramped muscles and knelt. "Take your time, lads, make the shots tell."

The riflemen aimed deliberately: their first shots would be the most important. As Harper had expected, Hagman, the Cheshire ex-poacher, was first, and the gunner who was on the point of inserting the fuse spun away from the barrel and fell. In the next two seconds three more of the French gun crew were slaughtered, the four survivors scrambling desperately for the scanty cover provided by the trail and the spokes of the gun's wheels. The gun could not be fired now. The canister was still not loaded: Harper could see it lying on the ground, and any man who dared try to thrust it into the barrel would be cut down by the rifles which, unlike the muskets, were deadly accurate at a hundred paces.

"Cease firing!" The riflemen looked at Harper. "Hagman!"

"Sarge?"

"Keep them busy. Gataker, Sims, Harvey! You load for Hagman. You others, with rifles, aim for the cavalry officers."

Knowles and the twenty men with muskets were there to protect the riflemen if the French horsemen charged them, as surely they must. Lieutenant Knowles ran and crouched beside the sergeant.

"Is there anything we can do?"

"Not yet, sir. We'll move in a minute."

The cavalry seemed as surprised as the gunners. Harper raised his first rifle, snapped the backsight into the upright position, and guessed the horsemen were three hundred yards away. It was a long shot for a rifle, but not impossible, and the French had conveniently bunched their senior officers in a small group forward of their first line. As he pulled the trigger he heard other rifles fire, he saw the group pull apart, a horse went down, two officers fell dead or wounded. The French were temporarily leaderless. The initiative, as Sharpe had planned, had gone totally to the British. Harper stood up.

"Hagman's group! Keep firing. You others! Follow me!"

He ran towards the gun, curving wide so that Hagman had an uninterrupted field of fire, and the men followed him. The plan had been for the riflemen to destroy the gunners and let Sharpe's company capture the gun, but Harper could see his lieutenant still had a long way to go. Now the surviving French artillerymen took one final look at the seeming dead who had come to life and fled. Harper sprinted the final few yards and then he was there, his hands actually on the brass muzzle, the men surrounding him.

"Sergeant?" Knowles was panting.

"Two ranks between the gun and the cavalry?" Harper made it sound like a request as the young lieutenant was nominally in charge, but Knowles nodded as if it had been an order. He had watched Sharpe and Sergeant Harper recover the regimental Colour and had been astonished by their action. Now he wanted to prove that his men could fight as effectively, so he lined up his small force.

It seemed as if a hundred horsemen were advancing towards them, the rest were slanting off towards Sharpe's group, and Knowles remembered the sabres, the smell of fear, and gripped his sword tightly. He thought of Sharpe's last words to him. "Wait!" Sharpe had said. "Wait until they're forty paces away, then fire the volley. Wait, wait, wait!" Knowles desperately wanted to fire his first volley now, to stop the French while they were still a hundred paces away. But he controlled the fear and watched the horses walk forward, watched as a hundred sabres rasped from their scabbards and caught the afternoon sun in ranks of curved light. Harper came and stood beside him.

"We've got a treat for the bastards, sir."

He sounded so cheerful! Knowles swallowed. Wait, he told himself, and was surprised to hear that he had spoken aloud and that his voice had sounded calm. He looked at his men. They were trusting him!

"Well done, sir. May I?" Harper had spoken softly. Knowles nodded, not sure what was happening.

"Platoon!" Harper was in front of the tiny line of men. He pointed to the ten men on the right. "Sideways, four paces, march!" Then on the left, the same order.

"Platoon! Backwards. March!"

Knowles stepped back with them, watching as the French eased their horses into a trot, and then understood. While he had been watching the French, the riflemen behind him had moved the gun! Instead of pointing down the track it was now aimed at the French cavalry; they had loaded it also, and the canister which should have swept the British off the road was now threatening the French instead. Harper went to stand at the back of the gun. The gunners had done most of the loading, the riflemen had simply thrust the canister into the barrel and found the slow match that burned red at the end of a pole. The fuse was in the touch-hole. It was a reed filled with fine powder and when Harper touched it the fire would flash down the tube and ignite the powder charge in its serge bag.

"Hold your fire!" Harper shouted clearly: he did not want the inexperienced men of the South Essex to fire when the gun went off. "Hold your fire!"

The cavalry were seventy yards away, just urging their horses into the canter, ten riders in the first rank. Harper guessed that fifty men were aimed at the tiny party round the gun and there were fifty more in reserve. He touched the fuse onto the reed. There was a fizzing, a puff of smoke from the touch-hole, and then the enormous explosion. Grey-white smoke belched from the muzzle; the gun lurched back. The thin metal canister split apart as it left the muzzle and Harper watched through the smoke as the musket balls and scrap iron snatched the cavalry off the field. The first three ranks were destroyed, the other two were shocked, unable to advance over the bloody corpses and the wounded.

Harper heard Knowles shouting. "Hold your fire! Hold your fire!"

Good lad, thought the Irishman. The cavalry had split either side of the carnage, some of the reserve was galloping forward, but the horsemen seemed dazed by the sudden blow. They came on towards the gun and Knowles watched as they drew nearer. He waited, waited until they put spurs to their horses for the last few paces, and slashed his sword down.

"Fire!" The muskets coughed out flame and smoke. The leading horses dropped, making a barrier to those behind. "Change muskets!" Knowles felt the stirrings of confidence. "Fire!"

A second volley destroyed the horsemen trying to close on the two sides of the gun. More horses fell, more men were pitched from their saddles. The horsemen behind came on, lapped round the back of the gun and the rifles started their sharper reports. Knowles was startled to see no more horsemen in front of the cannon; he turned his men round, changed to the third musket, and blasted a third volley over the heads of the kneeling riflemen.

"Thank you, sir!"

Harper grinned at the lieutenant. The cavalry had gone, shattered by the canister, bloodied by the close volleys, prevented from closing with the enemy because of the barriers of dead and wounded horses, forced back out of carbine range by the more accurate British rifles. He turned back to the captured cannon and summoned the riflemen to reload it.

Sharpe had seen the four-pounder fire, watched the horsemen cut down in a bloody swathe, then he had turned to the chasseurs attacking his own formation. As the cavalry had come closer he had halted his three ranks, turned them to face the French except for the rear rank that about-turned to deal with any horsemen seeking to envelop the small formation. The chasseurs were in savage mood. An easy victory had been snatched away from them, and still the insolent Colour waved from the small group of British infantry. They spurred on, their discipline ragged, their mood simply one of revenge. Sharpe watched them come. Forrest glanced nervously at him and cleared his throat but Sharpe shook his head.

"Wait, Major, always wait."

He and Forrest stood beneath the defiant Colour. The French spurred towards it, the trumpet rang out its curdling charge, the chasseurs screamed revenge, raised their sabres, and died.

Sharpe had let them come to forty yards and the musket volley destroyed the first line. The second rank of French horsemen clapped spurs to their mounts. They were confident. Had not the British fired their volley? They jumped over the writhing remains of the first rank and to their horror saw that the red-coated ranks were not busy reloading but were calmly aiming a second set of muskets. Its volley piled the horses beside the bodies of the first line.

And then the third volley. Sharpe's men were ringed with horses, dead and dying. Stunned and wounded chasseurs struggled from the mess and ran into the wide expanse of the field. The French had lost all chance of a further attack.

"Left turn! Forward!"

Sharpe ran on. He could see Harper and Knowles. Then the cannon fired again, shrouding the group in smoke, and more horsemen fell. A few still galloped round them; once Sharpe stopped and fired a volley to drive off a group of six. Then his men reached the gun. Sharpe pounded Harper on the back, and turned to congratulate Knowles. They had done it! Captured the gun, driven off the cavalry, inflicted terrible damage on men and horses, and without a single scratch to themselves.

The French dared not attack again. They circled well clear of the gun's range as the British formed square. Sharpe looked up at the Colour. A little honour had been regained. A French gun had been captured. But that was not all: lashed to the trail of the captured gun were long, tough ropes that could span a broken bridge—all he needed to start taking the wounded back across the river.

CHAPTER 7

"Damn you, Sharpe! I will break you! You will go back to the gutter you came from!" Simmerson's face was contorted with fury. He stood with Gibbons and Forrest, and the major tried ineffectually to stem Sir Henry's anger. The colonel shook Forrest's arm off his elbow. "I'll have you court-martialled, Sharpe!"

Sharpe stood on the other side of the room, his own face rigid with the effort of controlling his own anger and scorn. They were back in Plasencia, in the Mirabel Palace which was Wellesley's temporary headquarters, and he looked down the street at the huddled rooftops of the town. Carriages passed below, smart equipages with uniformed drivers, carrying veiled Spanish ladies on mysterious journeys. Sharpe had been under arrest, his sword taken from him, when the battalion had limped home the night before, its wounded carried in commandeered ox-carts.

Many had died; more would die of gangrene in the days ahead.

The door opened and Wellesley's aide, Lieutenant-Colonel Lawford, came into the room. His face had none of the animation Sharpe had seen at their reunion just five days before. Like the rest of the army he felt shamed by the loss of the Colour. "Gentlemen. Sir Arthur will see you now. You have ten minutes."

Simmerson marched through the open door, Gibbons close behind. Forrest beckoned Sharpe to precede him but he hung back.

The general sat behind a plain oak table piled with papers and maps. There was nowhere for the four officers to sit so they lined up in front of the table. Wellesley's face was unreadable.

"Well, Sir Henry?" His tone was cold.

Sir Henry Simmerson's eyes darted round the room. He licked his lips and cleared his throat. "We destroyed the bridge, sir."

"And your battalion."

The words were said softly. Sharpe had seen Wellesley like this before, masking a burning anger with misleading quietness.

Simmerson sniffed. "The fault was hardly mine, sir."

"Ah!" The general's eyebrows went up, he laid down his quill and leaned back in the chair. "Whose then, sir?"

"I regret to say, sir, that Lieutenant Sharpe disobeyed an order. Major Forrest heard me give the order to Lieutenant Gibbons who then carried it to Sharpe. By his action Lieutenant Sharpe exposed the battalion and betrayed it." Simmerson had found his rehearsed theme and he warmed to his task. "I am requesting, sir, that Lieutenant Sharpe be court-martialled . . . ."

Wellesley held up a hand and stopped the flow of words. He looked, almost casually, at Sharpe and there was something frightening about those inscrutable blue eyes over the great, hooked nose. The eyes flicked away. "You, Lieutenant Gibbons. What happened?"

Gibbons glanced at Sharpe. His tone was supercilious. "I ordered Lieutenant Sharpe to deploy his riflemen, sir. He refused. Captain Hogan joined in his refusal."

The general's fingers beat a brief tattoo on the table. "Ah, Captain Hogan. I saw him an hour ago." The blue eyes came round to Simmerson again, the tone of voice was still mild. "I have served with Captain Hogan for many years, Sir Henry. I have always found him a most trustworthy man." He raised his eyebrows in a query as though inviting Simmerson to put him right. Simmerson, inevitably, accepted the invitation.

"Hogan, sir, is an engineer. He was not in a position to make decisions about the deployment of troops." He sounded pleased with himself.

Somewhere in the palace a clock chimed ten o'clock. Wellesley sat, his fingers drumming the table. "Your request is denied, Sir Henry. I will not court-martial Lieutenant Sharpe." He paused. "We have decisions to take about your battalion, Sir Henry."

Simmerson exploded, his voice rising indignantly. "He lost my Colour! He disobeyed!"

Wellesley's fist hit the table with a crash. "Sir! I know what order he disobeyed! I would have disobeyed it! You proposed sending skirmishers against cavalry! Is that right, sir?"

Simmerson said nothing, aghast at the tumult of anger that was overwhelming him. Wellesley went on.

"First, Sir Henry, you had no business in taking your battalion over the bridge. It was damned foolish. Secondly, only a fool deploys skirmishers against cavalry. You have disgraced this army in front of our foes and our allies." Wellesley's voice was hard. "The only credit gained in this miserable engagement was by Lieutenant Sharpe. I understand, sir, that he regained one of your lost Colours and moreover captured a French gun and used it with some effect on your attackers. Is that correct?"

No one spoke. Sharpe stared rigidly ahead at a picture on the wall behind the general. Wellesley picked up a sheet of paper from the desk. His voice was lower.

"You have lost, sir, as well as your Colour, two hundred and forty-two men either killed or injured. You lost a major, three captains, five lieutenants, four ensigns and ten sergeants. Are my figures correct?" Again no one spoke. Wellesley stood up. "The next time, Sir Henry, I suggest you fly a white flag and save the French the trouble of unsheathing their swords!"

Simmerson had blanched. Sharpe had never seen Wellesley so angry. "You no longer have a battalion, Sir Henry. I wish I could send you home! But I cannot. My hands are tied, sir, by Parliament and by meddling politicians like your cousin. I am declaring your battalion, Sir Henry, to be a Battalion of Detachments. You will serve in General Hill's division."

"But sir—" Simmerson was overwhelmed. To be called a Battalion of Detachments? It was unthinkable! In every campaign there were small units of men, like Sharpe and his riflemen, who got separated from their units. They were the flotsam and jetsam of the army and the simplest solution, when there were enough of them, was for the general to tie them together as a temporary Battalion of Detachments. But by doing that now Wellesley was literally wiping the name "South Essex" from his army list; it was a punishment aimed at Simmerson's pride.

"I will attach new officers myself," Wellesley went on. Then, as Simmerson stammered a protest, "Are you telling me you have promised promotion already?"

Simmerson nodded. Wellesley looked at his sheet of paper. "To whom, Sir Henry, have you given command of the Light Company?"

"To Lieutenant Gibbons, sir."

"Your nephew?" Wellesley paused to make sure that Simmerson answered. The colonel nodded bleakly. Wellesley turned to Gibbons. "You concurred in your uncle's order to advance a skirmish line?"

Gibbons was trapped. He licked his lips, shrugged, and finally agreed. Wellesley shook his head.

"Then you are plainly not a fit person to lead a Light Company. No, Sir Henry, I am giving you one of the finest skirmishers in the British army. I can think of few men who are better leaders of Light Troops in battle than Mr. Sharpe. And I am gazetting him Captain."

Sharpe felt the flutter of hope. He had done it, he had become a captain! Captain Sharpe! The victory was complete, the enemy routed! What did it matter that the gazette was an artificial promotion needing official confirmation? It would do for a while.

Wellesley was bringing the interview to a close. Simmerson made one final effort, desperately clinging to whatever shreds of dignity he could. "I shall write, sir. I shall write to Whitehall, and they will know the truth of this!"

"You may do what you like, sir, but you will kindly let me get on with waging a war. Good day."

Lawford opened the door. Simmerson clapped on his cocked hat and the four officers turned to go. Wellesley spoke.

"Captain Sharpe! A word with you."

"Sir?" It was the first time he had been called "Captain".

Lawford closed the door on the other three. Wellesley eyed Sharpe, his expression still grim. "You disobeyed an order."

"Yes, sir."

Wellesley looked tired. "I have no doubt but that you deserve a captaincy. Whether you will keep it, Sharpe, is another matter. It is likely that London will cancel all these dispositions. Do you understand?"

"Yes, sir."

Wellesley looked up at Sharpe with a kind of wry distaste. "You have a habit, Sharpe, of deserving gratitude by methods that deserve condemnation. Am I plain?"

"Yes, sir." Sharpe kept his face expressionless.

Wellesley smiled ruefully. "I am glad to see you well. Your career is always interesting to watch, Sharpe, though I constantly fear it will end precipitately. Good day, Captain."

Sharpe left and Lawford followed him into the empty anteroom and put out his hand. "Congratulations."

"Thank you, sir. A Battalion of Detachments, eh?"

Lawford looked embarrassed. "That won't please Sir Henry." He walked across to the window and stared past the heavy velvet curtains at the plain beyond the walls; the whole scene doused in the relentless sun. "Simmerson is too powerful. I am afraid that he will damage you. He has friends in high places." He turned to Sharpe. "They will demand a scapegoat. When he writes from Spain and says the war is being conducted wrongly then his letter will be read in Parliament and people will listen! It doesn't matter that the man is as mad as a turkey-cock!"

Sharpe nodded wearily. "What you're saying is that pressure will be applied for me to be sacrificed so that Simmerson can survive?"

Lawford nodded. "I'm afraid so."

Sharpe knew he spoke the truth. For a few weeks he was safe, safe while Wellesley marched farther into Spain and brought the French to battle, but after that a letter would come from London. He was sure Wellesley would look after him, but he would still eke out his years under a cloud as the man named officially responsible for losing Simmerson's Colour.

"There is another way." He spoke quietly.

Lawford looked at him. "What?"

"When I saw the Colour being lost I made a resolution. I also made a promise to a dying man." It sounded desperately melodramatic but it was the truth. "I promised to replace that Colour with an Eagle."

In the last six years the French had appeared on the battlefields with new standards. In place of the old Colours they now carried gilded eagles mounted on poles. Each Eagle was personally presented to the regiment by the Emperor himself, so that the standards were more than just a symbol of the regiment, they were a symbol of all France's pride in its new order.

There was a moment of silence. Lawford whistled softly. He knew that the only thing that could stop the officials in Whitehall singling out Sharpe for punishment was if the rifleman performed a deed of such undoubted merit that they would look foolish trying to make him a scapegoat. It was not enough that he had regained a Colour and captured a gun. No, he had to go further, risk his life in an attempt to keep his job.

Sharpe laughed ironically. He slapped his empty scabbard. "Someone once said that in this job you're only as good as your last battle." He paused. "Unless of course you have money or influence. Now I'll go and join the happy throng. I presume my riflemen come with me?"

Lawford nodded. "Good luck." He watched Sharpe go. If any man could pluck an Eagle from the French he was that man. Lawford stood by the window. Down in the street he saw Sharpe step into the sunlight and put on his battered shako; a huge sergeant was waiting in the shade, the kind of man Lawford would happily wager a hundred guineas on in a bare-fisted prizefight, and he watched as the sergeant walked up to Sharpe. The two men talked for a moment and then the big sergeant clapped the officer's back and uttered a whoop of joy that Lawford heard two floors above.

THE BOOTS of the Coldstream Guards rang on the flagstones, echoing hollowly in the darkness, fading down the steep street to be replaced by the leading companies of the 3rd Guards. They were followed by the first battalion of the 61st, the second of the 83rd, and then by four battalions of the King's German Legions. Sharpe, standing in a church porch, watched the Germans march past.

"They're good troops, sir."

Major Forrest peered into the darkness. "What are they?"

"King's German Legion." The Germans were a foreign corps of the army and the law said they were allowed no nearer the British mainland than the Isle of Wight. Overhead the church clock struck. It was three o'clock on the morning of Monday, July 17th, 1809, and the British army was leaving Plasencia. Another German unit went past, a company of the 60th with the incongruous title of the Royal American Rifles. Forrest saw Sharpe staring ruefully at the marching riflemen with their green jackets and black belts.

"Homesick, Sharpe?"

Sharpe grinned in the darkness. "I'd rather it was my own rifle regiment, sir." He yearned for the sanity of the 95th rather than the worsening moroseness of Simmerson's battalion.

Forrest shook his head. "I'm sorry, Sharpe. He showed me the letter, you know."

Sharpe did know. Forrest kept apologizing and had described the letter twice already. Dereliction of duty, gross disobedience, even the word "treason" had found its place into Simmerson's scathing account of Sharpe's actions at Valdelacasa; but none of that was surprising. What had disturbed him was Simmerson's final request; that Sharpe be posted to a battalion in the West Indies. Sharpe had known men resign rather than go to the sun-drenched islands where fever reduced a man's life expectancy to less than a year.

"It may not happen, Sharpe." Forrest's tone betrayed that he thought Sharpe's fate was sealed.

"No, sir." Not if I can help it, he thought, and he imagined an Eagle in his hands. Only an Eagle could save him from the islands.

Almost every unit marched before them. There were over three thousand cavalry, followed by an army of mules carrying fodder. The cumbersome artillery with their guns, limbers, and portable forges added even more mules, more supplies, but mostly it was infantry who disturbed the quiet streets. Twenty-five battalions of unglamorous infantry, with stained uniforms and worn boots.

Simmerson's battalion finally took the road across the river well after sunrise, and if the previous days had been hot it now seemed as if nature was intent on baking the landscape into one solid expanse of terracotta. The army crept across the vast, arid plain and stirred up a fine dust that hung in the air and lined the mouths and throats of the parched infantry. There was no trace of wind, just the heat and glare, the sweat that stung the eyes, and the endless sound of boots hitting the white road.

The rest of the army shunned the new Battalion of Detachments as if the men were harbouring a repulsive disease. The loss of the Colour had stained the reputation of the whole army. Simmerson's men were sullen, and cowed by his brutality. Only the Light Company retained some vestiges of pride, particularly in their new captain. He was now believed to be a magic man, a man who would bring them luck in battle. Sharpe's riflemen agreed, they had always known their officer was lucky, and they revelled in his promotion. Sharpe had been embarrassed by their pleasure, and when they offered him drinks from hoarded bottles of Spanish brandy, he covered his confusion by pretending to have duties elsewhere.

On the first night of the march the battalion bivouacked near a nameless village and the woods were filled with soldiers hacking at branches to build the fires on which they could boil the tea leaves they carried loose in their pockets. Provosts guarded the olive groves: nothing made an army so unpopular as the French habit of cutting down a village's olive trees for fuel and Wellesley had issued strict orders that the olives were not to be touched. The officers of the South Essex were billeted in the village inn. It was a large building, and behind it was a courtyard with cypress trees beneath which were tables and benches. The yard opened onto a stream and on the far bank the men made fires and beds in a grove of cork trees. There had been pigs in the grove and as Sharpe stripped off his uniform to search the seams for lice he could smell pork cooking on various small fires. Such looting was punishable by hanging but nothing could stop it. Everyone was short of food and the tactful offer of some stolen pork would ensure that the provosts took no action.

The courtyard gradually filled with officers from the dozen battalions bivouacked in the village. The heat of the day mellowed into a warm, clear evening and the stars shone like the campfires of a limitless faraway army. From the main room of the inn came the sound of music and cheering as the officers egged on the Spanish dancers. Sharpe pushed his way through the crowded room and glimpsed Simmerson and his cronies playing cards at a corner table. Gibbons was there and for a second Sharpe thought about the girl. Her name was Josefina Lacosta. He had seen her once or twice since the return from the bridge and had listened to the rumours about her; that she was the widow of a rich Portuguese officer, or that she had run away from the Portuguese officer, no one seemed sure, but what was certain was that she had met Gibbons at a ball in Lisbon and, within hours, had decided to go to the war with him. It was said that they planned to marry once the army reached Madrid and that Gibbons had promised her a house and a life of dancing and gaiety.

Sharpe felt a surge of jealousy. He pushed the thought away; the officers of the battalion were split enough as it was. There were

Simmerson's supporters who toadied to the colonel and there were those who had publicly supported Sharpe. It was an uncomfortable situation.

In the courtyard he found Forrest, Leroy, and a group of subalterns sitting beneath one of the cypress trees. Forrest made room for him on the bench.

"Don't you ever take that rifle off?"

"And have it stolen?" Sharpe asked. "I'd be charged for it."

Forrest smiled. "Have you paid for the stocks yet?"

"Not yet." Sharpe grimaced. "But now I'm officially on the battalion's payroll I suppose it will be deducted from my pay, whenever that arrives."

Forrest pushed a wine bottle towards him. "Don't let it worry you. Tonight the wine's on me."

There was an ironic cheer from the officers round the gambling table. Unconsciously Sharpe felt the leather bag round his neck. It was heavier by six gold pieces, thanks to the dead on the field at Valdelacasa. He drank some wine, stretched his legs under the table and leaned back against the cypress trunk. Over the sound of talk and laughter he could hear the thousands of insects that chattered and clicked through the Spanish night. . . .

A hand hit him on the back.

"So they've made you a captain! This army has no standards!" It was Hogan. Sharpe had not seen him since the day they marched back from the bridge. He stood up and took the engineer's hand. Hogan beamed at him. "I'm delighted! Congratulations!"

Sharpe blushed and shrugged. "Where have you been?"

"Oh, looking at things." Sharpe knew that Hogan had been reconnoitring for Wellesley, coming back with news of which bridges could take the weight of heavy artillery, which roads were wide enough for the army to use. Forrest invited him to sit and asked for news.

"A lot of French are up the valley." Hogan poured himself some wine. "I reckon there'll be a battle within a week."

"A week!" Forrest sounded surprised.

"Aye, Major. They're swarming all over a place called Talavera." He pronounced it "Tally-verra", making it sound like some Irish hamlet. "But once you reach Oropesa and join with Cuesta's army you'll far outnumber them."

"You've seen Cuesta's troops?" Forrest asked.

"Aye." The Irishman grinned. "They're no better than the Santa Maria." He turned back to Sharpe. "The last time I saw you, you were under arrest! Now look at you. How's good Sir Henry?" There was a laugh round the table. Hogan did not wait for an answer but dropped his voice. "So what happens now?"

"I don't know." Sharpe spoke quietly. Only Hogan could hear him. "Simmerson has written home. I'm told that he has the power to stop London ratifying the gazette, so in six weeks I'll be a lieutenant again. But what about you? You were under arrest too."

Hogan shrugged. "Sir Henry forgave me. He doesn't take me seriously, I'm just an engineer. No, it's you he's after. You're an upstart, a rifleman, you're not a gentleman but you're a better soldier than he'll ever be." Hogan leaned nearer. "There'll be a battle soon. The—"

A woman's scream, terrifying and intense, came from one of the upper windows behind the balconies that ran round the courtyard, stopping all conversation beneath the trees. Sharpe got to his feet and reached instinctively for his rifle. Forrest put a hand on his arm. "It's not our business, Sharpe."

In the courtyard there was a moment's silence, some nervous laughter, and then the conversation started again. Sharpe felt uneasy, ashamed that he had done nothing.

Before Sharpe could move there came a man's bellow of rage. A door burst open, spilling yellow candlelight onto the balcony, and a woman ran out of the room and darted towards the stairs. A voice shouted. "Stop her!"

The girl tore down the stairs. The officers in the courtyard cheered her on and shouted abuse at the figure who emerged after her, Lieutenant Gibbons. He looked drunk and lurched as he blinked round the courtyard.

"It's Josefina." Forrest said.

Sharpe watched the girl half-run, half-fall down the stairs. For a second she looked desperately round for help. She was carrying a bag and Sharpe had a glimpse of what could have been a knife in her hand, and then she turned and ran into the darkness towards the lights of the battalion's fires. Gibbons stopped halfway down the stairs. One hand was clutching his unbuttoned shirt to his stomach, in the other hand was a pistol. "Come back, you lousy bitch!"

"What's the matter, Gibbons? Girl took your Colours?" The

voice came from one of the tables in the courtyard. Gibbons, his face furious, ran off towards the stream.

"There's going to be trouble." Sharpe climbed from the bench. "I'm going."

He threaded his way through the tables, Forrest and Hogan following. He splashed through the stream; there was no sight of the girl or her pursuer, just the lights in the cork grove and the occasional silhouette of a man crossing in front of the flames. Sharpe paused to let his eyes become accustomed to the dark, then ran ahead of the other two, keeping the silver track of the stream to his left, holding the rifle in his right hand.

In front Sharpe heard a scream. He ran faster, fearing the sound of a shot. Suddenly he saw Gibbons, trying to force the bag out of the hands of the kneeling girl. He heard him shouting at Josefina. "Let go, you bitch!"

Sharpe kept running. Gibbons looked up, startled, and then Sharpe hit him full tilt. The lieutenant was thrown backwards, the pistol flew from his hand and splashed into the stream, and Sharpe saw the bag fall from Josefina's hand and spill bright gold onto the dark grass. Gibbons tried to struggle to his feet but Sharpe pushed him with the rifle butt. "Don't move." He turned to see Forrest and Hogan arrive.

"Is she all right?" Forrest asked.

Sharpe looked at Josefina, at her bare shoulders and low-cut dress. He realized, irrelevantly, that it was the first time he had seen her not dressed in riding breeches. Her head was down; at first he thought she was sobbing, but then he saw her desperately picking up the scattered gold coins.

Forrest knelt at the girl's side. "Are you all right?"

The girl nodded.

His voice was paternal, kindly. "What's all this about?"

"We were playing cards. I won."

"So?"

"There was an argument. Christian hit me."

Sharpe turned towards Gibbons. The lieutenant had got to his feet. There was a small bloodstain on his shirt and Sharpe remembered the knife; Josefina had evidently cut at him but had done little damage. "Is it true?"

Gibbons's reply was invested with all the contempt he had for the lower classes. "Try to understand. We were playing cards. Miss

Lacosta lost her money and refused to pay up. Instead she decamped with the money. That is all."

"It's not true!" Josefina was crying. She came up to Sharpe, looked at him with eyes wet with tears, and clasped the bag between her hands. "It is not true. We were playing cards. I won. He tried to steal it from me! I thought he was a gentleman!"

Gibbons laughed. Sharpe turned on him. "You hit her?" He had seen a bruise on her cheek.

"You wouldn't understand how gentlemen behave, Sharpe." Gibbons sounded bored. "You'll believe her, because she's a whore, and you're used to whores. You're not used to gentlemen."

"Call me 'sir'."

Anger flared in Gibbons' face. "Go to hell."

Sharpe hit him in the solar plexus and as Gibbon's head came forward Sharpe lowered his own and butted him between the eyes. Gibbons reeled, blood dripping from his nose, and Sharpe dropped the rifle to hit him again. Gibbons folded up and vomited.

"Major Hogan?"

"Lieutenant?"

"Mr. Gibbons is a little the worse for drink, I believe."

The colonel's nephew got uncertainly to his feet, gasping, and turned to stammer at Forrest. "You saw him. He hit me!"

Hogan stepped forward, his voice crisp and authoritative. "Nonsense, lieutenant. You were drunk and fell. Go home to bed."

The lieutenant stumbled into the darkness. Sharpe watched him go. "Bastard!"

Hogan smiled sadly, and turned to the girl. "What are you going to do now?"

"Do?" She looked at Hogan and then at Sharpe. "I cannot go back. But all my clothes! They are in that room."

Forrest stepped forward, a concerned expression on his face. "Your clothes?"

"All my things! He'll kill me!"

Hogan's shrewd eyes flicked from the girl to Forrest. Then he took Josefina by the elbow. "Go with Major Forrest and rescue your things. Hurry!"

"But where do I spend the night?"

Sharpe cleared his throat. "She can use my room. I can double up with Hogan."

Forrest twitched at her elbow. "Come, my dear, we must hurry."

The two of them splashed through the stream and hurried towards the lights of the inn. Hogan watched them go. "You know what you're doing, Richard?" His voice was non-committal.

Sharpe leaned down to pick up his rifle. "What do you mean?"

The Irishman smiled. "She's beautiful. There aren't many as good-looking as that one; at least, not outside Cork." The small joke was made to lighten his tone, which was sad. "Well, you rescued her so she's yours for the moment. Will you be sending her home to Lisbon?" Sharpe started walking and said nothing. Hogan caught up with him. "Are you in love with her?"

"For God's sake!"

"And what's wrong with that?" They walked in silence for a few yards until Hogan felt in his pocket and held out a handful of guineas. "I'll wager you these against one rifle bullet that you won't double up with me tonight."

Sharpe stared down at Hogan's friendly, concerned face. It would be so easy to win the bet. All he had to do was put Josefina in his room and then walk to Hogan's billet and collect the handful of gold. There were six months' wages there, just for staying clear of the girl. Sharpe pushed the money away. "I don't gamble and I need all my bullets."

Hogan laughed. "That's true. But don't tell me I didn't warn you." He put a hand on Sharpe's belt, opened the ammunition pouch, and poured in the gold. Sharpe protested but Hogan forced the money inside. "Women don't come free. You'll need it, Richard. And don't worry. There'll be a battle soon and you'll shoot a rich man and then give me the money back."

They walked on in silence, back into the lights of the inn's courtyard. Hogan looked up at Sharpe and cuffed him gently on the arm. "Sleep well, Richard."

Sharpe grinned back. "Don't worry." He took the stairs three at a time, his boots squelching on the wooden steps.

CHAPTER 8

When the battalion arrived at Oropesa the Spanish army had been waiting for some days, and had long eaten any spare food from the surrounding countryside. The supply situation was hopeless and there was friction between the allies. British and German patrols had even ambushed Spanish supply wagons to get hold of the food Cuesta had promised to Wellesley but never delivered.

Sharpe felt his own hunger as he walked down the steep street. Josefina's servant had found food, at a price, and at least tonight he would eat. The two rooms she had found were costing a fortnight's pay every night but, he thought, the hell with it. If the worst came to pass and he was forced to choose between a West Indies commission and civilian life then damn the money and enjoy it. Rent the rooms, pay through the nose for a scrawny chicken, and carry into the fever ward the remembrance of Josefina and the extraordinary luxury of a shared bed. So far there was only the memory of the one night at the inn and then she had ridden ahead, grudgingly escorted by Hogan, while Sharpe spent two days marching through the dust and heat with the battalion. But now there was a whole evening, a long night, and no march tomorrow.

SHARPE WOKE with a start, sat up, instinctively reached for a weapon and then, realizing where he was, sank back on the pillow. He was covered with sweat though the night was cool and a small breeze stirred the edges of the curtains. Josefina sat beside the bed, watching him, a glass of wine in her hand. "You were dreaming."

"Yes."

"What about?"

"My first battle." He looked at the girl. "Why are you up?"

She shrugged. "I couldn't sleep." She had put on some kind of dark robe and only her face and the hand holding the glass were visible in the unlit room. "I was thinking. About what you said."

Somewhere in the town a dog barked but there were no other sounds. Sharpe thought back to the evening's long conversation with Josefina. She wanted to reach Madrid, and Sharpe had told her he thought it unlikely now that the allies would get as far as that.

"Why not go back to Lisbon?"

"My husband's family won't welcome me, not now."

"Then go home to your parents." She had been brought up in Oporto, the daughter of an important merchant. She had learned English because the rich families who dominated the port trade in her home town were English. Then she had married Duarte, ten years her senior, keeper of the King's Falcons in Lisbon. It was a courtier's job, and she had loved the glitter of the palace, the fashionable life. Then, two years before, Duarte had taken a mistress and Josefina had been left in the big house with his parents.

"Home? You don't understand. They will force me to wait for him just like his parents do." Her voice was edged with despair. "They want me to go into a convent. Can you believe that? That I should wait for him in a convent, a dutiful wife, while he fathers bastards on that woman?"

Sharpe rolled off the bed and walked to the window. He leaned on the black ironwork, oblivious of his nakedness, and stared towards the east, but there was nothing to be seen except the moonlight on the countryside and the falling roofs of the town. Josefina came and stood beside him and ran her fingers down the scars on his back. "You still don't understand. I'm a married woman and I've run away. The day I left Duarte's parents I became alone. I can't go back there, my parents will not forgive me. I thought in Madrid . . . ." She tailed away.

"And Christian Gibbons said he would look after you in Madrid?"

She nodded.

He tilted her face towards him. "Now you're worried. No Madrid and you're with someone who has no money and you're thinking of all those nights in the fields or flea-ridden cottages?"

She smiled up at him. "One day, Richard, you'll be a colonel with a big horse, and lots of money, and you'll be horrible to all the captains and lieutenants."

He laughed. "But not quickly enough for you?" He knew she would find a man richer than he, a cavalry officer with money to spare and an eye for a woman. He pulled her to him, feeling the night air chill on his skin. "I'll look after you."

"Promise?" Her voice was muffled.

"I promise."

"Then I won't be frightened." She pulled slightly away. "You're cold?"

"It doesn't matter."

"Come on." She led him back into the dark room. He knew that she was his for only a short time, and he was sad.

THE BATTALION paraded in companies, forming three sides of a hollow square. The fourth side, instead of the accustomed flogging triangle, was made up of two leaning poplar trees that grew beside a shallow pool. The fringes of the pond had been trampled by cavalry and the mud had dried into ochre lumps streaked with green scum. Between the trees lay the battalion's bass drum and on its grey stretched skin there rested an open Bible and prayer book. There was no wind to stir the pages, just the sun continuing its relentless assault on the plain and on the men who sweated at attention in full uniform. Simmerson was mounted in the centre of the square next to General Hill who, with his staff, had come to fulfil his duty of watching execution done. Two deserters had slipped past the guard in the night, and now they had been found.

Sharpe stood before the Light Company at the left of the line and stared over the heads of the Grenadier company opposite at the castle of Oropesa. Sweat stung his eyes, dripped onto his green jacket, trickled down his spine. He felt curiously light-hearted, not at all a fit state to watch deserters blown into eternity, and as he stared at the castle he thought of Josefina—she was his only for as long as she needed him, but in return she offered him her happiness and vivacity. And somehow, in the morning light, the bargain did not seem such a bad one.

He looked at Gibbons, paraded on his horse with the Light Company. Gibbons sat, stony-faced, and stared straight ahead. Sharpe could feel the hatred almost radiating from the man, the determination for revenge, for Sharpe had not only gained the promotion Gibbons wanted but, worse than that, the rifleman had the girl too.

Fourteen men, all defaulters, marched into the square and stood facing the trees. Their punishment was to act as the firing squad, and as the men stood there, their muskets grounded, they stared with fascination at the two newly-dug graves and the crude wooden coffins that waited.

Sharpe had seen many executions, and had seen men blown from the muzzles of decorated brass cannon, their bodies shredded into the Indian landscape. He had hanged men by a roadside himself, yet most often he had seen men shot in the full panoply of ritual execution. He had never enjoyed the spectacle, but he knew it was necessary. This execution was subtly different. It was not that the two men did not deserve to die: they had deserted, and there could be no end for them other than the firing squad. Yet coming on top of the fight at the bridge, coming on top of Simmerson's floggings, his repeated condemnation of his men for losing the Colour, the execution was seen by the battalion as summing up Simmerson's contempt and hatred for them. Sharpe had rarely felt such resentment from any troops.

In the distance, threading its way through the crowds of British and Spanish spectators, the provost-marshal's party appeared, prisoners and guard. Major Forrest walked his horse forward of Simmerson.

" 'Talion! Fix bayonets!"

Blades scraped out of scabbards and steel rippled round the ranks of the companies. The men must die with due ceremony. Sharpe watched Gibbons bend down to talk to the sixteen-year-old Ensign Denny. "Your first execution, Mr. Denny?"

The youngster nodded. He was pale and apprehensive.

Gibbons chuckled. "Best target practice the men can have!"

"Quiet!" Sharpe glared at them. Gibbons smiled secretly.

" 'Talion! Shoulder arms!"

The lines of men became tipped with bayonets. There was silence. The prisoners wore trousers and shirts, no jackets, and a chaplain walked with them. But they seemed to take no notice of him as they were marched to the trees, and Sharpe supposed them to be half full of rough brandy or rum. The drama moved inexorably forward. The men were tied to the trunks, blindfolded, and Forrest stood the firing squad to attention.

Forrest gave no commands. The firing party had been rehearsed to obey signals rather than orders, and they presented and aimed to jerks of the major's sword. He dropped the sword, the muskets banged, the bodies jerked, and a flock of birds burst screeching from the branches. Two lieutenants ran forward with drawn pistols but the musket balls had done their work.

A murmur, barely audible, went through the ranks of the battalion. Sharpe turned on his men. "Quiet!"

The Light Company stood silent. The smoke from the firing party smelt pungent in the air. The murmur became louder. Officers and sergeants screamed orders but the men of the South Essex had found their protest and the humming became more insistent. Sharpe kept his own company quiet by sheer force, glaring at them with drawn sword, but he could do nothing about the contempt that they showed on their faces. It was not aimed at him, it was for Simmerson, and the colonel twitched his reins in the centre of the square and bellowed vainly for silence.

Gradually, as the executioners' smoke thinned into the air, the moaning and humming died away. General Hill had not moved or spoken but now he motioned to his aides-de-camp and the small group trotted delicately away, past the firing squad who now lifted the bodies into the coffins. Hill's face was expressionless. He had a reputation as a kind and considerate officer and Sharpe wondered what he thought of Simmerson and his methods.

Simmerson rode his horse to the graves, wrenched the beast round, and stood in his stirrups. His face was suffused with blood, his rage obvious, his voice shrill. "You will pay for that display! There will be a parade for punishment at six o'clock this evening. Full equipment!" The men stood silent. Simmerson lowered his rump onto the saddle. "Major Forrest! Carry on!"

The battalion marched past the open coffins and the men were made to stare at the mangled bodies waiting by their graves. There, said the army, is what will happen to you if you run away.

ONE MAN IN TEN was to be flogged, six from each company, three dozen strokes each for sixty men, the captain of each company to deliver his men, stripped to the waist, ready to be tied to the flogging triangles that Simmerson was having made by local carpenters. The colonel made his announcement and then glared round the assembled officers. Were there any comments?

Sharpe took a breath. To say anything was useless, to say nothing was cowardly. "I think it a bad idea, sir."

"Captain Sharpe thinks it a bad idea." Simmerson dripped acid with every word. "Captain Sharpe, gentlemen, can tell us how to command men. Why is it a bad idea?"

"To shoot two men in the morning and flog sixty in the afternoon seems to me to be doing the work of the French for them, sir."

"Damn you, Sharpe, and damn your ideas. If the discipline in this battalion was as strictly enforced by the captains as I demand, then this punishment would not be necessary. I will have them flogged! And that includes your precious riflemen, Sharpe! I expect three of them in your six! There'll be no favouritism."

There was nothing to be said or done. The captains told their companies and, like Sharpe, cut straws and drew lots to determine who should be Simmerson's victims. By two o'clock the victims were scrounging for spirits that might dull their flesh and their sullen companions began the long afternoon of cleaning and polishing their kit for Simmerson's inspection. Sharpe left them to their work and went back to battalion headquarters. There was trouble in the air, a mood reminiscent of the heaviness before a thunderstorm, and Sharpe's earlier happiness was replaced by apprehension. He found himself wondering what might happen before he went back to the house where Josefina waited for him.

He spent the afternoon laboriously filling in the company books. Each month the Day Book had to be copied into the ledger and the ledger was due for Simmerson's inspection in a week. He found ink, sharpened a quill, and with his tongue between his teeth began writing the details. To Thomas Cresacre, Private, was debited the cost of one new shoe-brush. Fivepence. Sharpe sighed; the entry in the columns hid a small tragedy. Cresacre had hurled the brush at his wife and the wooden back had split against a stone wall. Sergeant McGivern had seen it happen and so on top of his marital troubles Thomas Cresacre would now lose fivepence from a day's pay of twelvepence. The next entry was for a pair of shoes for Jebediah Horrell. Sharpe hesitated. Horrell claimed the shoes had been stolen and Sharpe was inclined to believe him. Horrell was a good man, a sturdy labourer from the Midlands, and Sharpe always found his musket cared for and his equipment orderly. And Horrell had already been punished. For two days he had marched in borrowed boots and his feet had blistered. Sharpe crossed the entry from the ledger and wrote "Lost in Action". He had saved Private Horrell six shillings and sixpence. He drew the Accoutrement Book towards him and laboriously copied the information from the ledger into the book. He was amused to see that Lennox had already described every man in the company as having lost a stock "in Action", so officially the stocks, like Horrell's boots, were now a charge on the government rather than on the individual who had lost them.

For an hour he copied the small change of daily soldiering. When he had finished he drew the Mess Book towards him. This was easier. Against each name Sharpe wrote the figure three shillings and sixpence, the sum that was debited each week for the cost of their food. It was unfair, he knew: the men were already on half rations because their Spanish allies had failed to deliver a hundredth part of the supplies they had promised. But it was not in Sharpe's power to reduce the amount the men paid. Instead, he noted at the bottom of the page that the sum was double the food delivered and hoped that he would be ordered to redress the balance later. In the next column he wrote fourpence in each line, the cost of having the mens' clothes washed by the wives. Each private earned a shilling a day, but by the time he had been deducted for food, for washing, for pipeclay and blackball, for soling and heeling, and the one day's pay each year that went to the military hospitals at Chelsea and Kilmainham, each man was left annually with the three sevens: seven pounds, seven shillings and sevenpence a year. And Sharpe knew from bitter experience that they were lucky if they got even that. Most men lost further sums to replace missing equipment.

Sharpe finished with the books, shut them, laid the quill on the table and yawned as a clock in the town struck four. There was a knock on the door. "Who is it?"

"Me, sir." It was Harper's voice.

"Come in." Harper's face was bleak. "Well, Sergeant?"

"Trouble, sir. Bad. The whole bloody battalion refuses to parade."

Sharpe stood up. "Who knows about this?"

"Colonel does, sir. Men sent him a letter."

Sharpe swore under his breath. "Who signed it?"

"No one, sir. It just tells him that they won't parade and if he comes near they'll blow his bloody head off."

Sharpe slung on the big sword and picked up his rifle. There was a word for what was happening and the word was "mutiny". Simmerson's flogging of one man in ten could easily change—instead of being flogged men would be stood against trees and shot. He looked at Harper. "What's happening?"

"There's a lot of talk, sir. They're barricading themselves in the timberyard."

"All of them?"

Harper shook his head. "No, sir. There's a couple of hundred still in the orchard. Your company's there, sir, but the lads in the yard are trying to persuade them to join in."

Sharpe nodded. The battalion had been bivouacked in an olive grove, behind a walled timberyard with just one entrance.

Sharpe hurried out of the door. "Are there any officers at the timberyard?"

"No, sir."

"What about the sergeants?"

Harper's face was expressionless. Sharpe guessed that many of the sergeants were sympathetic to the protest but, like the big Irishman, knew better than the men what the result would be if the battalion refused to parade. "Wait here."

Sharpe ran to the officers' quarters. The rooms lay cool and empty. A woman looked at him from the kitchen, a string of peppers held in her hand, and quickly shut the door when she saw his face. Sharpe took the stairs two at a time and threw open the door of the room where the Light Company's junior officers were quartered. Ensign Denny was the only occupant, lying fast asleep on a straw mattress.

"Denny!"

The boy came awake, frightened. "Sir!"

"Where's Knowles?"

"Don't know, sir. In town, I think."

Sharpe thought for a second. "Join me in the courtyard as soon as you're dressed. Hurry."

Harper was waiting in the street. "Sergeant. I want the Light Company on parade in five minutes on the track behind the orchard. Full kit."

The sergeant opened his mouth to ask a question, saw the look on Sharpe's face, and threw a salute instead. He strode off. Denny came out of the courtyard buckling on his sword. Sharpe turned to him. "Listen carefully. You are to find out for me where Colonel Simmerson is and what he's doing. Understand?" The boy nodded. "And you're not to let him know that's what you're doing. Try the castle. Then come and find me. I'll either be on the track beside the orchard or on the square in front of the timberyard."

The boy went through his instructions. Sharpe nodded when he finished. "One more thing, Christopher." He deliberately used Denny's Christian name to give the lad reassurance. "You are not, in any circumstance, to go in the timberyard. Now, be off. If you see Lieutenant Knowles, or Major Forrest, or Captain Leroy, ask them if they'll join me. Hurry!"

Denny clutched his sword and ran off. Sharpe liked him. One day he would make a good officer if he was not first spitted on the bayonet of a French grenadier. Sharpe turned down the hill towards the timberyard. There was only one chance of averting a disaster and that was to get the battalion on parade as soon as possible, before Simmerson had time to react. There was a clatter of hooves behind him and he turned to see a rider waving at him. It was Captain Sterritt, the officer of the day.

"Sharpe! There's an officers' call at the castle. Now. Everyone."

"What's happening?"

Sterritt sketched in the events at the timberyard. Sharpe interrupted him. "I know about that. What's happening at the castle?"

"The colonel's asked to see General Hill."

There was still time. He looked up at the captain. "Listen. You haven't seen me. Understand?"

"But . . ." Sterritt's mouth dropped open. "The colonel's orders are that no one is to go near the timberyard."

"You haven't seen me so how could I have heard the order?"

"Oh." Clearly Sterritt did not know how to react. Sharpe turned, and went away down the street.

In front of the timberyard was a huge open space like an English village green except that the grass here was bleached yellow. The space was used for a weekly market but today the soldiers of a dozen battalions were using it as a football ground, the men cheering and jeering the players.

Sharpe swung left, beside the wall of the timberyard, and down towards the orchard. As he drew nearer he shouted for Harper and was rewarded by hearing a flurry of commands as the Light Company sergeants ordered the men onto the track. He stopped and watched as Harper paraded the company in four ranks. The men might be reluctant to parade, but none dared oppose him.

"Company on parade, sir!"

"Thank you, Sergeant."

Sharpe walked to the front of the company, his back to the trees and to the crowd of spectators drawn from the battalion's women mixed with men from other companies.

"We're going on parade early." They didn't move. Their eyes stared rigidly in front of them. "The six men detailed for punishment, one step forward."

There was a fractional hesitation. Then six men, three riflemen and three from the South Essex's original Light Company, took the forward pace. There was a murmur in the ranks.

"Quiet!"

The men went silent but a group of women began shouting insults and telling their men not to be cowards. Sharpe spun round. "Hold your tongues! Women can be flogged too!"

He marched the company to the market square and moved the footballers reluctantly from the thin turf. The six men to be flogged stood in the front rank wearing only trousers and shirt. Sharpe could tell from their faces that they were relieved that he had forced them onto parade. Whatever hot words had been spoken, Sharpe knew that no man really wanted to go through the hopeless business of taking on the full authority of the army. But now he had to persuade nine other companies. He walked up close to the six men.

"I know it's unfair." He spoke quietly. "You didn't make the noise this morning." He stopped. He was not sure what he wanted to say. Gataker, one of the unlucky riflemen, grinned cheerfully.

"It's all right, sir. It's not your fault."

Sharpe smiled back. He was grateful for Gataker's words. He stepped back five paces and raised his voice.

"Wait here! If any man moves he'll replace one of these six men!"

He walked towards the gates of the timberyard. As he went he wondered what trouble was brewing inside. And, more importantly, what trouble was being brewed behind the slab-like walls of the castle. He felt for his sword hilt and walked on.

"Sir! Captain! Sir!" Ensign Denny was running towards him, sword trailing, his face streaming with sweat.

"What did you find out?"

"Colonel's at the castle, sir. I think he's with the general. I met Captain Leroy and Major Forrest. Captain Leroy asked you to wait for him."

Over Denny's shoulder Sharpe saw Leroy, on his horse, coming from the steep streets that led to the castle. The American, thank God, was not hurrying: if the men in the timberyard saw panic among the officers they would think they were winning and merely become more obstinate.

Leroy walked his horse the last few yards. He nodded at Sharpe, took his hands off the reins, and lit a long black cheroot. "Sharpe."

Sharpe grinned. "Leroy."

Leroy slid off the horse and looked at Denny. "You ride a horse, young man?"

"Oh yes, sir!"

"Well, climb up on that one and keep her quiet for me. Here you are." Leroy cupped his hands and heaved the ensign up and into the saddle.

"Wait for us at the company," Sharpe said.

Denny rode away. Leroy turned to Sharpe. "There's bloody panic upstairs. Simmerson's turned green and is screaming mutiny. What's happening?"

"They've said they won't go on parade. But no one's actually ordered them to yet. My lads went easy enough. We've got to get the rest out there fast."

They walked on towards the timberyard. Leroy blew a thin stream of smoke into the air. "Simmerson's getting the cavalry."

"*What?*"

"General Hill didn't have much choice, did he? Colonel comes to him and says the troops are mutineers. So the general's ordered the KGL down here. They'll be some time, though; they weren't even saddled up."

The King's German Legion. They were the best cavalry in Wellesley's army; fast, efficient, brave, and a good choice to break up a mutiny. Sharpe dreaded the thought of the German horsemen clearing out the timberyard with their sabres.

"Where's Forrest?"

"He's coming down here. He went to look for the sergeant major. I don't think he'll wait for Sir Henry and his heavies." They were at the gates which were ajar. Leroy gestured to Sharpe. "Go ahead. I'll let you do the talking. They think you're some kind of a bloody miracle worker."

The yard was full of men lying, standing, sitting, their weapons piled, their jackets and equipment discarded. There was a fire burning in the centre of the yard which struck Sharpe as odd because of the heat of the day. Then he remembered the extra triangles which Simmerson had ordered for the mass flogging: the men had burned the timber which had been crudely nailed together ready for the punishments. As the two officers came through the gate there was a momentary hush, followed by a buzz of excited talk.

Leroy leaned against the entrance, Sharpe walked slowly through the groups of men, heading for the fire. The men were drinking, and as Sharpe went through the muttered comments and hostile looks a man ironically offered him a bottle. Sharpe knocked the man's arm with his knee as he walked past, and heard the bottle break on the ground. He came to the space in front of the fire and as he turned to face the bulk of the men the muttering died down.

He guessed there was not much fight in them: no ringleader had protested, there had only been sullen muttering.

"Sergeants!"

No one moved. There had to be sergeants in the yard. He shouted again. "Sergeants! On the double! Here!"

Still no one moved but in the corner of his eye he had the impression of a group of men, in shirts and trousers, stir uneasily. He pointed at them. "Come on. Hurry! Put your equipment on!"

They hesitated. For a moment he wondered if the sergeants were the ringleaders but then realized that they were probably afraid of the men. But they picked up jackets and belts. No one made a move to stop them. Sharpe began to relax.

"No!" A man stood up to the left. There was a hush, and the sergeants looked at the man who had spoken. He was a big man with an intelligent face. He spoke in a reasonable voice.

"We're not going. We decided that and we must keep to it!" His voice was educated. "The sergeants can go, sir, but we're not. It isn't fair."

Sharpe ignored him. This was not the time to discuss whether Simmerson's discipline was fair or unfair. Discipline existed and that was that. He turned back to the sergeants.

"Come on! Move yourselves!"

The sergeants, a dozen of them, came sheepishly to the fire. Sharpe was suddenly aware of the scorching heat of the blaze; his back was breaking out in a prickly sweat. He spoke loudly. "You've got two minutes. I want everyone on parade, properly dressed. The men to be flogged wearing shirts and trousers only. Grenadier company by the gate, the rest formed on them. Move!"

They hesitated. Sharpe took a step towards them and they suddenly snapped into action. He turned and walked into the crowded men. "On your feet! You're on parade! Hurry up!"

The burly man tried one last protest and Sharpe whipped round on him. "You want more bloody executions? Move!"

It was all over. The fight had gone out of them. Leroy joined Sharpe and, with the sergeants, they dressed the companies on the Grenadiers. They looked a mess. Their uniforms were unbrushed, their belts stained and muskets dirty. Sharpe had rarely seen a battalion in worse parade order but that was better than a mutinous rabble being chased by the efficient German cavalry.

Leroy swung open the gates, Sharpe gave the order, and the

battalion marched out in formation to line up on the Light Company. Forrest was outside. His mouth dropped as the first company emerged. He had a handful of officers and other sergeants with him and they ran to their companies and shouted orders. The battalion began to march crisply, the sergeant major hammered them into place, stood them at ease, stood them easy. Sharpe marched up to Forrest's horse, snapped to attention, and saluted.

"Battalion on parade, sir!"

Forrest looked down on him. "What happened?"

"Happened, sir? Nothing."

"But I was told they refused to parade."

Sharpe pointed at the battalion. The men were pulling their uniforms into shape, brushing the worst dirt off their jackets, punching their shakoes into shape. Forrest stared at them and back to Sharpe. "The colonel's not going to like this. He's coming here with the cavalry, Sharpe. And General Hill." He grinned, and Sharpe understood his amusement. Simmerson would be furious; he had disturbed a general, roused a regiment of cavalry, and all for a mutiny that had not happened. The thought pleased Sharpe.

The battalion stood in the heat, the bells in the town marked five o'clock and quarter past. As the clock struck the half hour there was the thunder of hooves, a cloud of dust, and the dragoons of the King's German Legion galloped onto the market square. They were splendidly turned out in their blue jackets, fur-trimmed pelisses and, on their heads, brown fur col-backs. Their sabres were drawn and they rode straight for the timberyard. Slowly it dawned on them that it was empty. Orders were shouted, horses turned, the cavalry subsided into an embarrassed silence and watched the red-coated horsemen that followed them onto the market place; Colonel Sir Henry Simmerson, with Major General Rowland Hill, aides-de-camps, officers of the battalion, and behind them other mounted officers. They all stopped. Simmerson peered into the timberyard, then looked back at the parade.

The sergeant major took his cue from Forrest. "'Talion! 'Shun!" The Battalion of Detachments snapped to attention. The sergeant major filled his chest. "'Talion! Shoulder arms!"

The three movements were perfectly timed. There was only the sound of six hundred palms slapping six hundred muskets in unison.

"'Talion will make the General Salute!" There was a general present. "Present arms!"

Sharpe swept his sword into the salute. Behind him the companies slammed the ground with their right feet, the muskets dipped in glorious precision. General Hill saluted back. The sergeant major ordered the battalion to shoulder arms, then stood the men at ease. Sharpe watched Forrest ride his horse to Simmerson and salute. He could hear nothing, but Hill seemed to be asking the questions and Sharpe saw Forrest turn in his saddle and point in the direction of the Light Company. The pointed arm turned into a beckoning one. "Captain Sharpe!"

Sharpe marched across the parade ground as though he were the regimental sergeant major on a royal parade. He cracked to a halt, saluted, and waited. Hill looked down on him, his round face shadowed by his large cocked hat.

"Captain Sharpe?"

"Sir!"

"You paraded the battalion? Is that correct?"

"Sir!" Sharpe had learned as a sergeant that repeating the word "sir" with enough force could get a man through most meetings with senior officers. Hill realized it too. He looked at his watch and then back at Sharpe. "The parade is thirty minutes early. Why?"

"The men seemed bored, sir. I thought some drill would do them good so Captain Leroy and myself brought them out."

Hill smiled. He looked at the ranks standing immobile in the sunlight. "Tell me, Captain, did anyone refuse to parade?"

"Refuse, sir?" Sharpe sounded surprised. "No, sir."

Hill looked at him keenly. "Not one man, Captain?"

"No, sir. Not one man."

Sharpe sensed Simmerson shifting uneasily on his saddle as Hill looked down shrewdly. "You surprise me, Captain."

"Surprise, sir?"

Hill smiled. He had dealt with enough sergeants in his life to know the game Sharpe was playing. "Yes, Captain. You see, your colonel received a letter saying that the men were refusing to parade. That's called mutiny."

Sharpe turned innocent eyes on Simmerson. "A letter, sir? Refusing to parade?" Simmerson glared at him. Once more he was looking foolish. He had cried "mutiny" to a general of division only to find that a junior captain had paraded the men. Sharpe looked back to Hill and let his expression change from innocent surprise to slow dawning of awareness. "I think that must be a prank, sir. You know how playful the lads get when they're ready for battle."

Hill laughed. "Good! Well, what a to-do about nothing! I think it's time I inspected your men, Sir Henry." Simmerson said nothing. Hill turned back to Sharpe. "Thank you, Captain. 95th, eh?"

"Yes, sir."

"I've heard of you, haven't I? Sharpe. Let me think." He peered down at the rifleman then snapped his fingers. "Of course! I'm honoured to make your acquaintance, Sharpe! What is it they say about the Rifles, eh, Captain?"

"First on the field and last off it, sir."

Hill nodded. "That's the spirit! Well, I'm glad you're in my division, Sharpe, very glad. Carry on!"

"Thank you, sir." He saluted, about-turned, and marched back towards the Light Company. As he went he heard Hill call out to the cavalry's commanding officer. "You can go home! No business today!"

The general walked his horse down the ranks of the battalion and talked affably with the men. Sharpe had heard much about "Daddy" Hill and understood now why he had been given the nickname. The general had the knack of making every man think that he was cared for, seemed genuinely concerned about each one. There was no way in which he could not have seen the state of the battalion. Even allowing for three weeks' marching the men looked hastily and sloppily dressed, but Hill turned a blind eye. When he reached the Light Company he nodded familiarly to Sharpe, joked about Harper's height, made the men laugh. He left the company and rode with Simmerson and his entourage to the centre of the parade ground.

"You've been bad lads! I was disappointed in you this morning!" He spoke slowly and distinctly so that the flank companies, like Sharpe's, could hear him clearly. "You deserve the punishment that Sir Henry ordered!" He paused. "But really you've done very well this afternoon! Early on parade!" There was a rustle of laughter in the ranks. "Well, because of your behaviour this afternoon Sir Henry has asked me to cancel the punishment parade. I don't think I agree with him but I'm going to let him have his way. So there will be no floggings." There was a sigh of relief. Hill took another deep breath. "Tomorrow we march with our Spanish allies towards the French! We're going to Talavera and there's going to be a battle! I'm proud to have you in my division. Together we're going to show the French just what being a soldier means!" He waved a benign hand at them. "Good luck, lads, good luck!"

They cheered him till they were hoarse, took off their shakoes and waved them, while the general beamed like an indulgent parent. When the noise died down he turned to Simmerson.

"Dismiss them, Colonel, dismiss them. They've done well!"

Simmerson had no alternative but to obey. The parade was dismissed and the men streamed off the field in a buzz of talk and laughter. Hill trotted his horse back towards the castle, and Simmerson and his group of officers rode after him.

Sharpe walked slowly away, head down to discourage conversation. He knew he had heaped too many insults on the colonel. Now, more than ever, Simmerson would need the satisfaction of seeing him broken. But there was more to it than that. There was the colonel's nephew also, and Josefina. He doubted if Gibbons would seek an honourable solution, and he felt a shiver of apprehension at what might happen. The girl would be Gibbons's target.

CHAPTER 9

In sixteen years' soldiering Sharpe had rarely felt such certainty that battle was about to be joined. The Spanish and British armies had combined at Oropesa and begun the march on to Talavera, twenty-one thousand British and thirty-four thousand Spanish, a vast army pouring eastwards. The wheels of one hundred and ten field guns ground the white roads to fine dust, the hooves of over six thousand cavalry stirred the powder into the air where it clung to the infantry who trudged through the heat while the leading Spanish skirmishers pushed aside the light screen of French voltigeurs. To left and right cavalry patrols rode parallel to the line of march. Closer by, in the fields, small groups of Spanish soldiers had fallen out of the march and now lay chatting with their women, smoking, watching the British infantry file past.

The men were hungry. Hard as Wellesley tried, there was simply not enough food for the whole army. The area between Oropesa and Talavera had already been scoured by the French; now it was vainly searched by Spanish and British, and the battalion had only eaten "Tommies", pancakes made from flour and water, since they left Oropesa the day before. It was a time for tightening belts, but the prospect of action raised men's spirits and when the battalion marched past the bodies of three French skirmishers they forgot their hunger. The men of the South Essex, who had not seen enemy infantry before, stared curiously at the blue-jacketed bodies that had been thrown down beside a church wall. Dark stains marked the uniforms, their heads were bent back in the strange attitude of the dead, one man had a finger missing where it must have been hacked off to get at a valuable ring.

The French made no resistance to the west of Talavera or in the town itself. The armies marched past the town and on a mile until they stopped at dusk where the vast, arid plain ended on the banks of the Alberche, a small river that flowed into the Tagus. On the far riverbank hundreds of smoke plumes mingled and shivered over the French camp of Marshal Victor. The armies had finally been brought together, and tomorrow they must fight.

Sharpe's company squatted by their fires in a cork grove that sloped down to the river and grumbled. They were tired and hungry and they resented being denied the pleasures of the town. They could see senior officers on horseback riding towards the old walls with their wives and children. Sharpe wondered how Josefina would find a room there. Still, Hogan had promised to look after her.

Now was the time for the rituals before battle. Sharpe walked through the trees and chatted with men who prepared themselves with the obsession for detail that all men thought might protect them in the chaos of the fight. Riflemen stripped their locks, pinned back the massive rifle mainsprings with nails, and brushed away every scrap of dirt. Infantrymen put new flints in their muskets, unscrewed them and put them in again, looking for the perfect fit that would never come loose or turn sideways. Pots of boiling water were carried carefully from the fires and poured into the barrels of the guns to flush out every last powder deposit, because tomorrow a man's life might depend on how fast he could reload. Joining the noise of the insects were the sounds of hundreds of stones rubbing endlessly on bayonets, sharpening the blades. Men repaired uniforms, sewed on buttons, made new laces, as though to be comfortable was to be safer. There were the same jokes: "Don't wear your hat tomorrow, Sarge, the French might see your face and die laughing"; other men were asked to go and sleep with the

French so their snoring would keep the enemy awake. The stale jokes were as much a part of the battle as the bullets which would begin to fly at first light.

Sharpe walked past the fires, swapping jokes, accepting tots of hoarded spirits, feeling the edges of bayonets, telling the men that the next day would not be bad. Nor should it be. The combined British and Spanish far outnumbered the French; the allies had the initiative, the battle should be short, swift, and victory almost a certainty. He listened to men boasting of the deeds they would perform next day and knew that the words covered their fear. Other men, more quietly, asked him what it would be like. He smiled and told them it would not be as bad as they feared, and shrugged away his knowledge of the panic they would all have to control when they walked into the storm of canister and musket shot.

He left the fires behind. In the last light of dusk he could see a farmhouse five hundred yards away where earlier he had seen the 16th Light Dragoons go with their horses. He crossed the fields and went into the yard. A line of troopers in blue and scarlet uniforms waited by the armourer. Sharpe waited for them to finish and then unsheathed his huge sword and carried it to the wheel. This was part of his own ritual, to have the sword sharpened by one of the cavalry armourers because they made a finer edge.

The armourer was an old soldier, too old to ride into battle, but he had seen it all. He took the blade from Sharpe, tested it with a broad thumb, and then pressed it onto the pedalled stone. The sparks flowed off the wheel, the blade sang, the man swept it lovingly up and down the edge and then wiped the sword with an oily piece of leather.

"Get yourself a German one, Captain." It was an old argument, whether the Kligenthal blades were better than the British. Sharpe shook his head. "I've eaten German swords with this one."

The armourer cackled toothlessly and peered down the edge. "There you are, Captain. Take care of it."

Sharpe put some coins on the wheel frame and held the sword up to the last light of the western sky. There was a new sheen on the edge, he felt it with his thumb. "You'll never get a Kligenthal as sharp as that."

He went back to his men. In the sky over the river he could see the glow of enemy fires where twenty-two thousand Frenchies were sharpening their own blades and wondering about the morning.

He himself lay awake for much of the night, rehearsing the next day in his head. The plan was simple enough. The Alberche ran in a curve to join the River Tagus and the French were on the inside of the bend. At dawn the Spanish trumpets would sound, their thirty guns be unleashed, and the infantry would splash across the shallow river to attack the outnumbered French. And as the French retreated, as assuredly they must, so Wellesley would throw the British onto their flank. And then the cavalry would come through the water and turn retreat into carnage. Marshal Victor's army would be destroyed, broken between the hammer of the Spanish and the anvil of the British. It was all so simple. Finally Sharpe slept, curled by the embers of a fire in his greatcoat, a gilded Eagle threatening his dreams.

There were no bugles to wake them, nothing that might alert the French to the dawn attack. Sergeants and corporals shook the men awake, soldiers cursed the dew and the cold air that rasped their throats. Every man glanced towards the river but the far bank was shrouded in mist and darkness, there was nothing to be seen or heard. They had been forbidden to relight the fires in case they should warn the French, yet somehow they managed to heat water and threw in the loose tea leaves and Sharpe gratefully accepted a tin mug of the liquid from his sergeants. Harper looked up at Sharpe and grinned. "Permission to go to church, sir?"

Sharpe grinned back. It was Sunday. He tried to work out the date. They had left Plasencia on the seventeenth and that had been a Monday and he counted the days forward on his fingers. Sunday, July 23, 1809. There was still no light in the eastern sky, the dawn was still two hours away. Behind them there was a rumbling and clanking and cursing as a battery of artillery unlimbered. Sharpe turned, the tea cradled in his hands, and watched the dim shapes as the horses were led away and the field guns pointed across the river. They would herald the second phase of the attack, after the Spaniards, hurling their round shot to tear holes in the French battalions as Sharpe led his skirmishers into the river. It was cold, too cold to feel any excitement. Now were the hours to feel apprehensive, to tighten belts and buckles, to feel hungry. Sharpe shivered slightly in his greatcoat, nodded his thanks to Harper, and made his way down between the lines of his men.

He left the trees and walked onto the grass beside the river. His boots swished through the dew and warned the sentries of his coming. He was challenged, gave the password, and was greeted as he jumped down onto the shingle at the water's edge.

"Anything happening?"

"No, sir."

The water slid blackly beneath the tendrils of mist. Sharpe peered over his cupped hands and blew on his fingers; there was the faintest dot of red light on the far bank that suddenly glowed brighter. The French sentry was smoking a cigar or a pipe. Sharpe looked to his left. The eastern sky at last had a suspicion of colour, a flat silver-grey that silhouetted the hills. He clapped one of the sentries on the shoulder. "Not long now."

He climbed the brief bank between the shingle and the grass and walked back to the trees. From the French lines he could hear the whinny of a horse, and then the sound of bugles. They would start lighting their fires—with luck they would be still eating their breakfast when the Spanish bayonets came at them from the west. He suddenly felt a longing for devilled kidneys and coffee, for any food other than the Tommies the battalion had lived on for a week. He remembered the garlic sausage they had collected from the enemy dead at Rolica and hoped he would find some that morning.

Back in the grove he took off his greatcoat, rolled it tight, and strapped it to his pack. He took the rag off the lock of his rifle that had protected it from the dew and tested the tension of the spring with his thumb. He slung it on his shoulder, slapped his sword, and started moving the Light Company forward. The skirmishers would go first, the thin line of riflemen and redcoats wading the Alberche to drive off the sentries and lock up the French voltigeurs so that they could not blunt the attack of the massed British battalions which would follow onto the French flank. He made the men lie down a few feet inside the grove where they merged into the shadows of the trees. Behind he could see the other nine companies of the battalion forming up for the assault.

Dawn crept over the mountains, shrinking the pools of shadow and revealing the shapes of trees and bushes on the far bank. It would still be a few moments, Sharpe decided, before the Spanish would break the silence and start the attack. He walked along the tree line, nodded to the captain of the Light Company of the 29th who was on his right flank, made polite small talk, and then strolled back to stand beside Harper. They did not speak but Sharpe knew the big Irishman would be thinking of the promise the dying

Lennox had extracted from them. If Sharpe could not pluck the Eagle from its perch today there might not be another chance for months. And that meant no chance at all, for in a few weeks, unless he could blunt Simmerson's letter, he might be on a ship for the West Indies. He thought of Josefina, asleep in the town, her black hair spread on a pillow, and wondered why suddenly his life had been enmeshed in such a series of unexpected problems.

Muskets banged erratically in the distance. The men cocked their ears, listened to the sporadic firing that rattled up and down the French lines. Lieutenant Knowles came up to Sharpe and raised his eyebrows in a question.

Sharpe shook his head. "They're clearing their muskets, that's all." The French sentries had been changed and the men going off duty were getting rid of their charges that might have become damp in the night air. Musket fire would not herald the attack. Sharpe was waiting for the red flashes that would show that the Spanish artillery was opening the battle. They could not be far off.

There were shouts from the river. Again the men pricked their ears, strained forward, but again it was a false alarm. A group of the enemy appeared, chasing and shouting at each other in horseplay, carrying buckets to the water's edge.

"Watering horses?" Knowles asked.

"No." Sharpe stifled a yawn. "Artillery buckets. There must be guns to our front." That was bad news. A dozen men were carrying buckets in which the sponges that damped out the sparks in discharged guns were dipped. If the guns were directly ahead Sharpe knew that the South Essex might be marching into a storm of canister fragments. He felt achingly tired, he wanted to begin the fight, he wanted the Eagle out of his dreams.

Simmerson and Forrest appeared, both on foot, and stared at the French artillerymen. Sharpe said good morning and Simmerson nodded back. He was doing his best to be civil and Sharpe wondered if suddenly he was regretting the letter he had written. Sometimes the imminence of battle made seemingly intractable quarrels appear unimportant. The colonel pulled out a vast watch, opened the lid, and shook his head. "Spanish are late."

The light began to lose its greyness. There was a sparkle on the river surface, leaves could be distinguished in the screen of trees on the far bank and behind them Sharpe could see the smoke of the French cooking fires. "Permission to relieve the picquets, sir?"

"Yes, Sharpe, yes." He looked as if he would say more but instead he shook his head again and led Forrest farther down the line.

The sentries were changed, the minutes passed, the sun climbed and the last vestiges of night disappeared like fading cannon smoke in the western sky. Damn the Spanish, thought Sharpe, as he listened to the bugles calling the French regiments to parade. A group of horsemen appeared on the far bank and inspected the British through telescopes. There would be no surprise now. The French officers would be able to see the batteries of guns, the saddled cavalry horses, the rows of infantry in the trees. The French would know now where the attack was planned.

The sound of church bells came from the town and Sharpe wondered what Josefina was doing; had the bells wakened her? He imagined her body stretching between warm sheets. The sound of the bells reminded him of England and he thought of all the village churches that would be filling with people. Would they be thinking of their army in Spain? He doubted it. The British were not fond of their army. They celebrated its victories, of course, but there had been no such celebrations for a long time. The navy was feted, Nelson's captains had been household names, but Trafalgar was a memory and Nelson was in his tomb.

The morning became warm, the men somnolent; they leaned against the cork trees and slept with their muskets propped on their knees.

"Sir!" A sergeant was calling him from one of the companies higher in the grove. "Company officers, sir. To the colonel!"

Sharpe waved his reply, left Knowles in charge and walked up the grove. He was late. The captains stood in a bunch listening to a lieutenant from Hill's staff. Sharpe caught snatches of his words. "Fast asleep . . . no battle . . . ."

There was a buzz of questions. The lieutenant sounded bored. "The general requests that we keep posted, sir. But we're not expecting the French to do anything."

He rode away, leaving the officers puzzled. Sharpe made his way towards Forrest to find out what he had missed when he saw a familiar figure riding hard down the track. It was Lieutenant-Colonel Lawford and he was furious. He saw Sharpe, reined in, and swore.

"Bloody hell, Richard! Bloody Spanish!"

"What's happened?"

Lawford could barely contain his anger. "They refused to wake up! Can you believe it?"

Other officers drew round. Lawford took off his hat and wiped his forehead; he had deep circles under his eyes. "We get up at two o'clock in the morning to save their bloody country and they can't be bothered to get out of bed!" Lawford looked round as though hoping to see a Spaniard on whom to vent his seething fury. "We rode over there at six. Cuesta's in his coach lying on cushions and says his army is too tired to fight! Can you believe it? We had them. Like that!" He pinched a finger and thumb together. "We would have murdered them this morning! We could have wiped Victor off the map. But no. It's *mãnana* . . . . And there won't be a bloody tomorrow! Victor's no fool, he'll march today. Damn, damn, damn." Lawford stared at Sharpe. "You know what happens now?"

"No."

Lawford pointed towards the east. "Jourdan's over there, with Joseph Bonaparte. They'll join up with Victor, then we'll have twice as many to fight! And there are rumours that Soult has scraped an army together and is coming from the north. God! The chance we lost today! You know what I think?" Sharpe shook his head. "I think the bastard wouldn't fight because it's Sunday. He's got priests mumbling prayers round his bloody bed on wheels. And there's still no bloody food!"

Sharpe felt the tiredness course through him. "What do we do now?"

"Now? We wait. Cuesta says we'll attack tomorrow. We won't because the French won't be there." Lawford dropped his shoulders and let out a sigh. "Do you know where Hill is?"

Sharpe pointed along the track and Lawford rode on. Damn the Spanish, thought Sharpe, damn everything. There would be no battle, no Eagle, not even a taste of garlic sausage. Damn.

CHAPTER 10

"I saw a man today . . . ."

"Yes?" Sharpe looked over at Josefina. She was sitting naked on the bed with her knees drawn up and was trying to shape her toe-nails on the edge of his sword. She was laughing at her attempts and then she dropped the blade and looked at him. "He was lovely. A red coat with white bits here." She brushed her breasts with her hands. "And lots of gold lace."

"On a horse?"

She nodded. "And there was a bag hanging down . . . ."

"His sabretache. And a curved sword?" She nodded again and Sharpe grinned at her. "Sounds like the Prince of Wales Dragoons. Very rich."

"How do you know?"

"All cavalrymen are rich. Unintelligent, but rich."

She cocked her head and frowned slightly. "Unintelligent?"

"All cavalry officers are. The horse has all the brains and they have all the money."

She shrugged her bare shoulders. "It doesn't matter. I have enough brains for two." She smiled. "You're jealous."

"Yes." He had picked up her penchant for honesty. She nodded.

"I'm bored, Richard. Not with you. You're good for me. But we've been in Talavera a week now and nothing is happening."

Sharpe leaned forward and tugged his boots up over the overalls. "Don't worry. Something will happen tomorrow."

"Are you sure?"

"Tomorrow we fight." This time though, he thought, we will be outnumbered.

She pulled her knees tight into her body, clasped them, and rested her chin on them. "Are you frightened?"

"Yes."

"Will you get your Eagle?"

"I don't know."

She smiled at him. "I'll have a present for you after the battle."

"I don't want a present. I want you."

"You have me already." She knew what he meant but she deliberately misunderstood him. He crossed the room for his sword and she laid it flat on the bed and uncurled herself to lie face down on top of it. "You can't have it." Her voice was muffled by the pillow. "Do you have to go?"

"I have to go. Give me the sword."

"Get it yourself . . . ."

IT HAD BEEN a strange week, he thought, as he walked through the streets of Talavera. A week of boredom mixed with passion and he had felt Josefina drawing away from him; not because she disliked him but because she was impatient to find the security she craved. A Prince of Wales Dragoon . . . ? He came to the crumbling town-wall, beside the gate where some of his men were mounting a guard. Hogan was there, on top of the wall, and Sharpe climbed the old stonework to look over the broken parapet. Towards the west the olive groves below the walls were full of Spanish soldiers filing into the positions that Wellesley had carefully prepared for them. Cuesta, after refusing to attack last Sunday, had impetuously marched after the retreating French. Now, four days later, his army was scuttling back, bringing after them a French army that had more than doubled its size. Tomorrow, Sharpe reflected, the Spanish would have to fight. The French would wake them up, and the allied army that could have taken its victory last Sunday must now fight a defensive battle.

Not, Sharpe thought bitterly, that the Spanish would have to do too much of the actual killing. Wellesley had drawn his army back to create a defensive line next to Talavera itself. The right-hand end of the line was made up of the town walls, olive groves, fields and woods, all made impregnable by Hogan's hard work. He had felled trees, thrown up earthworks, strengthened walls, and in the tangle of obstacles the Spanish troops took up their positions. No French infantryman could hope to fight his way across Hogan's breast-works as long as the defenders stayed at their posts; instead, the French army would swing north to the left side of Wellesley's line where the British would wait for the attack.

Sharpe looked at the northern plain. There were no obstacles there that an engineer could make more formidable; there was just a stream, the Portina, that a man could cross without the water coming over his boot-tops, and in the distance the Medellin, the hill which dominated the rolling grassland, that was an invitation for the massed French battalions and their long lines of splendid cavalry. And beyond it, across the Portina, a smaller hill, the Cascajal, ideal for the French guns. The Spanish troops, thirty thousand of them, could stay safely behind their breastworks and watch.

Sharpe looked down at Harper. The sergeant, with a dozen men, was guarding the gate of the town to stop any British or Spanish soldiers who might be tempted to lose themselves in Talavera's dark alleyways and avoid the fight. The battalion itself was on the Medellin and Sharpe waited for the orders that would send his company up the shallow Portina stream to find the patch of grass they would defend in the morning.

"And how's the girl?" Hogan was sitting on the powdery stone.

"She's bored."

"That's the way of women. Never content. Will you be needing more money?"

Sharpe saw the concern in his eyes. Already Hogan had lent Sharpe more than twenty guineas, a sum that would be impossible for him to repay unless he was lucky on the battlefield. "No. I'm all right for the moment."

Hogan smiled. "You're lucky. She's a beautiful creature, Richard." He asked again, "Are you in love?"

"She won't let me be."

"Then she's more sensible than I thought."

The afternoon passed slowly. Sharpe thought of the girl, bored in her room. Then, suddenly, there were flashes of light far away in the hazy trees and bushes that edged the plain to the east. It was the sun reflecting from muskets and breastplates. Sharpe nudged Hogan and pointed. "The French."

Hogan stood up and stared. "My God." He spoke quietly. "There's a good few of them."

The infantry marched onto the far plain like a spreading stain on the grass. Sharpe and Hogan watched battalion after battalion march into the pale fields, squadron after squadron of cavalry, the small squat shapes of guns scattered in the formations, the largest army Sharpe had ever seen in the field. He looked left to the British lines that waited beside the Portina. The smoke from hundreds of campfires wound into the early evening air, but the British force looked woefully small beside the massive tide of men, horses and guns that filled the plain. Napoleon's brother was there, King Joseph, and with him two full marshals of France, Victor and Jourdan. There were sixty-five battalions of French infantry, and they had come to swat this small British army and send it reeling to the sea.

Hogan whistled softly. "Will they attack this evening?"

"No." Sharpe scanned the far lines. "They'll wait for their artillery."

And in the morning, he thought, the French will open with one of their favourite cannonades, the massed artillery hurling its iron shot at the enemy lines before the dense, drummed columns followed the Eagles across the stream. French tactics were hardly subtle. They massed their guns and men and they hurled a terrifying hammer blow at the enemy line. Again and again it worked. He shrugged to himself. Who needed to be subtle? The guns and men of France had broken every army sent against them.

There were shouts from behind him and he peered down at the gate where Harper and his men were on guard. Lieutenant Gibbons was there, mounted, shouting at Harper. Sharpe leaned over the parapet. "What's the problem?"

Gibbons turned round slowly. It dawned on Sharpe that the lieutenant was slightly drunk and was having some difficulty in staying on his horse. Gibbons saluted Sharpe with his usual irony. "I didn't see you there, sir. So sorry." He bowed. "I was just telling your sergeant here that you can go back now, all right?"

"But you stopped on the way for refreshment?"

Gibbons bowed again. "You could say so, sir."

He urged his horse under the gateway and started up the road to the British lines to the north. Sharpe watched him go. "Bastard."

"Does he give you problems?" Hogan was sitting on the parapet again.

Sharpe shook his head. "No. Just insolence, remarks in the mess, you know." He wondered about Josefina. Hogan seemed to read his thoughts.

"You're thinking about the girl?"

Sharpe nodded. "Yes. But she should be all right. She keeps the door locked, and I can't see how he'd find her." He turned back to the spectacle on the plain. "What's that?"

Three-quarters of a mile away French horsemen were firing their carbines. Sharpe watched the puffs of smoke and listened to the faint crackle. "Dragoons."

"I know that." Hogan said. "But what are they firing at?"

"Snakes?" During his walks up the Portina Sharpe had noticed small black snakes in the dark grass. He had avoided them but he supposed it was possible the horsemen were merely amusing themselves with target practice. It was evening and the flames from the carbine muzzles sparkled brightly in the dusk. It was strange, Sharpe thought, how often war could look pretty.

Sergeant Harper had joined the two officers, and now he pointed down. "They've woken up our brave allies. Looks like a bloody ants' nest."

Below them Spanish infantry had lined themselves behind walls and laid muskets over the tree trunks Hogan had piled in the gateways. Officers stood on the wall, their swords drawn.

Hogan laughed. "It's so good to have allies."

The dragoons went on firing at their unseen targets, oblivious of the panic they were causing in the Spanish ranks. Every Spanish infantryman had crowded to the breastworks, and their muskets bristled towards the empty field. The officers barked out commands and Sharpe watched as the hundreds of muskets were loaded.

No order was given. Instead a single musket fired, its ball thrumming uselessly into the grass, and it was followed by the biggest volley Sharpe had ever heard. Thousands of muskets fired, gouted flame and smoke; the sound seemed to last for ever and mingled with it came the yells of the Spaniards. The dragoons looked up, startled, but no musket ball would carry even a third of the distance towards them so they sat their horses and watched the fringe of musket smoke drift into the air.

For a second Sharpe thought the Spanish were cheering their own victory over the innocent grass but suddenly he realized the shouts were not of triumph, but of alarm. They had been scared witless by the thunder of their own volley and now they ran for safety, throwing away muskets, screaming for help, running from their own noise. Sharpe shouted down to his men on the gate.

"Let them through!"

There was no point in trying to stop the panic. Sharpe's dozen men would have been swamped by the Spanish who streamed into the town. Others circled north towards the roads that led eastwards away from the French. Sharpe watched Spanish cavalry use their swords on the fugitive infantry. They would stop some of them, but the bulk of the infantry had evaporated, defeated by a handful of dragoons three-quarters of a mile away. Sharpe guessed it would take the Spanish cavalry all night to round up the fugitives and force them back to the breastworks, and even then hundreds would escape to spread rumours of a great French victory outside Talavera. Sharpe stood up. "Come on, Sergeant, time we were getting back."

A voice called up from the street. "Captain Sharpe! Sir!"

One of the riflemen was gesticulating and, next to him, stood Agostino, Josefina's servant. Sharpe's carefree mood disappeared. He scrambled down the broken stonework, Harper and Hogan following him, and strode across to the two men. "What is it?"

Agostino burst into Portuguese. Sharpe turned to Hogan. "What's he saying?"

The engineer licked his lips. "It's Josefina."

"What about her?" Sharpe had the inklings of disaster, a cold feeling of evil. He let Hogan take his elbow and walk him, with Agostino, away from the listening riflemen. Hogan asked more questions, and finally turned to Sharpe. His voice was low. "She's been attacked. He locked Agostino in a cupboard."

"He?" He already knew the answer. Gibbons.

Sergeant Harper crossed to them, his manner formal and correct. "Sir! Shall I take the men back, sir?"

Sharpe nodded. It occurred to him that Patrick Harper knew more of what was going on than Sharpe had assumed. There was a controlled anger in the Irishman. Your enemies, he was saying, are mine.

"Carry on, Sergeant."

"Yessir. And sir?" Harper's face was bleak. "You will let me know what happens?"

"Yes, Sergeant."

Sharpe and Hogan ran into the dark streets, pushing their way through the fugitives who were forcing the doors of wineshops and private houses. It would be a bad night in Talavera, a night of looting, destruction, and rape. Tomorrow a hundred thousand men would march into a maelstrom of fire. As Sharpe hurled two Spanish infantrymen out of his way, he feared for the evil that seemed to be welling up in preparation for the morrow. Then they were in the street where Josefina was living and he peered up at the quiet windows, the closed shutters, and prayed.

CHAPTER 11

Sharpe's boots crunched on broken plaster, as he paced up and down the tiny landing. Voices murmured in the room on the other side of the splintered door, and through a small window he saw high ragged clouds racing past the moon. Hogan sat on the top step of the steep stairs; beside him were the sheets, patterned in red, that they had taken from Josefina's bed. There was a cry from the room.

Sharpe spun round in irritation. "What are they doing to her?"

"The doctor's bleeding her, Sharpe. He knows what he's doing."

"As if she hasn't lost enough blood already?"

"I know, I know." Hogan sighed and picked up a tiny plaster head. The house belonged to a seller of religious statues and the stairs and corridors were stacked with his wares. When Gibbons had forced his way into the girl's room he had trampled on twenty or thirty images of Christ, each with a bleeding heart, and the scraps of statues still littered the landing. Hogan was a peaceful man. His war was fought with picks, shovels and powder, yet when he had burst into the attic room with Sharpe he had felt a searing anger and a need for revenge. The mood had passed. Now he sat, saddened and quiet but, as he watched the tall rifleman, he knew that in Sharpe the mood was being refined and fed. For the twentieth time Sharpe stopped.

"Why?"

"You know why. He was drunk. And he wanted revenge on you. So he beat her. It was all on the spur of the moment . . . . What will you do?"

"I don't know." Sharpe spoke irritably.

"What can you do, Richard? Call him out to a duel? That will ruin your career, you know that. Will you charge him with rape? For God's sake, Richard, who'd believe you? The town's full of Spanish tonight, raping anything that moves! And everyone knows the girl was with Gibbons before you. No, Richard, you must think before you do anything."

Sharpe turned on him and Hogan knew from his implacable face that there could be no argument. "I'll murder him."

Hogan sighed. "I didn't hear that. So you get hung? Shot? Beat the bones out of him if you must but no more, Richard, no more."

Sharpe did not answer, seeing in his mind the body they had found on the floor with the blood-soaked sheets. She had been raped and beaten. Now they waited while a doctor looked at the girl. New sheets had been carried into the room, water, and Sharpe had listened to the landlady tidy up the floor and he remembered the girl, bruised and bleeding, crawling among the broken saints and stained sheets.

The door opened, scrunching on the shards, and the landlady beckoned to them. The doctor was kneeling beside the bed where Josefina lay, her black hair fanned on the pillow, her eyes tight shut.

Sharpe sat beside her, saw the bruises spreading on her unnaturally pale skin, and he took one of her hands. She pulled away but he held on and her eyes opened. "Richard?"

"Josefina. How are you?" She closed her eyes and the faintest smile came and went.

She opened her eyes again. "I'll be all right."

Sharpe turned to the doctor. "How is she?"

The doctor shrugged. Hogan intervened and rattled at him in Spanish. Sharpe listened to the voices and as he did so he stroked the girl's face. All he could think of was that he had failed her. He had promised to protect her and now this had happened. Hogan sat beside him. "She'll be all right. She lost some blood. But she'll mend."

The girl's voice was very low. "Richard?"

"Yes?"

"Kill him." She spoke flatly.

Sharpe bent down and kissed her. "I will."

She squeezed his hand. "Will there be a battle tomorrow?"

"Yes."

"Be lucky."

"I'll come and see you afterwards." He smiled at her.

"Yes." But there was no conviction in her voice.

Sharpe turned to Hogan. "You'll stay?"

"Till daybreak. I'm not needed till then. But you should go."

Sharpe nodded. "I know." He kissed her again, stood up, and put on his rifle and pack. Hogan walked with him to the stairs.

"Be careful, Richard."

"I will."

Hogan put a hand on his shoulder to stop him moving. "Remember what you have to lose."

Sharpe nodded again. "Bring me news when you can."

He pushed his way into the street, and hurried up the track that led away from the town between the Portina stream and the Spanish lines. The frightened infantry were being forced back into their positions, and as he hurried through the trees he could hear the occasional musket shot from the town, the shouting, the coinage of Talavera's night of fear and rape. The moon had disappeared behind a bank of clouds but the lights of the Spanish fires showed the path and he half ran as he headed towards the Medellin hill. To his right the sky glowed deep red where thousands of French fires were reflected in the air. He should have been concerned for the morning, yet his mind was dominated by the need to find Gibbons. He came to the Pajar, the tiny hill that marked the end of the Spanish lines and the place where the Portina bent to his right and ran in front of the British position. He saw the field guns Wellesley had placed on the small hill and part of his mind registered how the fire of those guns would sweep protectively in front of the Spanish and deflect the massive French attack onto the British lines.

The track melted away into the grass. He could see the scattered fires of the British but he had no idea which was the South Essex. They were positioned at the Medellin hill, he knew that, so he ran by the stream, tripping over tussocks of grass, splashing through patches of marsh, keeping the silvered Portina as his guide to the hill. He was alone in the darkness. The British fires were far off to his left, the French to his right, the two armies still and quiet. Something was wrong. The old instinct prickled him and he stopped, sank to one knee and searched the darkness ahead. In the night the Medellin hill looked like a long, low ridge pointing at the French army. It was the key to Wellesley's left flank: if the French assaulted the hill they could turn and crush the British between the Medellin and Talavera. Yet there were no fires on the ridge. He could see a bright smear of flames at the western end, farthest from the enemy, but on the side facing the town, and on the summit nearest the enemy, there were no lights. He had thought the South Essex to be bivouacking on the gentle slope that faced him but it was empty.

He listened. There were the sounds of the night, and the far-off sounds of a hundred thousand men. Behind him Pajar hill was bright with fires. He stood up and walked softly on, his instincts alive to a danger he could not define, his mind searching for clues in the darkness. Why had he not been challenged? There should be picquets on the line of the Portina, sentries looking towards the enemy, but no one had stopped him. He kept by the stream until the black loom of the Medellin was above him, then turned left and began to climb the slope. By daylight it looked a gentle slope, but as he climbed with his pack and rifle the ground felt steep and each step made the muscles at the back of his legs ache. Tomorrow, he thought, this is precisely where the French columns will come. They will march up this slope, heads down, while the guns crack shot into their ranks and the muskets wait in silence at the crest.

Halfway up he stopped and turned round. On the far side of the stream was that other hill, the Cascajal. On its level top Sharpe could see the fires of the French, and he turned and hurried on. His mind was still alerted to danger, to a threat he did not understand, but continually he thought of the girl, of her terror in the attic when the drunken Gibbons had burst in.

The slope levelled out onto the plateau. Far off he could see the fires of the British and he ran slowly towards them, the pack bumping awkwardly, the rifle flapping at his side. He had still not been challenged. He was approaching the army from the direction of the enemy and there were no sentries in the darkness, as if the army had forgotten about the French. Two hundred yards from the line of fires he stopped and crouched low on the grass. He had found the South Essex. They were on the edge of the hill and he could see the bright yellow facings of their uniforms glowing in the light of the flames. He searched the fires and saw the green uniforms of his riflemen. His anger was turning into frustration. He had walked and run more than a mile to find the battalion, yet he knew that there was nothing he could do. Gibbons would be safe with the colonel and his cronies, sitting round a fire with the officers, secure from his revenge. Hogan was right. He would throw his career away if he fought the man, yet he had made a promise to Josefina, and he did not know how to keep the promise. And tomorrow he must try to keep the earlier promise to Lennox.

He tugged the great sword from its scabbard and laid its tip on the grass in front of him. The blade shone dully in the light of the fires; he stared at the length of steel and felt the sting of tears in his eyes as he remembered the girl's body lying teasingly naked along its flat blade. That had been only this afternoon. Now he cursed the fate that had led to this night, to the promises he could not keep. He thought of the girl, of Gibbons clawing at her and felt his helplessness. It was better, he knew, to concentrate on tomorrow but how was he to face Gibbons and see the triumph on his face without swinging the blade at him?

He turned round and stared back at the crest of the Medellin, and suddenly he froze. Had there been sentries there he had missed? Now he could see the silhouettes of a dozen men, carrying guns. He lay flat on the grass, put his ear to the ground, and heard the faint thump of marching feet. As he raised his head and kept looking, the dozen men turned into a misshapen mass. He remembered telling Hogan that the French would not attack at night, yet he suspected he was seeing just that: a night attack on the Medellin. The dozen men might be some of the skirmishers, and the solid mass a French column climbing the hill.

But how to be sure? It could as easily be a British battalion moving in the dark, finding a new place to camp. He wriggled forward on knees and elbows, keeping his body close to the earth. The sword rustled on the grass, he seemed to be making a deafening sound, but the men walked on towards him. He stopped when they stopped and he watched them kneel. He was almost sure they were voltigeurs, the skirmish line that had been sent ahead to flush out the sentries, and now that they were in sight of their targets they were waiting for the column so that the attack should crash home in unison. Sharpe held his breath. The kneeling men were calling softly to each other.

Their language was French. He turned and stared at the fires marking the British line. No one moved there; the men were sitting waiting for the morning, completely unaware that their enemy had found the plateau of the Medellin undefended and were about to attack. Sharpe had to warn the British, but how? A single rifle shot would be put down to a nervous sentry, seeing shadows in the night; he could not shout that far, and if he turned and ran then he would not reach the British fires much before the French. There was only one way. That was to provoke the French into firing a volley that would startle the British, and warn them of danger.

He gripped the sword, noted the nearest shadow of a kneeling voltigeur, then scrambled to his feet and sprinted towards the enemy. The man looked up as Sharpe neared him and put a finger to his lips. Sharpe screamed, a curdling yell of anger and challenge, and chopped sideways with the sword. He did not wait to see if he had caused any damage but ran on, screaming at the next man. This one stood up, shouted a question, and died with the blade in his belly. Sharpe wrenched the sword free, whirled it in the air so that it sang, spotted movement to his left and ran at yet another voltigeur. The suddenness of his attack had startled them, they had no idea how many men were among them. Sharpe saw two skirmishers together, their bayonets levelled at him, but he screamed, they faltered, and he cut at one man as he swerved past and disappeared in the night.

He dropped flat in the grass. He heard the French running, the moans of a wounded man, but no one had fired at him. He lay still, stared at the skyline, and waited until his eyes could see the dim shapes of the approaching column. Questions were shouted forward, he could hear the voltigeurs hissing back their answers. He laid the sword flat on the grass and pulled the Baker off his shoulder. He slid it forward, opened the pan and felt that the powder was still in its place, then eased the flint back until he felt it click into place.

The Baker spat its bullet towards the French and he heard a sharp cry. They would have seen the muzzle flash but Sharpe rolled to his right and snatched up the sword.

A dozen nervous soldiers pulled their triggers and he heard the bullets whirring over the grass. At last!

More muskets banged in the night. Officers shouted at their men to stop firing but the damage was done. The British had heard the firing, seen the musket flashes, and behind him Sharpe could see men grabbing weapons, fixing bayonets. It was time to be going. He sprinted towards the British lines. His body was silhouetted against the fires and he heard a crackle of musketry and felt the bullets go past him. He shouted as he ran.

"The French! Form line! The French!"

He saw Harper and the riflemen running down the line, away from the centre where the French would strike home, and out to the dimly lit edge of the plateau. That was sensible. Rifles were not for close work and the sergeant was hiding his men in the shadows where they could snipe at the enemy. Sharpe's breath echoed in his ears, he was panting, the run had become a struggle against tiredness and the weight of his pack. He watched the South Essex form small nervous groups that kept splitting up and reforming. To their right another battalion was in equal disarray and, behind, Sharpe could hear the steady sound of the French advance.

"The French!" He had no more breath. Harper had disappeared. Sharpe ran full tilt into a sergeant who supported him as he gasped for breath.

"What's happening, sir?"

"French column. Coming this way."

The sergeant was bewildered. "Why didn't the first line stop them?"

Sharpe looked at him, astonished. "You are the first line!"

"No one told us!"

Sharpe looked round him. Men ran to and fro looking for their sergeants or officers, a mounted officer rode forward through the fires and disappeared towards the column. Sharpe heard a shout, the scream of the horse as muskets fired, and the thump of the beast falling. The musket flashes showed where the French were; and Sharpe, with satisfaction, heard the crisp sound of the Baker rifles at the hill's edge.

Then the column was visible, their white trousers showing in the firelight, aiming at the centre of the British line. Sharpe screamed the orders. "Present. Fire!" A few muskets banged, the white smoke swallowed immediately in the darkness, and Sharpe was alone. The men had fled at the sight of the massive column. Sharpe ran after them, beating at men with his sword. "You're safe here! Stand still!" But it was no good. The South Essex had broken and panicked and were streaming back towards the fires in their rear where Sharpe could see men forming in companies, the ranks tipped with bayonets.

It was chaos. Sharpe cut across the fugitives, making for the edge of the hill and the darkness where his riflemen lay hidden. He found Knowles, with a group of the company, and pushed them ahead to join Harper. The French fired their first volley, a massive rolling thunder of shots that cracked the night with smoke and flame, and cut a swathe in the troops ahead of them. Sharpe crashed into fugitives, shook them off, struggled towards the comparative peace of the edge of the hill. He heard the distinctive sound of rifles firing to his right, as the last fugitives pounded past on the summit, the crackle of musketry, the shouts diminishing as the men ran back. He hurried towards the sound of the rifles, and sank down beside Harper. The sergeant looked at him and then turned back to face the hilltop and pulled his trigger. Smoke puffed from the pan, belched from the barrel, and Sharpe saw a voltigeur fall backwards into a fire. Harper grinned with satisfaction. "He's been annoying me, that one, so he has. Been jumping around like a regular little Napoleon."

Sharpe stared at the hilltop. It was like the paintings of hell he had seen in Spanish churches. Smoke rolled redly in weird patches across the hilltop, thickly where the column was pushing deeper through the fires that marked the British lines, and thinly where small groups fought the skirmishers. Hundreds of small fires lit the battle, muskets pumped smoke and flame into the night, the whole accompanied by the shouts of the French and the cries of the wounded. The French skirmishers had suffered badly from the riflemen. Harper had lined them in the shadows on the hill's edge and they picked off the blue figures long before the French were close enough to use their muskets with any accuracy. Sharpe pulled his own rifle forward and reached down for a cartridge.

"Any problems?"

Harper shook his head and grinned. "Target practice."

"The rest of the company?"

The sergeant jerked his head backwards. "Most of them are down below with Mr. Knowles, sir. I told him they weren't needed here." He grunted as he rammed another bullet into his rifle. "What happened to the lady, sir?"

Sharpe turned to the sergeant and told him, flatly and simply, and watched the Irish face turn bleak with anger. "How is she?"

Sharpe shook his head. "She lost a lot of blood. He beat her."

The sergeant searched the ground in front of him, sifting through the firelight and the humped shadows, the far musket flashes that could be French or English. When he spoke his voice was soft.

"What will you do?"

Sharpe remembered Josefina's words. And his reply. "Kill him," he said. "Unless the French do it for me."

Harper nodded and turned back to the battle. The enemy had been held. Judging by the position of the musket flashes, they had marched into a thickening opposition they at last could not break. Sharpe searched the darkness to his right. The French must have sent more troops but there was no sign of them. He turned round.

"Lieutenant Knowles!"

"Sir!" Knowles approached in the darkness.

"Tell the men to fix bayonets and come up here. It's time we joined in."

Knowles grinned. "Yes, sir."

"How many men do we have?"

"Twenty, sir, not counting the rifles."

"Good! To work then."

Sharpe stood up and walked to the hilltop. He waved the riflemen forward and waited for Knowles and his group to climb into the light. Sharpe waved left and right with the sword.

"Skirmish order! Then slowly forward. We're not trying to take on the column, just flush out their skirmishers."

The bayonets gleamed red in the firelight, as the line walked steadily forward, but the enemy skirmishers had disappeared. Sharpe took his men to a hundred yards from the enemy column and waved them down. There was nothing they could do except watch a demonstration of British infantry at its best. The French had ploughed their way almost to the end of the hill but had been checked by a battalion that had now stretched itself in line ahead of the French and was firing in controlled platoon volleys. It was superb. No infantry could stand against Britain's best and the battalion was shredding the column with musketry that rolled up and down the line, the platoons firing in sequence, an irresistible hammering of close-range fire that poured into the tight French ranks.

The enemy wavered. The column's commander tried to deploy into line also but he was too late. The men at the back would not go forward into the hail of lead that rippled methodically and murderously from the British muskets. Groups of blue-coated French began to melt into the dark, a mounted British officer saw it and raised his sword, the red ranks cheered and went forward with levelled bayonets and, as suddenly as it had begun, the battle was done. The French went backwards, stepping over the dead, retreating ever faster from the reaching blades. The enemy had done well but now they had to go back. As they drew level with the skirmish line some of Sharpe's riflemen lifted their weapons but Sharpe shouted to let them go. There would be killing enough tomorrow.

From the town came the bells of midnight and Sharpe thought briefly of the girl. Harper squatted beside him, his face black with powder smoke, and held out a bottle of spirits.

"Get some sleep, sir. You need it." Harper grinned briefly. "We have a promise to keep tomorrow."

Sharpe lifted the bottle towards the sergeant as if in a toast. "Two promises, Sergeant. Two promises."

CHAPTER 12

It was a short, bad night. After the repulse of the French the army rescued the wounded and, in the thin firelight, searched for and piled up the dead that could be found, to be buried before the sun rose high and made them offensive. Battalions that had thought themselves safe in an imaginary second line now posted sentries. The bugles sounded at two in the morning, the fires were restored to life, and hungry men shivered round the flames and listened to the distant French bugles rousing the enemy.

By four o'clock the army was in position. Hill's brigades were on the Medellin and the brigade majors lined the battalions back from the hill crest so that they would be invisible to the French gunners. The South Essex were on the flank of the hill overlooking the Germans and the Guards who would defend the flat plain between the Medellin and the Pajar. Sharpe was impatient for the battle to start, so that he could take his Light Company away from Simmerson and up to the skirmish line that would form in the mist-shrouded Portina valley.

Simmerson sat his grey horse and stared moodily at the smoke trails from the French camp that rose and mingled in front of the rising sun. Gibbons was beside him and it suddenly occurred to Sharpe that the two men were frightened. In front of them the solitary Colour drooped from its staff, a lonely reminder of the battalion's disgrace. If it did badly today then it would stay a Battalion of Detachments and dwindle away under the onslaught of disease and death until it would simply disappear from the army list; the battalion that never was. Simmerson would survive. He would sail home to his country estate, take his seat in Parliament, become an armchair expert on the war. But wherever soldiers met, the names of Simmerson and the South Essex would be scorned. Sharpe grinned to himself; ironically, on this day, Simmerson needed him far more than he needed Simmerson.

At last the signal came and the Light Companies went forward, spreading themselves into a thin screen of skirmishers to become the first men to meet the attack. As he walked down the slope towards the mist Sharpe stared at the Cascajal hill topped with French guns, the barrels pointing at the Medellin. Somewhere behind the guns the French battalions would be forming the huge columns that would be thrown at the British line, and behind them would be the cavalry, waiting to pour through the opening: more than fifty thousand Frenchmen preparing to punish the British for their temerity in sending Wellesley's small army into their empire.

Harper ran up to him and nodded cheerfully as he pulled the muzzle stopper from his gun. "Not a good day for us, sir."

The mist hid everything beyond a hundred paces and took away the advantage of the long-range rifles. Sharpe grimaced. "It will clear in an hour or so."

He walked upstream to where he suspected the attack would come, and found Knowles at the end of the line. "Lieutenant?"

"Sir?" Knowles looked nervously alert, as if half dreading, half enjoying his first day of real battle.

Sharpe grinned at him. "Any problems?"

"No, sir. Will it be long?"

"You'll hear the guns first." Sharpe stamped his feet against the cold. "What's the time?"

Knowles took out his watch and opened the case. "Nearly five, sir." He went on looking at the ornate watch face with its filigree hands. "Sir?" He sounded embarrassed.

"Yes?"

"If I die, sir, would you have this?" He held the watch out.

Sharpe pushed the watch back and shook his head gravely. "You're not going to die. Who'd take over if I went?"

Knowles looked at him fearfully and Sharpe nodded. "Think about it, Lieutenant. Promotion can be rapid in battle." He grinned, attempting to dispel Knowles's gloom. "Who knows? If it's a good enough day we may all end up generals."

A gun banged on the Cascajal. Knowles's eyes widened as he heard, for the first time, the rumbling thunder of iron shot in the air. The eight-pound ball struck the crest of the Medellin, bounced over the troops in a spray of dirt and stones, and rolled harmlessly to rest four hundred yards down the plateau. The sound of the shot echoed flatly from the hills. Knowles waited for another but there was only silence.

"What was that, sir?"

"A signal to the other French batteries. They'll be reloading the gun." Sharpe imagined the sponge hissing as it was thrust into the barrel, the steam rising from the vent, and then the new charge and shot being rammed home. "About now, I'd think."

The silence was over. Sharpe listened as the iron shot from seventy or eighty French guns screamed and thundered in the air. He could hear the crash of the guns, imagined them throwing their massive weights back onto the trails, bucking in the air and slamming back onto the wheels as the rammer was dipped in water and the men prepared the next shot. Behind was a different noise, the muted sound of the roundshot gouging the Medellin, the thud of iron on earth. He turned to Knowles. "This is my unlucky day."

Knowles turned a worried face on him. The company depended on the superstition that the captain was lucky. "Why, sir?"

Sharpe grinned again. "They're firing to our left." He was shouting over the sound of the massed cannons. "They'll attack there. I might have been the proud owner of a watch otherwise!" He slapped a relieved Knowles on the shoulder and pointed across the stream. "Expect them in about twenty minutes. I'll be back!"

He walked down the line of men, checking flints, making the old jokes, looking for Harper. He felt desperately tired, not just the tiredness of disturbed sleep, but the weariness of problems that seemed to have no end. He waved at Harper and, as the sergeant walked towards him, the noise of the battle changed. There was a whining quality to the roar of the shot overhead.

Harper looked up into the mist. "Shells?"

Sharpe nodded as the first one exploded on the Medellin, the crash of the shells echoing the thunder of the guns, and added to the din was the sharper sound of the British six-pounders firing back. Harper jerked a thumb at the unseen Medellin. "That's a rare hammering, sir."

Sharpe listened. "The bands are still playing." Through the incessant crashes that merged into one long rumble he could hear the sound of regimental bands. As long as the bandsmen were playing then the British battalions were not suffering overmuch from the French bombardment. If Wellesley had not pulled the British line behind the crest the French gunners would be slaughtering the battalions file by file and the bandsmen would be doing their other job of picking up the wounded. He stared across the stream at the empty grass, thinking of the promise to Lennox, of the Eagle.

Harper pointed ahead. "Hear that?"

It was the noise Sharpe had been waiting for, faint but unmistakable, the sound of the French attack. The enemy columns were not in sight, but through the mist he could hear the drummers beating the hypnotic rhythm of the charge. On and on it would go until the attack was won or lost, the drummer boys thrashing the endless rhythm that had carried the French to victory after victory. There was a relentless menace about the drumbeats, each repeated phrase bringing the French nearer by ten paces.

Sharpe smiled at Harper. "Look after the boy. Is he all right?"

"Denny, sir? Tripped over his sword three times but otherwise he's fine." Harper laughed. "Look after yourself, sir."

Sharpe walked back up the stream, the drumbeats nearer, the skirmish line peering apprehensively into the mist. Their job was about to begin. The French guns had failed to break the British battalions and now, spread out in front of the drums, the voltigeurs were coming. Their aim was to get as close to the British battalions as they could and snipe at the line with their muskets, to thin the ranks, so that when the column arrived the British line would be rotten and give way. Sharpe's skirmishers, with the other Light Companies, had to stop the voltigeurs.

He found Knowles standing by the stream. "See anything?"

"No, sir."

The drumming was louder, competing with the crash of the shells, and at the end of each drummed phrase Sharpe could hear a new sound as the drummers paused to let thousands of voices chant, "*Vive L'Empereur!*" It was the victory noise that had terrified the armies of Europe, the sound of Marengo, of Austerlitz, of Jena.

Then, upstream and out of sight, the Light troops met and Sharpe heard the first crackle of musketry; not the rolling volleys of massed ranks but the spaced, deliberate cracks of aimed shots.

Knowles looked at Sharpe with raised eyebrows. The rifleman shook his head. "That's only one column. There'll be at least another one, probably two, and nearer. Wait."

And there they were, dim figures running in the mist, dozens of men in blue jackets with red epaulettes, who angled across their front. The riflemen raised their muskets.

"Hold your fire!" He pushed a musket down. The voltigeurs ran into the fire of the 66th and the Royal Americans, a hundred paces upstream, and he waited to see if they would reach the South Essex. "Wait!"

He watched the first Frenchmen crumple on the turf, others knelt and took careful aim but it was still not his fight. He was glad to let his raw troops see real skirmishing before they had to do it themselves. The French, like the British, fought in pairs. Each man had to protect his partner, firing in turn. Sharpe could hear the shouts, the whistles that passed on commands, and in the background, insistent as a tocsin, the drumming. Knowles was like a leashed hound but Sharpe held him back. "Our turn will come."

The British line was holding. The French tried to rush the stream but fell as they reached the water. The British pairs moved in short rushes, changing position, confusing their enemy, waiting for them to come in range and then letting off their shots. The sound was rising to its first crescendo, the roar of cannon, the crash of shells, the drums and voices of the column, and the sound of bugles mixing with the musketry. The mist, thickening now with the smoke of the French batteries, would soon be burned off. Sharpe felt the faintest breeze and saw a great swirl of whiteness shiver and move, and in the gap was a mass of men, tight-packed marching ranks tipped with steel, one of the columns aiming for the stream. He heard Knowles draw breath with amazement before the mist closed down again. It was time to retreat.

Sure enough, Sharpe heard the whistles and bugles and saw the skirmishers to the left start to go backwards towards the Medellin. They left bodies, red and green, behind them.

He blew his own whistle, waved an arm, and listened for the sergeants to repeat the signal. As the line climbed out of the mist onto a hillside bright with the early sun, Sharpe turned, and heard his men gasp at the view they suddenly encountered.

Above them the crest of the Medellin was empty of soldiers, the French shells continuing to tear up the earth in gouts of soil and flame, while below them the French columns crawled out of the mist like great, strange animals emerging from the sea. The nearest column was two hundred yards to the left and to Sharpe's raw troops it must have seemed overwhelming. The voltigeurs were joining its ranks, the drummers beat it along relentlessly and the deep shouts of "*Vive L'Empereur!*" punctuated the grinding advance. There were three columns climbing the slope; each, Sharpe guessed, had close to two thousand men and over each there hung, glittering in the sun, three gilded Eagles reaching for the crest.

Sharpe turned his skirmish line to face the column and then waved the men down. There was little they could do at this range. He decided not to rejoin the battalion, the company would suffer less by staying on the hillside than if they tried to run through the barrage of shells. Ensign Denny came and knelt beside Sharpe and his face betrayed the fear that the drumming, chanting mass engendered. Sharpe looked at him. "What do you think?"

"Sir?"

"Frightening?" Denny nodded.

Sharpe laughed. "Did you ever learn arithmetic?"

"Yes, sir."

"Then add up how many Frenchmen can actually use their muskets."

Denny stared at the column and realization dawned on his face. The French column was a tried and tested battle winner, but against good troops it was a death trap—of the hundreds of men in the nearest column only the sixty at the front and the thirty or so men on the ends of the other ranks could actually fire at their enemies. The mass of men in the middle were there merely to look impressive, and fill up the gaps left by the dead.

The sound of the battle changed abruptly. The shelling stopped. The great marching columns were close to the crest of the Medellin and the French gunners were afraid of hitting their own men. For a moment there was just the drumming, the sound of thousands of boots hitting the hillside. And then, suddenly, the empty skyline was lined two deep with waiting men. It looked ridiculous, three great fists, enormous masses, aimed at a tenuous two-deep line. But the look was deceptive.

The nearest column was headed for the 66th and the 3rd. The British battalions were outnumbered two to one but every redcoat on the crest could fire his musket. The order was given, the British line took a quarter turn to the right as they brought their muskets to their shoulders. Instinctively the French column checked in the face of so many guns. The drums rattled, the French officers shouted, a kind of low growl came from the column, swelled to a roar, and the French charged towards the summit.

And stopped. The slim, steel blades of the British officers swept down and the relentless volleys began. Nothing could stand in the way of that musket fire. From right to left along the battalions the volleys flamed and flickered, a rolling fire that never stopped, the machine-like regularity of trained troops pouring four shots a minute into the dense mass of Frenchmen.

The drumming went on and, incredibly, the French tried to force their way on up the slope. The instinct of victory was ingrained, and as the front ranks were destroyed by the murderous fire the men behind struggled over the bodies to be thrown backwards in their turn. They faced an impossible task. The column was stuck, soaking up terrible punishment but refusing to accept defeat.

Sharpe was amazed that troops could take such losses. They tried to form into line and he could see the officers waving their swords to lead the rear ranks into the open flanks. Sharpe held his rifle up.

"Come on!"

His men cheered and followed him across the hillside. There was little danger that the French could form line but the appearance of a couple of hundred skirmishers on the flank would deter them. The Germans of the Legion went with Sharpe's company and they all stopped a hundred paces from the struggling mass of Frenchmen and began their own volleys, more ragged than the ordered fire from the crest, but effective enough. Sharpe yelled at his men to fix their bayonets. The sound of the drums faded. One boy gave a further determined rattle with his sticks but the attack was done. Broken and smashed by musket fire, the French did not wait for the bayonet charge. The mass split into small groups of fugitives, the Eagles drooped, the blue ranks broke and ran for the stream.

"Forward!"

The steel-tipped line marched down the slope. Sharpe looked for the Eagles but they were far ahead, being carried to safety, and he led his men diagonally down the hill to cut off the fleeing groups of Frenchmen. As the skirmishers cut into the blue mass the Frenchmen threw down their guns. One officer refused to surrender and flickered his blade towards Sharpe but the huge cavalry sword beat it aside and the man dropped to his knees. Sharpe ignored him. He wanted to get to the stream and stop his men pursuing the French onto the far bank where reserve battalions waited to punish the British victors.

Some Frenchmen stopped at the stream and turned their muskets on the British. A ball plucked at Sharpe's sleeve, another scorched past his face, but the small group broke and fled as he swept towards them. His boots splashed in the stream, he turned and screamed at his men to stop. He drove them back, away from the French reserve troops who waited with loaded muskets on the far bank.

It was done. The first attack was beaten and the slope of the Medellin smothered in a blue smear of bodies from the stream almost to the crest. There would be another attack, but first each side must count the living and collect the dead. Sharpe looked for Harper and saw, thankfully, that the sergeant was alive. Lieutenant Knowles was there, grinning broadly, and with red on his sword.

"What's the time, Lieutenant?"

Knowles tucked the blade under his arm and opened his watch. "Five minutes after six, sir. Wasn't that incredible?"

Sharpe laughed. "Just wait. That was nothing."

Harper ran down the slope towards them and held out a bundle in his hands. "Breakfast, sir?"

"Not garlic sausage?"

Harper grinned. "Just for you."

Sharpe broke off a length and bit into the pungent, tasty meat. He stretched his arms, felt the tenseness ease in his muscles.

Sergeant Harper turned to the men of the company, guarding their prisoners and boasting of their exploits. "All right, this isn't a harvest festival! Reload your guns. They'll be back."

AS THE SUN climbed higher and the battle died into silence, the Portina valley filled with men, British and French, who came to rescue the wounded and bury the dead. Sharpe took men down to the stream to find four members of the Light Company who were missing. All had been killed as they climbed back up the slope with their prisoners. The French cannon had opened fire and the shells blew apart in the loose ranks of the British trudging up the hill. Sharpe had watched one iron ball strike a rabbit hole and bounce into the air with smoke spiralling crazily from its fuse. The shell, small enough to pick up with one hand, landed by Gataker. The rifleman had bent down to pinch out the fuse but he was too late. It exploded, belching flame as it hurled his corpse backwards.

When the guns stopped the men were ordered back to bury the dead quickly, scraping shallow holes in the soft earth beside the stream. The French came as well. For a few minutes the troops avoided each other but soon someone made a joke, and within minutes the enemies shook hands, tried on each other's shakoes, and shared the meagre scraps of food. The valley was littered with the remains of battle: unexploded shells, weapons, looted packs.

"Sharpe! Captain!" Sharpe turned to see Hogan picking his way through the dead and wounded. "I've been looking for you!" The engineer slid from his horse and looked round. "Are you all right?"

"I'm all right." Sharpe accepted Hogan's offered water bottle. "How's Josefina?"

Hogan smiled. "She slept. I think she's all right." Hogan shook his head. "She's subdued; unhappy. But what would you expect after last night?"

Last night, thought Sharpe. Good God, it was only last night. He turned away and looked at the bloodied water of the Portina. He turned back to Hogan. "What's happening in town?"

Hogan took out his snuff box. "Everything's quiet. They rounded up most of the Spanish and they're back in their lines. There's a guard in the town to stop any more looting."

"So she's safe?"

Hogan looked at Sharpe's red-rimmed eyes, at the deep shadows on the face, and nodded. "She's safe, Richard."

He said no more. The two men began walking beside the stream,

between the bodies, and Hogan thought of the dragoon with a broken arm, a Captain Hardy, who had called at the house early in the morning. Josefina had been surprised to see him, but pleased, and told Hogan that she had met the cavalry officer in the town the day before. The dragoon had taken over Hogan's vigil and Hogan had liked the man: he could see how relieved Josefina was to have someone sitting beside her who told her jokes, talked blithely of balls and banquets, hunting and horses. Hardy was good for Josefina, Hogan knew, but this was not the time to tell Sharpe about him. "Richard?"

"Yes?"

"Have you done anything about . . . ?" Hogan broke off.

"Gibbons? Why?"

Hogan spoke hesitantly. "I was hoping that after a night to think about it you would be careful. It could destroy your career. A duel, a fight. Be careful."

Sharpe's face was unreadable. The Irishman waited, feeling an immense sadness. Finally he shrugged. "When will we see you, Richard?"

"I don't know." Sharpe indicated the waiting French army. "There's a hell of a fight still to come and I suspect we'll all have to stay on the field till one side goes home. Maybe tonight. Probably tomorrow. I don't know."

Bugles called the troops back to their positions, and Hogan gathered his reins in his hand and heaved himself into the saddle. "Be careful, Richard. We don't want to lose you." He put spurs to his horse and cantered back towards Talavera.

Sharpe walked up the slope of the Medellin with his men as they counted the spoils they had collected from the dead. For himself there would be richer pickings on the field before the sun fell; there was an Eagle to be plucked.

The morning crept on. No one seemed to be in a hurry. The first attack had been repulsed and now the French were doubly determined to break the small British army in front of them. Through his telescope Sharpe watched the blue battalions moving into place until he could see more than thirty Eagles gathering for the attack.

It was obvious what was about to happen. The French were planning a hammer blow of such weight that no troops in the world would be able to withstand it. Behind the French infantry Sharpe could see impatient cavalry waiting to pour through the gap and slaughter the defeated British.

At one o'clock, the French guns opened fire again.

CHAPTER 13

Sir Henry Simmerson had hardly moved all morning. He had watched the repulse of the first attack but, apart from the Light Company, the South Essex had not been needed. Now the eastern side of the Portina was filled with French troops preparing to come forward, and Sir Henry had silently inspected them with the telescope. Fifteen thousand men were about to launch themselves against the centre of the British position and, beyond them, another fifteen thousand were already beginning to approach the network of obstacles that sheltered the Spanish.

He grunted and shifted in his saddle. "We will not surrender."

Lieutenant Gibbons edged his horse closer to his uncle. It had not occurred to him that they might surrender but he had long known that the easiest way to stay in Sir Henry's favour was to offer agreement. "Quite right, sir."

Simmerson pushed his telescope shut. He had been right all along. It had been madness to let Wellesley have an army. "It will be a disaster, Christian. The army is about to be destroyed."

His nephew agreed again and Simmerson reflected what a waste of talent it was that Gibbons should only be a lieutenant. He had never heard anything but military sense from the boy.

A new battalion appeared in the French line, almost opposite the South Essex, and Simmerson opened the telescope again to look at them. "That's strange."

The fresh battalion was dressed in white jackets with red turnbacks and collars. Simmerson had never seen troops like them.

"Major Forrest! Do you know who these new troops are?"

"No, sir."

"Find out."

The colonel watched Forrest spur his horse down the line. "Going to see Sharpe. Thinks he knows it all." But not for long, thought Simmerson: this battle would see the end of military adventurers like Sharpe and Wellesley and return the army to prudent men, men like himself. He turned and watched the fall of the French shells.

Forrest came back. "Captain Sharpe thinks they're probably the Dutch battalions, sir. And he asks that the Light Company go forward. He thinks the Dutchmen will attack this part of the line."

Simmerson said nothing. Certainly the Dutch were very nearly opposite the South Essex, with a second battalion forming a separate column behind the first. But Simmerson had no intention of letting his battalion get involved in the death struggle of Wellesley's army.

"Sir?" Forrest prompted him.

Simmerson waved down the interruption. There was an idea in

his head. The army was doomed, that was certain, and in an hour or so Wellesley's force would be dead or prisoners. But there was no need for the South Essex to be part of that disaster. If he were to march them away from the Medellin to a position in the rear, then they would not be encircled by the French. More than that, they would be the rallying point for whatever fugitives managed to escape and he could then lead them back to Lisbon and to England. Such an action would be rewarded and Simmerson imagined himself in the lavish gold lace and cocked hat of a general. He gripped the pommel of his saddle in excitement. If he could salvage even a small part of this army then Whitehall would be forced to reward his initiative. His confidence soared.

"Major! Battalion will about turn and form column of march on the left!" Forrest did not move. The colonel wheeled his horse. "Come on, Forrest, we haven't much time!"

Forrest was appalled. If he did as Simmerson ordered, then the South Essex infantry would hinge back like a swinging gate and leave a gap in the British line through which the French could pour their troops. And the French columns had started their advance! Their voltigeurs were swarming towards the stream, the drums had begun their war rhythm. Simmerson slapped the rump of Forrest's horse. "Hurry, man! It's our only hope!"

The orders were given and the South Essex began the clumsy wheeling movement that left the flank of the Medellin an open slope to the enemy. A dragoon lieutenant, one of Hill's staff, slid his horse to a stop in a spray of earth. Simmerson looked at the newcomer. "Lieutenant?"

"General Hill's compliments, sir, and would you stay in position and deploy skirmishers."

Simmerson nodded benignly. "My compliments to General Hill, but he will find out I am doing the right thing. Carry on!"

Sharpe's company was the pivot of the movement and the ranks stared behind them, aghast, as the enemy columns began their advance. The skirmish line was already fighting: Sharpe could hear the muskets and rifles, and three hundred yards beyond the stream the Eagles were coming. Yet the South Essex were retreating!

Harper looked woefully at his captain. "What's happening, sir?"

"We're going forward, that's what's happening." Sharpe pushed through the ranks. "Light Company! Skirmish order. Follow me!"

He ran down the hill, his men following. Damn Simmerson! The skirmishers from the white-jacketed Dutch battalion were already over the stream. Shells burst among the Light Company and Harper, driving them from the back, saw two men fall. He watched Sharpe drag his sword from the scabbard and realized the captain planned to charge right into the skirmishers and push them back across the stream. Harper took a deep breath. "Bayonets! Bayonets!"

The men with muskets had little chance of fixing their bayonets in time, but the Baker rifle bayonet was long and equipped with a handle, so the riflemen held them like swords; the French saw them coming, turned, and fumbled with their ammunition. A bullet passed Sharpe, singing in his ear, and then he was swinging the sword at the nearest man, the rest of the company were stabbing and shouting, and the Dutchmen were scrambling back to the far side of the Portina.

"Down! Down! Down!" Sharpe yelled at his men and pushed two of them to the ground. "Aim low! Kill the bastards!"

The Dutch skirmishers reformed and started sniping across the stream. They were fifty yards away, and Sharpe's riflemen asserted their superiority thanks to the spiralling grooves in the barrels of their weapons. Sharpe's redcoat Light Company of the South Essex crept nearer to the stream to improve their aim; he watched them proudly, helping each other, pointing out targets, firing coolly and remembering the lessons he had pounded into them. Ensign Denny was standing up, shouting shrill encouragement, and Sharpe pushed him to the ground. "Don't make yourself a target, Mr. Denny. They like to kill promising young officers!"

Denny beamed at the compliment. "What about you, sir? Why don't you get down?"

"I will. Remember to keep moving!"

Knowles was sensibly watching the open end of the line, directing the fire of half a dozen men to stop the whitecoats outflanking the South Essex, and Sharpe was not needed there. The company was doing well, fighting like a veteran unit, and already there were a dozen bodies on the far side of the stream. There were two in red uniforms on their own side but the Light Company held the initiative and the Dutchmen did not want to risk coming too close.

But beyond the voltigeurs, advancing steadily, was the right-hand column of a series that filled the plain between the Cascajal and the town. The main attack was only minutes away and when it came, Sharpe knew, the skirmish line would be thrown back. The whole horizon was hidden by the clouds of dust thrown up by the French infantry, their drumming and cheering rivalled the sound of the guns and exploding shells.

Sharpe had never seen an attack on this scale: the columns covered half a mile in the width of their attack and behind them was a second line, equally strong, that the French would throw in if the British checked the first. Sharpe looked behind. Simmerson had swung the battalion and it was marching away, creating a great gap in the line. Sharpe could see a horseman riding recklessly towards the single Colour and he guessed that Hill or even Wellesley was dealing furiously with Simmerson.

He joined Harper. There were only seconds before the column would force them back and he stared at its slow advance and at the Eagle which flashed tantalizingly from its centre. As the column was drummed closer the enemy voltigeurs were making short dashes towards the stream in an attempt to force the British skirmish line back. Sharpe could now see half a dozen of his men lying dead or badly wounded.

The voltigeurs were firing faster, not bothering to aim, saturating their enemy with musket fire, and Sharpe saw another man go down—Jebediah Horrell, whose new boots had given him blisters. It was time to retreat. Sharpe blew his whistle twice and watched as his men squeezed off a last shot before running a few paces back, kneeling, and loading again. He rammed a bullet into his rifle, slid the steel ramrod back into the slit stock, looked for a target, and found him in a man wearing the single stripe of a French sergeant. Sharpe put the rifle to his shoulder, felt the satisfying click as the flat, ring-neck cock rode back on the mainspring, and pulled the trigger. The sergeant spun round, hit in the shoulder, and turned to see who had fired. Harper grabbed Sharpe's arm.

"That was a terrible shot. Now let's get the hell out of here! They'll want revenge for that!"

Sharpe grinned and sprinted back with the sergeant towards the new skirmish line seventy paces behind the stream. The air was full of drumming, and the columns were splashing through the stream, the whole plain engulfed in French infantry. The British guns had a target they could not miss, and time and time again the solid shot lanced into the columns, crushing men by the dozen. Spherical shot cases also, filled with musket balls—invented by a Colonel Shrapnell—detonated above the French ranks, shredding them. But there were too many men and the files closed, the ranks stepped over the dead, and the columns came on.

For Sharpe's company, there was no time to do anything but run and fire, run and fire, to try to keep the French skirmishers pinned back. Sharpe was taking the Light Company back towards the spot where the South Essex should have been. His company was down to less than sixty men and, at that moment, they were the only troops between the column and the empty plain at the rear of the British line. He had no chance of stopping the French, but as long as he could slow down the advance there was a hope that the gap might be filled and the sacrifice of his men justified. Sharpe fought with his rifle until it was so fouled he could hardly push the ramrod into the barrel.

Then, at last, the blessed sound of raking volleys, as the troops of the British battalions on either side tore apart the heads of the French columns and drove the ranks back. Sharpe could see nothing. The Dutch battalion had marched into the gap on the flank of the 7th Battalion of the King's German Legion, and the Germans there were fighting on two fronts, ahead of them, and to the side where the South Essex should have been. The voltigeurs had disappeared, and Sharpe and his company, black-faced and exhausted, were left watching the rear of the enemy column as it tried to roll up the flank of the Germans.

"Why don't they march on?" Knowles was beside him, bleeding from the scalp, and with the face, suddenly, of a veteran.

"Because the other columns are being defeated. They don't want to be left on their own." He accepted a drink from Knowles's canteen, his own was shattered, and the water was wonderfully cool in his parched throat. He wished he could see what was happening but the sound told its own story. The drumming from the twelve French columns faltered and stopped, the cheers of the British rose into the air, the volleys paused while bayonets scraped from scabbards and clicked onto muskets. Then the cheers became vengeful screams as the first line of the French attack disintegrated and the British line chased them back across the stream.

"Oh God." Sharpe groaned in disbelief.

"What?" Knowles looked towards the stream. At the stream was a second line of enemy columns, as large as the first, and the Frenchmen were able to find shelter behind the waiting guns of their reserve. The British, their blood roused, bayonets wet but muskets unloaded, ran straight into the fire of the reserve French troops and now it was their turn to be shattered by musket volleys. They fled in total disorder, and behind them the second line of enemy columns struck up the drumbeats and started to march onto the plain where Simmerson's gap had been widened to half a mile and where the only British troops were running from them.

Sir Henry, safe with the South Essex at the back of the Medellin, saw the second French advance and breathed a sigh of relief. For a moment he had been terrified. He had expected the French to carve their way through the British line as though it did not exist, and instead the British had driven twice their number in bloody chaos before them and with them, momentarily, went his dreams and hopes. But now this new French attack, even bigger than the first, was driving its way forward from the stream. He had been right after all.

He turned to point out his perspicacity to Christian Gibbons but, instead of his nephew, he found himself looking into the eyes of a strange lieutenant colonel.

"You are relieved, Sir Henry. The battalion is mine."

"What . . ?" The man did not wait to argue. He turned to Forrest and rapped out a stream of orders. The battalion was turning, heading back for the battle. Simmerson rode up behind the man and shouted a protest but the new lieutenant colonel wheeled on him with a drawn sword and bared teeth and Sir Henry decided that this was no place for an argument. The new man then looked at Gibbons.

"Who are you, Lieutenant?"

"Gibbons, sir."

"Ah yes. I remember. Of the Light Company?"

"Yes, sir."

The new colonel hit Gibbons's horse with the flat of his sword. "Then join the Light Company, Mr. Gibbons! Hurry! They need help, even yours!"

Sir Henry sat his horse and watched the South Essex march towards the battle, saw another battalion, the 48th, hurrying into the path of the enemy, while from the far side of the gaping hole other British battalions marched desperately to make a thin screen in front of the massing Eagles.

The battle was still not lost. Sir Henry looked round the hilltop and felt terribly alone.

"SIR! SIR!" Ensign Denny tugged Sharpe's jacket excitedly and pointed. Through the hanging smoke from the Medellin guns Sharpe saw a British battalion marching down the hill to the Light Company's rescue. "It's ours, sir! Ours!"

Behind them, dimly glimpsed through the smoke, Sharpe could see another battalion marching to put itself in front of this second, larger French attack. He could hear the drums again, and he sensed that the crisis of the battle was coming and, as if in confirmation, the French cannon started again, throwing shell after shell into the British battalions racing to form a new line to meet the fresh attack.

Sharpe's men were forgotten. They were a small band in the bottom of a shallow valley on the edge of a great fight. At any moment the French attack would strike stunningly home and Sharpe stood sword in hand, uncertain what to do. Harper tapped his arm and pointed to a horseman who was coming slowly towards them from the Medellin. "Lieutenant Gibbons, sir!"

Sharpe turned back to the fight. Presumably Gibbons was coming with orders from Simmerson following his inexplicable retreat from the battle and equally inexplicable return, but Sharpe was not particularly interested. The South Essex was still some moments away from opening fire on the white-coated battalion in the gap; when they did, Sharpe knew the Dutchmen would turn on their attackers and he had no trust in Simmerson's ability to lead the battalion. It was best to ignore the South Essex.

Sharpe turned to Harper and pointed. "Can you see what I see?"

Harper grinned, his white teeth brilliant against his powder-blackened face. "It's very tempting, sir. I was thinking of it myself."

Two hundred yards away, in the centre of the Dutch line, was an Eagle. It flashed gold in the light, its outstretched wings shadowing the pole on which it was mounted. Harper stared at the backs of the Dutch infantry who fired at an unseen target in the smoke beyond. "It would make a great story, so it would."

Sharpe plucked a blade of grass and chewed it, then spat it out. "I can't order you to come."

The sergeant smiled again, a big, happy smile. "I've nothing better to do. It will take more than the two of us."

Sharpe nodded and grinned. "Perhaps Lieutenant Gibbons might lend a hand?"

Harper turned and stared at Gibbons who now hovered anxiously, fifty yards behind the company. "What does he want?"

"God knows. Forget him." Sharpe walked in front of his men. They squatted on the grass, their faces filthy, their eyes red and sunken from the powder smoke and the strain of battle. They had done more than well. They looked at him expectantly.

"You've done well. I'm proud of you." They grinned, embarrassed at the praise, pleased by it. "I'm not asking a thing more of you. The battalion's on its way here and in a minute Mr. Denny will take you back and form you up on the left as usual." They were puzzled now, their grins gone. "Sergeant Harper and I are not coming with you. We think it's bad that our battalion only has one Colour so we're going to fetch another. That one." He pointed at the Eagle and saw the men look past him. "We're going now. Anyone who wants to come is a fool but they'll be welcome. The rest of you will go back with Mr. Denny. The sergeant and I will join you when we can."

Denny protested. "I want to come, sir!"

Sharpe shook his head. "Whoever else comes, Mr. Denny, you will not. I'd like you to have a seventeenth birthday."

Denny blushed, and Sharpe turned away. He heard Harper unsheathe his bayonet and then came the sound of other blades clicking into place. He began to walk towards the enemy, sword held low, and heard the steps behind him. Harper was beside him and they walked on towards the unsuspecting battalion.

"They've all come, sir. All."

Sharpe looked at him. "All?" He turned. "Mr. Denny? Go back to the battalion! That is an order!"

"But, sir . . . ."

"No, Mr. Denny. Back!"

He watched as the boy turned and took a few steps. Gibbons was still sitting on his horse and watching them. Sharpe went on, praying that the enemy would not notice them, praying that they would be successful. He had set his heart on an Eagle.

The noise of battle became louder. At last Sharpe could hear the regular platoon volleys and knew that away to the right the second French attack had met the new British line. The six-pound round-shot of the British cannon thundered overhead, but the drumming increased, the shouts of "*Vive L'Empereur!*" were unabated. Suddenly they were within a hundred yards of the Eagle. Sharpe twisted the sword in his hand and hurried the pace. Surely the Dutch would see them!

A drummer-boy, rattling his sticks at the rear of the enemy line, turned and saw the small group coming silently through the smoke. He shouted a warning, but no one heard. He shouted again and Sharpe saw men swivelling to face them but they were still loading, their ramrods half down their barrels. Sharpe raised his sword. "On! On!"

He began to run, oblivious of everything except the Eagle and the frightened faces of the enemy who were desperately hurrying to load their muskets. Around the standard bearer Sharpe could see Grenadiers wearing tall bearskins, some of them armed with axes, the protectors of French honour. Harper was beside him, the sword bayonet in his hand, and the two men screamed their challenge as they ploughed into the centre of the enemy line. Muskets exploded with a terrible crash, Sharpe had an impression of men in green uniforms being thrown backwards, and then he could see nothing except a tall grenadier, lunging at him in short professional jabs with a bayonet. Sharpe twisted to one side, let the blade slide past, grabbed the muzzle of the grenadier's musket with his left hand and pulled him onto his levelled sword blade. Someone cut at him from the left, a swinging down stroke with a clubbed musket, and though he turned so that it only thudded viciously into his pack, it threw him forward onto the body of the grenadier whose hands were clutching the blade embedded in his stomach. A gun deafened him, one of his own rifles, and suddenly he was clear and dragging the blade from the heavy corpse and screaming murder at the men who guarded the Eagle. Harper had cut his way through the first rank but his sword bayonet was too short and he was being driven back by two men with musket bayonets. Sharpe crushed them to one side with his sword, and Harper leaped into the gap, cutting left and right.

More muskets, more screams, the white-jackets were clawing at them, and the Eagle was retreating. But there was nowhere for the standard bearer to go except towards the musket fire of an unseen British battalion that was somewhere in the smoke. An axeman came at Sharpe, a huge man, smiling as he hefted the huge blade and swung it powerfully down. Sharpe wrenched himself out of the way, felt the wind of the blade, and saw the axe thud into the blood-wet ground. He stabbed the sword down into the man's neck, and watched as Harper plucked the axe from the earth and threw away his bayonet. The Irishman was screaming in the language of his ancestors, the axe searing in a circle, his lips wrenched back in his blackened face, his shako gone, his long hair matted with powder, the great silver blade singing in his hands and carving a path through the enemy.

The standard bearer jumped out of the ranks to carry the precious Eagle down the battalion to safety, but there was a rifle crack and he fell. Then there was a new sound, and the Dutch battalion reeled like a wounded animal as the South Essex arrived on their flank and began to pour in their volleys. Sharpe was faced by a crazed officer who swung at him with a sword, missed, and screamed in panic as Sharpe lunged with the point. A man in white ran out of the ranks to pick up the fallen Eagle but Sharpe kicked him in the ribs, bent, and plucked the staff from the ground. Men lunged at him with bayonets and he felt a blow on the thigh, but Harper was there and so was Denny.

Denny! Sharpe pushed the boy down, swung the sword to protect him but a bayonet was in the ensign's chest and even as Sharpe smashed the sword down on the man's head he felt Denny shudder and collapse. Sharpe screamed, swung the gilded Eagle at the enemy, watched the gold scar the air and force them back, screamed again and jumped the bodies with his bloodied sword reaching for more. The Dutchmen fell back, appalled; the Eagle was coming at them and they retreated in the face of the two huge riflemen who swung at them, who bled from a dozen cuts yet still came on. And now there were volleys coming from the right, from the front, and the Dutchmen who had fought so well for their French masters, had had enough. They ran, as the other French battalions were running. The whole French army went backwards, defeated by the line, by the musket that could be fired five times a minute on a good day, and by men who were not afraid of drums.

CHAPTER 14

It was still not over, but very nearly so. As the British troops in the centre of the field sank in exhausted lines by the edge of the discoloured Portina stream, flurries of firing and the shrill tones of cavalry trumpets came from the ground north of the Medellin. But nothing much happened; the 23rd Light Dragoons made a suicidal charge, the British six-pounders ground twelve French battalion squares into horror and then the French gave up. Silence fell. The British had the victory and the field.

And with it the dead and wounded. There were more than thirteen thousand casualties. The wounded cried for water, for their mothers, for a bullet, for anything other than the pain and helplessness in the heat. And the horror was not done with them. The sun had burned relentlessly for days, the grass on the Medellin and in the valley was tinder dry, and from somewhere a flame began that rippled and spread and flared through the grass and burned wounded and dead alike. The victors tried to move the wounded but it was too much, too soon, and the flames spread and the rescuers cursed and dropped beside the fouled Portina stream and slaked their thirst in its bloodied water.

Vultures circled the northern hills. The sun slanted shadows on the burning field, and on the blackened troops who stirred themselves to loot the dead and move the wounded. Sharpe and Harper wandered their own course, two men in the curtains of smoke and burning grass, both bleeding. Sharpe held the Eagle. It was not much to look at; a light blue pole eight feet long and on its top the gilded bird with wings outspread, its claws grasping the thunderbolts it was about to launch at the enemies of France. It was less than two hands' breadths across, and the same in height. But it was an Eagle and it was theirs.

Lieutenant Colonel the Honourable William Lawford sat his horse and stared at the bodies on the field. Sir Henry Simmerson was done. Wellesley had sworn, briefly and fluently, and sent Lawford to take over the battalion. He had led the South Essex down the slope and watched as they fired their muskets, slowly but calmly, into the enemy. He had seen the fight for the Eagle but the spreading smoke of the battalion's volleys had blotted out the scene. A lieutenant brought in forty-eight bleeding and stained riflemen, grinning like monkeys, who talked of the Eagle, but where was it? He wanted to see Sharpe, but the field was shrouded in flames and smoke so he started the battalion on the grisly task of stripping the dead and piling the naked bodies like cordwood for the fire. There were too many to bury.

Major Forrest rode up to Lawford and saluted.

"Major?"

"Except for the Light Company, sir, we've lost very few."

"How many?"

Forrest fetched a piece of paper from his pouch. "A dozen dead, sir, perhaps twice as many wounded."

Lawford nodded. "We got off lightly, Major. And the Light Company?"

"Lieutenant Knowles brought in forty-three, sir, and most of them are wounded. Sergeant Read stayed with the baggage with two others, that's forty-six. There were five men too sick to fight who are in the town." Forrest paused. "That's fifty-one accounted for, sir, out of a complement of eighty-nine."

Lawford said nothing. He leaned forward in his saddle and peered into the shifting smoke. Forrest cleared his throat nervously. "You don't think, sir . . . ?" He tailed the question away.

"No, Major, I don't. I've known Richard Sharpe since I was a lieutenant and he was a sergeant. He should have died a dozen times, but he crawls through somehow." Lawford grinned. "Don't worry about Sharpe, Major. It's much better to let him worry about you. Who else is missing?"

"There's Sergeant Harper, sir."

"Ah!" Lawford interrupted. "The legendary Irishman."

"And Lieutenant Gibbons, sir."

"Lieutenant Gibbons?" Lawford remembered the petulant blond lieutenant. "I wonder how he'll get on without his uncle?" The lieutenant colonel smiled briefly; Gibbons was his least concern. There was still much to do, many men to be rescued before the townspeople looted the bodies.

"Thank you, Major. We'll just have to wait for Captain Sharpe. In the meantime would you arrange a party to get water for the men? And let's hope these French dead have got food in their packs, otherwise we're in for a lean night."

The French did carry food, and gold, and Sharpe, as he always did, split his finds with Harper. The sergeant was carrying the Eagle and he peered at the bird thoughtfully.

"Is it worth money, sir?"

"I don't know." Out of habit Sharpe was reloading his rifle and he grunted as he forced the ramrod into the fouled barrel.

"But they'll reward us, sir, surely?"

Sharpe grinned at the sergeant. "I'd think so." He slid the ramrod back into place. "Perhaps they'll just say 'thank you'." He bowed ironically to the Irishman. "Thank you, Sergeant Harper."

Harper bowed back. "I can't wait to see Simmerson's face when you give him this," he said.

Sharpe laughed, he was looking forward to that moment. He took the Eagle from Harper. "Come on. We'd better find them."

Harper touched Sharpe's shoulder and froze, staring into the smoke above the stream. Sharpe could see nothing. "What is it?"

"Do you see it, sir?" Harper's voice was hushed, excited. "There! Damn! It's gone."

"What, for God's sake, what?"

Harper turned to him. "Would you wait, sir? Two minutes?"

Sharpe grinned. "Another bird?"

"Aye. The magpie with the blue tail. It went over the stream and it can't be far." Harper's face was lit up, the battle suddenly forgotten, the capture of the Eagle a small thing against the spotting of the rare bird.

Sharpe laughed. "Go on. I'll wait here."

The sergeant went silently towards the stream, leaving Sharpe in the drifting smoke among the bodies. Once a horse trotted past, its flank a sheet of blood. Far off, behind the flames, Sharpe could hear bugles calling the living into ranks. He stared at the Eagle, and felt a fresh surge of elation. They could not send him to the West Indies now! He smiled, held the bird up so its wings caught the light, and heard the hoof beats behind him.

His rifle was on the ground and he had to leave it as he rolled desperately to avoid Gibbons's charge. The lieutenant, curved sabre drawn, was wild-eyed, leaning from the saddle. The blade hissed over Sharpe's head, he fell, kept rolling, and knelt up to see Gibbons rein in the horse, turn it with one hand, urge it forward. The lieutenant was giving Sharpe no time to draw his sword, instead he pointed the sabre like a lance and spurred forward.

Sharpe dropped and the horse turned on its back legs, and Gibbons was high over him with the sabre stabbing downwards. The horse lashed with its feet, and Sharpe twisted away.

Sharpe swung with the Eagle, aiming for the horse's head, but Gibbons was too good a horseman, he easily avoided the wild blow. The lieutenant hefted the sabre in his hand. "She felt good, Sharpe. And I'll take that Eagle as well."

Sharpe looked round. The loaded rifle was five yards away and he ran towards it, knowing it was too far, hearing the hooves behind him, and then the sabre cut into his pack and threw him flat on the ground. He fell on the Eagle, twisted to his right, and the horse was pirouetting above him, the hooves like hammers and the sabre blade a curve of light behind the glinting horseshoes. He rolled again, felt a numbing blow as one of the hooves struck his shoulder, but kept rolling away from Gibbons's sabre. He was angry with himself for being caught, and he wondered how long the lieutenant had stalked him through the smoke.

He could hardly move his right arm, it seemed paralysed by the blow from the hoof, but he lunged up with the Eagle as if it were a quarterstaff, trying to keep the hooves away from his body. Damn that magpie! Couldn't Harper hear the fight? Then the sabre was over his stomach and Gibbons's face was above him.

Gibbons seemed to laugh at him, his mouth stretching and stretching, and still he did not stab downwards. Then his eyes widened and Sharpe saw the blood coming from his throat and falling, slowly and thickly, on the sabre. The lieutenant was dead. His body toppled towards Sharpe and in its back was a bayonet on a French musket, stuck there, swaying above the body. Sergeant Harper stood on the far side of the horse.

Gibbons's body slumped onto the ground and Sharpe moved, climbing to his feet. He looked at Harper. "Thank you."

"My pleasure." The sergeant was grinning broadly. "It was worth being in this army just to do that."

Sharpe leaned on the Eagle's staff, catching his breath, appalled at the closeness of death. He shook his head at Harper. "The bastard nearly got me!"

"He would have had to finish me off first, sir." It was said lightly enough, but Sharpe knew the sergeant had spoken the truth and he smiled in acknowledgment and then went to pick up his rifle.

He and the sergeant walked away, stamping through the flames, until they saw the solitary yellow Colour of the South Essex.

Lieutenant Knowles saw them first, shouted, and suddenly the Light Company were round them, slapping their backs. Sharpe looked past a beaming Forrest to see Lawford.

"Sir? Where is Sir Henry?"

Lawford shrugged his elegant shoulders. "Shall we just say that Sir Henry suddenly felt a burning desire to return to the good burghers of Paglesham. You now have the honour to command *my* Light Company."

Sharpe wanted to laugh. The Eagle was low at his side, hidden in the press of men, so he dragged it clear and it suddenly flashed in the light. He handed it up to Lawford. "The battalion's missing Colour, sir. It was the best Sergeant Harper and I could do."

Lawford stared at the two men, at the tiredness beneath the powder stains, at the lines on their faces grooved with blood from scalp wounds, and at the black patches of blood on their green jackets. He took the Eagle and hoisted it high into the air. The South Essex, so long scorned by the army, saw it and cheered until other battalions stopped to see what the noise was about.

Above them, on the Medellin, General Hill heard the excitement and trained a telescope on the battalion that had so nearly lost the battle. He caught the Eagle in the lens and his mouth dropped open. "I'll be damned! Bless my soul! The strangest thing! The South Essex have captured an Eagle!"

There was a dry laugh beside him and Hill turned to see Sir Arthur Wellesley. "Sir?"

"I'll be damned too, Hill. That's only the third time I've ever heard you swear." He took the glass and looked down the slope. "God damn it! You're right! Let's go and see this strange bird."

THE WINE was dark red in the crystal glasses, the deep-polished table shone from a score of candles in their silver holders, the paintings showed grave and eminent ancestors of the Spanish family in whose Talavera mansion Sir Arthur Wellesley was host to a dinner party. Even the food was fairly equal to the occasion. The troops were still on meagre half-rations, but Wellesley, as befitted a general, had done better than most and Sharpe had sipped chicken soup, enjoyed jugged hare, eaten amply of Wellesley's favourite mutton, and listened to his fellow guests grumble about the diet as they drank unending bottles of wine.

"Daddy" Hill was there, rubicund and happy, smiling at Sharpe, shaking his head and saying, "Bless me, Sharpe, an Eagle."

There was laughter round the table. Lawford, confirmed, at least temporarily, as commanding officer of the South Essex, leaned back, fixed Sharpe with a cynical eye and thumped the table.

"You were lucky, Sharpe, lucky!"

"Yes, sir."

"Don't you 'yes sir' me." Sharpe saw Wellesley watching with an amused eye. Lawford pushed a bottle of red wine towards Sharpe. "You lost damn near half your company! If you hadn't come back with the Eagle you would have deserved to have been broken right back to private again. Aren't I right?"

Sharpe inclined his head. "You are, sir."

Satisfied, Lawford raised his glass to the rifleman. "But it was damn well done, all the same . . . ."

There was more laughter. Sharpe leaned back and listened to the talk round the table and let the meal rest heavy in his stomach. The servants were bringing in brandy and cigars, which meant that the evening would soon be over, but he had enjoyed it. He sipped his wine, and reflected again on his good fortune. Perhaps he really was lucky, as his men said, but he wished he knew how to preserve that luck. He remembered Gibbons's falling body, the bayonet deep in his back, and the sight of Harper back from his bird-watching just in time to stop the sabre stabbing down into Sharpe. The next day all traces of the crime had been burned away. The dead, Gibbons among them, had been stacked in naked piles and the living had thrust wooden faggots deep into the corpses and set fire to them. There had been far too many for burial, and for two days the fires were fed with more wood and the stench hung over the town until the ashes were scattered across the Portina valley. "Sharpe?"

He started. Someone had spoken his name and he had missed what was said. "Sir? I'm sorry."

Wellesley was smiling at him. "Captain Hogan was saying that you've been improving Anglo-Portuguese relations?"

Sharpe glanced at Hogan who raised his eyebrows impishly. All week the Irishman had been determinedly cheerful about Josefina. Now, with three generals watching him, Sharpe had no option but to smile and give a modest shrug.

"Fortune favours the brave, eh, Sharpe?" Hill grinned.

"Yes, sir."

He leaned back and let the conversation flow on. He missed her. It was only just over two weeks since the night he had followed her from the inn courtyard into the darkness by the stream, and since then he had spent only five nights with her. And now there would be no more. He had known as soon as he had reached Talavera, on the morning after the battle. There she had kissed him and smiled, and while Agostino packed her leather saddlebags, she had walked with him through the town.

"It would never have lasted, Richard."

"I know." He believed otherwise, but she wanted him to say

goodbye to her gracefully and it was the least he could do.

They walked into a small, sunlit square and stared at a convent which formed one side of the plaza. Fifteen hundred British wounded were in the building and the army surgeons were working on the first floor. Screams came clearly down from the windows and, with them, a grisly flow of severed limbs that piled up beside a tree. There he told her about Gibbons; about the final look before Harper's bayonet took its revenge.

Josefina plucked his elbow and they turned away. "I have a present for you." She gave him a tiny paper packet.

Inside the paper was a ring, made of silver, engraved with an eagle. She looked up at him, pleased at his expression. "I bought it in Oropesa. For you."

Sharpe had stammered his thanks and now, sitting with the generals, he let his fingers feel the silver ring. They had walked back to the house and, waiting outside, there had been a cavalry officer with two spare horses. "Is that him?"

"Yes."

"And he's rich?"

She smiled. "Very. He's a good man, Richard. You'd like him."

Sharpe laughed. "I doubt it." He wanted to tell her how much he would not like the dragoon, with his rich uniform and his thoroughbred horses.

"I can't stay with the army, Richard."

"So you're going back to Lisbon?"

She nodded. "He has a house in Belem—a big one. I'm sorry, Richard. I can't follow an army." She was looking up at him, pleading for understanding.

"I know. But armies follow you, yes?" It was a clumsy attempt at gallantry and it had pleased her, but now it was time to part and he did not know what to say. "Josefina? I'm sorry . . . ."

She touched his arm, and there was a gleam of tears in her eyes. "One day, Richard, you will fall in love with the right girl. You promise. You—"

A knock on the dining-room door interrupted his thoughts and Sharpe watched as a staff captain entered and gave Wellesley a sealed paper. Wellesley opened the paper. Then he tapped the table and the conversation tailed away.

The hook-nosed general lifted the paper into the air. "The Austrians have made peace with Bonaparte." He waited for the exclamations to die down. "Effectively, gentlemen, we are on our own. We can expect more French troops, maybe even Napoleon himself. But we have beaten three marshals this year, gentlemen, so let the rest come on!"

The officers pounded the table. Abruptly, Sir Arthur Wellesley got to his feet and held up his wineglass. "Gentlemen, I give you the King."

Sharpe scraped his chair back, took his glass, and joined in the murmuring. "The King, God bless him."

He was sitting down again, looking forward to the brandy and one of the general's cigars, when he noticed that Wellesley was still standing. He straightened up, cursing his lack of manners.

Wellesley waited for him. "I remember one other battle, gentlemen, which almost matched our recent victory in carnage. After Assaye I had to thank a young sergeant—today we salute the same man, a captain."

He raised his glass to Sharpe who was convulsed with embarrassment. He watched the officers smile at him, raise their glasses to him, and he looked down at the silver eagle. He wished Josefina could see him at this moment, that she could hear Wellesley's toast.

"Gentlemen. I give you Sharpe's Eagle."

Bernard Cornwell

When Bernard Cornwell gave up a successful career as a television producer and editor in June 1979 he did so to write the books he had been meticulously researching and planning for over seven years: a series covering the adventures of a soldier in the Peninsular Wars. *Sharpe's Eagle* is the first novel in the series, and Richard Sharpe has already staked his claim as the most exciting new fictional hero to arrive on the literary scene for many years.

Cornwell, who was born in London in 1944, first became interested in this period through his enjoyment, as a teenager, of C.S. Forester's *Hornblower* books. He subsequently became fascinated by Wellington's military campaigns—he thinks Wellington was our greatest-ever general—and always hoped someone would write a series of books about the adventures of a soldier that would parallel the naval exploits of Horatio Hornblower. When none appeared, he decided to write the series himself. First he read everything he could find on the subject, and during this research formed invaluable friendships with the Tower of London armourer and the curators of many regimental museums. Then he moved to New Jersey, USA, to write his novels, taking 146 books on the Peninsular Wars with him! He wanted to set his stories against a background of regimental life in the rich, realistic detail that few authors had attempted before. Significantly, he now feels that the best scenes in *Sharpe's Eagle* are those suggested by true events described in contemporary diaries and letters.

Richard Sharpe possesses a physical courage that Bernard Cornwell envies; unfortunately poor eyesight disappointed his own ambitions for an army career, but that does not mean he has not seen action: as a television journalist he has been under fire in Africa, the Middle East and Northern Ireland. It is no coincidence that two important characters in *Sharpe's Eagle* are Irishmen, both of whom are based on people Cornwell met while he was working in Belfast.

Cornwell is already far ahead with the next novel in the series, and is planning some research on the spot in Spain and Portugal, for descriptions of the siege of Badajoz. After that he feels that he will have earned a holiday!

MAN WOMAN and CHILD

A CONDENSATION OF THE BOOK BY

Erich Segal

ILLUSTRATED BY MITCHELL HOOKS

PUBLISHED BY GRANADA

The Beckwiths seemed a very ordinary family: Bob and Sheila's marriage was a good one, and their two daughters were growing up with the usual joys and troubles.

Then something totally unexpected happened—the disclosure of a guilty secret from the past—and suddenly the family unity was threatened with collapse.

Erich Segal, author of the bestselling *Love Story*, shows a new depth and maturity in this sensitive exploration of a family's reaction to crisis.

CHAPTER ONE

"I have an important message for you, Dr. Beckwith."

"I'm tied up right now. Can I get back to you?"

"Actually, Professor, I'd prefer to speak to you in person."

A phone call had summoned Robert Beckwith from the final departmental meeting of the term. It was the French consulate.

"Can you get to Boston before five?" the under-secretary asked.

"It's almost four thirty now," said Bob.

"I will wait for you."

"Is it *that* important?"

"Yes, I believe so."

Totally mystified. Bob walked back to where five other senior members of the Massachusetts Institute of Technology's statistics department were waiting. Citing the unimportance of their agenda when compared to the excellence of the June weather, he moved that they adjourn until the fall. As usual, there was one objection.

"I must say, Beckwith, this is rather unprofessional," huffed P. Herbert Harrison.

"Let's put it to a vote, Herb," Bob replied.

The score was five to one in favour of vacation.

Bob hurried to his car. As he began threading his way across the Charles River through the heavy rush-hour traffic, he had plenty of time to speculate on what could possibly be so urgent. And the more he thought, the more the odds seemed to suggest one thing: They're giving me the Legion of Honor.

It's not so impossible, he told himself. After all, I've lectured lots of times in France—twice at the Sorbonne.

That must be it. Sheila and the girls will be proud.

"THIS MESSAGE came to us by telex," said M. Bertrand Pelletier the moment Bob sat down in his elegant high-ceilinged office. He held a narrow slip of paper.

The award, thought Bob. He tried not to smile too soon.

"It requests that Dr. Beckwith of MIT contact a Monsieur Venarguès in Sète immediately." He handed Bob the paper.

"Sète?" repeated Bob. And thought, It can't be.

"Charming town," said Pelletier. "Do you know the south of France?"

"Uh—yes." Bob grew even more uneasy when he noticed that the consular official wore a rather solemn expression.

"Monsieur Pelletier, what's this all about?"

"I was only informed that it concerns the late Nicole Guérin."

Nicole. So long ago, so well suppressed he had almost convinced himself it never happened. The single infidelity in all his years of marriage. Why *now*? Why after all this time? And hadn't she herself insisted they would never meet again, never contact one another? Wait a minute.

"Monsieur Pelletier, did you say the *late* Nicole Guérin? She's dead?"

The under-secretary nodded. "I regret that I have no details. May I offer my *condoléances*, Dr. Beckwith?"

Bob stood up. "Thank you, Monsieur Pelletier." They shook hands, and, a bit unsteadily, Bob walked out onto Commonwealth Avenue. He was parked right near the Ritz. Should he get a quick shot of courage at the bar? No. Better make that phone call first. From somewhere private.

THE CORRIDOR was silent. Everyone seemed to have left for the summer. Bob closed his office door, sat at the desk and dialed France.

"*Wuy?*" croaked a sleepy voice with a thick Provençal accent.

"This is Robert Beckwith. May I speak to Monsieur Venarguès?"

"Bobbie—it is me, Louis! At last I've found you. What a task!"

Even after all these years, that voice was unmistakable. The rasp created by the smoke of fifty million Gauloises.

"Louis the mayor?"

"*Ex*-mayor. Can you imagine? They put me out to pasture like some ancient dinosaur. The council—"

Bob was much too tense for lengthy anecdotes.

"Louis, what is this about Nicole?"

"Oh, Bobbie, what a tragedy. Five days ago. Head-on collision. She was coming from a cardiac emergency. The whole town is in mourning. She was so young. A saint, unselfish."

He paused to sigh. Bob seized the opportunity.

"Louis, this is terrible news. But I don't see why you wanted me to call you. It's been ten years since I saw her."

Suddenly a silence on the line. Then Louis answered almost in a whisper: "Because of the child."

"Child? Was Nicole married?"

"No, no. Of course not. She was an independent mother, so to speak. She raised the boy herself."

"I still don't see what this has to do with me," said Bob.

"He is your child, too," said Louis Venarguès.

For a moment there was silence on both sides of the Atlantic. Bob was stunned. Then anger helped him to regain his powers of speech. "I don't believe it," he replied.

"But it's true. I was her confidant in everything."

"But what makes you so sure that *I'm* the father?"

"Bobbie," Louis answered gently, "you were here in May. The little boy came, so to speak, on schedule. There was no one else in her life at the time. She would have told me. Of course, she never wanted you to know."

Bob thought, This is incredible. "Louis, even if it's true, I'm not responsible for—"

"Bobbie, tranquilize yourself. No one's saying that you have responsibility. Jean-Claude is well provided for. Believe me—I am the executor. But there is one small problem."

Bob trembled at the possibilities.

"What?" he asked.

"Nicole had no other family. The boy is all alone." Louis paused. "Ordinarily we would take him in, Marie-Thérèse and I. We are his guardians. But my wife is gravely ill, Bob. She doesn't have much time."

"I'm sorry," Bob interjected softly.

"What can I say? We had a honeymoon of forty years. But now

you see why it's impossible. Unless we can find some alternative—and quickly—the authorities will take the boy away."

At last Bob sensed where this was leading. He grew angrier with every breath. And frightened.

"The child is inconsolable," Louis continued. "His grief is so great he cannot even cry. He just sits there—"

"Get to the point," said Bob.

Louis hesitated. "I want to tell him that you exist."

"No! Are you crazy! How could that possibly help?"

"I just want him to know that somewhere in this world he has a father. It would be *something*, Bobbie."

"Louis, I'm a married man with two young daughters. I'm truly sorry about Nicole. I'm sorry about the boy. But I refuse to get involved in this. I can't. I *won't*. That's final."

There was a pause. "All right," said Louis at last. "I'll trouble you no more. But I do confess I'm very disappointed." Yet another pause (for Bob to reconsider), and then capitulation. "Good-by, Bobbie," he mumbled, and hung up.

Bob put down the receiver and buried his head in his hands. This was too difficult to take in all at once. After so many years, Nicole Guérin, back in his life. And could their brief affair really have produced a child? A son?

Oh, God, what should I do?

"Evenin', Perfesser." It was Lilah Coleman, on her daily rounds of tidying the offices. "How's yer statistics?"

Bob looked up, startled. "Oh, pretty good."

"Say, you ain't run across some likely numbers, have ya? Rent's due an' my luck's been pretty lousy lately."

"Sorry, Mrs. Coleman, I don't feel too lucky myself."

"Well, as they say, Perfesser, 'if you don't feel it, don't play it.' That's my philosophy. You gotta trust your gut."

She emptied his wastebasket and whisked a cloth across his desk. Then she left. But something she had said stuck with him. Trust your gut. Quite unprofessional. But very human.

He sat frozen, staring at the telephone, long after Mrs. Coleman's footsteps faded down the corridor. He felt a desperate inward struggle, heart and mind at war. Don't be crazy, Bob. Don't risk your marriage. Nothing's worth it. But an impulse he could not control made him pick up the phone.

"Hello, Louis. It's me, Bob."

"Ah, good. I knew that you would reconsider."

"Listen, I need time to think. I'll call you back tomorrow."

They hung up. Now Bob was terrified. He had placed his whole existence in jeopardy. What had made him call again?

Affection for Nicole? No. All he felt for her now was enormous rage.

A little boy he'd never met?

He left his office and walked like a zombie to the parking lot.

He was panicked and confused. He had to talk to someone. But in the entire world he had only one close friend; one person who really understood him. His wife, Sheila.

CHAPTER TWO

By now Route 2 was fairly empty and he reached Lexington too quickly. He had really needed more time. To gain control of himself. Organize his thoughts. What am I going to say? How am I even going to face her?

"How come you're home so late, Bob?"

Paula, his nine-year-old daughter, was in constant training to take over as his wife.

"Departmental meeting," Bob replied, deliberately ignoring her unlicensed use of his first name.

In the kitchen Jessica Beckwith, twelve-and-a-half going on twenty-five, was discoursing with her mother. Subject: creeps, wonks and nerds. "Really, Mom, there's not one decent male in the whole Upper School."

"What's all this?" asked Bob, as he entered and kissed the two older women in his family. He was determined to act naturally.

"Jessie's lamenting the quality of the opposite sex at school—or actually the lack of it."

"Then maybe you should transfer, Jess," he said, teasing her.

"Oh, Father, you are hopelessly obtuse. All of Massachusetts is the boonies. It's a province in search of a city."

"Well, Ms. Beckwith, what is your solution?" asked Bob.

Jessie blushed. Bob had interrupted her sales pitch.

"Mom knows," said Jessica.

"Europe, Bob," said Sheila. "Your daughter wants to take a Garber teenage tour to France this summer."

"But she's not actually a teenager yet," retorted Bob.

"Oh, Daddy," sighed Jessica. "I'm old enough to go."

"But you're also young enough to wait a year."

"Oh, you are hopeless," sighed Jessica once again, and slouched disdainfully from the kitchen.

They were alone. Why did she have to look so beautiful tonight? thought Bob.

"I wish they'd outlaw puberty," said Sheila, going to her husband for the daily evening hug she had looked forward to since breakfast. She put her arms around him. "How come you're late? More memorable orations from the 'colleague'?"

"Yeah. He was in a rare stupefying form."

After so many years of talking to each other, they'd evolved a kind of code. For example, Bob's department had three men, two women, and a colleague—P. Herbert Harrison, a pompous ass with lengthy and dissenting views on everything.

The Beckwiths had a marriage very much in synch. And Sheila had flawless antennae when it came to sensing Bob's emotions.

"Are you okay?" she asked. "You look a little pale."

"Just academic pallor. Two days on Cape Cod and I'll be absolutely golden."

"Still, promise me you won't do any work tonight."

"Okay," said Bob. (As if he would be able to concentrate on anything.) "Have you got any work from the Press?"

"Nothing urgent. I'm still wading through that Russo-Chinese diplomatic thing. I tell you, for a professor, Reinhardt's prose has more starch than a laundry."

"Honey, if all authors wrote like Churchill, you'd be unemployed. But anyway, let's neither of us work tonight."

"Fine. What'd you have in mind?" Her green eyes were shining. His heart ached thinking of what she would have to hear.

"I love you," he said.

"Good. But in the meanwhile set the table, huh?"

HE WAITED until the girls were fast asleep. Sheila was curled up on the couch with "a ridiculously trashy" Hollywood novel, and Bob was pretending to read *The New Republic*. The tension he felt was unbearable.

"Want a drink, hon?"

"No, thanks," said Sheila, without looking up.

How can I do this? he thought. He made himself an unusually tall Scotch and sat down near her. "Honey, I gotta talk to you."

"Sure. Is something wrong?" She put her book down.

"Well, sort of. Yes."

He lowered his head. Sheila was suddenly frightened. How many of her friends had heard their husbands open conversations with preambles just like this? We have to talk. About our marriage. And from the grim expression on Bob's face, she feared that he too was about to say, "It isn't working anymore."

"Bob," she said with candor, "something in your voice scares me. Have I done anything?"

"No. It's me. I've done it." Bob took a breath. He was shaking. "Sheila, remember when you were pregnant with Paula?"

"Yes?"

"I had to fly to Europe—Montpellier—to give that paper. . . ."

"And . . . ?"

"I had an affair." He said it as quickly as he could. Like ripping off a bandage fast, to cause less pain.

Sheila's face went ashen. "No," she said, shaking her head violently as if to drive out what she had just heard. "This is some terrible joke." She looked at him for reassurance. "Isn't it?"

"No. It's true," he said tonelessly. "I—I'm sorry."

"Who?" she asked.

"Nobody," he replied. "Nobody special."

"*Who*, Robert?"

"Her—her name was Nicole Guérin. She was a doctor." Why does she want to hear these details?

"And how long did it last?"

"Two, three days."

"Which—two days or three days? I want to know."

"Three days," he said. "Does all this matter?"

"Everything matters," Sheila answered.

He watched her fight to keep control. This was worse than he had imagined. Then she looked at him and said, "I thought our marriage was based on total honesty. Why didn't you ever tell me?"

"I—I was waiting for the right moment." He knew it sounded absurd, but it was true. He had really wanted to tell her. But not like this.

"And ten years was the right moment?" she said sardonically. "No doubt you thought it would be easier. On *whom*?"

"I—I didn't want to hurt you," he said, knowing any answer would be futile. And then he added, "Sheila, if it's any consolation, that's the only time. I swear. It was the only time."

"No," she answered softly, "it isn't consolation. Once is more than never."

She bit her lip to hold back tears. And he had more to say.

"Sheila, that was so long ago. I had to tell you now because—I mean—" And then he blurted out, "She's dead."

"For God's sake, Bob, why are you telling me all this?"

"Sheila, I am telling you because she had a child."

"And we have *two*—so what?"

Bob hesitated. And then whispered, barely audible, "He's mine. The boy is mine."

She stared in disbelief. "Oh, no, it can't be true."

Bob nodded sadly. "Yes, it's true."

And then he told her everything. The meeting with Nicole. Their brief affair. Then this afternoon. The call from Louis. And the boy. The problem with the boy.

"I didn't know about it, Sheila. Please believe me."

"Why? Why should I believe anything you tell me now?"

He couldn't answer that.

In the awful silence that ensued, Bob suddenly remembered what he'd long ago confessed to her—so unimportant then. That he would like to be the father of a boy.

"*I wouldn't mind a little quarterback.*"

"*And what if it's another girl?*"

"*Well, then we'll keep on trying. Isn't that the best part?*"

At the time they laughed. The quarterback, of course, was Paula. And the operation at her birth made further children impossible. Sheila felt unlovable for many months. But Bob kept reassuring her, till gradually she again believed that what they shared was too strong for anything to change. They healed into an even tighter bond. Until tonight, which was a requiem for trust. Now everything was a potential source of pain.

"Sheila, listen—"

"No. I've heard enough."

She rose and fled into the kitchen. Bob hesitated for a moment, then went after her. She was seated at the table, sobbing. He reached out to stroke her blond hair. She moved away.

"Bob, why'd you have to tell me, *why?*"

"Because I don't know what to do." And because I somehow thought you'd help. He sat down at the table.

"You can't know how much it hurts," she said. "I trusted you. I trusted—" She broke down again.

He longed to embrace her, but he was afraid.

"Please, honey," he said. "I'll do anything to make it right."

"You can't."

He was scared by the finality of her statement. "You don't mean that you want to split. . . ."

"Robert, I don't have the strength right now. For anything." She rose from the table. "You could do me a big favor."

"Anything."

"Sleep in your study, please," she said.

"WHO DIED last night, for heaven's sake?" For once the gloomy philosopher Jessica had been wiser than she knew. They were in the kitchen eating—or in Jessie's case—dieting. She was ingesting Special K and half-and-half (half skim milk, half water), and commenting on the familial ambiance.

"Eat your breakfast, Jessie," Sheila ordered.

"You look awful, Dad," said Paula with solicitude.

"I worked late," he answered.

"You work much too hard," said his junior wife.

"He wants world renown," said Jessie to her sister. "And a free trip to Sweden."

"What's there?" asked Paula, taking Jessie's bait.

"The Nobel Prize, birdbrain."

"Jessie," Sheila remonstrated, "don't insult your sister."

"Mother, her existence is an insult to any person of normal intelligence."

"Want this peanut butter in your face?" asked Paula.

"Stop it, both of you,"said Bob. "The Nobel committee takes family manners into consideration."

For a moment sibling rivalry allowed Bob and Sheila to forget their marital abrasions. They smiled at one another. Then they both remembered that this wasn't quite a normal morning. They withdrew their smiles—and hoped the children didn't notice.

"Ladies," said Bob, "I'm driving you to the bus. Hurry up!"

He hovered by the door while the girls got ready. "Will you be here when I get back?" he asked Sheila uneasily.

"I don't know," she answered.

When he returned from ferrying the girls, she was still seated at the kitchen table, staring at her empty coffee cup.

I did this to her, he told himself, and was filled with self-loathing. He sat down across from her. She wouldn't start the conversation, so, after a long silence, he said, "Sheila, how can I make it up to you?"

She slowly raised her head and looked at him.

"I don't think you can," she said.

"You mean we're gonna bust up over this?" he asked.

"I don't know," she said. "I just wish I had it in me to really hurt you back for this. I wish I could. . . ." Her voice trailed off. She had almost let slip that she was still, despite it all, in love with him. But that, at least she would withhold.

"I wish I hadn't told you," he said.

So do I, she thought.

"Why *did* you tell me, Bob?"

"I don't know."

"You *do*, Bob. You *do!*" Her fury was erupting. Because she knew now what he wanted from her. "It's the child," she said.

It struck him with a force that frightened him.

"I—I'm not sure," he said.

"Look, Bob, I know you inside out. You didn't want it, you didn't plan it, but since you have it, you feel responsible."

"Yeah," he admitted, "I do. I can't explain it, but I feel I should do something to help. Find an alternative to—you know, sending him away. Maybe if I flew there. . . ."

"To do what? Do you know anyone who'd take him in? Do you even have a plan?"

"No, Sheila. No, I don't."

"Then what's the point of flying over?"

He could not defend his impulse. He could barely fathom it.

And then she staggered him.

"I guess there's only one solution, Robert. Bring him here."

He stared at her in disbelief. "Do you realize what you're saying?"

She nodded. "Isn't that really why you told me?"

He wasn't sure, but he suspected she was right. Again. "Could you bear it?"

She smiled sadly. "I have to, Bob. If I don't let you try to help him now, you'll blame me someday for allowing your—your child to be put in an orphanage."

"I wouldn't. . . ."

"Yes, you would. So do it, Bob, before I change my mind."

And so he let his lovely wife ignore the outrage and the imposition of it all as they discussed the visit of his son from France. The boy could join them when they moved down to the Cape.

"But just a month," she said. "Not one day more. That should give this Louis person time to make some permanent arrangement."

"What would we tell the girls?"

"We'll manufacture something."

How could she be so generous? "You're incredible," he said.

She shook her head. "No, Robert. I'm just thirty-nine years old."

CHAPTER THREE

Two weeks later, Bob was pacing back and forth in the corridor of the international arrivals building at Boston's Logan Airport.

In the anxious days before, there had been many conversations with Louis Venargues to make arrangements for the boy's brief visit to America. A month, not one day more. And Louis would have to use this grace period to find some alternative to a state orphanage.

Louis had to tell Jean-Claude that he had been invited by old friends of his mother's. The idea was not totally implausible, since Nicole would surely have spoken to him about her year of residency in Boston. But under no circumstances could Louis tell the boy that Robert Beckwith was his father.

Then there had been the not inconsiderable matter of telling the girls. After much agonizing, Bob convoked a family meeting. "A friend of ours has died," he said. "A lady in France. She had a son roughly Paula's age, and. . ."

"And he's an orphan," Sheila added with emphasis.

"Oh, gee," said Paula sympathetically.

"That's why," said Bob, "—since he's alone—we'd like to ask him over, for a while. Maybe a month. When we're in the big house at the Cape. That is, if neither of you minds."

"Oh, wow," chirped Paula. Her voice was clearly yes.

"Jessie?"

"Well, there's justice in the world. If I can't visit France, at least I'll have a native to discuss it with."

Sheila had made herself go through the motions of a normal day. Her act worked well enough for the girls, who seemed to sense nothing awry. She worked furiously, and completed the editing of Reinhardt's book. Bob, of course, could see behind this façade of industry, but could do nothing. Say nothing. As she grew more distant he felt increasingly helpless. They had never been estranged like this. At times when he was yearning for her smile, he would hate himself. At other times, he would hate the boy.

The Arrivals board now announced that TWA 811 from Paris had just landed. A crowd began to form around the double-doored exit from the customs area. And Bob suddenly was very scared. During the past weeks his mind had been occupied with making arrangements. He'd been too distracted to think what he might feel when those metal doors would open and a son of his would walk into his life. Not a theoretical dilemma he'd discussed by telephone, but flesh and blood. A living child.

The double doors parted for an instant. Out came the flight crew. Bob craned his neck to glimpse inside. He saw the lines of passengers waiting for customs inspection. But no little boy.

The doors opened again. This time a stewardess emerged, carrying a green leather valise and leading a tousle-haired little boy who was clutching a red flight bag close to his chest. The stewardess found Bob immediately.

"Professor Beckwith?"

"Yes."

"Hi." She turned over the boy. "Have a good time," she said, and slipped off.

Now the two of them were on their own. Bob glanced down at the little boy. Does he look anything like me? he thought.

"Jean-Claude?"

The boy nodded and held out his hand. Bob shook it.

"*Bonjour, monsieur,*" the child said politely.

Though his French was reasonably fluent, Bob had prepared some remarks in advance. "*Est-ce que tu as fait un bon voyage?*"

"Yes, but I speak English. I have taken private lessons since I was small. I thank you for inviting me."

Bob sensed the boy's remarks had also been rehearsed. He picked up the green suitcase. "Can I take your flight bag?"

Mitchell Hooks

"No, thank you," said the boy, clutching his red bag even tighter.

"My car's just outside," said Bob. They began to walk. Through the doors and into the parking area, where the bright sun was now dimming into the late afternoon. The heat was still intense. The boy followed silently, half a step behind.

"Uh—how was the movie?" Another question Bob had prepared.

"I didn't watch it. I was reading a book."

"Oh," said Bob. They had now reached his car. "Look, Jean-Claude, a Peugeot. Doesn't that make you feel at home?"

The boy glanced up at him and gave a tiny smile. Did that mean yes or no?

"Would you like to sleep in back?" Bob asked.

"No, Mr. Beckwith. I would prefer to see the sights."

"Please don't be formal, Jean-Claude. Just call me Bob."

Inside the car, Bob helped him with the seat belt. As he fastened it, his hand brushed the little boy's chest.

My God, Bob thought. He's real. My son is real.

In a matter of minutes Jean-Claude was fast asleep. As they headed south on Route 93, Bob kept the car under the speed limit. The trip would normally take at least an hour and a half. But he wanted as much time as possible to look at the boy. Simply look.

The boy was curled up, leaning his head against the car door.

He looks a little frightened, Bob thought, as he drove into the growing darkness. Well, it's only natural. But he has such poise for a nine-year-old. *Nine.* He had been alive for almost a decade without Bob's knowing he existed. But then *he* doesn't know that *I* exist. Bob wondered what Nicole had told him of his father.

He looked at the sleeping child and thought, You are a stranger in a foreign land, thousands of miles from home and unaware that I, sitting right beside you, am your father. What would you say if you knew? Did you miss not knowing me? He looked at him again. Did I miss not knowing you?

The boy awakened just as they were passing Plymouth. He saw the road sign. "Is that where the rock is?" he asked.

"Yes. We'll visit it sometime. We'll visit all the famous places while you're here."

Then the Cape Cod Canal. And Sandwich. The boy laughed.

"There is a place called *Sandwich*?"

"Yes." Bob chuckled with him. "There's even an *East* Sandwich."

"Who made up such a funny name?"

"Somebody hungry, I guess," said Bob. The boy laughed again.

Good, thought Bob, the ice is broken.

Later they passed another road sign: WELLFLEET 6 MILES. In a few short minutes, the trip would end.

"Do you know about my children, Jean-Claude?" Bob asked.

"Louis said you have two daughters. And your wife is kind."

"She is," said Bob.

"Did she know my mother too?" the child asked.

"Uh—yes. But distantly."

"Oh. Then you were her closer friend."

"Yes," Bob answered softly. Just then they reached the corner of Pilgrim Spring Road. In sixty seconds they'd be home.

THEY ALL STARED at him with differing emotions.

Sheila felt an inward tremor. She thought she had prepared herself for this. But she was not prepared. The little boy now standing in her living room was his. Her husband's child. The impact exceeded everything she had imagined. Because, she realized, a part of her had been refusing to accept the truth. But now proof was standing there before her, four feet tall.

"Hello, Jean-Claude. We're glad to have you." That was the most she could manage. Every syllable took painful effort. Would he notice that she couldn't smile?

"Thank you, madame," he answered. "I am very grateful for your invitation."

"Hi, I'm Paula."

"Very glad," he answered with a smile. Her heart was his.

At last the one aristocrat among them spoke. "*Jean-Claude, je suis Jessica. Avez-vous fait un bon voyage?*"

"*Oui, mademoiselle. Votre français est éblouissant.*"

"What?" Jessie had prepared herself to speak French, not to understand it.

And Bob watched as the youngsters spoke. He thought, They're all my children.

"His English is terrific," said Paula to her sister, "and your French is terrible."

"Paula!" Jessie snarled.

"*Terrible* is slang in French," said Jean-Claude diplomatically. "It also means terrific." Jessica was reassured. This would be a splendid *continental* summer.

Jean-Claude now approached Sheila. Reaching into his flight bag, he withdrew a chunk of . . . clay? It looked like a heavy wad of ossified chewing gum. He offered it to her.

"Oh—thank you," Sheila said.

"What is it?" Paula asked.

Jean-Claude searched his vocabulary, but could not find the word.

He turned to Bob. "How do you say *cendrier?*"

"Ashtray," Bob replied, and recalled that Nicole had smoked.

"Thank you," Sheila repeated. "Is it—handmade?"

"Yes," said the boy. "In our ceramics class."

Sheila took the gift and looked at it. He'd meant well, after all. It was a touching gesture. A ceramic ashtray, signed by the craftsman who had made it: GUERIN 16.6.78.

"*Voulez-vous boire quelque chose?*" asked Jessica, ready to sprint for whatever beverage the Frenchman would fancy.

"*Non, merci, Jessica. Je n'ai pas soif.*"

"*Je comprends,*" she said proudly.

"How're things in France, Jean-Claude?" asked Paula, anxious to preserve her share of the guest's attention.

Bob thought it prudent to abridge this conversation. "We'll have lots of time to discuss things, girls. But I think Jean-Claude's pretty tired. Aren't you, Jean-Claude?"

"A bit," the boy conceded.

"I'll take his baggage up," said Bob to Sheila.

"No, I will" she replied, and picked up the green valise (did it belong to *her?*). "This way, Jean-Claude."

"Good night," he said shyly, and followed her upstairs.

As soon as they were out of sight, Bob went to the liquor cabinet.

"Wow, he's cute!" gushed Paula. "And his English is fantastic."

"He's had a private tutor," explained Bob, who had now fortified himself with Scotch.

"How come?" asked Jessie hopefully. "Is he noble?"

"No," said Bob. "His mother was a country doctor."

"What about his father?"

"I'm not sure," said Bob evasively, "but he wasn't noble."

"HE'S VERY independent," Sheila said.

"In what way?" They were now in their bedroom. The rest of the household was already asleep.

"He wouldn't let me help him unpack. He insisted on doing it by himself," she said, and then added, "Was I cold to him?"

"You were wonderful," said Bob, and reached out for her hand. She moved away. His eyes followed her as she went into the bathroom.

She emerged a few minutes later in her nightgown and bathrobe. Lately Bob had had the disconcerting feeling that she was uneasy about undressing in front of him.

She sat down on the bed and started to adjust the alarm clock. (What for—wasn't this vacation?) He wanted to reach over and embrace her, but the gap of sheets and pillows separating them seemed much too wide to bridge.

"Sheila, I love you."

Her back to him, she kept playing with the clock. Finally she turned. "He's got your mouth," she said.

"Does he?"

"I'm surprised you didn't notice."

Sheila slipped her robe off and burrowed under the covers. She lay silent for a moment. Then, "She must have had brown eyes."

"I really don't remember."

With a melancholy smile Sheila said, "Come on, Bob."

Then she took her pillow and curled herself around it in the corner of the bed. "Good night," she said.

He kissed her on the cheek. She did not respond. He had vaguely hoped that if they made love, it would somehow make things better. He now saw that they were much too far apart for that.

He picked up the *American Journal of Statistics* and idly leafed through a piece on stochastic processes.

"Bob?" Her voice startled him.

"Yes, honey?" He turned toward her. There was such pain on her face. Yet somehow she looked younger and so vulnerable.

"You never really told me why you had an affair," she said. "What exactly was wrong with me?"

Damn, thought Bob. Why doesn't she understand that it was—what? Weakness? Chance? What could he say?

"Sheila, nothing was wrong with you. . . ."

"With us, then. I thought we were happy."

"We were. We are." He said the last words with as much hope as conviction.

"We were," she said, and turned away again. To sleep.

CHAPTER FOUR

"Hey, Beckwith, there's some fantastic stuff at the mixer."

"I'm studying, Bernie."

"On a Saturday night, with two hundred Vassar lovelies gracing our campus?"

Robert Alan Beckwith, Yale '59, put his math book down on the table and sat up on the moth-eaten couch of the Branford College suite he shared with Bernie Ackerman.

"Bernie, I came to Yale to get an education."

"Listen, this mixer's free of charge. Doesn't that imply that Yale considers girls a part of the educational experience?"

"Bernie, I know myself. I'm shy. I lack your amazing charm and wit. I'm not competitive. . . ."

"In other words, you're scared."

"No, Bern. In those very words. I am scared. Now go back to the mixer." And he buried himself once again in numerical analysis. Bernie simply stood there.

"Beckwith, I'm gonna help you. I have a secret weapon."

"Then you use it."

"I can't. I'm too short."

Bob looked up. Bernie had snared his interest.

"Willya come if I lend you my secret weapon?"

"Okay. The evening's shot anyway, I might as well get a beer."

Bob went into his bedroom, got his college blazer and combed his hair. Then, after spilling Old Spice in every conceivable place, he re-entered the living room, where Bernie stood like a midget colossus on the coffee table, holding . . . a tie.

"That's a secret weapon?" Bob asked, frowning. "A *tie?*"

"—which signifies that the wearer has won a varsity *Y* in *football!*"

"But I haven't," Bob protested.

"I have," Bernie said. He was the team manager.

"Bernie, I am a hundred-and-forty-five-pound weakling."

"But you're six one, Beckwith. Put two or three sweaters on under your jacket and you could be a tight end. Believe me, the girls know a football tie when they see one. It turns them on."

"Bernie, forget it."

"Come on, Beckwith. This is your big chance."

"*YOU AIN'T NOTHIN' but a hound dog . . .*"

It was pitch-black, and the deafening sounds of Rumple and the Stiltskins shook the panels of the Branford College dining hall. Bodies rocked and rolled. From either side, the opposing sexes glanced across at one another while pretending not to.

"Oh, Beckwith, lookit all the talent," said Bernie, surveying the populous scene. "I'm dying from the pulchritude. See the short, cute one. I've gotta make my move."

And for the final time he fixed Bob's tie and sprinted off.

Bob was on his own. Self-consciously, he walked toward the female side. His eye chanced upon a tall and slender girl with long blond hair. Boy, thought Bob, I wish I had the guts. But three Yalies were already paying court to her. No chance, thought Bob. Besides I'm really boiling in these sweaters. Maybe I should head back to my room.

"Beckwith!" someone bellowed.

It was one of the trio romancing the young lady.

"Yes?"

"What is that around your scrawny neck?"

To his horror, Bob now realized that the voice belonged to Terry Dexter, captain of the undefeated football team. Dexter then said to the Vassar girl, "He shouldn't be wearing that tie."

"Why not?" she asked, then turned to Bob. "What is it?"

"The Morons' Club," he said, smiling. Boy, she's beautiful.

"Like hell," said Terry. "It's the football team."

"Not much difference," Bob replied.

The Vassar girl laughed. This enraged the football captain.

"Beckwith," snarled Terry, "take off that tie."

Bob was sweating profusely; he pulled it off and handed it over. Then, making swift retreat, he casually tossed a "Nice meeting you" in the direction of the lovely Vassar girl who had witnessed this horror show.

In the coatroom area, Bob tore off his blazer. Thank you, Bernie, for this mortification. Dexter would doubtless never forget it. And you won't get your tie back, either. As Bob was pulling the first of his sweaters over his head, he heard a muffled "Excuse me."

He peered out. It was the girl.

"Yes?" said Bob, whipping the sweater back down.

"You forgot something," she said. And in her left hand she held out the football tie.

"Thank you. I guess I looked pretty stupid wearing it."

"No," she said gently. "I think it was the sweaters that made you look a little weird."

"Oh," he said. And then, "I'm just getting over a cold."

"Oh," she answered, perhaps believing him. "Why'd you leave so early?"

"I don't function well in mobs."

"Me either," she said.

"Then would you like to take a walk?" I hope she doesn't think I want to lure her to my room. "I mean in the courtyard."

"Good idea," she said. "It's incredibly stuffy in there."

As they descended the stone stairway and strolled out into the chilly autumn evening, they introduced themselves.

"I'm Bob Beckwith. And I'm a math major."

"Sheila—Sheila Goodhart. And I haven't picked a major yet." They walked slowly around the courtyard. The band was barely audible.

"Are you busy next weekend?" Bob asked impulsively.

"Yes," she said.

He was crushed. "Oh."

"I mean with midterms. I've got to cram. How about the week after?"

"How about if I came up to Vassar next weekend and we studied together? I really mean study, Sheila, 'cause I'm a grind and I've got midterms, too."

"Okay, Bob. I'd like that."

"Great." His heart was pirouetting.

Half an hour later, he walked her to Chapel Street, where the buses were waiting to transport the girls back to Poughkeepsie. Bob was in turmoil. To kiss or not to kiss, that was the question. At length he concluded that it would be best to play it safe.

"Well," he said as she was about to board the bus, "I look forward to next weekend."

"So long."

She smiled and darted up the steps.

He watched her walk toward the back of the bus. She found a seat on his side, sat down and looked out at him. She was gorgeous, even through a dirty windowpane.

He stood transfixed as the bus moved away from the curb, then down the street into the New Haven night.

"BECKWITH, where've you been?"

"Out, Bernie."

"I was looking everywhere for you. What happened?"

Bob waited. Finally he smiled and said, "Let's just put it this way, Bernie: The tie worked."

WHEN HE KISSED HER the next weekend, it was all over. He knew for certain she would be the love of his life. He was just absolutely sure.

In the few minutes preceding that fateful embrace, as they were walking from the Vassar canteen to her dorm, he made a final frantic attempt to dry his palms. Again and again he rubbed them against his sweater—to no avail. He could not, therefore, reach for her hand. Instead he very casually put his right arm around her shoulder. This was followed by a startling and unexpected development: She put her left arm around his waist.

What does this mean? thought Bob.

To any casual observer, it had been an ordinary college date. They sat opposite one another in the library reading all afternoon, went to Francesco's for pasta and returned to the library, where they both, true to their words, really studied. Not just their books, but each other.

There were the inevitable biographical details. Sheila was the youngest of three daughters of a Connecticut physician. Her mother was second-string art critic for the Stamford *Gazette*. Not only had her parents never divorced, they didn't even want to.

Bob's father had taught math at Penn for nearly forty years, during which time he published two textbooks and assembled a vast collection of jokes. ("Oh, that's where you get your sense of humor.") Bob's mother had died when he was barely seven, and Dan Beckwith thought it best to send his son to boarding school. Fortunately Lawrenceville was less than an hour from Philadelphia, so they spent all their weekends together. Weekdays were pretty dismal, though, until the first form, when Bernie Ackerman arrived upon the scene. Even then he was a walking sports encyclopedia and a fanatically loyal friend.

"Thanks to Bern, I met my future wife," Bob said to Sheila over coffee.

"Oh?" Her face was quizzical.

"You," he said.

She laughed. "We've just met."

"Sheila, by their third date, Romeo and Juliet were already dead."

"You're crazy."

"Yes. About you."

No further mention of matrimony was made that evening. Bob felt he had said it all. And Sheila felt he'd just been teasing her.

But she really liked him. Which is why she put her arm around him. And why she kissed him on the doorstep of Josselyn Hall.

"ALL RIGHT, Sheila, tell me about the boy you were kissing."

"His name is Bob."

"Bob who, what, how and since when?"

The interrogator was Margo Fulton, self-styled *femme fatale,* purveyor of news and dispenser of worldly advice. She was Sheila's roommate in Josselyn Hall.

"Well, Sheil, I want all the details. How did you meet him?"

"Last weekend at Yale. At a mixer, if you can believe it."

"A mixer! I haven't been to one of those in ages. Though I did meet Rex at one freshman year. You remember Rex?"

"I think so." Margo had gone through a string of beaux.

"Is your Yalie sincere or just another sex maniac?"

"He's nice," Sheila answered. And thought to herself, He's really *really* nice.

"He looks like a basketball player. Is he?"

"I didn't ask him, Margo."

"Well, what on earth did you talk about?"

"Things," Sheila said, not wanting to betray a syllable of what they had said to one another.

"Oh," said Margo. "When are you seeing him again?"

"Next weekend. I'll be going there." Then Sheila yawned to give her friend a hint.

"Sweet dreams," said Margo. "We'll chat tomorrow."

Sheila lay back in her bed and smiled. I wonder if he's serious, she thought.

"THANKS FOR THE CAR, Bern."

"How did it go?"

It was after three and this was midterm week, but nonetheless Bob sat and fed his friend a few vague details.

"I'm getting the impression that you like her, Beckwith."

"Well, I think I do." (To say the least!)

"Is she that great-looking?"

Of course she is. You'd faint if she just looked at you with those green eyes. But I'm not giving you specifics. So Bob hid behind a little erudition.

"Remember Spenser's *Epithalamion*? Well, she has 'that inward beauty which no eye can see.'"

"In other words, she's ugly, right?"

Bob smiled. "Don't you think I can pick a winner, Bern?"

"Frankly, no. I mean, what would she see in you?"

"I don't know," Bob answered, poker-faced. He rose and headed toward his bedroom. "Good night." He closed the door.

Inside his tiny cubicle, Bob took out a piece of Branford College stationery and wrote:

16 November 1958 (3:45 a.m.)

Sheila—

I meant every word I said.

Bob

THE FUNNY THING is that they did get married. Not as soon as either of them wanted, but in June of 1960, one week after Sheila's graduation. Everyone was happy, even though at times during their long engagement Sheila's mother, who "thought the world" of Bob, tried to convince her daughter not to hurry into matrimony.

"You're both so young. Why not live a little first?"

"I want to, Mother. But I want to live with *him*."

ON THEIR SECOND anniversary, Bob asked his twenty-three-year-old wife if she had any regrets.

"Yes," she answered. "I should've married you the day you first proposed."

"You're together all the time," said Bernie once, when he came up from Yale Law School to visit. "Don't you ever get bored?"

"No," said Bob. "What makes you ask?"

"I mean, I sometimes get bored after two or three dates."

"Then you just haven't met the right girl yet."

Bernie was inspired. Three months after that he got engaged to

Nancy Gordon. Everybody crossed his fingers. But the marriage worked, and they had a son within the year.

In Cambridge, Bob worked on his doctorate at MIT and Sheila was hired by Harvard University Press. Twice a month they'd have a bunch of friends for dinner. They all yearned for a relationship like Bob and Sheila's.

Unlike their former classmates, they never had to scrounge. The US government was paying Bob's tuition and the US army paid him every summer just for the fun of solving statistical puzzles. With what Sheila earned they could even afford such luxuries as season tickets to the symphony. Sheila loved her job. She quickly rose from typing letters to proofreading galleys and then to editing books. On their fourth anniversary, she took Bob to dinner at Chez Dreyfus, insisting that it go on her newly acquired expense account.

"All you have to do is to promise us your next book," she said.

Next book? He hadn't written any yet. In fact he hadn't even completed his thesis. But he felt so indebted to the Press for that $27.50 banquet that he flogged himself to finish it that summer. He made a book of it while teaching in the fall and had it accepted by Harvard Press before their next anniversary dinner.

"TO RESPOND to another person when you are in pain, there must be a lot of trust between you."

Bob scribbled furiously.

"You don't have to write it *all* down," Sheila whispered.

"Shh—listen," Bob replied, and kept on scribbling.

A dozen pregnant women sat on the floor of the Cambridge Adult Education Center as an instructor told them how to breathe their way through childbirth. Their husbands sat next to them.

Bob was already feeling uneasy about this avant-garde approach to parenthood. What if I faint? he thought. He gazed at his lovely wife, now rhythmically expanding and contracting, and heard the subsequent instruction with growing anxiety.

"And don't forget your husband is the coach. He regulates and controls your breathing."

Great, Bob thought. Now I'm really gonna pass out.

As he was practicing the sacrolumbar massage on Sheila's back, Bob glanced around the room. Only in Cambridge could there be such an odd assemblage: a cabbie, several students, a nervous neurosurgeon and an East African prince. The women shared a pride in their impending motherhood and the feeling that they looked like dancers in an elephants' ballet. The men shared the brotherhood of fear.

After that first session, Sheila and Bob grabbed a quick burger. "How did I do?" he asked.

"Robert, you're the loveliest husband in the whole world."

He kissed her and got relish on his lips.

THEY HAD BARELY moved into the new house in Lexington. They had their furniture, but less than half the books were put away. New Year's Day 1966 was gusty with Arctic cold. Bob was staring out the window. I would hate to go out into that, he thought.

Five hours later they were speeding down Route 2 toward Boston. "Breathe easy, honey, and drive very carefully," he said.

"I am breathing, Bob. *You're* driving. So calm down."

He drove, but he could not calm down. By the time they reached the Lying In, his stomach cramps were synchronized with her labor pains. She squeezed his hand as he helped her from the car. "It's gonna be okay," she said.

In the labor room he timed her contractions. Through every one of them he tightly held her hand. Sometimes he stared up at the clock because he couldn't bear the sight of her in pain.

"Bob, you're a great coach," Sheila whispered.

As they wheeled her down the corridor he kept her hand in his. "This is the homestretch, honey. Now I know we're gonna make it." Which meant that he didn't think he'd faint.

She bore down when Dr. Selzer told her to, and soon a tiny head appeared. It's really happening, Bob thought. Our baby's real.

"Congratulations," Dr. Selzer said. "You've got a little girl."

Since they had long ago decided on the names, she whispered to her husband through her tears. "Oh, Bob, it's Jessica."

"She looks like you," he said. "She's beautiful."

He kissed the mother of his child.

CHAPTER FIVE

There were five of them at breakfast the next morning. Sheila fought to suppress the anger she felt. "Did you sleep well, Jean-Claude?" she asked.

"Yes, thank you, Mrs. Beckwith."

He was looking wistfully into his chocolate milk.

"Is there something more you'd like?" Sheila asked.

"Well, at home we would drink coffee in the morning."

"Really?" Paula gasped, in awe of this sophistication.

"Of course," said Sheila. "I should have asked." She got up to get him some.

"Today we're going to a barbecue," said Jessie. "Do you know what that is, Jean-Claude?"

"I think so," he replied. He seemed intimidated at the prospect. More strange new faces, he was doubtless thinking.

Paula continued enthusiastically. "There'll be hot dogs and hamburgers and corn on the cob with melted butter."

"Paula, you sound like a commercial for McDonald's," Jessie said sarcastically.

"Do you know what McDonald's is?" Paula asked Jean-Claude.

"Yes. It is a restaurant in Paris. I have eaten there."

THE PEUGEOT was crowded as they all embarked for Truro, and the seaside home of Bernie Ackerman.

"He's been my pal since we were just about your age," said Bob to Jean-Claude. "Bernie is a lawyer. He represents a lot of big-league athletes. Baseball, hockey, football—"

"Football?" Jean-Claude's eyes lit up.

"The American version," Jessie said disdainfully. "The breaking of empty heads."

As they reached Bernie's place, it suddenly occurred to Bob that his wife had not said a word during the entire ride.

SHEILA GAZED at the patchwork quilt of T-shirts, jogging suits and summer dresses, and wondered if her friends would notice her unhappiness. Fortunately everybody seemed preoccupied—sunning, tossing Frisbees, drinking, laughing, grilling, yelling at their children not to throw food. It was not a day for psychic scrutinizing. Probably she'd pull it off.

Bernie was the first to notice their arrival. He tapped his wife, Nancy, on the shoulder, and they hurried toward them.

"Beckwith—Did you bring your catcher's mitt?"

"I left it in your garage last summer. How are you, Bern?"

The two old friends embraced. As the salutations subsided, the

Ackermans noticed an extra member of the Beckwith party. Bob hastened to explain.

"This is Jean-Claude Guérin, a visitor from France."

"Hi. I'm your Uncle Bernie, this is Aunt Nancy—and the tall kid over there sinking hook shots is my son, Davey."

"Very pleased to meet you," Jean-Claude said to them both.

"He's very cute," whispered Nancy Ackerman to Sheila.

"Does he play ball?" Bernie asked Bob confidentially.

"Uh, he's kind of tired from the plane trip, Bern. Besides I don't think softball's big in France."

"Oh," said Bernie, and then loudly and slowly told the visitor: "You see, every year the fathers and the sons play softball. It's an annual event. Held every year."

"Oh," the boy replied politely.

"You're gonna love it," said the host, and added, "Beckwith, take your squad to the feeding station. Give Jean-Claude a burger."

Bernie chugged off. Bob led Paula and Jean-Claude to the barbecue pit. Jessica had already wafted off. And Sheila was—or seemed—deep in conversation with Nancy Ackerman.

"WANNA go to a movie sometime, Jess?" asked Davey Ackerman.

"The name is Jessica. And no, I wouldn't. I don't go out with juveniles."

"I'm fourteen months older than you."

"Chronology's irrelevant."

"You think you're hot stuff, but you're not, Jessie. Besides, there are lotsa fish in the sea." A pause. "I'm gonna be a professional ballplayer."

"I couldn't care less," Jessica retorted. Then, "What sport?"

"I haven't decided. Maybe pro soccer. My dad says soccer's gonna be huge in the '80s. I can kick with both feet."

"Not at once, I assume," said Jessica.

When it came to Jessica Beckwith, the normally pugnacious Davey Ackerman had the patience of a saint. If only Jessie hadn't been so darn good-looking, he might cure himself of the painful crush he had on her. Or if only she'd recognize his many athletic virtues. But as things stood, he was violently jealous of everything that caught her attention, even inanimate objects like books. Small wonder, then, that he now fixed upon Jean-Claude Guérin.

"Who's that foreign kid?"

"He's from abroad. A visitor."

"Where's his parents?"

"None of your business. Actually, he's an orphan," she said.

"No kidding," said Davey. "You guys gonna adopt him?"

This had never occurred to Jessica.

"I'm sorry, but I'm not at liberty to say."

"PLAY BALL!"

At last the annual Bernie Ackerman Cape Cod Invitational Softball Game was under way. Parents and children had been split into two teams, led by Bernie and Jack Ever, a computer scientist. Bernie won the toss and got first draft choice. Purely on ability and killer instinct, he selected Davey Ackerman.

Bob was chosen by Jack Ever on the seventh round. Though a distinguished academic, he was, as Bernie had to tell him candidly, a pretty mediocre catcher. The signing-up of Nancy Ackerman as short-center fielder made the contest nominally coed. Paula and Jean-Claude joined the cheering section on the first-base line. Jessica sought solitude beneath a tree with Baudelaire (in English). Hardly in a sporting mood, Sheila went to walk along the beach.

She had realized something the moment they reached the party. Seeing all their friends, she knew at once that things would never be the same. Not just because they all looked up to her and Bob. Who cared about images? But because Bob was no longer funny, loving, faithful Bob. Ever since she'd seen that child, the one certainty that had defined her life had disappeared.

TENSION was mounting. The score was 12–12 and they were into extra innings. Both teams were wilting from the heat, but no one more than Bob, who had been roasting in his catcher's mask. It was bottom of the tenth and Bernie's team was batting. Davey Ackerman had lined a double to left field and was now dancing boldly from the base. Bernie came to the batter's box.

"Come on, Dad, send me home!" called Davey, as he hopped up and down and whistled to distract the pitcher.

Bernie popped a fly to center. The instant Patsy Lord caught it, Davey Ackerman was off and flying toward third base. It was clear that he would try to score. Patsy fired the ball to Bob, who had thrown off his mask and stood blocking home plate. But Davey rounded third and fearlessly charged homeward.

"Knock his head off, Davey!" This counsel came from Bernie, shrieking like a maniac. As Davey drew near, Bob lunged to tag him, but couldn't. Davey dodged, and slid right into him. Bob fell backward on the ground. The softball trickled from his glove. The other team was cheering. They had won!

"No hard feelings," Bernie crowed at Bob. "Are you okay?"

"Yeah," Bob said, slowly getting up. He gritted his teeth as he wiped the dirt and sweat off his face with his sleeve. His shins ached.

While the players stampeded for the beer and Cokes, Bob took off his sneakers and walked toward the beach. He saw the visitor from France perched on a dune. Jean-Claude looked concerned.

"Did he hurt you, Bob?" he asked.

"No, it's nothing. Let's go get our feet wet."

They walked together to the water's edge and waded in. Bob grimaced when the water reached his shins.

"I would like to hit that boy," said Jean-Claude.

Bob laughed. And thought, Me too.

"HOW WAS your day?"

"Not bad," Sheila answered tonelessly. She was combing her hair as they both prepared for bed.

"Not good, either, huh?"said Bob, studying her. Even in her faded bathrobe and with night cream on her face, she was beautiful. He wanted her so badly.

"No, Robert, certainly not good." It was only in times of extreme emotion that she called him Robert. "You haven't any notion how hard this is for me." She sat down on the bed and stared across at him. "I can't take it, Robert."

He was about to remind her that she had volunteered, but stopped himself. After all, he was the culprit.

"Maybe we should send him home?" He gazed at her hopelessly.

"Look, I said I would, and I will," she replied as she examined the ends of her long hair. "But I need a little relief. I'm going to have to get away now and then."

"Of course." What could she mean? Her words unsettled him.

"Tomorrow. I want to go to Boston for the day."

"Oh, good. A good idea," said Bob, relieved that she had not demanded even more time.

She put her hairbrush down on the night table and climbed under the bedcovers, her back to him. She was still wearing her bathrobe. He put his hand on her shoulder. Just a friendly touch, he told himself.

"I took a sleeping pill, Bob," she said softly, without turning.

In a minute she was asleep. He felt too restless to remain in bed. He got up quietly, left the room and started down the stairs.

In the living room he saw the boy. He was seated in pajamas on the sofa, staring out the window at the ocean.

"Jean-Claude, are you all right?" Bob said softly.

The boy turned, startled. "*Oui*—yes. I couldn't sleep."

"That makes two of us," Bob answered. "Aren't you cold?"

"A little."

Bob led Jean-Claude to the kitchen. He sat at the table as Bob poured some milk into a pan and started heating it. While it warmed, he opened up a beer. Then he gave Jean-Claude the milk and sat down with him at the table. It was very quiet in the house.

"Did you enjoy today, Jean-Claude?"

The little boy looked lost and sad. "I am sorry that I don't know baseball."

"It's not important," Bob replied, and added, "As you could see, I don't know too much baseball, either."

Silence. Jean-Claude sipped his milk.

"What were you looking at when I came down? The sea?"

Jean-Claude hesitated, and then answered, "Yes. I was wondering how far it was to France."

"Too far to swim." Bob smiled, and then, "Are you homesick?"

"Well, a little. When I look out at the water, I imagine that I see Sète."

Bob felt sorry for him.

"Come on. Let's go back and look out at France."

The boy padded after Bob back to the living room. He sat on the sofa once again, Bob in the easy chair right near him.

"It's a lovely town, Sète."

"Do you know it?" asked Jean-Claude.

Bob sensed this would be the first of many innocently probing questions. But he felt a need to talk, if only indirectly.

"I was there once," he replied, "many years ago."

The next question made Bob's heart beat faster. "Did you know my mother there, or just in Boston?"

Bob hesitated. "Uh—just in Boston. When she was a resident at Mass. General. We met at someone's house."

The little boy's eyes brightened. "Did you like her?"

"She was very nice," Bob offered.

"She was a very good doctor," the little boy added. "We could have lived in Paris, but she preferred the south."

"I know," said Bob. And wondered suddenly if these two syllables had not been too revealing. But the boy said nothing. Bob drained his beer and wanted to get another. But he couldn't leave the boy alone.

"Did you know my father?"

Though he knew it had to come, it sent shivers up Bob's spine. What did the child know really? Had Nicole, had Louis . . . ?

"Uh—what did your mother tell you about him?"

"That he was married." The boy lowered his head.

"And?" Bob's heart was hammering.

"That she loved him. And they loved each other and decided to have me. But, of course, he could not stay in France."

"Uh—did she ever tell you who he was?"

"No. But I think perhaps he was an Englishman."

"Why do you say that?"

"Because if he was Italian, I think she would have made me learn Italian. So I could talk to him."

How logical he is, Bob thought. Sort of like me. The boy continued wistfully.

"I always hoped that when I was grown up, *Maman* would . . ."

". . . tell you all about him?"

"Yes. But now she's dead." For the first time since he'd arrived, the child had explicitly referred to his mother's death. And the words caused him to burst into tears.

Silent, choking sobs that shook his little body.

Bob's heart was aching for the child. He picked him up. The little boy responded instantly. He threw his arms around Bob's neck and clung to him.

"*Maman,*" he murmured, crying all the while.

"I know," Bob answered softly, rocking him. "I know."

They held each other tightly, neither wanting to let go. Until their intimate embrace was interrupted.

"Bob?" It was Sheila, standing sleepily on the first step.

To Bob, his wife's expression seemed to reflect betrayal.

Slowly, he let the boy slide onto his feet.

"I woke up and you were gone," she said.

"I couldn't sleep. Jean-Claude was here when I came down. We'll go to bed now."

"Oh. That's all right. I was just a little worried."

As she walked back up the stairs, Bob's eyes followed her. He wondered what his wife might be thinking and feeling.

Then something touched his hand. He looked down.

"Bob," the little boy said, "I think I will go to bed now."

"Good. A good idea." Bob bent down and once again the boy embraced him. He was too much in conflict to respond.

CHAPTER SIX

"Sheila, darling, what a lovely surprise. I thought you'd be stuck on the Cape for the whole month."

"Thanks. You're the best thing that's happened to my ego this week."

"Lovely, ego boosting is my middle name."

Well, not exactly. Sheila's former college roommate was now Margo Fulton Andrews Bedford van Nostrand. She was nursing a martini in the patio of Harvest, the new restaurant behind the Brattle Theater, where she had a daily noontime table.

"Is this mine?" asked Sheila, indicating the glass of tomato juice sitting before her.

"Yes. Your usual."

"I think I'd like it spiked today," said Sheila.

"Good," said Margo, and signaled for the waiter. "Well, how's Bob and the girls?"

"Fine. They all send their love," Sheila answered. In fact, she had told the children she had business at the Press. And had told Bob nothing. "How's Hal?"

"Hal is Hal, to paraphrase Gertrude Stein, and he always will be. That's why I married him. No risk of surprises."

"And the gallery?"

Margo grinned. "It gets more successful every week. Hal is flabbergasted. He really thought I was too scatterbrained to be anything but a pretty face. Now he says I have a better business head than he does. Anyway, what brings you back to Cambridge?"

"I had some things to take care of. Uh—is that a new dress? It's very chic."

"It is, but you've seen it half a dozen times. What's with you today? You look preoccupied."

"Nothing," said Sheila, taking a sip of her Bloody Mary.

"Come on, Sheila, 'fess up. Is something wrong?"

"Yes." As Sheila removed her sunglasses and covered her face with her hand, Margo could see she had been crying.

"What happened?" Margo asked apprehensively.

"Bob had an affair." Sheila said it quietly and quickly.

"Sheila, I don't believe it. Bob is simply not the type. He thinks he's Adam and you're Eve. He wouldn't."

"He did," Sheila said almost inaudibly.

"Well," Margo temporized, "women sometimes imagine—"

"It's not my imagination. He told me."

"Oh." Margo looked at her former roommate and, with genuine shock in her voice, added, "This is really upsetting, Sheil. You've always been so happy." Margo sounded as though the news had shattered her few remaining illusions. "Who did he fall for?"

"She was French."

"Ah, I might have known," said Margo. She sat silent for a moment. At last she said, "I'm really sorry, Sheila."

Then Sheila gave voice to her greatest agony.

"They had a child."

"Oh, no," Margo said, as quietly as she could manage, and then, "You'd better tell me everything. From the beginning."

As she recited the events in sequence, Sheila grew more and more angry. This is so monstrous. What am I doing in this nightmare? Margo took it all in, her eyes widening. When Sheila got to Nicole's death and Bob's confession, Margo could no longer suffer in silence.

"Sheila, this beats everything I've ever heard. I thought Bob was perfect."

"So did I," said Sheila sadly.

There was a pause. Neither woman knew quite what to say.

"Well," said Margo desperately, "maybe you could pretend it was World War II and Bob was a GI in Europe and let the matter drop."

"I can't. Bob wanted to see the boy."

Margo was offended. "Men are so pathetic. They really get

turned on by the idea of boy children. I hope you put your foot down, Sheila. Him or you."

"That's precisely what I didn't want, Margo. If I made him choose, there'd always be a chance I'd lose him."

Margo eyed Sheila with mounting anxiety. "What did you do?"

She told Margo the rest of the story.

"But in your own *home*, Sheil. Where can it lead?"

"Look, we made a bargain. One month and the boy goes back to France. There are people trying to make arrangements for him. Better thirty days of suffering than a lifetime of uncertainty."

"But how can you stand it?"

Sheila shrugged. "I don't know. Sometimes I can't. Sometimes, when we're sitting there at night pretending to listen to Bach and pretending that everything is the way it always was, I feel such *rage* that I could kill Bob—"

"Maybe you should," Margo interrupted sardonically.

"—and yet there are other times when I feel I need him more than ever. Strange, isn't it? Even after what he's done, he's still the only one who can really comfort me."

Margo shook her head. "I can't understand you, Sheil."

"Neither can I," she replied. "But love and hate don't seem to cancel each other out. They can co-exist and drive you mad."

Margo sighed. "Do you really believe that it'll be all wrapped up neatly at the end of the month?"

"Yes," said Sheila. But in her heart she was no longer sure of anything.

"What do the girls think?"

"We didn't tell them who he was. They think he's cute."

"Is he?"

"I don't know. I look at him as little as possible, frankly. And when I do my only reaction is, what did she look like? Am I crazy, Margo?"

"No, darling." She reached across the table and touched Sheila's hand affectionately. "You're the wisest woman I know. If Hal ever did that to me, the only thing I could do is go out and have an affair or shop. Or both. I'd never have the strength to face it the way you have. It's a gamble, but knowing you, you'll shame Bob into line with your generosity. Now, can I help?"

Sheila shook her head. "Margo, you're a friend. But this is my problem."

"I envy you," said Margo.

"Why, for heaven's sake?" Sheila asked.

"I wish I could love a man as much as you love Bob."

"Thanks, Margo. Thanks for understanding."

THE SUN WAS SOFT and warm. Gentle waves nuzzled the shore of Cape Cod Bay. The little boy was sitting by himself, one of Bob's baseball caps on his head, a book in his hands.

"Hi, Jean-Claude."

He looked up. It was Paula Beckwith. "Hello."

"Whatcha reading?" she asked, peering at his book.

"*Histoire Générale*—world history," he replied.

"Wow! You must be very intellectual."

"Not really." He smiled. "Would you like to sit down?"

"Sure." Paula plopped on the sand. "What's new in history?"

"I am reading about Vercingetorix."

"What's that?"

"He was the first French hero. He led a revolt against Julius Caesar. Then Caesar had him strangled."

"Ugh." Paula clutched her neck in empathy for the valiant dead man. "Is there a picture of the strangling in that book?"

"Uh—no. I'm sorry."

Paula pondered for a moment. "We take hygiene next year."

"What is that?"

"Do you know what sexual education is?"

"I think so." He wasn't sure and didn't want to admit it.

"Well, do you know where babies come from?" she asked, enjoying the thrill of grown-up dialogue.

"Uh—yes. My mother told me. She was a doctor."

"Yeah, I know. How come your dad didn't tell you, though?"

Paula had innocently trespassed onto Jean-Claude's most private anxiety. "My father was not there," he said, and hoped she'd change the subject.

"You mean he was dead already?"

"What?"

"My father said your father was dead."

"Oh," said Jean-Claude, wondering why Bob's version should have contradicted what his mother had always told him. "Well . . ."

Meanwhile Paula was preparing to probe deeper. "Was that French you were speaking on the phone this morning?"

"Yes," the little boy replied, a trifle uneasy.

"It sounds terrific. I'm gonna start it in school this year. Then I'll be able to visit you sometime."

"That would be very nice."

"Yeah," said Paula, happy to receive the invitation. "Uh—were you talking to a friend?"

"Yes. An old friend of my mother's. Louis Venarguès. He was mayor of our town for many years. He says he will call every week to ask me how I am."

"Gee, I wish I had a friend like that."

The boy looked wistful and his eyes were saying, You have parents. But Paula didn't notice. In fact, just then she bounded up.

"I gotta help Jessie cook. We're making dinner to surprise my mom when she gets home. You wanna watch?"

"Yes," replied Jean-Claude, who was now not anxious to be alone.

As they started toward the house, side by side, their arms occasionally brushed. And Paula Beckwith inscribed the joy she felt upon a special page of memory. To prize forever.

JESSICA was poring over the Julia Child cookbook which was spread out on the kitchen table surrounded by open jars, boxes and assorted vegetables. Bowls and spoons were scattered everywhere.

"Yuck," said Paula. "What a mess! Whatcha doing, Jessie—cooking or finger painting?"

"Paula, I am trying to make a *blanquette de veau.*"

Paula turned to Jean-Claude and explained, "Jessie's studied cooking in school."

"Oh," said the visitor.

"What's that junk?" Paula asked Jessie. She pointed to four pots, all steaming away on the stove.

"Well, Jean-Claude obviously knows, but for your information, right now I'm working on the *sauce velouté.*" She was stirring some white viscous lumps with a wooden spoon.

"But it's just a veal stew, Jessie. Couldn't you have made everything in one pot?"

Jean-Claude sensed he was caught in a magnetic field between the two sisters.

"May I help you, Jessica?" he asked.

"Oh, that's *très gentil.* Do you know how to make a salad?"

"Yes," Jean-Claude replied. "That used to be my job. To have the salad ready when my mother came home from the clinic."

In a few moments both girls stopped working and stared at Jean-Claude. He had meticulously separated the lettuce leaves and immersed them one by one in water. Scrutinizing every leaf for imperfections, he placed those that passed onto a towel, patting them with care. After this he reached for the olive oil and vinegar. Instants later he was scientifically measuring ingredients into a bowl. He then looked up at his enraptured audience and said, "I need—I do not know the English for *de l'ail.*"

"Jessie?" Paula asked her sister.

"We haven't had that word yet. I'll look it up." And she sprinted toward the French dictionary in the living room. There were sounds of ruffled pages and at last a triumphant shout of "Garlic!"

"Wow," said Paula to Jean-Claude. "Are you gonna be a French chef when you grow up?"

"No," the boy replied. "A doctor."

Jessie re-entered in search of garlic and a garlic press.

"When will Mom and Dad be home?" asked Paula.

"Well, Dad is jogging on the high-school track with Uncle Bernie. He won't be late. Mom should be here around seven."

"She'll be real excited when she sees you've made the blanket stew for her."

"*Blanquette.* I hope so. I—uh—Jean-Claude, could I ask you to—uh—taste the sauce?"

"Of course, Jessica." He walked over to the pot, dipped the wooden spoon in and brought it to his mouth.

"Mmm," he said softly, "very interesting."

"But is it good, is it *good?*" Jessica persisted.

"Superb," the little boy replied.

It was a triumph of international diplomacy.

"DO YOU SEE that fantastic son of mine? Isn't he great?"

As the two fathers circled the Nanuet High School track, Bernie kept touting his son's athletic talents. At this moment, Davey was scrimmaging with some of the older soccer honchos.

"He's pretty good," Bob conceded. His legs still bore some bruises from that collision with Bernie's pride and joy.

"Good? Beckwith, the kid's fantastic. He's got all the moves. I mean, he's really pro material. Don't you agree?"

"Yeah," Bob answered.

Bernie glanced at his friend. His voice was sympathetic. "You know, women's sports are getting big too. If you started your girls on a program now, they'd have a chance for athletic scholarships. I could maybe even help."

"They hate sports, Bern."

The men jogged along for another half mile, their increasingly labored breaths punctuated by Bernie's gasps of "Great" and "Fantastic" whenever Davey showed his style.

"Good workout," Bernie said when they reached the finish line and began to walk. "You should run during the year too, Beckwith. I mean, how do you stay so thin? You don't even play squash."

"I worry a lot," said Bob, and kept walking.

"You seem down, Beckwith. Is anything wrong?"

Bob looked at him. "I gotta talk to someone, Bern."

"What am I here for, Beckwith?"

They picked up their sweat clothes, wandered over to the wooden bleachers, climbed to the highest step and sat down.

"Okay, okay," said Bernie. "What's the matter?"

"You know the French boy I brought over yesterday?"

"Yeah. Nice-looking."

"He's mine."

"What do you mean?" Bernie was normally far from obtuse, but something visceral prevented him from understanding Bob's statement.

"He's my son." Bob repeated.

Bernie's jaw dropped. "Good Lord," he said. "You mean you've been cheating on Sheila all this time?"

"No, no. This was ten years ago. It wasn't even an affair. I mean, more like a fling. The woman died last month. That was the first I ever heard about the boy."

"Are you really sure he's yours?"

"Yes."

"Good Lord," Bernie repeated, and then, "Was she good-looking?"

"I suppose so."

"Have you got a picture?"

Bob glared angrily at Bernie. "Will you be serious?"

"It was a reasonable question, Beckwith. If I ever cheated on Nancy—which I'd never have the guts to do, 'cause it would kill her—it'd have to be with something like Raquel Welch or better. And the least I'd do is save a picture."

Bob turned to him and said quietly, "Her hair was darker, but she looked a lot like the boy."

Something else dawned on Bernie. "What is he doing *here?*"

"He's got no other family. If we didn't take him, he'd already be in an orphanage. A guy in France is trying to fix up something else."

The soccer team had now disbanded, and sunset cast long shadows on the field. The only sound was Davey Ackerman kicking his ball into the nets. Bernie was at a loss for words. He slowly shook his head and stared down through the wooden slats at the ground below. What could he say?

"Bob, I never dreamed a guy like you would mess around. I mean, you and Sheila were like those little figures on a wedding cake. What made you do it?"

"I don't remember, Bernie. It was so long ago."

"Did you love the girl?"

Bob looked wounded. "Of course not," he shot back.

"I'm sorry," Bernie retorted. "I don't believe you. I don't believe a guy married to someone like Sheila would have an affair with a woman he didn't at least *think* he loved."

"The important thing is," Bob said quietly, "I don't know what to do now."

"Get rid of the kid, Bob. Pronto. Amputate the relationship or your marriage will get gangrene. How's Sheila taking it?"

"She agreed to a month's visit. But it's getting to her."

"I'll bet. That's why you've gotta ship that kid off now, Bob. You've got too much to lose. Hey, I just thought of something ironic."

"What?"

"Here you are, a professor of statistics. You have one lousy affair in your whole life. A little fling. And you get a kid as evidence. What are the odds of that happening to anybody?"

"Oh," said Bob bitterly, "about a billion to one."

"THE VEAL IS PERFECT, Jessie."

"Do you really think so, Mom?"

"I think so, too," said Bob unasked. All during dinner he had been trying to read Sheila's face, but found it curiously indecipherable. They'd talk later, he reassured himself.

"What a nice surprise," Sheila added. "Did you make the salad dressing too?"

"Actually Jean-Claude made it," said Jessie.

Sheila tried to seem pleased. "It's very good, Jean-Claude."

"Thank you," he answered shyly.

"He used to do it for his mom, every day," Paula added. "He can cook a lot of other stuff too."

"Oh," said Sheila, "that's nice." She was doing her best, and Bob wasn't helping at all.

"Anyone care for more *blanquette?*" asked Jessica.

At first there seemed no takers. Everybody's appetite was satisfied. But there was so much left.

"Uh—I would like some," said Jean-Claude. Jessie was delighted. Better to please one French palate than a dozen provincial know-nothings. For dessert she had prepared Black Forest cake à la Sara Lee. Provincial taste buds suddenly reawakened.

"May we go watch television?" Paula asked her father.

"Can't you ever read a book?"

"Books are too scary," Paula protested.

"What are you talking about?" asked Bob.

"Jean-Claude has a schoolbook about *strangling*," Paula said.

"What's this?" Bob asked the boy.

"I was reading the history of France. That is how Julius Caesar disposed of Vercingetorix, the revolutionary."

"Oh," said Sheila. "Do you enjoy history, Jean-Claude?"

"Not when it's sad. I was hoping Vercingetorix would win."

Bob smiled. "Why don't you go watch TV with the girls, Jean-Claude? It'll take your mind off strangling."

The two girls scampered off, but the French boy did not move. "If you don't mind, Bob," he said politely, "I would prefer to read. I want to finish Julius Caesar." He got off his chair and started out toward the stairway.

"You'll like what happens to him, Jean-Claude," Sheila called. "Brutus and Cassius get revenge for Vercingetorix."

"I know," he answered with a smile. "There is a picture."

When he had left the room, Sheila said something that totally astonished Bob. "He's very cute."

They lingered over coffee in the dining room.

"How was Cambridge?" Bob inquired.

"Hot and tiring," she answered. "The Square was swarming with summer school kids. . . ." Their dialogue was strangely awkward.

"See anyone?" Bob asked.

"Yes. Margo."

"How is she?" Bob asked, wondering if Sheila had confided in her friend as he had in his.

"The same."

They finished their coffee in silence. Bob was now pretty sure she had told Margo. Then they began to talk again. Not really communicating, merely lobbing words over the net.

"Anything happen today?" Sheila asked.

"Nothing much. Oh, yeah—Louis Venarguès called."

"Has he made any progress?"

"Not yet. He just wanted to see if the boy was okay."

"I think he's adjusted rather well, don't you?"

"Seems to have. Good kid," he said tentatively, "don't you think?"

"Yes," she said, "considering."

And then it suddenly occurred to Bob. We are talking like unhappily married people.

EVEN DURING VACATION time, lights out was ten p.m. for the Beckwith children. Jessie and Paula, all cooked out and viewed out, were more than willing to go to bed. Sheila tucked them in, then joined Bob in their own room.

"How're the kids?" he asked.

"In the arms of Morpheus. He's still reading, though."

"I missed you today," Bob whispered. She was tying her hair up, her back to him. "I don't want us to grow distant, Sheila."

"No," she said tonelessly.

"Will we?" he asked, a silent plea in his voice.

"I hope not," Sheila answered. She turned and started for the door. "I want to check on the boy."

And she left her husband alone with his uncertainties.

A soft light was still emanating from Jean-Claude's room. Sheila tiptoed down the hallway and stopped at his door. He had fallen asleep while reading. *Histoire Générale* was open across his chest. She looked down at him. There is nothing like a sleeping child to stir affection in the beholder.

And Sheila was by no means ill-disposed toward him. During the drive back to the Cape, she had become absolutely determined about one thing. The child was innocent. Whatever anger she might feel should be restricted to her husband. None of this was Jean-Claude's fault. None.

She watched him sleep. His brown hair had fallen across his brow. Should she brush it back? No, it might wake him. And he would be frightened to find himself so far from home. What if he should have a nightmare? Whom would he turn to?

You could come to me, she told him with her thoughts. I'd comfort you, Jean-Claude. I hope you haven't found me cold. I like you. Yes, I really do.

She went to turn off the light next to him. Almost accidentally her glance strayed to the night table. And then she froze.

Right by Jean-Claude's pillow was a picture in a silver frame. Taken several months ago at most. It was Jean-Claude sitting in an outdoor restaurant, smiling at a woman. A lovely, raven-haired woman in a low-necked blouse, who was smiling back at him.

It was *she*. And she was beautiful. Very beautiful.

Evidently Jean-Claude only took the picture out at night.

Sheila turned away and left the light on.

"Was he asleep?" asked Bob when she returned to their room.

"Yes," she answered. And her voice felt numb.

"Sheila," Bob said tenderly, "we'll work it out between us. I love you. Nothing's more important in the whole world."

She didn't answer.

She wanted to believe it. But no longer could.

CHAPTER SEVEN

The next morning Bob woke up before Sheila. Sunshine flooded the room. It was a glorious day. He looked over at his sleeping wife and wondered, How can I make her smile? He went downstairs to the kitchen, brewed coffee and brought it up to her.

"Oh, thank you," she said drowsily. (Almost smiling?)

He sat on the edge of the bed. "Hey, Sheila, it's gorgeous out. Why don't we take a little trip to Provincetown?"

"The two of us?"

"Everybody." Damn. The instant he'd replied, Bob realized he had blown a unique opportunity.

Still, once they had all arrived in the quaint fishing village-artist-

colony-tourist trap, his spirits again lifted. Everybody seemed happy to be there. Narrow Commercial Street (an apt name, Bob thought) was teeming with tourists in loud summer shirts and even louder sunburns. At the first appropriate shop, Jessica insisted upon buying a pair of garish pink sunglasses.

"Wow," said Bob. "You look like Dracula's daughter."

"I resent that," said Sheila, a twinkle of humor in her voice.

Then they climbed up to the Pilgrim Monument, looked with the requisite reverence and started down again. The two girls walked ahead with Sheila, stopping to peer at antiques. Jean-Claude remained at Bob's side. Touched by this, Bob began pointing out the sights. All the while he was studying a contemporary attraction just ahead of them.

"See that chick in the white shorts? She's got the nicest legs we've seen all day."

Just then the leggy beauty—Sheila Beckwith—turned and smiled at them. Had she heard Bob? He hoped so.

By midafternoon, they were at MacMillan Wharf, where they all ate clams. Then Bob bought everybody soft ice cream, and they strolled out on the pier to watch the fishermen unload the day's catch. For Jean-Claude this was the best part of the day.

As they climbed back in the car, he remarked, "I like this place. It reminds me of my home."

Minutes later, they were cruising along the ocean on Route 6A. Bob was pleased. The excursion had been a success. Not only were the kids elated, but even Sheila seemed to have enjoyed herself. He glanced at his watch. It was nearly five o'clock.

"Hey guys," he said, "I promised to meet Uncle Bernie at the track about now for a run. Why don't we all go?"

Jessie and Paula groaned.

"I don't think so, Bob," Sheila said gently, "but we could drop you off and Bernie could give you a lift home."

They drove for several miles without further conversation. Then Jean-Claude spoke. "May I come, please?" he asked.

Bob was delighted. "You mean you'd like to run?"

"No," the boy replied, "but I would like to watch you."

BERNIE WAS WARMING UP, his eyes constantly on the infield, where Davey was once again outclassing the high-school soccer stars. Then he noticed his friend walking toward him.

"Ho, Beckwith!" he called, without interrupting his jumping jacks. "Ho, kid! You gonna run with us?"

"No," said Jean-Claude. "I will just wait for Bob."

"Sports are crucial for growing boys," stated Bernie, and then turned to indicate the action on the field. "Lookit Davey He's gonna grow up to be a regular Tarzan."

"Maybe Jean-Claude doesn't want to swing from trees," Bob interposed. "C'mon, Bern, let's get on the road."

The men chugged off. The boy walked to the stands, climbed to the fourth tier and sat down.

"When's he leaving?" whispered Bernie on the curve.

"I told you, Bern. Sheila agreed to a month's visit."

"Okay, okay. Just remember, I warned you that what a wife thinks and what she says don't always match."

"Let's run, huh?" Bob picked up the pace.

"That reminds me," Bernie puffed. "You know, what you've told me is buried in the Fort Knox of my brain. But—"

"But what?"

"I'd really like to tell Nance. Husbands and wives shouldn't have secrets from each other. Besides, she'll notice I'm holding out on her. Heaven knows what she'll think it is."

"She'd never guess," Bob said wryly.

"That's just the point. Please, Beckwith, Nance'll be discreet."

"Okay, Bern," he sighed. "When'll you tell her?"

Three strides later, Bernie answered sheepishly, "Last night."

THE HIGH SCHOOL soccer stars began to disband, bidding farewell to Davey Ackerman. Today he decided to practice dribbling. So he began to trot around the field, nudging the ball before him with alternating feet.

When he reached the stands, he noticed the Beckwiths' visitor seated by himself. He trapped the ball under his foot, stopped short and pivoted toward the stands.

"Hey!" he called. "How come you're always with Jessica Beckwith, huh?" Davey's tone was distinctly belligerent.

"Uh—I am her guest," Jean-Claude replied. "She is my friend." He vaguely sensed that he was being challenged to something.

"She's *my* girl, Frenchie, do you understand that? *My* girl," Davey insisted, thumbing his expanded chest for emphasis.

"My name is not Frenchie," the boy said quietly.

Ahh, thought Davey, I've found a sore point.

"Yeah? Well, I'll call you whatever I want, whenever I want, how many times I want—plus ten more. Frenchie, Frenchie . . ."

Davey was standing there, his right foot on the soccer ball, his right hand making a sophisticated gesture in conjunction with his nose. He was appreciably taller than the younger boy.

Jean-Claude stood up and descended from the stands. "My name is Jean-Claude Guérin," he said quietly, walking slowly toward Davey. He was now less than a foot away.

"And I say it's Frenchie. Sissy Frenchie Fruitcake."

Then Jean-Claude kicked. Not Davey, but the ball beneath his foot. Davey fell back onto his behind. His departing buddies saw the superstar's tumble and began to laugh. Davey rose from the ground, infuriated, and lunged for the ball. Jean-Claude deftly tapped it away.

Now the French boy dribbled toward midfield. Davey gave chase. He sprinted and lunged again. Jean-Claude feinted and dodged. Davey could not get anywhere near the ball. The team guys now began to whistle and applaud. They had never seen such ball handling by so young a kid. They hadn't learned in school that European children begin kicking as soon as they begin walking.

The cheers became audible to the joggers on the far side of the field. Bernie was the first to notice. He could not believe his eyes. "Good grief!" he exclaimed. "The kid's an athlete!"

At first Bob did not bother to look up, assuming it was yet another of Bernie's panegyrics on his son. Then he did. And he saw Jean-Claude feinting as Davey Ackerman tackled for the ball—and this time landed face down in the dust.

He felt a shiver, and thought, *My son's* fantastic! He stopped running to watch. "Bravo, Jean-Claude!" he shouted. "*Bien joué, bien joué!*"

"Beckwith," Bernie said quietly, "you've gotta get rid of that kid before it's too late."

"What do you mean, too late?"

"Before you fall in love with him."

"HOW WAS YOUR RUN?" Sheila asked.

"Not bad," said Bob. "Jean-Claude played some soccer," he added, unable to conceal his pride. "You should have seen him. He's really very good."

Jean-Claude beamed. Bob felt a further joy that his praise had so pleased the boy.

"How about washing up for dinner, Jean-Claude?"

"Okay, Bob," he said, and skipped out of the kitchen.

Bob kissed Sheila on the cheek. "Dinner smells great. Can I help?"

"Yes. Peel some potatoes."

"Sure." He was happy to be doing something with her again—even if it was only KP. He put on an apron and began to peel.

One potato later, Sheila mentioned, "Evelyn called. She asked me to come to Cambridge tomorrow."

"Honey, Evelyn Unger is a workaholic and a slave driver. The Harvard Press is *not* the *New York Times*. What is so important that it couldn't wait three weeks?"

"Gavin Wilson," she replied.

"Isn't he in Washington with the National Security Council?"

"Yes. But he'll be in Cambridge tomorrow. Only tomorrow. Evelyn wants to reissue his books. And she wants me to convince him to do some revisions and updating."

"For this you have to sacrifice a chunk of your vacation?"

She said quietly, "I'm flattered to be asked, Bob."

He understood. At this delicate moment she wanted some reaffirmation of her worth. He should be glad for her.

"Yeah," he said, after another potato, "it is flattering, isn't it? Well, haven't I always said you were the best editor they had? I say it's about time they acknowledged it."

"And I say keep peeling," she replied cheerfully.

BOB AND SHEILA were sitting peacefully in the living room, listening to the music of the waves. "Hey," he said suddenly, "I've got an idea. Why don't we drive up to Cambridge together?"

"What about the kids?"

"We could get a baby-sitter to sleep over."

"Sleep over?"

"Well, I thought we might give ourselves a break and stay over at the Lexington house. Just the two of us." Please Sheila, he was thinking. Please.

She mulled it over. "Not this time, Bob," she said at last.

At least it was a conditional rejection. "Not this time" implied perhaps another time.

She stood up. "I'd better get a good night's sleep," she said.

Then she walked over to him, and whispered, "Thanks for asking," and kissed him lightly on the forehead.

It was the best thing that had happened to him in weeks.

"HI SHEILA," called Maureen, the receptionist. "He's in Evelyn's office. Lucky you."

Funny, thought Sheila, as she started down the corridor toward the editorial department. Maureen's usually blasé, accustomed to the likes of Kissinger and Galbraith parading by.

When she turned the corner, she saw him having coffee with Evelyn at her desk. He was long and lanky, with graying hair and square tortoiseshell glasses. He was wearing jeans and a T-shirt reading GO BOSTON RED SOX! She was somewhat startled, for she had prepared herself to meet a three-piece suit (the Washington influence) with a cultured English accent (the Oxford influence).

He stood up as she approached. Evelyn introduced them. "Gavin, this is Sheila Beckwith, our number one editor."

"How do you do," said Wilson. (At least the accent was still there.) "I understand you've had to interrupt your holiday on my account. I'm terribly sorry."

"I'm happy to have the chance of working with you, Dr. Wilson."

"Gavin, please. And may I call you Sheila?"

"Of course. I know you're on a tight schedule. Would you like to come right to my office and begin?"

He smiled and turned to Evelyn. "You didn't exaggerate. She's a harsh taskmaster." And then, turning to Sheila, "May I get you a coffee en route?"

"Please," said Sheila. "White, no sugar."

By the time he entered her office, Sheila had already placed his three books on her desk and was spreading out some sheets of yellow paper.

He put the container of coffee on the corner of the desk and then sat down across from her.

"Thank you," she said. And then, to break the ice, asked, "Do you miss Cambridge at all?"

"Yes, I do. Though Washington does have its compensations. At the White House, one has the scintilla of power. Which I confess I quite enjoy."

"I admire your candor."

"In any case, if and when this administration's voted out, I do hope Harvard will welcome back the Prodigal Son."

"Oh, they will," Sheila said, smiling, "especially since your books will have been reissued and updated."

"Well, I can see I'm being buttered up to do serious revisions," he said. "But I was really thinking of a 'Preface to the second edition sort of thing. And then I could plead Washington pressures for not being able to revamp the whole business."

"Well, in that case, you don't need me," Sheila replied pleasantly but firmly, "and I don't think the Press would reissue your books with nothing but cosmetic changes."

Wilson shifted a bit uneasily in his chair. "You're not too bad in the candor department, either," he said. "Uh—what sort of things did *you* have in mind?"

"Well, I've only been able to skim the books since Evelyn called me. But take *The Re-emergence of Postwar Germany.* It was the best thing published in its time. It's not your fault that it came out just before Brandt began his *Ostpolitik.*"

He frowned. "If I understand your drift, you're about to ask for an enormous amount of work."

"Yes, I'm sorry. But if I were you, I'd take the time. Now that you're in the papers a little more than the average Harvard professor, some of your academic colleagues—which is to say everybody who didn't get appointed to the National Security Council—will start trying to punch holes in your scholarship."

He laughed. "How do you know university politics so well?"

"My husband's a statistics professor at MIT."

"Oh, a real brain. I'm always self-conscious when I meet that sort of mind. I can barely add a column of figures."

"Neither can Bob," Sheila said, grinning. "That's my job at the end of every month."

"Oh," said Gavin Wilson. "Then my admiration for you knows no bounds." And his smile did not seem to be solely for Sheila's arithmetical ability.

In any case, considering the ice fairly well broken, Sheila got back to business. By the end of the morning Gavin had agreed to make revisions, and Sheila had agreed to have lunch with him at Harvest.

Margo would doubtless be at her daily corner table. But so what, thought Sheila, this was business, wasn't it?

Gavin dressed for lunch. Which is to say he put a dungaree jacket over his Red Sox T-shirt. When they got to the restaurant, it was rather late. Most people were having coffee and dessert—and Margo seemed to have left.

It was July, and Cambridge was an oven. So they ordered iced tea instead of an aperitif. Facing a long afternoon of editorial negotiations, they restricted the conversation to small talk.

"Do you have any children?" he asked.

"Uh—yes," she replied after a split second. "Two girls, nine and twelve. You?"

"Two. My son's reading medicine at Oxford, Gemma's still at home with my ex-wife, in England. I don't think they miss their father much. My wife's propaganda has done its work."

"Are you on bad terms—or shouldn't I ask?"

"Not at all. Yes, we are on extremely bad terms. She's never forgiven me for joining the British brain drain. She told me to choose between her and Harvard—never expecting I would take the latter—she's been a bit ill-disposed toward me ever since. I'm still fond of her, if that counts for anything. And I miss the children. Oh—but forgive me for babbling on about boring domestic matters."

"You're not boring me at all," she answered, genuinely happy to be discussing someone else's domestic problems. And then she asked him, "Are you bitter?"

He seemed unprepared for her question. "Do I seem bitter?"

"No, of course not," she said quickly, "and it was impolite of me to ask."

"Not at all," he protested. "You're a perceptive lady. Let's just say my pride was—sprained. Why else would I have told you, when we could have been discussing things of interest to us both?"

Sheila had never considered herself perceptive about anyone except Bob and the children. But Gavin was obviously trying to flatter her. He had a reputation for suavity.

As she was reaching for the credit cards in her purse, he put his hand on hers. "What do you think you're doing?" he asked.

"Paying the check," she replied. "I like to use my expense account. It makes me feel important." She removed her hand. signaled the waiter and settled the bill.

"Thank you." He smiled. "Are you always this persuasive?"

"Only when it comes to my job." She smiled back.

BY FIVE THIRTY they had worked their way painstakingly through four chapters, marking in the margins where revisions or at least rechecking would be necessary. By now Sheila was tired.

"You'll have to excuse me, Gavin," she said, barely suppressing a yawn, "but I've got a long drive back to the Cape. I can go through the rest of the chapters, make copies of the pages that need revisions and send them on to you in Washington. . . ."

He looked up. "Must you?"

She nodded. "I've got a family waiting." She started to gather her papers and put them into her zippered case.

"Sheila?" He was now standing, gazing down at her. "Since the Press so graciously invited me to lunch, I'd like to reciprocate by asking you to dinner."

She paused for a moment. What had impressed her all afternoon was not his good looks, but his manner. Patient and good-humored. Irony without cynicism. What was her hurry to return to the minefield that she once called home?

"Well, I might be able to stay with friends in Cambridge."

"Splendid. You ring them from here, and I'll nip into Evelyn's office and book a table."

As soon as she was alone, she dialed Margo at the gallery.

"Sheila—are you in Cambridge again? Have things exploded at the Cape?"

"No. I had to do some work at the Press. In fact, I called to ask if I can stay over with you. I have to work late."

"Oh, that's wonderful. Hal's off fishing. All he'll probably catch is the tuna I packed for him. That means we can have a midnight party like the old days."

Then Sheila called Bob. He did not conceal his disappointment. "What about the kids?" he asked plaintively.

"You're there," she replied. "They can manage without me for one night."

"*I* can't manage without you," he answered.

THE PLACE WAS dimly lit, the checkered tables crowded with young college couples.

During dinner they relaxed easily into friendly conversation.

"You seem to enjoy your work," Gavin remarked.

"I do," Sheila replied.

"Well, you're good at it. I mean, it's a rare editor who doesn't hide behind coy euphemisms when they think a paragraph is total rubbish."

"Tell me about Washington," she said.

"Tell me more about you," he countered.

"I've told you everything, really. My life's pretty conventional compared to yours."

Again she had shifted the topic back to him. I'm not *that* fascinating, he told himself. Still, it was refreshing to encounter someone who could resist talking about herself.

As he gazed at Sheila across the candles, he wondered why this lovely woman seemed to emanate such sadness.

"You know, you're extremely attractive, Sheila," he said.

She tried desperately to look happily married.

"Do you think I'm just flattering you?" he asked.

"Yes," she said.

"Don't believe everything you read. I'm not playing the devious roué. And I hope you'll accept my invitation for a nightcap without any superfluous qualms."

"No, really, I can't. My friends are expecting me."

"The Sheraton-Commander's midway between there and here."

His hotel. What a line! Did he ever actually succeed with it? Of course he did. Because in other circumstances he might well succeed in making her believe she was attractive and desirable. How ironic that it happened now, when she was at the nadir of her confidence as a woman.

"Sheila?" Gavin repeated, still awaiting her response.

"Really, I'm exhausted. I wouldn't be much fun." He could construe that in accordance with his own intention.

"Some other time, then," he said good-naturedly, and rose to help her from her chair.

They drove in silence to the Harvard Press. He waited while she got into her car.

"Thank you, Gavin," Sheila said.

And he replied, "I can't tell you how much I look forward to working with you."

"AH! YOU WEREN'T working overtime. You had a date!"

"I had dinner with an *author*, Margo."

"I don't care if he was a trapeze artist. He was a man and you were out with him. By my definition, that's a date."

As Sheila sat down on the couch, Margo poured her some wine. "Now tell me *everything*," she said.

"Well . . ." Sheila began, "we're reissuing three of Gavin Wilson's books."

"Couldn't that have waited till the end of your holiday?"

"Not really. Gavin was only up in Cambridge for the day."

"Gavin?" Margo grinned. "We're already on a first-name basis, are we? Is he as handsome as his photographs?"

"I suppose so."

"Did he like you?"

Sheila paused. "Well, he thinks I'm a good editor."

"Editor shmeditor. Where did he take you for dinner?"

"La Groceria in Central Square."

"Ah, candlelight—very romantic. And when did he make his pass?"

"What?"

"Come on, Sheil. He's gorgeous, eligible and notorious."

"But I'm—"

"And you're a *very* pretty lady."

"I was about to say I'm married."

Margo raised an eyebrow. "And the world is round," she stated. "None of which has anything to do with Gavin Wilson. Now tell me about the postprandial pitch."

"Well, he did ask me for a drink at his hotel."

"Then what are you doing *here*?"

"That sort of thing is hardly my life-style," Sheila answered.

Margo got up and sat next to her on the couch. "Listen, lovey," she said, taking Sheila's hand, "you've always been the perfect wife and you've just had your ego flattened with a steamroller. Doesn't it make you feel good to find out that a really super guy thinks you're terrific?"

"I . . . I was sort of flattered, yes. Anyway, it doesn't matter, Margo. Despite this wretched mess, I still love Bob and I don't want my marriage to suffer any more than it has."

"Look, Sheil, Bob doesn't ever have to know. And you could use some distraction. Be honest with yourself. Weren't you the least bit tempted?"

What was the point of denying it now?

"Margo, where could it lead?"

"Nowhere, probably. But it might just make you a little less unhappy. Anyway, you'll never know unless you follow it up. Call Gavin now. Before you lose your nerve."

"What could I say? It's so embarrassing."

"Just tell him you had a lovely evening. Let him make the next move. Where's he staying?"

"The Sheraton-Commander."

In an instant, Margo was leafing through the phone book. She found the number, scratched it on a piece of paper and handed it to Sheila. "Come on, honey, call," she said.

"I can't."

"Okay, Sheila, it's your life. I don't want to be Mephistopheles. Be unhappy on your own terms." She started to scrunch the paper into a ball.

Then Sheila blurted out, "Wait. I—I'll do it."

Her fingers trembled slightly as she pressed the buttons on the telephone. The next moments seemed endless, while the hotel operator rang Gavin's room.

There was no answer. Sheila let the receiver slide from her hand back onto the phone. Thank God.

CHAPTER EIGHT

Jean-Claude was seated in his usual spot on the beach, studying *Initiation à la Géographie*. He had been there since early morning, having risen before the rest of the family.

Jessica appeared some time later, carrying her paperback of *Anna Karenina*, and walked to a dune far down the beach. They sat like bookends for two hundred yards of silent sand and driftwood.

The sun was nearing its meridian when an unwelcome shadow cut off Jessie's reading light.

"Whatcha doing, Jess?"

She looked up. It was that Philistine, Davey Ackerman.

"Reading," she replied. "And I'd be grateful if you'd quit blocking my sun."

"I got a secret to tell you, Jess," he said.

She eyed Davey with her customary disdain. "What?"

"Walk with me to the cove," he answered. "We gotta talk in private, Jess. I could get killed if anyone found out."

The thought of a man risking his life to impart something to her piqued Jessie's interest. She stood up. "Okay," she said, brushing the sand off her shorts. "This better be worth it."

They walked till they had rounded a dune in the cove.

"Well?" asked Jessica impatiently.

He took a deep breath to summon up his courage. "I heard my parents talking last night about your parents. . . ."

Jessie grew anxious. She had lately noticed a slight coolness between Bob and Sheila, but had refused to ascribe any importance to it. Not them, she had told herself. They're happy.

"What about my parents?" she asked, biting her nail.

"Well, it was about the French kid, actually." Davey paused, then blurted nervously, "He's your father's son."

"What?" demanded Jessie, frightened that she understood.

"Your father is his father. You get it?"

"You're a filthy liar!" Jessie shouted, on the verge of tears.

"Cool it, Jess," he pleaded. Her unexpected tantrum was upsetting him. He had hoped for something more like gratitude. But she turned away and ran down the beach.

"WHAT WAS he like, Mom?" Paula asked, as Sheila unpacked her briefcase, piling Gavin Wilson's three books on her desk.

"Nice," she replied. "I expected him to be a little conceited, but he wasn't." She was careful to place the volumes with the front covers facing upward. So Gavin's photograph would not stare up to remind her of what had almost happened yesterday.

"What did you have for dinner last night?" she asked, hoping her daughter would not notice the blatant shift of subject.

"Dad took us out for pizza. It was fun," and then, realizing her lapse in tact, Paula added, "Of course, it woulda been better if you were there too, Mom."

"Thanks." Sheila laughed and kissed her on the forehead. Just then the front door slammed.

"Mom, where are you?" Jessie shouted.

"In here, Jess. I just got back this instant—"

Jessica entered the room, her face flushed and sweating.

"What's the matter, honey?" Sheila asked.

"Is it true about Daddy?" Jessie demanded, her voice quavering.

"Uh—I don't know, Jessie." At least I hope I don't.

"What's going on?" inquired Paula.

"Davey told me that Jean-Claude is Daddy's *son!*"

"What? You're crazy!" said Paula.

"Please," said Sheila, frantically trying to preserve all their sanity, "let me try to explain. . . ."

Jessie turned angrily on her mother.

"First admit it's true, Mom. Tell me Dad is really Jean-Claude's—" Jessie couldn't bring herself to say the word.

"Yes," Sheila said quietly, "it's true."

Now Paula began to cry. "No." She shook her head. "It's some big lie. He's *our* daddy."

Jessie exploded at her sister. "Don't you understand, you little idiot? He had an affair with Jean-Claude's mother."

Paula looked helplessly at her mother and voiced her deepest fear. "Is Daddy gonna leave us?" she asked.

Sheila took the two girls in her arms. "It'll be all right," she murmured, hoping to make herself believe it.

Just then the front door slammed again. They froze. And Jean-Claude, book in hand, walked into the room. "Good afternoon." He smiled. He was especially happy to see Sheila again.

"He's *our* daddy," Paula shrieked at him. "He's ours!"

Jean-Claude was confused. "What do you mean?" he asked.

"Our daddy is your father, and you want to take him away," she screamed.

"But no—" Jean-Claude protested.

"I'll bet your mother isn't even dead," snarled Jessica, wanting to hurt him. To make him go away.

Paula rushed toward the boy and began to pummel him. He did not raise a hand to defend himself. For he was beginning to feel that he was, in some inexplicable way, guilty of a crime.

"Paula, stop hitting him this instant!"

Sheila pulled the two children apart. Jean-Claude was crying softly. He glanced fearfully at everyone, then retreated swiftly up the stairs. They heard his bedroom door close.

Sheila looked at her traumatized daughters. This was all Bob's fault. They were innocent victims whose lives had just been permanently disfigured by the shrapnel of his infidelity. And I was wrong too, she thought with anguish. I made the wrong decision.

Just then a car pulled up outside. It was Bernie, dropping Bob off from their tennis match. The girls fled up the stairs, leaving Sheila all alone.

She sighed as she heard her husband open the front door.
"Sheila, honey?"
"I'm in here, Robert," she said quietly. And knew she sounded like a stranger.

THEY SAT facing one another.
"What're we gonna do?" Bob asked Sheila.
"Not *we*," she said firmly. "This is *your* problem."
"What do you expect me to do?" he said, unwilling to understand what she was making crystal clear.
"Send him home, Robert," she said curtly. "Now. Today."
She was right.
"Otherwise I'll take the girls and go," Sheila added.
"Okay." He rose, went numbly to the phone and dialed.
"They have one seat on tonight's flight," he reported, putting his hand over the receiver, "but it leaves at seven. . . ."
"You can make it if you hurry," she said quietly.
"Okay," she heard him tell the airline. "The name is Beckwith—uh—I mean Guérin. Yes, we'll get there an hour before." He hung up and walked over to Sheila. "I'll go tell the boy."
She did not respond. He turned, started out of the room and up the stairs. He was too preoccupied with what he had to say to notice that the phone was ringing.
Sheila answered. It was Gavin Wilson.
"Could I call you back?" she asked. "Are you in Washington?"
"No, that's just the point. I can postpone Washington, if you are free—that is, willing to keep forging ahead with the revisions. I'd come down to you, of course."
"Gavin, I can't," she said.
"You sound upset. Is everything all right?"
"I'm sorry. Things are too confused. I can't talk now."
She hung up. And for a split second almost laughed. This can't be happening, she thought.

BOB KNOCKED. "Jean-Claude, may I come in?"
"Yes," he answered softly. Bob opened the door. The boy was curled up on his bed. He cast a furtive glance at Bob.
"Uh—okay if I sit down?" asked Bob.
Jean-Claude nodded. And again glanced fleetingly at Bob.
He chose the chair farthest from the bed. "I can't tell you how

sorry I am about the . . . fight with Jessie and Paula. They really wouldn't want to hurt you. You know that, don't you?"

Without looking up, the boy nodded. Slightly. "Would you like me to go home?" he asked.

Bob was embarrassed. "We think it might be best for you."

"Do you want me to go now?"

Oh, God, thought Bob, he's being so good about this.

"Well, yes," Bob answered. "That would make it easier. Why don't I help you pack?"

"There is no need," Jean-Claude said. "I have only a few things."

Bob hesitated. "I'll be back in a while, okay?"

He got up, crossed the room, touched the boy's shoulder and went out.

He stood for a moment outside Jessica's door, gathering his courage. Then he knocked.

"Who is it?" Jessie snapped belligerently.

"Me. Your father. I want to talk to you."

"I have no father. Go away."

"Please, Jess, open up. Is Paula there?"

"No," Paula retorted through the door. "Leave us *alone!*"

Heartsick, Bob walked away and went downstairs to the living room.

Sheila was curled up in the easy chair, hugging her knees.

"He'll be ready in a little while," Bob said softly. "He's packing by himself. He didn't want my help."

Sheila did not reply. But she had a selfish thought: I won't ever have to see that picture in the silver frame again.

"The girls won't talk to me," he added. "I've devastated them. haven't I? I mean, what can they believe in now? They'll never get over this." Then he asked his wife a favor. "Can you speak to them while I'm gone?"

She looked at him and asked simply, "What could I say?"

INSTEAD OF TAKING Route 6 all the way across the Cape, Bob turned off onto 6A at Orleans. Slower, but prettier. The Cranberry Highway, with a view of the sea.

The boy had been stoically silent during the last hours before departure. He had packed and then dutifully waited in his room for Bob to come and get him. Bob had carried the green valise, Jean-Claude his flight bag. They walked down the stairs to the kitchen.

where Sheila had prepared cheese sandwiches and coffee to fortify them for the journey to the airport.

While the girls remained in Jessie's room, Sheila had pulled herself together. It could not get worse. There was even a part of the summer left to try to make things better. She watched the man and the boy eat their sandwiches, and spoke the commonplaces the occasion called for.

"It was nice having you, Jean-Claude."

His mouth was full. He swallowed and politely answered, "Thank you, *madame*."

"I'm sure the girls are sorry for that . . . misunderstanding."

"Please say good-by for me," said Jean-Claude.

When it was time to go, Jean-Claude extended his hand. Sheila took it, and then leaned down to kiss him on the cheek. As Bob watched her, he thought: Am I going to be doing that at the airport, in just three more hours?

THEY HAD BEEN riding for thirty minutes. Bob tried to make conversation. "When we passed Orleans, I forgot to tell you something. That's where they built the first cable station for telegrams to France. There weren't any phones in those days. . . ."

"Oh," said the boy quietly.

What am I babbling about? Bob wondered. Cables? Yes, he then realized, it wasn't all that irrelevant. You were trying to tell him somehow that you'd still keep in touch. Did he understand?

The boy said nothing.

"We'll miss you, Jean-Claude," said Bob.

Coward, don't you even have the guts to use the singular?

"I've grown really fond of you," Bob added. There, I've done it. I've expressed my feelings. Some of them anyway.

For a long while, the boy did not reply.

At last, when they were scarcely an hour away from Logan airport, he spoke.

"Are you really my father?"

Bob looked at him. "Yes, Jean-Claude, I am your father."

All right, curse me out, kid, I deserve it. For not telling you the minute I first met you, to assuage your grief. For not even telling you today, until you made me.

And now, knowingly this time, abandoning you once again.

"That makes me happy," said the little boy. Yet there was a

tinge of sadness in his voice. "My mother used to talk about my father. That he was kind and good. And funny. And . . ."

"Yes?"

"And when I met you, even when I saw you the first time at the airport, I hoped that my father might be someone like you."

This was my worst fear, thought Bob. Or was it my best hope? That I would meet my son and he would like me—no, love me, imperfect as I am. He reached over and touched the little boy. Jean-Claude took Bob's hand with both of his and held it tightly.

Very tightly. And Bob said to himself, I can't let him go back.

I can't let go.

CHILDHOOD HAD ENDED abruptly for Jessica and Paula.

Sheila stood at the top of the stairway and heard them talking to one another.

"He's never gonna come back to this house," Paula insisted. "Never, never, never."

Jessie sounded strangely less agitated. "That's really up to Mom," she said. "I just hope they don't split."

A silence, while Paula tried to ponder the grown-up realities. "Oh, Jessie. I'm so scared. Everything's different."

"Don't worry. I'll take care of you."

Yet another pause. "But who'll take care of Mom?"

Sheila knocked, and opened the door. The girls looked relieved to see her. She sat down on the bed.

"Well, it's been quite a day, hasn't it?" And she made an effort to smile.

"What's gonna happen, Mom?" asked Paula anxiously.

"Well, Daddy will be back soon," she replied, "and we'll start to pick up the pieces. Look, the most painful part of growing up is discovering that nobody's perfect. Not even your parents."

"You still love Daddy, don't you?" Jessie asked.

Sheila nodded. "Jess, we've been happy for nearly twenty years. Happier than almost anyone."

"Life stinks, Mom," Jessie said painfully.

Sheila weighed this judgment for a moment.

"Yes, darling," she acknowledged. "Sometimes it does."

Just then the doorbell rang. "I'll get it," Sheila said, rising.

She went downstairs and opened the door. It was Gavin Wilson. Sheila was speechless.

"Forgive me for intruding, Sheila," he said, looking ill at ease, "but you sounded a bit strange on the phone. I was rather concerned. Are you certain everything is all right?"

"Oh, yes. It's just that when you called, the children were . . ." She groped for a plausible excuse.

"Yes. Quite," he said, agreeing with her incompleted thought. "Well, I'm afraid I've been presumptuous in rushing down. But I'm glad everything's all right. I'm staying at the Inn. If I can be of any help, just ring. But don't feel obliged to."

"That's very kind of you," said Sheila. Then added vaguely, "My husband ought to be back soon. He had to go to the airport."

"Oh?" said Gavin. "Some sort of emergency?"

"You might say so."

"Yes. Well. Uh—you know where to reach me, then," he answered shyly. He turned and started back toward his car.

"Gavin," Sheila called. "Would you like to come for a drink this evening—say, nine thirty? Bob will be glad to meet you."

"That would be splendid. Well, till then." He waved in a kind of half salute, turned and walked to his car.

How nice he is, thought Sheila. Going to all this trouble. Just for me.

SHEILA AND THE GIRLS were having dinner when the phone rang.

"Sheila?"

"Bob—is everything okay?"

"Uh—yes and no. We ran into an incredible traffic jam. We're still not at Logan and the flight's already taken off. I think we should stay over in Lexington so he can take the flight tomorrow evening. Don't you agree?"

She hesitated, and then said, "I suppose it makes sense."

"How are the girls?"

"A bit calmer."

Just then a nasal voice intruded on the line. "Deposit another forty cents, please."

"Listen, Sheil," Bob said hastily. "I'll call you from the house." Then he added, "I love you," just as the phone went dead. He hoped she had heard him. Because he had done a lot of rehearsing before making the call.

He hung up and started back into the dining area of the Howard Johnson's on Route 128. Jean-Claude was in a corner booth, picking at his fried clams (it was eat-all-you-want fish night). Bob sat down across from him.

"How would you like to stay another day?" he asked. "We could sleep at our house in Lexington. What do you think?"

"Oh, yes," said the boy.

SHEILA FELT RESENTFUL. Even when he had called the airline, Bob seemed to be looking for excuses to stall. Maybe he had deliberately missed the flight. To steal another day with his son.

She was so angry because he had left her alone to deal with the girls, taking for granted, as usual, that she would handle it. He didn't even sound apologetic about staying away for the night. Don't we matter anymore? Where are his priorities?

Gavin Wilson arrived at the stroke of nine thirty.

"Hello, Sheila." The tone of his voice matched the formality of his dress. He was wearing a tie and jacket.

"Come in," she said. "Can I get you something to drink?"

"Please. Scotch and water, if that's convenient." He followed her into the living room and glanced around uneasily.

"Uh—Bob had to stay in Boston," Sheila said, and tried to sound casual. "Please sit down. I'll get the drinks."

She went to the kitchen and opened the fridge. All at once the strain of all the pretense was too much for her. She closed the door, leaned on it and began to cry. Softly, steadily. It was a relief. Now she realized just how much she'd wanted to break down. And for how long.

Suddenly she felt someone's arms around her.

Gavin had come into the kitchen without her hearing him. As he continued to hold her, he whispered, "Now, Sheila, are you or are you not going to tell me what the matter is?"

She could not move, trapped by the crosswinds of emotion.

"I don't know you," she said without turning.

"If it will make it any easier," he answered gently, "I've been checked for security by the FBI. That means I can be trusted with the most vital secrets."

She gave a little laugh. Then he said, "Anyway, for what it's worth. I think I'm falling in love with you."

She did not reply.

"I know you've got every reason not to believe me. We've just met. And then, of course, I made that clumsy pass in the restaurant.

You don't know how sorry I am. I was so furious afterward that I walked for nearly two hours along the Charles."

Is this man trying to say he really cares for me?

"Sheila, it was awful of me not to realize that something was troubling you."

"It's all right," she said.

"Listen," he continued, "I came here not just to apologize but to try to comfort you. Do you feel a little better now?"

"Yes."

"Good. Now then, I'll fix us both that drink."

Back in the living room he sat down in the chair opposite her.

"Well?" he said.

She looked down into her glass and then again at him. "Gavin, I don't fool myself. You're—how can I put it?—a kind of intellectual pinup. I, on the other hand—"

"Don't finish that sentence, Sheila. You are not only intelligent and beautiful, you're extremely sensitive, and, if my instinct is correct, like myself a member of FOBS."

"What's FOBS?"

"The Fellowship of Bruised Souls. I'm the founder, actually."

"You don't seem at all wounded to me."

"I've just learned to hide it better." He paused. "I didn't really tell you the whole story the other day. When I left England and my wife didn't, it wasn't exactly Oxford she preferred as much as a certain Oxford don. A very nice professor of philosophy. So you see my being a pinup, as you so flatteringly call it, can't really compensate for the fact that my own wife didn't think so."

"Oh," said Sheila. "I'm sorry. I don't know what to say, except that I think I know the feeling. Do you ever get over it?"

"I really haven't. But time does help regenerate one's capacity for hope. After a while you begin to believe you might meet someone you trust." He looked at her.

"I really don't know where I am," she said. "I mean, so many things have happened to me all at once."

He took a breath, and then asked gently, "Is there someone else in your husband's life, Sheila?"

She was unable to find words for a moment. "Gavin, things aren't quite the way they look. I mean—" She shook her head. "I just couldn't explain it if I tried."

"Sheila, I withdraw my question—with apologies. It's really none of my business. We'll talk some other time, when you feel you can. Or want to." He stood up. "I should really go now. . . ."

She was about to protest, when he added, "Really, it's the right thing for both of us."

She hesitated, and at last said, "Thank you, Gavin."

He took out his address book, tore a page from it and began scribbling. "I'm giving you my home number in Washington and my White House extension. Promise me you'll call if you need me. Now are you sure you'll be all right on your own?"

"Yes," she answered. She went with him to the door. He stopped and looked down at her.

"I would like very much to kiss you, but this is not the time. Good night, Sheila." He gently touched her cheek. And walked out into the night.

Sheila watched his car drive off and thought, I wonder what would have happened if he'd kissed me.

CHAPTER NINE

Bob awakened to the sound of rain. At first glance it seemed like a winter day. And felt like it, as he closed the window. The thermometer actually read fifty-eight degrees. Winter on the Fourth of July. A statistical impossibility—except in Boston.

He padded down the hallway and peered into Jessie's room, where he had put Jean-Claude to bed for the night. The boy was still sleeping peacefully. Bob stared at the tranquil face. What am I to do? he thought.

When Jean-Claude woke, they shared some rolls and coffee. And since the energetic rain showed no signs of fatigue, Bob abandoned plans to tour the sights in Lexington and Concord. Instead he drove to Cambridge and parked in the MIT faculty lot.

"This is where I teach," said Bob, as they splashed toward the entrance of his building.

Their footsteps echoed as they marched down the corridor to Bob's door. Bob unlocked the office.

"May I sit at your desk?" the boy asked.

"Sure." Bob smiled.

The boy plopped onto Bob's chair and began to swivel from side to side.

"I am Professor Beckwith," he pronounced in a kind of soprano baritone. "Would you like to ask me some statistics?"

"Yes," replied Bob. "What are the chances of this rain stopping today, Professor?"

"Mmmm," said Jean-Claude, pondering earnestly. "You'll have to see me tomorrow about that." And then he giggled, enjoying his own joke. And sitting in his father's leather chair.

"I like it here," Jean-Claude went on. "You can see the sailboats on the river. Look—there are even some out in the rain."

Bob was usually so wrapped up in work that he rarely glanced out the window. But the boy was right. His view was wonderful.

It was almost three p.m.

"I have an idea," said Bob. "If you don't mind a little walk, we could visit the Museum of Science."

"Okay."

Bob found an old umbrella and they went out to brave the elements. They crossed Memorial Drive and walked along the Charles River to the museum.

As Bob expected, it was packed because of the bad weather. Jean-Claude stood hypnotized by the gaze of Spooky the Owl, the avian host of the place. Bob bought him a Spooky T-shirt, which he immediately put on over his other clothes.

They then waited their turn so that Jean-Claude could explore the lunar surface and climb up into the Apollo landing module. He waved at Bob, who now stood several hundred thousand miles away.

"*Salut* from the moon."

Bob smiled. He offered Jean-Claude his hand to help him out of the spaceship, and after that the little boy did not let go. They went up to the second floor, bought ice cream cones and engaged the plexiglass Transparent Woman in conversation. Bob was impressed with how much anatomy the boy already knew.

"Do you want to be a doctor when you grow up?" he asked.

"Perhaps. Or maybe a professor."

In the museum souvenir shop, Bob bought some postcards for Jean-Claude and a newspaper. By now he had almost banished the evening's flight from his mind, and wanted to find something to do. "Hey," he said, looking at the paper, "there's supposed to be an outdoor concert tonight. I wonder if they've canceled it."

The lady at the shop overheard, and answered, "Not *this*

concert, sir. It's Arthur Fiedler's golden anniversary with the Boston Pops."

"Thanks, ma'am," said Bob, and then turned to Jean-Claude. "We might get a little wet, but it could be fun."

"Is it jazz?"

"No. Does it matter?"

"No," said the boy.

They walked back to Bob's car and he took out the ancient blanket he kept in the trunk. Then, after a detour to buy submarine sandwiches, they crossed the Harvard Bridge and strolled to the green grass of the Esplanade.

Several thousand diehard fans were camped in defiance of the elements, having improvised tents, tepees, lean-tos and the like. Bob spread the blanket as close as possible to Hatch Shell, the hemispheric shelter for the musicians. He offered Jean-Claude an enormous sandwich.

"Must I?" asked the boy. "My stomach hurts a little."

"Don't worry," Bob assured him, thinking it was probably nerves. "Eat what you can."

"Okay," he sighed, and began pecking away desultorily.

About an hour later, a storm of applause drowned out the drizzle. The venerable conductor, Arthur Fiedler, was striding to the podium. The crowd rose to its feet and shouted, "We love you, Arthur."

Bob explained. "The man with all the white hair is a big celebrity. He's even more important than the music."

"He looks like *Père Noël*," said the boy.

"You're right," Bob said. "He does look like Father Christmas.

Then Bob had a curious thought. There's something about Fiedler that reminds me of my dad.

And he remembered the many happy excursions he had taken with his own father. The Phillies games. Saturday matinees with Ormandy and the Philadelphia orchestra. Camping in the Poconos. Just the tow of them.

Suddenly he missed his father terribly.

Fiedler raised his baton and the concert began. The opening number was "When Johnny Comes Marching Home."

During the next half hour the rains intensified.

"I think we should go," said Bob.

"Oh, no, please," said the boy.

"Okay," said Bob with some reluctance. He glanced at his watch. Eight forty. The plane for Paris was already over the Atlantic.

The finale was the "1812 Overture," complete with pealing church bells and cannon shots from a little howitzer. Jean-Claude was ecstatic, especially when he recognized the melody.

"It's 'La Marseillaise,'" he shouted, leaping to his feet.

"Yes," said Bob. "It's a surprise for you."

The boy was clapping even before it ended, and continued to applaud as the orchestra glided into "Stars and Stripes Forever." Now the whole waterlogged crowd rose to its feet, singing, shouting and marching in place. A glorious pandemonium.

Suddenly the sky exploded with lights—red, white, green, yellow, blue. "*Regarde, Papa,*" cried the boy. "*Les feux d'artifice!*"

Bob picked him up and put him on his shoulder, so he could have a better view of the dazzling fireworks. As he did, he could not help noticing that although the air was cold, the boy seemed strangely warm. Too warm.

"Come on, Jean-Claude, let's go back to the car."

Still carrying the boy, Bob began to walk toward the bridge. Jean-Claude's gaze remained transfixed by the multicolored bombs bursting in the air. By the time they reached the MIT parking lot, Jean-Claude was shivering, but his forehead was very hot.

"Let's change you into some dry clothes," Bob said.

"Okay," said the boy, sounding subdued.

Bob opened the trunk, grabbed the green valise and the two of them hurried toward the entrance to his office. Upstairs, he dried Jean-Claude with paper towels from the men's room. The boy suddenly seemed so small and frail, all bony shoulders and skinny legs. But every limb was blazing.

"Would you like some tea from the machine?" Bob asked.

"I don't want anything," replied Jean-Claude.

Oh, no, thought Bob, I've given him cramps from junk food and now I've frozen him into a fever. Great father. And then he realized. I can't take him back to Lexington. I don't know how to handle a sick child. He put his windbreaker around the boy and, before he lost his nerve, dialed Sheila at the Cape.

"Bob, where are you? It's pouring here."

"Here too," he replied, "and the fog is terrible. I couldn't let him fly in this weather."

"Oh," she said blandly. "I suppose that's wise."

"Listen, Sheil, he's been soaked and I think he's got a fever. Can I bring him back just for tonight?"

There was a pause.

"Bob, the girls are still very upset." She sighed. "But I don't think it's good for you to stay away anymore. It's beginning to look like you've left."

Bob was enormously relieved.

THE ROAD WAS slick and dark. Bob drove too fast. The boy was clearly getting sicker by the minute. He sat quietly, holding his stomach, now and then emitting a barely audible moan.

The storm seemed to have discouraged traffic on the highway. He reached the Cape Cod Canal in record time. And he continued to push the car along Route 6.

The nearer they got, the angrier the heavens became.

He skidded as he turned onto Pilgrim Spring Road. Fortunately he spun off into heavy mud and regained control almost immediately. Jean-Claude didn't notice the near accident. He was oblivious to everything except his stomach pains.

Bob braked sharply in front of the house. Rain pelted the windshield. He looked over at the boy. His eyes were closed, his head leaning against the door.

"We're here, Jean-Claude," he whispered, stroking his hair. "Do you feel well enough to walk—or should I carry you?"

"I can walk," the boy said slowly.

"Good. When I count to three, we each get out our own side and hurry into the house. Okay?"

"Okay."

Bob counted, and then stepped out into the downpour. He looked quickly across to the other side of the car, saw Jean-Claude's door open and then rushed for the shelter of the porch.

Sheila was waiting alone in the living room. Though it had been only a day since they had seen one another, their awkwardness made it feel like years. She looked at her husband, soaked with rain and remorse.

"Are you okay?" she asked.

"Yeah. Where are the girls?"

"I sent them upstairs. I didn't think this was the time for confrontations." She glanced over his shoulder. "Where's Jean-Claude?"

"He's—" Bob turned. The boy was not behind him. He turned back to Sheila. "Maybe he was too scared to come in."

They rushed to the porch and saw nothing but the ink-black storm. Then a bolt of lightning briefly illuminated the driveway.

The boy was laying face down, a few steps from the car, the rain slapping his motionless body.

"My God!" Bob gasped. He ran to the boy and turned him over.

"He's unconscious," he shouted to Sheila, who was standing on the porch.

"Bring him in. I'll call a doctor!" she shouted back.

"No—it looks bad. I'm gonna take him to the hospital."

In an instant she was by his side. The child opened his eyes. She felt his forehead as Bob lifted him.

"He's absolutely boiling!" She opened the car door as Bob gently placed him inside. "I'll come with you."

"No. Go in and warn the hospital."

She nodded and ran back toward the house.

From a lighted window on the second floor, two pairs of eyes watched Bob's car splash down the road. Jessica and Paula wondered what new catastrophe had just entered their lives.

BOB DROVE to Hyannis like a man possessed. The boy was silent, his breathing short and rapid. And his forehead began to grow disturbingly cold. Now and then he uttered a single word: "*Maman.*"

The emergency room was a madhouse. The stormy holiday roads had yielded many traffic accidents. But as Bob, holding Jean-Claude in his arms, announced himself, a harried-looking intern rushed out.

"Bring him right into the examining room," he said.

Bob watched him check Jean-Claude's pulse and then begin palpating the boy's abdomen. Suddenly he snapped an order to a hovering nurse. "Get an IV into him immediately. Put two g.ms of ampicillin and sixty m.gs of gentamicin. And have somebody get John Shelton fast."

She rushed off. The intern took the thermometer from Jean-Claude's mouth, squinted at it and turned to Bob.

"Can you step outside, sir?"

"I'll be right back," Bob said to Jean-Claude, touching his cheeks. "Don't be afraid." The boy nodded. He looked terrified.

"What's wrong?" Bob demanded, the instant they had left the room.

"Peritonitis," said the intern. "A burst appendix. His fever's 105 degrees. We've got to operate as soon as possible. We're sending for our best general surgeon. We think he's out on his boat—"

"Isn't there anybody here?" Bob asked, praying that there was someone on the grounds more competent than this nervous kid.

"Dr. Keith is in the OR with a patient. Besides, he's an orthopedic surgeon. Our best bet is to wait for Dr. Shelton."

"What do we do in the meanwhile?"

"He's very dehydrated, so I'm giving him intravenous fluid. And a large dose of antibiotics."

"And that's it?" Bob asked. "Can't we do anything else while we're waiting for this big shot?"

"We could be calm," said the intern pointedly. "Perhaps you might want to register him while you're waiting. . . ."

Bob paused. Take it easy, he told himself. This kid's got a lot on his hands. "Yeah," he said. "Sorry." He turned away.

"PATIENT'S NAME?" Bob told the registering clerk.

"Address?" He gave the Wellfleet house.

"Occupation?"

"Child," said Bob sarcastically, then gave the boy's age.

"Religion?" He didn't know. The clerk looked displeased.

"Uh—I suppose Catholic," Bob said. That answer, it seemed, was satisfactory. Less so was the fact that there was no Blue Cross or other medical plan. Bob's offer to pay was looked at askance.

"Mr Beckwith," a voice called from down the corridor. "Good news!" It was the intern, who ran up, breathless and sweating. "Dr. Shelton was home on account of the weather. He's just come in."

"Great," Bob replied. And they both charged down the hall.

Dr. Shelton had streaks of gray in his hair and looked, thank heavens, calm and experienced. "Have we permission to operate?" the surgeon asked the intern.

"I haven't gotten around to it, sir."

Shelton turned to Bob. "Where are the boy's parents?"

"They're . . . dead," Bob answered.

"Well someone has to sign *in loco parentis*. Are you his guardian?"

"No. It's a man named Venarguès in France."

"Well, then he'll have to give us permission by telephone. That's legal if there's a second person listening."

No, thought Bob, there isn't time. I haven't even got Louis's number with me.

"Can't I sign?" Bob asked.

"You have no legal authority," said Shelton. "Surgeons, like everyone else, must live by the rules."

"Don't worry about a malpractice suit," Bob said angrily. "I'll indemnify you. Just operate."

The surgeon was persistent. "Mr. Beckwith, my French is fluent. I can explain the entire situation to this Monsieur Venarguès on the phone. The child is very sick."

Bob was desperate.

"Doctor, may I tell you something in confidence?"

"Uh—I'll check on the OR," said the young man. And he dashed off. Bob and Shelton were alone.

"I can sign," Bob said, steeling himself. "I—I'm his father."

"But you just told me—"

"Out of wedlock," Bob said quickly. "His mother is Dr. Nicole Guérin. She's on the medical faculty at Montpellier, France. I mean, was. She died a month ago."

Bob's intuition was right. The irrelevant fact that the boy's mother had been a medical colleague made a curiously positive impression on Dr. Shelton.

"Is this really the truth?" Shelton asked.

"Call my wife, she'll verify it," said Bob.

The doctor was convinced.

THE OPERATION DRAGGED on and on. Bob sat on a plastic chair in the waiting room and tried to control his feeling of helplessness. It was impossible. He blamed himself for everything. At about a quarter to three he caught sight of the intern.

"Doctor," he called out meekly. "May I see you for a moment?" His attitude toward the young physician had changed markedly.

"Yes, Mr. Beckwith?"

"How serious is peritonitis?"

"Well, in young children it can be a pretty dicey thing. But Dr. Shelton is a fine surgeon."

"Still, there's a chance he could die, isn't there?"

"Yes, Mr. Beckwith," he said quietly.

"HELLO, SHEILA?"

"Bob—I've been so worried. Is he all right?"

"He's got a burst appendix. They're still operating."

"Will he be okay?" she asked, hearing the panic in his voice.

"Yes, of course," he replied, trying to believe it.

"Well, call me the instant you know. Please, honey."

"Yeah. Try not to worry."

Bob hung up and walked back to his chair. He sat down and put his head in his hands. And at last gave in to the terrible sorrow he had been suppressing for the past few hours.

CHAPTER TEN

"Brilliant lecture, Bob," said Robin Taylor of Oxford.

"Especially considering the hardships of your journey," added Daniel Moulton, chief of IBM in Montpellier, France. "To make your way here during the strikes was nothing short of heroic."

Indeed, for Robert Beckwith of MIT to reach southern France during the turbulent days of May 1968 had been a herculean task. But the hardest labor was not so much having to fly to Barcelona, then rent an asthmatic car to drive across the Pyrenees all the way to Montpellier. It was that the entire expedition had been in the company of his colleague, P. Herbert Harrison.

For instead of marveling at the beauty of the Mediterranean or the splendors of the Côte Vermeille, Harrison had held forth incessantly on academic politics. Or more specifically, why he disliked everyone in the profession. Why, Bob thought to himself, couldn't Sheila have come? She seems to have a way of charming Harrison into silence.

Now, having given his lecture on the final morning of the conference, Bob was too relieved and euphoric to care what Harrison might say about *him*. And so he began to ease away from the group of well-wishers.

"Aren't you coming to lunch with us, Bob?" called Harrison.

"Thanks, Herb. But I'd like to unwind a bit with a walk."

"But Bob," the colleague protested, "it's dangerous. They threw a bomb last week. And the concierge told me there's some big march today. Thousands of rabid students in the streets." (Harrison always cringed when he said students.)

"That's okay," Bob replied, "I've had rabies shots." And he started down the cobblestone street.

He headed toward the Palace de la Comédie, stopping every so often to admire the elegant eighteenth-century town houses. The closer he came to the center of town, the louder became the noise of the marching students. Police vans were crouched in the tiny side-streets, like tigers waiting to pounce.

Ahead of him a pair of policemen had stopped two female students in jeans and were frisking them. What kind of bust was this? Bob wondered. The girls can't be carrying weapons. Their pants were too tight.

He drew closer. The dialogue between the police and the women was acrimonious. Bob stopped about ten feet away to watch.

"*Hé, toi—qu'est-ce que tu fais là?*" One of the policemen had noticed Bob and asked him what he was doing.

"Nothing," he replied in his best Yale French. But now both officers were moving toward him.

"*Tes papiers,*" ordered the larger one.

His papers? Both his passport and his driver's license were at the hotel. And his tie and jacket were in the lecture hall.

"I'm an American," said Bob in French. "A professor."

This did not deter the officers, who slammed Bob against a wall. "Where are your papers?" they demanded.

"In my hotel," he said angrily. "Métropole, room 204."

"Bull," snarled the larger cop, grabbing Bob by the shirt.

Bob was now frightened and put up his hand to fend off a blow he sensed was imminent. And he was right, for he suddenly felt a sharp crack on his forehead, which stunned him.

One of the girls ran up and began a torrent of abuse, which somehow made an impression on Bob's aggressors. They backed off, warning, "Next time carry your papers." Then they marched to their car and, ignoring the women, sped off.

"Thanks," Bob said to the girl who had saved him. She was slender and raven-haired. "What exactly did you tell him?"

"I just showed the pig you were wearing your hello card." She pointed to his conference name tag pinned to his shirt pocket.

HELLO! MY NAME IS:
Robert Beckwith
MIT, USA

"Sorry about your head," said the girl. "You'd better let me take a look at it."

Bob put his hand to his temple. It was swollen and bleeding. And starting to throb. "Maybe I should go to the hospital."

"No need. I'm a doctor. And Simone over there is a third-year student. Come on, I've got my stuff in the trunk."

Bob walked, a bit unsteadily, to the red Dauphine convertible the girls were driving. Simone opened the trunk and handed her friend her kit. The doctor opened a bottle and began to dab Bob's wound.

"It's fairly superficial," she said as she placed several gauze sponges on the injured area and wrapped a pressure dressing around his forehead. "But I'd better take a closer look. That wasn't his fist he hit you with—it was his club."

She took out an ophthalmoscope and peered into Bob's eyes.

"Am I okay?" he asked.

"I'm pretty sure, but I suggest you go back to your hotel and lie down with a cold compress. And take two aspirins."

"Ah, aspirin—now I know you're a serious doctor."

The blue-jeaned physician laughed. As he started down the street, she called after him.

"Listen, if you don't feel better, be sure to come to the hospital. Ask for Dr. Guérin. Nicole Guérin."

BOB AWOKE in his hotel room a few hours later and heard the tolling of bells. Five o'clock. His head was throbbing. He decided he ought to go to the hospital, after all.

The taxi let him off just outside the emergency entrance of the Hôpital Général. Inside it was extremely crowded. Bob was told to sit and wait. Which he did. On a hard wooden bench. After forty minutes he ran out of patience. Maybe he should ask for that young doctor. What was her name—Guérin?

"We do have a Dr. Guérin," said the nurse in charge. "But she is in Pathology."

"Could you page her anyway? Say it's Professor Beckwith."

She reluctantly complied. Soon Nicole Guérin breezed into the emergency room, clad in a white coat, her dark hair tied back in a ponytail. She briskly ordered cranial X-rays for the patient.

Some fifteen minutes later, she was studying them.

"Are my brains intact?" Bob quipped, to cover his anxiety.

"I'm not a psychiatrist," she smiled. "But I don't see any signs of fracture. You might have a mild concussion, but basically I think you're just shook up, as you say in America."

As she wrapped a new bandage around his head, Bob made polite conversation. "I guess you don't do this sort of thing too often. I mean, being a pathologist."

"I'm only a specialist two days a week," she replied. "The rest of the time I'm a real doctor. You know, broken arms, measles, crying babies. In Sète, where I live. Do you know Sète?"

"Doctor, all I've seen is a lecture room and the chamber of commerce tour. You know—Roman ruins, the aqueduct. . ."

She was horrified. "You can't leave without seeing the lovely fishing village where the poet Valéry was born and died. Look, I'm off duty—let me take you now. It's the perfect time of day."

"Uh—I don't think I could," said Bob.

"A previous engagement?"

"Well, sort of . . ." (I'm not only engaged, I'm married.)

Her dark brown eyes fixed on him. She spoke good-humoredly. "If I were a middle-aged man, you would have accepted, right?"

He was embarrassed.

"Come on, Professor, the sea air will do you good. And, if you like, that's a medical order."

Before he knew it, they were in her red Dauphine, speeding south on the N108. And she was right. The breeze coming off the ocean did clear his head considerably. And his mood.

"Where'd you learn such fluent English, Doctor?"

"Nicole," she corrected him. "I spent a wonderful year in Boston. I did my residency at Mass. General."

"Why didn't you stay on?"

"Oh, I was tempted. And my departmental head was willing to pull strings. But in the end I decided that even the greatest medical facilities couldn't compensate for what I have in Sète."

"You mean family?"

"No. They're all gone. The townspeople are my family. But I was born here and I want to die here. Besides, they needed a young doctor. Also my clinic is above the best bakery in France."

"What about Montpellier?"

"I just keep the affiliation in case I need to hospitalize my Sètois."

"You seem very happy," said Bob.

She smiled. "Oh, some people think I'm crazy. I actually turned down a post in Paris. But since I live by my own definitions, I can say I'm a very happy woman. Are you happy, Bob?"

"Yes," he replied, and, seizing the opportunity, added, "I'm very happily married."

They flew along the highway, the Mediterranean on their left.

Sète was like a little Venice. Except for three small bridges, the old port was completely encircled by canals. They stopped at a restaurant that reverberated with loud conversations, raucous laughter and the clinking of glasses.

"What are they celebrating?" Bob asked as they sat at an outdoor table.

"Oh, the day's catch, the revolution—or maybe just life," she replied. She ordered a *bourride*, the local fish stew, and a white wine from Narbonne. Bob grew increasingly uneasy. This was getting more and more like a date.

"Are you married?" he asked.

"No. And I never will be," she replied softly. Then she reached across the table and touched his hand. "But I don't steal husbands, Bob. I have been involved with married men, but only by mutual consent."

"Nicole! *Salut, ma jolie professeur de médecine!*" A voice more like the growl of a bear heralded the arrival of a red-faced old man wearing an open shirt.

"Ah," Nicole whispered to Bob. "We're about to be honored by a visit from the mayor himself."

The older man threw his arms around Nicole and they kissed each other on both cheeks. He then turned to Bob.

"*Salut. Je m'appelle Louis. Et toi?*"

"This is Bob," said Nicole, "a professor from America."

"America?" said Louis, sitting down uninvited. "This calls for a drink." And he signaled the owner to bring out some of his usual muscat. He then lit a cigarette and turned back to Nicole's guest.

"So, Bobbie, what do you think of our revolution, eh?"

"Well, I haven't seen more than the end of a cop's club."

"They struck him," Nicole said, and she explained what had happened.

"*Salauds*," muttered Louis. Then he brightened. "I tell you, Bobbie, the workers are going to win this one. For once they have made those big shots in Paris wake up." Louis now rose precipitously. "I have to go off and meet some of my *enragés*. You two come by tomorrow for lunch with Marie-Thérèse and me."

"I'll be going back to the US," said Bob.

"Not unless you grow wings," said the mayor. "The proletariat has got the country shut tight. So there's nothing to do but drink and talk politics. And we'll do both tomorrow over lunch. *Ciao, Bobbie. Bon soir, ma petite.*" He kissed Nicole and ambled off.

"Quite a character, eh?" said Nicole to Bob. "Can you imagine what France would be if he replaced de Gaulle?"

"Yes," Bob said, smiling. "It would be Italy."

She laughed. "You're funny."

"No, I just think I'm a little high." He took another sip of Louis's muscat and then looked inquisitively at Nicole. "You were just starting to explain why you would never marry."

She shrugged. "I don't think marriage is for everybody. At least not for me. I enjoy being independent too much. That doesn't necessarily mean being lonely."

"I'm sure," Bob interrupted, "someone as attractive as you—" He stopped himself. He had not wanted to reveal how strongly he was affected by her beauty. "Don't you ever want children?" he asked.

"I've thought of it. I think I will. If I find someone I like enough to make a child with."

"That's pretty . . . avant-garde."

"You mean un-bourgeois, don't you? Anyway, I think I'm strong enough to be a parent on my own. And Sète is certainly not bourgeois. Shall we have another drink?"

"Thanks. I've had more than my share." Not that he was drunk. But in a way he felt himself losing control. He struggled to keep the conversation innocuous. The meeting at Montpellier. P. Herbert Harrison. The book Sheila was editing.

"You must love her very much," said Nicole.

"She's why I believe in marriage," Bob replied.

"I envy you that faith," said Nicole, her manner for the first time slightly wistful. They drank coffee. It was getting late.

"I should really be heading back," said Bob.

"Yes." She stood up. "You're starting to look uncomfortable. It's either fatigue, your bruise—or my personality."

He thought he should protest. But her diagnosis was irrefutable.

The highway was lit only by the moon. She had taken the Route de la Corniche out of Sète to show him the tranquil shore before returning to Montpellier.

"Tomorrow I'll show you some extraordinary limestone formations we call *causses.* They're not quite the Grand Canyon, but they do have a certain savage beauty. Anyway, you'll see."

Will I? thought Bob. Do I have to face temptation again in the light of day? He did not reply, hoping his silence would discourage her from making plans for them.

"Can you see those beaches we're passing?" she asked.

"Yes." He was being polite. "They're nice and white."

"And deserted. Why don't we take a swim?" She turned to smile at him.

He could not answer yes. He did not want to answer no. He simply let her pull the car onto a small dirt road above the beach. They got out and walked to the edge of the sea without speaking.

Unselfconsciously she slipped out of her clothing till it was all in a tiny pile at her feet. He gazed at her beauty, silhouetted against the sea and sand. "Come on, Bob," she said softly.

He removed his clothes and followed her into the sea.

As the gentle waves splashed over them he wondered what would happen next. And yet he knew. It was inevitable now. He was swimming in a starlit sea, thousands of miles from all his values. He knew very well what would happen. And he wanted it.

She took his hand as they walked out of the water. They stopped, the ocean still swirling around their ankles. She put her face very close to his. They kissed.

"Come back to Sète with me, Bob," she whispered. "No strings, just because tonight we both want to be with one another."

And he answered, "Yes."

CHAPTER ELEVEN

Bob heard footsteps coming toward him. He looked up. It was Dr. Shelton, still dressed in surgical greens. Bob stood up, his heart pounding.

"I think we were in time," said Shelton. "We'll know in about twelve hours, but I'm pretty optimistic. I suggest you go home and get a little rest."

"Can I see him?"

"Go ahead. He's in room 400."

Bob started to run. He was out of breath when he reached the room. The little boy was propped up in bed, one tube in his nostril, another in his arm. His eyes were half closed.

"Jean-Claude?" he whispered.

The boy turned his head. "Bob," he said hoarsely, "it hurts when I speak."

"Then I'll talk and you just nod your head." Bob walked toward the bed. "You had a burst appendix," he said. "They had to operate, but you're gonna be okay. The doctor told me."

For a minute the boy just looked at him.

Then, despite the discomfort, he spoke. "I'm sorry to cause you so much trouble."

"Shh. Don't be silly." Bob stroked his hair to reassure him. "Now go to sleep, and I'll see you in a few hours."

Jean-Claude tried to smile. "Don't worry. I am not afraid."

HE DROVE BACK slowly. The storm had ended, but there were puddles everywhere. By the time he reached the house, he could feel a hot, humid day beginning.

Sheila came onto the porch when she heard the car.

"How is he?" she asked.

"It looks pretty good."

"Thank God. We were all so worried."

He looked at his wife. There were a million things he longed to tell her. "I love you, Sheila," he said. And she put her arm around him as they walked into the house.

The girls were sitting on the steps in their pajamas.

"How is he?" they burst out.

"He'll be okay," said Bob. He wrapped his daughters in his arms and held them tight. He could feel their fright and confusion. "We're gonna be together," he said. "Always. Nothing will ever change that."

He felt a tender touch on the back of his neck. "You're exhausted, honey," Sheila said. "You ought to get some sleep."

He nodded, kissed the girls and started up the stairs with Sheila. She helped him off with his clothes and into pajamas. He could barely manage a thank you as he crawled under the covers and closed his eyes. Sheila bent over and kissed his cheek.

"I missed you," she whispered, thinking he was already asleep.

But he had heard and, eyes still shut, reached for her hand. She grasped his. He brought her fingers to his lips, hugging them, thinking, Please don't let go, Sheila. Never, never, never.

BOB AND SHEILA visited Jean-Claude in the hospital every day. One morning Sheila came to see him alone. Jean-Claude looked uneasy when he noticed she was by herself.

"I've brought the books you asked for." She smiled, sitting near his bed. "*Histoire Générale*, *Spider-Man* and *The Incredible Hulk*."

"You are very kind," he said. Then he looked away. "As soon as I am well I will go back to France."

"Of course not. You'll come and stay with us."

He turned toward her. His eyes were sad. "When I came here, I did not know . . . who Bob was." A pause, "But you did?"

Sheila hesitated for a moment, then decided honesty was better than awkward diplomacy. "Yes," she said. "He told me."

"Were you angry with him?"

"Yes."

"Then you must also have been angry with me."

How could she respond to this? She took his hand.

"I suppose I was, at first," she said gently. "But now we know each other. Now we're friends."

He had listened very carefully. She could not tell if he believed her. At last he said, "You are very kind, Sheila."

JESSICA HAD BECOME quiet and withdrawn. She spent a lot of time out of the house. Bob preferred to think it was a stage of adolescence and assumed—at least he hoped—she would get over it. And he made frequent efforts at conciliation.

"Say, Jess, why don't we all go to the flicks tonight? I hear *Silent Movie* is hilarious."

"Sorry. I've got a previous engagement. A date, actually."

"Oh. Anyone I know?"

"David Ackerman," said Jessie.

"Oh—*Davey*. Oh. Nice boy."

There was only one movie house in the vicinity, a gray barn with ancient wooden seats. Bob took Paula and Sheila that night, sitting between them, with an arm around each. After the film, as they were buying ice cream cones, he caught sight of Jessica and Davey, walking side by side. Did she notice him? He couldn't tell.

As they were driving home Paula asked, "How much longer will Jean-Claude be in the hospital?"

"Dr. Shelton thinks about another five days," said Sheila.

"What happens then?" Paula asked uneasily.

"Your mother and I think he should come home and stay with us till he's stronger," Bob said.

"Oh," said Paula. "Have you told Jessica?"

"Yes," said Bob.

"What did she say?"

"Nothing," Sheila answered.

JEAN-CLAUDE was pale and thin, but otherwise looked healthy. It was difficult to tell how he felt about returning to the Beckwith house. For there, two weeks ago, the nightmare had begun for him. Bob wondered as he drove him from the hospital if the boy was apprehensive about confronting Jessica and Paula.

Sheila met them at the door and kissed Jean-Claude.

"Where are the girls?" Bob asked.

"They've been upstairs all morning," Sheila answered, glancing at Bob as if to say, I don't know what's going on. She turned to the boy again. He looked a little tired.

"Why don't you take a nap before lunch, Jean-Claude?"

"Okay." He went slowly up to his room. When he opened the door he was stunned. Pelé was staring straight at him. That is, a life-size poster of the great Brazilian soccer star.

"Do you like it?" asked Paula, jumping from her hiding place.

Before he could respond, Jessie added, "It's personally autographed to you."

He was incredulous. "To me?" He stepped closer to read the inscription. "To my pal Jean-Claude, Best Wishes, Pelé."

"How did you obtain such a thing?" he asked, his eyes full of wonder.

"David Ackerman's father is his lawyer," Jessie answered.

The three children stood there for a moment. Then Paula said, "We—uh—really missed you."

And Jessie added, "Welcome home."

IT WAS NEARLY the end of July when Jean-Claude arrived home from the hospital. Sheila was due to return to work on the first Monday in August. And Bob grew increasingly uncomfortable at the prospect of having the whole brood on his hands alone. He said nothing to Sheila, but she knew what he was thinking.

"Why don't I ask Evelyn for another month's holiday? Even if she says no, she might at least let me bring work back here."

He was touched by her offer. For he knew this might raise hackles at the office. The next day they drove up to Cambridge together. He waited for her outside the Harvard Press. When she emerged she was beaming.

"I'm an idiot, do you know that?" she stated cheerfully. "Evelyn said I should have asked her for some time off years ago."

"Haven't I always told you that you were the best editor they had?"

"Yes, but I didn't believe you."

"Well, this ought to teach you to trust my judgment a little more. Now let's celebrate," he said, taking her hand. "What would you say to a candlelight dinner?"

"What about the kids? We've got to get home soon."

"Tomorrow morning's soon enough," he said. "I've made arrangements for the sitter to stay overnight."

She smiled at him mischievously. "Do you have any other surprises in store?"

"You'll see," he answered. And he felt a surge of joy. Joy born of hope. She hadn't objected to any of his arrangements. So far, anyway.

THE CANDLELIGHT DINNER was not at any restaurant. While she was confronting Evelyn Unger, he had dashed to Mass. Avenue and bought canned vichyssoise, frozen chicken divan, salad in a bag and two bottles of very good champagne. As for the candles, there were plenty in the house in Lexington.

They sat in the flickering candlelight and talked for a long time. Then he moved close to her, brushed back her hair and kissed her forehead. She did not move away. He took that as a hopeful sign.

"Do you believe I'll always love you?" he asked softly.

She bent her head down. And then answered, "I think so."

He put his arm around her and said firmly, "You *believe* it. Take it as an article of faith. I love you more than life."

Tears began to trickle slowly down her cheeks.

Both of them were silent. His heart ached for her. He had caused her so much pain, and he was desperate to make it right again.

"Sheila, do you think you might in time be able to forget the way I've hurt you?"

"I'll try," she whispered. "I can't promise more, Bob." He took her in his arms. As she leaned back she spilled her champagne.

"That's good luck," he said, kissing her eyes. Her cheeks. Her lips.

At last she responded, embracing him. "I've missed you terribly," she said. "I couldn't bear the thought of losing you. Oh, Robert . . ."

"QUICK, JOHNNY, I'm free—pass me the ball!"

It was the final week of August, and Davey Ackerman and his new friend, "Johnny" Guérin, were scrimmaging with the varsity soccer boys on the Nanuet High School field. Ever since Jean-Claude had been well enough to kick a ball again, he and Davey had worked out together, evolving a terrific give-and-go which would always get one of them past the defense into a clear shot at the goal. Their teamwork made Bernie ecstatic.

"What a combo," he shouted, slapping Bob on the back as they watched the boys score their second goal. Then he added, "Too bad the kid's gotta leave. He's got great potential. In seven years those two coulda made Yale invincible."

"Yeah," said Bob, thinking, Bern, you have the soul of a soccer ball.

That night dinner conversation at the Beckwiths seemed a bit subdued. Jean-Claude wasn't there. He was sleeping over at Davey's.

"Gosh," said Paula, "it feels funny without him here."

"Well, better start getting used to it," said Jessie to her sister. "Jean-Claude will be gone for good soon. Won't he, Dad?"

"Yes," said Bob, "any day now." He said it as matter-of-factly as he could. He wanted Sheila to know he had no qualms.

The girls went to bed about nine thirty. Bob went upstairs to kiss them good night. Paula clung to him, but Jessica, though she accepted his embrace, let him know she was getting too old for this sort of thing.

When he came back downstairs, Sheila was putting on a sweater.

"Feel like a little walk?" she asked.

"Sure." He got a flashlight, and they went out to stroll beneath the trees. It was silent except for the sea behind the house. Peaceful. He felt close to her. He took her hand.

"You want him to stay, don't you?" she said gently.

"Of course not," he said very quickly. "It's out of the question. We agreed—"

"That isn't what I asked. I wanted to know how you feel."

They walked for a few steps before he answered.

"Well, I'm not overjoyed at his leaving. But it's a fact of life. I mean—" he hoped this admission wouldn't hurt her "—I do like him a lot."

"We all do," she said softly.

They had reached a small clearing in the woods. She stopped and looked at his face, with its stoic expression.

"He doesn't have to go, Bob," she said.

Though they were standing very close, he wasn't certain he had actually heard her.

"Look," she went on, "something terrible happened to us. It will take a long time for the scars to heal." She paused. "But it has nothing to do with him, Bob. Besides, he's your child. Do you think you'd ever forget him if he went away?"

He hesitated. "No. I guess not."

Then she continued his thoughts for him.

"There would always be a part of you that would be wondering how he was, what had become of him. And he'd be thinking of you. He adores you."

Bob refused to let himself surrender to the impulse of the moment. "Honey, the most important things in my life are you and the girls. They're both in pretty fragile shape. Especially Jessie with that whole not-caring act. Paula seems to be taking it better, for some reason."

"Bob, she's obsessed with losing you. Haven't you noticed that every morning she peeks into our room and looks at your side of the bed. She's petrified."

Bob took a deep breath. He realized how desperately Paula had been clinging to him. "But if he did stay. . . ?"

"Bob, we'd all have a better chance if he were here instead of somewhere in the corner of everyone's imagination. I mean yours and mine—and especially the girls'. They'd always be afraid that you might go away."

He thought, I've really put them in a no-win situation.

"There's one more thing," Sheila said gently. "You love him."

"Yes," he answered. And thought, Thank you, Sheila.

HE BROACHED IT the next morning while Jean-Claude was still at Bernie's. "Girls, your mother and I were considering asking Jean-Claude to stay on with us. We'd like to know what you think."

Paula pondered for a moment. "We start French this year," she said. "It would be neat to have Jean-Claude around to help."

"Jessie?" Bob inquired.

"I have no objection," she said tonelessly. And then added, "Actually I like him quite a lot."

Bob looked across at Sheila. They smiled at one another.

About noon, Bob drove to Bernie's to pick up Jean-Claude, who seemed happy to see him. Bob asked the boy to take a walk with him along the beach.

"Summer's almost over," Bob said as they strolled by the water.

"I know," the boy replied. "I must be leaving soon."

"That's just what I wanted to talk to you about. Uh—how would you feel about staying on with us?"

The boy stopped, a surprised look on his face.

"I mean sort of joining the family," Bob continued.

"That's impossible," said the boy.

"Oh, I know what you're thinking. But everyone is sorry for what happened. All of us want you to stay. Wouldn't you like to?"

Jean-Claude did not know how to answer. At last he spoke. Very shyly. "Bob, I cannot. School starts in fifteen days."

"But you could go to school here, Jean-Claude. Besides, where would you live in France?"

"At St. Mâlo," the boy replied. "That is the school where my mother wanted me to go when I was eleven. To be with other boys. But Louis has been speaking to the director. He says I can start now if I pass certain examinations. And I have studied hard."

So that explains all his reading.

"But we want you to live with us," said Bob. "We . . . love you."

The boy's voice quavered. "Bob, I must go to St. Mâlo. It is what my mother planned. And it is the right thing."

Bob gazed down at his son. "Is that really what you want . . . to be alone?" Please change your mind, Jean-Claude.

The boy seemed at the limit of his strength. "Bob, I must go . . . for many reasons."

"Are you positive, Jean-Claude?"

"Yes," he said softly, and turned his gaze toward the sea.

THERE WAS NOTHING more to say, really. Bob booked a flight for three days later. The leave-taking was subdued. Sheila and the girls stood on the porch and watched the car go off. No one cried. Yet each had the vague sensation that the others would, eventually.

Bob wanted the ride to Logan to last forever. There was so much he wanted to tell the boy. To clarify his feelings. Establish their relationship. Express his love. And yet they barely spoke during the journey.

He parked the car and took the green valise out of the trunk. Jean-Claude carried his red flight bag, and they walked to TWA, where the boy was checked in for Flight 810. Bob walked him to the gate. It was only six thirty. They still had some time. Outside, the big white 747 was waiting to take on passengers. Since it was the end of summer, not many people were flying to Europe. The departure lounge was quiet. Now and then a flight was called.

They sat side by side in white plastic chairs.

"Do you have enough to read, Jean-Claude?"

"I have my books."

"Of course. Good luck in the exams. Are you nervous?"

"A little."

"You'll be sure and let me know how they turn out?"

"Yes."

"And we'll stay in touch. . . ."

The boy hesitated slightly, then said, "Yes."

"*TWA announces its final call for Flight 810, nonstop 747 service to Paris. Immediate boarding Gate 17.*"

They stood up without a word and started slowly toward the gangway door. But Bob still had something important to say.

"Uh—if you like, you could visit us again next summer. Or even Christmas. I mean, anytime."

"Thank you," he said.

"So maybe you'll come next summer, huh?"

"Maybe."

Or maybe not, thought Bob. *Very likely not.*

The lady taking tickets seemed to be signaling.

"I should go, Bob," said the little boy.

No, please, thought Bob. Not yet. Not yet.

Now Jean-Claude held out his hand and, as if preparing for the life awaiting him across the ocean, spoke his final words in French. "*Au revoir, papa.*"

Bob swept the little boy into his arms. He longed to say, I love you, but was scared of breaking down. So he simply held his son. And hugged him, wanting never to let go.

On the periphery of his awareness, someone said the door was going to close. He put the little boy down. "Go on," he whispered hoarsely, unable to say more. His throat was tight.

The boy looked up at him for a split second and, without another word, turned toward the door. Bob watched him hand his ticket to the hostess, watched her tear a page off. Watched him walk straight-backed, carrying his flight bag, down the gangway onto the plane. And disappear.

The door closed. A few minutes later, the white jumbo jet slowly backed away, then headed toward the runway into the growing darkness. Bob stood there for a long while.

At last he turned and started walking slowly down the now deserted corridor.

I love you, Jean-Claude. Please don't forget me.

Erich Segal

In what spare time he has left from his many academic and literary pursuits, Erich Segal is an accomplished marathon runner. Apart from an appropriately wiry physique, he also possesses the other attributes so vital for success in his chosen sport: the love of a challenge together with the determination and perseverance to see it through. These qualities have influenced the whole of his life.

Born in Brooklyn in 1937, Erich Segal has had a distinguished academic career, and his first published book, a study of the Roman playwright Plautus, firmly established him in the esoteric field of classical literature. Then, in 1967, he accepted the challenge to write the screenplay of *Yellow Submarine* for the Beatles, and its success led him to wonder if he could write a novel.

The result was *Love Story*, which has sold over 21 million copies since it was first published ten years ago. It brought him international fame and financial security for life but presented yet another challenge. Could he write a second novel, or was he just a "one-off" storyteller? *Oliver's Story*, the sequel to *Love Story*, was enormously popular, but Erich Segal was not content with this, and wondered if he would ever be able to create a novel with an entirely fresh set of characters. Now, with the publication of *Man, Woman and Child*, he has proved that he can.

When I visited Professor Segal this summer, he was completing a year as Visiting Fellow at Wolfson College, Oxford. He and his English wife Karen were living in a spacious flat overlooking Hampstead Heath, owned by a London University professor who was staying at the Segals' home in Vermont. He told me that his one extravagance—his "Rolls Royce"—is an eighty-volume set of *The Encyclopaedia of Classical Knowledge.* To his delight he found that the owner of the Hampstead flat had indulged in an identical luxury, so that Erich Segal, whether in London or Vermont, need never lack his treasure.

I asked him what challenge he most looked forward to in the future. He smiled as he told me, "Karen and I are expecting our first child this autumn. The answer to your question is: to be a good father."

NDB

A CLASSIC OF OUR TIME

ILLUSTRATED BY GARY KEANE
PUBLISHED BY GOLLANCZ

The Citadel

A condensation of the book by

A. J. CRONIN

When Dr. Andrew Manson arrived in the small Welsh mining town he was full of youthful hopes and ideals, but ill-prepared for the challenges his first job would offer him. In the bad days of the depression, he had to do his best with heartbreaking cases caused by poverty, appalling living conditions, and a lack of understanding of the lung diseases which afflicted so many of the miners. Only his belief in his vocation and the love of his young bride sustained him during those difficult years.

Then fortune smiled, when Manson's humble new London practice expanded into a fashionable and prosperous one. Or was it such good fortune? It took tragedy to make Andrew realize how far he had lost sight of his earlier goals and to give him the determination never to forget them again.

A.J. Cronin—himself a doctor—wrote this classic novel in 1937. Time has not dimmed the courageous ideals which shine from its pages.

PART ONE

Chapter 1

Late one October afternoon, in the year 1924, a shabby young man gazed intently through the window of a third-class compartment in the almost empty train labouring up the Penowell Valley from Swansea. All that day Andrew Manson had travelled from the North, yet the final stage of his tedious journey to Drineffy found him still strung to great excitement by the prospect of the first post of his medical career in this strange, disfigured country.

Outside, a heavy rainstorm came blinding down between the mountains which rose on either side of the single railway track, their tops hidden in a grey waste of sky, their sides black and desolate, blemished by ore workings and great heaps of slag on which a few dirty sheep wandered in vain hope of pasture. The trees, seen in the fading light, were gaunt and stunted spectres. At a bend of the line the red glare of a foundry flashed into sight, illuminating a score of workmen stripped to the waist, their torsos straining. Manson drew a long breath.He felt a sudden overwhelming exhilaration springing from the hope and promise of the future.

Darkness had fallen when, half an hour later, the engine panted into Drineffy. Gripping his bag, Manson leaped from the train and walked quickly down the platform, searching eagerly for some sign of welcome. At the station exit, beneath a wind-blown lamp, an old man in a groom's square hat and a long mackintosh stood waiting. He inspected Manson. "You Dr. Page's new assistant?"

"That's right. Manson is the name."

"Huh! Mine's Thomas. Old Thomas they mostly call me, dang 'em. I got the gig here. Set in—unless you'd rayther swim."

Manson slung his bag up, climbed into the battered gig, and they drove off through the town. For several minutes the wizened old groom did not speak but continued to dart pessimistic glances at Andrew from beneath the dripping brim of his hat. At last he said: "Only jest got your parchment, eh?" Andrew nodded. "I knowed it." Old Thomas spat. "Last assistant went ten days ago. Mostly they don't stop."

Despite his nervousness, Andrew smiled. "Why?"

"Work's too hard for one thing, I reckon."

"And for another?"

"You'll find out!"

The main street ended and, turning up a side road, they entered the narrow drive of a house which stood amongst the adjacent rows behind a stunted ash tree. On the gate was the name Bryngower.

"This is us," said Thomas, pulling up the horse.

Andrew descended. While he gathered himself for the ordeal of his entrance, the front door was flung open by a tall, spare, smiling woman of about fifty with a calm face and clear blue eyes.

"Well! well! This must be Dr. Manson. Come in, please, come in. I'm doctor's sister, Miss Page. I *am* pleased to see you. I been out of my mind, nearly, since the last fellow we had left us. Come along, I'll show you to your room myself."

Andrew's room was small, with a brass bed, a yellow varnished chest of drawers and a bamboo table bearing a basin and ewer. He said, anxiously polite: "This looks very comfortable, Miss Page."

"Yes, indeed." She patted his shoulder maternally. "You'll do famous here, I'm sure. Now come along and meet doctor." She paused, her tone striving to be offhand. "I don't know if I said so in my letter but doctor hasn't been too well lately."

Andrew looked at her in sudden surprise.

"Oh, it's nothing much," she went on quickly, "he's been laid up a few weeks. But he'll soon be all right."

Perplexed, Andrew followed her to the end of the passage where she threw open a door, exclaiming blithely: "Here's Dr. Manson, Edward— our new assistant. He's come to say 'ow do."

As Andrew went into the rustily furnished bedroom with chenille curtains closely drawn and a small fire burning in the grate, Edward Page turned, with an effort, upon the bed. He was a big man of perhaps sixty, his harshly lined features stamped with suffering and a kind of weary patience. And there was something more. The light of the oil lamp revealed one half of his face expressionless and waxen. The left side of his body was also paralysed and his left hand was contracted. Observing these signs of a severe stroke, Andrew was conscious of a sudden dismay. There was an odd silence.

"I hope you'll like it here," Dr. Page remarked, slurring his words a little, "I hope it won't be too much for you. You're very young."

"I'm twenty-four, sir," Andrew answered awkwardly. "I know this is my first job—but I'm not afraid of work."

An even deeper immobility settled on Page's face. He gazed at Andrew. Then his interest seemed to fade. He said in a tired voice: "I hope you'll stay."

"My goodness!" cried Miss Page."What a thing to say!" She turned to Andrew, smiling and apologetic. "It's only because he's a morsel down today." Bending, she kissed her brother fondly. "There! I'll send your supper up when we've had ours."

Page did not answer. His gaze strayed to the book that lay on the table beside his bed. Andrew saw that it was entitled *The Wild Birds of Europe*.

As Andrew went down to supper his thoughts were painfully confused. He had applied for this assistantship in answer to an advertisement in the *Lancet*, and in the correspondence conducted with Miss Page there had been no mention of Dr. Page's illness. Yet it would be months before Page would be fit for work, if he were ever fit for work again.

"You're lucky, doctor," remarked Miss Page brightly as she came into the dining room. "You can have your bit of snap straight off tonight. No surgery. Dai Jenkins done it."

"Dai Jenkins?"

"He's our dispenser," Miss Page said casually. "A handy little feller. He's done the surgery and visits also, these last ten days."

Andrew stared at her in fresh concern. All the warnings he had received regarding the questionable ways of practice in these remote Welsh valleys flashed into his mind.

When Miss Page seated herself comfortably in her chair at the head of the table she tinkled the little cowbell in front of her. A middle-aged servant brought in the supper.

"Come along, Annie," cried Miss Page. "This is Dr. Manson."

Annie did not answer. She served Andrew with a slice of cold boiled brisket. Miss Page had a cut from the same joint with, in addition, a pint of fresh milk.

As she lifted the glass to her lips, she explained: "I have to watch my diet, doctor. It's the blood. I have to take a drop of milk for my blood."

Andrew chewed the uninteresting brisket and drank cold water determinedly. After all, he could not expect to find luxury upon the tables of these spartan valleys.

During the meal Miss Page ate in silence. Studying Manson, she saw a gawky youngster, dark, rather tensely drawn, with high cheekbones, a fine jaw and blue eyes. These eyes, when raised, were extraordinarily steady and inquiring. But what pleased her most of all was his acceptance, without demur, of that three days' old heel of brisket. She reflected, that, though he looked hungry, he might not be hard to feed.

"I'm sure we'll get on famous, you and me," she again declared with quite a genial air. "It's been awful, my dear. What with Dr. Page's illness, wicked bad assistants—well! you wouldn't believe it! And the job I've had to keep the manager and mine officials sweet—it's them the practice money comes through—what there is of it. You see, the Company deducts so much from the wages of every man they employ and pays that out to the listed doctors according to how many of the men sign on with them. The Company has three doctors on its lists, and these doctors can have assistants if they like—Dr. Page has you, and Dr. Nicholls has a fellow called Denny—but the assistants don't ever get on the Company's list. . . ." She broke off, gazing at him quizzically.

"I think I see how the system works, Miss Page."

"Well, then!" She gave her short laugh. "You don't have to bother about it any more. All you've got to remember is that you're working for Dr. Page."

With a glance at the clock, she straightened herself. "By the way, there's a call for number seven Glydar Place. It came in at five o'clock. You better do it straight away."

ANDREW WENT OUT to the call immediately, glad of the opportunity to disentangle himself from the conflicting emotions stirred up by his arrival at Bryngower. Already he had a suspicion that he would be called upon to run the practice for his disabled principal. It was a strange situation. Yet, after all, his work was the important thing, and he longed to begin it. So he hastened his pace, exulting in the realization—this, this was his first case.

It was still raining when he struck along Chapel Street in the direction indicated by Miss Page. Darkly the town took shape before him. Shops and chapels—he passed a round dozen of them—then a big Co-operative store and the Western Counties Bank, all lining the main thoroughfare, lying deep in the bed of the valley. The sense of being buried, far down in this cleft of the mountains, was singularly oppressive. At the head of the gorge, beneath a glow that spread like a great fan into the opaque sky, were the Drineffy hematite mine and ore works.

He reached 7 Glydar Place, knocked breathlessly, and was at once admitted to the kitchen where, in the recessed bed, the patient lay. While her husband stood by in the cramped, ill-lit room he examined the young woman with scrupulous care. She complained that her head ached intolerably. Temperature, pulse, tongue, they all spoke of serious trouble. What was it? Andrew asked himself with a strained intensity as he went over her again. His first case. Suppose he found himself unable to make a diagnosis? He struggled to group the symptoms under the heading of some recognized disease.

At last he straightened, folding his stethoscope, "Did she have a chill?" he asked, his eyes upon the floor.

"Yes, indeed," the husband answered eagerly. He had looked scared during the examination. "Three, four days ago."

Andrew nodded, attempting painfully to generate a confidence he did not feel. He muttered, "We'll soon have her right. Come to the surgery in half an hour. I'll give you some medicine."

He trudged back to the surgery, a ramshackle wooden erection at the entrance to Page's drive. Inside, he lit the gas light and began to pace backwards and forwards beside the blue and green bottles. There was nothing symptomatic. It must be a chill, but, in his heart he knew that it was not. He groaned in anger at his own inadequacy. He was forced to temporize. Unhappily, he took a bottle from beneath the counter and began to compound a mixture. Spirits of nitre, salicylate of sodium. He tried to cheer himself by reflecting that they were excellent drugs, bound to get the temperature down, certain to do good.

He had just finished his compounding and was writing the label when the surgery bell went "ping", and a short, thick-set, red-faced man of thirty strolled in, followed by a muddy black and tan mongrel. The man, who wore pit stockings, hobnail boots and an old velveteen suit with a sodden oilskin cape over his shoulders, looked Andrew up and down. His voice was politely ironic and annoyingly well-bred.

"I saw your light and thought I'd look in to welcome you. I'm Denny, assistant to Dr. Nicholls, LSA. That, if you haven't met it, is the Licentiate of the Society of Apothecaries, the highest qualification known to God and man."

Andrew stared back doubtfully. Denny lit a cigarette and strolled forward insolently. He picked up the bottle of medicine, read the label, uncorked it, sniffed it, and put it down, his face turning blandly complimentary.

"Splendid! You've begun the good work already! One table-spoonful every three hours. God Almighty! It's reassuring to meet the dear old mumbo-jummery." He paused, becoming more offensive than ever. "Now tell me, doctor, what's in it? Spirit of nitre by the smell. Wonderful stuff, my dear doctor! Carminative, stimulant, diuretic, and you can swill it by the tubful."

Suddenly he laughed, a mocking appreciation of the blank expression on Andrew's face. He said derisively: "Science apart, doctor, you might satisfy my curiosity. Why have you come here?"

Andrew's temper was rising. He answered grimly. "To turn Drineffy into a health resort—a sort of spa, you know."

Again Denny laughed insultingly, and Andrew longed to hit him. "Witty, my dear doctor. Unfortunately I can't recommend the water here as being ideal for a spa. As to the medical gentlemen—they're the rag, tag and bobtail of a truly noble profession."

"Including yourself?"

"Precisely." Denny nodded. Then he dropped his mocking irony, and his tone, though bitter, was serious. "Look here, Manson! There are one or two things you ought to know about this place. There's no hospital, no ambulance, no X-ray. If you want to operate you use the kitchen table. The town's sanitation won't bear looking at. Page, your boss, was a damn good doctor, but he's finished. Nicholls, my owner, is a tight little money-chasing midwife. Bramwell knows nothing but a few sentimental recitations and the Song of Solomon. As for myself, I drink like a fish. I think that's about all. Come, Hawkins," he said to the dog, "we'll go." He moved towards the door and paused. "By the way, I should look out for typhoid in Glydar Place if I were you."

"Ping" went the door again. Before Andrew could answer, Denny and Hawkins disappeared into the darkness.

IT WAS NOT the lumpy mattress which caused Andrew to sleep badly that night, but growing anxiety about the case in Glydar Place. Was it typhoid? Denny's parting remark had started a fresh train of doubt in his already uncertain mind, as he tossed and turned through the long restless night.

His nature was extraordinarily intense. Probably this derived from his mother, a Highland woman. His father, a small Fifeshire farmer, had been painstaking and steady. He had never made a success of the land and when he was killed in the last year of the Great War, he had left the affairs of the little steading in a sad muddle. For twelve months Jessie Manson had struggled on, then the cough which she had endured for a period of years turned worse and she surrendered to consumption.

At eighteen Andrew found himself penniless and alone, a first-year student at St. Andrews University, with a scholarship worth £40 a year. His salvation had been the Glen Endowment, a foundation which loaned needy students £50 a year for five years provided they reimbursed such loans after they qualified.

The Glen Endowment had sent Andrew through his course at university, where he had taken the Hunter Gold Medal, awarded annually to the best student in clinical medicine. Although in his heart he would have preferred a clinical appointment, gratitude to the Endowment, allied to an inconvenient honesty, had sent him hurrying down to South Wales, where assistants could command the highest remuneration.

And now he was in Drineffy, rising, shaving, dressing, in a haze of worry over his first patient. He ate his breakfast quickly, then hurried out for morning surgery and his first meeting with the dispenser, Dai Jenkins, who turned out to be a quick little whippet of a man, with hollow cheeks and an ingratiating manner.

Fortunately there were few people waiting in the wooden shanty, and at half past ten Andrew could set out for 7 Glydar Place.

Twenty minutes later he came out of No. 7, his lips tightly compressed. He went two doors down, into No. 11, which was also on his list of visits. Altogether, he made seven such calls in the immediate vicinity. Five of them, including 7 Glydar Place, which was now showing a typical rash, were clear cases of typhoid.

The remainder of his round he accomplished as quickly as possible, in a state dithering towards panic. At lunch, of plain boiled fish, he brooded upon the problem in frozen silence. He decided he must speak to Dr. Page.

But when he went up to the doctor's room the curtains were drawn and Edward Page lay prostrate with a painful migraine. Andrew felt it would be cruelty to thrust this trouble upon him. He confined himself to asking: "Dr. Page, if we get an infectious case, what's the best thing to do?"

There was a pause. Page replied with closed eyes, "It's always been difficult. If anything very nasty arises ring up Griffiths at Toniglan. He's the district medical officer."

Andrew hastened down to the hall and rang up Toniglan. "Hello! Hello! Is that Dr. Griffiths?" He got through at last.

A woman's voice answered very guardedly. "Who wants him?"

"This is Dr. Page's assistant. I've got five cases of typhoid up here. I want Dr. Griffiths to come up immediately."

The reply came back in a sing-song intonation, very Welsh and apologetic, "I'm powerful sorry, doctor, indeed I am, but Dr. Griffiths has gone to Swansea. Important official business."

"When will he be back?" shouted Manson. This line was bad.

"Indeed, doctor, I couldn't say for certain."

"But listen . . . ."

There was a click at the far end. The other had rung off.

Cursing, Manson visited his cases once more, returning for evening surgery. For an hour and a half he sat in the little consulting room, wrestling with a packed surgery until the place was choked with the steam of damp bodies. Yet all the time he was reaching his decision, thinking, as he wrote prescriptions or sounded chests, "It was he who put me on to the thing. I hate him. But I can't help that, I'll have to go to him."

At half past nine, when the last patient had left the surgery, he came out of his den. "Jenkins, where does Dr. Denny live?"

The little dispenser turned with a look of horror that was almost comic. "You aren't goin' to have anything to do with that fellow, doctor? Miss Page—she don't like him." Jenkins paused, then, reading Andrew's look, added reluctantly, "Oh, well, if you 'ave to know, it's 49 Chapel Street."

If Denny was surprised to see Andrew at his lodgings he concealed it. He merely asked, standing in the doorway of his untidy sitting room, "Well! Killed anybody yet?"

Andrew reddened. But conquering his temper and his pride, he said abruptly: "You were right. It was typhoid. I've got five cases. I rang the district MO and couldn't get a word out of him, so I've come to ask your advice."

Denny at last made a grudging gesture. "You'd better come in and take a look at that, if you like!"

On the table stood a fine Zeiss microscope and some slides. Andrew focused a slide and immediately picked up the rod-shaped clusters of the bacteria.

"It's very clumsily done, of course," Denny said quickly. "I'm no lab. merchant, thank God! If anything I'm a surgeon. But there's no mistake, even to the naked eye. I cooked them on agar myself."

"You've got cases too?" Andrew asked with tense interest.

"Four! All in the same area as yours." He paused. "And these bugs come from the well in Glydar Place. It's the main sewer that's to blame. It leaks into the wells at the bottom of the town. I've hammered at Griffiths about it till I'm tired. He's a lazy, evasive, incompetent, pious swine."

"It's a damned shame," Andrew burst out, forgetting himself in a sudden rush of indignation.

Denny shrugged his shoulders. "He's afraid to ask the Council for anything in case they dock his salary to pay for it."

There was silence. Andrew had a warm desire that the conversation might continue, yet now he had no pretext on which to prolong his stay. He got up from his seat and moved towards the door. "I'm much obliged for the information. I thought I might be dealing with a carrier, but since you've localized it to the well it's a lot simpler."

Denny rose also. "Now, no touching thanks, doctor, if you please. We shall probably have to endure a little more of each other before this thing is finished. Come and see me any time you can bear it. We don't have much social life in this neighbourhood." He prodded his dog with the toe of his burst slipper and concluded rudely, "Even a Scots doctor would be welcome."

Yet, going home via Glydar Place, where he left strict instructions to boil all water from the well, Andrew realized that he did not detest Denny so much as he had thought.

ANDREW THREW HIMSELF impetuously into the typhoid campaign, counting himself fortunate to have been afforded such an opportunity so early in his career. He had all the ordinary routine of the practice on his hands, yet somehow he got through with it, then turned exultantly to his typhoid patients. As the end of the month drew near, they were all doing well and he seemed to have confined the outbreak. When he thought of his precautions, so rigidly enforced—the boiling of the water, the carbolic-soaked sheet on every door, the pounds of chloride of lime he had himself shot down the Glydar drains—he exclaimed in elation: "It's working. I don't deserve it. But by God! I'm *doing* it!"

He saw Denny often because of the proximity of their cases. At times Andrew came near to liking him—for the hours he spent in the sickrooms of his patients, if nothing else—but then the whole thing would be shattered by a sneering word. Hurt and baffled, Andrew turned one day in the hope of enlightenment to the Medical Directory. It showed Philip Denny, MS, as an honours scholar of Cambridge and Guy's.

Then, one day, Denny unexpectedly rang him up. "Manson! Can you come to my place at three o'clock? It's important."

"Very well. I'll be there."

Andrew went into lunch with Miss Page thoughtfully. As he ate his cottage pie he felt her inquiring eyes fastened on him.

"Who was that on the phone? So it was Denny, eh? You don't have to go around with that fellow. He's no use at all. Mostly he's drunk. He's an insulting devil also. You leave him alone, doctor, and remember you're workin' for Dr. Page."

Andrew felt a quick rush of anger sweep over him. But he went on with his lunch in silence, reflecting sadly on the relations which existed between Miss Page and himself. From the first moment that he had entered Bryngower, he had sensed that they were unsympathetic to one another. Yet he did his utmost to please her.

Andrew left the house in a smouldering irritation, but when he saw Dr. Bramwell approaching his mood lightened. He was already on friendly terms with Dr. Bramwell. His practice was not extensive, and did not permit him the luxury of an assistant.

Bramwell came slowly, majestically, white hair sweeping over his soiled collar, eyes fixed on the book he held at arm's length. When he reached Andrew he gave a theatrical start of recognition. "Ah! Manson, my boy! I was so immersed, I almost missed you!"

He closed his book, then thrust his free hand picturesquely into the breast of his faded coat. He was so theatrical he seemed hardly real. No wonder locals had named him the Lung Buster.

"And how, dear boy, are you liking our little community? It isn't so bad as it might appear at first sight. We have our talent, our culture. My dear wife and I do our best to carry the torch, even in the wilderness. You must come to us one evening. Do you sing?"

Andrew had an awful feeling that he must laugh. Bramwell was continuing with unction: "Of course, we have all heard of your work with the typhoid cases. I only wish the chance had come my way. If there is any emergency in which I can be of service to you, call upon me!"

A sense of compunction prompted Andrew to reply. "As a matter of fact, Dr. Bramwell, I've got a really interesting secondary mediastinitis in one of my cases, very unusual. You may care to see it with me if you're free."

"Yes?" queried Bramwell, with a slight fall in his enthusiasm. "I don't wish to trouble you."

"It's just round the corner," Andrew said hospitably. "And I've got half an hour to spare before I meet Dr. Denny."

Bramwell hesitated, then made a damped gesture of assent. They walked down to Glydar Place and went in to see the patient.

But Dr. Bramwell seemed unattracted by the opportunity to see such a rare condition of the thymus gland. He haltingly approached the bed where, at a safe range, he made a very cursory investigation. Only when they left the house did his normal glowing eloquence return.

"I'm glad to have seen your case with you, my boy. Believe it or not, this is the best case of inflammation of the pancreas I have ever seen!"

He shook hands and hurried off, leaving Andrew utterly nonplussed. To think that a qualified practitioner, in whose hands lay hundreds of lives, did not know the difference between the pancreas and the thymus, when one lay in the belly and the other in the chest—why, it was nothing short of staggering!

He walked slowly up the street towards Denny's lodging, where Philip received him in gloomy silence.

Then, after a moment, he said quietly, with a still, cold fury, "Young Jones died this morning. Perforation. And I have two new entries in Ystrad Row."

Andrew dropped his eyes, hardly knowing what to say. "We must write to the Ministry of Health," he said at last.

"We could write a dozen letters," Philip answered grimly, "and all we'd get would be a doddering commissioner down here in six months' time. No! There's only one way to make them build a new sewer. We must blow up the old one!"

For a second Andrew wondered if Denny had taken leave of his senses. Then he perceived something of the other's hard intention. He stared at him in consternation and muttered: "There'll be a heap of trouble—if it's found out."

Denny glanced up arrogantly. "You needn't come in with me."

"Oh, I'm coming in with you," Andrew answered slowly.

All that afternoon though, he went about his work fretfully, regretting his promise. He cursed Philip violently, yet, for some complex reason, he could not draw back.

At eleven o'clock that night, Denny and he started out in company with the mongrel Hawkins. It was very dark with a gusty wind and a fine spatter of rain which blew into their faces at the street corners. Denny had timed his plan carefully; the late shift at the mine had gone in an hour ago.

The two men and the dog moved quietly. In the pocket of his heavy overcoat, Denny had six sticks of dynamite stolen for him that afternoon from the quarry by Tom Seager, his landlady's son. Andrew carried six cocoa tins, each with a hole bored in the lid, an electric torch, and a length of fuse.

Immediately above Glydar Place they reached the main manhole of the sewer, and there they set to work. The iron cover had not been disturbed for years but, after a struggle, they prised it up.

Then Andrew shone the torch into the odorous depths, where, on the crumbled stonework, a dirty stream flowed slimily.

"Pretty, isn't it?" Denny rasped. "Take a look at the cracks in that pointing. Take a *last* look, Manson."

No more was said. People were dying of this festering abomination and petty officialdom had done nothing. Andrew was conscious of a wild upswing of elation and determination.

They slipped a stick of dynamite into each of the cocoa tins. Fuses of graduated lengths were cut and attached. A match flared in the darkness, and one by one the cocoa tins were floated down the sluggish currents, those with the longest fuses going first. Andrew's heart was thudding with excitement. As the last tin went in, they flung the manhole cover back and raced frantically thirty yards up the street.

They had barely reached the corner and stopped to look round when bang! the first can went off.

"By God!" Andrew gasped, exultantly. "We've done it, Denny!"

Then swiftly, beautifully, the muffled explosions followed, the last a glorious detonation that must have been at least a quarter of a mile down the valley.

"There!" said Denny in a suppressed voice, as though all the secret bitterness of his life escaped into the single word. "That's the end of one bit of rottenness!"

He had barely spoken before doors and windows were flung open, and in a minute the street was thronged. The hubbub and confusion made the night ring. Under cover of the darkness and the noise, Denny and Manson dodged home.

Before eight o'clock next morning Dr. Griffiths arrived upon the scene by car, summoned with much blasphemy from his warm bed at the angry command of Councillor Glyn Morgan. And indeed, Glyn Morgan had cause for anger. His new villa half a mile down the valley had, overnight, become surrounded by a moat of more than mediaeval squalor. For half an hour the councillor told his medical officer exactly what he thought of him.

At the end of it, wiping his forehead, Griffiths tottered over to Denny who, with Manson, stood amongst the interested crowd. In the cold light of morning, abashed by the havoc of the torn-up road, Andrew was again uncomfortable, nervously perturbed. But Griffiths was in no condition to be suspicious.

"Man, man," he quavered. "We'll have to get that new sewer straight off now."

Denny's face remained expressionless. "I warned you about that months ago," he said frigidly. "Don't you remember?"

"Yes, yes, indeed! But how was I to guess the wretched thing would blow up?"

Denny looked at him coolly. "Where's your knowledge of public health, doctor? Don't you know these sewer gases are highly inflammable?"

The construction of a new sewer was begun on the following Monday.

Chapter 2

It was three months later and a fine March afternoon. The promise of spring scented the soft breeze blowing across the mountains. Under the crisp blue sky even Drineffy was beautiful.

As he went out to pay a call, Andrew felt his heart quicken to the day. Gradually he was becoming acclimatized to this primitive town, isolated by the mountains, with no places of amusement, nothing but its grim mine, its quarries and ore works, its string of chapels and bleak rows of houses.

And the people, they also were strange; yet Andrew, though he saw them so alien to himself, could not but feel stirrings of affection towards them.

The position in regard to Dr. Page's practice was now clear to Andrew. Edward Page would never see another patient. But the devoted Blodwen, bringing her forces to bear upon Watkins, the mine manager, had succeeded in keeping her brother on the Company's list, and was in consequence receiving a good income, perhaps one sixth of which she paid out to Manson.

Andrew was profoundly sorry for Edward Page. He was a gentle, simple soul, who had never had much enjoyment in his lonely bachelor life. It was impossible not to love him, he had so manifestly the spiritual qualities of sacrifice and unselfishness. He had literally worked himself out in the unswerving pursuit of duty in this harsh valley. Now he would spend hours lying absolutely still, watching his windowsill, where every morning Annie placed breadcrumbs for the birds.

A frequent visitor to the house was the manager of the Western Counties Bank, Aneurin Rees, a shifty-eyed man whom Andrew at first sight distrusted. He spent a perfunctory five minutes with Dr. Page and was then closeted for an hour at a time with Miss Page, discussing money. Andrew judged that Blodwen had a good deal of it invested, under the admirable direction of Aneurin Rees, in sound stocks. Money held no significance for Andrew. It was enough that he was regularly paying off his obligation to the Endowment. He had a few shillings in his pocket for cigarettes. Beyond that he had his work.

Now, more than ever, he appreciated how much his clinical work meant to him. Medically, he had begun to think for himself.

Perhaps Denny, with his radical outlook, was mainly responsible for this. He had sneered at him, that first night, for naively compounding a bottle of medicine: Denny held that only half a dozen drugs were any use, the rest he cynically classed as "muck". It was something, that view of Denny's, to wrestle with in the night.

At this point in his reflections, Andrew arrived at 3 Riskin Street, his first call of the day. Here he found the patient to be a nine-year-old boy, named Joey Howells, who had a mild attack of measles. The case was of little consequence, yet because of the circumstances of this poor household, it promised inconvenience to Joey's mother. Howells himself, a day labourer at the quarries, had been laid up for three months with pleurisy, for which no compensation was payable, and now Mrs. Howells, already run off her feet attending to one invalid, in addition to her work of cleaning Bethesda Chapel, was called upon to make provision for another. At the end of his visit Andrew remarked with regret: "You have your hands full. It's a pity you must keep Idris home from school." Idris was Joey's younger brother.

Mrs. Howells raised her head quickly, "But Miss Barlow said I needn't keep him back."

In spite of his sympathy Andrew felt a throb of annoyance. "Oh?" he inquired. "And who is Miss Barlow?"

"She's the teacher at Bank Street School," said the unsuspecting Mrs. Howells. "She's let little Idris stop on in her class. Goodness only knows what I'd have done if I'd had him fallin' over me as well!"

It was a distinct contravention of the regulations to keep Idris at school when his brother was suffering from measles. Andrew had a sharp impulse to tell her that she must obey his instructions and not those of a meddling schoolmistress. As he took his leave his face wore a resentful frown. He decided suddenly to have the matter out with this officious Miss Barlow.

Five minutes later he was outside the classroom of Standard I. He knocked at the door, then entered. It was a large room, well ventilated, with a fire burning at one end. All the children were under seven and, as it was the afternoon break, each was having a glass of milk—part of an assistance scheme introduced by the local branch of the Mine Workers Union. His eyes fell upon the mistress at once. She was busy writing out sums upon the blackboard, her back towards him. Suddenly she turned round.

She was so different from the intrusive female of his indignant fancy that he hesitated. Or perhaps it was the surprise in her brown eyes that made him immediately ill at ease. He flushed and said: "Are you Miss Barlow?"

"Yes." She was a slight figure in a white blouse, brown tweed skirt, woollen stockings and small stout shoes. She was about twenty-two, he guessed. She inspected him, faintly smiling, as though she welcomed distraction on this fine spring day.

"I am Dr. Manson," he said stiffly. "I believe you have a contact here. Idris Howells. You know his brother has measles."

Her eyes, though questioning now, were persistently friendly. Brushing back untidy hair she answered: "Yes, I know."

Her failure to take him seriously was sending his temper up again. "Don't you realize it's against the rules to have him here?"

At his tone her colour rose. He could not help thinking how clear and fresh her skin was, with a tiny brown mole on her right cheek. Now she was breathing rather quickly, yet she spoke slowly: "Mrs. Howells was at her wit's end. Most of these children have had measles. If Idris had stopped off he'd have missed his milk which is doing him such a lot of good."

"It isn't a question of his milk. He ought to be isolated."

Tiny points of light glinted in her eyes. "You may be able to order people about in more exalted spheres, but here it's my word that counts."

He glared at her, with raging dignity. "You're breaking the law! You can't keep him here. If you do I'll have to report you."

He could see her hand tighten on the chalk she held. She said disdainfully: "Then report me. Or have me arrested. I've no doubt it will give you immense satisfaction."

Furious, he did not answer, feeling himself in an utterly false position. He tried to rally himself, raising his eyes, and for an instant they faced each other, so close he could see the gleam of her teeth between her parted lips.

"There's nothing more, is there?" she said and swung round tensely to the class. "Stand up, children, and say: 'Good afternoon, Dr. Manson. Thank you for coming.'"

A clatter of chairs as the infants rose and chanted her ironic bidding. His ears were burning as she escorted him to the door. He had an exasperating sense of discomfiture and added to it the wretched suspicion that he had behaved badly in losing his temper while she had so admirably controlled hers.

MANSON, AFTER AN EVENING during which he composed and tore up three vitriolic letters to the medical officer of health, tried to forget about the episode. Following a sharp struggle with his stiff Scots pride, he decided he had been wrong, he could not dream of reporting the case. Yet he could not so easily dismiss Christine Barlow from his mind. It was absurd that he should be concerned by what she might think of him. At unguarded moments, the scene in the classroom would flash back to him with renewed vividness and he would find himself frowning. He still saw her, crushing the chalk, her eyes warm with indignation. He did not ask himself if she were pretty. It was enough that she stood before the screen of his sight.

A fortnight later he was walking down Chapel Street in a fit of abstraction when he almost bumped into Mrs. Bramwell. She stopped at once, dazzling him with her smile. "Why, doctor! The very man I'm looking for. I'm giving a little social evening tonight. You'll come, won't you?"

Gladys Bramwell was a corn-haired lady of thirty-five, showily dressed, with a full figure, baby-blue eyes and girlish ways. As Andrew scanned her he sought hurriedly for an evasion.

"I'm afraid, Mrs. Bramwell, I can't possibly get away tonight."

"But you must, silly. I've got such nice people coming. Mr. and Mrs. Watkins from the mine, Dr. Gabell from Toniglan—oh, and I almost forgot, the little schoolteacher, Christine Barlow."

A shiver passed over Manson. He smiled foolishly. "Why, of course I'll come, Mrs. Bramwell. Thank you very much for asking me." And for the remainder of the day he could think of nothing but the fact that he was going to see Christine Barlow again.

Mrs. Bramwell's "evening" began at nine o'clock, but it was, in fact, a quarter past nine by the time Andrew finished his last consultation.

Hurriedly, he splashed himself in the surgery sink, combed his hair, and hastened out. But he was still the last arrival. Mrs. Bramwell chided him brightly, then led the way in to supper.

It was a cold meal, spread out on paper doilies on the dark oak table. Mrs. Bramwell prided herself upon being a hostess, something of a leader in style in Drineffy, and her idea of "making things go" was to talk and laugh a great deal. As they sat down she glittered: "Now! Has everbody got what they want?"

Andrew, embarrassed and breathless from his haste, dared not look at Christine. He kept his eyes lowered, conscious of her sitting at the far end of the table between Dr. Gabell, a dark-complexioned dandy, and Mr. Watkins, the elderly mine manager.

Defensively, scarcely knowing what he said, he began to devote himself to his neighbour, Mrs. Watkins, a little wisp of a woman, enduring the anguish of talking to one person when he longed to talk to another.

He could have sighed with relief when Dr. Bramwell viewed the cleared plates benevolently and made a napoleonic gesture. "Shall we adjourn to the drawing room?"

It was plain that music was expected. Bramwell beamed fondly on his wife and led her to the piano. She played and sang while her husband, one hand behind his back, the other advanced as in the motion of snuff-taking, stood beside her and deftly turned the sheets. Gladys had a full contralto voice, bringing all her deep notes up from her bosom with a lifting motion of her chin. After the "Love Lyrics", she gave them "Wandering By", and "Just a Girl".

There was a generous applause. Andrew saw an impish glint in Watkins's eye. The old mine manager, a true Welshman, had last winter helped his men to produce a Verdi opera. Andrew could not help thinking that it must afford Watkins deep amusement to observe these strangers affecting to dispense culture in the shape of worthless, sentimental ditties.

Dr. Gabell was then persuaded to his feet to bellow fruitily, "Love in Sweet Seville". And so, finally, to the highlight of the evening. Dr. Bramwell took the centre of the stage. Clearing his throat, he stuck out one foot, threw back his head, placed his hand inside his coat and announced: "Ladies and gentlemen. 'The Fallen Star', A Musical Monologue." The recitation was glutinous with sentiment and Bramwell gave it with soulful anguish. When the drama rose, Gladys at the piano pressed bass chords. When the pathos oozed, she tinkled on the treble. As the climax came, Bramwell drew himself up, his voice breaking on the final line, "There she was . . ." a pause, "starving in the gutter . . ." a long pause, "only a fallen star!"

By this time it was after eleven o'clock and, on the tacit understanding that anything following Bramwell's effort would be sheer anticlimax, the party prepared to break up. As Andrew pulled on his coat in the hall, he reflected miserably that he had not exchanged a word with Christine all evening.

Outside, he stood at the gate. He felt that he must speak to her. The thought of the wasted evening, in which he had meant to put things right between them, weighed on him like lead. His pulse raced suddenly as she came down the steps and walked towards him, alone. He gathered all his strength and stammered: "Miss Barlow, may I see you home?"

"I'm afraid, . . ." she paused, "I've promised to wait for Mr. and Mrs. Watkins."

His heart sank. He felt like turning away, a beaten dog. Yet something held him. His face was pale but his chin had a firm line. The words came tumbling out with a rush.

"I only want to say that I'm sorry about the Howells affair. I ought to be kicked—hard. What you did about the kid was splendid. After all, it's better to observe the spirit than the letter of the law. Sorry to bother you with this but I had to say it. Good night!"

He did not wait for her answer, but swung round and walked down the road. For the first time in days he felt happy.

THE HALF-YEARLY return of the practice came in from the Company's offices. For the first time in eighteen months the figures showed an upward jump. There were over seventy more men on "Dr. Page's list" than there had been before Manson's arrival. It was flattering to know that the people of Drineffy liked him. And he took it as an especial tribute when, a few days later, John Morgan, a foreman driller at the hematite mine, came to the surgery to see him with his wife.

The Morgans were a middle-aged couple, not well off, but highly thought of, who had been married for nearly twenty years. They were leaving shortly for South Africa, where the drill work in the gold mines was similar and the pay much better. Yet no one was more surprised than Andrew when Morgan self-consciously explained the purpose of their visit.

"Well, sir, we have done it at last, it seems. The missus here is goin' to have a baby. We are plain delighted, man. And we've decided to put off our leavin' till after the event. For we come to the conclusion that you're the doctor we must have to handle the case. It'll be a hard job too, I fancy. Missus here is forty-three."

Andrew entered up the case with a warm sense of having been honoured. It was a strange emotion, which in his present state was doubly comforting. Lately he had felt curiously lost. Extraordinary currents were moving within him, disturbing and painful.

He had never before thought seriously of love. He had been too poor, too badly dressed and far too intent on getting through his examinations to come much in contact with the other sex. He had always prided himself on being practical, and he attempted, violently and with determined self-interest, to argue himself out of his emotion for the schoolmistress. He tried, coldly and logically, to examine her defects. She was not beautiful, her figure was skimpy, too small and thin. In addition she probably detested him.

But try as he would, Andrew could not get Christine out of his mind. What did she think of him? Did she *ever* think of him? It was so long since he had seen her that he despaired of ever seeing her at all. Then, one Saturday afternoon in May, he received a note which ran as follows:

Dear Dr. Manson,

Mr. and Mrs. Watkins are coming to supper with me tomorrow, Sunday evening. If you have nothing to do, would you care to come too? Half past seven.

Sincerely,

Christine Barlow

He gave a cry which brought Annie hurrying from the scullery.

"Eh, doctor, *bach*," reprovingly. "Sometimes you do act silly."

"I have done, Annie," he answered. "But I—I seem to have got away with it. Listen, Annie, dear. Will you press my trousers for me? I'll sling them outside my door tonight when I go to bed."

On the following evening he presented himself in tremulous expectation at the house of Mrs. Herbert, with whom Christine lodged. It was Christine herself who opened the door for him, her face welcoming, smiling towards him.

Yes, she was smiling, actually smiling. And he had felt that she disliked him! He was so overwhelmed he could barely speak.

"It's been a lovely day, hasn't it?" he mumbled as he followed her into her sitting room.

"Lovely," she agreed. "And I had such a grand walk this afternoon. I actually found some celandines."

They sat down. "Mrs. Watkins has just sent word," she remarked. "She and her husband will be a little late. He's had to go down to the office. You don't mind waiting a few minutes?"

Mind! A few minutes! If only she knew how wonderful it was to be here with her. Surreptitiously he looked about him. It was a simple room, unlike any he had seen in Drineffy. In the centre of the supper table was a plain white dish in which floated, like masses of tiny water-lilies, the celandines she had gathered. The effect was beautiful.

He began to ask her about herself and she answered him simply. She was from Yorkshire. Her mother had died when she was fifteen. Her father had then been under-manager at one of the big Yorkshire collieries. Four years later, when she was nineteen and her teaching course completed, her father had been appointed manager of a pit twenty miles from Drineffy. She and her brother John had come with him, she to keep the house, John to assist his father. Six months after their arrival there had been an explosion in the pit. John had been killed instantly. Her father had gone down after him only to be met by a rush of black damp. A week later his body and John's were brought out together.

When she concluded Andrew was sympathetic. "I'm sorry."

"People were kind to me," she said soberly. "Mr. and Mrs. Watkins especially." She paused, her face lighting up again. "I'm like you, though, I'm still strange here."

He looked at her, searching for a remark which might tactfully dispose of the past and hopefully open out the future. "It's easy to feel cut off down here. I often feel I want someone to talk to."

She smiled. "What do you want to talk about?"

He reddened, felt cornered. "Oh, my work, I suppose." He halted, then felt obliged to explain himself. "I seem just to be blundering about, running into one problem after another."

"Do you mean you have difficult cases?"

"It isn't that." He hesitated, went on. "I came down here full of the things that everybody believes, or pretends. Well, I'm finding out that some of them are wrong. Take medicine. It seems to me that some of it does more harm than good. A patient comes into the surgery. He expects his 'bottle of medicine', and he gets it, even if it's only burnt sugar, soda carb. and good old aqua. It isn't scientific." He broke off. "I'm sorry! I'm boring you!"

"No, no," she said quickly. "It's awfully interesting."

"I'm just beginning, just feeling my way," he went on tempestuously, thrilled by her interest. "But I do honestly think, even from what I've seen, that the textbooks I was brought up on have too many old-fashioned ideas in them. You might say it doesn't matter to the average GP. But why should the general practitioner be just a medicine slinger? I believe that the outlying GPs have opportunities to *see* things, and a better chance to observe the first symptoms of new disease than they have at any of the hospitals."

She was about to answer when the doorbell rang. She rose, suppressing her remark, saying instead, with her faint smile, "I hope you'll talk of this another time."

Watkins and his wife came in, apologizing for being late. And almost at once they sat down to supper. They had veal cooked in a casserole and potatoes mashed with butter, followed by rhubarb tart with cream, then cheese and coffee. After the skimpy meals served to him by Blodwen Page it was a great treat to Andrew to find hot, appetizing food before him. He sighed: "You're lucky in your landlady, Miss Barlow. She's a marvellous cook!"

Christine coloured slightly. "That's the nicest compliment I've ever had. You see, as it happens, I cooked the supper. I have the run of Mrs. Herbert's kitchen. I like doing for myself."

The evening passed quickly. When Andrew looked at his watch he saw to his amazement that it was nearly eleven o'clock. As he rose, regretfully, to take his leave, Christine accompanied him to the door. In the narrow passage his arm touched her side. A pang of sweetness went over him. She was so different from anyone he had ever known, with her quietness, her fragility, her dark intelligent eyes. Heaven forgive him having thought her skimpy!

Breathing quickly, he mumbled: "I can't thank you enough for tonight. Please can I see you again? Would you—Christine, would you come to the Toniglan cinema with me, sometime?"

Her eyes smiled up at him. "Try asking me."

A long silent minute on the doorstep under the high stars. The dew-scented air was cool on his hot cheek. He longed to kiss her. Fumblingly he pressed her hand, turned, clattered down the path and was on his way with dancing thoughts, walking on air. Oh! She was a wonderful girl! How well she had understood his meaning when he spoke of his difficulties! What a marvellous cook too! And he had called her Christine!

THOUGH CHRISTINE now occupied his mind more than ever, he no longer felt despondent but happy, elated, hopeful.

More than once he found Denny's satirical eye upon him.

But he did not care. In his intense, idealistic way he linked Christine with his ambitions. He admitted to himself that he still knew practically nothing. Yet he was learning to think for himself, and prayed that he might never become slovenly or mercenary, never come to write "the mixture as before". He wanted to be worthy of Christine. The sort of opportunity he longed for came towards the end of the last week in June. As he came over the station bridge he encountered Dr. Bramwell, and they walked up the street together talking shop. Bramwell was always ready to discuss his cases and now, with an air of gravity, he told Andrew that Emlyn Hughes, Annie's brother-in-law, had been acting strangely lately. He had turned quarrelsome and violent.

"I don't like it, Manson." Bramwell nodded sagely. "I've seen mental trouble before. And this looks uncommonly like it."

Andrew expressed his concern. He had always thought Hughes a stolid and agreeable fellow, but he recalled that Annie had looked worried lately.

On the following Friday, at six o'clock in the morning, he was awakened by a knocking on his bedroom door. It was Annie herself, fully dressed and very red about the eyes, offering him an envelope, a message from Bramwell. *Come round at once. I want you to help certify a dangerous lunatic.*

Annie struggled with her tears. "It's Emlyn, doctor, *bach.* A dreadful thing has happened. I do hope you'll come down quick."

Andrew threw on his things in three minutes. Accompanying him down the road, Annie told him that during the night Emlyn had set upon his wife with a bread knife. Olwen had just managed to escape by running into the street in her nightgown. When they reached the Hughes's house Andrew found Dr. Bramwell, unshaven, without his collar and tie, seated at the table in the front room, pen in hand. Before him was a bluish paper form, half filled in.

"Ah, Manson! Good of you to come so quickly. A bad business this. Hughes has gone mad. Acute homicidal mania." Bramwell rolled the words over his tongue with tragic grandeur. "We'll have to get him into Pontynewdd straight away. That means two signatures on the certificate, mine and yours. You know the procedure, don't you?"

"Yes." Andrew nodded. "What's your evidence?"

Bramwell began to read what he had written on the form. It was a full account of certain of Hughes's recent actions, all of them indicative of mental derangement. "Clear evidence, I think!"

"It sounds pretty bad," Andrew said slowly. "Well! I'll take a look at him."

"Thanks, Manson. You'll find me here when you've finished." And he began to add further particulars to the form.

Emlyn Hughes was in bed and seated beside him—in case restraint should be necessary—were two of his mates from the mine. Standing by the foot of the bed was Olwen, her pale face ravaged by weeping. The atmosphere of the room was so dim and tense that Andrew had a momentary thrill of fear.

He went over to Emlyn and at first he hardly recognized him. His face seemed swollen, the skin waxy, except for a faint reddish patch that spread across the nose. His whole appearance was heavy, apathetic. Andrew spoke to him. He muttered an unintelligible reply. Then, clenching his hands, he came out with a tirade of aggressive nonsense, which seemed to make the case for his removal only too conclusive.

A silence followed. Andrew, inexplicably, was not satisfied. *Why*, he kept asking himself, should Hughes talk like this? He had always been a happy, easy-going man. Why had he changed to *this?* There must be a reason. Instinctively, Andrew reached out and touched Hughes's swollen face, noting that the pressure of his finger left no dent in the cheek.

All at once, a terminal vibrated electrically in his brain. *Why* didn't the swelling pit on pressure? He had it, by God, he *had* it! Curbing his excitement, he lifted Emlyn's hand. Yes, the skin was dry and rough, the fingers slightly thickened at the ends. Methodically he finished the examination, fighting back each successive wave of elation. Every symptom fitted superbly.

Rising, he went down to the parlour where Dr. Bramwell greeted him.

"Well? Satisfied? The pen's on the table."

"I don't think we ought to certify him, Bramwell." Andrew averted his eyes, battling to keep triumph from his voice.

"But the man's out of his mind!" Bramwell exclaimed in hurt astonishment.

"That's not my view," Andrew answered in a level tone. He must try not to antagonize Bramwell. "In my opinion Hughes is suffering from thyroid deficiency—a straight case of myxoedema. He's only sick in his mind because he's sick in his body."

Bramwell stared at Andrew glassily. He was dumbfounded.

"After all," Andrew went on persuasively, "Pontynewdd asylum is such a sink of a place. Once Hughes gets in there he'll never get out. Suppose we try pushing thyroid into him first."

"Why, doctor," Bramwell quavered. "I don't see—"

"Think of the credit for you," Andrew cut in quickly, "if you should get him well again. Come on now, I'll call in Mrs. Hughes. You can explain we're going to try a new treatment."

Before Bramwell could protest Andrew went out of the room. When he came back with Mrs. Hughes, the Lung Buster had recovered himself. Planted on the hearth-rug he informed Olwen "that there might still be a ray of hope", then he went out to telephone to Cardiff for thyroid.

There were several days of agonized suspense before Hughes began to respond to the treatment. But once it had started, that response was magical. He was out of bed in a fortnight and back at his work at the end of two months. He came round one evening to the surgery at Bryngower, accompanied by the smiling Olwen, to tell Andrew he had never felt better in his life.

Olwen said: "We owe everything to you, doctor. We want to change over to you from Bramwell. He'd have had my Emlyn in the—well, you know what—if it hadn't been for you."

"You *can't* change, Olwen," Andrew answered. "It would spoil everything." He dropped his professional gravity and broke into genuine youthful glee. "My friend Dr. Denny tells me I'm too conceited to live with as it is!"

Chapter 3

In July of that year the annual conference of the British Medical Union was held in Cardiff. Splendidly organized, it offered social and scientific enjoyments to members and their families. Andrew was not a member of the Union, since the subscription was beyond his means, but he viewed it enviously from a distance.

But midway through the week a letter arrived, bearing the address of a Cardiff hotel, which caused Andrew a more pleasurable sensation. It was from an old St. Andrews classmate, Freddie Hamson. Freddie was attending the conference and he asked Manson to come and see him. He suggested Saturday, for dinner.

Andrew showed the letter to Christine. It was instinctive now for him to take her into his confidence. Since that evening, nearly two months before, when he had gone round to supper, he was more than ever in love, and happier than he had been in his life. Christine was a practical little person, perfectly direct and entirely without coquetry. She had a lively sense of humour, and she never flattered him. Occasionally, too, they had long arguments, for she had a mind of her own. He often felt that she had great courage, which made him long to protect her.

When it was fine on Saturday or Sunday afternoons they took long walks. Once, they went to a film in Toniglan. But most of all he enjoyed the evenings when Mrs. Watkins was visiting her and he was able to enjoy her companionship in her own sitting room. It was then that most of their discussions took place, with Mrs. Watkins a respectable buffer state between them.

Now, with this visit to Cardiff in prospect, he wished her to accompany him. When she had read Freddie Hamson's letter he said, impulsively: "Will you come with me? It's only an hour and a half in the train. I'll get Blodwen to unchain me on Saturday evening. I'd like you to meet Hamson."

She nodded. "I'd love to come."

On Saturday they took the train to Cardiff. Andrew was in high spirits. With a smile he looked across at Christine on the opposite seat. She wore a navy blue coat and skirt which intensified her usual air of trimness. Her eyes were shining. A wave of tenderness came over Andrew. He wanted to take her in his arms, to feel her, warm and breathing, close to him. It was on his tongue to tell her that he loved her, to ask her to marry him. But something, an intuition that the moment was not right, restrained him. He decided he would speak to her in the train coming home.

The train ran into Cardiff at a quarter past six, and they made directly for the Palace Hotel. Hamson had promised to meet them there at half past.

They stood together watching the scene. The place was crowded with doctors and their wives, talking and laughing. There were also palms and a string orchestra. "Pretty social, eh?" Andrew remarked, feeling that they were rather left out of the general hilarity. "And Freddie's late as usual, hang him."

At that moment Freddie Hamson arrived, leaping from his taxi and entering the hotel with a page-boy carrying his golf clubs behind him. He saw them at once and advanced with a wide and winning smile on his fresh-complexioned face.

"Hello, hello! Here you are! Sorry I'm late. Well, well! It's good to see you again, Manson!" He clapped Andrew on the back, affectionate, his glance smilingly including Christine. "Introduce me, stick-in-the-mud! What are you dreaming about?"

They sat down at one of the round tables. With a snap of his fingers Hamson had a waiter running for drinks. Then, over the sherry, he told them about the golf match he had been playing.

They went into the grill room rather than the restaurant for dinner, since none of them was formally dressed. Freddie told them he would have to get into tails later on. There was a dance, a confounded nuisance, but he must show up at it.

Having nonchalantly ordered the food he began recalling the old days at university with dramatic ardour. "I'd never have thought, then," he ended with a shake of his head, "that old Manson would have buried himself in the South Wales valleys."

"Do you think he's buried?" Christine asked, with a rather forced smile. There was a pause. Freddie surveyed the crowded room, grinned at Andrew.

"What do you think of the conference?" he said.

"I suppose," Andrew answered doubtfully, "it's a useful way of keeping up to date."

"Up to date, my uncle! I haven't been to a meeting all week. No, no, old man, it's the contacts you make that matter. You've no idea the really influential people I've met. When I get back to town I'll ring them up, play golf with them."

"I don't quite follow you, Freddie," Manson said.

"Why it's as simple as falling off a log. I've got my eye on a nice little room up West with a smart little brass plate with Freddie Hamson, MD, on the door. When the plate does go up, these fellows, my pals, will send me cases. You know how it happens. You scratch my back and I'll scratch yours." Freddie took a slow appreciative sip of hock. "Why, in a year or two, you old dog, you'll be sending me patients from your stick-in-the-mud Drin—whatever you call it."

Christine glanced quickly at Hamson, made as if to speak, then checked herself. She kept her eyes fastened upon her plate.

"And now tell me about yourself, Manson, old son," Freddie continued, smiling. "What's been happening to you?"

"Oh, nothing out of the ordinary. I consult in a wooden surgery, average thirty visits a day—mostly miners and their families."

"Doesn't sound too good to me." Freddie said condolingly.

"I enjoy it," Andrew said mildly.

Christine interposed. "And you get in some real work."

"Yes, I did have one rather interesting case lately." Andrew gave Hamson a short account of the case of Emlyn Hughes.

Though Freddie made a great show of interested listening, his eyes kept rolling round the room. "That was pretty good," he remarked when Manson concluded. "Anyhow, I hope you socked in a whacking good bill. And that reminds me. A fellow was telling me today the best way to handle this fee question . . . ." And he was off again. They had reached the end of the dinner before his dissertation was over.

At a quarter to ten, Freddie looked at his watch, but Christine was before him. She glanced at Andrew brightly, and remarked: "Isn't it almost our train time now?"

Manson was about to protest that they had another half-hour when Freddie said: "And I suppose I must think about this confounded dance. I can't let the party I'm going with down."

He accompanied them to the swing doors. "Well, old man," he murmured with a final shake of the hand. "When I put the little plate up in the West End I'll remember to send you a card."

Out in the warm evening air Andrew and Christine walked along Park Street in silence. Vaguely, he was conscious that the evening had not been the success he had anticipated. At last, diffidently, he said: "It was pretty dull for you, I'm afraid, listening to all those old hospital yarns."

"No," she answered. "I didn't find that dull in the least."

There was a pause. He asked: "Didn't you like Hamson?"

"Not a great deal." She turned, her eyes sparking with honest indignation. "The idea of him, sitting there, all evening, with his waxed hair and his cheap smile, patronizing you. It was unbearable. 'A fellow was telling me the best way to handle the fee question.' Just after you'd told him about your wonderful case! Oh! I could hardly stand it, the way he put himself above you."

"I don't think he put himself above me," reasoned Andrew, puzzled. "I admit he seemed rather full of himself tonight, but he's the best-natured fellow you could hope to meet. We were great friends at college."

"Probably he found you useful to him," Christine said with unusual bitterness. "Got you to help him with his work."

He protested unhappily. "Now, don't be mean, Chris."

"It's you," she flared, bright tears of vexation in her eyes. "You must be blind not to see the kind of person he is."

They trudged towards the station some distance apart. It was the first time he had seen Christine angry. And he was angry too—angry at himself, at Hamson, yes, at Christine. The evening had been a dismal failure.

They entered the station and made their way towards the up platform. He longed with all his soul to have a long quiet talk alone with Christine, to open his heart to her. But the train, when it came in, was packed with miners, loudly discussing the Cardiff City football match.

It was late when they reached Drineffy and Christine looked very tired. There was nothing for it but to see her to Mrs. Herbert's and unhappily bid her good night.

THOUGH IT WAS nearly midnight when Andrew reached Bryngower he found Joe Morgan waiting for him, anxiously walking up and down outside the house.

"Eh, doctor, I'm glad to see you. I been here this last hour. The missus wants ye—before time too."

Andrew, abruptly recalled from the contemplation of his own affairs, told Morgan to wait. He went into the house for his bag, then they set out in silence for Morgan's home. The night air was cool and deep with quiet mystery. At the door of No. 12, Joe drew up short. "I'll not come in," he said, and his voice showed signs of strain. "But, man, I know ye'll do well for us."

Inside, a narrow stair led up to a small, clean bedroom, lit only by an oil lamp. Here Mrs. Morgan's mother, a tall grey-haired woman of nearly seventy, and the stout midwife waited beside the patient.

"Let me make you a cup of tea, doctor," said the former quickly.

Andrew smiled faintly. He saw that the old woman knew there must be a period of waiting and was afraid he would leave the case, saying he would return later. "Don't fret, mother. I'll not run away."

Down in the kitchen he drank the tea which she gave him. Overwrought as he was, he knew that this case would demand all his attention. A queer lethargy came upon him.

An hour later he went upstairs again, noted the progress, came down once more, sat by the kitchen fire. The old woman opposite him sat quite motionless, her eyes never leaving his face.

He let his chin sink upon his chest, stretched out his legs, stared broodingly into the fire, his thoughts filled with Christine. He started when the nurse called from the top landing. Andrew rose and went up to the bedroom. He perceived that he might now begin his work.

An hour elapsed. It was a long harsh struggle. Then, as the first streaks of dawn strayed past the broken edges of the window blind, the child was born, lifeless.

A shiver of horror passed over Andrew. After all that he had promised! He stared at the baby with a haggard frown. It was a boy, perfectly formed. The limp warm body was white and soft as tallow. The skin was of a lovely texture, smooth and tender. The head lolled on the thin neck. The limbs seemed boneless. The whiteness meant only one thing: asphyxia pallida, and his mind raced back to a case he had once seen. Instantly he was on his feet.

"Get me hot water and cold water," he threw out to the nurse. "And basins too. Quick! Quick!"

"But, doctor—" she faltered, her eyes on the child's pallid body.

"*Quick!*" he shouted.

Snatching a blanket he laid the child upon it and began the special method of respiration. The basins arrived, the ewer, the big iron kettle. Frantically he splashed cold water into one basin; he mixed water as hot as his hand could bear into the other. Then he hurried the child between the two, now plunging it into the icy, now into the steaming bath.

Minutes passed. Sweat was running into Andrew's eyes, blinding him. No breath came from the body of the child.

A desperate sense of defeat pressed on him. He felt the midwife watching him in stark consternation. "For mercy's sake," she whimpered, "it's stillborn."

Andrew did not heed her. Beaten, despairing, he still persisted in one last effort, rubbing the child with a rough towel, crushing and releasing the little chest with both his hands, trying to get breath into that limp body.

And then, as by a miracle, the tiny chest gave a short convulsive heave. And another. Andrew turned giddy. The sense of life springing beneath his fingers was so exquisite it almost made him faint. He redoubled his efforts feverishly. The child was gasping now, a bubble of mucus came from one tiny nostril. The head no longer lay back spinelessly. The blanched skin was slowly turning pink. Then, unbelievably, came the child's cry.

"Dear Father in heaven," the nurse sobbed hysterically, "it's come . . . it's come alive."

In a daze, Andrew handed her the child. About him the room lay littered: blankets, towels, basins, the ewer knocked over, the kettle on its side in a puddle of water. Upon the huddled bed the mother still dreamed her way quietly through the anaesthetic. Now he attended to her needs, and when he had done so pulled on his jacket mechanically, and picked up his bag. He went downstairs, through the kitchen into the scullery, where he took a long drink of water. He reached for his hat and coat.

Outside he found Joe standing on the pavement with a tense, expectant face. "All right, Joe," he said thickly. "Both all right."

It was quite light. Nearly five o'clock. A few miners were already in the streets; the first of the night shift moving out. As Andrew walked back he kept thinking blindly, "I've done something, oh, God, I've done something real at last."

AFTER A SHAVE and a bath he felt less tired. But Miss Page, finding his bed unslept in, was dryly ironic at the breakfast table.

"You seem a bit of a wreck this mornin', doctor. Been out on the tiles, my boy? Didn't get back from Cardiff till this mornin', eh? You're all the same, you assistants. I never found one yet that didn't drink or go wrong somehow!"

After morning surgery Andrew dropped in to see his case. The instant he placed his foot on the doorstep the door was swung open and the old woman, beaming all over her wrinkled face, made him welcome. She patted him upstairs with tremulous old hands.

He entered the bedroom. The little room had been scoured and polished until it shone. The bed had been changed, and there, upon it, was the mother, her plain middle-aged face gazing in dumb happiness towards him, the babe sucking quietly at her full breast.

Warmly inarticulate, Susan Morgan tried to stammer out her gratitude. "Has my Joe been to see you yet, doctor?" she asked timidly. "No? Well he's comin', you may be sure. He's fair overjoyed. He was only sayin' though, doctor, that's the thing we will miss when we're in South Africa, not havin' you to 'tend to us."

Leaving the house, fortified with seed cake and elderberry wine—it would have broken the old woman's heart had he refused to drink her grandson's health—Andrew continued on his round with a queer warmth round his heart. They couldn't have made more of me, he thought, if I'd been the King of England.

A fortnight later Joe Morgan came round to see him. Having laboured long with words, he said explosively: "Dang it all, doctor, *bach,* I'm no hand at talkin'. The missus and I want to make you this little present." He handed over a slip to Andrew. It was an order on the Building Society made out for five guineas.

Andrew stared at the cheque. The Morgans were far from being well-off, and this amount must represent a great sacrifice. Touched, Andrew said: "I can't take this, Joe, lad."

"You *must,*" Joe said with grave insistence, "or missus and me'll be mortal offended. It's for yourself, not Dr. Page. He's *well* paid. This is for *yourself,* doctor, *bach.* You understand."

"Yes, I understand, Joe," Andrew nodded, smiling.

He folded the cheque, placed it in his waistcoat pocket and forgot about it until the following Tuesday. Passing the Western Counties Bank he paused, then went in. As Miss Page always paid him in notes, which he forwarded by registered letter to the Endowment offices, he had never had occasion to deal through the bank. But he decided to open a deposit account with Joe's gift.

He filled in some forms and handed them to the young cashier, remarking with a smile: "It's not much, but it's a start."

Meanwhile, he had been conscious of Aneurin Rees watching him in the background. And, as he turned to go, the manager came forward to the counter. In his hands he held the order.

"Afternoon, Dr. Manson. How are you?" Pause. Sucking his breath in over his yellow teeth. "You want this paid into your account?"

"Yes." Manson spoke in some surprise. "Is it too small an amount to open with?"

"Oh, no, no, doctor. 'Tisn't the amount, like." Rees hesitated, then raised his small suspicious eyes to Andrew's face. "Eh—you want it in your *own* name?"

"Why—certainly."

"All right, all right, doctor. I only wanted to make sure. What lovely weather we're havin' for the time of year. Good day to you, Dr. Manson."

Manson came out of the bank puzzled, asking himself what that bald, buttoned-up devil meant. It was some days before he found an answer to the question.

CHRISTINE had left for her vacation more than a week before. He had been so occupied by the Morgan case that he had only seen her for a few moments on the day of her departure. But now that she was gone he longed for her with all his heart.

The summer was exceptionally trying in the town. When the daily shotfiring from the mines re-echoed on the still, spent air it seemed to enclose the valley in a dome of burnished sound. Old Thomas, the groom, had jaundice and Andrew had to make his rounds on foot. As he slogged through the baking streets he thought of Christine. Was she thinking of him? And what of the future, their chance of happiness together?

And then, quite unexpectedly, he received a message from Watkins asking him to call at the Company Offices.

The mine manager received him in agreeable fashion, invited him to sit down. "I've been wantin' to talk to you for some time, doctor," he said in a friendly tone. "There's been a number of the lads at me askin' me to put you up for the Company's list."

Andrew straightened in his chair. "You mean—arrange for me to take over Dr. Page's practice?"

"Why no, not exactly, doctor," Watkins said slowly, "I can't put Dr. Page off the list. What I was meanin' was to squeeze you in, quiet-like, then them that wanted to slip away from Dr. Page to yourself could easily manage it."

Andrew's eagerness faded. He frowned. "But surely you see I couldn't do that. If I set up in opposition to Page—no decent doctor could do that! Why don't you let me take over the practice? I'd willingly pay something for it, out of receipts."

Watkins shook his head bluntly. "Blodwen won't 'ave it. I've put it up to her afore. She knows she's in a strong position. Nearly all the older men here are on Page's side. They believe he'll come back. I'd have a strike on my hands if I even tried to shift him." He paused. "Take till tomorrow to think it over, doctor. I send the annual return to Swansea head office then. Once it's gone in we can't do anything for another twelve months."

Andrew stared at the floor a moment, then slowly made a gesture of negation. "What's the use. I couldn't do it."

It cost him a bitter pang to reach this decision. For the rest of the day he was sadly cast down, wishing the offer had not been made to him at all. In the evening he went dejectedly to call on Denny. He reached his lodging about half past eight and, as was now his custom, entered the house without knocking.

Philip lay on the sofa in the sitting room, sprawled on his back, breathing heavily, his arm across his face. He was dead drunk.

Andrew turned to find the landlady at his elbow, watching him apprehensively. "I heard you come in, doctor. He's been like this all day." Andrew simply did not know what to say.

Vaguely he knew that Denny had had a wife, socially his superior, who had tried to mould him to the demands of a county practice, where there was no credit in operating well four days of the week if one did not hunt the other three. After five years of effort on Denny's part she had left him for another man, and Denny had fled to the backwoods.

"It's ten months now since his last bout," Mrs. Seager went on. "And he don't touch it in between. But when he do begin, he goes at it wicked."

With the help of her son Tom, a young miner who seemed to regard the matter as a joke, they got Philip into his pyjamas. Then they carried him, heavy as a sack, to the bedroom.

"The main thing is to see that he doesn't get any more of it, you understand." Andrew addressed the landlady as they came back into the sitting room. "Turn the key in the door if necessary."

Next morning, immediately after surgery, he went round to the lodgings. Philip was drunker than before, heavy, insensible. After prolonged efforts to restore him Andrew took Philip's list of calls as Dr. Nicholls was on holiday. Cursing the heat, the flies, and Denny, he did double work that day.

In the late afternoon he came back, angrily resolved to get Denny sober. He found him astride a chair in his pyjamas, still drunk, delivering a long address to Tom and Mrs. Seager.

As Andrew entered, Denny stopped short and gave him a lowering stare. He spoke thickly. "Ha! The Good Samaritan. I understand you've done my round for me. Extremely noble. But why should you? Why should that blasted Nicholls leave us to do the work?"

"I can't say." Andrew's patience was wearing thin. "All I know is, it would be easier if you did your bit of it."

"I'm a surgeon. I'm not a blasted general practitioner. GP. Huh! It's the worst, stupidest system ever created. Dear old GP! And dear old BP!—that's the British Public!" He laughed derisively. "They made him. They love him. They weep over him." He swayed in his seat, his inflamed eyes again bitter and morose.

Suppressing his irritation, Andrew said: "Oughtn't you to get back to bed now? Come on, we'll help you."

"Let me alone," said Denny sullenly. "Don't use your blasted bedside manner on me." He rose abruptly and, taking Mrs. Seager by the shoulder, he thrust her into the chair. Then, swaying on his feet, he addressed the frightened woman. "And how are you today, my dear lady? A leetle better, I fancy."

There was, in the ludicrous scene, an alarming note—the stocky, pyjama-clad figure of Philip aping the society physician before the shrinking miner's wife. Tom gave a nervous gulp of laughter. In a flash, Denny turned on him. "That's right! Laugh! Laugh your blasted head off. But I spent five years of my life doing that. God!" He glared at them, seized a vase that stood on the mantelpiece, and dashed it upon the floor. He started forward, red destruction in his eye.

"For mercy's sake," whimpered Mrs. Seager. "Stop him—"

Andrew and Tom Seager flung themselves on Philip who struggled wildly. Then he suddenly relaxed. "Manson," he drooled, "you're a good chap. You and I—if we stuck together we could save the whole bloody medical profession." He stood, his gaze wandering, lost. Then his body sagged. He allowed Andrew to help him to the next room and into bed.

Next morning he was drunker than ever. Andrew gave up. All that week he struggled through Denny's calls in addition to his own. On Sunday, after lunch, he visited Philip. He was up, dressed, immaculate in appearance and, though drawn and shaky, cold sober.

"I understand you've been doing my work for me, Manson." His manner was icily stiff. "It must have put you to a great deal of trouble."

Andrew flushed. Not a word of gratitude, he thought, nothing but arrogance. "If you do want to know the truth," he blurted out, "it put me to a hell of a lot of trouble! And if it hadn't been for me

Mrs. Seager would have wired Dr. Nicholls and you'd have been thrown out on your neck. And what you need is a damned good punch on the jaw."

Denny lit a cigarette, his fingers shaking so violently he could barely hold the match. He sneered: "Nice of you to choose this moment to offer physical combat."

"Oh! Shut up!" said Andrew. "Here's your list of calls for tomorrow." He flung out of the house in a fury.

On the way home his resentment slowly cooled. He was genuinely fond of Philip and he had by now a better insight into his complex nature: shy, talented, inordinately sensitive. The memory of how he had exposed himself during his recent bout must be causing him excruciating torture.

Nevertheless, when Andrew reached home he still smarted from his impact with Philip's coldness. And so he was scarcely in the mood to hear Miss Page's voice exclaiming: "Is that you, doctor? I want you!" He swung round to see her sail out of the sitting room, her blue eyes sparkling with emotion. "What is it, Miss Page?" he said irritably.

"What is it, indeed." She could scarcely breathe. "It's *this*, my smart young gentleman! Maybe you'll be kind enough to explain this." From behind her back she produced a slip of paper and fluttered it menacingly before his eyes. He saw it was Joe Morgan's cheque. Then, raising his head, he saw the bank manager standing in the doorway of the sitting room.

"Ay, you may well look!" Blodwen went on. "You better tell us quick how you came to bank that money for yourself when it's Dr. Page's money and you know it."

Andrew felt the blood rise behind his ears in quick surging waves. "It's mine. Joe Morgan made me a present of it."

"A *present!* Indeed! I like that. He's not here now to deny it! Comin' down here and thinkin' you can get the practice into your own hands when you should be workin' for Dr. Page. But this shows what you are, all right."

She flung the words at him, half-turning for support to Rees, standing in the doorway. Andrew, indeed, saw Rees as the instigator of the whole affair. His hands clenched fiercely. He advanced towards them, his eyes fixed on Rees's thin bloodless mouth with threatening intensity.

"Miss Page," he said, livid with rage. "You've made a charge against me. Unless you apologize within two minutes I'll sue you for defamation of character. And I've no doubt Mr. Rees's board of governors will be interested to hear how he discloses his official business."

"I—I only did my duty," stuttered the bank manager.

"I'm waiting, Miss Page." Andrew's words came with a rush.

She saw she had gone too far. His ominous attitude sobered her. It was almost possible to follow her swift reflection: Heavy damages! She choked, swallowed, stammered: "I—I take it back. I apologize."

It was almost comic, the gaunt angry woman, so suddenly and unexpectedly subdued. But Andrew found it singularly humourless. He realized, with a great flood of bitterness, that he could not put up with this impossible situation any longer. He took a quick deep breath. "Miss Page, there is just one thing I want to tell you. Last week a deputation of the men approached the manager, who invited me to put my name on the Company's list. On ethical grounds I refused. And now, Miss Page, I'm so absolutely sick of you, I couldn't stay on. I give you a month's notice here and now."

She gaped at him, her eyes nearly bursting from her head, then she said: "It's all lies. You couldn't get near the Company's list. And you're *sacked*. No assistant has ever given me notice in his life. The impudence, the insolence, talking to me like that. I said it first. You're sacked, you are, sacked—"

At the height of the outburst there was an interruption. Upstairs, the door of Edward's room swung slowly open and, a moment later, Edward himself appeared, a strange, bleak figure in a nightshirt. Dragging his paralysed leg behind him, he came slowly, painfully, to the topmost stair. "Can't I have a little peace?" His voice, though agitated, was stern. "What's the matter?"

Gazing upwards, Blodwen gulped and launched into a tearful diatribe against Manson. She concluded, "And so—and so I gave him his notice."

Manson did not contradict her version of the case.

"You mean he's going?" Edward asked, trembling all over with agitation and the exertion of keeping himself upright.

"Yes, Edward." She sniffed. "I did it for your sake. And, anyhow, you'll soon be back."

There was a silence. Edward's eyes dwelt blankly upon Andrew, moved to Rees, passed quickly on to Blodwen. A look of hopelessness formed upon his stiff face. "No," he said at last. "I'll never be back. You know that—all of you." Turning slowly, he dragged his way back into his room.

Chapter 4

Remembering the joy, the pure elation which the Morgan case had given him and which his quarrel with Miss Page had now turned to something sordid, Andrew brooded angrily, wondering if he should not take the matter further. In the end, however, he picked a local charity and, in a mood of determined bitterness, posted five guineas to the secretary and asked him to send the receipt to Aneurin Rees. After that he felt better.

He began immediately to look for another position, combing the back pages of the *Lancet*. But at the end of two weeks he had received not a single answer to his applications. He was disappointed and astounded. He still owed £50 to the Glen Endowment and he really began to worry. If he could not find another job how was he to live? He had no reserves. He had moments of sheer terror when he saw himself sinking to destitution.

Surrounded by difficulties and uncertainty he longed for Christine. Yet she was not returning until the first week in September.

On the evening of August 30, three weeks after he had given Miss Page his notice, he was walking dispiritedly along Chapel Street when he met Denny. They had remained on terms of highly strained civility during the past few weeks and Andrew was surprised when the other man stopped him.

Knocking out his pipe on the heel of his boot, Philip inspected it as though it demanded all his attention.

"I'm rather sorry you're going, Manson. It's made quite a difference you being here." He hesitated. "I heard this afternoon that the Aberalaw Medical Aid Society is looking for a new assistant. It's quite a decent Society, as these things go. And it's only thirty miles away. Why don't you try?"

Andrew gazed at him doubtfully. His expectations had recently been so hopelessly dashed that he had lost all faith in his ability to succeed. "Well, yes," he agreed slowly. "I may as well try."

On September 6, a full meeting of the Committee of the Aberalaw Medical Aid Society took place for the purpose of selecting a successor to a Dr. Leslie who had recently resigned. Seven candidates had been asked to attend at four p.m.

It was a perfect summer afternoon and the time was close on four o'clock. Prowling up and down on the pavement outside the Medical Aid offices, darting nervous glances at the six other candidates, Andrew longed with all his heart to be successful.

From what he had seen of Aberalaw he liked it. The town was considerably larger than Drineffy, with good streets and shops, two cinemas, and a sense of spaciousness conveyed by green fields on its outskirts. After the sweltering confines of the Drineffy ravine, Aberalaw appeared a perfect paradise.

"But I'll never get it," he fretted as he paced up and down—"never, never, *never.*" All the other candidates looked far better turned out, more confident than himself. Especially a Dr. Edwards, a stoutish, prosperous, middle-aged man who had freely intimated that he had just sold his own practice down the valley in order to "apply" for this position. Damn him, grated Andrew inwardly, he wouldn't have sold up if he hadn't been sure of this one!

Four o'clock at last. As he turned towards the entrance a fine car drew up silently. From the back seat a short, dapper man emerged, smiling affably at the candidates. Before mounting the stairs he recognized Edwards, nodding casually.

"How do, Edwards." Then aside: "It'll be all right, I fancy."

"Thank you ever so, Dr. Llewellyn," breathed Edwards.

"Finished!" said Andrew to himself bitterly.

Andrew was the third to go in for interview. He entered the committee room with a blank expression and took the seat offered him. If the post was already promised he was not going to cringe for it.

About thirty miners filled the room, seated, gazing at him with blunt, but not unfriendly, curiosity. At a small side table was Owen, the secretary, a pale man with an intelligent face. Lounging on the edge of the table, smiling good-naturedly, was Dr. Llewellyn.

The interview began. Owen, in a quiet voice, explained the conditions of the post. "It's like this you see, doctor. Under our scheme, the workers in Aberalaw pay a certain amount to the Society out of their wages every week. Out of this the Society provides a nice little hospital, surgeries, medicines, et cetera. In addition the Society engages doctors: Dr. Llewellyn, the head physician and surgeon, and four assistants, together with a dentist, and pays them so much per head according to the number on their list. I believe Dr. Leslie made something like five hundred pounds a year." He paused. "Altogether we find it a good scheme." Owen raised his head and faced the committeemen. "And now, gentlemen, have you any questions to ask?"

They began to fire questions at Andrew. He tried to answer calmly, truthfully.

At last it was over. "Thank you very much, Dr. Manson," Owen said, and Andrew was out again in the sour-smelling waiting room, watching the other candidates go in.

Edwards, the last man called, was absent a very long time. He came out smiling broadly. Then followed an interminable wait. But at last the door of the committee room opened and out came Owen, the secretary.

"Would you come in a minute, Dr. Manson? The committee would like to see you again," he said with real friendliness.

Pale-lipped, his heart pounding in his side, Andrew followed the secretary back into the committee room.

Back in the prisoner's chair again, he faced smiles and encouraging nods. Dr. Llewellyn, however, was not looking at him. Owen commenced: "Dr. Manson, we may as well be frank with you. The committee is in some doubt. In fact, on Dr. Llewellyn's advice, it had a strong bias in favour of another candidate.

"'E's too fat, that Edwards," interrupted a member at the back. "I'd like to see 'im climb to the houses on Mardy Hill."

Andrew was too tense to smile.

"But today," the secretary went on, "the committee has been very taken with you. It wants young, active men!"

Laughter, with cries of "'Ear! 'Ear!"

"Moreover, Dr. Manson," continued Owen. "I must tell you that the committee has been exceedingly impressed by two testimonials, testimonials *unsolicited* by yourself, which makes them of more value in the eyes of the committee. These are from two practitioners in Drineffy. One is a Dr. Denny, who has the MS, a very high degree, as Dr. Llewellyn, who should know, admits. The other, enclosed with Dr. Denny's, is signed by Dr. Page, whose assistant I believe you now are."

Andrew bit his lip, his eyes lowered, aware for the first time of this generous thing that Denny had done for him.

"There is just one difficulty, Dr. Manson," Owen paused, diffidently moving the ruler on his table. "This position is one for a married man. You see, apart from the fact that the men prefer a married doctor to attend their families, there's a house that goes with the position. It wouldn't be very suitable for a single man."

Andrew drew a tense breath, his thoughts focused upon the image of Christine. He heard himself declaring calmly: "As a matter of fact, gentlemen, I'm engaged to someone in Drineffy. I've—I've just been waiting on a suitable appointment—such as this—to get married."

Owen slapped down the ruler in satisfaction. There was approval, signified by a tapping of heavy boots.

"I take it you're agreed then, gentlemen," Owen's voice rose above the noise. "Dr. Manson is unanimously appointed."

There was a vigorous murmur of assent. Andrew experienced a wild thrill of triumph.

"When can you take up your duties, Dr. Manson? The earlier the better, so far as the committee is concerned."

"I could start the beginning of next week," Manson answered. Then he turned cold as he thought: "Suppose Christine won't have me. Suppose I lose her, and this wonderful job as well."

"That's settled then. Thank you, Dr. Manson. I'm sure the committee wishes you every success in your new appointment."

Applause. They were all congratulating him. Then he was out in the waiting room, trying not to show his elation, trying to appear unconscious of Edwards's crestfallen face.

As he walked to the station his heart swelled with excited victory. On his right as he strode down the hill was a small green public park with a fountain and a bandstand. Think of it!—a bandstand!—when the only feature of the landscape in Drineffy was a slag heap. And hadn't Owen said something about a hospital too? Ah! Thinking of what the hospital would mean to his work, Andrew drew a deep, excited breath.

The train back to Drineffy would simply not go fast enough. Andrew's mood had altered now. Sunk in the corner seat, his thoughts tormented him.

For the first time he saw that all his hesitations about marriage had selfishly centred on his own feelings. But suppose Christine did not love him? He saw himself, rejected, writing a letter to the committee telling them that owing to circumstances over which he had no control he could not accept the position. A pang of longing shot through him. Dear Christine! If he had to forgo her, he did not care what happened to him.

At nine o'clock the train crawled into Drineffy. In a flash he was out and moving up Railway Road towards her lodgings. Though he didn't expect her until the morning there was just a chance that—a light in the front room sent a pang of expectation through him. Telling himself that it was probably only her landlady preparing the room for her return, he swept into the house, burst into the sitting room.

Yes! it was Christine. She was kneeling over some books in the corner arranging them on a shelf.

"Christine!"

She swung round, a strand of hair fallen over her brow, then with a little cry of surprise and pleasure she rose. "Andrew! How nice of you to come round."

Advancing towards him, her face alight, she held out her hand. But he took both her hands in his and held them tightly. He gazed down at her. His heart was throbbing. "Chris! I've got to tell you something."

Concern swept into her eyes. "What has happened? Is it more trouble with Miss Page? Are you going away?"

He shook his head, and then, all at once, he broke out: "Christine! I've got the most wonderful job. At Aberalaw. I saw the committee today. Five hundred a year and a house. A house, Christine! Oh, darling—Christine—could you—would you marry me?"

She went very pale. "And I thought—I thought it was bad news you were going to tell me."

"No! no!" he cried impulsively. "It's the most marvellous news, darling. Oh! if you'd just seen the place. All open and clean with decent shops and a park and—oh! Christine, a hospital. If only you'll marry me, darling, we can start there straight away."

Her lips were soft, trembling. But her eyes smiled with a shining lustre towards him. "Is this because of Aberalaw or because of me?"

"It's you, Chris. Oh, you know I love you, but then—perhaps you don't love me."

She gave a little sound in her throat, buried her head in his breast. As his arms went round her she said brokenly: "Oh, darling, darling. I've loved you ever since I saw you walk into that stupid classroom."

PART TWO
Chapter 1

Gwilliam John Lossin's decrepit pantechnicon banged and boiled its way up the mountain road. In front, jammed in gaily with Gwilliam John were Dr. Manson and his wife.

They had been married that morning. This was their bridal carriage. In the van were Christine's few pieces of furniture, several new pots and pans, and their suitcases. Since they were without pride they had decided that this was the cheapest way to bring their worldly goods and themselves to Aberalaw.

The day was bright, with a fresh breeze blowing, burnishing the blue sky. They laughed and joked with Gwilliam John, who obliged occasionally with his special rendering of Handel's *Largo* upon the motor horn. At last they crested the final rise and coasted down into Aberalaw. It was a moment tinged with ecstasy. The town lay before them with its long lines of roofs reaching up and down the valley, its shops, churches and offices clustered at the upper end and, at the lower, its mines and ore works, the chimneys smoking steadily, and all spangled by the midday sun.

"Look! Chris, look!" Andrew whispered, pressing her arm. "It's a fine place, isn't it? A gas works, too. No more oil lamps!"

They stopped a passing miner and were soon directed to Vale View. Another minute and they were there.

"Well!" said Christine. "It's—it's nice, isn't it?"

"Yes, darling. It looks—it looks a lovely house."

"By Cor!" Gwilliam John shoved his cap to the back of his head. "That's a rum lookin' shop."

Vale View was, indeed, an extraordinary edifice, something between a Swiss chalet and a Highland shooting box, with a great profusion of little gables, standing in half an acre of desolate garden choked with weeds through which a stream tumbled over tin cans beneath a mouldering rustic bridge.

Whatever their impression of the outside, however, the house was sound and cleanly papered within, even though alarmingly large. They both perceived instantly that Christine's few pieces would barely furnish two of the rooms.

"Let's see, darling," Chris said, as they stood in the hall after their first breathless tour. "I make it a dining room, drawing room, and library downstairs, and five bedrooms upstairs."

"No wonder they wanted a married man." Andrew's smile faded to compunction. "Honestly, Chris, I feel rotten about this—me without a bean using your nice furniture, taking everything for granted, dragging you over here at a minute's notice. I'm a selfish ass. I ought to have come over first and got the place decently ready for you."

"Andrew Manson! If you'd dared to leave me behind."

"Anyhow, I'm going to do something about it," he frowned at her doggedly. "Now listen, Chris—"

She interrupted with a smile. "I think, darling, I'm going to make you an omelette according to Madame Poulard."

The omelette—Gwilliam John had been sent for the eggs before he took his departure—came out of the pan, hot, savoury and a delicate yellow. They ate it sitting together on the edge of the kitchen table. He exclaimed vigorously: "By Jove! You can cook! Is there a little more omelette? Gosh! You don't know how keen I am to get started. There ought to be opportunities here. *Big* opportunities!" He broke off suddenly, his eyes resting on a varnished wooden case which stood in the corner. "I say, Chris! What's that?"

"Oh, that!" She made her voice sound casual. "That's a wedding present—from Denny!"

"Denny!" His face changed. Philip had been stiff and offhand when Andrew had thanked him for his help in getting the new job and told him he was marrying Christine. It had hurt Andrew that he had not even come to see them off. He advanced slowly, rather suspiciously, to the case, and opened it. Then he gave a gasp of sheer delight. Inside was Denny's microscope, the exquisite Zeiss, and a note: "I don't really need this, I told you I was a sawbones. Good luck."

There was nothing to be said. Thoughtful, almost subdued, Andrew finished his omelette. Then, reverently, he took up the microscope and, accompanied by Christine, went into the empty room behind the dining room. He placed the microscope solemnly in the middle of the bare floor.

"This isn't the library after all, Chris. Thanks to our good friend Philip Denny, I hereby christen it 'the lab'."

He had just kissed her, to make the ceremony really effective, when the phone rang shrilly.

It was Dr. Llewellyn, telephoning his welcome. His voice came urbanely over the wire, and Chris, at Andrew's shoulder, could hear the conversation perfectly. "Hel-*lo*, Manson. I wanted to be the first to welcome you and your wife to Aberalaw."

"Thanks, thanks, Dr. Llewellyn. It's awfully good of you."

"Look here, if you're not doing anything tonight come over and have dinner with us, no formality, half past seven. We'll be delighted to see you both. That's settled then? Goodbye."

Andrew put down the receiver, his expression deeply gratified.

"Wasn't that decent of him, Chris? Asking us over like that! The head doctor, mind you! And he sounded so friendly. Believe me, Mrs. Manson, we're going to make a big hit here." Slipping his arm round her waist he began jubilantly to waltz her round the hall.

THAT NIGHT, at seven o'clock, they set out through the busy streets for Dr. Llewellyn's house, Glynmawr. They had no difficulty in finding it, a solid villa with well-tended grounds, for Dr. Llewellyn's beautiful car stood outside and Dr. Llewellyn's beautifully polished plate, his qualifications displayed in small chaste letters, was bolted to the wrought-iron gate. Suddenly nervous, they rang the bell and were shown in.

Llewellyn greeted them, dapper in frockcoat and stiff gold-linked cuffs, his expression beamingly cordial. "Well! well! This is splendid. Delighted to meet you, Mrs. Manson. Hope you'll like Aberalaw. Come along in. Mrs. Llewellyn'll be down in a minute."

Mrs. Llewellyn, a red-haired woman of about forty-five, with a pale freckled face, was as beaming as her husband. Having greeted Manson, she turned towards Christine with an affectionate gasp. "Oh, my de-ar, you lovely little thing! I declare I've lost my heart to you already." Without pausing, she embraced Christine.

Dinner was an excellent meal—tomato soup, two roast fowls with stuffing and sausages, sultana pudding.

"You'll soon get the hang of things, Manson," Llewellyn said.

"I'll help you all I can. You'll be at the West Surgery—that's your end of town—with old Dr. Urquhart—he's a card, I can tell you—and Gadge, the dispenser. Up here at the East Surgery we've got Dr. Medley and Dr. Oxborrow. Of course, I have a lot to do here. Yes, yes, indeed. Myself, I don't bother about the surgeries. I have the hospital on my hands. I do the compensation cases for the Company, I'm medical officer for the town, I'm surgeon to the workhouse and public vaccinator as well. I do a good deal of county court work. Oh! and I'm coroner, too. And besides"—a gleam escaped his guileless eye—"I do a goodish bit of private practice at odd times."

"It's a full list," Manson said.

Llewellyn beamed. "We've got to make ends meet, Dr. Manson. That little car you saw outside cost a little matter of twelve hundred pounds. There's no reason why you shouldn't make a good livin' here. Say around three to four hundred for yourself."

"Dr. Manson!" Mrs. Llewellyn called sweetly from her end of the table. "I'm just telling your dear wife we must see a lot of each other. She must come to tea sometime and run down to Cardiff with me in the car."

"Of course," Llewellyn proceeded glossily, "Leslie, the feller that was here before you, was a slack devil. Oh, he was a rotten doctor. He couldn't give a decent anaesthetic anyhow! You're a good anaesthetist, I hope, doctor? But, bless my soul, it isn't fair to bother you with that yet."

"Idris!" cried Mrs. Llewellyn to her husband, with a kind of delighted sensationalism. "They were only *married* this morning! Mrs. Manson just told me. Why, would you believe it, the dear innocents."

"Well, now!" beamed Llewellyn.

Mrs. Llewellyn patted Christine's hand. "My poor lamb! To think of the work you'll have getting straight. I must come sometime and give you a hand."

Manson reddened slightly. He felt as though Christine and he had become moulded into a soft little ball, played back and forward between Dr. and Mrs. Llewellyn.

They drank their coffee in the drawing room and Llewellyn offered cigarettes from his gold cigarette case—"Take a look at that, Manson. From a grateful patient! Worth twenty pounds if it's worth a penny."

Towards ten o'clock Llewellyn beamed at his fine half-hunter watch with that bland cordiality which was especially his own. "I've got to go to the hospital," he remarked. "Gastro-duodenal I did this morning. How about runnin' round with me in the car and taking a look at it?"

Andrew sat up eagerly. "Why, I'd love to, Dr. Llewellyn."

Since Christine was included in the invitation also, they said good night to Mrs. Llewellyn and stepped into the waiting car, which moved away with silent elegance.

"Here we are, then," said Llewellyn only two minutes later. "This is my spiritual home."

The hospital was a well-constructed red-brick building and immediately they entered Andrew's eyes lit up. Though small, the place was modern, beautifully equipped. As Llewellyn showed them round the theatre, the X-ray room, the two fine airy wards, Andrew kept thinking exultantly, this is perfect! I'll get my cases well in here!

They picked up the matron on their travels, a tall, raw-boned woman who melted into adoration before Llewellyn.

"We get pretty well all we want here, don't we, matron?" Llewellyn said. "We just speak to the committee. Yes, they're not a bad lot. How's my gastro-enterostomy, matron?"

"Very comfortable, Dr. Llewellyn," she murmured.

"Good! I'll see it in a minute!" He escorted Christine and Andrew back again to the vestibule. "Yes, I do admit, Manson, I'm rather proud of this place. I regard it as my own. You'll find your own way home, won't you?"

Walking down the road together they kept silence for a while, then Christine took Andrew's arm. "Well?" she inquired. Andrew could feel her smiling in the darkness.

"I like him," he said quickly. "Did you spot the matron, too? As if she was going to kiss the hem of his garment. But by Jove! That's a marvellous little hospital."

The lights of the town lay behind, and an odd silence fell between them as they approached Vale View. A great wave of love swept over Andrew. He thought of her, married in a mining village, dragged in a lorry across the mountains, dumped into a half-empty house—and sustaining these hardships with courage and a smiling tenderness. She loved him, trusted him, believed in him. A great determination swelled in him to show her, by his work, that her faith in him was justified.

They crossed a wooden bridge. The murmur of the stream was sweet in their ears. He took the key of their house from his pocket, and fitted it in the lock. In the hall it was almost dark. He closed the door and turned to her. Her face was faintly luminous, her slight figure expectant, yet defenceless. He put his arm round her gently. He whispered, strangely: "What's your name, darling?"

"Christine," she answered, wondering.

"Christine what?"

"Christine Manson." Her breath came quickly, quickly, and was warm upon his lips.

WALKING DOWN from Vale View the next morning, Andrew felt the crisp, cool breeze strike invigoratingly on his cheek. He saw his work stretching out before him here, work always guided by his principle, the scientific method.

The West Surgery was only four hundred yards from his house. A high-vaulted building, white-tiled, with a faint air of sanitation, its central portion was the waiting room. At one end, cut off by a sliding hatch, was the dispensary. At the other were two consulting rooms, one bearing the name of Dr. Urquhart and the other, freshly painted, Dr. Manson.

It gave Andrew a thrill of pleasure to see himself identified, already, with his room, which had a good desk and a leather couch for examinations. He was flattered, too, by the number of people waiting on him. Seating himself, he signalled for his first case to come in. This was a man who asked simply for a certificate, adding, as a kind of afterthought, beat knee. Andrew examined him, found him suffering from beat knee, gave him the certificate.

The second case came in. He also demanded his certificate, nystagmus. The third case: certificate, bronchitis. The fourth case: certificate, beat elbow.

These certificate examinations were taking a great deal of time. He went to his door and asked: "How many more men for certificates? Will they stand up, please."

There were perhaps forty men waiting outside. They all stood up. Reluctantly, Andrew decided to abbreviate his examinations. Even so, it was half past ten when Andrew got through his last case. Then there stamped into his room a medium-sized, elderly man with a brick-red face, stooping slightly so that his head had a forward belligerent thrust. He wore cord breeches, gaiters, and a tweed jacket, the side pockets stuffed to bursting point. About him hung the odour of drugs, carbolic and strong tobacco. Andrew knew before he spoke that it was Dr. Urquhart.

"Thank God ye look sound in mind an' limb," said Urquhart without a handshake or a word of introduction. "Do ye smoke a pipe?"

"I do."

"Thank God for that also! Can ye play the fiddle?"

"No."

"Neither can I—but I can make them bonny. I collect china too. I'll show ye some day when ye come to my house. And now, come away and meet Gadge. Our dispenser's a miserable devil. But he knows his incompatibles."

Andrew followed Urquhart into the dispensary where Gadge greeted him with a gloomy nod. He was a long, lean, cadaverous man, wearing a short alpaca jacket, green with age and the stains of drugs. His air was sad, caustic, tired; his attitude that of the most disillusioned man in the whole universe.

"Well," said Urquhart spryly, after the introduction. "Ye've met Gadge and ye know the worst. Is there anything I can tell ye?"

"I'm worried about the number of certificates I had to sign. What can anyone think of a doctor who hands out certificates like cigarette coupons?"

Urquhart darted a glance at him. He said bluntly: "Be careful how you go. They're liable not to like it if you sign them off."

Gadge interjected, "Ruddy scrimshankers . . . ."

All that day while he did his rounds Andrew worried about the certificates. In the end he came to a decision: he could not, on any account, give a slack certificate. He went down to evening surgery with an anxious yet determined line between his brows.

The crowd was larger than at the morning surgery. And the first patient to enter was a fat lump of a man, who smelled strongly of beer and looked as if he had never done a full day's work in his life. He had small, pig eyes which blinked down at Andrew.

"Certificate," he said, without minding his manners.

"What for?" Andrew asked.

"'Stagmus." He held out his hand. "The name's Ben Chenkin."

The tone alone caused Andrew to look at Chenkin with quick

resentment. Even from a cursory inspection he felt convinced that Chenkin had no eye trouble. However, he would soon make sure. "Take your things off. I'm going to examine you."

Ben Chenkin's jaw dropped. Sulkily he pulled off his jacket and shirt, revealing a hairy torso, swathed in adiposity.

Andrew made a thorough examination. Then, sharply, he said: "Dress up, Chenkin." He began to write out a certificate.

"Ha!" sneered old Ben. "I thought you'd let us 'ave it."

"Next please," Andrew called out.

Chenkin almost snatched the pink slip from Andrew's hand. Then he strode triumphantly from the surgery.

A minute later he was bellowing like a bull, his face livid. "Hey! What's the meanin' of this?" He flourished the certificate in Andrew's face.

Andrew affected to read the slip. It said, in his own handwriting: *This is to certify that Ben Chenkin is suffering from the effects of over-indulgence in malt liquors but is perfectly fit to work. Signed A. Manson, MB.*

"Well?" he asked.

"'Stagmus," shouted Chenkin. "Compensation money for 'stagmus. You can't play the fool on us. Fifteen year us got 'stagmus!"

"You haven't got it now," Andrew said. A crowd had gathered round the open door. He was conscious of Urquhart's head popping out curiously from the other room, of Gadge inspecting the tumult with relish through his hatch.

"For the last time—are ye going to give us 'stagmus certificate?" Chenkin bawled.

Andrew lost his temper. "No, I'm not," he shouted back.

Ben looked as if he might wipe the floor with Andrew. Then he turned and, muttering profane threats, walked out of the surgery. The minute he was gone Gadge shuffled across to Andrew. He rubbed his hands with melancholy delight. "You know who that was? Ben Chenkin. His son's a big man on the committee."

THE SENSATION of the Chenkin case hummed round Manson's district in a flash. Some people said it was "a good job" that Ben had been pulled up in his swindling, but the majority were on his side, particularly those drawing compensation money for disabilities. As he went on his rounds Andrew was conscious of black looks directed towards him. And at night, in the surgery, he had to face an even worse manifestation of unpopularity.

The workmen had the right of free choice of doctor. Each man had a yellow card and by demanding that card and handing it to another doctor he could effect a change. It was this ignominy and humiliation which now began for Andrew. Every night that week, men dropped into his surgery to say, without looking at him: "If you don't mind, doctor, I'll 'ave my card." And every card he gave away meant ten shillings subtracted from his salary.

On Saturday night Urquhart invited him into his house. The old man began by exhibiting his treasures. He had perhaps a score of yellow violins, all made by himself, but these were as nothing compared with his collection of old English china. He had a superb collection—Spode, Wedgwood, and best of all, old Swansea—they were all there. They filled every room in the house and overflowed into the bathroom where it was possible for Urquhart to survey with pride an original willow-pattern tea service.

The old man passed, in the town, as a character. He gave his age as sixty but was possibly nearer eighty. Tough as whalebone, his sole vehicle shoe leather, he covered incredible distances, swore murderously at his patients, and could yet be tender as a woman, lived by himself—since the death of his wife eleven years before—and existed almost entirely upon tinned soup.

This evening, having proudly displayed his collection, he suddenly remarked to Andrew with an injured air: "Dammit, man! I don't want any of your patients. I've got enough of my own. But what can I do if they come pestering me?"

Andrew reddened. There was nothing that he could say.

"You want to be more careful, man." Urquhart went on in an altered tone. "Oh, I know, I was young myself once. But all the same, go easy."

With Urquhart's words sounding in his ear, Andrew made every effort to steer a cautious course. But, even so, a greater disaster immediately overtook him.

On the Monday following he went to the house of Thomas Evans, a hewer at the Aberalaw colliery. He had upset a kettle of boiling water over his left arm. It was a serious scald, covering a large area around the elbow. When Andrew arrived he found that the district nurse had already dressed the scald with carron oil.

Andrew examined the arm, suppressing his horror of the filthy dressing. Out of the corner of his eye he observed the carron oil bottle, corked with a plug of newspaper.

"Nurse Lloyd done it pretty good, eh, doctor?" said Evans nervously. He was a dark-eyed, highly-strung youngster.

"A beautiful dressing," Andrew said with a great show of enthusiasm. "Only a first dressing, of course. Now I think we'll try some picric." He knew that if he did not quickly use the antiseptic the arm would almost certainly become infected. And then heaven help that elbow joint! With scrupulous gentleness, he cleansed the arm and slipped on a moist picric dressing.

"There now," he exclaimed. "Doesn't that feel easier?"

"I don't know as how it does," Evans said dubiously. "Are you sure it's goin' to be all right, doctor?"

"Positive!" Andrew smiled reassuringly. "You must leave this to nurse and me."

He left a note to the district nurse, taking extra pains to be tactful. He thanked her for her splendid emergency treatment and asked her, as a measure against sepsis, to continue with the picric dressings.

Next morning when he arrived at the house, he found the arm had been redressed with carron oil. Waiting upon him, prepared for battle, was the district nurse. "What's all this about, I'd like to know?" She was a middle-aged woman with untidy, iron-grey hair and a harassed face.

Andrew's heart sank. But he forced a smile. "Come now, Nurse Lloyd, suppose we talk this over together in the front room."

The nurse swept her eyes to where Evans and his wife were listening, wide-eyed and alarmed. "No, indeed, we'll talk it over here. I've got nothing to hide. I've worked here in Aberalaw twenty years as district nurse, and nobody ever told me not to use carron oil on a burn or scald."

"Now listen, nurse," Andrew pleaded. "Carron oil is all right in its way. But there's a great danger of contracture here. That's why I want you to try my dressing."

"Never 'eard of the stuff. I don't hold with new-fangled ideas of somebody that's been here no more nor a week!"

Andrew felt ill at the thought of the repercussions of this scene, but he could not risk his patient with that antiquated treatment. He said in a low voice: "If you won't do the dressing, nurse, I'll come in morning and evening and do it myself."

"You can then, for all I care," Nurse Lloyd declared, moisture flashing to her eyes. "And I 'ope Tom Evans lives through it."

The next minute she had flounced out of the house.

In dead silence Andrew patiently attended to the damaged arm. When he left the house, he promised to return that night.

That same evening as he entered his consulting room the first person to enter was Mrs. Evans. Her eyes avoided his. "I hate to trouble you," she stammered, "but can I have Tom's card?"

A wave of hopelessness passed over Andrew. He rose without a word, searched for Tom Evans's card, handed it to her. Then as she made for the door he asked, "Is the carron oil on again?"

She gulped, nodded and was gone.

After surgery, Andrew, who usually tore home at top speed, made the passage to Vale View wearily. He was silent during supper. But afterwards, in the sitting room, while they sat together on the couch before the cheerful fire, he laid his head close to Christine's soft young breasts. "Oh darling," he groaned, "I've made an awful muddle of our start!"

As she soothed him, gently stroking his brow, he felt tears smarting behind his eyes.

Chapter 2

Winter set in early with a heavy fall of snow. Aberalaw lay so high that hard and bitter frosts gripped the town almost before the leaves had fallen from the trees.

Though they had to bear many things, Christine and Andrew were happy. Andrew had only pence to jingle in his pockets, but the Endowment debt was almost settled and the instalments on the furniture they had bought were being paid. Christine, for all her fragility and inexperience, had the attribute of the Yorkshire woman, she was a housewife. With the daily help of a young girl named Jenny, a miner's daughter, she kept the house shining.

The work of the practice was desperately hard—not alas! because he had many patients, but because of the difficult climbs in the snow to the high parts of Andrew's district. When it thawed and the roads turned to slush he came in so often with sodden trouser ends that Christine bought him a pair of leggings. At night, when he sank into a chair exhausted, she would kneel and take off these leggings, then his heavy boots, before handing him his slippers. It was not an act of service, but of love.

The people remained suspicious, difficult. All Chenkin's relations —and they were numerous—had become welded into a hostile unit, and Nurse Lloyd was Andrew's bitter enemy.

In addition, Dr. Llewellyn was using him for anaesthetics far oftener than seemed fair, and Andrew was increasingly irritated by this. He hated giving anaesthetics—it demanded a slow and measured temperament which he did not possess. He did not in the least object to serving his own patients, but when he found himself requisitioned three days a week for cases he had never seen before, he began to feel that he was shouldering a burden which belonged to someone else.

One evening in November Christine noticed that something unusual had upset him. Though he made pretence of unconcern, she loved him too well not to detect that he had received an unexpected blow.

After supper she began to busy herself with some sewing beside the fire. He sat beside her, biting on his pipe, then all at once he declared: "I hate grousing, Chris! God knows I try to keep things to myself!" This, considering that he poured his heart out to her nightly, was highly diverting. But Christine did not smile as he continued: "You know the hospital, darling. Remember how I raved about opportunities of doing fine work there, and everything? I needn't have deluded myself. It isn't the Aberalaw Hospital. It's Dr. Llewellyn's Hospital."

She was silent, her eyes concerned, waiting for him to explain.

"I had a case this morning, Chris!" He spoke quickly now. "You'll note that I say *had!*—a really early apical pneumonia. In an anthracite driller, too! I thought to myself—here's my first chance for charting and scientific recording. I rang up Llewellyn, asked him to see the case with me, so that I could get it into the ward!"

He took a swift breath, then rushed on: "Well! Down came Llewellyn, limousine and all. Nice as you please, and damned thorough in his examination. He confirmed the diagnosis, and agreed to take the case into hospital there and then. I began to thank him, saying how much I would appreciate having such good facilities." He paused again, his jaw set. "At that Llewellyn gave me a look, Chris, very friendly and nice. 'You needn't bother coming up, Manson,' he said, '*I'll* look after him now. We couldn't have you assistants clattering around the wards'—he took a look at my leggings—'in your hobnail boots—' " Andrew broke off. "What it all boils down to is this—I can go tramping into miners' kitchens, treating my cases in bad conditions, but when it comes to the hospital—ah! I'm only wanted there to give the ether!"

He was interrupted by the ringing of the telephone. Gazing at him with sympathy she rose to answer it. He could hear her speaking in the hall. Then, very hesitatingly she returned. "It's Dr. Llewellyn. I'm—I'm terribly sorry, darling, he wants you tomorrow at eleven for—for an anaesthetic."

He did not answer, but remained with his head bowed.

"What shall I tell him, darling?" she murmured anxiously.

"Tell him to go to hell!" he shouted; then passing his hand across his brow. "No, no. Tell him I'll be there at eleven," he smiled bitterly, "at eleven *sharp*."

When she came back she brought him a cup of hot coffee, and as he drank it he smiled at her wryly.

"I'm so dashed happy here with you, Chris. If only the work would go right. Oh! I admit there's nothing personal or unusual in Llewellyn's keeping me out of the wards. It's the system. But why should a doctor be dragged off his case when it goes into hospital, Chris? It's all wrong!"

But at the end of the week he had an unexpected visitor, late in the evening. At the door was Owen, the secretary to the Society.

Andrew paled. Did the committee want him to resign? Was he to be sacked, a wretched failure? His heart contracted as he gazed at the secretary's diffident face, then suddenly expanded with relief and joy as Owen produced a yellow card.

"I'm sorry to call so late, Dr. Manson, but I didn't have time to look in at the surgery today. I was wondering if you would care to have my medical card. I haven't bothered to fix up before. Last time I visited a doctor it was down in Cardiff. If you'll have me, I'd greatly appreciate to be on your list."

Andrew could scarcely speak. He had handed over so many of these cards that to receive one, and from the secretary himself, was overwhelming. "Thank you, Mr. Owen—I'll—I'll be delighted to have you."

Christine, standing in the hall, was quick to interpose.

"Won't you come in, Mr. Owen. Please?"

Protesting that he was disturbing them, the secretary seemed nevertheless willing to be persuaded into the sitting room. Seated in an armchair, he had an air of extraordinary tranquillity. After some moments he said: "I'm glad to have the opportunity of talking to you, doctor. Don't be downhearted if you're havin' a bit of a setback to begin with, like. They're a little stiff, the folks here, but they'll come!" Before Andrew could intervene he continued: "You haven't heard of Tom Evans, like? No? His arm has turned out very bad. Aye, that stuff you warned them against did exactly what you was afraid of. His elbow's gone all stiff and he can't use it; he's lost his job at the pit. Aye, and since he scalded himself at home, he don't get compensation."

Andrew muttered an expression of regret. He felt no rancour, merely a sense of sadness that this case had gone wrong so needlessly.

Owen fell silent, then in his quiet voice he began to tell them about his own early struggles, of how he had worked underground as a boy of fourteen, attended night school and gradually "improved himself", and finally secured the secretaryship of the Society.

Andrew could see that Owen's life was dedicated to improving the lot of the men, and his work in the Society was an expression of his ideals. But he wanted more than mere medical services. He wanted better housing, better sanitation, better and safer conditions not only for the miners, but for their families.

But, besides talking, he listened. He showed a deep interest in Andrew's view that the anthracite workers were more liable to lung trouble than other underground workers.

Stimulated, Andrew launched into this subject with great ardour. It had struck him how large a percentage of the anthracite miners he had examined suffered from insidious forms of lung disease. He had begun to ask himself if there was not some direct connection between the occupation and the disease.

"You see what I mean?" he exclaimed eagerly. "These men are working in dust all day—their lungs get choked with it. Now I have my suspicions that it's injurious. It may even cause tuberculosis. And what excites me so much is—oh well—it's a line of investigation nobody has covered much. The Home Office does not list any such industrial disease, so when these men are laid up they don't get a penny piece of compensation!"

Owen bent forward, a vivid animation kindling his face. "My goodness, I never heard anything so important for a long time."

They fell into a lively discussion and it was late when the secretary rose to go. He pressed Andrew wholeheartedly to proceed with his investigation, promising him all the help in his power.

As Andrew closed the front door behind Owen he thought, as at the committee meeting when he had been given the appointment, that man is my friend.

THE NEWS THAT the secretary had lodged his card with Andrew spread quickly through the district, and did something to arrest the run of the new doctor's unpopularity. Apart from this material gain, both Christine and he felt better for Owen's visit. So far the social life of the town had completely passed them by. Though Christine never spoke of it there were moments during the day when she felt lonely. Mrs. Llewellyn, who had promised undying affection, and delightful little motor trips to Cardiff, was not heard of again, while the wives of the other doctors had proved singularly uninspiring. There seemed indeed to be no sense of unity or social intercourse amongst the medical assistants or their wives.

One December afternoon, when Andrew was returning to Vale View, he saw approaching a lanky yet erect young man of his own age whom he recognized at once as Richard Vaughan, the managing director of the Aberalaw Company. His first impulse was to cross to the other side to avoid him, and then, doggedly, came the thought: Why should I? I don't care a damn who he is!

With eyes averted he prepared to pass Vaughan when, to his surprise, he was addressed in a friendly, half-humorous tone. "Hello! Aren't you the chap who put Ben Chenkin back to work?"

Andrew stopped, his gaze lifting warily. Though he answered civilly enough he told himself he would not be patronized by a Vaughan. The Vaughans were the virtual owners of the Aberalaw Company—rich, exclusive, unapproachable.

Now, considering Andrew and tugging at his moustache, Richard Vaughan said: "I'd have enjoyed seeing old Ben's face."

"I didn't find it particularly amusing."

Vaughan's lip twitched behind his hand at the stiff Scots pride. He said easily: "You're by way of being our nearest neighbours. My missus—she's been away in Switzerland these last weeks—will be calling on yours, now that you're settled in."

"Thanks!" Andrew said curtly, walking on.

At tea that night he related the incident sardonically to Christine:

"What was his idea? Perhaps he thought he'd mug me into sending a few more men back to work at his dashed mines!"

"Now, don't, Andrew," Christine protested. "You're frightfully suspicious of people."

"Think I would be suspicious of him? Stuck up blighter, rolling in money, old-school tie under his ugly phiz—my missus—been yodelling on the Alps while you pigged it on Mardy Hill—will be calling on yours! Huh! I can *see* her looking near us, darling! And if she does," he was suddenly fierce, "take jolly good care you don't let her patronize you."

Chris answered him more shortly than he had ever heard her in all the tenderness of those first months: "I think I know how to behave."

Mrs. Vaughan did call upon Christine. When Andrew came in the evening after her call he found Christine gay, slightly flushed, with everv appearance of having enjoyed herself.

"I suppose you had out the best china," he mocked.

"No. We had bread and butter," she answered equably. "And the brown teapot."

Something rankled queerly in Andrew after this conversation, an emotion which, had he tried, he could not quite have analysed. Ten days later when Mrs. Vaughan rang to ask them to dinner he was shaken. Christine was in the kitchen at the time baking a cake, and he answered the phone himself.

"I'm sorry," he said. "I'm afraid it's impossible. I have surgery till nearly nine every evening."

"But not on Sunday, surely." Her voice was light, charming. "Come to supper next Sunday. We'll expect you then!"

He stormed into Christine. "These dashed high-blown friends of yours have raked us in to supper. We can't go!"

"Now you listen to me, Andrew Manson!" Her eyes had sparkled at the invitation but nevertheless she lectured him severely. "You've got to stop being silly. We're poor and everybody knows it. But you're a doctor and a good doctor, too, and I'm your wife." Her expression relaxed momentarily. "Are you listening to me? The Vaughans have got a lot of money but that's just a detail beside the fact that they're kind, charming, intelligent people. We're marvellously happy together here, darling, but we must have friends. Forget about money and position and learn to take people for what they really are!"

"Oh, well—" he said grudgingly.

He went on Sunday with apparent docility, merely remarking, as they walked up the well-laid-out drive to the large modern house overlooking the town: "Probably won't let us in, seeing I haven't got on a dinner jacket."

Contrary to his expectation they were well received. Vaughan's bony, ugly face smiled hospitably and Mrs. Vaughan greeted them with effortless simplicity. There were two other guests, a Professor and Mrs. Challis, who were staying for the weekend.

Over the first cocktail he had ever encountered Andrew took stock of the long, fawn-carpeted room with its flowers, books, beautiful old furniture. Christine was talking light-heartedly with Vaughan, his wife and Mrs. Challis, an elderly woman with humorous wrinkles around her eyes. Feeling isolated and conspicuous, Andrew found himself approached by Challis.

"Will some bright young physician kindly undertake an investigation," he smiled at Andrew, "as to the exact function of the olive in the martini? Mind you, I warn you beforehand—I have my suspicions. But what do you think, doctor?"

"Why—" Andrew stammered. "I—I hardly know—"

"My theory!" Challis took pity on him. "A conspiracy of bartenders and inhospitable fellows like our friend Vaughan. An exploitation of the law of Archimedes:" He blinked rapidly under his bushy brows. "By the simple action of displacement they hope to save the gin!"

Andrew could not even smile for thinking of his own awkwardness. He did not know what to do with his empty glass, his cigarette ash, even his own hands! He was glad when they went in to supper.

It was a simple but beautifully presented meal—a cup of hot bouillon stood waiting on each plate and this was followed by a chicken salad, all white breast and heart of lettuce and strange delicate flavours. Andrew was next to Mrs. Vaughan.

"Your wife is charming, Dr. Manson," she remarked quietly as they sat down. She was a tall, slim, elegant woman, with wide intelligent eyes and a distinguished manner.

She began to talk to him about his work. She tried kindly to draw him out, asking how he felt the conditions of practice could be improved.

"Well—I don't know—" clumsily spilling some soup. "I suppose —I'd like to see more scientific methods used." Stiff and tongue-tied, he kept his eyes upon his plate until, to his relief, Mrs. Vaughan slipped into conversation with Challis.

Challis—presently revealed as Professor of Metallurgy at Cardiff, and a member of the exalted Mines Fatigue Board—was a gay and stimulating talker. He talked with his body, his hands, arguing, laughing, meanwhile throwing great quantities of food and drink into himself like a stoker deliriously raising steam.

Andrew, however, listened grudgingly as the conversation turned to the qualities of Bach, and then, by one of Challis's prodigious leaps, to Russian literature. The names of Tolstoy, Chekhov, Turgenev, Pushkin, set his teeth on edge.

Christine, however, was enjoying herself thoroughly. Glaring sideways, Andrew saw her smiling, heard her taking part in the discussion. It amazed him how well she stood up to the professor, how quickly, unselfconsciously she made her points. He began to see his wife in a strange new light. Seems to know all about these Russian bugs, he grated inwardly, funny she never talks to me about them!

Once or twice he caught Christine's eyes offering him a bright interchange of intimacy and several times she diverted the conversation in his direction. "My husband is very interested in the anthracite workers, Professor Challis. He's started an investigation into dust inhalation."

Challis turned an interested glance on Manson.

"Isn't that so, darling?" Christine encouraged. "You were telling me all about it the other night."

"Oh, I don't know," Andrew growled. "Perhaps this TB doesn't come from the dust at all. I haven't enough data yet."

He was furious with himself. Perhaps Challis might have helped him; the fact that he was connected with the Mines Fatigue Board certainly seemed to offer a wonderful opportunity. Involuntarily his anger became directed towards Christine. As they walked home at the end of the evening he was jealously silent.

While they undressed, usually a communicative and informal proceeding, he kept his gaze studiously averted.

When Christine pleaded: "We did have a nice time, didn't we, darling?" he answered with great politeness. "Oh! An excellent time!" In bed he kept well away from her, resisting the slight movement which he felt her make towards him.

Next day the same sense of constraint persisted between them.

While they were having tea there was a ring at the front door. It was the Vaughan chauffeur with a pile of books and a great bunch of pheasant's eye narcissi laid on top of them.

"From Mrs. Vaughan, madam," he said, smiling.

Christine returned to the sitting room with heaped arms and a glowing face. "Look, darling," she cried excitedly. "The whole of Trollope loaned me by Mrs. Vaughan. I've always wanted to read him right through! And such lovely—lovely flowers."

He stood up stiffly, sneering: "Very pretty! Books and flowers from the lady of the manor! You've got to have them, I suppose, to help you endure living with me! I'm too *dull* for you. I'm not one of those flashy talkers that you seemed to like so much last night. I'm just one of these bloody ordinary medical aid assistants!"

"Andrew!" All the colour went from her face. "How can you!"

"It's true, isn't it? You're sick of me already. I'm only fit for slogging round in the slush, turning over dirty blankets, collecting fleas. I'm too much of a lout for your taste now!"

Her eyes were dark and pitiful in her pale face. But she said steadily: "How can you talk like that! It's because you *are* yourself that I love you. And I'll never love anybody else."

"Sounds like it," he snarled and banged out of the room.

For five minutes he skulked in the kitchen, tramping up and down. Then all at once he dashed back to where she stood, forlornly staring into the fire. He took her fiercely in his arms.

"Chris, darling!" he cried, in hot repentance. "Darling, darling! I'm sorry! For heaven's sake forgive me. I didn't mean a word of it. I'm just a jealous fool. I adore you!"

They clung to each other. The scent of narcissi was in the air. "Don't you know," she sobbed, "that I'd just die without you!"

Afterwards, as she sat with her cheek pressed against his, he said sheepishly, reaching for a book: "Who is this Trollope, anyway? Will you teach me, darling? I'm just an ignorant hog!"

THE WINTER PASSED. He had now the added incentive of his work on dust inhalation, which he had begun with a systematic examination of every anthracite worker on his list. After his late surgery Christine helped him to transcribe his notes. Often they had long talks, and he began to discern in her a fineness of instinct which made her judgment of literature, music, and especially of people, uncannily correct.

As the days lengthened she began on the wilderness that was the garden. Jenny, the maid, had a great-uncle, an elderly, disabled miner, who for tenpence an hour became Christine's assistant. Manson, crossing the dilapidated bridge one March afternoon, found them starting an assault on the rusty salmon tins that lay on the stream bed there.

"Hey, you below," he shouted from the bridge. "What are you doing? Spoiling the fishing?"

She answered his gibes with a brisk nod: "You wait and see."

In a few weeks she had grubbed out the weeds and cleared the neglected paths. The bed of the stream was clean, its edges trimmed, and a new rockery stood at the foot of the glen. Vaughan's gardener brought over bulbs and cuttings, offering advice. With real triumph Christine led Andrew to view the first daffodil.

Then, on the last Sunday in March, without warning, Denny visited them. They fell upon him, delighted to see him again. When they had shown him round, fed him, and thrust him into their softest chair they eagerly demanded news.

"Page died a month ago," Philip announced. "Another stroke. And a good thing too!" He drew on his pipe, the familiar cynicism puckering his eyes. "Blodwen Page and your friend Rees seem all set for matrimony."

"So that's it," Andrew said without bitterness. "Poor Edward!"

There was a pause while they thought of Edward Page, and all his drudging years amidst the slag heaps of Drineffy.

"And how about you, Philip?" Andrew asked at last.

"Oh, I don't know! I'm getting restless." Denny smiled drily. "Drineffy hasn't seemed quite the same since you people cleared out. I think I'll take a trip abroad somewhere. Ship's surgeon, maybe—if some cheap cargo boat will have me."

Andrew was silent, distressed by the thought of this talented man deliberately wasting his life.

AS THE DAYS passed after Philip's visit Andrew became gradually aware of a gap existing in his work. In Drineffy with Philip near him he had always been aware of a shared purpose. But in Aberalaw he felt no such purpose amongst his fellow doctors.

Then, one day early in April, Andrew discovered a cavity in a back tooth and went, in consequence, in search of the Society's dentist. He had not yet met Con Boland. When he reached the little surgery, he found a notice pinned upon the closed door: *Gone to Extraction. If Urgent apply at House.*

Andrew decided that since he was here, he might at least call to make an appointment so, having inquired the way, he set out for the dentist's house.

This was a small semi-detached villa on the outskirts of the town. As Andrew walked up the untidy front path he heard a loud noise and peering into a dilapidated wooden shed at the side of the house he saw a red-haired, rangy man in his shirtsleeves, violently hammering at something. The man caught sight of him. "Hello!" he said. "What are ye after?"

"I want to make a dental appointment. I'm Dr. Manson."

"Come in," said the man, hospitably. He was Boland.

The shed was littered with portions of an incredibly old motor-car. In the middle stood the chassis, supported on wooden egg boxes, and presenting the evidence of having been sawn in half. Andrew glanced from this extraordinary spectacle to Boland.

"Is this the extraction?"

"It is," Con Boland agreed in his thick Irish brogue. "When I'm slack in the surgery I just put a little bit in on my car. I've had her five year, this little car of mine, and, mind ye, she was three year old when I got her. Ye mightn't believe it seeing her *sthripped* but she goes like a hare," he said with unmistakable pride. "But she's small by the size of my family now. So I'm in the process of extendin' her by a good two feet of insertion. Wait till ye see her finished, Manson!" He reached for his jacket. "Come away now, to the surgery, and I'll fix your tooth."

At the surgery, which was almost as untidy as the garage, Con filled the tooth, talking so much and so violently that his bushy red moustache was always dewed with beads of moisture. He was a careless, impetuous, good-natured, generous fellow, and Andrew was utterly captivated by him. He was mad on "mechanics" and he idolized his motorcar. The fact that Con should possess one at all was in itself a joke, as he had not a penny to his name.

The filling complete, Con demanded that Andrew should return to the house with him to tea. "Come on, now," he insisted hospitably. "You've got to meet the family."

Con's family was, in fact, in the process of having tea when they arrived. In the warm, disordered room Mrs. Boland sat at the head of the table with a baby at her breast. Next came Mary, fifteen, quiet, shy—"the only dark-haired one and her dad's favourite," was Con's introduction—who was already earning a decent wage as a clerk. Sitting beside Mary was Terence, twelve, then three other younger children sprawling about, crying out to be taken notice of by their father.

There existed about this family a careless gaiety which entranced Andrew. The room itself spoke with a gorgeous brogue. Above the fireplace, beneath a coloured picture of the Pope, the baby's napkins were drying. The canary's cage stood on the dresser beside Mrs. Boland's rolled-up stays—previously removed in the cause of comfort—and a split bag of puppy biscuits. Six bottles of stout were upon the chest of drawers, also Terence's flute.

Andrew was fascinated by Mrs. Boland. Pale, dreamy, unperturbed she sat silently imbibing endless cups of tea while the children squabbled about her. She possessed a kind of abstracted placidity, as though years of din, dirt, drabness—and Con's ebullience—had in the end exalted her to a plane of heavenly lunacy where she was isolated and immune.

He almost upset his cup when she addressed him, gazing over the top of his head, her voice meek, apologetic, "I meant to call on Mrs. Manson, doctor. But I was so busy—"

"In the name of God!" Con rolled with laughter. "Busy, indeed! She hadn't a new dress—that's what she means. I had the money laid by—but damn it all, Terence or one of them had to have new boots. Never mind, mother, wait till I get the car lengthened and we'll whirl ye up in style."

Andrew raced home to Christine after the meal, eager to tell her about his new friends.

Chapter 3

The following Saturday afternoon Llewellyn asked if he would give an anaesthetic at the hospital. Resentfully, he agreed. As he watched Llewellyn go through with the operation, a long and complicated abdominal case, he could not repress a feeling of admiration, despite himself. Llewellyn was amazingly clever, not only clever but versatile. From public health administration to the latest radiological technique, the whole range of his duties found Llewellyn expert and prepared.

On Sunday morning, usually devoted to long and peaceful repose, Andrew suddenly blurted out, "Why don't I like Llewellyn, Chris? At least, why do I like him one minute and hate him the next? Tell me honestly, Chris. Am I jealous? What is it?"

Her answer staggered him. "Yes, I think you are jealous! And why shouldn't you be? I don't want to be married to a saint. There's enough cleaning in this house already without you setting up a halo."

"Go on," he growled. "Give me all my faults when you're about it." A pause during which he waited for her to continue the argument. Then, irritably, "Why should I be jealous of Llewellyn?"

"Because he's frightfully good at his work, knows so much, and well—chiefly because he has first-class qualifications."

"While I have a scrubby little MB from a Scots University!" Furious, he flung out of bed and began to walk about the room in his pyjamas. "What do qualifications matter anyway? It's method, clinical ability that counts. I believe in what I hear through the end of my stethoscope, and, in case you don't know it, I hear plenty. I'm beginning to find out real things in my anthracite investigation. Damn it all! It's a fine state of affairs when a man wakes up on Sunday morning and his wife tells him he knows *nothing!*"

Sitting up in bed, she took her manicure set and began to do her nails. "I didn't say exactly that, Andrew." Her reasonableness aggravated him the more. "It's just—darling, you're not going to be an assistant *all* your life. You want people to pay attention to your work, your ideas—oh, you understand what I mean. If you had a really fine degree—an MD or—or the MRCP, it would stand you in good stead."

"The MRCP!" he echoed blankly. "Don't you understand they only give that to the crowned heads of Europe!"

He banged the door and went into the bathroom to shave. Five minutes later he was back again, one half of his chin shaved, the other lathered. He was penitent, excited. "Do you think I could do it, Chris? You're absolutely right. We need a few pips on the old name plate so we can hold our end up! But the MRCP—it's the most difficult medical exam. It's—it's *murder!*"

Breaking off, he dashed downstairs for the Medical Directory. When he returned with it his face had fallen to acute dejection.

"Sunk!" he muttered dismally. "I *told* you it was an impossible exam. There's a compulsory preliminary paper in four languages.

Latin, French, Greek, German. All the Latin I know is dog lingo—*mist. alba mitte decem.* As for the others. . . ."

She did not answer. He stood at the window gloomily considering the empty view. At last he turned, frowning, worrying. "Why shouldn't I—*damn* it all, Chris—why shouldn't I learn these languages *for* the exam?"

She jumped out of bed and hugged him. "Oh, I did want you to say that, my dear. That's the real *you.* I could—I could help you perhaps. Don't forget your old woman's a retired schoolmarm!"

They made plans excitedly all day. They cleared the sitting room for action. All that evening he went to school with her. The next evening, and the next . . . .

Sometimes Andrew felt the sublime bathos of it. Sitting over the table with his wife, in this remote Welsh mining town, muttering after her *Madame, est-il possible que?*, wading through declensions, irregular verbs, reading aloud from Tacitus, he would jerk back suddenly in his chair, morbidly conscious—"If Llewellyn could see us here—wouldn't he grin! And to think that this is only the beginning, that I've got all the medical stuff after!"

Towards the end of the following month, parcels of books began to arrive from the International Medical Library. Andrew began to read where, at college, he had left off. He discovered, quickly, how early he had left off.

"Chris! I know nothing. And this stuff is killing me!"

He had to contend with the work of his practice; he had only the long nights in which to study. Sustained by black coffee, he battled on, reading into the early hours of the morning. When he fell into bed, exhausted, often he could not sleep.

He smoked to excess, lost weight. But Chris was always there, letting him talk, draw diagrams, explain, in tongue-twisting nomenclature, the astounding selective action of the kidney tubules. She also permitted him to shout, gesticulate and, as his nerves grew more ragged, to hurl abuse at her.

She was a better soldier than he. She had a quality of balance which steadied them through every crisis. She made sacrifices, refused all invitations. No matter how badly she had slept she was always up early, neatly dressed, ready with his breakfast when he came dragging down, unshaven, the first cigarette of the day already between his lips.

Suddenly, when he had been working six months, her only

relation, an aunt in Bridlington, took ill with phlebitis and wrote asking her to come North. She declared immediately that it was impossible for her to leave him, but he, hunched sulkily over his bacon and egg, growled out: "I wish you'd go, Chris! Studying this way, I'd get on better without you. We've been getting on each other's nerves lately. Sorry—but—it seems the best thing to do."

She went, unwillingly, at the end of the week. Before she had been gone twenty-four hours he found out his mistake. It was agony without her. He found himself gazing dully at his books, losing hours, while he thought of her.

At the end of a fortnight she wired that she was returning. He dropped everything and prepared for the celebration of their reunion. He sped to the town on a mission of extravagance. He bought first a bunch of roses. In the fishmonger's he found a lobster, fresh in that morning, which he seized quickly, lest Mrs. Vaughan—for whom all such delicacies were intended—should ring up and forestall him. Then he bought ice in quantity, salad stuff and finally, with trepidation, a bottle of moselle.

After tea he told Jenny, the maid, she might go, then set to work and lovingly composed a lobster salad. The zinc pail from the scullery made an excellent ice bucket.

At last his preparations were complete. After surgery, at half past nine, he raced to meet her train at the station.

It was like falling in love all over again, fresh, wonderful. Tenderly, he escorted her to the love feast. The evening was hot and still; the moon shone. He told her they might be in Provence, or some place like that, in a great castle by a lake. He told her he had been a brute to her but that for the rest of his life he would be a carpet—not red, since she objected to that colour—on which she might tread. He told her much more than that.

AUGUST ARRIVED, dusty and scorching. With the finish of his reading in sight he was confronted with the need to brush up his practical work, an apparently insuperable difficulty without the use of a laboratory. It was Christine who thought of Professor Challis and his position at Cardiff University. When Andrew wrote to him, Challis immediately replied, stating that he would use his influence with Doctor Glyn-Jones of the Department of Pathology.

"I've got to hand it to you, Chris! It does mean something to have friends. But all the same, I hate asking favours."

There were, in the slackness of summer, three hours each afternoon which Andrew regarded as his own. So, later that month a second-hand motorcycle—a low, red, wickedly unprofessional machine—made its appearance at Vale View. Immediately after lunch every day, a red streak would roar down the valley towards Cardiff, thirty miles away. And every day at five o'clock a slightly dustier red streak, would move back towards Vale View.

These sixty miles in the heat with an hour's work at Glyn-Jones's specimens and slides made heavy going of the next few weeks, but the final journey was made at last. Glyn-Jones had nothing more to show him. He knew every slide and every single specimen by heart. All that remained was to enter his name and send up the heavy entrance fees for the examination.

On October 15 Andrew set out for London. Now that the actual event was at hand a queer calmness had settled upon him. His brain was inactive, almost dull. He felt that he knew nothing.

Yet, on the following day, when he began the written part of the examination he found he wrote and wrote, never looking at the clock, filling sheet after sheet. Between his papers he lived in a kind of daze; occasionally, to clear his head, he took a ride on the top of a bus.

After the written papers, the practical and oral part of the examinations began and Andrew found himself dreading this more than anything which had gone before. There were perhaps twenty other candidates, all of them with an unmistakable air of assurance and position.

His practical at the South London Hospital went, he thought, well enough. His case was one of bronchiectasis in a young boy of fourteen, which, since he knew lungs so intimately, was a piece of good fortune. But when it came to the oral examination his luck seemed to change completely. This procedure at the college had its peculiarities. On two successive days each candidate was questioned, in turn, by two separate examiners. If at the end of the first day the candidate was found inadequate he was handed a polite note telling him he need not return.

Andrew's first examiner, Dr. Maurice Gadsby, was a spare, undersized man with a ragged black moustache and small, mean eyes. Recently elected to his fellowship, he had none of the tolerance of the older examiners, but seemed to set out deliberately to fail the candidates who came before him. He considered Andrew with a supercilious lift of his brows and placed before him six slides. Five of these slides Andrew named correctly but the sixth he could not identify. For five minutes Gadsby harassed Andrew on this section—which, it transpired, was the ovum of an obscure West African parasite—then passed him on to the next examiner, Sir Robert Abbey.

Andrew crossed the room with a heavily beating heart. He was desperate to succeed, but he was convinced that Gadsby would fail him. He raised his eyes to find Robert Abbey contemplating him with a friendly smile.

"What's the matter?" said Abbey unexpectedly.

"Nothing, sir," Andrew stammered. "I think I've done rather badly with Dr. Gadsby—that's all."

"Never mind about that. Have a look at these specimens. Then just say anything you think about them." Abbey smiled encouragingly. He was perhaps the third most distinguished physician in Europe, a ruddy-complexioned man of about sixty-five with a high forehead, and a long, humorous upper lip. As he gazed at Andrew, observing his ill-cut suit, the soft collar and shirt, and above all, the look of strained intensity upon his serious face, the days of his own provincial youth came back to him. Instinctively his heart went out to this unusual candidate and his eye, ranging down the list before him, noted with satisfaction that his markings were above pass level.

Meanwhile Andrew, his eyes fixed upon the glass jars before him, had been stumbling unhappily through his commentary.

"Good," Abbey said suddenly. He took up a specimen—it was an aneurism of the ascending aorta—and began in a friendly manner to question Andrew. His questions became more searching until finally he asked: "Do you know the history of aneurism?"

"Ambrose Paré"—Andrew answered, and Abbey had already begun his approving nod—"is presumed to have discovered the condition."

Abbey's face expressed surprise. "Why presumed, Dr. Manson? Paré did discover aneurism."

Andrew plunged on: "Well, sir, that's what the textbooks say." A quick breath. "But I happened to be reading Celsus, brushing up my Latin, when I came across the word *aneurismus*. Celsus described aneurism in full. And that was thirteen centuries before Paré!"

There was silence. Andrew raised his eyes, to see Abbey looking at him with a queer expression on his ruddy face. "Dr. Manson," he said at length, "you are the first candidate who has ever told me something original, something true, and something which I did not know. I congratulate you."

Andrew turned scarlet. "Just tell me one thing more—as a matter of personal curiosity," Abbey went on, "what do you regard as the main principle which you keep before you when you are exercising the practice of your profession?"

There was a pause while Andrew reflected desperately. At length he blurted out: "I suppose—I suppose I keep telling myself never to take anything for granted."

"Thank you, Dr. Manson."

As Andrew left the room, Abbey reached for his pen. He thought: "If he'd told me he went about trying to heal people, trying to help suffering humanity, I'd have failed him out of sheer damned disappointment." As it was, Abbey traced the unheard-of maximum, 100, opposite the name of Andrew Manson.

A few minutes later Andrew went downstairs with the other candidates. At the foot of the stairs a liveried porter stood with a little pile of envelopes before him. As the candidates went past he handed one to each of them. Andrew could barely read. Dazedly he heard someone congratulate him. His chances were still alive. He walked down to the ABC café and treated himself to a malted milk. He thought tensely, if I don't get through now, after all this, I'll—I'll walk in front of a bus.

The next day passed grindingly. Andrew had no idea whether he was doing well or badly: he knew only that his head ached abominably, that his feet were icy, his inside void.

At last it was over. At four o'clock in the afternoon he came out of the cloakroom, spent and melancholy, pulling on his coat. Then he became aware of Sir Robert Abbey standing before the big open fire in the entrance hall. He was holding out his hand, smiling, telling him—telling him that he was through.

Dear God, he had done it! He had *done* it! He was alive again, his headache gone, all his weariness forgotten. As he dashed to the nearest post office his heart sang wildly, madly. It hadn't been for nothing after all: those long nights, those mad dashes down to Cardiff, those racking hours of study. On he sped through the crowds, missing the wheels of taxis and buses, his eyes shining, racing to wire news to Christine.

IT WAS NEARLY midnight when the train got in. All the way up the valley the engine had been battling against a high head wind and at Aberalaw, as Andrew stepped out on the platform, the force of the hurricane almost bowled him off his feet. The station was deserted. Andrew started along Station Road, his body braced against the wind. Full of his success, his ears ringing with Sir Robert Abbey's words, he could not reach Christine fast enough to tell her everything. His telegram would have given her the good news; but now he wished to pour out in detail the full exciting story.

As he swung, head down, into Talgarth Street he was conscious, suddenly, of a man running, the noisy clatter of his boots upon the pavement so lost in the gale that he seemed a phantom figure. Instinctively Andrew stopped. As the man drew near he recognized him, Frank Davis, an ambulance man from Anthracite Sinking No. 3. At the same moment Davis saw him.

"I was comin' for you, doctor. This wind's knocked the telephone lines all to smash." A gust tore the rest of his words away.

"What's wrong?" shouted Andrew.

"There's been a fall down at Number Three." Davis cupped his hands close to Manson's ear. "A lad got buried there. Sam Bevan, he's on your list. Better look sharp, doctor, and get to him."

"I've got to have my bag," he bawled to Davis. "You go up to my house and fetch it for me. I'll go on to Number Three." He added, "And Frank!—tell my missus where I've gone."

He was at No. 3 Sinking in four minutes, blown there on the following wind. In the rescue room he found the under-manager and three men waiting on him. At the sight of him the under-manager's worried expression lifted slightly.

"Glad to see you, doctor. We've had a nasty fall. Nobody killed, thank God, but one of the lads pinned by his arm. We can't shift him an inch. And the roof's rotten."

They went to the winding shaft, two of the men carrying a stretcher with splints strapped to it and the third, a wooden box of first-aid materials. As they entered the cage, Davis came bundling across the yard with the bag.

"You've been quick, Frank," Manson said as Davis squatted beside him in the cage, panting.

Davis simply nodded; he could not speak. There was a clang, an instant's suspense, and the cage rocketed to the bottom.

Andrew had been underground before, he was used to the high-vaulted caverns of the Drineffy mines. But this sinking was an old one with a low-roofed, tortuous haulage way leading to the workings. They crawled, often on their hands and knees, for nearly half a mile along the dripping, clammy passage. Suddenly the light borne by the under-manager stopped, just ahead of Andrew.

Slowly, he crept forward. Three men, cramped together on their bellies in a dead end, were doing their best to revive another man whose body slewed sideways, one shoulder pointing backwards, lost seemingly in the mass of fallen rock.

"Well, then, lads?" asked the under-manager in a low voice.

"We can't shift him, nohow." The man who spoke turned a sweat-grimed face. "We tried everything."

"Don't try," said the under-manager, with a quick look at the roof. "Here's the doctor. Get back a bit, lads, and give us room."

Sam Bevan was quite conscious, but his features were haggard beneath a powdering of dust. Weakly, he smiled at Manson. "Looks like you're goin' to 'ave some amb'lance practice on me proper!" Bevan had been a member of a first-aid class and had often been requisitioned for bandage practice.

By the light of the under-manager's lamp Andrew ran his hands over the injured man. His body was free except his left forearm, which lay under an enormous weight of rock. Andrew saw instantly that the only way to free Bevan was to amputate the forearm. And Bevan, straining his pain-tormented eyes, read that decision immediately. "Go on, then, doctor," he muttered. "Only get me out of here quick."

"Don't worry, Sam," Andrew said. "I'm going to send you to sleep now. When you wake up, you'll be in bed."

Stretched flat in a puddle of muck under the two-foot roof he slipped off his coat, folded it, and put it under Bevan's head. He rolled up his sleeves and asked for his bag. As the under-manager handed it forward he whispered: "For God's sake hurry, doctor. We'll have this roof down on us before we know where we are."

Andrew opened the bag. Immediately he smelt the reek of chloroform. Frank Davis in his haste to reach the mine, must have dropped the bag, and the chloroform bottle was broken. A shiver passed over Andrew. This meant he had no anaesthetic.

For perhaps thirty seconds he remained paralysed. Then automatically he felt for his hypodermic, gave Bevan a maximum of morphine. He bent over the man, and tightened the tourniquet which was already on his arm. "Shut your eyes, Sam!" he said.

The light was dim and the shadows moved with flickering confusion. At the first incision Bevan groaned between his shut teeth. Then, mercifully, he fainted. A cold perspiration broke on Andrew's brow as he worked. He could not see what he was doing. He felt suffocated here in this rat-hole, lying in the mud. He wasn't a surgeon. He would never get through the arm. The roof would crash upon them all. A slow drip of water falling cold upon his neck. His fingers, working feverishly, stained and warm. The grating of the saw. Oh, God! would he never get through!

At last. He almost sobbed with relief. He slipped a pad of gauze on the bloodied stump. Stumbling to his knees he said: "Take him out."

Fifty yards back, in a clearing in the haulage way, with space to stand up and four lamps round him he finished the job. He tidied up, ligatured, drenched the wound with antiseptic. Bevan remained unconscious, but his pulse was steady. Andrew drew his hand across his forehead.

"Go steady with the stretcher. Wrap these blankets round him. We'll want hot bottles when we get out."

The slow procession, bent double in the low places, began to move. They had not gone sixty paces when a low rumbling subsidence echoed in the darkness down behind them. The under-manager said to Andrew with quiet grimness: "That's the rest of the roof."

The journey back to the shaft bottom took close upon an hour. Up, up they shot, out of the depths. The keen bite of the wind met them as they stepped out of the cage. With a kind of ecstasy, Andrew drew a long breath.

It was still dark, but in the mine yard they had hung a big naphtha flare which hissed and leaped, illuminating a small crowd of waiting figures. Suddenly, Andrew heard his name called wildly and the next instant Christine's arms were about his neck. Sobbing hysterically she clung to him in the darkness, bare-headed, with only a coat over her nightdress. She was a waif-like figure.

"What's wrong?" he asked, startled, trying to disengage her arms so that he might see her face.

But frantically clinging to him, she said brokenly: "They told us the roof was down—that you wouldn't—wouldn't come out."

Her skin was blue, her teeth chattering with cold. He carried her into the warmth of the rescue room, ashamed, yet deeply touched. They drank hot cocoa from the same scalding cup. It was a long time before either of them remembered about his grand, new degree.

Chapter 4

The rescue of Sam Bevan was commonplace to a town which had known, in the past, the agony and horror of major mine disasters. Yet in his own district it did Andrew a vast amount of good. He began to receive nods and even smiles from people who had never seemed to look at him before; he found the off-shift men ready for a word with him, the women ready to "call him in", as he went by. Cards began to come back to Andrew, gradually at first and then, when it was seen that he did not abuse his returned renegades, with a rush.

Llewellyn had affected great delight at the result of the examination. He congratulated Andrew effusively then blandly raked him in for double duty at the theatre. "By the way," he remarked, beaming, at the end of the long session, "uid you tell the examiners you were an assistant in a medical-aid scheme?"

"I mentioned your name to them, Dr. Llewellyn," Andrew answered sweetly. "And that made it quite all right."

Dr. Urquhart, at least, was genuinely glad of Andrew's success, though his comment took the form of vituperative explosion. "Dammit to hell, Manson! What d'you think you're doin'? Trying to put my eye out!"

Denny, now abroad, knew nothing of the new degree. But a final and somewhat unexpected congratulation came in a long letter from Freddie Hamson. Freddie had seen the results in the *Lancet,* chided Andrew on his success, and then detailed his own exciting triumphs in Queen Anne Street where, as he had predicted that night at Cardiff, his neat brass plate now shone.

"It's a shame the way we've lost touch with Freddie," Manson declared. "I must write to him oftener. Nice letter, isn't it?"

"Yes, very nice," Christine answered drily.

With the approach of Christmas the weather turned colder—crisp, frosty days and still, starry nights. The iron-hard roads rang under Andrew's feet. Already shaping in his mind was the next step in his great assault on the problem of dust inhalation. He had obtained permission to make a systematic examination of all the anthracite workers—a marvellous opportunity. He planned to use the pit workers and surfacemen as controls.

On Christmas Eve, he returned from the surgery to Vale View with an extraordinary sense of spiritual anticipation and physical well-being. The miners made much of Christmas here. For the past week the front room in each house had been locked against the children, festooned with paper streamers, toys hidden away and a steady accumulation of good things to eat, all bought with the club money paid out at this time of year.

Tonight as he came into the house he saw at once an extra excitement upon Christine's face.

"Don't say a word," she said quickly, holding out her hand. "Not a single word! Just shut your eyes and come with me!"

He allowed her to lead him into the kitchen. There, on the table lay a number of parcels, some merely wrapped in newspaper, but each with a little note attached. In a flash he realized that they were presents from his patients.

"Look, Andrew!" Christine cried. "A goose! And two ducks! And a lovely iced cake! And a bottle of elderberry wine! Isn't it wonderful they should want to give them to you?"

He simply could not speak. It overwhelmed him, this kindly evidence that the people of his district had at last begun to appreciate, to like him. He read the notes, the handwriting laboured and illiterate. "Your grateful patient at 3 Cefan Row." "With thanks from Mrs. Williams." One gem from Sam Bevan, "Thanks for gettin' me out for Christmas, doctor"—so they went on.

When Andrew had recovered his normal loquacity—a glass of home-made elderberry assisted him—he paced up and down the kitchen while Christine stuffed the goose. He raved: "That's how fees should be paid, Chris. No money, no damned bills, but payment in kind. You get your patient right, he sends you something that he has made, produced. Coal if you like, a sack of potatoes from his garden, eggs maybe, if he keeps hens—see my point? If every doctor was to eliminate the question of *gain* the whole system would be purer."

"Yes, dear. Would you mind handing me the currants? Top shelf in the cupboard!"

Christmas Day was fine and clear. Tallyn Beacons in the blue distance were pearly, with a white icing of snow. After morning surgery, Andrew went on his round, a short one. He did not tire of the Christmas greetings he gave and received all along the Rows. He could not help contrasting this present cheerfulness with his bleak passage up those same streets only a year ago.

Perhaps it was this thought which made him draw up, hesitantly, outside No. 18 Cefan Row. Of all his former patients, apart from Chenkin, whom he did not want, the only one who had not come back to him was Tom Evans, whose scalded arm he had been called in to treat all those months ago. Today he had a sudden impulse to wish Evans a merry Christmas.

Knocking once, he opened the front door and walked through to the kitchen. Here he paused, taken aback. The kitchen was very bare, and in the grate there burned only a spark of fire. Seated on a broken-backed wooden chair, with his crooked arm bent out like a wing, was Tom Evans. The droop of his shoulders was dispirited, hopeless. On his knee sat his little girl, four years of age. They were silently gazing, both of them, at a branch of fir planted in an old bucket. Upon this diminutive Christmas tree were three tiny tallow candles, as yet unlighted. And beneath it lay the family's Christmas treat—three small oranges.

Suddenly Evans turned and caught sight of Andrew. He started, and a slow flush of shame and resentment spread over his face. Andrew sensed that it was agony for him to be found out of work, crippled, by the doctor whose advice he had rejected. At that moment Mrs. Evans came into the kitchen with a paper bag under her arm. She was so startled at the sight of Andrew that she dropped her paper bag, which fell to the stone floor and burst open revealing two meagre beef faggots. The child, glancing at her mother's face, began suddenly to cry.

"What's the matter, sir?" Mrs. Evans ventured at last, her hand pressed against her side. "He hasn't done anything?"

Andrew gritted his teeth together. He was so moved by this scene that only one course would satisfy him. "Mrs. Evans!" He kept his eyes down. "I know there was a bit of a misunderstanding between your Tom and me. But it's Christmas—and—oh! I'd be awfully pleased if the three of you would come round and help us eat our Christmas dinner."

"But, doctor—" she wavered.

"You be quiet, lass," Evans interrupted her fiercely. "We're not goin' out to no dinner. If faggots is all we *can* have it's all we *will* have. We don't want any bloody charity from nobody."

"What are you talking about!" Andrew exclaimed in dismay. "I'm asking you as a friend." He turned towards Mrs. Evans, distressed yet determined. "You persuade him, Mrs. Evans. I'll be really upset now if you don't come. Half past one. We'll expect you." Before any of them could say another word he swung round and left the house.

Christine made no comment when he blurted out what he had done. Andrew watched her lay the extra places. "You're cross, Chris?" he said at last.

"I thought I married Dr. Manson," she answered. "Not Dr. Barnardo. Really, darling, you're an incorrigible sentimentalist!"

The Evans arrived exactly upon time, washed and brushed, desperately ill at ease. Andrew, striving nervously to generate hospitality, had a dreadful premonition that the entertainment would be a dismal failure. Evans proved to be clumsy at the table because of his bad arm; his wife was obliged to butter his roll for him. And then by good fortune, the top fell off the pepper pot as Andrew was using it and the entire contents shot into his soup. There was a hollow silence, then the little girl gave a sudden delighted giggle. The mother bent to rebuke her, when the sight of Andrew's face restrained her. The next minute they were all laughing.

Free of his dread of being patronized, Evans revealed himself as a staunch rugby football supporter and a great music lover. He discussed with Christine the oratorios of Elgar, while the child pulled crackers with Andrew.

Later, Christine drew Mrs. Evans and the little girl into the other room. Left alone, a strange silence fell between Andrew and Evans. Finally with a kind of desperation, Andrew said: "I'm sorry about that arm of yours, Tom. Don't think I'm trying to crow over you or anything like that. I'm just damned sorry."

"You're not any sorrier than I am." Evans said.

There was a pause, then Andrew resumed: "I wonder if you'd let me speak to Mr. Vaughan about you. Shut me up if you think I'm interfering—but I've got a little bit of influence with him and I feel sure I could get you a job on the surface—timekeeper—or something—"

He broke off, not daring to look at Evans. At length Andrew raised his eyes only to lower them again immediately. Tears were running down Evans's cheeks, his entire body shaking. He laid his good arm on the table, buried his head in it.

Andrew crossed to the window where he remained for a few minutes. By the end of that time Evans had collected himself, and at half past three the family departed in a mood contrasting cheerfully with the constraint of their arrival.

"You know, Chris," Andrew philosophized, "all that poor fellow's trouble—his stiff elbow, I mean—isn't *his* fault. He distrusted me because I was new. He couldn't be expected to know about that carron oil."

"Darling!" protested Christine, smiling at him from the sofa. "I've put up with your philanthropy all day. Come and sit by me here. I had a really important reason for wanting us to be alone."

"Yes?" Doubtfully; then, indignantly. "You're not complaining, I hope. After all—Christmas Day—"

She laughed silently. "Oh, my dear, you're just too lovely. Another minute there'll be a snowstorm and you'll take out the St. Bernards to bring in somebody off the mountain. Sit here." She stretched out her arm. "I want to tell you something."

He went over to seat himself beside her when suddenly there came a loud braying of a Klaxon from outside.

"Damn!" said Christine concisely. It had to be Con Boland.

"Don't you want them?" Andrew asked in some surprise. "Con half said they'd be round for tea."

"Oh, well!" Christine said, accompanying him to the door.

The Bolands sat, opposite the front gate, in the reconstructed motorcar. Con was upright at the wheel in a bowler hat and enormous gauntlets with Mary and Terence beside him, the three other children packed around Mrs. Boland in the rear, like herrings in a tin.

"How are you, Manson, my boy? How d'you like the old car now? I've lengthened her a good two feet. Isn't she grand? Mind you, there's still a little bother with the gearbox."

"Come in, Con," Christine smiled. "I like your gloves!"

"Christmas present from the wife," Con answered, admiring the flapping gauntlets. "Ah! what's gone wrong with this door?"

Unable to open it he threw his long legs over, helped the children and his wife from the back, surveyed the car—fondly removing a lump of mud from the windscreen—then followed the others to Vale View.

They had a cheerful tea party. Con was in high spirits. Mrs. Boland abstractedly drank six cups of strong tea. The children emptied every plate on the table.

After tea, Andrew played with the baby on the hearthrug. It was the fattest baby he had ever seen, a Rubens infant, who tried repeatedly to poke a finger into his eye. Every time it failed a look of solemn wonder came upon its face. Christine sat with her hands in her lap, watching him playing with the baby.

But Con and his family could not stay long. Con had doubts concerning the functioning of his lamps.

When they rose to go, he delivered the invitation: "Come out and see us start."

Andrew and Christine stood at the gate while Con packed the car with his offspring. After a couple of swings the engine obeyed and Con, with a triumphant nod towards them, pulled on his gauntlets and adjusted his bowler to a more rakish tilt. Then he heaved himself proudly into the driving seat.

At that moment the car's elongated middle collapsed slowly to the ground with a groan, like some beast of burden perishing from sheer exhaustion. The stupefaction on Con's face was irresistible.

Andrew and Christine gave out a shriek of laughter. Once they began they could not stop. They laughed till they were weak.

"In the name of God," Con said, picking himself up. Observing that no one was hurt, he considered the wreckage, pondering dazedly. Then his face brightened. He took the helpless Andrew by the arm and pointed proudly to the crumpled bonnet, beneath which the engine still feebly emitted a few convulsive beats. "See that, Manson! She's still runnin'."

Somehow they dragged the remains into the backyard of Vale View. In due course the Boland family went home on foot.

"What a day!" Andrew exclaimed when they had secured peace for themselves at last. Then, turning to Christine, he asked: "You did enjoy your Christmas?"

She replied oddly: "I enjoyed seeing you play with baby Boland."

He glanced at her. "Why?"

She did not look at him. "Oh, can't you guess, darling?—I don't think you're such a smart physician after all."

SPRING ONCE MORE. And early summer. The garden at Vale View was a patch of tender colours. Chiefly these colours came from flowering shrubs planted the previous autumn, for now Andrew would allow Christine to do no manual work at all.

Her favourite seat was at the end of the little glen where she could hear the soothing converse of the stream. An overhanging willow offered a screen from the rows of houses above. Beneath the willow, Andrew defined his policy.

"You see, Chris, we've got to keep calm. After all you're a doctor's wife and I'm—I'm a doctor. I've seen this happen hundreds, at least scores of times before. It's a very *ordinary affair*. Now don't misunderstand me, darling, it's *wonderful* for us, of course. But we're not going to get sentimental. No, no! It would be rather idiotic, wouldn't it, for me, a doctor, to start—oh, say—to start mooning over those little things you're knitting or crocheting, or whatever it is. And all this junk about what colour of eyes she—er—it, will have and what sort of rosy future we'll give her—that's right off the map!" He paused, frowning, then gradually a reflective smile broke over his face. "I say, though, Chris! I wonder if it *will* be a girl!"

She laughed till the tears ran down her cheeks. She laughed so hard that he sat up, concerned.

"Now stop it, Chris! You'll—you might bring on something."

Early one May morning as they lay in bed he became aware, through his light sleep, of a gentle thrusting, the first movement of the child within Christine. He held himself rigid, suffocated by a rush of feeling, of ecstasy. Oh, hell! he thought a moment later, perhaps I'm just a sentimentalist after all. I suppose that's why they make the rule a medico can't attend his own wife.

The following week he felt it time to speak to Llewellyn whom they had decided should undertake the case. Llewellyn was pleased and flattered. He came down at once, made a preliminary examination, then chatted to Andrew in the sitting room.

"I'm glad to help you, Manson," accepting a cigarette. "Believe me, I'll do my best. By the way, it's pretty stifling in Aberalaw at present. Don't you think your little missus ought to have a change of air while she can?"

Christine did not wish to go away but Andrew was gently insistent. "I know you don't want to leave me, Chris, but it's for the best. We've got to think of—oh! everything. Would you rather have the seaside or maybe you'd like to go up to your aunt? Dash it all, I can afford to send you, Chris. We're pretty well off now!"

They had paid off the Glen Endowment and the last of the furniture instalments and now they had nearly two hundred pounds saved in the bank. But she was not thinking of this when, pressing his hand, she answered steadily: "Yes! We're pretty well off, Andrew."

She decided to visit her aunt in Bridlington, and a week later he saw her off at the station. He missed her beyond belief, their comradeship had become such a part of his life. Their talks, discussions, squabbles, their silences together—he came to see how much these meant to him. His meals, conscientiously served by Jenny according to the programme written out by Christine, were arid snatches behind a propped-up book.

Wandering round the garden she had made, he was struck, suddenly, by the dilapidated condition of the bridge. He had several times told the committee the bridge was falling to pieces, but they were always hard to move when it came to repairs. Now, however, he rang up the office and pressed the point strenuously. The clerk assured Andrew that the matter had been referred to Richards the builder, who would soon put the work in hand.

In the evenings he betook himself to Boland, twice to the Vaughans and once, to his surprise, he found himself playing golf with Llewellyn. But he sought distraction, chiefly, in his work.

His clinical examinations at the anthracite sinkings were, by this time, well under way. Already the results were adding further to his excitement. He saw, without jumping to any immediate conclusion, that the incidence of pulmonary trouble amongst the anthracite workers was positively in excess of that existing in the other underground workers in the coal mines.

He went through the literature on the subject, and its paucity astounded him. Few investigators seemed to have concerned themselves greatly with the pulmonary occupational diseases. Andrew felt himself on the track of something definitely unexplored. He thought of the enormous social importance of this line of investigation. What a chance, what a wonderful chance! Striding up and down the sitting room before the dead fire long after midnight, he suddenly seized Christine's photograph from the mantelshelf. "Chris! I really believe I'm going to *do* something!"

In the card-index he bought for the purpose, he carefully began to classify the results of his examinations. In the changing room at the minehead baths the men stood before him, stripped to the waist, and with fingers, his stethoscope, he plumbed skilfully the hidden pathology of those living lungs: a fibroid spot here, the next an emphysema, then a chronic bronchitis.

At the same time he took sputum samples from each man and, working with Denny's microscope, tabulated his findings. He found that most of these samples contained bright angular particles of silica. This riveted his attention. He could not escape the thrilling idea that the changes in the lungs were fundamentally dependent on this factor.

This was the extent of his advance when Christine returned at the end of June and flung her arms round his neck. "It's so good to be back. Yes, I enjoyed myself, but oh! I don't know!"

Her holiday had done her good, her cheeks had a fine bloom upon them. But she was concerned about him, his lack of appetite.

She asked him seriously. "How long is this special work going to take?"

"I don't know." It was a wet day, and he was unexpectedly moody. "It might take a year, it might take five."

"Well, listen to me. Don't you think that if it's going on as long as that you should work systematically, keep regular hours, not stay up late and kill yourself?"

"There's nothing the matter with me."

But in some things she had a peculiar insistence. She brought an armchair and a rug into the lab. and would sit, sewing and knitting while he worked at the table. Bent over the microscope he quite forgot about her, but she was there, and at eleven o'clock every night she got up. "Time for bed!"

"Oh, I say . . . ." Blinking at her near-sightedly over the eyepiece. "You go up, Chris! I'll follow you in a minute."

"Andrew Manson, if you think I'm going up to bed alone, *in my condition* . . . ."

This last phrase had become a comic byword in the household.

Towards the end of July an outbreak of chickenpox kept him busy and on August 3 his list had kept him out from morning surgery until well after three o'clock. As he came up the road, tired, hungry, he saw Llewellyn's car at the gate of Vale View.

The implication caused him to hasten towards his house. He

threw open the front door and saw Llewellyn. Gazing at the other man with nervous eagerness he stammered: "Hello, Llewellyn. I—I didn't expect to see you here so soon."

"No," Llewellyn answered.

Andrew smiled excitedly. "Well?"

Llewellyn did not smile. After the faintest pause he said: "Come in here, my dear chap." And he drew Andrew into the sitting room. "We've been trying to find you all morning."

Llewellyn's manner, the sympathy in his voice, shot a wave of coldness over Andrew. He faltered: "Is anything wrong?"

"Manson," Llewellyn said gently, "this morning—as your wife was going over the bridge—one of the rotten planks gave way. *She's* all right now, quite all right; but I'm afraid—"

He understood even before Llewellyn finished. A great pulse of anguish beat within him.

"We did everything," Llewellyn went on. "I came at once, brought matron from the hospital, we've been here all day . . . ."

A sob broke in Andrew's throat, another, then another. He covered his eyes with his hand.

"Please, my dear fellow," Llewellyn entreated, "who could help an accident like that? I beg of you—go up and console your wife."

His head lowered, Andrew went upstairs. Outside the door of the bedroom he paused, then, stumblingly, he went in.

Chapter 5

By the year 1930, Dr. Manson of Aberalaw had a somewhat unusual reputation. His practice was not prodigious, but everyone on his list had a convincing belief in him. There were, however, still those on the committee who had never completely forgiven him for his agonized outburst over that matter of the bridge, nearly three years before. They sympathized, of course, with Mrs. Manson and himself in their bereavement, but they could not hold themselves responsible. Len Richards, who had been given the job, had been busy with the new houses on Powys Street.

As time went on Andrew had many heartburnings with the committee for he had a stubborn desire for his own way. In addition there was a certain clerical prejudice against him. Though his wife often went to church he was never seen there. And he had, moreover, a deadly enemy amongst "the chapel" folk—no less a person than the Reverend Edwal Parry, pastor of Sinai.

In the spring of 1929 the good Edwal, newly married, had sidled, late, into Manson's surgery with an air, thoroughly Christian, yet ingratiatingly man of the world.

"How are you, Dr. Manson! I just happened to be passing, and you're a very up-to-date doctor by all accounts. And I'd be glad . . . mind you, I'll pay you a nice little fee too . . . if you could advise me . . . ." Edwal masked a faint priestly blush by a show of worldly candour. "You see the wife and I don't want any children for a while yet, my stipend bein' what it is, like . . . ."

Manson considered Parry in cold distaste. He said carefully: "Don't you realize there are people with a quarter of your stipend who would give their right hand to have children?"

With a queer twist of his face Parry had slunk out. Andrew knew he had spoken too violently. But then, Christine, since that tragic stumble, would never have the children they both desired with all their hearts.

Walking home this May afternoon, Andrew was inclined to ask himself why he and Christine had remained in Aberalaw since the loss of their child. The answer was his work on dust inhalation which bound him to the mines. He reviewed what he had done. His clinical survey and the tabulation of his findings showed the marked preponderance of lung diseases amongst the anthracite workers. He found also that the deathrate from lung troubles amongst the older anthracite miners was nearly three times that of miners employed in all coal mines.

Next, he set out to show that the silica dust he had found in the sputum was actually present in the anthracite headings, which he was able to demonstrate conclusively. Now he had actually to *prove* that the dust was destructive to lung tissue. It was necessary for him to conduct pathological experiments on guinea pigs, to study the action of the silica dust on their lungs.

Here his real troubles began. He already had the spare room, the lab. It was easy to procure a few guinea pigs and equipment. But though his ingenuity was considerable, he was not a pathologist. He swore angrily at having to work without assistance and pressed Christine to his service, teaching her to cut and prepare sections which, in no time at all, she did better than he.

Next he constructed, very simply, a dust chamber, in which, for certain hours of the day, the animals were exposed to concentrations of the dust, others being unexposed—the controls. In spite of mistakes, setbacks and delays he got his specimens, proving in progressive stages the deterioration of the lung and induction of fibrosis from the dust.

Now he asked himself if there was not some chemical action beyond the mere physical irritation of the silicate crystals. He devised a fresh series of experiments.

He injected colloidal silica under the skin of one of his animals. The result was an abscess. Similar abscesses could be induced, he found, by the injection of solutions of amorphous silica which was, physically, a non-irritant, while the injection of a mechanically irritating substance, such as carbon, produced no abscess at all. The silica dust *was* chemically active.

He was almost out of his mind with excitement. Feverishly he collected his data, the results of his three years' work. He had decided, months ago, not only to publish his investigation but to send it in as his thesis for the degree of MD. But when he had posted it, he slumped into a backwash of despair. And yet, through it all, there were shining moments when he knew he had accomplished something after all.

ONE MAY afternoon, when Andrew reached home after work, his preoccupation and listlessness caused him to miss the look of distress upon Christine's face. When he had finished tea, however, he suddenly observed her expression. He asked, as he reached out for the evening paper: "What's the matter?"

She appeared to examine her teaspoon for a moment. "I had some visitors this afternoon. A deputation from the committee, including Ed Chenkin, and escorted by Parry—you know, the Sinai minister."

An odd silence fell. "What did they want?"

She met his scrutiny for the first time, fully revealing the anxiety in her eyes. "They came about four o'clock—asked for you. I told them you were out. Then Parry said they wanted to come in. Of course I was quite taken aback. Ed Chenkin said it was the committee's house and that in the name of the committee they could and would come in." She paused, drew a quick breath. "I was angry—upset. But I managed to ask them *why* they wished to come in. Parry took it up then. He said it had come to his ears that you were performing experiments on animals, vivisection, he had the cheek to call it. And because of that they had brought Mr. Davies, the Prevention of Cruelty to Animals man, to look at your workroom."

Andrew had not moved. "Go on, my dear," he said, quietly.

"Well, I tried to stop them, but they just pushed past, into the lab. When they saw the guinea pigs Parry let out a howl!—'Oh, the poor dumb creatures!' They prowled round everything, and then Parry said, 'I'm not leavin' those poor suffering creatures to be tortured any more. I'll put them out of their pain.' He shoved them all into a bag. I tried to tell them there was no question of suffering, and that in any case those five guinea pigs were not going to be used for experiments, that we were going to give them to the Boland children for pets. But they simply wouldn't listen to me. And then they—they went away."

There was a silence. Andrew's face was now deeply flushed. "I never heard such rank impertinence in all my life. It—it's damnable you had to put up with it, Chris! But I'll make them pay for it!" He started towards the telephone, but just as he reached it the instrument rang. He snatched it from the hook. "Hello!" he said angrily, then his voice altered slightly. It was Owen. "Yes, Manson speaking. Look here, Owen—"

"I know, I know, doctor," Owen interrupted Andrew quickly. "Now listen. No, no, don't interrupt me. We're up against a nasty bit o' business, doctor. I'm comin' down to see you now."

When Owen arrived, there was nothing reassuring in his face. Before Andrew could speak he said: "Doctor, did you have a Home Office licence? You've got to have one for experimental work on animals. You knew that, didn't you?"

"But damn it all!" Manson protested hotly, "I'm not a pathologist, never will be. I only wanted to do a few simple experiments to tie up with my clinical work."

Owen's troubled eyes were averted. "You ought to have had that licence, doctor. You see a chap like you, who's honest enough to speak his mind, he's bound to—well, you must know there's a section here that's dyin' to put a knife in you. There now!—it'll be all right. But you'll have to come before the committee."

Andrew stormed, "I'll bring a counter-action. I'll sue them for—for illegal entry. No, damn it, I'll sue them for stealing my guinea pigs. I want them back, anyway."

"You can't have them back, doctor. Reverend Parry and Ed Chenkin said they'd have to put them out of their misery, so they drowned them. In the name of humanity."

Sorrowfully, Owen went away. And the following evening Andrew was summoned to appear before the committee in one week's time, on the Sunday.

Meanwhile the case had flared into prominence; nothing so exciting, so scandalous, had startled Aberalaw since Trevor Day, the solicitor, was suspected of killing his wife with arsenic. Sides were taken, violent factions formed. From his rostrum at Sinai, Edward Parry thundered the punishments meted out, in this life and the hereafter, to those who tortured animals and little children. Even the women were aroused to action. Members of the Welsh Ladies Endeavour League, normally active in the streets only on flag days, could be seen distributing gruesome anti-vivisection folders. Though Andrew's district was solidly behind him, round the East Surgery there was a block of contrary opinion. Fights broke out in the pubs between Andrew's supporters and his enemies.

Dr. Urquhart made few remarks. But once, squinting across at Andrew's constrained, tense face, he declared: "Dammit to hell! When I was your age I'd have enjoyed a scrap like this, too. But now I suppose I'm getting old."

Andrew could not help thinking that Urquhart misjudged him. He was far from enjoying the "scrap". Yet, although his vitality was low, he had a desperate desire to be vindicated.

The following Sunday afternoon the committee assembled for the disciplinary examination of Dr. Manson. There was not a vacant place in the committee room and outside the offices groups of people were hanging about as Andrew entered. He felt his heart bumping rapidly. He had told himself he must be calm. Instead, as he took his seat he was stiff, dry-lipped, nervous.

The proceedings began with a fiery speech from Ed Chenkin. "I'm going to put the full facts of this case," said Chenkin, jumping up, "before my fellow members of this committee." He proceeded to enumerate the complaints in a loud, illiterate speech. Dr. Manson had no right to do this work in the committee's time, and on the committee's property. Also it was vivisection, or near neighbour to it. And it was all done without the necessary permit, a very serious offence in the eye of the law!

Here Owen intervened swiftly. "As regards that last point, I must advise the committee that if it reports Dr. Manson's failure to secure this permit any subsequent action taken would involve the Medical Aid Society as a whole. As he is our assistant we are legally responsible!"

There was a murmur of assent at this and cries of, "We don't want any trouble. Keep it amongst ourselves."

"Never mind the permit, then," bawled Chenkin, still upon his feet. "There's enough other charges to hang anybody."

"Hear! Hear!" called out someone at the back. "What about all them times he sneaked off to Cardiff on his motor bike—that summer three years back?"

"He don't give medicine," came another voice. "You can wait an hour outside his surgery and not get your bottle filled."

"Order! Order!" Chenkin shouted. When he had stilled them he proceeded to his peroration. "All these complaints are bad enough! They show that Dr. Manson 'as never been a satisfactory servant to the Society. But we got to keep our minds on the main item. Here we have an assistant who's turned our property into a slaughter-'ouse. Fellow members, I know you are with me one and all, when I say that here and now we demand Dr. Manson's resignation." Chenkin sat down amidst loud applause.

"Perhaps you'll allow Dr. Manson to state his case," Owen said palely, and turned to Andrew.

There was a silence. Andrew sat still for a moment. The situation was worse, even, than he had imagined. His heart burned. He would not, simply would not resign. He got to his feet. He was angry now, his nervousness lost in a swelling indignation at the intolerant stupidity of Chenkin's accusation. He began:

"No one seems to have said anything about the animals Ed Chenkin drowned. That was cruelty if you like—useless cruelty. Why do you men take white mice and canaries down the mine? To test for black damp—you all know that. And when these mice get finished by a whiff of gas—do you call that cruelty? No, you don't. You realize that these animals have been used to save men's lives, perhaps your *own* lives.

"That's what I've been trying to do for you! I've been working on these lung diseases that you get from the dust of the mine headings. You all know that you get chest trouble and that when you *do* get it you don't get compensation. For these last three years I've spent nearly every minute of my spare time on this problem. I've found out something which might give you a fairer deal, keep you in health. What if I used a dozen guinea pigs? Don't you think it was worth it? You don't believe me, perhaps." Then, diving into his breast pocket he produced the letter he had received earlier in the week. "But this'll show you what people who are qualified to judge think of it."

He handed over a letter from the Clerk of the Senate at St. Andrews informing him that, for his thesis on dust inhalation, he had been awarded his MD. Owen read the letter with a sudden brightening of his face. Thereafter it was passed slowly from hand to hand. After a few further remarks, Owen said: "Perhaps you'll leave us now, doctor, please."

Waiting outside, while they voted on his case, Andrew kicked his heels, simmering with exasperation. He had the conviction that on this occasion even Owen's goodwill would not save him.

But the secretary, when Andrew went in again, was smiling. Others on the committee were regarding him at least without hostility. And Owen immediately stood up and said: "I'm glad to tell you, Dr. Manson that the committee has decided by a majority to ask you to remain."

He had won, but the knowledge, after one swift throb of satisfaction, gave him no elation. There was a pause. They obviously expected him to express his relief, his gratitude. But he could not. He felt tired of the whole business, of the committee, Aberalaw, medicine, silica dust, guinea pigs and himself.

At last he said: "Thank you, Mr. Owen. I'm glad that the committee doesn't wish me to go. But, I'm sorry, I can't stay on in Aberalaw any longer; I give a month's notice from today." He spun round and walked out of the room.

There was a dead silence. Ed Chenkin was the quickest to recover himself. "Good riddance," he called half-heartedly after Manson.

Then Owen startled them all with the first burst of anger he had ever shown in that committee room. "Shut your senseless mouth, Ed Chenkin. We have lost the best man we ever had."

ANDREW WOKE UP in the middle of that night groaning.

"Am I a fool, Chris? Chucking away a sound job? After all, I *was* getting a few private patients lately. And Llewellyn has been pretty decent. Did I tell you?— he half-promised to let me consult at the hospital. I believe in time, when Llewellyn retired, the committee might have made me head doctor in his place."

She comforted him, quiet, reasonable, lying beside him in the darkness. "You don't really want us to stay in a Welsh mining practice all our lives, my dear. We've been happy here, but it's time for us to move on."

"But listen, Chris," he worried, "we've only just got enough money to buy a practice."

She answered sleepily. "What has money got to do with it? Besides, we're going on holiday before we do anything else."

Her spirit infected him. He felt adventurous, prepared to take his chance with life. Besides, the cautious side of him could not avoid glancing at the assets side of his balance sheet. He had his MRCP, and an honours MD. With this behind them, surely they would not starve. Even after their planned holiday in France.

It was strange how lightly his thesis appeared to have shaken the outer world in the face of all these local reverberations. It had gained him his MD. It had been printed in the *Journal of Industrial Health* in England and published in the United States by the Association of American Hygiene. But beyond that it brought him exactly two letters.

The first was from Professor Challis, an enthusiastic letter of congratulation and appreciation, and the second was an unusual, stimulating communication which had crossed the Atlantic from Oregon. Andrew read and re-read the typewritten sheets then took them in excitement to Christine.

"This is rather decent, Chris! It's from a fellow called Stillman, Robert Stillman—you've probably never heard of him, but I have—it's full of the most exact appreciation of my inhalation stuff. More, much more than Challis. Apparently the active destructive ingredient in my silica is secrecite. I hadn't enough chemistry to get to that. It's a marvellous letter—and from Stillman!"

"Yes?" She peeped inquiring. "Is he some doctor out there?"

"No, he's a physicist really. But he runs a clinic for disorders of the lungs, near Portland, Oregon. And he's a big man."

He was so thrilled to receive Stillman's letter he sat down and answered it on the spot.

They were now overwhelmed by preparations for their holiday, arrangements for storing their furniture in Cardiff—and by the doleful processes of leave-taking. Their departure from Drineffy had been abrupt, but here they suffered much lingering sentiment. When the actual day of departure arrived Jenny, in tears, told them—to their consternation—that they were to be given a "platform send-off".

They hurried to the station, engulfed by the crowd who waited there, shaken by the hand, patted on the back, embraced, and finally hustled into their train compartment. As they steamed off, their friends lustily sang "Men of Harlech".

Andrew's eyes were glistening as he said: "I wouldn't have had us miss it for anything, Chris. Aren't people *decent*. And to think that a month ago half the town was after my blood!"

They reached Southampton that evening, took their berths in the cross-channel steamer. Next morning they saw the sun rise behind St. Malo and, an hour later, Brittany received them.

The wheat was ripening, the cherry trees were heavy with fruit, goats strayed on the flowering pastures. It had been Christine's idea to come here, to get close to the real France.

They reached Val André. Their little hotel was within sound of the sea, within scent of the meadows. Their bedroom had plain scrubbed boards, and their morning coffee came to them steaming, in thick blue bowls. They lazed the whole day long.

"Oh, Lord!" Andrew kept repeating. "Isn't this wonderful, darling? I never, never, never want to look a lobar pneumonia in the face again." They drank cider, ate langoustines, shrimps, pastries and whiteheart cherries. In the evenings Andrew played billiards with the proprietor on the antique octagonal table. A whole month slipped past in blissful happiness.

PART THREE

Chapter 1

They decided to search for a London practice. It was a jagged business—wild peaks of expectation followed by wilder plunges of despair. Stung by a consciousness of two successive failures—at least so he construed his departures from Drineffy and Aberalaw—Andrew longed to vindicate himself at last. But their total capital was no more than five hundred pounds. Though they haunted the medical agencies and chased every opportunity offered in the *Lancet* it appeared that this sum was scarcely adequate to purchase a London practice.

Because of his MD, MRCP, he wanted a non-panel, non-dispensing practice. But as the weeks went on he wanted anything and he inspected practices all over London.

And then, after two months, when they had reached the point of desperation, all at once heaven relented and allowed old Dr. Foy to die, painlessly, in Paddington. His obituary notice, four lines in the *Medical Journal*, caught Andrew's eye. They went to No. 9 Chesborough Terrace. They saw the house, a tall, leaden-hued sepulchre with a surgery at the side. They saw from the books that Dr. Foy had made perhaps five hundred pounds a year. They met the widow, who assured them that Dr. Foy's practice was sound and had once been excellent with many "good patients" coming to the "front door". They thanked her and left without enthusiasm.

"It's full of disadvantages." Andrew worried. "It's a baddish locality. But it's on the *fringe* of a decent neighbourhood. And on a main street. And near enough our price. What do you say, Chris? It's now or never. Shall we chance it?"

Christine's eyes rested upon him doubtfully. She loved the country and now she longed for it with all her heart. Yet he was so set upon a London practice she could not bring herself to even try to persuade him from it. She nodded slowly. "If you want to, Andrew."

The next day he offered Mrs. Foy's solicitors £500 in place of the £650 demanded. The offer was accepted, the cheque written. On October 10 they moved their furniture into their new home. It was Sunday before they had collected themselves from the frantic eruption of straw and sacking. Andrew took advantage of the moment to launch into one of his rare lectures.

"We are properly up against it here, Chris. We've paid out every stiver we've got. We've got to live on what we earn. You've got to spruce things up, Chris, economize . . . ."

To his dismay she burst into tears, standing in the gloomy, dirty-ceilinged, and as yet uncarpeted, front room. "For mercy's sake!" she sobbed. "Leave me alone. Economize! Don't I always economize? Do I cost you *anything*?" She flung herself frantically against him. "It's this house! That basement, the stairs, the *dirt*—"

"But hang it all, it's the practice that really matters!"

In the end he apologized. Then they went, his arm still round her waist, to fry eggs in the basement.

Next morning, at nine o'clock sharp, he opened his surgery. His heart was beating with excitement and a greater, far greater, expectation than on that almost forgotten morning when he took his first surgery at Drineffy.

Half past nine came. His plate shone on the door. He waited anxiously. Since the little surgery, which had its own door to the side street, was connected by a short passage to the house, he could control both it and his consulting room—the main room on the ground floor—to which the "good" patients, by Mrs. Foy's account, were admitted through the front door of the house. He had, in fact, a double net cast out. Tense as any fisherman, he waited for what that double cast might bring. Yet it brought nothing, nothing!

Then suddenly, when he had almost abandoned hope, the bell on the surgery door tinkled sharply and an old woman in a shawl came in. Chronic bronchitis—he saw it, before she spoke, in every rheumy wheeze.

Tenderly he seated and sounded her. In the tiny cubbyhole of a dispensary, he made up her physic. He returned with it. And then, as he prepared, tremblingly, to ask her for it, she handed him the fee, three shillings and sixpence.

The thrill of that moment, the sheer relief of these silver coins in the palm of his hand was unbelievable. It felt like the first money he had ever earned in his life. He ran to Christine, thrust the coins upon her. "First patient, Chris. It mightn't be a bad old practice after all!"

Sensing that Christine wished to wrestle with her domestic worries in solitude, he spent the rest of the morning walking round the district, viewing the peeling houses, the drab, private hotels, the sooty squares, and at a sudden turn of North Street, a squalid patch of slum—pawnshops, hawkers' barrows, pubs. It was a dingy district, yet there were signs of new life springing up amidst the fungus—a new block of flats, some good shops and offices and, at the end of Gladstone Place, the famous Laurier's. Even he, who knew nothing of women's fashions, had heard of Laurier's and it did not require the long line of elegant motor cars standing outside to convince him of its exclusiveness.

That night in the surgery there were three patients, two of whom paid him the three-and-sixpenny fee. The third promised to return and settle up on Saturday. He had, in his first day's practice, earned the sum of ten and six.

But the following day he took nothing at all. And the day after, only seven shillings. Thursday was a good day, Friday just saved from being blank, and on Saturday, he took seventeen and six at the evening surgery.

On Sunday Andrew morbidly reviewed the week. Had he made a horrible mistake in taking this derelict practice? What was *wrong* with him? He was over thirty. He had an MD honours, and the MRCP. He had clinical ability, and a fine piece of research work to his credit. Yet here he was, taking barely enough three and sixpences to keep them in bread.

Never before had the financial side of practice so obtruded itself upon him. And no subtler method of converting him to materialism could have been devised than those genuine pangs of hunger which he felt many days of the week.

About a hundred yards down the main bus route stood a small delicatessen shop kept by a fat little woman, a naturalized German, called Schmidt. The little shop was typically continental, its narrow marble counter loaded with soused herrings, sauerkraut, pastries, salami, and a delicious cheese named Liptauer. Also it had the virtue of being very cheap. Since money was so scarce at 9 Chesborough Terrace, Andrew and Christine dealt a great deal with Frau Schmidt. On good days they had hot frankfurters and apfelstrudel; on bad, they would lunch on a soused herring and baked potatoes.

Frau Schmidt soon developed an especial liking for Christine. Her pastry-cook's face would wrinkle up beneath her high dome of blonde hair, as she smiled and nodded to Andrew: "You will be all right. You have a good wife. She iss small, like me. But she iss good. Chust wait—I will send you patients!"

Almost at once, the winter was upon them and fogs hung depressingly about the streets. They pretended their struggles were amusing, Christine did her utmost with their chill barracks. She whitewashed the ceilings, made new curtains for the waiting room, and repapered their bedroom.

But never in all their years at Aberalaw had they known such hardship.

ANDREW BEGAN to hunger for medical friendship. One evening he went to a meeting of the local medical association and found himself standing next to a young man with glossy brushed black hair, singularly at variance with the upturned collar of his shabby coat. He decided to introduce himself. "My name's Manson. I've just bought Dr. Foy's practice in Chesborough Terrace."

"I feared as much." A pause. "I'm Dr. Hope—at least I used to think I was Hope. Now I am definitely Hope deferred."

Andrew laughed. "What do you do?"

"God only knows! I work for the Coal and Metalliferous Mines Fatigue Board—the MFB—so occasionally they send me chunks of decomposed miner and ask me the cause of the explosion."

They went out for a drink together. Dr. Hope explained that he was a Backhouse Research Scholar from Cambridge, via Birmingham, and that he had been loaned to the Metalliferous Board. He had nothing to do but sheer mechanics, a routine which any lab. attendant could have tackled. He implied that he was surely going mad through indolence and the inertia of the Board.

After that first meeting Andrew and Hope took many lunches together. Hope, despite his undergraduate humour and a tendency to flippancy, was well endowed with brains. Indeed, in his serious moments, he often exposed his eagerness to get back to the real work he had planned for himself, on the isolation of gastric enzymes.

Occasionally Christine joined them for lunch. Afterwards, Hope confided to Andrew that he was a less likely candidate for the straitjacket since meeting Mrs. Manson.

Meanwhile, Denny was still abroad. After working as a ship's surgeon, he had found Tampico to his liking and had remained there, taking a post as surgeon to the New Century Oil Company. For the present at least, he was lost to Andrew.

Many times Andrew was taken by the impulse to get in touch with Freddie Hamson, who was still in Queen Anne Street, but always the reflection that he was still unsuccessful restrained him. Andrew found himself wondering more and more how Freddie had got on, until suddenly he found the compulsion too strong for him. He rang Hamson.

"You've probably forgotten all about me," he said, half prepared for a snub. "This is Andrew Manson. I'm in practice here in Paddington."

"Manson! You old warhorse!" Freddie was lyrical. "Good Lord, man! *Why* haven't you rung me?"

"Oh, we've barely got settled," Andrew smiled into the receiver. "I'm married now, you know."

"So am I! Look here, we've got to get together again. Soon! I can't get over it. You, here, in London. Marvellous! Where's my book . . . . How about next Thursday? Can you come to dinner then? Yes, yes. That's great. So long then, old man."

Christine seemed to lack enthusiasm when he told her of the invitation. "You go, Andrew," she suggested after a pause.

"Oh! that's nonsense! Freddie wants you to meet his wife. I know you don't care for him much but we've had so little fun lately. Black tie, he said. Lucky I bought myself that dinner jacket last year. But what about you, Chris? You ought to have something new to wear."

"I ought to have a new gas cooker," she answered a trifle grimly. These last weeks had taken toll of her. She had lost a little of that freshness which had always been her greatest charm.

But on that Thursday night he could not help thinking how sweet she looked in a white dress from their Aberalaw days, altered in some way which made it seem newer, smarter. Her hair was done in a new style too, closer to her head, so that it lay darkly about her pale brow. He noticed this as she tied his bow for him, meant to tell her how nice it was, then forgot, in the sudden fear that they would be late.

They were not late, however, but early. Freddie came gaily in, both hands outstretched, telling them that his wife would be down in a second, offering drinks, pounding Andrew on the back. Freddie had put on weight, there was heavy prosperity in the pink roll of flesh on the back of his neck.

"It's wonderful to see you again!" He elevated his glass. "How do you like my place here, old man? I've the whole house, not just rooms, bought the freehold last year. And did it cost money?" He patted his tie approvingly. "No need to advertise the fact, of course, even if I am successful."

It looked expensive, there was no doubt: modern furniture, a baby-grand piano. Andrew was preparing to voice admiration when Mrs. Hamson entered, tall, cool, with clothes extraordinarily different from Christine's.

"Come along, my dear." Freddie greeted her with affection,

and darted to pour her a drink. Then the other guests—Mr. and Mrs. Charles Ivory, Dr. and Mrs. Paul Deedman—were announced. Introductions followed, and much talk and laughter. Then they went in to dinner. The table appointments were superfine. The food tasted extremely well. And there was champagne. After two glasses Andrew felt more confident. He began to talk to Mrs. Ivory, a slender woman in black with an extraordinary amount of jewellery around her neck.

Her husband was Charles Ivory, the surgeon—she laughed in answer to his question, she thought everyone knew Charles. They lived in New Cavendish Street round the corner. It was nice being near Freddie and his wife. Charles and Freddie and Paul Deedman were all such good friends.

He turned to Mrs. Deedman on his other side, finding her softer, friendlier. He encouraged her to talk of her husband. He said to himself: "I want to *know* these fellows, they're so dashed prosperous and smart."

Paul, said Mrs. Deedman, was a physician, with rooms in Harley Street. He had a wonderful practice, she said, chiefly at the Plaza Hotel. So many wealthy Americans and film stars and—she broke off, smiling—oh, everybody came to the Plaza, which made it rather wonderful for Paul.

Andrew liked Mrs. Deedman. He let her run on until Mrs. Hamson rose, when he jumped up and drew back her chair.

"Cigar, Manson?" Freddie asked him with a knowledgeable air when the ladies had gone. "You'll find these pretty sound. And I advise you not to miss this brandy. Eighteen ninety-four."

With his cigar going and a glass of brandy before him, Andrew drew his chair nearer to the others. It was this he had really been looking forward to, a lively medical palaver. He hoped Hamson and his friends would talk. They did.

"By the way," Freddie said, "I ordered an Iradium lamp today. Eighty guineas, but it's worth it."

"It ought to pay for its keep," said Deedman thoughtfully. He was slight, dark-eyed, with a clever Jewish face.

Andrew took an argumentative grip of his cigar. "I don't think much of these lamps, you know. Abbey's paper on bogus heliotherapy proves they have no infra-red content."

Freddie stared, then laughed. "They've got a lot of three-guinea content. Besides, they bronze nicely."

"Mind you, Freddie," Deedman cut in, "I'm not in favour of expensive apparatus. Honestly, old chap, nothing beats the good old hypo for profit. There's no getting away from it," he continued, "in good-class practice, oral administration is definitely demoded. If I prescribed—oh, say a veripon powder—it wouldn't cut one-guinea's worth of ice. But if you give the same thing hypodermically, swabbing up the skin, sterilizing and all the rest of the game, your patient thinks that you are the cat's pyjamas!"

Andrew's head rocked. Here was an argument for the abolition of the medicine bottle which staggered him with its novelty.

For the next ten minutes the three friends talked shooting, golf, cars and tailors, while Andrew listened and smoked his cigar and drank his brandy. He felt, a trifle muzzily, that they were extraordinarily good fellows. As they stood up, Ivory clapped him on the shoulder. "I must send you a card, Manson. It'd be a real pleasure to see a case with you—any time."

In the taxi, returning home, he proclaimed happily: "First-rate chaps these, Chris! 'Sbeen a wonderful evening, hasn't it?"

She answered in a thin, steady voice: "It's been a hateful evening!"

"Eh—what?"

"As your medical friends, Andrew, I like Denny and Hope—not these, these flashy—"

He broke in, "Wha's wrong with—"

"Oh! couldn't you see," she answered in an icy fury. "It was everything. The food, the furniture, the way they talked—money, money all the time. Perhaps you didn't see the way Mrs. Hamson looked at my dress. You can't guess what it was like—the conversation—before you came in. Smart-set gossip, what the hairdresser told her, the latest society abortion, not one word of anything *decent.*"

Mistaking her outburst for jealousy he babbled: "I'll make money for you, Chris. I'll buy you plenty of expensive clothes."

"I don't want money. And I hate expensive clothes."

"But—darling." Tipsily he reached for her.

"Don't!" Her voice struck him. "I love you, Andrew. But not when you're drunk."

He subsided in his corner, fuddled, furious. "All right, my girl," he muttered. "If that's the way of it."

He paid the taxi, let himself into the house before her. Then without a word he marched up to the spare bedroom. Everything seemed squalid and dismal after the luxury he had just quitted.

"Damn it," he thought, as he flung himself into bed. "I'm going to get out of this hole. I'll show her. I *will* make money."

Until now, in all their married life, they had never slept apart.

AT BREAKFAST next morning Christine behaved as though the whole episode were forgotten. But after he had grunted a few surly replies, Christine stopped being nice to him and retired within herself. Stubborn little devil, he thought, I'll show her!

His first action in his consulting room was to take down the Medical Directory. He was eager to have more information about his friends of the previous evening. Yes, there it was—Frederick Hamson, Queen Anne Street, MB, ChB, assistant to out-patients, Walthamwood.

Andrew's brows drew into a frown of perplexity. Freddie had talked a great deal about the hospital appointment—nothing like it for helping a fellow in the West End, he had said. Yet surely this was a poor-law institution in one of the outer suburbs?

Andrew looked up Ivory and Deedman, then he rested the big red book on his knees, his expression puzzled. Paul Deedman was, like Freddie, an MB. And Ivory? He had the lowest surgical qualifications, the MRCS, and no hospital appointment whatsoever.

Andrew rose and put the book on its shelf. There was no comparison between his own qualifications and those of the prosperous fellows he had dined with last night. What they could do he could do also. Better. He was more determined than ever to make a success of himself. But first he must get himself attached to one of the London hospitals. But how?

For three days he brooded, then he went shakily to Sir Robert Abbey, who received him with twinkling kindness. Andrew began nervously, diffidently.

"I was wondering—that's to say—could you help me, Sir Robert, to find an out-patients hospital appointment?"

"Hmm! That's difficult. Do you know how many fellows there are waiting on honorary appointments? You ought to be going on with your lung work too—and that narrows the field. The Victoria Chest Hospital should be your target. Suppose I make some inquiries. I don't promise anything, but I'll keep an eye open." Abbey made him stay to tea. Afterwards, as he showed Andrew to the door, he said: "Even if I do get you into the Victoria, mind you don't develop a bedside manner." His eyes twinkled. "That's what has ruined me."

Andrew went home treading the clouds. He was so pleased he neglected to maintain his dignity with Christine. He blurted out: "I've been to Abbey. He's going to try and fix me up at the Victoria! That practically gives me a consultant's standing." Her gladness made him suddenly feel shamefaced. "I've been pretty difficult lately, Chris! Let's—oh! let's make it up, darling."

She ran to him, protesting it had all been her fault. Then, for some strange reason, it appeared entirely to be his.

He flung himself into his work with renewed vigour and optimism. There was no doubt that his practice was increasing. It was not—he told himself—the class of practice he wanted, these three-and-sixpenny consultations and five-shilling visits. Yet it was genuine. The people who came to him were far too poor to dream of troubling the doctor unless they were really ill. Thus he met diphtheria in queer stuffy rooms above converted stables, rheumatic fever in damp servants' basements, pneumonia in the attics of lodging houses.

Many of his cases were urgent—surgical emergencies which cried aloud for immediate admission to hospital. Andrew encountered great difficulty in securing admission, even for the worst, the most dangerous cases. These had a way of happening late at night. Returning, coat and jacket over his pyjamas, he would hang over the telephone, ringing one hospital after another, entreating, threatening, but always met with the same refusal, the curt, often insolent: "Dr. who? Who? No, no! Sorry! We're full up!"

He went to Christine, livid, blaspheming. "They're not full up. They've plenty of beds for their *own* men. Isn't it hell—Chris! Here am I with this strangulated hernia and I can't get a bed. And this is London, the heart of the British Empire. This is our voluntary hospital system."

Whatever his difficulties, no matter if he railed against the dirt and poverty, she always had the same reply. "It's *real* work anyway. That makes all the difference."

"Not enough to keep the bugs off me," he growled, going up to the bath to shake himself free.

She laughed; for she was back again to her old happiness. Though the task had been formidable she had at last subdued the house. She had her new gas cooker, new shades for the lamps, had the loose chair-covers freshly cleaned. After weeks of worry with servants who preferred to work in the local boarding houses because of the tips, Christine had chanced on Mrs. Bennett, a widow of forty, who because of her daughter, a child of seven, had found it almost impossible to secure a "living-in" position. Together Mrs. Bennett and Christine had turned the basement into a comfortable bed-sitting room, where Mrs. Bennett and little Florrie felt themselves secure.

The early spring flowers which made the waiting room so bright reflected the happiness of Christine's house. She bought them at the Mussleburgh Road street market for a few pence, as she went on her round of morning shopping. She often stopped at Frau Schmidt's on the way back for a few minutes' conversation and a wedge of the Liptauer cheese which Andrew liked so well.

Andrew was still waiting for those "good" patients who did not come, longing to hear from Abbey about the appointment, fretful because their evening at Queen Anne Street had produced no subsequent opportunity. In this condition he sat in his surgery one evening towards the end of April when a young woman entered. She gazed at him uncertainly: "I didn't know whether to come this way—or by the front door."

"It's exactly the same," he smiled sourly. "Except that it's half price this end. Come along. What is it?"

"I don't mind paying the full fee." She came forward with a peculiar earnestness and sat down. She was about twenty-eight, he judged, stockily built, dressed in dark olive green.

He relented, saying: "Don't let's talk about the fee! Tell me your trouble."

"Well, doctor! It was Frau Schmidt who recommended me to come to you. I work at Laurier's, quite near. My name is Cramb. But I must tell you I've been to a good many doctors round here." She pulled off her gloves. "It's my hands."

He looked at her hands, the palms of which were covered by a reddish dermatitis. With sudden interest he took up a magnifying-glass and peered more closely. Meanwhile she went on talking.

"I can't tell you what a disadvantage this is to me in my work. I've tried every kind of ointment under the sun. But none of them seem to be the slightest use."

"No! They wouldn't," he said, feeling the thrill of an obscure yet positive diagnosis. "This is rather an uncommon skin condition, Miss Cramb. It's due to a blood condition and the only way to get rid of it is by dieting."

"No one ever told me that before," she said doubtfully.

"I'm telling you now." He laughed and wrote out a diet for her, which she accepted hesitatingly. "Well! Of course I'll try it, doctor. I'd try *anything*." Meticulously she paid him his fee, then went away.

Ten days later she returned, entering the consulting room with such an expression of suppressed fervour that he could barely keep from smiling.

"Would you like to see my hands, doctor?"

"Yes." Now he did smile. "I hope you don't regret the diet."

"Regret it!" She surrendered her hands to him in a passion of gratitude. "Look! Completely cured. You don't know how much it means to me—I can't tell you—such cleverness—"

"That's all right," he said lightly. "It's my job to know these things. You run away and don't worry. Keep off those foods I told you about and you'll never have it again."

She rose. "And now let me pay you, doctor?"

"You've already paid me." Right gladly would he have taken another three and six from her, but the temptation to dramatize the triumph of his skill proved irresistible.

"But, doctor—" Unwillingly she allowed herself to be escorted to the door where she paused for the final earnestness. "Perhaps I'll be able to show my gratitude some other way."

He nodded and closed the door upon her. He was tired, already half regretful at refusing the fee, and, in any case, he had little thought of what a shopgirl might do for him. But here at least he did not know Miss Cramb.

MARTHA CRAMB was known as the "Half-Back" to the juniors at Laurier's. Sturdy, unattractive, she seemed a strange person to be one of the senior assistants in this unique shop which dealt in smart gowns, exquisite undergarments and expensive furs. It was esteemed an honour to be allowed to work at Laurier's, to wear the dark-green dress which was the uniform of the establishment. Sweated employment and the bad living-in conditions which ordinary shop assistants often endured simply did not exist at Laurier's, where the girls were admirably fed and housed and chaperoned. Mr. Winch, the elderly male buyer, especially saw to it that they were chaperoned.

But the fact was that the Half-Back's earnest sincerity made her an admirable saleswoman, highly valued by her customers. And her cure caused a mild sensation, the first result of which was that more and more of the Laurier girls began to come to Andrew's surgery. By the end of May it was not uncommon for half a dozen of them to be waiting to see him—very smart, modelled upon their customers, lipsticked, young.

The smartness of his new patients forced him one evening after surgery to take stock of himself, his nondescript worsted and uncreased trousers. Hang it all, he thought testily, how can I attract first-class patients if I look like this? The next day he went to Rogers, in Conduit Street, Freddie Hamson's tailor.

Chapter 2

He was as self-conscious as a schoolboy when, a fortnight later, he came downstairs in one of his two new suits. It was a dark, double-breasted grey, worn on Rogers's suggestion, with a wing collar and a dark bow-tie. The tailor knew his job, and the mention of Hamson's name had made him do it thoroughly.

This morning, as it fell out, Christine was not looking her best. She had a slight sore throat and had wound her old scarf protectively around her throat. She was pouring his coffee when the radiance of his presence burst upon her. "Why, Andrew!" she gasped. "You look wonderful. Are you going anywhere?"

"Going anywhere? I'm going on my rounds, of course!" Being self-conscious made him snappy. "Do you like it?"

"Yes," she said, not quickly enough to please him. "It's frightfully smart . . . but," she smiled, "it doesn't quite seem *you!*"

"You'd rather keep me looking like a tramp, I suppose."

She hesitated. "Please don't misunderstand me, darling, but I'd rather you didn't care *how* you looked."

He stared at her, then turned abruptly away.

ONE AFTERNOON, a week or so later, he was sitting in the consulting room, totalling his receipts for the past month, when suddenly the phone rang.

"Yes, yes! Dr. Manson speaking."

An anguished voice came back to him. "Oh, Dr. Manson! This is Mr. Winch!—Mr. Winch of Laurier's. We've had a slight mishap to one of our customers. Could you come at once?"

"I'll be there in four minutes." Andrew clicked back the receiver and in four minutes and a half he was inside the revolving doors of Laurier's, met by an anxious Miss Cramb, and escorted over swimming surfaces of green-piled carpet, past long gilt mirrors against which, as if by chance, there could be seen one small hat on its stand, a lacy scarf, an ermine evening wrap. As they hastened, Miss Cramb explained: "It's Miss le Roy, one of our customers. I spoke to Mr. Winch about you, Dr. Manson—"

"Thanks!" he said brusquely. "What's happened?"

"She seems—oh, Dr. Manson—she seems to have had a fit in the fit . . . fitting room!"

At the head of the broad staircase she surrendered him to Mr. Winch, pinkly agitated, who fluttered: "This way, doctor—I hope you can do something. It's most unfortunate—"

Into the exquisite fitting room; a crowd of twittering girls, a gilt chair upturned, a towel thrown down, a spilled glass of water, pandemonium. And there, the centre of it all, Miss le Roy, the woman having the fit. She lay on the floor, rigid, with spasmodically clutching hands. From time to time a strained crowing broke from her throat.

"Oh dear. Oh, dear," muttered Mr. Winch. "This is dreadful, dreadful. Shall I—shall I ring for the ambulance?"

"No, not yet," Andrew said. He bent down beside Miss le Roy. She was very young, about twenty-four, with blue eyes and washed-out silky hair. Her convulsive spasms were increasing. On the other side of her knelt a woman with dark, concerned eyes.

"Please clear the room," Andrew said. "Everyone out but—" his eye fell upon the dark young woman "—but this lady."

"This is an extremely serious case," Andrew said, when the others had removed themselves from the room. Miss le Roy's eyeballs rolled towards him. "Get me a chair, please."

The fallen chair was righted by the other woman. With great sympathy, Andrew helped Miss le Roy into the chair.

"There," he said with even greater sympathy. Then, with the flat of his hand, he hit her a resounding smack upon the cheek. Miss le Roy stopped crowing, the spasm ceased, her rolling eye-

balls righted themselves. She gazed at him in pained bewilderment. Before she could relapse he struck her on the other cheek. Smack! The surprise in Miss le Roy's face was ludicrous. She began, gently to cry. Turning to her friend she wept: "Darling, I want to go home."

Andrew gazed apologetically at the dark young woman who now regarded him with restrained yet singular interest.

"It was the only way," he muttered. "Bad hysteria—she might have harmed herself. . . . Anyway—it worked."

"Yes—it worked."

"Let her cry this out," Andrew said. "Good safety valve. She'll be all right in a few minutes."

"Wait, though"—quickly—"you must see her home."

"Very well," Andrew said, in his busiest professional tone.

They left the fitting room a few minutes later, and their progress through the long showroom was sheer sensation. Wonder and relief left Mr. Winch almost speechless. He followed, babbling deferential words.

The taxi took them along Bayswater Road in the direction of Marble Arch. Miss le Roy was sulking. From time to time her hands and the muscles of her face gave slight involuntary twitches. She was, now that she could be seen more normally, very thin and almost pretty. Andrew was himself nervous, conscious of the awkward situation, yet determined to take full advantage of it.

The taxi drew up before a house in Green Street, Mayfair. Inside, it took Andrew's breath away—the cabinets gorgeous with jade, the lacquer chairs, the wide settees, the skin-thin faded rugs.

Toppy le Roy flung herself down on a satin-cushioned sofa, still ignoring Andrew. "Press the bell, darling, I must have a drink. Thank God, father isn't home."

Quickly, a manservant brought cocktails. When he had gone, Toppy's friend considered Andrew thoughtfully, almost smiling. "I think we ought to explain ourselves to you, doctor. I'm Mrs. Lawrence. Toppy here had rather a row over a dress she's having specially designed and—well!—she's been doing too much lately. We're frightfully indebted to you for getting us back here."

"That bloody Laurier woman," said Toppy peevishly. "I'll tell father to ring up and get her sacked! Oh, no I won't!" As she tilted her cocktail a smile of gratification slowly overspread her face. "I did give them something to think about, though, didn't I,

Frances? I simply went *wild!*" Her scraggy little frame shook with laughter. She met Andrew's eyes without ill-will. "Go on, doctor—laugh! It was priceless."

"No, I don't think it was so amusing." He spoke quickly, anxious to establish his position, convince her she was ill. "You really had a bad attack. And please don't imagine that I think you tried to bring it on. Hysteria—well, that's what it was—is a condition of the nervous system. You see, you're extremely run down, Miss le Roy. You're in a very nervous state."

"That's perfectly true," Frances Lawrence nodded. "You've been doing far too much lately, Toppy."

"You sound like father," Toppy said, losing her good humour.

There was a pause. Andrew had finished his cocktail. There seemed nothing more for him to do. "Well!" he said eventually, "I must get on with my work. Please take my advice, Miss le Roy. Go to bed, and—since I cannot be of any further service to you—call in your own doctor tomorrow. Goodbye."

Mrs. Lawrence accompanied him into the hall. She was tall and slim with a small elegant head. In her dark, beautifully waved hair, a few iron-grey strands gave her a curious distinction. Yet she was quite young, not more than twenty-seven. She gave him her hand, her greenish hazel eyes fixed upon him in that faint, friendly, unhurried smile.

"I only wished to tell you how I admired your new line of treatment." Her lips twitched. "Don't give it up on my account. I foresee you making it a crashing success."

Walking down Green Street to pick up a bus he saw to his amazement that it was nearly five o'clock. He had spent three hours with these two women. He ought to be able to charge a really big fee for that!

And yet, despite this elevating thought, he felt strangely dissatisfied. Suddenly he gritted his teeth in angry exasperation. Not only had he omitted to leave his card, he had forgotten even to tell them who he was.

THE FOLLOWING MORNING, as he was on the point of going out on his rounds, the telephone rang. A manservant's voice purred at him. "Dr. Manson, sir! Ah! Miss le Roy wishes to know, sir, what time you will be calling on her today. Ah! Excuse me, sir, hold on—Mrs. Lawrence will speak to you herself."

Andrew hung on with excitement while Mrs. Lawrence explained that they were expecting him to call.

He dropped all his other calls and went straight up to Green Street. He found Joseph le Roy impatiently awaiting him, a bald, thickset figure, who abused his cigar like a man who has no time to lose. For one second his eyes bored into Andrew, then he spoke forcibly in a colonial accent.

"See here, doc, I'm in a hurry. I understand you're a clever young fellow and you don't stand any nonsense. Now you take my girl in hand. Get her right, get all this damn hysteria out of her system. Don't spare anything. I can pay. Goodbye."

Joseph le Roy was born Joe Leary, a New Zealander. And despite his money, his Green Street house, and his exotic little Toppy, it was not difficult to believe that his first job had been that of "milker" on a farm. But as he said himself, he'd been born to milk more than cows. And thirty years later it was Joseph le Roy who put his signature to a deal unifying New Zealand's dairy farms into a single great dried-milk combine.

It was a magic scheme—the Cremogen Combine. It was le Roy who saw the possibilities in dried-milk goods, advertising them worldwide as God-given nourishment for infants and invalids. The achievement lay in Joe's audacity. All surplus skim milk, which had previously been poured down the drain or given to the pigs was now sold in Joe's brightly packaged tins as Cremogen, Cremax, and Cremafat at three times the price of fresh milk.

Mrs. Lawrence's husband was manager of the English le Roy interests. Yet it was more than the bare association of commerce which drew Mrs. Lawrence and Toppy together. Frances, far more at home in the smart society in London than Toppy, had an amused affection for the girl. When Andrew went upstairs after his interview with le Roy she was waiting for him outside Toppy's room. Indeed, on subsequent visits she was usually present, helping with his exacting, wilful patient.

Grateful to Mrs. Lawrence, he was still diffident enough to feel it strange that this exclusive person should have even this mild interest in him. He had an extraordinary desire to fathom her character, her personality. She was always at ease, watchful in everything she did, despite the graceful casualness of her speech.

He hardly realized that the suggestion was hers, yet he began to ask himself impatiently how any doctor could develop a high-class practice without a smart car. Three weeks later a brown, folding-roof coupé, brand new and darkly glittering, drew up at 9 Chesborough Terrace. Easing himself from the driving seat Andrew ran up the stairs of his house. "Christine!" he called out, trying to suppress the gloating excitement in his voice. "Christine! Come and see something!"

He had meant to stagger her. And he succeeded. "Goodness!" She clutched his arm. "Is it *ours?* Oh! what a beauty!"

"Isn't she! Look *out*, dear, don't handle the paintwork! It's—it's liable to mark the varnish!" He smiled at her in quite his old way. "Pretty good surprise, eh, Chris? Me getting it and licensing it and everything and never saying a word to you. Step in, lady, and I'll demonstrate. She goes like a bird."

She could not admire the little car enough as he took her, bareheaded, for a short spin. Their moments of intimacy, of understanding and happiness together, were so rare now that she was loath to relinquish this one. She murmured: "It'll be so easy for you to get about now, dear." Then, again, diffidently, "And if we could get out a little bit into the country, say on Sundays, into the woods—oh, it would be *wonderful.*"

"Of course," he answered absently. "But it's really for the practice. We can't go getting mud all over it!"

On Thursday of the following week, as he came out of 17a Green Street, he ran straight into Freddie Hamson.

Hamson's expression was frankly nonplussed. "Why, hello!" said Freddie. "What are you doing here?"

"Patient," Andrew answered, jerking his head in the direction of 17a. "I've got Joe le Roy's daughter on my hands."

"Joe le Roy!"

That exclamation alone was worth much to Andrew. He put a proprietary hand on the door of his beautiful new coupé.

"Which way are you going? Can I drop you anywhere?"

Freddie recovered himself quickly. Indeed, in thirty seconds, his whole idea of Manson's usefulness to him had undergone a swift and unexpected revolution. "Yes," he smiled companionably. "I was going along to Ida Sherrington's Nursing Home. Walking to keep the old figure down. But I'll step in with you."

Hamson was thinking hard. Looking astutely ahead, Freddie suddenly saw a profitable basis for cooperation between Andrew and himself. He would go carefully, of course, for Manson was a touchy, uncertain devil. He said: "Come in and see Mrs. Raeburn with me. You're strong on lungs, aren't you? Come along and examine her chest. It'll please her enormously. And it'll be five guineas for you."

"What—you mean—? But what's the matter with her?"

"Nothing much," Freddie smiled. "She's probably got a touch of senile bronchitis! And she'd love to see you! That's how we do it here. Ivory and Deedman and I. You really ought to be in on it, Manson—it would amaze you how it works out."

Andrew drew up at the house indicated by Hamson, an ordinary town house, tall and narrow, in a noisy street. It was difficult to imagine how any sick person could find peace here. Andrew mentioned this to Hamson as they mounted the steps to the front door.

"I know, my dear fellow," Freddie agreed. "But all the nursing homes are the same. This little bit of the West End is jammed with them. You see, we must have them convenient to ourselves. Now you must meet Ida."

With the air of a man who knows his way about, he led the way into a constricted office on the ground floor, where a little woman in a mauve uniform and a stiff white headdress sat at a small desk. "Morning, Ida," Freddie exclaimed, between flattery and familiarity. "Doing your sums?"

She raised her eyes and smiled good-naturedly. She was short and stout, with a look of coarse bustling vitality.

Yet Ida Sherrington's Nursing Home was the most fashionable in London. Half the peerage had been to Ida, society women, racing men, famous barristers and diplomats. The prices which she charged her patients were fantastic.

Ida had a soft side for the younger members of the profession and she greeted Manson agreeably as Freddie babbled: "Take a good look at him. He'll soon be sending you so many patients you'll overflow into the Plaza Hotel."

"The Plaza overflows into me," Ida replied knowingly.

"Ha! Ha!" Freddie laughed. "That's pretty good—I must tell old Deedman that one. Come on, Manson. We'll go up top."

The cramped lift, just wide enough to hold a wheeled stretcher diagonally, took them to the fourth floor. The passage was narrow, trays stood outside the doors, and vases of flowers wilted in the hot atmosphere. They went into Mrs. Raeburn's room.

She was a woman of over sixty, propped up on her pillows, holding a slip of paper on which she had written certain symptoms experienced during the night, together with questions which she wished to ask. Seated on the bed, Freddie felt her pulse, listened to her and gaily reassured her. He asked her to allow his colleague, Dr. Manson, whose speciality was lungs, to examine her chest. Mrs. Raeburn enjoyed it all very much. She was wealthy, without relatives, and spent her time equally between exclusive hotels and West End nursing homes.

"Lord!" Freddie exclaimed when they had left the room. "You've no idea what a goldmine that old woman has been to us."

Andrew did not answer. The atmosphere of this place slightly sickened him. There was nothing wrong with the old lady's lungs and only her touching look of gratitude towards Freddie saved the matter from being downright dishonest.

At the end of the month, when he received a neatly written cheque from Mrs. Raeburn—with her best thanks—for five guineas, he laughed at his silly scruples.

Chapter 3

The practice now began a rapid, almost electrifying expansion in all directions. Andrew's surgery receipts began to soar and soon he managed to have the front of the house repainted and to refurnish his surgery and consulting room with a new couch, a padded swing-chair, a rubber-tyred trolley, and sundry elegantly scientific cabinets in white enamel and glass.

The manifest prosperity of the freshly cream-painted house, of his car, of this glitteringly modern equipment, soon brought back many of the "good" patients who had consulted Dr. Foy in the past but had gradually dropped away. The days of hanging about were finished for Andrew. At the evening surgeries it was as much as he could do to keep going, the front bell purring, the surgery door "pinging", causing him to dash between the surgery and the consulting room. So evolved a scheme to save his time.

"Listen, Chris," he said one morning. "I've just struck on something that's going to help me a lot in these rush hours. It's a shocking waste of time for me to make up the medicine after I've seen a patient in the surgery—when I might be using it to polish off one of the 'good' patients waiting to see me in the consulting room. Well, from now on, you're my dispenser!"

She looked at him with a startled contraction of her brows.

"But I don't know anything about making up medicine."

He smiled reassuringly. "That's all right. I've prepared a few nice stock mixtures. All you have to do is to fill the bottles, and label them."

"But—" Christine's perplexity showed in her eyes. "Oh, I want to help you, Andrew—only—do you really believe—"

"Don't you see I've *got* to!" His gaze avoided hers.

In the old days she would have taken a firm stand. But now, sadly, she reflected on the reversal of their earlier relationship. She no longer influenced, guided him. It was he who drove ahead.

She began to stand in the dispensary during those hectic surgery periods, waiting for his tense exclamation, in his rapid transit between "good" and surgery patients: "Iron!" or "Alba!" or "Carminative!" When she would protest that the iron mixture had run out, a strung-up bark: "Anything! Damn it! *Anything!*"

After surgery they made up the ledger. "My God! What a day, Chris!" he would gloat. "We took over eight pounds *cash*." He tucked the money, heavy piles of silver and a few notes, into the little tobacco sack which Dr. Foy had used as his money bag, and locked it away. "We've got it absolutely gilt-edged every way, Chris," he exulted. "A paying surgery and a sound middle-class connection. And on top of that I'm building up a first-rate consultant practice on my own."

One evening after surgery Mrs. Lawrence rang him up. He always enjoyed the graceful inconsequence of her telephone conversations, but today, after mentioning that her husband was fishing in Ireland, she asked him to luncheon on the following Friday.

"Toppy'll be there. And one or two other people. It might do you some good—perhaps—to know them."

He hung up the receiver feeling something between satisfaction and an odd irritation. In his heart he was piqued that Christine had not been invited too. Then, gradually, he came to see that it was not a social but really a business occasion. And, in any case, Christine need know nothing at all of the affair. When Friday came he told her that he had a luncheon engagement with Hamson and jumped into his car, relieved. He forgot that he was an extremely bad liar.

Frances Lawrence's house was in a quiet Knightsbridge street. Andrew was late in arriving and most of the guests were already there: Toppy, Rosa Keane, the novelist, Sir Rumbold Dudley-Blane, MD, FRCP, and member of the board of Cremo Products, Nicol Watson, traveller and anthropologist, and several others.

He found himself at a table beside a Mrs. Thornton who lived in Leicestershire, and who came up periodically to Brown's Hotel for a short season in town. Though he was now able calmly to sustain the ordeal of introductions, he was glad to regain his assurance under cover of her chatter.

Giving one ear to Mrs. Thornton, who took his mute listening for interest, he still managed to hear something of the suave and witty conversation around him—Rosa Keane's acid pleasantries, Watson's fascinating account of a recent expedition through the Paraguayan interior. "Of course," Watson concluded his narrative with a deprecatory smile. "Easily one's most devastating experience was to come home and run straight into an attack of influenza."

"Ha!" said Sir Rumbold. "So you've been a victim too." By the device of clearing his throat, he gained the attention of the table. Sir Rumbold was at home in this position—for many years now the attention of the great British public had been focused upon him. It was Sir Rumbold who, a quarter of a century before, declared that a certain portion of man's intestine was not only useless but definitely harmful. Hundreds of people had rushed straight away to have the dangerous section removed and the fame of the operation established Sir Rumbold's reputation as a dietitian.

He now said, glancing paternally at Frances: "One of the most interesting features of this recent epidemic has been the spectacular therapeutic effect of Cremogen. We have no cure for influenza, but we have proved incontestably the phenomenal power of Cremogen in organizing the vital antagonism of the body."

Watson turned to Andrew with his odd smile. "What do you think of Cremo productions, doctor?"

Caught unawares, Andrew found himself saying: "It's as good a way of taking skim milk as any other."

Rosa Keane, with a swift, approving side glance, was unkind enough to laugh. Frances was smiling too. Hurriedly, Sir Rumbold passed to a description of a recent visit to the Trossachs.

Otherwise the luncheon was harmonious. Andrew eventually

found himself joining freely in the conversation. Before he took his leave Frances had a word with him.

"You really do shine," she murmured, "out of the consulting room. Mrs. Thornton hasn't been able to drink her coffee for telling me about you. I think you've bagged her as a patient."

On the following morning, however, at half past ten, he had an unpleasant shock. Freddie Hamson rang him to inquire briskly: "Enjoy your lunch yesterday? How did I know? Why, you old dog, haven't you seen this morning's *Tribune*?"

Dismayed, Andrew went directly into the waiting room, where the papers were laid out when Christine and he had finished with them. He slowly went through the *Tribune*. There, on the society gossip page, was a photograph of Frances Lawrence with a paragraph describing the luncheon party, his name amongst the guests.

With a chagrined face he slipped the sheet from the others, crushed it into a ball, flung it in the fire. Then he realized that Christine had already read the paper. Had she seen this paragraph? He frowned in an access of vexation.

Christine *had* seen the paragraph. And, after a momentary bewilderment, the hurt of it struck her to the heart. Why had he not told her? She would not have minded his going to this stupid lunch. She tried to reassure herself—it was all too trivial to cause her such anxiety and pain. But she saw, with a dull ache, that its implications were not trivial.

It was Saturday morning and she had promised to take Florrie Bennett shopping. Florrie was a bright little girl and Christine had become attached to her. She was waiting now, sent up by her mother from the basement, clean and wearing a fresh frock.

Christine felt better in the open air with the child holding her hand, walking down the market, talking to her friends amongst the stall holders, buying fruit, flowers, trying to think of something especially nice to please Andrew. Yet the wound was still open. Why, why had he not told her?

But actually her concern was less for herself than for him. She knew that it was possible for him to be as fine a doctor in Green Street, Mayfair, as in Cefan Row, Aberalaw. Yet she did feel that in those days in Aberalaw his idealism had been pure, illuminating both their lives with a clear white flame. Now the flame had turned yellower and the globe of the lamp was smudged.

As she went into Frau Schmidt's, she tried to erase the lines of worry from her brow. Nevertheless, she found the old woman looking at her sharply. And presently Frau Schmidt grumbled: "You don't eat enough, my dear! Look! I will make you taste this. It iss good!" She cut a slice of her famous boiled ham and made Christine eat a soft bread sandwich. At the same time Florrie was provided with an iced pastry.

Frau Schmidt kept talking. "And now you want some Liptauer. Herr Doctor—he has eaten pounds of my cheese and he never grows tired of it." Chuckling, Frau Schmidt ran on until they left her.

Outside, Christine and Florrie stood on the kerb waiting till the policeman on duty—an old friend called Struthers—should signal them across the busy road.

They were home at last and Christine began to unwrap her purchases. As she put the chrysanthemums she had bought into a vase, she began to feel sad again. Suddenly the telephone rang.

She answered it, her face still, her lips slightly drooping. Afterwards her expression was transfigured, her eyes bright and excited. From time to time she glanced out of the window, eager for Andrew's return, her despondency forgotten in the good news she had received. Nothing could have been more propitious.

When he arrived she ran to meet him in the hall. "Andrew! Sir Robert Abbey had just been on the telephone."

"Yes?" His face which had drawn into sudden compunction at the sight of her, cleared.

"Yes! He rang up himself, he was terribly nice. Darling! You're to be appointed to out-patients at the Victoria Hospital!"

His eyes filled slowly with excited realization. "Why—that's good news, Chris."

"Isn't it, isn't it," she cried, delighted. "Your own work again—chances for research—" She put her arms round his neck and hugged him.

He looked down at her, indescribably touched by her love, her generous unselfishness. He had a momentary pang. "What a good soul you are, Chris! And—and what a lout I am!"

THE FOLLOWING MONTH Andrew began his duties at the Victoria Chest Hospital. His days were Tuesdays and Thursdays, the hours from three until five o'clock in the afternoon. It was exactly like his old surgery days in Aberalaw except that now all the cases which came to him were specialized lung and bronchial conditions. And he was, of course, now an honorary physician in one of the oldest and most famous hospitals in London.

The Victoria Hospital was unquestionably old. Situated in Battersea in a network of streets close to the Thames, it seldom caught, even in summer, more than a stray gleam of sunshine.

The out-patients department was, in part, a relic of the eighteenth century. The untiled walls were painted dark chocolate, the uneven passages, though scrupulously clean, were so ill-ventilated that they sweated, and throughout there hung the musty odour of sheer old age.

On his first day, he went round with Dr. Eustace Thoroughgood, the senior honorary, a kindly man of fifty, rather like an agreeable churchwarden. After their tour of the hospital he took Andrew to the basement commonroom. A fine fire blazed in the grate and on the walls there hung portraits of distinguished physicians to the hospital.

They had a pleasant tea and much hot buttered toast with the other members of the staff. Andrew thought the house physicians were likeable youngsters. Yet, as he noted their deference to Dr. Thoroughgood and himself, he could not refrain from smiling at the recollection of his clashes with their like not so many months ago, in the frequent struggles to get his patients into hospital.

Dr. Thoroughgood was a sympathetic and helpful colleague, and a sound physician. But in treatment, his tidy mind resented the intrusion of the new. He would have nothing to do with tuberculin, holding that its value was still unproved, and was chary of using pneumothorax, an operation to collapse a diseased lung artificially.

Andrew forgot about Thoroughgood in beginning his own work. He gave, at the outset, quite a good imitation of his old ardour and enthusiasm, but yet his heart was not in the work. He could not recapture the spontaneous enthusiasm of his silica inhalation investigations. He had far too much on his mind, too many important cases in his practice, to be able to concentrate upon obscure signs which might not even exist. And he was always in a hurry. Soon he fell into an attitude of admirable logic—humanly speaking, he simply could not do everything.

The poor people who came to the hospital dispensary did not demand much of him, and, so long as he prescribed generously and made an occasional joke, his popularity was never in doubt. He soon adopted the habit of having his regular patients up, in a bunch, to his desk at the beginning of dispensary, then rapidly initialling their cards. As he scribbled Rep. Mist—the mixture as before—he had no time to recollect how he had once derided this classic phrase.

SIX WEEKS after he had taken over at the Victoria, as he sat at breakfast with Christine, he opened a letter which bore the Marseilles postmark. Gazing at it unbelievingly for a moment, he gave a sudden exclamation: "It's from Denny! He's sick of Mexico at last! Coming back to settle down—I'll believe that when I see it! But, Lord! It'll be good to see him again. Have you got the paper there, Chris? Look up when the *Oreta* gets in."

She was as pleased as he at the news, but for a rather different reason. She had always recognized that Denny, and indeed, in a lesser degree, Hope, exerted a beneficial effect upon Andrew. No sooner had this letter arrived than her mind was at work planning a meeting which would bring these three together.

The day before the *Oreta* was due at Tilbury she broached the matter. "I wonder if you'd mind, Andrew—I thought I might give a little dinner next week—just for you and Denny and Hope."

He gazed at her in some surprise. In view of the vague constraint between them it was strange to hear her talk of entertaining. He answered: "Hope's probably in Cambridge. And Denny and I might as well go out somewhere." Then, seeing her face, he relented quickly. "Oh! All right. Make it Sunday though; that's the best night for all of us."

On the following Sunday Denny arrived, stockier and more brick-red of face and neck than ever. He seemed less morose, more contented in his manner. Yet he was the same Denny, his greeting to them being: "This is a very grand house. Sure I haven't made a mistake?"

Seated, a moment later, he refused a drink. "No! I'm a regular limejuicer now. Strange as it may seem I'm going to set to now. I've had enough of the wide and starry sky."

Andrew considered him with affectionate reproof. "You really should settle down, Philip," he said. "After all, you're on the right side of forty. And with your talents—"

Denny shot him a glance from beneath his brows.

"Don't be so smug, Professor. I may still show you a few tricks."

He told them he had been appointed Surgical Registrar of the South Hertfordshire Infirmary, three hundred a year and all found. He did not consider it a permanency, but he would be able to refresh his surgical technique there.

"Don't know how they gave me the job," he argued. "It must be another case of mistaken identity."

"No," said Andrew rather stolidly, "it's your MS, Philip. A first-class degree like that will get you anywhere."

"What have you been doing to him?" Denny groaned. "He don't sound like the bloke what blew up that sewer with me."

At this point Hope arrived. He had not met Denny before. But five minutes was enough for them to understand one another. At dinner they were agreeably united in being rude to Manson.

"Of course, Hope," Philip remarked, as he unfolded his napkin. "You needn't expect much food here. Oh, no! They were thrown out of their last home for starving their guinea pigs."

"I usually carry an egg in my pocket," said Hope. "But unfortunately Mother's hens are not laying at the moment."

There was more of this as the meal went on—Hope's facetiousness seemed especially provoked by Denny's presence—but gradually they settled down to talk. Denny related some of his experiences overseas; and Hope detailed for them the latest activities of the Mines Fatigue Board.

"Thank heaven my scholarship has only another nine months to run. Then I'm going to *do* something. I'm tired of working out other people's ideas. I wish to God I had a lab of my own!"

Then, as Christine had hoped, the talk became violently medical. After dinner when coffee was brought in, she sat, her elbows on the table, chin on her hands, listening silently, forgotten, her eyes fixed earnestly on Andrew's face.

At first he had appeared stiff and reserved. Though it was a joy to see Philip again he felt that his old friend was a little casual towards his success, even mildly derisive. And after all, what had Denny done? When Hope chipped in with his attempts at humour he had almost told them to stop being funny at his expense.

Yet now that they were talking shop he was drawn into it unconsciously. They were discussing hospitals which caused him suddenly to express himself upon the whole hospital system.

"The way I look at it is this." He took a long breath of smoke—

it was not now a cheap cigarette but a cigar—"the whole structure is obsolete. Mind you, I'm not knocking my own hospital. I love it down there at the Victoria and I can tell you we do great work. But it's the system. The Victoria is falling down. And what are we doing about it? Collecting pennies. At the Victoria, if we're lucky, in ten years' time, we'll start to build a new wing. But what *is* the use of a lung hospital in the centre of a foggy city like London? And it's the same with most of the other hospitals, *and* the nursing homes. They're bang in the middle of roaring traffic—the patients' beds rattle when the buses go past."

"Well, what's the remedy?" Philip lifted an eyebrow.

"Decentralization is the remedy," Andrew answered. "Why shouldn't our big hospitals stand in a green belt outside London? Take a place like Benham, for instance, only ten miles out, where there's still green country, fresh air, quiet. The tube could take you out there in exactly eighteen minutes, and considering that it takes our fastest ambulance forty minutes on the average to bring in an emergency, that sounds to me an improvement. But what's being done? Zero, absolute zero. We just drag on, in the old, old way. Lord, if I had my way I'd raze the Victoria flat and have a new chest hospital out at Benham. And by God! I'd show a rise in our recovery rate!"

This was merely by way of introduction. The crescendo of discussion rose.

Philip got on to his old contention—the folly of asking the general practitioner to pull everything out of the one black bag, the stupidity of making him carry everything on his shoulders until that moment when, for five guineas, some specialist he has never seen before tells him it is too late to do anything at all.

Hope expressed the case of the young bacteriologist, sandwiched between commercialism and conservatism—on the one hand, the bland firm of chemists who would pay him a wage to make proprietary articles, on the other a hospital board of blithering dotards.

They did not stop until after twelve o'clock when they found sandwiches and coffee before them on the table.

"Oh, I say, Mrs. Manson," Hope protested with a politeness which showed that, in Denny's gibe, he was a Nice Young Man at Heart. "We must have bored you stiff. Funny how hungry talking makes one."

After Hope had left, Denny remained a few minutes longer. Then, Andrew having gone to ring for a taxi, he apologetically brought out a small, very beautiful Spanish shawl. "The Professor will probably slay me," he said. "But this is for you." He arrested Christine's gratitude by saying, "Extraordinary how all these shawls come from China. They're not really Spanish. I got that one in Shanghai on my way home."

A silence fell. They could hear Andrew coming back from the telephone in the hall.

Denny got up, his kind, wrinkled eyes avoiding hers. "I wouldn't worry too much about him, you know." He smiled. "But we must try to get him back to Drineffy standards."

Chapter 4

At the beginning of the Easter school holidays, Andrew received a note from Mrs. Thornton, at Brown's Hotel, telling him that since she had been much struck by his interest at Mrs. Lawrence's, she was anxious to have his advice about her daughter Sybil's foot.

He made the visit promptly, and found the condition was perfectly simple. Yet it was one which demanded an early operation. He straightened himself, with a smile to the solid Sybil, and explained this to Mrs. Thornton.

"The bone has thickened. Might develop into a hammer toe if it's left untreated. I suggest you have it seen to at once."

"That's what the school doctor said." Mrs. Thornton was not surprised. "Sybil can go into a home here. I want you to undertake all the arrangements. Whom do you suggest should do it?"

The direct question momentarily stumped Andrew. Suddenly he thought of Ivory. He said pleasantly: "Mr. Ivory might do this for us—if he's available."

Mrs. Thornton had heard of Mr. Ivory. Of course! Wasn't he the surgeon who had been in all the newspapers the month before, through having flown to Cairo to attend a case of sunstroke? She thought it an admirable suggestion.

Andrew went home and hesitantly rang Ivory. But Ivory's manner—friendly, confident, charming—reassured him. They arranged to see the case together on the following day.

Next morning, when Ivory had agreed emphatically in Mrs.

Thornton's presence with all that Andrew had said, Sybil was transferred to Ida Sherrington's Nursing Home and two days later the operation was performed.

Andrew was there. Ivory insisted that he be present, in the most genuine and friendly fashion imaginable.

The operation was not difficult—indeed in his Drineffy days Andrew would have tackled it himself—and Ivory accomplished it with imposing competence. Andrew watched him from the other side of the table with grudging respect.

A fortnight later, when Sybil Thornton had left the home, Ivory asked him to lunch at the Sackville Club. Ivory was an entertaining conversationalist, with a fund of up-to-the-minute gossip. The high dining room of the Sackville, with its Adam ceilings and crystal chandeliers, was full of famous people. Andrew found the experience flattering, as no doubt Ivory intended it should be.

"You must let me put your name up at the next meeting," the surgeon remarked. "You'd find a lot of friends here—Freddie, Paul, myself—by the way, Jackie Lawrence is a member. Interesting marriage that, they're perfect good friends and they each go their own way! By the by, we'll be hearing from the Thorntons presently. You leave all that to me. They're first-class people. And incidentally, while I speak of it, don't you think Sybil ought to have her tonsils seen to? No end of septic absorption. I took the liberty of saying we might do them for her when the warm weather comes in!"

Three weeks later, as he sat at tea with Christine, the afternoon post brought him a letter from Ivory.

My dear Manson,

Mrs. Thornton has just come nicely up to scratch. As I am sending the anaesthetist his bit I may as well send you yours—for assisting me so splendidly at the operation.

Ever cordially yours,

C.I.

Enclosed was a cheque for twenty guineas.

Andrew stared at the cheque in astonishment—he had done nothing to assist Ivory at the operation—then gradually the warm feeling which money always gave him now stole round his heart. With a complacent smile he handed over the letter and the cheque for Christine's inspection.

"Damned decent of Ivory, isn't it, Chris? I bet we'll have a record in our receipts this month."

"But I don't understand." Her expression was perplexed. "Is this your bill to Mrs. Thornton?"

"No—silly," he chuckled. "It's a little extra. I earned this fee for assisting, for being *there*, just as the anaesthetist earned his fee for giving the anaesthetic. Ivory sends it all in with his bill."

She laid the cheque upon the table, subdued, unhappy.

"It seems a great deal of money."

"Well, why not?" He closed the argument in a blaze of indignation. "The Thorntons are rich. This is probably no more to them than three and six to one of our surgery patients."

When he had gone, her eyes remained fastened upon the cheque with strained apprehension. How terribly fond he now was of money. Tears welled slowly to her eyes. She must speak to him, oh, she must, she must.

That evening, after surgery, she approached him diffidently. "Andrew, could we go out to the country on Sunday in, the car? We haven't been able to go all winter."

He glanced at her queerly. "Well—oh! all right."

Sunday was a soft spring day. With a rug and a picnic basket in the back of the car they set off. Christine's spirits lifted as they ran across Hammersmith Bridge. Soon they were through Dorking, turning onto the road to Shere. The village, with its stream quietly wandering amongst the watercress beds, was as yet untroubled by summer tourists. They parked the car near one of the close-turfed bridle paths. There, in the little clearing where they spread the rug, was a singing solitude which belonged only to them and the birds.

They ate sandwiches in the sunshine, drank the coffee from the thermos. Around them primroses grew in great profusion. Christine longed to gather them, to bury her face in their cool softness. Andrew lay with half-closed eyes, his head resting near her. A sweet tranquillity settled upon the dark uneasiness of her soul. If their life together could always be like this!

His drowsy gaze had been resting on the car and suddenly he said: "Not a bad old bus, is she, Chris?—I mean, for what she cost us. But we shall want a new one at the Motor Show."

She stirred—her disquiet renewed by this fresh instance of his restless striving. "But we haven't had her any time."

"Hum! She's sluggish. Didn't you notice how that Buick kept ahead of us. I want one of these new Vitesse saloons."

"But why?"

"Why not? We can afford it." He lit a cigarette and turned to her with every sign of satisfaction. "Yes! My dear little schoolmarm from Drineffy, we are rapidly getting rich."

She did not answer his smile. She felt her body, peaceful and warm in the sunshine, chill suddenly. She said: "Dear, do we really want to be rich? When we had scarcely any money we were —oh! we were deliriously happy. We never talked of it then. But now we never talk of anything else. Don't you remember how you used to speak of life—as though you had to take some castle that you knew was there, but couldn't see, on the top—"

He muttered uncomfortably. "Oh! I was young then—foolish. That was just romantic talk."

She took a shaky breath. "Darling! Please listen to me. I've been so unhappy at this—the change in you. It's dragging us away from one another."

"What have I done?" he protested irritably. "Do I beat you, do I get drunk? Give me one example of my *crimes*."

Desperately, she replied: "It's your whole attitude, darling. Take that cheque Ivory sent you. It's a small matter on the surface perhaps, but underneath—oh, underneath it's cheap and grasping and dishonest."

She felt him stiffen, then he sat up, offended, glaring at her! "For God's sake! What's wrong with my taking it?"

"Can't you see?" All the accumulated emotion of the past months overwhelmed her, causing her suddenly to burst into tears. "For God's sake, darling. Don't . . . don't *sell* yourself!"

Furious with her, he spoke slowly, with cutting deliberation. "For the last time! Can't you stop nagging?"

"I haven't nagged you," she sobbed. "I've wanted to speak before, but I haven't."

"Then don't." He lost his temper and suddenly shouted, "Do you hear me. *Don't*. You talk as if I was some kind of dirty crook. I only want to get on. People judge you by what you are, what you have. If you're one of the have-nots you get ordered about. In future I'm going to do the ordering. Now don't even mention this damned nonsense to me again."

"All right," she wept. "But I tell you—some day you'll be sorry."

The excursion was ruined for them, and most of all for her. Though she dried her eyes and gathered a large bunch of primroses, all the rapture of the day was dead.

His anger turned gradually to indignation. Why should Chris, of all people, set upon him? Other women, and charming women too, were enthusiastic at his rapid rise.

A few days later, Frances Lawrence rang him up. She had spent the winter in Jamaica, but now she was back, eager to see her friends. He went round to tea. She was beautifully tanned, her spare face stained as a faun's. The pleasure of seeing her again was intensified by the welcome in her eyes.

They talked as old friends. She told him of her trip, of the coral gardens, of the heavenly climate. He gave her, in return, an account of his progress. Perhaps some indication of his thoughts crept into his words for she answered lightly: "You're frightfully solemn and disgracefully prosy. Frankly, I think it's because you're doing too much. For my part I should have thought it time for you to take a consulting room up West."

At this point her husband entered, tall, lounging, mannered. He nodded to Andrew, and gracefully accepted a cup of tea.

Half an hour later, as Andrew drove home, Mrs. Lawrence's suggestion firmly occupied his mind. Why shouldn't he take a consulting room in Welbeck Street? He wouldn't give up his profitable practice but he could easily combine it with a room up West, use the better address for his correspondence, his bills.

Without saying anything to Christine he began to look for a West End consulting room. And when he found one, about a month later, it gave him great satisfaction to declare in assumed indifference, over the morning paper: "By the way, I've taken a place in Welbeck Street now. I shall use it for my better-class consultations."

THE ROOM at 57a Welbeck Street gave Andrew a new surge of triumph—I'm there, he secretly exulted, I'm there at last!

On the day the lease was signed, Hamson accompanied him round to take possession. Freddie had proved extraordinarily helpful in all the preliminaries and had found him a useful nurse. Nurse Sharp was not beautiful. She was middle-aged, with a sour, yet capable expression. Freddie explained her concisely:

"The last thing a fellow wants is a pretty nurse. You know what

I mean, old man. Fun is fun. But business is business. And you can't combine the two."

While Freddie and he stood discussing the arrangement of the room, Mrs. Lawrence unexpectedly appeared. She had been passing and came in, gaily, to investigate his choice. She did not stay long but she had ideas, suggestions for decoration, for the window hangings and the curtains, far more tasteful than the crude plannings of Freddie and himself.

Bereft of her vivacious presence the room was suddenly empty. Freddie gushed: "You're a lucky devil, if ever I met one. She's a nice thing."

Andrew pretended he didn't know what Freddie was driving at.

He had not many patients at the start. But by dint of writing politely to every doctor who sent him cases at the Chest Hospital he soon had a network reaching out all over London which began to bring private patients to his door.

In June, Sybil Thornton's tonsils came out. They were, to a certain extent, enlarged. Ivory did the enucleation with care.

"I prefer to go slow with these lymphoid tissues," he said to Andrew as they washed up. "I daresay you've seen people whip them out. *I* don't work that way."

When Andrew received his cheque from Ivory, Freddie was with him. "You know, Manson," Freddie now remarked. "I'm glad you've chucked your old holy-willy attitude. Even now, you know," he squinted at the cheque, "you're not getting all the juice out of the orange. You hang in with me, my lad, and you'll find your fruit more succulent."

That evening, as he drove home, he was in an unusually light-hearted mood. When he reached Chesborough Terrace and entered the front room he found Christine knitting there, with his tea—which she had rung for at the sound of his car—set out upon a tray. When he had accepted a cup of tea she said quietly:

"Mrs. Lawrence rang you again this afternoon. No message."

"Oh!" He flushed. "How do you mean—again?"

"This is the fourth time she's rung you in a week."

"Well, what of it? Can *I* help it if she rings me?"

She was silent, her eyes downcast. If he had known the tumult in that still breast he would not have lost his temper as he did.

"You would think I was a bigamist the way you go on. She's a perfectly nice woman. Why, her husband is one of my best friends. They're charming people. They don't hang about looking like a sick pup. Oh, hell—"

He gulped down the rest of his tea and got up. Yet the moment he was out of the room he was sorry. He flung into the surgery, reflecting wretchedly that things were going from bad to worse between Christine and himself. Their growing estrangement was the one dark cloud in the bright sky of his success.

Christine and he had been ideally happy in their married life. He did not idolize her as he once had done, but he was—oh, damn it all!—he was *fond* of her. As he stood there he had a sudden desire to please, propitiate her. Suddenly his eye brightened. He glanced at his watch, found that he had just half an hour before Laurier's closed. The next minute he was in his car on his way to see Miss Cramb.

Miss Cramb was immediately and fervently at his service. They walked into the fur department where various "skins" were modelled. Miss Cramb stroked them with expert fingers, pointing out all that one should look for in this special pelt. In the end he made a selection which she cordially approved, saying, "They're beautiful skins. Your wife will be proud to wear them."

On the following Saturday at ten o'clock, Andrew took the distinctive dark, olive-green box and went into the drawing room. "Christine!" he called. "Here a moment!"

She was upstairs but she came at once, her eyes wondering a little at his summons.

"Look, dear!" Now that the climax approached he felt awkward. "I bought you this. I know—I know we haven't been getting on so well lately. But this ought to show you—" He broke off and, like a schoolboy, handed her the box.

She was very pale as she opened it. Her hands trembled upon the string. Then she gave a cry: "What lovely, lovely furs."

There, in the tissue paper, lay a double stole of silver fox, two exquisite skins shaped fashionably into one.

"Do you like them, Chris? The good old Half-Back helped me choose them. They're absolutely first-class quality. You see that sheen on them and the silver marking on the back—that's what you want specially to look for!"

Tears were running down her cheeks. She turned to him quite wildly. "You do love me, don't you, darling? That's all that matters to me in the world."

Reassured at last, she tried on the furs. They were magnificent. He could not admire them enough. He wanted to make the reconciliation complete. He smiled. "Look here, Chris. We'll have a little celebration today. Meet me at one o'clock at the Plaza Grill."

All morning he was gayer than he had been for months. Fool that he'd been!—neglecting Christine. All women liked to have attention paid to them. The Plaza Grill was just the place—all London, or most of it that mattered, could be seen there.

He waited for her in a small lounge, watching as all the best tables became occupied. It was twenty minutes past one when she came hurrying in, flustered by the ornate flunkeys and the fact that, for the last half-hour, she had been standing in the wrong lounge.

"I'm so sorry, darling," she gasped. "I waited and waited. And then I found it was the restaurant lounge."

Late now, they were given a bad table wedged against a pillar beside the service. The place was grotesquely crowded.

"Now, Chris, what would you like?" Andrew said.

"You order, darling," she answered faintly.

He ordered a rich, expensive lunch: caviare, *soupe Prince de Galles, poulet riche,* asparagus, *fraises de bois* in syrup, and a bottle of Liebfraumilch.

"We didn't know much about this in our Drineffy days." He laughed. "Nothing like doing ourselves well, old girl."

Nobly, she tried to respond to his mood, but the smart vulgarity of the place was hateful to her. All at once she began to lose her poise. She felt other women staring at her, conscious of the discrepancy between her new furs and her inexpensive dress.

"What's the matter?" he asked suddenly. "Aren't you enjoying yourself?"

"Yes, of course," she protested, wanly trying to smile. But her lips were stiff. She could barely swallow the creamed chicken.

"You're not listening to a thing I say," he muttered resentfully. "Damn it all, when a man takes his wife out—"

"Could I have a little water?" she asked feebly. She could have screamed. She didn't belong there. Nervously she lifted an asparagus stalk. As she did so the head broke and fell, dripping with sauce, on the new fur. The blonde at the next table turned to her companion with an amused smile. Andrew saw that smile. He gave up the attempt at entertainment.

They went home drearily. They were wider apart than before.

The pain in Christine's heart was intolerable. She began to ask herself if she was the right wife for him. That night she put her arms round his neck and kissed him, thanking him again for the furs and for taking her out.

"Glad you enjoyed it," he said flatly. And went to his own room.

AT THIS POINT an event occurred which diverted Andrew's attention from his difficulties at home. He read in the *Tribune* that Richard Stillman, the lung expert from Portland, Oregon, was staying at Brooks Hotel, London.

He pondered over the *Tribune*, glad that he could now approach Stillman with the standing of a Welbeck Street consultant. He typed a letter recalling himself to the American and asking him to lunch at the Plaza on Wednesday.

The following morning Stillman rang him up. His voice was quiet, friendly. "Glad to be talking to you, Dr. Manson. I'd be pleased for us to lunch. But don't let's make it the Plaza. I hate that place already. Why don't you lunch with me here?"

Andrew found Stillman in his suite at Brooks, a quietly select hotel. The American was about fifty, small and slight. His complexion was a boyish pink and white, his light-coloured hair thin and parted in the middle. It was only when Andrew saw his eyes, pale, steady and glacially blue, that he realized the driving force behind this insignificant frame.

"Hope you didn't mind coming here," said Stillman in his quiet manner. "I know we Americans are supposed to like the Plaza." He smiled, revealing himself human. "But a lousy crowd goes there." He paused. "And now let me congratulate you again on that splendid inhalation paper."

They descended to the restaurant, gave their orders and Andrew turned with respect to his companion. It was impossible to remain in Stillman's presence long without acknowledging the compelling interest of his personality. His history too was unique.

Richard Stillman came of an old Boston family which had, for generations, been connected with the law. But young Stillman managed to persuade his father to allow him to study medicine at Harvard. After two years his father died suddenly, leaving the family in unexpectedly poor circumstances. At this point Richard's grandfather insisted that his grandson should abandon his medical studies in favour of the family tradition of the law. Richard was forced to take a legal degree, and in 1906 he entered the family company and, for four years, devoted himself to it.

It was, however, a half-hearted devotion. Bacteriology was his passion, and he set up a small laboratory in the attic of his Beacon Hill home. When, in the winter of 1908, his sister Mary, to whom he was much attached, died of consumption, he concentrated his forces against the tubercle bacillus.

In the year 1910, when his grandfather died, Richard had at last succeeded in curing tuberculosis in guinea pigs. The results of this double event were immediate: he disposed of his Boston law practice, purchased a farm near Portland, Oregon, and flung himself at once into the real business of his life.

So many years had already been wasted he made no attempt to take a medical degree. Soon he succeeded with a vaccine in the immunization of a herd of Jersey cows. At the same time he was developing the treatment of damaged lungs through immobilization. From this he launched straight into therapeutics.

His success with reputably adjudged incurable cases immediately earned for him the determined antagonism of the medical profession. Stillman had sunk every dollar he possessed in establishing his institute and often it seemed that material difficulties, allied to the bitterness of the opposition, would submerge him. Yet with magnificent courage he survived every crisis.

Gradually the storm of controversy subsided, and Stillman began to receive large donations from private individuals, and even from public bodies. His institute became, with its superb equipment and situation, a show place.

And now, seated in the restaurant of Brooks Hotel, unspoiled by success, he gazed across at Andrew with quiet friendliness.

"It's very pleasant," he said, "to be in England. I like your countryside. Our summers aren't as cool as this."

"I suppose you've come over on a lecture tour?" Andrew said.

Stillman smiled. "No! I don't lecture now. As a matter of fact I'm over here to start a small clinic on the lines of our place at Portland. The clinic—we're calling it Bellevue—is pretty near completion—out on the Chilterns near High Wycombe. I'll get it started, then hand it over to one of my assistants. Frankly, I look upon it as an experiment, a very promising experiment."

Andrew leaned forward. "That sounds interesting. What are you specially concentrating on? I'd like to see over your place."

"You must come when we are ready. We shall have our radical asthma regime, and I have particularly specified a few early tuberculosis cases. This will interest you. I have a new method of inducing pneumothorax. It is really an advance."

"You mean the Emile-Weil?"

"No, no. Much better. Without the disadvantages of negative fluctuation." They plunged deep into technicalities, and only stopped when Stillman looked at his watch and discovered he was half an hour late for his next appointment.

Andrew left Brooks Hotel with a stimulated and exalted mind. But, on the heels of that, came a queer reaction of confusion, dissatisfaction with his own work.

He was not in a particularly amiable frame of mind when he arrived home yet, as he drew up outside his house, he composed his features. Christine now presented to him a face so expressionless that he felt he must answer it in kind.

It seemed to him that she had retired within herself. She read a great deal, wrote letters. She began also, with unobtrusive regularity, to go to church. And this exasperated him most of all, seeing it only as a further slight upon himself.

This evening, as he entered the front room, she was seated alone at the table, wearing the glasses she had recently taken to, a book before her like a scholar at her lesson. A feeling of exclusion swept over him. Reaching over her shoulders he picked up the book which, too late, she attempted to conceal.

"Good God!" He was staggered, somehow furious. "Is this what you've come to? Taken to Bible thumping now."

"Why not? I used to read it before I met you." A look of pain was in her eyes. "Possibly your Plaza friends wouldn't appreciate the fact. But it is good literature."

"Is that so! Well, let me tell you this in case you don't know it—you're developing into a blasted neurotic woman!"

"Quite probably. But I'd rather be a blasted neurotic woman and be spiritually alive than a blasted successful man—and spiritually dead!" She broke off suddenly. With a great effort she took control of herself. Looking at him steadily, she said, "Andrew! The Vaughans have taken a house in Newquay for the summer. Don't you think it would be a good thing if I went away for a while? Mrs. Vaughan has written asking me to spend some time with her."

"Yes! Go! Damn it all! Go!" He swung round and left her.

Chapter 5

Christine's departure was a relief, an exquisite emancipation. For three whole days. Then he began to brood, to fret for her return. He felt the same sense of incompleteness as before, in Aberalaw, when she had left him to study for his examinations.

He went out a great deal, played bridge at the club. He frequently saw Stillman, who was moving between Brooks Hotel and the nearly completed clinic at Wycombe.

Fitfully he tried to concentrate on his clinical research at the hospital, but he was too restless. He woke during the still hot nights, his mind seething with schemes, his nerves overwrought, missing Christine, his hand reaching out automatically for a cigarette.

Finally, he rang up Frances Lawrence. "You wouldn't care to run out somewhere in the evening? It's so hot in London."

Her voice was soothing. "That would be frightfully nice. I was hoping you might ring. Do you know Crossways? Jazzed-up Elizabethan, I'm afraid. But the river is too perfect there."

The following evening after surgery, he picked her up and set the car in the direction of Chertsey. She sat beside him, saying little yet filling the car with her charming presence. He was overwhelmingly conscious of her gracefulness.

Crossways was an exquisite Elizabethan house set in perfect gardens on the Thames, with topiary work and lovely formal lily ponds, all outraged by the conversion from mansion to roadhouse.

They went into the restaurant. It was smart, full, with tables placed round a square of polished floor and a head waiter who might have been brother to the grand vizier of the Plaza. One swift glance from him and they were shown to the finest table.

Frances wanted very little: a salad, toast melba, no wine, only iced water. Undisturbed, the head waiter seemed to see in this frugality a confirmation of her caste. Andrew realized with a sudden qualm that had he walked in here with Christine and ordered such a trivial repast he would have been treated with scorn. He was aware of people at the adjoining tables viewing them with interest, of masculine admiration to which Frances was calmly oblivious.

He recollected himself to find her smiling at him. She said:

"Would it flatter you too much if I told you I had put off a previous theatre engagement to come here? Nicol Watson—do you remember him—was taking me to the ballet."

"I remember Watson. And his ride through Paraguay. Clever fellow."

"He's frightfully nice."

"But you felt it would be too hot at the ballet?"

She smiled without answering, took a cigarette from a flat enamel box on which there was an exquisite miniature.

"Yes, I heard Watson was running after you," he persisted vehemently. "What does your husband think of that?"

She lifted an eyebrow as if mildly deprecating some lack of subtlety. Then she said: "Surely you understand? Jackie and I are the best of friends. But we each have our *own* friends."

They danced. She moved with a fascinating grace, light in his arms, impersonal.

Back at the table he was driven by a sudden curiosity and exclaimed: "Please tell me something. Why have you been so kind to me—all these months?"

She looked at him, faintly amused yet without evasion. "You are extraordinarily attractive to women. And your greatest charm is that you do not realize it."

"No, but really—" he protested, flushing; then he muttered, "I hope I'm some kind of a doctor as well."

She laughed, slowly fanning away the cigarette smoke with her hand. "Of course, you're an excellent doctor. We were talking of you only the other night at Green Street. Le Roy and others are getting a little tired of our company dietitian. They want someone younger, with more drive, on the board. Apparently they plan a big campaign to interest the medical profession—from the scientific angle—as le Roy put it. Now don't frown. You look exactly as you did that first day—when you came into the fitting room—very proud and nervous—even a little ridiculous. And then—poor Toppy! By the ordinary convention it is *she* who should be here."

"I'm very glad she's not," he said with his eyes upon the table.

"Please don't think me banal. I couldn't bear that. We are fairly intelligent I hope—and I for one—just do not believe in the grand passion. But I do think life is so much gayer if one has—a friend." She picked up her cigarette case. "It's stuffy here, and I want you to see the moon on the river."

He paid the bill and followed her onto the terrace. Before them a wide avenue of turf led down to the river between dark borders of clipped yew. The moon glinted palely upon the silver water.

They strolled down to the river, seated themselves upon a bench. He kissed her. She gave no sign either way. In a minute she said: "That was very sweet. And very badly done."

"I can do better," he mumbled, staring in front of him. He was awkward, ashamed and nervous. Angrily he told himself that it was wonderful to be here on such a night with such a graceful, charming woman. Finally he kissed her again in defiance.

"I thought possibly you were taking another twelve months to make up your mind." Her eyes held amusement. "And now, don't you think we should go, doctor. These night airs are treacherous to the puritanical mind."

He helped her to her feet and she retained his hand, holding it lightly as they walked to the car. As he drove towards London her silence was eloquently happy.

But he was not happy. His brain was a mass of tormenting thoughts, swept by recollections of the agonizing sweetness of his first love for Christine.

They arrived at her house. "You'll come up, won't you? I'm afraid the servants are in bed."

He hesitated, stammered. "It's very late, isn't it?"

She did not seem to hear him, but went up the steps with her key in her hand. As he followed, he had a fading vision of Christine walking down the market, carrying her old string bag.

THREE DAYS LATER Andrew sat in his Welbeck Street consulting room. It was a hot afternoon and he was tired from having coped with six three-guinea patients in the space of one hour, knowing that he must rush his surgery to take Frances out to supper. He glanced up impatiently as Nurse Sharp entered.

"There's a man called to see you, a dreadful person. He's not a patient and he says he's not a traveller. His name's Boland."

"Boland?" Andrew echoed blankly; then his face cleared suddenly. "Con Boland? Show him in, nurse! Straight away."

"But you have a patient waiting."

"Oh! never mind that!" he said irritably. "Do as I say."

Nurse Sharp flushed at his tone. She sniffed and went out with her head in the air. The next minute she showed Boland in.

"Why, Con!" said Andrew, jumping up.

"Hello, hello, *hello*," shouted Con, as he bounded forward with a broad and genial grin. The red-headed dentist was no different, as real and untidy in his oversized shiny blue suit and large brown boots as if he had that moment walked out of his wooden garage. He pounded Andrew vehemently on the back. "In the name of God, Manson! It's great to see ye again. Ye're lookin' marvellous, marvellous. How are ye, now?"

He refused to relinquish Andrew's hand, but pumped it up and down. It was a rare tonic to see Con again on this devitalizing day. When Andrew at last freed himself, he flung himself into his swivel chair. Then Con, becoming more serious, sketched the reason for his coming.

"Listen, Manson, my boy! It's Mary—you'll remember my daughter surely, for I can tell you she remembers you! She's been poorly lately—not up to the mark at all. We've had her to Llewellyn and devil the bit of good he's doin' her." Con grew heated suddenly, his voice was thick. "Damn it all, Manson, he's got the sauce to say she's got a touch of TB. Now look here, Manson, will ye do something for old friendship's sake? Will ye take a look at Mary for us? If you're too busy ye've only got to say so and I can easy sling my hook."

Andrew's expression had turned concerned. "Don't talk that way, Con. I'll do everything I can for Mary, everything. How long are you up for, Con? Three or four days—that's fine! Why don't you come and stop with me? We've loads of room. Christine's away, but she'll be back on Friday. She'll be delighted to see you, Con, delighted. We can talk over old times together."

On the following day Con brought his bag round to Chesborough Terrace. In the evening they went together to the Palladium music hall. It was amazing how good every turn seemed in Con's company. Afterwards they had a steak and beer at the Cadero; then they returned, stirred up the fire in the front room and sat down to talk. Momentarily, Andrew forgot the complexities of his super-civilized existence.

But the next day came. And it brought, inexorably, the moment of reunion with Christine. Andrew dragged the unsuspecting Con to the station, irritably aware of the inadequacy of his self-possession. He knew one shattering moment of anguish at the sight of Christine's face advancing amongst the crowd of strangers,

straining in expectation towards his own. Then he put everything into the effort to achieve cordial unconcern.

"Hello, Chris! Thought you were never coming! Yes, you may well look at him. It's Con all right! He's staying with us, Chris—we'll tell you all about it in the car. Did you have a good time? Oh, look here!—*why* are you carrying your case?"

Swept away by this platform reception Christine lost her wan expression. Ensconced in the back of the car, colour flowed back into her cheeks. She also had been apprehensive, nervously keyed, longing for a new beginning. She felt almost hopeful now.

"Oh, it is good to be home." She took a deep breath inside the front door of the house; then, quickly, wistfully, "You have missed me, Andrew?"

"I should think I have. We *all* have. Eh, Mrs. Bennett? Eh, Florrie? Con! What the devil are you doing with that luggage?"

He was out in a second, helping Con unnecessarily with suitcases. Then, before anything more could be done or said, he had to leave on his rounds. As he slumped into the seat of his car he groaned: "Thank God that's over! She doesn't look a lot better for her holiday. Oh, hell!—I'm sure she didn't notice anything."

He was late in returning and his cheerfulness was excessive. Once or twice he felt Christine's eye upon him. He perceived that Mary's illness was distracting her. She had asked Con to wire Mary to come up at once, so that everything would be done without delay.

When Mary appeared the following day, it was evident that she was not well. Now a lanky girl of twenty, she had that almost unnatural beauty of complexion which spoke an immediate warning to Andrew. She was tired out by her journey and was persuaded to go to bed about six o'clock. It was then that Andrew went up to examine her chest.

When he came down to Con and Christine in the drawing room his expression was genuinely disturbed. "I'm afraid Llewellyn was perfectly right, Con. But don't worry, it's in the primary stage."

"You mean it can be cured?" said Con apprehensively.

"Yes. But it means constant observation, every care." He reflected, frowning deeply. "Why don't you let me get her into the Victoria? I could keep my eye on her there."

"Manson!" Con exclaimed impressively. "That's a true act of friendship. If any man'll get her right it's yourself."

The next two days were fully occupied. By Saturday afternoon, when Mary had been admitted to the Victoria and Con had boarded his train at Paddington, Andrew's self-possession was at last equal to the occasion. He was able to press Christine's arm, and exclaim lightly on his way to the surgery: "Nice to be together again, Chris! Lord! What a week it has been."

It sounded perfectly in key. But it was as well he did not see the look upon her face. She sat down in the room, alone, her head bent slightly, very still. She had been so hopeful when first she came back. But now, within her, was the dreadful foreboding: Dear God! When and how is this going to end?

Chapter 6

On and on rushed the spate of his success, sweeping him irresistibly forward in an ever-swelling flood.

How flattering for Andrew was the patronage of Joseph le Roy. Twice in the last month he had lunched with him. At their last meeting le Roy had tentatively remarked:

"You know, doc, I've been feeling my way with you. It's a pretty large thing I'm going on to and I'll need a lot of clever medical advice. I believe the time has come to expand our interests and go in for more scientific derivatives: Cremo with vitamin B, Cremofax and lecithin for malnutrition, rickets, deficiency insomnia—you get me, doc? And further, I believe if we tackle this on more orthodox professional lines we can enlist the help of the whole medical profession. Now, this means scientific advertising, doc, and that's where I believe a young scientific doctor could help us all along the road."

Andrew did not pause to consider that there were probably more vitamins in one fresh green pea than in several tins of Cremofax. He was excited at the thought of le Roy's interest.

It was Frances who told him how he might profit by le Roy's spectacular market operations. Ah! it was pleasant to drop in to tea with her, to feel that this charming sophisticated woman had a special glance for him, a swift, provoking smile of intimacy!

It was no longer an embarrassment to face Christine, he could come into his house quite naturally, following an hour spent with Frances. By way of recompense he went out of his way to be nice to Christine. She never argued with him now, never recriminated. She seemed altogether passive.

And then, out of high heaven, the bolt fell.

On an evening at the beginning of August, the wife of a neighbouring tradesman came to his consulting room at Chesborough Terrace. She was Mrs. Vidler, a small sparrow of a woman, middle-aged. Andrew knew her family well, he had attended the little boy for some childish complaint. The Vidlers, respectable, hard-working tradespeople, kept a double shop at the head of Paddington Street, one half devoted to boot repairs and the other to the cleaning and pressing of wearing apparel.

It was of her husband, Harry, that Mrs. Vidler now spoke.

"Doctor," she said in her brisk way, "for weeks now my husband's been poorly. I've been at him and at him to come, but he wouldn't. Will you call tomorrow, doctor?"

Next morning Andrew found Vidler in bed, giving a history of internal pain and growing stoutness over the last few months. He had several ways of accounting for it: he had been taking a drop too much ale, or perhaps his sedentary life was to blame.

But Andrew, after his investigation, was convinced that the condition was cystic and, although not dangerous, it was one which demanded operative treatment. He proposed that Vidler should go into hospital at once.

Here, however, Mrs. Vidler held up her hands. "No, sir, I won't have my Harry in a hospital!" She struggled to compose her agitation. "We're not well-off people, doctor, as you know, but we 'ave got a little bit put by. And now's the time to use it. I won't have Harry goin' into a public ward like he was a pauper."

"But, Mrs. Vidler, I can arrange—"

"No! You can get him in a private home. So long as I'm here no public hospital shall 'ave Harry Vidler."

He saw that her mind was firmly made up. And indeed Vidler himself also wanted the best treatment that could be had.

That evening Andrew rang Ivory. "I'd like you to do something for me, Ivory. I've an abdominal that wants doing—decent hard-working people but not rich, you understand. It would oblige me if you did it for—say a third of the usual fee."

Ivory was very gracious. Nothing would please him more than to do his friend Manson this service.

Ivory saw the case with Andrew and on the following day Harry

Vidler moved into a nursing home not far away. Miss Buxton, the proprietress, was a qualified sister and a hard-working woman. Whatever its defects, the Brunsland was spotlessly aseptic.

The operation was fixed for Friday at two o'clock, and Ivory arrived punctually. The surgeon plainly thought little of the home, but his manner remained as suave as ever. Within the space of ten minutes he had reassured Mrs. Vidler, made the conquest of Miss Buxton and her nurses, then, gowned and gloved in the little theatre, he was imperturbably ready.

The patient walked in with determined cheerfulness, slipped off his dressing-gown and climbed upon the narrow table. Before the anaesthetist placed the mask over his face, he smiled at Andrew.

"I'll be better after this is over." The next moment he had closed his eyes and was almost eagerly inhaling deep draughts of ether. Ivory commenced the operation. His medial incision was large and immediately, almost ludicrously, the trouble was revealed. The cyst bobbed through the opening like a fully inflated, wet, rubber football. Andrew reflected that Vidler would do nicely when detached from this uncomfortable accessory.

Meanwhile Ivory, in his masterly manner, was playing with the football, imperturbably trying to get his hands round it to its point of attachment and imperturbably failing as the ball slithered away from him. If he tried once he tried twenty times.

Andrew glanced irritably at Ivory, thinking—what is the man doing? There was not much space in the abdomen in which to work, but he had seen Llewellyn, Denny, a dozen others manipulate expertly with far less latitude. Suddenly he realized that this was the first abdominal operation Ivory had ever done for him. He drew nearer, rather rigidly, to the table.

Ivory was still straining to get behind the cyst, still calm, unruffled. Miss Buxton and a young nurse stood trustfully by, not knowing very much about anything. There was no high sense of tension, but for some reason a sense of coldness fell on Andrew.

Ivory, with a faint smile, gave up the attempt to find the cyst's point of attachment and asked for a knife. Before Andrew knew what he was about, he made a generous puncture of the glistening wall of the cyst. After that everything happened at once.

The cyst burst, exploding a great clot of venous blood into the air, vomiting its contents into the abdominal cavity. Frantically, Miss Buxton felt in the drum for swabs. The anaesthetist sat up abruptly. The young nurse looked like fainting. Ivory said gravely: "Clamp, please."

A wave of horror swept over Andrew. Ivory had blindly, wantonly, incised the cyst. And it was a haemorrhagic cyst.

"Swab, please," Ivory said in his impassive voice. He was fiddling about in the mess of gurgling blood, swabbing out the blood-filled cavity, failing to control the haemorrhage. Realization broke on Andrew in a blinding flash. He thought: God Almighty! He can't operate at all.

The anaesthetist, with his finger on the carotid, murmured; "I'm afraid—he seems to be going, Ivory."

Ivory, relinquishing the clamp, began to suture up his great incision. Vidler's stomach had an empty, caved-in look, the reason being that Vidler was dead.

"Yes, he's gone now," said the anaesthetist finally.

Ivory put in his last stitch, clipped it methodically and laid down his scissors. Andrew felt paralysed. By great force of will Miss Buxton seemed to collect herself. She went outside.

Ivory spoke at last. "Very unfortunate," he said in his calm voice as he stripped off his gown. "I imagine it was shock—don't you think so, Gray?"

Gray, the anaesthetist, mumbled an answer.

Andrew could not speak. He suddenly remembered Mrs. Vidler, waiting downstairs. It seemed as if Ivory read that thought. He said: "Don't worry, Manson. I'll attend to the little woman. Come. I'll get it over for you now."

Andrew found himself following Ivory down to the waiting room. He was still stunned, weak with nausea, wholly incapable of telling Mrs. Vidler. Ivory rose to the occasion. "My dear lady," he said compassionately, placing his hand gently on her shoulder. "I'm afraid—I'm afraid we have bad news for you."

She clasped her hands together. Terror and entreaty were mingled in her eyes. "What?"

"Your poor husband, Mrs. Vidler, in spite of everything which we could do for him—"

She collapsed into the chair, her face ashen, her hands still working together. "Harry!" she whispered heartrendingly.

"I can only assure you," Ivory went on, sadly, "that no power on earth could have saved him. And even if he had survived the operation—" He shrugged his shoulders significantly.

She looked up at him, sensing his meaning, aware even at this frightful moment of his condescension, of his goodness to her.

"That's the kindest thing you could have told me, doctor." She spoke through her tears.

"I'll send sister down to you. Do your best to bear up. And thank you, thank you for your courage."

He went out of the room and once again Andrew went with him. Ivory walked into the office at the end of the hall. There he lit a cigarette. His hand was steady, his nerve absolutely unshaken.

"Well, that's over," he reflected coolly. "I'm sorry, Manson. I didn't dream that cyst was haemorrhagic. But these things happen in the best-regulated circles, you know."

Andrew sank down on the leather-covered fender that surrounded the fireplace. He was sick, shattered, on the verge of a complete collapse. He could not escape the vision of Harry Vidler, walking unaided to the table and then ten minutes later, a mutilated, butchered corpse. He covered his eyes with his hand.

"Of course, he didn't die on the table. I finished before that—which makes it all right. No necessity for an inquest."

Andrew raised his head. He was infuriated by Ivory's cold-blooded nerve. He said, in a frenzy: "For Christ's sake stop talking. You know you killed him. You're the worst botcher I've seen in all my life."

There was a silence. Ivory gave Andrew a pale, hard glance. "I don't recommend that line of talk, Manson."

"I know you don't!" A painful hysterical sob shook Andrew. "But it's the truth. All the cases I've given you up till now have been child's play. But this—the first real case we've had—Oh, God! I should have known—"

"Pull yourself together, you hysterical fool. You'll be heard."

"What if I am?" Another weak burst of anger seized Andrew. He choked: "You bungled so much—it was almost murder!"

For an instant it seemed as if Ivory would knock him senseless. But with a great struggle he controlled himself, turned and walked out of the room. But there was an ugly look on his face which spoke, icily, of unforgiving fury.

How long Andrew remained in the office, his forehead pressed against the cold marble mantelpiece, he did not know. But at last he rose, compelled by machine-like habit to perform his duties. In this fashion he managed to drag round his remaining visits. Then, with a leaden heart, he returned home for his evening surgery.

The surgery was packed to the door. Heavily, like a dying man, he dropped into his swing chair, began with a mask-like face the usual evening rite.

"How are you? Yes, I think you're looking a shade better! Yes. Pulse has much more tone. The physic is doing you good."

Out to the waiting Christine, handing her the empty bottle, forward along the passage to the patients in the consulting room, stringing out the same interrogative platitudes there, then back along the passage, picking up the full bottle, back into the surgery. In a daze he kept asking himself: Where am I going? Where, in God's name, am I going?

At last, it was finished. Christine waited in the consulting room, ready to call out the lists, to help him make up the book.

For the first time in many weeks he gazed deeply into her face. Piercing even his numbness, the change in her shocked him. Her expression was still and fixed, her mouth drooped. There was a mortal sadness in her eyes.

Seated at the desk before the heavy ledger he felt a frightful straining in his side. But his body, that outer covering of deadness, allowed nothing of that inner throbbing to escape. Before he could speak Christine had begun to call out the list. When it was finished she asked, in a voice whose wincing satire he only then observed: "Well! How much today?"

He could not answer. She left the room. He heard her go upstairs, heard the sound of her closing the door. He was alone: dry, stricken, bemused. Suddenly his eyes fell upon the tobacco sack, bulging with the day's takings. A wave of hysteria swept over him. He flung the bag into the corner of the room.

HE TOSSED RESTLESSLY in bed all through the night until, at six in the morning, he at last fell asleep. Awakening late he came down to find that Christine had already breakfasted and gone. Normally this would not have upset him. Now, with a pang of anguish, it made him feel how far they were apart.

He drank a cup of coffee, then he mixed himself a stiff whisky and soda, drank that too. He then prepared to face the day.

Though the machine still held him, his movements were less automatic than before. He knew that he was on the verge of a colossal breakdown. He knew also that if he once fell into that abyss he would never crawl out of it. Cautiously he opened the garage and took out his car. The effort made the sweat spring out on his palms.

His main purpose this morning was to reach the Victoria. He had made an appointment with Dr. Thoroughgood to see Mary Boland. At the hospital he went up to the ward and passed along to Mary's bed, picking up her chart on the way. Then he sat down on the edge of the bed, aware of her welcoming smile, of the big bunch of roses beside her, but all the while studying her chart. It was not satisfactory.

"Good morning," she said. "Aren't my flowers beautiful? Christine brought them yesterday."

He looked at her. No flush, but a little thinner than when she came in. "Yes, they're nice flowers. How do you feel, Mary?"

"Oh!—all right." Her eyes avoided his momentarily. "Anyway I know it won't be for long. You'll soon have me better."

Her trust sent a great throb of pain through him. He thought, if anything goes wrong here it will be the final smash.

At that moment Dr. Thoroughgood arrived. "Morning, Dr. Manson," he said pleasantly, then turned to Mary's bed. "I'm glad you asked to see this case with me. Let's have the screens, sister."

They examined Mary together, then went to the end window, where they could not be overheard. "Well?" he said.

Out of the haze, Andrew heard himself speak. "I don't know how you feel, Dr. Thoroughgood, but it seems to me that the progress of this case isn't quite satisfactory. It seems to me that there's some slight extension."

"Oh, I don't think so, Manson."

"Excuse me for suggesting it—I appreciate our relative positions perfectly, but would you not consider pneumothorax? You remember I was very anxious we should use it when Mary came in."

Thoroughgood glanced sideways at Manson. His face altered, set into stubborn lines. "No, Manson. I'm afraid I don't see this as a case for collapsing the lung. I didn't then—and I don't now."

There was a silence. Andrew could not utter another word. He felt spent, unable to pursue the argument. It was nearly one o'clock. He had two appointments this afternoon at Welbeck Street. He drove there slowly.

Nurse Sharp was in a bad temper, as always when asked to work on Saturdays. Yet she inquired if he felt ill.

When she went out of the room he sat at his desk staring straight in front of him. The first of his patients arrived at half past two—a young clerk, who was genuinely suffering from a valvular complaint. He spent a long time over the case, taking especial pains. At the end, as the other fumbled for his thin pocket-book he said quickly: "Please don't pay me now. I'll send a bill."

The thought that he would never send the bill, that he had lost his thirst for money, comforted him strangely.

Then the second case came in, Miss Basden, one of the most faithful of his followers. He listened wearily while she launched into an account of all that had happened to her symptoms since her last visit. Suddenly he raised his head. "Why do you come to me, Miss Basden?"

She broke off in mid-sentence, her mouth dropping open.

"Oh, I know I'm to blame," he said. "I told you to come. But there's really nothing wrong with you."

"Dr. Manson!" she gasped, unable to believe her ears.

He realized, with cruel insight, that all her symptoms were due to money. She had never done a day's work in her life, her body was soft, pampered, overfed.

"I'm sorry I can't be of any further service to you, Miss Basden—I may be going away. I've no doubt you'll find another doctor around here."

She opened her mouth several times like a fish gasping for air. Then she rose and hurried from the room.

He prepared to go home, shutting the drawers of his desk with an air of finality. But before he got up Nurse Sharp bounced into the room, smiling. "Dr. Hamson to see you!"

The next minute Freddie was there, flinging himself into a chair with an air of purpose. His tone had never been friendlier.

"Sorry to bother you on a Saturday, old man. Now look here, I heard all about the operation yesterday and I don't mind telling you I'm darn well glad you've had an inside slant on Ivory." Hamson's voice took on a sudden vicious twist. "I think you ought to know, old chap, that I've been rather falling out with Ivory and Deedman lately. We've been running a little pool together, and very profitable it was, but now I'm pretty well sure those two are twisting me out of some of my share. Besides which, I'm about sick of Ivory. He's nothing but a damned abortionist. You didn't know that, eh? There's a couple of nursing homes where they do nothing else and Ivory's the chief scraper! Now you listen to me, old man, you've been too damn green. You haven't been getting your proper whack. Here's my scheme. Let's ditch them altogether, you and me, and start a little partnership of our own."

Freddie broke off to light a cigarette, then he smiled, expansively. "You wouldn't believe the stunts I've pulled. D'you know my latest. Three guineas a time injections—*of sterile water!* Patient came in one day for her vaccine. I'd forgotten to order the damn thing, so rather than disappoint, pumped in the H_2O. She came back the next day to say she'd had a better reaction than from any of the others. *So I went on.* And why not?"

Andrew remained motionless and stiff. He had no anger against Hamson, only a bitter loathing of himself. Nothing could have shown him more blastingly where he had been going than this suggestion of Hamson's. At last he mumbled: "I can't go in with you, Freddie. I've—I've suddenly got sick of it. I think I'll chuck it here for a bit. There are too many jackals in this square mile of country. There's a lot of good men, trying to do good honest work, but the rest of them are just jackals. It's the jackals who give all these unnecessary injections, whip out tonsils that aren't doing any harm, play ball amongst one another with their patients."

Hamson's face had reddened. "What about yourself?"

"I know, Freddie," Andrew said heavily. "I'm just as bad. But I'm going to try to stop thinking of money."

"You bloody fool," said Hamson distinctly. He swung round and went out of the room.

Andrew sat woodenly at his desk, desolate. He got up at last and drove home. As he approached his house he was conscious of the rapid beating of his heart. The whole trend of the day seemed working towards its climax.

Christine was in the front room. The sight of her pale face sent a great shiver through him. He longed for her to show some concern as to how he had spent these hours away from her. But she merely said, in that non-committal voice: "You've had a long day. Will you have some tea before the surgery?"

He answered: "There won't be any surgery tonight."

She glanced at him: "But Saturday—it's your busiest night."

His answer was to write a notice stating that the surgery was closed tonight, and then he pinned it on the surgery door. His heart was now thumping so violently he felt that it must burst.

When he returned her face was paler still, her eyes distraught. "What is the matter?" she asked in a strange voice.

He looked at her. The anguish in his heart tore at him, broke through in a great rush that swept him beyond all control.

"Christine!" Everything within him went into that single word. Then he was at her feet, kneeling, weeping.

Chapter 7

Their reconciliation was the most wonderful thing that had happened to them since they first fell in love. Next morning, he lay beside her, as in those days at Aberalaw, talking, talking, pouring out his heart to her. Outside, the quiet of Sunday was in the air, the peaceful sound of bells. But he was not peaceful.

"How did I come to it?" he groaned restlessly. "I can't believe it when I look back on it. Me—getting in with that crowd—after Denny, and Hope—I should be executed."

She soothed him. "It all happened with such a rush, dear. It would have swept anyone off their feet."

"No, but honestly, Chris. I feel like going off my head when I think about it. And what a hell of a time it must have been for you! Lord! it ought to be a *painful* execution!"

She smiled, actually smiled. It was the most marvellous experience to see her face stripped of that frozen blankness, tender, happy. Oh, God! he thought: we're both *living* again.

"There's only one thing to be done," he brought his brows together determinedly. "We've got to clear out of here. We can easily sell the practice. And oh! Chris, I've got a wonderful idea."

"Yes, darling?"

He smiled at her diffidently, tenderly. "How long is it since you called me that? I like it. Chris!—this idea, this scheme—it hit me when I woke up this morning. I was worrying about Hamson having asked me to join up with his rotten team idea—then suddenly it struck me, why not a genuine team? You see, Chris, even in quite a small provincial town you could have a clinic, a little team of doctors, each doing his own stuff. Why don't I get Denny and Hope together and form a genuine threesome? Denny does all the surgical work—and you know how good he is!—I handle the medical side, and Hope is our bacteriologist! Wouldn't it be wonderful, dear, if we could form a little front-line unit, a kind of pioneer force to try to break down prejudice, maybe start a complete revolution in our whole medical system."

She gazed at him with shining eyes. "It's like old times to hear you talk that way. I can't tell you how I love it. I am happy, darling, *happy*."

"I've got a lot to make up for," he reasoned sombrely. "I've been a fool. And worse." He pressed his brow with his hands. "I can't get poor Harry Vidler out of my head. And I won't, either, till I do something to make up for it. I believe Denny's really dying to get back into the rough and tumble of a practice again, and Hope—if we give him a little lab where he can do original work—he'll follow us anywhere."

He jumped out of bed and began to pace up and down the room in his old impetuous style. "I've so much to settle up, Chris," he cried, "and one thing I must see about. Chris, I have a fearful weight on my mind over Mary Boland. She's not getting on well at the Victoria. She ought to be out in the country, in the fresh air, in a good sanatorium."

"Yes?"

"I want us to run out to Stillman's clinic. Bellevue's the finest little place you could ever hope to see. If only I could persuade him to take Mary in—"

She said with decision: "We'll leave the minute you're ready."

When he had dressed he went downstairs, wrote a long letter to Denny and another to Hope. Then, after a light meal, he and Christine set out for Wycombe.

The journey was a happy one. More than ever it was borne upon him that happiness was an inner state, wholly spiritual, independently of worldly possessions. All these months, he had been existing in a kind of delirium!

He glanced sideways at Christine. How she must have suffered because of him! But now, if he had wished for any confirmation of the sanity of his decision, the sight of her altered, glowing face was evidence enough. He swore he would never again in all his life do anything to make her sad.

They reached Bellevue towards three o'clock. Its location was superb, on a little plateau which, though sheltered on the north, afforded an outlook over two valleys.

Stillman was cordial in his reception. He was a self-contained little man, yet he showed his pleasure in Andrew's visit by demonstrating the full beauty and efficiency of his creation. As Andrew walked round he could not help contrasting its ultra-modern perfection with the antique buildings which served as many of the London hospitals and nursing homes.

Afterwards, Stillman gave them tea. And here Andrew brought out his request with a rush. "I hate asking you a favour, Mr. Stillman, but I wonder if you'd take in a case for me here? Early TB. Probably requires pneumothorax. You see, she's the daughter of a great friend of mine and she's not getting on where she is."

Something like sadness gathered behind Stillman's pale blue eyes. "I'm afraid I am full up, my friend. In spite of the antipathy of your medical fraternity I have a long waiting list."

"Well!" Andrew muttered—Stillman's refusal was a great disappointment to him. "I was more or less banking on it. When I think of that old ward in the Victoria where Mary's lying now, listening to the cockroaches scramble behind the skirting . . . ."

"So! I see you are worried. Well, I have no vacant room until Wednesday but I'll take your case." Stillman's lip twitched at Andrew's blank expression. "I don't mind dealing with the profession when I'm obliged to. Why don't you smile?—that's a joke. Never mind. Even if you've no sense of humour you're a darn sight more enlightened than most of the brethren. Let me see. Bring your case to me a week on Wednesday and I promise you I'll do the best I can for her!"

Andrew's face reddened with gratitude. "I . . . I can't thank you enough . . . I . . . ."

"Then don't. And don't be so polite. I prefer you when you look like throwing things about."

Driving home, Andrew meditated to Christine: "That's a big load off my mind, Chris. I'm positive it's the right place for Mary. He's a great chap, is Stillman. I like him a lot. I wonder if ever we could have a clinic on those lines—Hope and Denny and me. That's a wild dream, eh?"

By way of answer she leaned sideways, and, greatly to the common danger on the public highway, she soundly kissed him.

NEXT MORNING he rose early, after a good night's rest. He put the practice in the hands of Fulger & Turner, medical transfer agents. After a scrutiny of the books lasting all that morning, Mr. Gerald

Turner, the head of the firm, assured Andrew that he would have not the slightest difficulty in effecting a quick sale.

At lunchtime Christine produced two telegrams which had come for him. He had asked both Denny and Hope to wire him in reply to the letters he had written the day before.

The first, from Denny, said simply: *Impressed. Expect me tomorrow evening.*

The second declared with typical flippancy:

Must I spend all my life with lunatics. Feature of English provincial towns pubs stocks cathedrals and pig markets. Did you say laboratory. Signed *Indignant Ratepayer.*

Later in the week Andrew drove down to the Victoria. Seated beside Mary's bed he explained privately to her what he wished to do. "You'll find a big difference when you get to Bellevue, Mary," he patted her hand reassuringly. "But they've been very kind to you here, there's no need to hurt anybody's feelings. You must just say you want to go out next Wednesday, discharge yourself. Then I'll take you out myself by car to Bellevue. I'll have a nurse with me and everything."

That evening in his surgery he set himself sternly to weed out the chronics. A dozen times in the course of an hour he declared firmly: "This must be your last visit. You're quite better now. And it doesn't do to go on drinking medicine!"

It was amazing, at the end of it, how much lighter he felt. He went in to Christine with a step almost boyish. "Now I feel less like a salesman for bath salts!"

It was then that the telephone rang. She went to answer it, and when she returned her expression was again oddly strained.

"Someone wants you on the phone."

"Who . . . ?" All at once he realized it must be Frances Lawrence. There was a bar of silence in the room. Then, hurriedly, he said, "Tell her I'm not in. No, wait! I'll speak to her myself."

He came back in five minutes to find that Christine had seated herself with some work in her familiar corner. He walked to the window, and with his back to her he said: "That's finished too. It may interest you to know it was only my stupid vanity. And self-interest. I loved you all the time. And while I was at the phone I rang up le Roy. I've wiped myself off Cremo products, too, Chris."

She did not answer but the click of her needles made, in the silent room, a brisk and cheerful sound.

Next morning he brought her home a great bunch of chrysanthemums. He strove with all his old intensity to show his affection for her, not by that showy generosity which she had hated but in the small, considerate, almost forgotten, ways.

That evening Denny arrived for supper. He brought a message from Hope, who had rung him from Cambridge, to say that he would be unable to get to London that evening.

"Did he say anything about my idea?" Andrew asked quickly.

"Yes, he's keen, and I'm keen too." Denny helped himself to salad. "I can't imagine how a first-class scheme like this came out of your fool head. Especially when I fancied you'd become a West End soap merchant. Tell me about it."

Andrew told him, fully, and then they began to discuss the more practical details. They suddenly realized how far they had progressed when Denny said: "My view is that we don't want to pick too large a town. Look at a map of the West Midlands. You'll find scores of industrial towns of under twenty thousand inhabitants served by four or five doctors who are politely at each other's throats. It's just there that we can demonstrate our idea of specialized cooperation. We won't be very grand at first, but I've a feeling we'll take root."

Andrew bounced the cutlery as he brought down his fist. "The scheme's good. But it's the ideal behind the scheme! A new interpretation of the Hippocratic oath; an absolute allegiance to the scientific ideal, no shoddy methods, no stock prescribing, no soft-soaping of hypochondriacs!"

They talked on until one o'clock in the morning. Andrew's tense excitement was a stimulus felt even by the stoic Denny.

As he left next day he promised to come to town again on the following Friday. Meanwhile he would see Hope and buy a large-scale map of the West Midlands.

"It's on, Chris, it's on!" Andrew came back triumphant from the door. "Philip's as keen as mustard."

That day they had the first inquiry for the practice and that was followed by others. On Monday, a Dr. Noel Lowry called twice, and thereafter Turner rang up Andrew, suavely confidential: "Dr. Lowry is interested, doctor, *very* interested I may say. He's particularly anxious we don't sell till his wife has a chance to see the house. She's coming up on Wednesday."

Mary was due to leave the hospital at two o'clock that Wednesday. He had fixed up with Nurse Sharp to accompany them in the car. At half past one he started off by driving to Welbeck Street to pick up the nurse. She was in a sulky humour; since he had told her he must dispense with her service at the end of the month her moods had been even more uncertain than before.

Fortunately he had no difficulty with Mary. He drew up as she came through the porter's lodge and the next moment she was in the back of the car with Nurse Sharp, warmly wrapped in a rug with a hot bottle at her feet.

At half past three they reached Bellevue. Andrew found Stillman in the office. He was anxious to see the case with him at once, for the question of pneumothorax induction weighed heavily on his mind.

"Very well," Stillman nodded. "We'll go up right now."

He led the way to Mary's room. She was now in bed, pale from her journey. Stillman examined her meticulously. Afterwards he said nothing to Mary but took Andrew beyond the door.

"Pneumothorax," he said. "There's no question. That lung should have been collapsed weeks ago. I'm going to do it right away."

While he went off to see to the apparatus, Andrew returned to inform Mary of their decision. He spoke as lightly as he could, but it was evident that the prospect of the induction upset her.

"It's nothing, Mary. You won't feel the slightest pain. I'll be here. I'll be helping him! I'll see that you're all right."

He had meant to leave the operation to Stillman. But as she was so nervous, he offered his assistance.

Ten minutes later they were ready. When Mary was brought in he gave her local anaesthesia. Stillman skilfully inserted the needle, controlling the flow of sterile nitrogen gas into the pleura. The apparatus was exquisitely delicate and Stillman undoubtedly a master of the technique.

After an early phase of acute nervousness Mary's anxiety gradually faded. She submitted to the operation with increasing confidence and at the end she could smile at Andrew, completely relaxed. Back again in her room she said: "It was nothing. I don't feel as if you'd done anything at all."

"No!" He lifted an eyebrow; then laughed. "That's how it should be. We've immobilized your lung. It'll have a rest now. And when it starts breathing again it will be healed."

IT WAS NEARLY seven o'clock when he left Bellevue. He had remained longer than he had anticipated, talking to Stillman, enjoying the cool air and the quiet conversation of the other man. As he drove off he was pervaded by an extraordinary sense of tranquillity. He was now easy in his mind about Mary. For the first time in many months he felt that he had done something which, to his own belief, was worthy.

He drove slowly, enjoying the quiet of the evening. Nurse Sharp sat quietly in the back seat of the car. She asked him to drop her at Notting Hill Tube Station, and he was glad to be rid of her. She was a good nurse but her nature was repressed and unhappy. She had never liked him. He decided to post her month's salary to her the next day. Then he would not see her again.

Strangely, his mood altered as he approached his house and he went in with a curious sadness pressing upon him.

Christine met him joyfully in the hall. Whatever his mood might be, hers was vivid with success. Her eyes were shining with her news. "Sold!" she declared gaily. "Knocked down, lock, stock, and basement. They waited and waited for you, darling—they've only just gone. Dr. and Mrs. Lowry, I mean. He got so agitated," she laughed, "because you weren't here for the surgery that he did it himself. You've to meet him at Mr. Turner's office tomorrow at eleven to sign the contract."

He followed her into the front room. He was pleased, naturally, that the practice should be sold, yet he could not, at present, summon any great show of elation.

"It is good, isn't it," Christine went on, "that it should all be settled up so quickly. If only we could have a little holiday before we start work—" She broke off, gazing at him. "Why, what's the matter, dear?"

"Oh, nothing," he smiled, sitting down. "I'm a little tired, I think. Probably because I missed my dinner—"

"What!" she exclaimed, aghast. "I felt certain you'd have had it at Bellevue." Her glance swept round. "And I've cleared everything away, and let Mrs. Bennett go to the pictures."

"It doesn't matter."

"But it *does*. Now you just sit there one minute and I'll bring up a tray. Is there anything you'd especially like?"

He considered. "Scrambled egg, I think, Chris. Oh! but don't bother. Well, if you like . . . and a bit of cheese afterwards."

She was back in no time with a tray on which stood a plate of scrambled egg, bread, biscuits, butter and the cheese dish. He ate his scrambled egg. The food was certainly making him feel better.

"You know, darling," she said, placing her hands beneath her chin in her characteristic way, "I've thought such a lot these last few days. It's only when you've got to fight for things that they really become worth while. Don't you remember those days at Aberalaw, when we had to go through all those rough times together? Well! now I feel that the same thing is starting for us all over again. And oh! I'm so happy about it."

He glanced towards her. "You're really happy, Chris?"

She kissed him lightly. "Never happier in my life."

There was a pause. He buttered a biscuit and lifted the lid of the cheese dish, revealing not his favourite Liptauer but a barren end of cheddar. The instant she saw it, Christine gave a self-reproachful cry.

"And I meant to call at Frau Schmidt's today!" She jumped up, her eye upon the clock. "I've just time to rush across for it now before she closes."

"Don't bother, Chris—"

"*Please*, darling." She silenced him gaily. "I *want* to do it. I want to—because I—I love you."

She was out of the room before he could protest again. He heard the light closing of the outer door. His eyes were faintly smiling—it was so like her to do this.

The house was very still: Florrie sleeping downstairs and Mrs. Bennett at the cinema. He began absently to eat a buttered biscuit. He'd lose his appetite if she didn't hurry up. She must be talking to Frau Schmidt. Suddenly the doorbell rang violently. He glanced up, went into the hall to open the front door.

Immediately he was conscious of the commotion outside, a crowd of people on the pavement. The policeman, their friend Struthers, loomed up before him.

"Doctor—" He breathed with difficulty, like a man who has been running. "Your wife's been hurt. She ran, oh! God Almighty! She ran right out of the shop in front of the bus."

A great hand of ice enclosed him. Before he could speak the commotion was upon him. Suddenly the hall was filled with people. Frau Schmidt weeping, another policeman, strangers, all pressing in. And then, through the crowd, carried by two men, the figure of his Christine. Her head dropped backwards upon the thin white arch of her neck. Still entwined by its string in the fingers of her left hand was the little parcel from Frau Schmidt. She was quite dead.

Chapter 8

He broke down completely and for days was out of his mind. In moments of lucidity he became aware of Mrs. Bennett, of Denny, and of Hope. But for the most part he went through the days like an automaton, and the nights in long nightmares of despair.

How the arrangements for the funeral were made he did not know, but they all came mysteriously to pass. As he drove to Kensal Green his thoughts kept darting back through the years. In the dingy cemetery he remembered the wide and windswept uplands behind Vale View. She had loved to walk there, to feel the breeze upon her cheeks. And now she was being laid in this grimy city graveyard.

That night he tried to drink himself insensible. But the whisky only seemed to goad him to fresh anger against himself. He paced up and down the room, drunkenly apostrophizing himself. "You thought you were getting away with it. But my God, you weren't! Crime and punishment, crime and punishment! You're to blame for what happened to her. You've *got* to suffer."

He staggered upstairs, hesitated, went into her room. There on the dressing-table lay her bag. He picked it up, pressed it against his cheek, then fumblingly opened it. Some coppers and loose silver lay inside, a small handkerchief, a bill for groceries. And then, in the middle pocket, he came upon some papers—he recognized them with a throbbing pang—those little notes he had received at Christmas from his patients at Aberalaw: *With grateful thanks*—she had treasured them all those years. He fell on his knees by the bed in a passion of weeping.

Denny seemed to be about the house almost every day. Andrew's nerves had gone to pieces. The sound of the doorbell made his heart palpitate madly. He sat upstairs in his room staring at the fire, knowing that when night came he must face the spectre of insomnia.

This was his condition when Denny walked in one morning.

"I'm free at last, thank God. Now we can go away," he said.

In silent apathy, he watched Denny pack a suitcase for him. Within an hour they were on their way to Paddington Station.

They travelled all afternoon through the southwest, changed at Newport and struck up through Monmouthshire to Abergavenny. Here Denny hired a car, and as they drove out of the town, across the River Usk and through the rich autumnal-tinted countryside, he said: "We're going to a small place I once used to come to—fishing. Llantony Abbey. I think it ought to suit."

They reached their destination at six o'clock. Round a square of close green turf lay the abbey ruins, a few arches of the cloisters still upstanding. And adjoining was a guest-house, built entirely from the fallen stones. Nearby, a small stream flowed with a constant soothing ripple.

Next morning, Denny dragged Andrew out to walk. It was a crisp dry day but Andrew, sick from a sleepless night, his flabby muscles failing on the first hill, soon made to turn back. Denny, however, was firm. He walked Andrew eight miles that day and on the next he made it ten. By the end of the week they were walking twenty miles a day and Andrew fell immediately into insensibility upon his bed at night.

During their walks they rarely spoke. At the beginning Andrew was quite unconscious of the countryside, but as the days passed the beauty of its woods and rivers, of its bracken-covered hills penetrated gradually through his numbed senses.

The progress of his recovery was not sensationally swift, yet by the end of the first month he was able to eat and sleep normally and face the future without cowering.

He began to talk. The topics of their discussion were inconsequential at the outset. But gradually, imperceptibly, he learned from Denny the progress of events.

His practice had been sold to Dr Lowry, and Hope had at last completed the full term of his scholarship at Cambridge. Denny also was free. The implication was so clear that Andrew suddenly lifted up his head. "I ought to be fit for work at the beginning of the year."

Now they began to talk in earnest and within a week his listlessness was gone. He felt sad that the human mind should be capable of recovering from such a mortal blow, yet recovery was there.

At night, Denny and he pored over a large-scale map. They

made a list of towns in the Midlands, then narrowed their selection down to eight. On the following Monday, Denny took his departure and was away nearly a week.

Returning from a walk on Saturday afternoon, Andrew found a small Ford drawn up at the guest-house. Inside, in the lamp-lit refectory, Denny and Hope sat at a ham and egg tea.

Philip's report, delivered during the meal, was a fiery prelude to their excited discussions. Two of the towns visited by Denny—Franton and Stanborough—were, in Hope's phrase, ripe for medical development. Both were solid semi-agricultural towns upon which industry had recently been grafted. But in each case the medical services had lagged behind the increase in population.

These bare details were enough to set them off like hounds upon a scent. But Denny had information even more stimulating. He produced a plan of Stanborough and as they bent their heads over it, he said, "That is the market square—only for some reason they call it the Circle. It's bang in the centre of the town. You know the kind of thing, a ring of houses and shops and offices, rather a Georgian effect. The chief medico of the place, a whale of a fellow, I saw him, red face and mutton chops, has his house in the Circle." Denny's tone was gently ironic. "Directly opposite him are two empty houses, large rooms, frontage *and* for sale. It seems to me—"

"And to me," said Hope with a catch in his breath.

They went on talking. "Of course," Denny concluded, "we are probably all quite mad. We none of us have a lot of cash. We shall also probably fight like hell amongst ourselves. But somehow—"

"God help old mutton chops!" said Hope, stretching himself.

With the prospect of a full day before him, Hope left early next morning, dashing off in his Ford before the others had finished breakfast. After breakfast the post arrived, a pile of letters forwarded from London.

Andrew's first letter was from Mary Boland. She began by sympathizing with him, hoping he had now recovered fully. Then briefly she told him she was better, almost well again. Her temperature had been normal for the last five weeks. She was up, taking exercise. She could not thank him enough for having sent her to Bellevue.

Andrew laid down the letter, his expression bright with the thought of Mary's recovery. Then he picked up his next letter.

This was a long official-looking envelope. He opened it, drew out the stiff sheet of notepaper within.

Then the smile left his face. He stared at the letter with disbelieving eyes. He turned deadly pale. For a full minute he remained motionless, staring, staring at the letter.

"Denny," he said, in a low voice. "Look at this."

Chapter 9

Eight weeks before, when Andrew set down Nurse Sharp at Notting Hill Station, she went on by tube to Oxford Circus and from there walked rapidly in the direction of Queen Anne Street. She had arranged with her friend Nurse Trent, who was Doctor Hamson's receptionist, to spend the evening at the Queen's Theatre. But since it was now eight fifteen and the performance began in half an hour, time was short. So instead of having a nice hot meal at the Corner House, they would have to snatch a sandwich on the way. Nurse Sharp's mood was that of a woman bitterly ill-used. As the events of the afternoon kept turning in her mind she seethed with indignation and resentment. Mounting the steps of No. 170 she hurriedly pressed the bell.

Nurse Trent opened the door, her expression patiently reproachful. But before she could speak Nurse Sharp pressed her arm. "My dear," she said, speaking rapidly, "I'm ever so sorry I'm late. But *what* a day I've had! I'll tell you later."

As the two nurses stood together in the passage Hamson came down the stairs, groomed, shining. Seeing them, he paused. Freddie could never resist an opportunity to demonstrate the charm of his personality. "Hello, Nurse Sharp! You look weary. And why are you both so late?"

"I was detained over one of Dr. Manson's cases," said Nurse Sharp.

"Oh?" Freddie's tone held just a hint of interrogation.

It was enough for Nurse Sharp. Rankling from her injustices she suddenly let herself go. "I've never had such a time in all my life, Dr. Hamson. Never. Sneaking a patient out from the Victoria to that Bellevue place and Dr. Manson keeping me there while he does a pneumothorax with an unqualified man . . . ."

There was a silence when she concluded her story. Freddie's

eyes held an odd expression. "That was too bad, nurse," he said at length. "But I hope you won't miss your theatre. Look, Nurse Trent—you must take a taxi and charge it to me."

"*There's* a gentleman," Nurse Sharp murmured, following him admiringly with her eyes. "Come, dear, get the taxi."

Freddie drove thoughtfully to the club. Since his quarrel with Andrew he had fallen back to a closer association with Deedman and Ivory. Tonight the three were dining together. And as they dined, Freddie airily remarked: "Manson seems to be playing pretty parlour tricks since he left us. I hear he's started feeding patients to that Stillman fellow."

"What!" Ivory laid down his fork.

"And cooperating, I understand." Hamson sketched a graceful version of the story.

A pause followed. Beneath his outward calm, Ivory felt a savage elation. He had never forgiven Manson for that final remark after the Vidler operation. He knew deep in his heart that he was an incompetent surgeon. But no one before had ever told him so with such cutting violence. He hated Manson for that bitter truth.

"It seems to me," Ivory reflected coolly, "that something ought to be done about this. Gadsby happened to be speaking to me about this Stillman only the other evening. He's getting into the papers. Some ignorant jackass in Fleet Street has got together a list of alleged cures by Stillman, cases where doctors had failed, you know, the usual twaddle. Now! Just what is going to happen if members of the profession are going to *support* this rank outsider? I'm going to get in touch with Gadsby straight away."

Hamson, for once, looked uncomfortable. He had no ill-will towards Manson, whom, in his easy, egotistic fashion he had always liked. He muttered: "Don't bring me into it."

"Don't be a fool, Freddie. Are we going to let that fellow sling mud at us and then get away with *this?*"

Later that evening Ivory called upon Gadsby, and when he mentioned the object of his visit, Gadsby leaned forward in his chair, and listened intently.

"Well! I'm damned!" he exclaimed with unusual vehemence at the end of it. "I examined this Manson for the MRCP. Do you mean to tell me that he took a case from the Victoria and turned it over to Stillman? It must have been one of Thoroughgood's cases—we'll hear what Thoroughgood has to say about *that*."

"More than that, he assisted Stillman at the operation."

"If that is true," Gadsby said, "the case is one for the General Medical Council."

"Well," Ivory hesitated becomingly. "That was precisely my own view. But I knew Manson at one time rather well, and didn't really feel like lodging the complaint myself."

"If what you tell me is indeed a fact, I will lodge it personally," said Gadsby authoritatively. "The point at issue is a vital one, Ivory. This man Stillman threatens our status, our training, our tradition. And if he can secure professional collaboration then we're lost. Fortunately the GMC have always come down like a ton of bricks upon that sort of thing in the past. If you'll excuse me one minute now, I'll ring Thoroughgood."

He rose and telephoned Thoroughgood. On the following day he took a signed statement from Nurse Sharp. So conclusive was her testimony he immediately got in touch with his solicitors. The process raised against Andrew moved steadily upon its way.

Later, the Penal Cases Committee, having considered that complaint, summoned Andrew to attend at the November meeting of the council to answer the charge. This was the letter which he now held in his hand:

"*That you, Andrew Manson, knowingly and wilfully, on August 14, assisted one Richard Stillman, an unregistered person practising in a department of medicine, and that you associated yourself in a professional capacity with him in carrying out such practice. And that in relation thereto you have been guilty of infamous conduct in a professional respect.*"

The case was due to be heard on November 10 but Andrew was in London a full week before that date. He was alone, for he had asked Hope and Denny to leave him entirely to himself.

Though outwardly controlled, his state of mind was desperate. Six weeks ago this crisis would have found him still benumbed by the agony of Christine's death, heedless, uncaring. But now, eager and ready to begin work again, he felt the shock of it with cruel intensity. Why did the council wish to strike him off the register? All that he had done was to cure Mary Boland of TB.

His defence was in the hands of Hopper & Co., a firm of solicitors Denny had strongly recommended. At first sight Thomas Hopper was not impressive, a sallow-faced man with gold-rimmed glasses and a fussy manner. Nevertheless, he had decided views upon the conduct of the case. When Andrew, in his first burst of agonized indignation, had wished to rush to Sir Robert Abbey, his one influential friend in London, Hopper had wryly pointed out that Abbey was a member of the council. With equal disapproval the solicitor had vetoed Andrew's frantic plea that they cable Stillman, who was now back in America, to return immediately. The presence of the unqualified practitioner could serve only to exasperate the council members.

Andrew's frenzied logic, as he protested his innocence, caused the solicitor concern. At last Hopper was forced to declare: "There is one thing I must beg of you, Dr. Manson, that you will *not* express yourself in such terms during the hearing on Wednesday. I assure you nothing would be more fatal to our case."

Andrew stopped short, his eyes burning. "But I want them to know the *truth*. I want to show them that curing this girl was the best thing I'd done for years."

Hopper's eyes behind his glasses were deeply concerned. "Please, Dr. Manson. You don't *understand* the gravity of our position! I must take this opportunity to tell you frankly that at the *best* I consider our chances of success to be slender. Now, I entreat you to answer questions simply in the affirmative or negative, or, failing that, as briefly as possible. If you launch into one of your digressions we will unquestionably lose our case."

Andrew saw dimly that he must try to control himself. But the idea that he must forgo all attempt at self-exoneration and dully answer "yes" or "no" seemed more than he could bear.

On the morning of Wednesday, November 10, Andrew woke to a sense of sick anxiety. He ate no breakfast, but fretted nervously with the newspapers in the lounge of his hotel until half past ten. His case was at eleven and Hopper had asked him to be early, but his taxi was caught in a traffic jam in Oxford Street, and it was striking eleven when he reached the GMC offices.

He hurried into the council chamber where the council sat at a high table with the president, Sir Jenner Halliday, in the chair. Seated at the far end were the participants in his own case. Hopper was there, Mary Boland, accompanied by her father; Nurse Sharp, Dr. Thoroughgood, Ward Sister Myles from the Victoria—his glance travelled along the lines of chairs. Then hastily he seated himself beside Hopper.

The president was pronouncing judgment on the case before his own, an adverse judgment, erasure from the register. The next minute his own case was called. His heart contracted as the proceedings began.

The charge was formally read through. Then Mr. George Boon, the prosecuting solicitor, rose to open. He was a thin, precise, frock-coated figure. His voice came deliberately.

"Mr. President, gentlemen, the case which you are about to consider exhibits a clear-cut instance of professional association with an unregistered person. The facts are these. The patient, Mary Boland, suffering from apical phthisis, was admitted to the Victoria Chest Hospital on July 18. There she remained under the care of Dr. Thoroughgood until September 14, when she discharged herself on the pretext that she wished to return to her home. I say pretext because instead of returning home, the patient was met at the lodge of the hospital by Dr. Manson and taken to an institution by the name of Bellevue which purports to undertake the cure of pulmonary disorders.

"On arrival at this place, the patient was put to bed and examined by Dr. Manson in conjunction with the proprietor, Mr. Richard Stillman, an unqualified alien. It was decided in consultation—I particularly call the council to mark that phrase—in consultation, by Dr. Manson and Mr. Stillman, to induce the condition of pneumothorax. Thereupon Dr. Manson administered the local anaesthetic and the induction was performed by Dr. Manson and Mr. Stillman.

"Now, gentlemen, having outlined the case I propose to call further evidence. Dr. Eustace Thoroughgood, please."

Dr. Thoroughgood rose and came forward and Boon began his interrogation. "Dr. Thoroughgood, is it not a fact that on Saturday, September 3, Dr. Manson pressed you to a consultation upon this patient Mary Boland?"

"Yes."

"And is it not also a fact that during this consultation he pressed you to adopt treatment which you thought to be unwise?"

"He wished me to perform APT, and I refused."

"Was Dr. Manson's manner in any way peculiar when you refused?"

"Well—" Thoroughgood hesitated. "He didn't seem altogether himself that morning. He seemed to disagree with my decision."

"Thank you, Dr. Thoroughgood. You had no reason to imagine that the patient was dissatisfied with her treatment at the hospital?"

"None whatever. She always seemed happy and contented."

"Thank you, Dr. Thoroughgood." Boon picked up his next paper. "And now, Ward Sister Myles, please."

Dr. Thoroughgood sat down. Ward Sister Myles came forward. Boon resumed: "Sister Myles, on the forenoon of Thursday, September 8, five days after that consultation, did Dr. Manson call to see the patient?"

"He did."

"And tell us, Sister, what took place subsequent to Dr. Manson's departure."

"About half an hour later, Mary Boland said to me, 'Sister, I've been thinking things over and I've made up my mind to go. You've been very kind to me. But I want to leave next Wednesday'."

Boon interrupted quickly. "Next Wednesday. Thank you, Sister. It was that point I wished to establish. And now—Nurse Sharp, please." A pause. "Nurse Sharp, can you bear out the statement relating to Dr. Manson's movements on the afternoon of Wednesday, September 4?"

"Yes, I was there!"

"I gather from your tone that you were there unwillingly."

"When I found out where we were going and who this man Stillman was, not a doctor or anything, I was shocked."

"Exactly," Boon purred. "Now, Nurse Sharp, did Dr. Manson actually cooperate with Mr. Stillman in performing this operation?"

"He did," Nurse Sharp answered vindictively.

At this point Abbey leaned forward and, in his capacity as a member of the council, put a question suavely, through the president. "Is it not the case, Nurse Sharp, that when the events in question took place you were under notice to Dr. Manson?"

Nurse Sharp reddened violently, lost her composure and stammered: "Yes, I suppose so."

As she sat down a minute later Andrew was conscious of a faint spark of warmth—Abbey, at least, remained his friend.

Boon now turned to the council table. "Mr. President, gentlemen, I submit that I have proved my case conclusively. There seems no doubt that the patient Mary Boland was removed, entirely through the connivance of Dr. Manson, from the care of an eminent specialist in one of the best hospitals in London to this questionable institute and that there Dr. Manson deliberately associated himself with its unqualified proprietor in the performance of a dangerous operation, already stated to be contraindicated by Dr. Thoroughgood. Mr. President, gentlemen, here, I submit, we are not dealing with an accidental misconduct, but with a planned infringement of the medical code."

Mr. Boon sat down, well pleased. Then Andrew's solicitor came forward and prepared to address the council.

As usual, Hopper seemed flustered, and he had difficulty in arranging his papers. Yet, strangely, this seemed to gain him the indulgence of the council. The president said: "Yes, Mr. Hopper?"

Hopper cleared his throat. "May it please you, Mr. President, gentlemen—I am not in dispute with the evidence brought by Mr. Boon. But the manner of its interpretation gravely concerns us. There are, besides, certain additional points which throw a complexion upon the case, much more favourable to my client.

"It has not yet been stated that Miss Boland was primarily Dr. Manson's patient, since she consulted him, previous to seeing Dr. Thoroughgood, on July 11. Further, as Miss Boland is the daughter of a close friend, Dr. Manson regarded her all along as his responsibility.

"We have heard of the slight difference of opinion over the question of treatment between Dr. Thoroughgood and Dr. Manson. Bearing in mind Dr. Manson's great interest in the case it was not unnatural for him to wish to take it back into his own hands. Naturally, he wished to cause his senior colleague no distress. That, and nothing more, was the reason for his subterfuge."

Here Hopper paused. "And now we come to the matter of association with Mr. Stillman. Although unqualified, he enjoys a certain reputation. It so happens that he introduced himself to Dr. Manson many years ago through a letter complimenting Dr. Manson upon some research work he had done. The two met later, on a purely personal basis, when Mr. Stillman came here to establish his clinic. Thus, though it was ill-considered, it was not unnatural that Dr. Manson, seeking a place where he could himself treat Miss Boland, should avail himself of the convenience offered him at Bellevue. Mr. Boon has referred to Bellevue as a 'questionable' establishment. On that point I feel the council might be interested to hear evidence. Miss Boland, please."

As Mary rose, the curious scrutiny of the council members fell upon her. Though nervous, she seemed well, in normal health.

"Miss Boland," said Hopper. "Tell us frankly—did you find anything to complain of while you were at Bellevue?"

"No! Quite the reverse." Andrew saw that she had been carefully instructed beforehand. Her answers came with guarded moderation.

"You suffered no ill effects?"

"On the contrary. I am better."

"In fact the treatment carried out was the treatment Dr. Manson suggested at your first interview on July 11."

"Yes."

"I have finished with this witness, sir," Hopper said quickly to the council. "What I am venturing to suggest, gentlemen, is that the treatment effected at Bellevue was in actuality Dr. Manson's treatment carried out—unethically perhaps—by other persons. There was, I contend, within the meaning of the act, no professional cooperation between Stillman and Dr. Manson. I should like to call Dr. Manson."

Andrew rose, acutely conscious that every eye was directed towards him. Cold emptiness lay in the pit of his stomach.

"Dr. Manson, you received no financial gain in respect of this alleged cooperation with Mr. Stillman?"

"Not a penny."

"You meant no reflection on your senior colleague, Dr. Thoroughgood?"

"No. It was just—our opinions did not coincide on this case."

"Exactly," Hopper intervened rather hastily. "Then you can assure the council honestly and sincerely that you had not the remotest idea that your conduct was in any degree infamous."

"That is the absolute truth."

Hopper suppressed a sigh of relief as, with a nod, he dismissed Andrew. Now it was safely over he felt that they might have a chance of success. He said, contritely, "I have no wish to keep the council further, I have tried to show that Dr. Manson merely made an unhappy mistake. I appeal, not only to the justice, but to the mercy of the council. And I should like finally to draw the council's attention to my client's considerable attainments. His past record is one of which any man might be proud."

Almost at once Boon was on his feet again, craving the

indulgence of the president. "With your permission, sir, there are one or two questions I should like to put to Dr. Manson." He swung round. "Dr. Manson, you say you had no knowledge that your conduct was in any degree infamous. Yet you *did* know that Mr. Stillman was not a qualified gentleman."

Andrew considered Boon from beneath his brows. He said distinctly: "Yes, I knew he was not a doctor."

A wintry smirk of satisfaction showed on Boon's face. He said goadingly: "I see. Yet even that did not deter you."

"Even that didn't," echoed Andrew with sudden bitterness. He felt his control going. "Mr. Boon, I've listened to you asking a great many questions. Will you allow me to ask you one? Have you heard of Louis Pasteur?"

"Yes," Boon was startled into the reply. "Who hasn't?"

"Exactly! Who hasn't? However, you are probably unaware of the fact that Louis Pasteur, the greatest figure of all in scientific medicine, was *not* a doctor. Nor was Metchnikoff, inferior only to Pasteur in his greatness. These facts may show you that every man fighting disease, whose name is not on the register, isn't necessarily a knave or a fool!"

Electric silence.

Hitherto the proceedings had dragged along in an atmosphere of pompous dreariness, but now every member at the council table sat erect. Abbey, in particular, had his eyes upon Andrew with a strange intentness.

Hopper groaned in dismay. Now, indeed, he knew the case was lost. Boon, though horribly discomfited, made an effort to recover himself. "Yes, yes, these are illustrious names, but surely you don't compare Stillman with them?"

"Why not?" Andrew rushed on in burning indignation. "They're only illustrious because they're dead!"

"Are we to take it," Boon managed a sneer, "that you have an ardent admiration for Richard Stillman?"

"Yes! He's a great man, a man who has devoted his whole life to benefiting mankind. He's had to fight jealousy and prejudice and in his own country he has overcome it. But apparently not here. Yet I'm convinced that he's done more against tuberculosis than any man living in this country."

The president intervened. "Do you realize what you are saying?"

"I do." Andrew gripped the back of his chair tensely, aware of his grave indiscretion, yet determined to stand by his opinions. Breathing quickly, a queer kind of recklessness took hold of him. "I've listened to the pleading that's been going on today on my behalf and all the time I've been asking myself what harm I've done.

"I know I am speaking more strongly than I should, but I can't help it. If we go on trying to make out that everything's wrong outside the profession and everything is right within, it will mean the death of scientific progress. It's high time we started putting our own house in order. Think of the training doctors get. When I qualified, all I knew was the names of a few diseases and the drugs I was supposed to give for them. Anything I know I've learned since then. But how many doctors do learn anything beyond the ordinary rudiments they pick up in practice? There ought to be a great attempt to bring science into the front line, to do away with the old bottle-of-medicine idea. We never give our pioneers a chance. I know I have made plenty of mistakes, and bad mistakes, in practice. And I regret them. But I made no mistake with Richard Stillman. All I ask you to do is to look at Mary Boland. She had apical phthisis when she went to Stillman. Now she's cured. If you want any justification of my infamous conduct here it is, in this room, before you."

Quite abruptly he ended and sat down. At the Council table there was a queer light upon Abbey's face. Boon, still upon his feet, gazed at Manson in confusion. Then he bowed to the president and took his chair.

For a minute a peculiar silence filled the chamber, then the president declared: "I ask all strangers to withdraw."

Andrew went into the cloakroom, desiring only to be alone, and sat on the edge of one of the washbasins, mechanically feeling for a cigarette. But the smoke was tasteless on his parched tongue and he crushed the cigarette beneath his heel. He knew he had behaved like a fool. Despite the things he had said of the profession a few moments ago, it was strange how miserable he felt at the thought of being cast out from it. The future stretched out before him desolately.

The sound of people moving in the corridor brought him wearily to his feet. As he re-entered the council chamber he prayed that he would show no sign of weakness. With his eyes fixed firmly on the floor immediately before him, he remained passive, motionless. All the trivial sounds of the room re-echoed maddeningly about him—the scraping of chairs, the coughing, whispering, even someone tapping idly with a pencil.

But suddenly there was silence and then the president spoke, slowly, impressively.

"Andrew Manson, I have to inform you that the council has given very careful consideration to the charge brought against you. The council is of the opinion that, despite your own particularly unorthodox presentation of the case, you were acting in good faith and were sincerely desirous of complying with the spirit of the law demanding a high standard of professional conduct. I have to inform you, accordingly, that the council has not seen fit to direct the registrar to erase your name."

For one dazed second he did not comprehend. Then a sudden shivering thrill passed over him.

He was free, clear, vindicated.

He raised his head shakily towards the council table. Of all the faces turned towards him, the one he saw most distinctly was that of Robert Abbey. He knew, in one illuminating flash, that it was Abbey who had got him off. He muttered feebly—and though he addressed the president it was to Abbey that he spoke: "Thank you, sir."

The president said: "That terminates the case."

Andrew stood up, instantly surrounded by his friends. He saw Mary gazing up at him, her eyes filled with tears. "If they'd done anything to you—after all you've done for me, I'd—oh! I'd have killed that old president."

Andrew smiled weakly, doubtfully, joyously.

When Andrew and the Bolands reached the hotel just after one o'clock, Denny was waiting in the lounge. He sauntered towards them, gravely smiling. Hopper had telephoned the news. But he had no comment to make. He merely said: "I'm hungry. Come along, all of you, and have lunch with me."

It was a happy celebration. After lunch Denny said to Andrew: "Our train leaves at four o'clock. Hope's already in Stanborough. We can get that property dirt cheap. I'll meet you at Euston at ten to four!"

Andrew gazed at Denny, conscious of his friendship, of all that he owed him since the first moment of their meeting in the little Drineffy surgery. "Supposing I'd been struck off?"

"You're not." Philip shook his head. "And I'll see to it that you never will be."

Andrew accompanied Con and Mary to their train at Paddington. As they waited on the platform, rather quiet now, he repeated the invitation he had already given them. "You must come and see us at Stanborough."

"We will that," Con assured him. "In the spring—whenever I get the little bus tuned up."

After their train had steamed out, he still had an hour to spare. Instinctively, he boarded a bus and soon he was in Kensal Green. He entered the cemetery, stood a long time at Christine's grave. It was a bright, fresh afternoon, with that crisp breeze she always loved. When at last he turned away, hastening for fear he should be late, there, in the sky before him, a bank of cloud lay brightly, bearing the shape of battlements.

A. J. Cronin

It was fifty years ago that a successful London doctor, forced to retire from medicine because of ill-health, published his first novel. The doctor was A. J. Cronin, and the book was *Hatter's Castle*, the first of a long line of extraordinarily successful novels.

A. J. Cronin was born in Cardross, Scotland, in 1896 and studied medicine at Glasgow University. He served in the Royal Navy in the Great War, and afterwards worked as Medical Inspector of Mines, visiting over five hundred collieries. It is the author's firsthand experience of medical practice in Welsh mining towns which gives the story of Andrew Manson so much immediacy and realism. Like Andrew, young Dr. Cronin made his rounds by day in dirty oilskins and hobnailed boots, and sat up all night studying for higher medical examinations. He and his wife and baby (the first of their three sons) lived in two rooms in a miner's cottage.

Also like Andrew Manson, Cronin later became a West End physician, and it was his personal knowledge of some of the dubious practices of fashionable doctors that made his attack on Harley Street so blisteringly effective.

Over and over, Dr. Cronin has used his own experiences to give life and reality to his books, and the Tannochbrae of the long-running television series *Dr. Finlay's Casebook* could be the very Scottish town where the author once worked as the assistant to the original Dr. Cameron.

A. J. Cronin now lives in Switzerland, and can look back with pride on a series of novels, written over many years, which are still as fresh and popular as when they were first published. *The Citadel* is the seventh of his books to appear as a Condensed Books selection.

Hell and High Water
A CONDENSATION OF THE BOOK BY
Thomas Thompson
ILLUSTRATED BY HOWARD TERPNING
PUBLISHED BY ANDRÉ DEUTSCH

On July 2, 1973, the *Triton*, a thirty-one-foot trimaran, sailed out of Tacoma, Washington, bound for Costa Rica. For Jim Fisher, the boat's skipper, this was a voyage ordained by God. Fisher was answering a long-awaited call to missionary work, and he believed he shared the *Triton*'s wheel with the Lord.

For the other two people aboard, Bob Tininenko and his beautiful young wife, Linda, the trip was simply to be a pleasant, adventurous way to spend a long summer vacation.

Then in a howling gale the *Triton* capsized, hurling its three crew members into a purgatory of survival. In the long days that followed, their physical endurance was tested to the utmost; but it was their spiritual and emotional struggles that nearly tore them apart. *Hell and High Water* is a true and fascinating account of human souls engaged in the ultimate conflict.

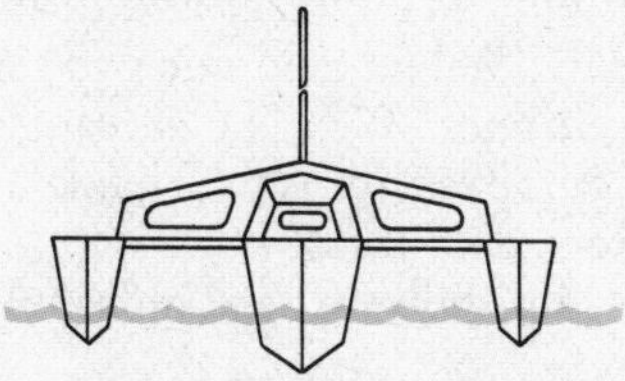

Chapter One

The soft summer wind abruptly died and it became eerily still, almost an omen. James Fisher stood in the bow pulpit of the thirty-one-foot trimaran he had built with his own hands, and he called out mightily to the God who dominated all of his days and nights. "Dear Lord," he cried, his voice carrying across the windless hush of the Tacoma marina so that the other yachtsmen looked up, "we ask for Your protection and guidance. We ask for Your hand upon the wheel, and a fair wind to fill our sails and hurry us to Your work. We ask that You watch over my brother-in-law, Bob, and his wife, Linda, and me, for we are Your children, going forth on a mission in Your blessed name. . . ."

The prayed-for brother-in-law, Robert Tininenko, glanced up. He would tolerate with courtesy any man's prayer, but he disliked being included when he no longer believed in that specific God. A decade before, Bob Tininenko had quit the church into which he had been born, the Seventh-Day Adventists. If he had any intention of interrupting the prayer to disclaim membership in the family of his brother-in-law's God, tactfully he did not.

As soon as the prayer was done, the Tininenkos were to leave on a sea journey of perhaps fifty days with Jim Fisher, a man so unwavering in Adventist faith that he did not attend movies, watch television, drink coffee, utter curses, or even read the newspaper. Jim Fisher lived this life in preparation for a second, and better one, in the arms of Christ, and he considered it his obligation to enlist others to do the same.

"Get on with it, Jim," Bob muttered under his breath. Already they had been delayed most of the day while Jim and a friend tinkered with the radios. If the prayer stretched on much longer, darkness would cover their leave-taking. And Bob did not relish threading through harbor and into Puget Sound at night.

Still, Jim prayed on. "We further ask, dear Lord, that You look after my beloved wife, Wilma, and our two sons, our unborn child and all of our loved ones. We, Thy servants, dedicate this boat, this voyage, and our lives to You. Thank You for hearing and answering our prayers, dear Jesus."

Standing beside him, Bob's wife, Linda, felt his impatience and squeezed his elbow.

"Amen!" they heard. The prayer was concluding. Jim's body trembled, as if a force had passed from the unseen into his outstretched hand and down into the muscles of his husky body.

"Ready?" asked Bob.

"Let's go," said Jim, in a voice now reticent and soft.

Thus at day's end on Monday, July 2, 1973, the *Triton* and its crew of three eased out of the Tacoma, Washington, marina and into Puget Sound. From there the graceful white craft with blue hull and yellow trim would sail into the Juan de Fuca Strait to enter the Pacific Ocean. Then it would make a broad turn to the south, follow a carefully prescribed course down the western coast of the United States, past Mexico, and—if their calculations were accurate and the winds benevolent—tie up finally in Costa Rica thirty to fifty days hence.

IT HAD arisen suddenly, the idea for this adventurous summer voyage. In early May, as the academic year neared its end at the Adventist high school in Auburn, Washington, where Jim served as registrar and occasional instructor of German, a letter arrived. Upon reading it, the stocky, blond young man bowed his head and prayed with sudden happiness. At long last God had answered his prayer. An invitation for missionary work!

That night Jim's wife, Wilma, shared her husband's excitement and together they prayed their thanks. "Well," asked Jim, when their prayer was over, "what do you think?"

"I have never interfered in what you want to do," she said. "You must follow what you believe is the Lord's will."

The letter was from Elder Fleck, a retired Adventist minister who was establishing a bakery in San José, Costa Rica. He planned to use any profits to start other small industries, such as broom and mattress factories, and to spread Adventist doctrine. It was a way of combining missionary and business activities, two objectives in which the Adventists are traditionally strong.

Elder Fleck wanted Jim Fisher to be his administrative aide. If Jim accepted, it would be a four-year commitment. The pay would be meager, the living conditions hard.

The Fishers had always lived frugally, both by religious intent and because Jim earned only four hundred dollars a month. They rented their home from the church for fifty dollars a month. Their clothes Wilma sewed or bought second-hand, their vegetables (they ate no meat) came from a home garden, their furniture was built by Jim. They budgeted nothing for entertainment other than family outings. But even with a strict ten percent of their income going to the Adventist tithe, the Fishers were not in debt nor did they consider their lives barren. Theirs was the good and hard life of an unfrilled America, an America where credit cards and installment buying did not exist, an America where family roles were sharply defined—father as wage earner and disciplinarian, mother as homemaker and teacher of the young.

The Fishers' simple, puritan tastes and harsh economies had even left them enough extra, by meticulous budgeting, for Jim to build the thirty-one-foot trimaran.

Trimarans are sea creatures of grace and beauty, descended from the Polynesian outrigger canoes which sliced across the Pacific for thousands of years. Jim chose the design over more conventional sailboats because he could construct one for a third as much as a keelboat. And, Jim pointed out to Wilma, trimarans are supposed to be virtually unsinkable.

Two years and several thousand dollars later, the boat was built. Its name, *Triton*, which Jim selected, held two meanings. One was clever—the craft had three hulls and weighed one ton; the other was more romantic—triton was a brightly colored seashell that Jim loved to collect. That Triton was also the name of a minor Greek deity, son of Poseidon, god of the sea, Jim did not know, for his education had been firmly within the framework of his church, and he rarely wandered into fiction or pagan culture.

The *Triton* served splendidly as a family diversion on Puget Sound during the summer of 1972. Four could sleep comfortably on the two double beds, two more could pass the night on cushioned benches, and the spacious top deck was perfect for sunbathing and fishing.

It was the only possession of the Fisher family worth much materially. Jim adored his boat so much that sometimes, in conversations with God, he would promise that if his pleasure in the *Triton* ever encroached on his love and service to God, he would banish it. Immediately.

One week after the letter from Costa Rica arrived, a week filled with prayer, Jim told his family that he would accept the call. It was an order from God.

To move their furniture would have been too expensive, so Wilma held a garage sale. Everything was bought, even their ancient Volkswagen. "God *does* mean for us to go," she told Jim, happily counting the almost one thousand dollars realized.

But what of the *Triton*? "Tell me what to do, Lord," Jim prayed. Should he sell the boat? The trimaran was worth between fifteen and twenty thousand dollars, and Jim could invest this money in his missionary endeavors. Or should he sail the *Triton* to Costa Rica, where she could take students on outings to show them the beauties of God's world?

He put it to God squarely, as was his custom. If You want me to sell my boat, he prayed, then send me a buyer. He believed not only in the real power of prayer, but also that God always made His will known. Perhaps Jim stretched this point a little, for he dearly wanted to keep the boat. Consequently he did not advertise that his trimaran was for sale. And when, after a month or so, the Lord had not produced a buyer, Jim decided that he was meant to sail the *Triton* to Costa Rica.

Now the question arose, how would he get her there? Wilma and his small sons could not sail as crew, because his wife was pregnant with their third child.

Then why not, suggested Wilma, ask her brother, Bob Tininenko, and his wife, Linda? An excellent sailor, Bob was a man who seized life and attacked it, whether skiing down a precipitous slope or backpacking into remote regions. He and Linda had no children and were prone to do things impulsively. Their marriage stood radically apart from the Fishers' frugality and piousness. The Tininenkos lived in a world of candlelight and good Burgundy and a sleeping bag thrown down on pine needles beside a rushing stream. They were a striking couple: he with dark good looks and a compact, muscular body; she possessed of the exquisite beauty and slim figure of a high-fashion model. The blood of the East flowed in both. Bob's parents had come from Russia. Linda's mother was Japanese, a Tokyo girl who had fallen in love with an American navy man during the occupation following World War II.

Though shy, Linda gamely followed her husband up his cliffs and into his wildernesses. They had even met on the side of a mountain, where Bob was teaching a ski class. Linda showed up the first day with her bindings so loose that Bob laughed. But she was determined to learn, and within the few months that it took her to become one of the best and most daring skiers on the mountain, he was irrevocably in love with her. They were married six months later.

Because both were teachers—he an instructor of history at Lower Columbia Junior College, she about to go to a first-grade assignment—they would be free for the summer. Bob was interested in Jim's invitation, but he wanted to know what navigational equipment and radios the *Triton* would have. Having sailed to Vancouver on the boat during the summer of 1972, Bob knew that she was not equipped for long-range ocean communication.

"The best there is," promised Jim. He was in the process of getting his license to send and receive over ham radio.

A few days later, with Linda's enthusiastic consent, Bob called his brother-in-law and said they would go, the one proviso being that the radio lifeline between ship and shore be satisfactory to him. Once again Jim promised an excellent radio setup, with an elaborate system of communications to friends along the coasts of the United States and Mexico. There was, however, a shadow on his voice, something Bob could not place. He quickly put it away, this pinprick of concern, for Bob had never known Jim Fisher to lie.

INDEED THERE WERE RADIOS—three of them.

On the afternoon they sailed, Jim enthusiastically showed Bob and Linda the communications shelf he had erected at the forward end of the main hull.

The first and simplest radio was a receiver. It would be used to pick up marine broadcasts, Greenwich time, and small-craft warnings from coastal weather stations. It could receive radio broadcasts from coastal towns, and thus serve as a navigational aid. When the *Triton* neared Portland, for example, that city's radio stations would come in clear.

As the men talked, Linda moved to the icebox and began coating four dozen eggs with Vaseline to prolong their freshness. Her hope was that the radios were a little more modern than the icebox. For it was the old-fashioned kind which required a large chunk of ice.

The second radio system, explained Jim, was the ship-to-shore.

Bob interrupted. "That's only good up to twenty-five miles out."

"Forty," stated Jim. Their course would sometimes take the *Triton* as far as a hundred miles offshore. There the ship-to-shore would be useless. But, Jim insisted, it would be helpful for, say, entering the harbor of Los Angeles ten days hence.

The journey was to be divided into three parts of approximately a thousand nautical miles each: Tacoma to Los Angeles; from there to an unspecified stop in Mexico; then the final leg to Costa Rica. Because Jim estimated the *Triton* could average a hundred miles a day, each segment was budgeted at ten days.

Now Jim moved to his main pride—a new Hallicrafters ham radio in which he had invested almost a thousand dollars. For weeks Bob had been hearing from his brother-in-law about the examinations he was taking for the federal radio license required to send and receive Morse code and voice messages.

"The Hallicrafters," said Jim, "is the insurance policy. If any trouble arose, help could be summoned in a matter of minutes."

To keep their families informed of their progress, Jim had established a radio liaison with Wes Parker, a teaching colleague in Auburn, who held a ham license. Each morning sharp at seven Jim would reach Wes and report the *Triton*'s position and any other news. And every Friday morning Bob and Linda were to talk to their families via telephone patches established by Wes. This weekly link was especially important to Linda's mother, Hisako Elliott, who was bitterly opposed to the journey.

"Trust me, Mother," Linda had said. "Bob's been sailing for seven years. He's an expert." She recited his credentials: racing a twenty-five-foot Cal, skippering a sixteen-foot sailboat on the Columbia River with its tricky currents, pleasure sailing on Puget Sound.

Unsatisfied, Hisako wept and implored her daughter not to go. But Linda sighed and closed the subject. She was an adult. She would do what she and her husband wanted to do.

NOW, FINISHED coating the eggs, Linda thought about asking Jim to call her mother, but the men were so absorbed that Linda dismissed the idea and started preparing supper. She was serving fresh salmon steaks, green peas, a salad, and root beer. No wine or liquor was on board in deference to Jim's rigid abstinence.

The men had decided to stand six-hour shifts at the cockpit instead of the usual four, to allow longer periods of uninterrupted sleep. Bob, who was standing the evening shift, took his dinner topside. Below, Linda and Jim ate quickly, then Jim began to read his Bible, one of four he had brought with him. Linda put away the dishes and checked the provisions again. The *Triton* would make a stop the next day at the marina of a small village, just before she left the Sound and entered the Pacific. There Linda could pick up any last-minute necessities.

Linda, though weary now, took out her shopping list to check what she had purchased: freeze-dried peas and potatoes, beans, rice, macaroni, cans of Veja-Links and packs of VegeBurgers—vegetable substitutes for frankfurters and meat patties—canned vegetables, soups, soda, fruit juices, the four dozen eggs, cheese, fresh fruit, and meat for herself and Bob. In another cabinet she counted powdered milk, Kool-Aid, cookies, spices, and five pounds each of red licorice rope and jelly beans—Bob's indulgences. He thought the candy would be helpful in his vow to stop smoking.

When Linda had finished her inventory, she went to the compartment where she and Bob would sleep behind curtains, drawn to separate the double bed from the rest of the main hull. Suddenly a wave of nausea swept over her. Remembering Bob's admonition to use their water supply sparingly, she drank just half a glass and felt better immediately. If the nausea returned she would open a can of soda. There were only sixty gallons of water on board for all their needs—twenty in each of the two outriggers and another twenty in the main hull.

One hour after midnight Bob turned the wheel over to Jim and hurried below. He found Linda asleep, her copy of *Anna Karenina* open on her chest. This was to be her summer for Russian novels. Bob lifted the book gently, then undressed and slipped in beside his wife. Linda's beauty refreshed him. If she did nothing each day but let him look at her, that would be a positive contribution to the world, he thought. His arms around his wife, Bob drifted off to sleep.

SHORTLY AFTER midnight at the end of that first day Jim tried to ease his *Triton* into Juan de Fuca Strait, a notorious bottleneck that links Puget Sound with the Pacific Ocean. But sudden heavy winds from the west hurled the boat back, and treacherous currents thwarted Jim's attempt to tack. Wisely he sailed to a secluded cove and dropped anchor for the rest of the night.

The next morning Bob took over and, though the winds still behaved contrarily, guided the trimaran to the marina where the last-minute purchases were to be made. Linda hurried to the pay telephone and called her parents in Kelso, Washington. Her report was cheerful: weather warm and cloudy, the water calm, the *Triton* performing beautifully.

"You can get off at Los Angeles, you know," said Mrs. Elliott. "If you don't like it, if you don't feel safe, promise me you'll get off."

"If anything goes wrong, Mother, I will. I promise."

Her mother's voice broke. "I have a bad feeling about this trip, Linda. Why won't you listen to me?"

Annoyed, Linda made a rushed good-by, reminding her mother that she would talk to her on Friday morning via the radio-phone patch. She hung up. Never before had she heard her mother so worried, so near hysteria.

The admonition hung over Linda while she prepared dinner. As she did so, she had to run to the toilet and vomit. This time the attack did not go away until she went topside to take a cup of tea to Bob at the wheel.

She found her husband bathed in the reflection of a spectacular northwest sun. His face was so somber that Linda quickly forgot her illness. "Okay, skipper?" she asked.

Nodding, Bob pointed to the Pacific, stretching forever beyond them. Respectfully, Linda looked at the expanse of water spreading the scarlet fire evenly across the horizon. At that moment they were transfixed less by the beauty of the Pacific sunset than by the enormous challenge: the *Triton* was very small, and the sea beyond imagination.

"What are you thinking?" asked Linda.

"About a line from 'The Rime of the Ancient Mariner,'" he answered. "The one that goes, *Alone, alone, all, all alone, Alone on a wide wide sea!*"

"Well, please tell the mariner that dinner's ready in ten minutes," Linda said, before disappearing through the hatch.

Laughing, pleased at the easy manner in which Linda could lift his mood, Bob began preparations for a southwesterly tack.

When Bob turned the wheel over to Jim that night, the brisk west winds abruptly eased, fell silent for half an hour, then, almost arrogantly, began anew, this time from the south. They seemed to be challenging the *Triton*.

On the fourth day, Thursday, July 5, as they sailed about seventy miles off the coast of Washington, the men decided to test their skills. Bob was the better sailor, having a seat-of-the-pants feel for the *Triton* and how she handled. On the other hand, Jim was the better navigator, far more sophisticated with sextants, compasses and charts.

Jim plotted a test course that required Bob to tack east, then back west, then east again. If the calculations were correct, the *Triton* should by nightfall be at the mouth of the Columbia River, on the Washington-Oregon border. At day's end they were elated to see a Coast Guard lightship at the river, meaning that they were less than a quarter of a mile off course.

"If you were a drinking man," cried Bob exuberantly, "this would call for a glass of champagne."

Jim's expression turned serious. He would not tolerate even in jest an intrusion on the severe code that governed his life.

LINDA WAS UP early the next morning, anxious to get breakfast over so she could talk to her parents on the first Friday radio-phone patch. All week long she had watched and listened as Jim tapped out his Morse code messages to Wes Parker. That Jim had never used voice transmission did not seem unusual to her.

When Jim finished his cereal he went directly to the radio shelf and began transmitting—in Morse code. Linda joined him, but he did not look up or acknowledge her. In a few minutes he shut down the radio and started to climb the hatch steps.

Puzzled, Linda stopped him. "Aren't we going to call Wes and put in the phone patch? My parents are standing by."

Jim shook his head. "I've already talked to Wes," he said.

Now Linda was confused. "But it's Friday," she persisted. "It's all arranged."

"Well, it can't be done today," said Jim, hurrying topside.

Linda followed him into the cockpit, where Bob was guiding the boat. He looked up, catching the concern on her face.

"Jim says we can't call our parents," said Linda.

"Why, Jim?" asked Bob. "Radio on the blink?"

Instead of answering, Jim turned and looked out at the morning sunlight. Clouds were moving in, and before long the day would turn gray.

Bob pressed on. "Something wrong with the set, Jim?"

His face reddening, Jim slowly turned back. For a time there was no sound other than the waves slapping against the *Triton*'s hull. Finally he cleared his throat and, with difficulty, spoke.

"I don't have a license," he said bluntly.

Bob's mouth fell open. "But you said you'd passed the Morse code test and were about to get the voice-transmission license."

"I *did* pass the test. But I didn't get the certificate in time to leave. So I—I—borrowed someone else's number."

"What about the voice-transmission license?" demanded Bob.

Jim shrugged. He pushed his fingers together the way a child forms a church steeple, only he pushed them so hard that they turned green-white.

"I know you've got a voice number," insisted Bob. "I heard you using it the day we left, when you were checking the radios."

Jim buried his face in his hands. He was close to tears. "I guess I just made up a Costa Rican number," he said in a muffled voice. "I'm sorry, Bob. I really am sorry."

Linda did not grasp what it all meant. "But you know how to use the radio," she said brightly. "Can't we call my folks anyway?"

"It's a federal crime," said Jim. "The penalty could be two years in jail."

Bob rose in anger. "You know that was the condition for our coming on this cruise," he said. "It was the *number one* condition. You think I'd be here risking my life—and Linda's—without that?"

"I never said I had a license."

"You never said you *didn't* have one, either. Isn't there anything in that moral code of yours that prohibits lying by omission?" Bob was shouting now. "You're a hypocrite," he cried, "a religious hypocrite! You and your no-smoking, no-drinking, no-dancing, no-movies, no-new-ideas, no-nothing way of life! If this is the kind of hypocrisy your church teaches, I only wonder why it took me so long to get out of it!"

"Bob, please. I said I was sorry." Jim turned to Linda with an imploring look.

"Let's have a cup of tea," she suggested.

"I'll tell you one thing, brother Jim," Bob said, ignoring Linda. "I don't belong to your church anymore. But I do believe in telling the truth. By your standards I'm a lost soul. But my code is more moral than yours!" He turned back to the wheel.

No one said anything for a time, an awkward time. Jim was obviously in deep distress. They watched the grayness settling over the day. Then Bob gestured in the direction of unseen land. "If there was a port over there," he said, "we'd be off this boat in about ten seconds!"

THE QUARREL between the men, one-sided as it was, had raged for almost two hours. Finally, Bob had finished his shift and wordlessly turned the wheel over to Jim. Now he sat on the bed, Linda beside him. Above their heads the winds were rising.

"I do think we should get off," said Bob, quieter now.

Linda giggled. "I don't think I can swim that far."

Bob smiled. "I mean," he said, "get off at the first possible port. We could probably make Coos Bay tomorrow."

"Can't we go as far as San Francisco?" asked Linda. "I'd like to at least touch ground in California."

Bob shook his head doubtfully. "We have no business being out in the Pacific Ocean without a usable radio. It's insanity."

As they talked, the *Triton* lurched in the sharpening new winds.

THE NEXT morning was a Saturday, the Sabbath and most holy day of the week for Jim's religion. It was a day when he had hoped to enlist Bob and Linda for informal worship services. Before departure Jim and his wife, Wilma, had prayed together that the *Triton*'s missionary voyage to Costa Rica would somehow, someway, bring Bob back to the church of his family.

Instead Jim knelt alone in the cockpit during his shift and prayed, one hand on the wheel, the other holding his Bible. It was impossible not to mark Jim's agony, and occasionally Bob felt guilty over his outburst, bitter though he still was. To please Linda, he had decided to stay on the boat until San Francisco. But under no condition would he go on after that. If Jim still wanted to sail to Costa Rica, he would have to find himself another crew.

Linda stayed in bed most of that day, feigning a headache—but in reality contending with nausea that would not go away.

The winds continued to rise until they reached twenty miles an hour, contrary winds that confounded the *Triton*'s progress. Less than twenty miles were made that day, a fifth of what had been charted.

At sundown, feeling better, Linda turned on the kerosene burners to cook dinner. As the fumes rose she grew dizzy again. At that moment Bob appeared in the cooking area and saw his wife's pale face and trembling hands.

"You've got more than a headache," he said. "Little seasick?"

Linda shook her head in denial. "I just figured it out," she said. "It's the fumes from this stove. I've been sick every day, only I didn't want to mention it because I thought I was a bad sailor."

Bob reached for the skillet. "I'll do the cooking. I'm a liberated man."

Linda embraced her husband and sat down gratefully on the nearby bench. "I'm sorry the trip turned out this way," she said.

"I'm sorry, too. . . . I feel awkward about Jim and me splitting up as enemies."

"I don't know him very well," Linda said thoughtfully.

"Neither do I. And he's married to my sister. I don't think anybody really knows Jim, except maybe Wilma."

A decade before, Bob had met Jim at Walla Walla College, an Adventist school where Bob taught history and Jim was majoring in German. Jim was the poster-perfect Aryan—hair the color of fresh wheat, piercing blue eyes—all forming into a sturdy, muscular youth of remarkable beauty.

When Jim married Wilma Tininenko, Bob had only brief conversations with his reticent new brother-in-law. But then Bob had had scant contact with his large family after his renunciation of their church. "It was pretty cold there for a while between me and them," Bob had told Linda. "Not until I married you did things thaw."

Bob dropped the VegeBurger patties into the skillet. "Jim is still the most religious man I know," he said. "Probably he was just so anxious to get to Costa Rica that he cut a few corners. And now he's going through the tortures of the damned."

THE WEATHER BUREAUS that watch the sea off the western coast of the United States report that the summer months are normally benevolent to sailors. Gale-force winds—those that blow from thirty-nine to forty-seven miles an hour—occur only one percent of the time from late June until early September. But that doesn't rule out those freak storms that rear up, shriek their furies for several hours, and then vanish.

During the first few days of July, 1973, a series of weather fronts advanced across the North Pacific, edging slowly onshore in Washington, but losing punch as they dropped down toward California. By July 6, the day that Jim made his revelation about the radio, the summer storm seemed to be disintegrating.

But on July 10 the storm was reborn, smearing the seascape a scowling gray, creating winds that reached nearly thirty miles an hour, commanding the waves to twelve-foot swells.

At midafternoon on that day Jim took a reading with his sextant and estimated that the *Triton* was about forty miles off the coast of northern California, near a place called Cape Mendocino.

An hour later, near five p.m., the receiver picked up a small-craft warning issued from Eureka, a port in northern California, predicting winds gusting to twenty miles per hour, and seas up to eight feet. Jim hurried up to the cockpit to inform Bob, who was encountering weather far more dangerous than that forecast. The men agreed to prepare the *Triton* for a storm and make all due speed for Eureka.

Quickly they dressed the boat for foul weather, dropping the mainsail, stowing the jib, raising a smaller storm jib, dropping anchor with a hundred yards of line from the stern, and rigging two drag anchors. These drag anchors, lashed to the outriggers, would slow the boat if the winds hit hard. They hoped to go downwind rather than tack, riding the waves like a roller coaster.

During the preparations Jim made directional readings and frowned. The *Triton* had made but five miles toward shore in three hours. Jim relieved Bob at the helm a little after five p.m.

Later, as Bob pulled on two pairs of jeans, two shirts, a ski parka, and his foul-weather gear, Linda lay on the bed, apprehension in her eyes. Winds were slamming into the *Triton*, causing it to roll and pitch with stomach-wrenching violence. Bob put his arms around her. "I'll probably be up there most of the night," he said. "At least until things quiet down. I can handle her better than Jim."

When Bob relieved Jim at the wheel, the night sky was oddly clearing, but the wind-indicator needle was hovering near 30 mph, with gusting up to 35 mph, just short of gale force.

"I'll stay until this thing dies down a little," Bob yelled above the wind, and he tied himself into the safety harness. "Get some rest."

Jim looked surprised. "Can you take her that long?" he shouted.

"Just stay near the radios in case we need help. And if I holler, come running!"

At ten past nine the wind-indicator needle jumped to an astonishing 60 mph, and the waves became mountains.

Quickly Bob determined there were two wave systems spawned by the freak storm, which together were squeezing the *Triton* in a crushing vise. He planned to ride the forty-foot swell from the northwest first, then turn and try to ascend the fifty-foot swell from the north. The principal peril to this course was the larger wave, exploding with a violent fifteen-foot chop of white water, smashing the *Triton* and drenching her with angry froth. Each time Bob encountered one of the great waves, the cockpit filled to his chest; then the churning water drained out in great sucking, whooshing noises, only to return moments later.

But the *Triton* held. Shuddering, groaning as she fought the storm, the trimaran fairly flew. She went rocketing on the winds across lakes of foam a thousand yards across—lakes that were born and lived and died in seconds—in a pageant that seemed to have no end. Bob had never felt a sailboat go so fast.

Within an hour the wind indicator showed about 40 mph, frightening under normal conditions, but a blessing after what had passed. The *Triton*, to Bob's anguish, progressed farther and farther away from land. By midnight his guess was that the boat was at least ten miles farther out into the Pacific than when the storm had begun. He had no idea how far south they'd gone; the distance indicator wasn't working.

All night long the storm shrieked, but as long as Bob held to a compass reading between 165 and 185 degrees, the *Triton* seemed capable of riding out the weather. Often during that night Bob blessed Jim's craftsmanship in building such a strong boat.

Jim sat at the radio shelf, straining to pick up weather reports, receiving instead only static or an occasional maddening fragment of dance music. Most of the time he kept his head buried on his hands in prayer. He felt that he had unleashed God's wrath with his radio lie, that the storm was his punishment. It was the most terrifying night of his life, for he was not prepared to die with a sin staining his soul.

Near dawn, as the skies lightened from black to mauve, Bob witnessed the birth of a new terror—whirlpools a hundred feet across, on the port side. If the *Triton* were lured into one of these gaping holes, she would be pulled into the depths of the sea. Bob dared not take his eye off the compass for an instant, for if it slipped below 165 degrees, there was the danger of broaching—turning the *Triton* sideways to the high winds and the main wave. If the boat broached, she would surely capsize.

At seven a.m., after a marathon of praying and repentance, Jim turned on his radio and argued silently with himself. It was time for him to take the helm. Would he have the strength to bear the winds as Bob had done? He had confidence in the seaworthiness of his boat, but would he be interfering with God's will, His plan for the *Triton*, by challenging the storm?

On the other hand, Jim reasoned, as skipper he was responsible for Bob and Linda. He must get them to safe harbor. Help and rescue were but a few miles away in California. It would be simple to call the Coast Guard for assistance. But if he did, how would he explain his fraudulent use of the radio?

He reached for the knobs to begin vocal transmission, but his fingers failed him. He could not face the disgrace of answering for such a crime. The storm would surely die soon. The best thing, he decided, was to alert Wes Parker in Auburn that they had encountered a storm, but that the *Triton* had bested it.

Quickly Jim tapped out a message to Wes, reporting that there had been high seas and winds, but that they were subsiding. Twice he repeated, "We are okay." Then he signed off abruptly.

A noise behind him made Jim turn. Linda, still in her nightclothes, her slim body shaking in sickness and fear, stumbled to the hatch steps to see if Bob needed his thermos jug filled with hot tea. At that moment another giant wave slapped the *Triton*, and Linda grabbed a beam to keep from pitching forward onto the wet floor.

The sight of her convinced Jim to find help. He began announcing his fictitious call letters, T12JF, interspersing with the triple break. In amateur radio a triple break means emergency. The first operator to pick up his plea was so far away that Jim could barely hear him, but within ten minutes another response was heard, this one from a seventy-two-year-old amateur named N. C. DeWolfe in San Carlos, California, seventeen miles south of

San Francisco. While chatting idly with fellow hams DeWolfe heard a weak voice crying, "Break! Break! Break!" He answered the distress call immediately.

DeWolfe could barely hear, but he was able to determine that the caller was aboard a ship and was requesting a telephone patch to the nearest Coast Guard office. "Stand by," he shouted, quickly finding the number for Search and Rescue in south San Francisco. Then, accomplishing the patch, DeWolfe anxiously monitored the conversation from sea to the Coast Guard.

Jim gave his name, the identity of his boat, his destination as Los Angeles, and said the *Triton* carried a crew of three. High winds and waves were being encountered, he said, but the storm was easing. He estimated the *Triton* was seventy-five miles southwest of Cape Mendocino. The duty officer at the Coast Guard asked if they needed assistance. Jim replied, "Negative. Do not need assistance at this moment. . . . We are becalmed." Then, after a few moments of crackling, suspenseful silence, transmission went dead.

DeWolfe could not let a mystery like that go unpursued. He had picked up an emergency call, heard someone in distress at sea asking to be linked to the Coast Guard, then heard the caller contend that, after all, he needed no assistance! It's crazy, thought DeWolfe. Immediately he notified WESCARS, an emergency network of California amateur radio operators who are on constant standby for disasters. DeWolfe told of the strange call from the *Triton* and advised them to be alert for another distress message. Then he tried to raise the *Triton* again. All morning long he broadcast Jim's name, his call letters, his boat. But he was unable to elicit a sound from her.

Just before nine that same morning Jim climbed to the cockpit to relieve Bob, now exhausted to the point of numbness. He had been on the radio, Jim said.

Over the winds Bob cried, "It doesn't seem to be slacking any." A wave crashed into the cockpit, drenching both men to their waists. "Who did you call?" yelled Bob.

"First I talked to Wes Parker. I told him we were in a storm, but that we didn't need any help right now. Then I reached a man named DeWolfe in San Carlos and he phone-patched me to the Coast Guard."

"What did the Coast Guard say?"

After a time came Jim's reply, a soft and hollow one, as if the words were located in a forbidden, even sinful place. Later Bob would wonder if he had heard them correctly. "They said they'd probably have a plane out sometime today," said Jim. "But I told them that no assistance was needed."

Bob stared at Jim incredulously. "You don't think we need any help?" Bob felt anger growing. "Jim, this is serious. I've held this boat all night; I'm beat. I think you'd better call the Coast Guard again and get some help out here."

"I can't. The battery's low. It won't work the radio."

Bob clenched his fist. "Then start the motor and recharge the battery. Dammit, Jim, move!"

Jim shook his head helplessly. "The battery's too low to start the motor. Maybe later this morning." The color was drained from Jim's face now, and his voice seemed curiously separate from his body. Bob wondered if Jim really understood the severity of the situation.

"I've got to get some rest, Jim. Do you think you can take her for a while? I'll come back as soon as I can."

Jim nodded. Carefully, twice, Bob explained the dual wave systems still at war with the *Triton*. He showed Jim how vital it was to keep the compass between 165 and 185 degrees. "If she falls below a hundred and sixty-five, we'll broach. Do you understand that, Jim?" Bob fairly screamed the warning at Jim.

"She's mine," said Jim. "I built her. I understand her."

Without stripping off his wet clothes, Bob went below and fell onto the bed, throwing an arm about Linda. For a moment he was silent; then he turned and, gripping her tightly, he broke down, tears falling on his cheeks. Linda knew what he had gone through, and she was proud of him.

"I'm glad we're getting off in San Francisco," she said.

At that moment on the morning of Wednesday, July 11, the *Triton* broached for the first time.

Only five minutes after taking the wheel, Jim let the compass reading slip below 165, and his boat turned sideways against a giant wave, a force that sent a rendering shudder across its timbers. Realizing exactly what had happened, Bob ran to the hatch steps and cried, "Jim, watch it! Don't let her broach again. We lucked out that time!"

By the time Bob got back to bed, the *Triton* broached a second time. Another sickening scream of uncountable tons of water crashing against one ton of sailboat. Bob started to rise. "I've got to go back up there," he said. "Jim can't handle her."

"But you've got to have some sleep—" began Linda. She was not allowed to finish her sentence. Without a sound the *Triton* broached for the third and last time.

The wave flipped the boat completely over. In the cockpit Jim was hurled out and down into the violent sea. Below, Bob and Linda were thrown out of their bed onto a floor that seconds before had been the ceiling. And the sea rushed in and over their upside-down world, quickly filling the doomed trimaran.

Chapter Two

Bob watched helplessly as the water poured into the *Triton*. Linda backed into a corner, holding out her hands as if she could forbid the water to reach or touch her. Then Bob collected his senses and dived for his wife. In an almost fluid action he ripped off her pajama bottoms, helped her into a pair of jeans, pulled a sweat shirt over her head, strapped her into a life jacket, found a rope, lashed her to him, and began swimming for an exit.

"Take a big breath," he ordered. Linda gulped air and held her nose. Down they plunged into the shockingly cold water, through the open hatch door, plunging farther into the depths to avoid the broken pieces of mast and railing. They swam, their lungs aching, until Bob felt they were clear enough of the *Triton* to surface.

When they came up, the overturned *Triton* was but an arm's length away, helpless as a dead whale, only the hump visible above the water, with two smaller whales—the outriggers—in escort. Bob grabbed the slippery boards and pulled Linda and himself onto what had been the *Triton*'s cerulean blue bottom, now the only visible part unclaimed by the sea. Everything else—mast, sails, cockpit, cupboards, supplies, clothing, charts—all were under water.

When the shock began to wear away, Bob remembered that Jim had been at the wheel at the moment of capsizing. He and Linda began to call for Jim. Finally she spotted him swimming frantically toward the upturned hull. He was fighting his way along the safety line that bound him to the cockpit. Choking, flopping at last onto the overturned boat, he collapsed, grabbing Bob's leg.

But none of them could last here long. Their hands were cold, their fingers were numbing, and soon they would lose their grip. Desperately, Bob looked about for a better place. At the stern, the steel railings of the cockpit were visible, not yet totally submerged. "Over there!" Bob shouted. He began to inch his way, Linda still lashed to him. In the journey of ten feet the ropes trailing from each of them became entangled, and Bob felt for his knife to cut his line. But while he sawed, the knife fell from his numb hands. Cursing, he watched it vanish. A Swiss knife, with numerous tools and gadgets, by day's end it would have been priceless.

Jim offered no apologies for his seamanship, but his face reflected his shame and agony. Nor were there suggestions to right the overturned boat, for that would be impossible without a block and tackle, a pulley, and the labor of several men in a calm marina. Instead, the three survivors could only huddle together, half submerged in the still angry sea.

Linda was first to spot the debris floating away. She called out, pointing to the bobbing red corks with the precious rods and fishing reels beneath them, gasoline cans, clothing and boxes of food.

"We won't need them," said Jim. He looked at his watch, which still worked. It was almost ten a.m.

"Do you think they're sending a plane?" asked Bob.

Jim nodded. But the nod lacked conviction, and though Bob wanted to wrestle the precise words of the Coast Guard from him, he feared to press the subject lest it shatter under examination. Until almost noon they hung to the railings—watching, waiting, listening for the sound of the plane.

BOB HAD HELD Linda so long that he did not realize her body was limp in his arms. Only when she thrashed convulsively out of his grasp did he know that something terrible was happening to his wife. Her face turned bluish white and her eyes rolled to the top of their sockets.

"Linda's out!" cried Bob, pulling her down onto the arching surface of the *Triton*. He flung his body over her, pressing his mouth to hers, gulping the salt-flecked wind and blowing it into his wife's lifeless form. Linda's dead! he sobbed inwardly.

But abruptly she gasped, and tiny bubbles of air appeared on her lips. Her eyes burst open and stared wildly. She pushed Bob away from her and tried to rise on the slippery incline. Standing uncertainly, her eyes darkened. An odd mask of anger dropped across them. She flung out her hands in a don't-come-near-me attitude. "You're killing me!" she shrieked at the two men watching her helplessly. Then she lashed out in fury at the master of the *Triton*. "Why are you trying to murder me, Jim? Why? *Why?*"

Bob moved toward her, but she shoved him away. Her screams quieted into a jumble of weeping, cursing pleas.

"She's hallucinating," murmured Bob, while Jim edged backward in horror. To Linda, Bob said gently, "Please, baby, let me hold you."

But Linda's shrieks intensified. "I know what you want. You want to kill us. I won't let you kill us."

"Us?" said Jim, puzzled. Why say *us* to her husband?

But Bob understood. His young wife was pressing her hands against her stomach, and in a flash of revelation he knew that Linda was pregnant. Her seasickness and her revulsion at the kerosene fumes were clues, but he had been unwilling, or unable, to recognize them. Now, with her mind as turbulent as the sea, she unknowingly betrayed the secret.

This time when Bob moved to her, trying to contain his own tears, she beat her fists against his chest. But he locked himself forcibly about her for more than an hour, not caring about her screams. Finally, by midafternoon, he found more rope and tied her securely to the steel railing.

Thus did they endure the last hours of daylight that July 11—the woman on the edge of madness, the husband tortured by helplessness, the zealot in a passion of prayer. Around five p.m. Bob called out to Jim as he had done so often this day, "Is the plane coming?"

But Jim either could not, or would not, answer.

"I'M COLD, BOB." Linda's voice was normal, her face composed. "What happened? I don't remember a thing," she said. "Except turning over and swimming. After that . . ." Linda shook her head.

"Poor baby, you blacked out on us," said Bob kindly.

"Is the plane coming?" asked Linda.

Bob shrugged noncommittally. He knew there would be no plane today. Search missions did not waste time at sea in twilight and darkness. But he did not say this, fearful of setting her off

again. "I've been thinking," he said instead, "we'd better figure out some way to get through the night. If that storm comes up again, we'll have a hard time hanging on here."

He tapped his foot against the arching bottom of the *Triton*, riding but a foot above the waves. "What do you suppose it's like under here?" he said.

Jim looked down at where Bob was tapping. It had been the floor of the main hull before the trimaran capsized. Almost simultaneously it occurred to the men that the hull might not be completely filled with water. Maybe an air pocket existed, with room enough to shelter them, at least for the night. But the sea still felt shockingly cold, and neither man had the will to plunge in and swim underneath to explore the hull.

"Why couldn't we cut a hole?" said Jim, thinking out loud.

"Wouldn't we sink?" asked Linda.

Jim shook his head quickly. The *Triton* was well lined with flotation material. "If she's lasted this long, she won't sink."

The memory of the lost pocketknife came back to Bob, and he cursed his clumsiness.

Then Jim had a sudden inspiration. He removed the metal buckle from his life jacket and pried it apart. Patiently he pushed the buckle back and forth against the *Triton*, trying to chew a hole in its overturned hull.

Within minutes he had made a small hole in the center of the hull. He began enlarging it with his hands, tearing his flesh as he worked. Soon the hole was big enough for him to squeeze through, and within seconds, from below, came his exultant shout, "Air! At least a foot and a half of air pocket! Come on down."

Wriggling through first, Bob fell into cold black water up to his shoulders. He held up his arms to aid Linda into the darkness. For a moment all three stood uneasily in the upside-down cabin, on what had been the ceiling of their living quarters. Pieces of wood bumped against their bodies. Now that they were sheltered, they were hungry and ready for sleep, but there was no time for anything except ensuring survival. They could not stand in the water all night; it might rise and drown them. The men sought for some way to raise themselves above the waterline and stay there, hoping the air pocket would remain until morning.

Bob found some plywood from a cupboard door floating near him and he wedged it into the narrow end of the hull, where the sides came together in a V. He lifted Linda onto the platform, just big enough for her to crouch in a fetal position, her face inches from the boards above her. It seemed to her like a very small cave.

Then the men found smaller planks to wedge against the walls. By jamming their backs against one wall and their feet against the opposite one, they were able to keep the upper parts of their bodies out of the water. Suddenly something brushed against Bob and he reached for it. A can of root beer!

"Here's dinner," he said, pulling the snap tab and passing it around.

Each drank carefully, savoring the taste, trying to wash away the taste of salt. When it was gone and there was nothing left to do but listen to the waves whooshing in and out of the chamber, Jim asked if he could pray.

"I don't mind," said Bob, preferring anything to silence.

Jim's voice rang out in the darkness. "Dear Jesus," he prayed, "please hear me in our hour of need. If You have it in Your design to rescue us, then we are ready. We want to be rescued, Jesus. . . ." He prayed on, asking blessings for his wife and children, his voice continuing with a curious power.

When the prayer was done, Jim began singing "A Mighty Fortress Is Our God." Bob and Linda joined in, both surprised that they remembered the words.

Later, when they began their attempts at sleep, sliding in and out of consciousness, each frightened at the black water surrounding them, Linda screamed. Instantly Bob called out comfort to her, and she quieted. She slept only eight feet away from him, but he did not have the strength left to swim to her.

After midnight Jim's board gave way and he fell into the water. But he was too weary to put it back. He stood in the sea for the rest of the night, shivering and dozing and talking to his God.

THE NEXT MORNING, in a gray dawn, Jim climbed out of their watery quarters and looked for rescue. But his searching eyes found only the sea, still menacing with eight-foot swells.

Below, Linda seemed remarkably chipper after her night on the plywood wedge. A little backache was her only complaint. Half walking, half swimming, Bob worked his way to her. "I love you," she said, "but you do get me to do the darndest things." They laughed and kissed.

Jim dropped back through the hole and joined them. "Anything?" asked Bob.

Jim shook his head.

"Well, let's look around," suggested Bob, setting forth in a modest breaststroke. He was not a very good swimmer.

"I've already checked out the radios," said Jim gloomily. "They're ruined." The communications equipment, which had been set up on a high shelf, was now totally submerged.

The men began to move cautiously about the cabin, a space roughly twenty feet long and eight feet wide. All of it was filled with seawater except the air pocket, which seemed to be constant, extending approximately eighteen inches from the water level to what was now the ceiling.

Jim felt a cupboard door with his feet and dived down quickly to open it. He came up with a prize—the *Triton*'s bag of tools. He placed the precious implements out to dry—a hammer, file, screwdrivers, pliers, drill, nails, screws, bolts and a saw with which he began smoothing out the edges of the jagged entrance hole.

While he worked, Linda talked privately with Bob. Her question was one that Bob had considered most of the night—where were they? The night the storm broke the *Triton* had been approximately forty miles off the coast of northern California, near Cape Mendocino. During the twelve hours he fought the storm, the *Triton* had made little progress, probably no more than thirty miles south, perhaps fifteen miles farther west from shore. Calculating rapidly in his head, Bob said, "I'd estimate that we're about a hundred miles above San Francisco, maybe fifty miles offshore."

"There'll be ships, won't there?" Linda wondered. "I mean, even if the plane doesn't come." In the *Triton*'s nine days at sea they had seen more than a score of tankers and cargo ships. Only now, in their ordeal, were they suddenly alone.

"Linda," began Bob haltingly, for he did not want to alarm her, "I don't think we should count on that Coast Guard plane. Jim is kind of vague about it. Maybe he heard them wrong. He was in a state of shock because of the storm."

She nodded in agreement. Her courage satisfied him.

"So I think we'd better spend today rigging up some way to live inside here and conserve our energy. It will just be for a little while, I'm sure. Yesterday Jim told Wes Parker we were in a storm, and when we don't check in with him today, he's bound to notify the authorities."

"They'll come," said Linda with confidence. "I mean, it's not like we're out in the *middle* of the ocean. I'll bet if it cleared up we could probably see California."

Bob smiled, but he could not risk telling Linda what he really believed, that the winds were shoving them farther and farther away from shore. Besides, something else was on his mind.

"Honey, why didn't you tell me about the baby?" he asked gently.

Linda's eyes opened wide in surprise. "How did you know?"

"You said something about it before you blacked out."

"I was afraid you wouldn't want me to come if you knew. Besides, I'm barely pregnant, only since around the first of June."

Quickly Bob began counting the months on his fingers. Linda stopped him. "February!" she said happily.

LATER THAT MORNING Bob stood looking at the water-filled room, attempting to devise a way to keep three people permanently above the waterline. Every few moments a wave would rush in through an opening and out another. Although there always was that constant air pocket, sometimes it was as much as three feet; other times it narrowed to eighteen inches.

Rummaging among the tools, Bob pulled out the hand drill and commenced to bore holes in one side of the hull, placing them six inches apart in a horizontal line. When he had drilled holes along roughly twelve feet of one side, he swam to a center beam and did the same. Then he took the ropes that had been used for the drag anchors during the storm and began weaving a latticework hammock just above the waterline. By working the half-inch-thick rope back and forth from the holes in the hull to the holes in the center beam, Bob rigged a perch strong enough for them all.

But there remained a serious drawback. The ropes would cut into their bodies and make sleep difficult, if not impossible. Suddenly Bob snapped his fingers in inspiration! Ducking under the water and swimming into what had been his and Linda's bedroom, he found some sheets and their double mattress, waterlogged, but —miraculously—still there.

He would place a few boards down on the hammock, and on top of them the foam mattress, sawed into two long, narrow strips. Jim's place on the ropes would be approximately five feet long and two feet wide. Bob and Linda would share a strip about six feet long and a little more than a foot and a half wide. They would lie along the starboard side of the hull, but Bob left a few inches between the two mattresses as a sort of dividing line between Jim and the two of them.

Jim eyed the handiwork skeptically. "Will it hold us?"

"There's only one way to find out," said Bob, climbing onto his mattress, positioning Linda beside him. They had just enough room to lie facing one another in a lover's embrace.

When Jim got onto his bed, it sagged perilously, but stopped just short of the water. Bob and Linda decided to stretch out with their feet pointed toward the stern. Jim's feet faced the other way—toward the bow, and their heads were almost touching. But because the two men did not have to face each other, a frontier of privacy was established.

An immediate surge of claustrophobia enveloped all three. Their heads were but an inch or two from the ceiling, and below them the water lapped at their mattresses. Still, these conditions could be tolerated.

It took Bob most of the day to construct the beds. Jim, meanwhile, spent his time exploring the cabin—a grim treasure hunt—looking for food and supplies. Taking deep breaths, submerging, feeling around the cupboards and shelves, he would burst out of the water sputtering. "Hey, just what we need, vanilla extract!" With each discovery Linda cheered from her plywood perch. Her task was to listen for the Coast Guard plane, although Bob now privately doubted that one would come.

Once during the day Bob noticed a gallon metal container of rice bobbing in their quarters. Happily he threw it over to Jim to store along with the other food. Jim had created a makeshift shelf at the end of what was to be his bed. But less than a quarter of an hour later Bob saw the same metal container float past him, sucked out of the boat by a departing wave.

"We just lost the rice, Jim!" he called out testily.

Jim apologized, but Bob noted once more that curious hollowness to his words, not unlike the way he had spoken of the rescue plane. For one absurd moment Bob imagined that Jim *wanted* to lose the rice. But that idea was foolish and Bob dismissed it.

Then Bob spied two balls of Gouda cheese, retrieved them from the water and tossed them to Jim. Later, Bob would remember that Jim definitely caught them.

Just before dark Bob made a major find—the water-distillation kit. Before leaving Tacoma, Jim had demonstrated the kit to Bob and Linda, pointing out that it had been developed by the U.S. Navy and was simple to operate. A large balloon, it could be inflated by mouth up to six feet across, set down on the sea, and tied to the boat. It made use of the sun to separate out the salt and produce fresh, drinkable water. The kit had no battery, and no parts had been damaged in the capsizing. It would be invaluable if rescue did not reach the *Triton* soon. The twenty-gallon supply of water in the main tank was now lost, and the forty gallons in the outriggers were probably washed out, too.

"Put this kit up in a safe place," said Bob sharply. "It's essential." Jim took the kit and looked at it strangely.

"TWO CANS of creamed corn, two cans of string beans, one jar of peanut butter, one can with no label, probably peas . . ." Jim was taking inventory of food found that day. Rather than risk having it washed off the shelf by a sudden high wave, Jim announced that he had burrowed a hole at the foot of his foam mattress, and there the food would stay. No one had elected him captain of the food supply, but Jim was the skipper as long as there was a *Triton*. Neither Bob nor Linda complained.

"Let's see," Jim went on. "Five cans of sardines . . ." He grimaced; Jim detested sardines. "One can apple-pie filling, one can chop-suey mix, one jar vegetable oil, six packs Kool-Aid, four packets powdered milk, one pack chicken-bouillon powder, one pack freeze-dried peas, one bag caramel-candy chips, three packs VegeBurgers, three cans Veja-Links." Then Jim held up a handful of condiment bottles—salt, vanilla, peppermint extract.

Bob frowned. "You didn't count the two balls of Gouda cheese."

Jim shook his head. "There aren't any cheese balls."

"I threw them at you, Jim. I saw you catch them."

Jim said stubbornly, "Well, there aren't any cheese balls here. Maybe you imagined it."

Bob elected not to argue. Everyone was tired. Flaring tempers would help nothing. Instead he watched carefully as Jim put away the food. Making a rapid calculation, he estimated that roughly four pounds of usable food had been salvaged. "We've got enough to last for quite a while if we're careful," he said. "You're sure that's everything, Jim? You didn't find anything else?"

Jim pursed his lips in recollection. He thought of something. "Oh, I forgot. I did find that big can of jelly beans and licorice."

Bob brightened. "Fantastic. We can use the sugar for energy."

"But I threw them out."

"Why did you do that?" Bob flared. "We need every drop of food we can get. God knows when anybody's going to find us out here."

The nerve was at last exposed. Jim leveled somber eyes at his brother-in-law. "That's just it, Bob," he said. "God *does* know when we're going to be rescued."

"Don't start that on me, Jim. I want to know why you threw out those jelly beans."

"They were waterlogged. You wouldn't have wanted them."

"I would have wanted to make that decision myself."

As she had done before and would do again, Linda moved between the two men as buffer. "Now, about dinner, you guys," she began, taking a can of peas from Jim.

But Jim cut across her words. "I want us to understand one thing," he said. "This isn't going to be one of those men-against-the-sea endurance contests. It just isn't going to be that way."

Bob raised his eyebrows. "And what *is* it going to be?"

"We'll be rescued when God is ready for us to be rescued," said Jim, his voice building with the fervor of prayer. "There's nothing we can do to bring on that moment."

Exasperated, Bob swung his legs around, wishing for a place where he could move and let off steam. He felt as confounded as he had in childhood when teachers had rebuked him for questioning the Bible. Well, here I am again, he thought, and I will get no further with Jim than I did with them.

Bob began his rebuttal softly, but he made sure that Jim both heard and understood.

"I don't agree with you, Jim," Bob said, measuring his words. "I feel sure we will be rescued soon. But until that happy moment, this isn't going to turn into some sort of religious, mystical experience for me and Linda. We will ration our food; we will also conserve our energy and try our damnedest to keep our spirits up. If you want, we can divide the provisions three ways right now, and you can make a banquet out of yours—eat it all for dinner. But don't ask us for handouts tomorrow if Jesus decides not to come."

BOB OPENED the can of peas with a screwdriver, and they split the contents three ways, carefully dividing the juice, which was their only liquid of the day. But one more job needed to be done before they could sleep. The exit hole was open to the sky, and when waves broke across the *Triton*, a shower of salty spray fell onto the beds. Finding another cupboard door, the men sawed it to fit the hole. But when the wood was wedged in place, their quarters became a pressure chamber and the sound of the sea a roar. So Bob cut a six-inch hole in the exit cover, enough to relieve the pressure and allow moonlight to enter—if the moon ever broke through the heavy overcast.

After the good-nights were said, Jim prayed silently. All four of his Bibles were lost in the capsizing, but he had found his copy of *The Great Controversy*, an Adventist book that traced the history of his denomination. He had read its pages a hundred times before, but he could still draw strength and comfort from it.

Snuggling close to her husband, Linda quickly found sleep. But within an hour she was awake, shrieking in hysteria that the *Triton* was disintegrating, that they would all drown. Bob drew her into his arms and rocked her until the terror went away. Hallucinating again, he thought. We'll have to watch it, all of us.

Perhaps if Linda had more room, she would sleep more tranquilly. Bob scooted down a few feet and curled himself into a ball at the foot of the mattress. He stayed in that cramped position until claustrophia overtook him. The darkness, the clammy, creaking walls, the chill water that waited below him—all coalesced to frighten him. A scream building, he pushed past Linda and craned his neck to peer through the little hole that led to the world above their heads.

He could see the grayness of early dawn; the night was almost over. Reassured, he eased back to the foot of the mattress. Whispering courage to himself, listening to the waves, waiting for the sun, he finally slept.

Chapter Three

On Friday, July 13, the third day inside the overturned sailboat, Jim opened a can of Veja-Links. "Three each," he said as he handed a portion to Linda. Bob stopped him.

During the long night Bob had come to the realization that if they were to survive, they could not function as individuals, each clinging desperately to life. Only by a full-scale cooperative effort, could they hold out until rescue came.

"Before we eat, I want to say something," began Bob. He knew now that he must couch his remarks with diplomacy. "We may be rescued today, and if not today, then tomorrow. And if we're not picked up this week, then I feel we will sooner or later drift into the coast of California." As best as he could determine, Bob went on, the winds continued to blow from the north and west, pushing them on a southeasterly course that would eventually lead to land.

"But," he continued, "these are only probabilities. So I believe we've got to formulate a long-range plan that will conserve our food and liquid and also give us a daily schedule to keep our minds occupied."

Pausing to see what effect his notions were having, Bob saw that Linda was attentive. But Jim seemed uninterested. He wanted breakfast done with, so he could drop into the water beneath their beds and make further explorations. Moreover, this was Friday, eve of the Seventh-Day Adventist Sabbath, and by nightfall he would cease all activity save prayer and meditation. He was impatiently transferring the can of Veja-Links back and forth between his hands.

"I feel," Bob snapped, "that what I'm saying might be important, Jim."

Linda quickly reached over and placed her hand across the can. "Come on, Jim," she said lightly, "you promised Wilma you were going to lose twenty pounds on this cruise and be all skinny and handsome when she and the boys come down to Costa Rica."

Jim brightened. It was true. At almost two hundred and twenty pounds he was growing potty at the waist, and although his body was still well developed, the excess weight made him look older than thirty. Jim laughed. "I didn't mean this kind of diet," he said.

"Okay," continued Bob. "I figure we've got enough food to last us thirty days, but that means no more than a cup for each person per day." He took the can of Veja-Links from Jim and fished one out. "This one rip-off frankfurter, for example, will be breakfast *and* dinner for me. Half now, half tonight. When we finish these links we open a can of, say, creamed corn. We split the can three ways, and that one-third of a can must last each of us two meals."

After a few moments of reflection Jim asked how the food distribution system would be controlled.

Bob had a quick answer. "The honor system. You keep the food, Jim. We don't even know exactly where it is, only that you've got that storage place at the foot of your bed. Each of us is on his honor not to eat a single bite of food unless the others know about it. The same goes for the three cans of soda we've got. And if the sun ever comes out, we can set up the water-distillation kit and apply the same rules to any fresh water we make."

Bob stopped. His throat was dry, and so many words delivered so quickly made him hoarse. He still had the second half of his plan to offer—a daily schedule of activities.

But Jim, fishing out a Veja-Link, had tuned out his brother-in-law. He quickly ate half of his link and went topside.

THAT MORNING several important discoveries were made in the water beneath their beds. In their flooded former bedroom Bob found Linda's purse, and she squealed with delight as she set out her cosmetics, comb and brush to dry.

Jim found a pair of waterlogged binoculars and a compass, not the *Triton*'s expensive navigational compass but one that could still designate rough directions. The major find of the morning was a medicine kit containing aspirin, vitamins, penicillin salve and mercurochrome, all unharmed from their submersion.

In a cupboard that Bob took three dives to force open, he happily found two cans of white paint, a brush, a container of kerosene, a can of diesel fuel, rags, motor oil, and three knives. Two Bob kept for himself—a Boy Scout knife with contraptions, and a seven-inch kitchen knife. The other kitchen knife he gave to Jim.

Linda suddenly remembered the icebox. Immediately Jim plunged into the cold water, and after a long minute came up triumphant. The cooler still contained perfectly edible fresh cherries, two grapefruits, and two dozen Vaseline-coated eggs. In celebration, a grapefruit was eaten.

In the afternoon the men went topside and painted the once blue bottom of the *Triton* a glistening white. They left two-foot letters spelling HELP in the original blue, and an enormous six-foot blue arrow leading to the plea. The arrow lent a nice pop-art quality, Bob thought. Finally they took the orange curtains from the bedrooms and orange life jackets that Jim's children had used and nailed them about the overturned main hull for contrast. Certainly the gaudy trimmings could be seen by a searching airplane from miles away.

When they were done, Bob found a large piece of wood and, with some of the remaining white paint, painted a message.

THE TRITON—CAPSIZED JULY 11, 1973, OFF CAPE MENDOCINO, CAL. THREE PEOPLE. ALL SAFE. PLEASE CALL COAST GUARD IN SAN FRANCISCO OR L.A. TODAY IS JULY 13, 1973.

When the sign was dry, Bob hurled it into the sea.

DINNER WAS THE second half of the Veja-Link. Bob and Linda chewed slowly, savoring each morsel, but Jim disposed of his in two rapid bites. He was anxious to begin observation of his Sabbath eve.

"Do you mind if I have an informal Friday evening service?" asked Jim.

Bob nodded agreeably. The day had been a productive one, and he did not want friction just before they must try to sleep.

With his harmonica Jim began playing Sabbath school songs. Bob had learned the tunes three decades ago, and they washed memories over him—of other Friday nights, of brothers and sisters warmed by a blazing hearth, of a father reading from the family Bible, his grandmother reading hers in Russian. He could almost taste the fried buns and the borscht that the women had prepared to last through the Sabbath hours, for it was forbidden to work or cook between sundown on Friday and sundown on Saturday.

Now, lost somewhere in the world's largest ocean, Bob found temporary harbor in the memory of those bonds.

"*Jesus in the family . . . happy, happy home,*" sang Jim. It was a song every Adventist child could sing. When it was over Linda requested one from her young years—"Jesus Loves Me"—which Jim played, followed by "Row, Row, Row Your Boat," which gave them a secular round of fun.

When the singing ended, Jim read silently from his Adventist book for a while; then he asked if he could pray aloud.

"If you want," said Bob, warmed by the memories.

"Dear Lord, dear Jesus," prayed Jim, his eyes tightly closed. How quickly the power filled him, swelling his voice! Blessings were asked for his family, for Bob's and Linda's families. And then he stopped, as if finished. But Bob knew more would come.

"And if it is Your will, dear Jesus, that we be rescued," continued Jim, "we are ready. We do not want to rush You, for we know that Your heavenly plan will be unfolded. But we want You to know that we are waiting. Thank You, dear Jesus. Amen."

Beside him Linda said, "Amen." Her benediction surprised Bob, for he knew her religion was even more casual than his.

After the prayer Linda went to sleep quickly, passing the entire night, for the first time, without trembling or screaming.

THE NEXT MORNING brought yet another first. A brilliant sun illumined Jim's Sabbath, a hopeful Saturday dawn that contained none of the dark gloom that had commenced each of their days since the capsizing.

Linda awoke excitedly, anxious to climb outside where she could dry her clothing and bedcovers. For two days and three nights she had not left her damp bed.

But first, suggested Jim, why not join him in Sabbath services and thank God for the sun and its promise? Linda agreed to wait. His service followed the same format as the night before: hymns on the harmonica, a text from *The Great Controversy*, and a concluding prayer. Linda paid little attention to the words, but Bob heard, and what he heard disturbed him.

"Dear Jesus," intoned Jim, "help us prepare ourselves for the hour of rescue. Now it is clear. Now we understand that You will *not* rescue us until each of us is prepared. Speak to our hearts, dear Jesus, make our hearts right so You can rescue us. Thank You for hearing and answering our prayers. Amen."

With that Jim took his half of Veja-Link and hoisted himself into the sunlight. But the prayer troubled Bob. It seemed that Jim was edging closer and closer to a point he wished to make. Bob decided not to bring the matter to a head now. He, too, pulled himself up and out into the air. A dozen feet away, Jim faced him. But they did not speak. The current between them, however, was electric.

The discovery of her purse had buoyed Linda's spirits, and she combed her hair carefully and put on makeup, peering into the tiny mirror built into her bag. Then she called out to Bob to help her topside.

Bob whistled in appreciation when he peered down at her. "You're beautiful," he said. He noticed a line of pain around her eyes that the makeup could not hide, but he did not remark on it.

Linda smiled flirtatiously and raised her arms for a lift through the hole. In the few seconds it took to help her onto the surface of the boat, her newly decorated face became masked with intense pain. She lay on the arching slope of the overturned trimaran and breathed heavily.

"What is it, honey?" asked Bob, bending down beside her.

"It's nothing," lied Linda. "My legs hurt a little. Probably cramps. They'll go away."

"Maybe I'd better take a look."

"No!" said Linda, grabbing her husband's hand.

"Linda, let Dr. Tininenko examine you."

Reluctantly she allowed Bob to pull off her jeans, which had not been removed since the *Triton* flipped over. And then Bob saw. It was all he could do to avoid recoiling in horror.

Covering Linda's hips, thighs, calves, all the way to her ankles, were sores—some as large as a tennis ball, others the size of a quarter, all puckering with infection. Obviously she had been, and still was, in intense pain.

"Poor baby," Bob said, trying to sound calm, "you've got a bunch of lousy sores. Must be an allergy or something."

Linda knew their cause. Ever since the boat had turned over, there had been no discussion of toilet needs. The men had been urinating inside their pants, automatically rinsing their clothes when they dropped into the water to search for supplies. And they had made trap holes in their mattresses, which made it easy to urinate into the sea, flushing continuously beneath them.

But Linda had not left her bed. Her urine had stayed inside her jeans, where it combined with the salt water that always dampened her clothing. The result was this eruption of infected sores.

Bob took the bed sheet and dried it in the sun and placed it over Linda's legs so that she could—modesty's dues paid—feel the warmth. But within an hour she had grown so weary that he had to take her back through the hole and lower her gently onto their bed. From the medicine kit he took penicillin salve and spread it over her legs. As he worked he wished for fresh water to bathe the sores.

And then he remembered. The water-distillation kit! It would be usable today because the sun was out. They could have an inexhaustible supply of water.

Bob called to Jim, who was staring pensively out at the sea. He had caught only a glimpse of Linda's sores, then turned away quickly. But he seemed deeply affected by her suffering. Now he sat alone in brooding silence.

"Let's set up the water-distillation kit," Bob shouted.

"Where is it?" Jim called down, as if the existence of the apparatus were a revelation to him.

"Where is it?" Bob echoed. "What do you mean, '*Where is it?*' I gave it to you. You put it up somewhere, remember?"

Jim gave a noncommittal shrug, and came slowly down through the hole to his bed. For a few moments he rummaged brusquely through the food and supplies he had stored. Then he turned and shook his head. "Can't find it." He spoke casually, as if he could not find a missing button.

"You're kidding me," said Bob in disbelief.

"It's simply not there, Bob. I guess it fell off."

Rage leaping within him, Bob lunged across the space dividing the two mattresses. Desperately, he pawed through the possessions. The book. The knife. A can of peanut butter. Not there!

A scream escaped Bob, and as he thrashed wildly in search of the missing kit, he rolled into the water beneath the beds.

"Help me, dammit! Help me find it!" Bob yelled at Jim, reaching up with wet hands and trying to pull him into the water.

But Jim drew back, and in a voice of calm and serenity he said, "Maybe it is the will of God that we no longer have the kit."

"No! It must be here somewhere." Bob gulped air and plunged under, staying until his lungs ached. Defeated, his body throbbing from the cold, he swam to his bed and dragged himself up, collapsing beside Linda, trying to expel the terrible thought that consumed him. But he could not.

It seemed impossible, cruel, and Bob sought to dismiss the disturbing idea from his consciousness. But it lodged there, refusing to go away. It seemed that Jim had deliberately thrown away the water-distillation kit. Perhaps he had even destroyed the cheese and cast off the rice.

Perhaps, thought Bob, Jim is systematically denying us nourishment, denuding us in the eyes of his omniscient God.

Jim's next intonement made it all but clear. "We must be totally dependent upon God," he said softly. "If we distilled water, then we would congratulate ourselves and perhaps live a long time and think that we did it all."

Bob bit into his mattress to keep from screaming.

Chapter Four

Linda heard the sound first, a faint drone. She raised up on her elbows, wanting to believe her ears yet almost fearful to do so. But the noise held. She shook Bob, daydreaming beside her.

"Listen!" she commanded in a hushed whisper. Bob strained his attention. The drone was louder, and was not the familiar sound of the sea. This was the sound of man. Rescue!

Bob fairly leaped through the exit hole, shouting at Jim to follow him. The two sprang onto the *Triton*'s surface.

On the horizon, bearing directly at them from the south, was a two-seater airplane. It seemed to be in search of something. And below, moving stately across the waves, was a ship. Obviously they were partners in a rescue team.

Had the seascape been a clockface, both the plane and the ship would first have been seen at ten o'clock. And by the time they reached an imaginary high noon Bob and Jim were leaping, dancing and waving on the sloping bottom of the *Triton*. Below them, in her bed, Linda wept with happiness. She looked at the wall where Bob was carving a daily calendar. July 18, 1973. Eight days lost at sea. He would never carve the ninth!

But the plane banked east and disappeared in a shelf of clouds. Never mind, thought Bob, the ship is coming to get us. Ten minutes dragged by, the men growing tired from their leaping and waving. The ship seemed to stop less than two miles from them. Then it executed a right-angle turn. The plane reappeared, circled over the ship in some sort of reunion salute; then both the plane and the boat moved off into the horizon and vanished.

The men screamed and implored with their aching arms for the rescuers to return. But they were left exactly as they had been at the moment Linda first heard the faraway drone. Alone.

"Now they'll figure they've searched this area," Bob said bitterly. "They won't come back."

Jim nodded knowingly.

THAT NIGHT Linda said she could not take solid food. She had neither the strength to chew it nor the will to keep it down. In despair Bob remembered the powdered-milk packets. Dreading the reply, he asked Jim, "Do we still have the powdered milk?"

Jim looked in the storage place and held up four packs.

"Tomorrow," said Bob, "I'm going to swim to the outrigger and see if there's any water left. I wedged some of the containers pretty tightly in the forward hull."

In the eight days since they had capsized they had drunk only the liquids from the canned goods. The seas had been too choppy and cold to risk plunging in and prowling underneath the *Triton*. Now Bob had to try. He needed water to make milk for Linda.

Before they went to sleep on this disappointing night, Jim prayed again. "Dear Jesus," he began, "we come to You tonight with understanding in our hearts. We know now that one of us on board is not ready for Your coming. . . ."

Bob tensed. This third prayer's theme was now clear to him.

"One of us on board has not given his heart to You," the prayer continued. "And we know that when that person does these things, dear Jesus, then You will rescue us. . . ."

There was to be more, but Bob cut in sharply. "I don't like what you just prayed." His voice was cold. "It isn't true."

Opening his eyes, Jim transferred his attention from God to his brother-in-law. "I believe what I pray," he said. "I believe that God brought the storm, that God's hand caused us to capsize, and that God will rescue us when we are all ready. And not until then."

A racing began in Bob's head. "That's nonsense, Jim. Do you really believe God caused that great storm just to punish me because I stopped going to church ten years ago? God didn't capsize your boat, Jim," Bob continued. "You did. I kept her sailing for twelve hours. And fifteen minutes after you took the wheel, we were upside down."

Linda put her hand out. "Bob, please, let's go to sleep."

He shook her away. One more thing remained to be said, and he said it so coldly that Jim could not possibly misconstrue its meaning. "I don't want to hear that prayer again, Jim. I can't stop you from praying to yourself, but I warn you—don't say it out loud. Understand?"

Jim turned on his side and faced the wall.

None of them slept well that night.

THE SUN held for another day, yet when Bob dived in the next morning, July 19, to search the outriggers, the shock and cold sent pricks of pain and cramps through his body. Through startlingly clear blue-green water he swam hurriedly under the hull to the starboard outrigger fifteen feet away, where twenty gallons of water had been stored. He found a large jagged hole had been ripped in the outrigger's belly, probably caused by a chunk of the mainmast when it splintered and fell that stormy morning. The water containers were gone.

On his way back out the jagged hole, Bob's foot brushed against Jim's scuba-diving suit and a bag of gear. He grabbed them, burst to the surface, and wearily paddled to the main hull, where Jim was standing.

"No water," he gasped, as he held up the scuba equipment.

Jim seemed unconcerned at the bad news, so eager was he to get into his wet-suit, mask, and fins. Quickly he dropped into the sea, as eager as a man on a yachting holiday. When he came up he was grinning, happier than he'd been since the day they set sail.

Bob cupped his hands and called, "Check the other outrigger. Maybe there's water in that one."

Jim shook his head. He pulled off his mask. "There's no water, Bob," he said. "It won't do any good to look. I told you how I feel about interfering with the Lord's will."

"God helps those who help themselves, dammit! Now go and look. I found your scuba outfit. Return the favor." It was more of an order than a request.

Reluctantly Jim paddled to the port outrigger and peered through the open hatch. He emerged a few minutes later, holding up a one-gallon Purex bottle which Bob knew contained fresh water. Then, pleased in spite of himself, Jim dived under once again.

Within half an hour thirteen one-gallon jugs of fresh water were transferred from the port outrigger to the main hull. Not all of them were full, as there had been leakage and evaporation. Bob touched each with awe. When Jim came up with the last one, Bob leaned down to the water's edge. "Did you see anything else we might use in there?"

Jim shook his head. "Nothing. Everything washed out except the water jugs and that anchor."

Bob shrugged. "We might find some use for the anchor."

Within three weeks Bob would find a use, and it would be unbearably poignant.

DISCOVERY OF THE WATER cheered the three and eased the crackling tension between Bob and Jim. Everyone celebrated with a greedy cupful. Then Bob set about concocting a drink for Linda—powdered milk, a raw egg, vanilla extract and a drop of peppermint. Mixing it all together in a plastic juice container, he presented her his "milk shake *extraordinaire*." Within an hour Linda had taken the whole cup and there was new color in her cheeks. "Hey, you guys," she said, "I feel much better."

After dinner, which for the men was a few teaspoons of chop-suey mix, Bob picked up a piece of plywood and began to paint another message, which he would throw into the sea the next morning. As he wrote the date, July 19, 1973, he paused. "Nine days," he said to himself. But Linda heard him.

"They haven't given up on us, have they?" she whispered.

"Of course not," Bob said quickly. "By now they've got an alert to the Coast Guard and the civilian fleet and every airplane owner who flies anywhere in the vicinity. They'll find us."

Bob put his arms about Linda lightly, carefully, because of her painful sores. Before dinner he had bathed her thighs and legs in the cool fresh water, then put on a new application of penicillin salve. He hoped the sea would remain calm, so that waves would not splash salt water onto her bed and irritate her further.

Above them Jim watched the last drops of the sunlight meld with the blue-black sea, and he reluctantly closed his book. Then he dropped through the hole and onto his bed. This was the hour when their spirits ebbed; they dreaded the darkness. Bob tried not to look at his watch during the night, for it was maddening to wake up and feel dawn to be near, only to discover that a scant five minutes had passed since his last look at the hour.

"I tied the water jug here," said Jim, his voice breaking the quiet. This was the third time today he had showed them the container, lashed by ropes between their beds. But he still seemed anxious for them to know where the water supply was kept. They had agreed that, starting immediately, the daily ration would be one cupful per person. This was Bob's idea, and though Jim grumbled about rationing God's generosity, he went along.

It was further agreed that the water jug would be in full view at all times and that no one would take even the slightest sip without informing the others.

The water level in the jug would become as familiar to each as their profiles.

Chapter Five

More than a week went by after the *Triton* capsized before someone on land grew worried enough to sound an alarm. The astonishing truth was that no one even began to look for the *Triton*'s three passengers until July 22, the twelfth day of their ordeal. The plane and its companion ship were not in search of the trimaran, but were engaged only in summer naval maneuvers. Nor had a Coast Guard plane been dispatched the morning of July 11 in the hours after the capsizing.

Certainly one of the first people to have become worried should have been Wes Parker, the radio liaison in Auburn, to whom Jim spoke in Morse code each day up to and including the morning of the capsizing. But three days went by after July 11 with no word from the *Triton*, and Parker did not notify the Coast Guard. Instead he rang up Jim's wife and mentioned rather casually that the boat was out of contact.

What did that mean? asked Wilma. Not much, suggested Parker. Perhaps the radio had broken down. Perhaps Jim, whom he described as a "rank novice" at communications, was unable to tune the set properly. Or even more likely, the winds were blowing so favorably that the *Triton* was making record progress to Los Angeles, with no time for radio reports.

Wilma accepted this. She believed in Jim's craftsmanship and her brother Bob's sailing ability. Moreover, her faith in God was as unshakable as her husband's, and she believed that a divine hand was sharing the wheel with Jim and Bob. She never thought of calling the Coast Guard.

Linda's parents, Mr. and Mrs. Elliott, were on vacation during this week, and when they returned on July 15, no one seemed to know anything about their daughter and her sailing mates. By the schedule that Linda had left for her mother to follow, the boat should have been docked in Los Angeles by now. But the telephone had not rung with Linda's cheerful voice.

"I'm very worried," fretted Mrs. Elliott. "Can't we do something?" Her husband, Joe, a veteran navy man, counseled his wife not to get upset. But soon he, too, found himself waiting for the telephone to ring.

Finally, in Los Angeles, Bob's sister, Carol Lilley, grew concerned when the *Triton* did not dock at Marina Del Rey around July 14, as scheduled. She made several calls to the harbor master at Marina Del Rey, getting increasingly brusque responses. Finally she telephoned the Coast Guard in Long Beach on the afternoon of July 18. The *Triton* was long overdue, she said. Had the boat been heard from?

The Long Beach office bucked the *Triton* request up to San Francisco, where the Search and Rescue unit began a long-established drill. First, Wilma Fisher was interrogated to determine the boat's size, coloring, navigational equipment, and course. With that information each harbor from Cape Mendocino to Los Angeles was contacted by telephone—hundreds of them, from the great marinas choked with yachts to remote restaurants with moorings for one or two speedboats.

At the same time attempts were made to raise the *Triton* by radio. A distress report was also broadcast to all boats in the area, telling them to be on the lookout. All of this took three days. Not until July 22 would a Coast Guard unit actually set out on the ocean to look.

As usually happens, numerous false leads were turned in. One well-meaning sharp eye claimed to have seen the *Triton* tied up to a luxurious restaurant in Sausalito, where its owner was buying gin and tonics for the bar crowd and telling of his exploits. But such nonsense had to be checked out.

On the evening of July 21 all of the available information was assembled by the Search and Rescue unit in its San Francisco office. A computer in Washington had digested weather reports, the *Triton*'s description, her last known position, and had coughed up a mechanical notion of where the boat could be found. It was decided to launch a major search at dawn the next day.

At sunrise on July 22 a C-130 four-engine plane took off from San Francisco and spent all day flying low over a thirty-mile circle of sea, near where Jim had last reported the *Triton*.

When the plane returned with a negative report, the search was widened. Another C-130 went up as well—now there were two planes and ten men trained to scan the ocean with the naked eye rather than binoculars. These searchers work only fifteen-minute shifts before relief, because the eye grows weary when it focuses on nothing but the monotonous sea.

The Air Force contributed two more planes, which joined three Coast Guard helicopters and two cutters. The Navy sent still more equipment and personnel. All told, more than six hundred men in six ships and thirty-four aircraft spent the next three days searching for the *Triton* in an ever-widening swath. Eventually they covered more than two hundred thousand square miles, from the Oregon border to Punta San Antonio, Mexico, and from the shore to four hundred miles out. The search, which cost $208,000, was one of the Coast Guard's most massive in 1973.

On the peak days of the search, July 24, 25, and 26, the capsized trimaran was drifting almost due west in a straight line from San Francisco, between a hundred and a hundred and fifty miles from shore. But no planes or ships spotted her, for the *Triton* rode only eighteen inches above the waves. On the evening of July 28, convinced that the territory had been checked and rechecked, that no further expense was warranted, the Coast Guard's public-affairs office issued a terse statement to the news media.

> SAN FRANCISCO, July 28, 1973. An extensive four-day search for the missing sailboat *Triton*, from Tacoma, was suspended today at dark. The search, which covered approximately 200,000 square miles, was a combined effort by the U.S. Coast Guard, Air Force, and Navy. Last contact with the missing vessel and its crew of James Fisher, owner and operator from Auburn, Wash., and Robert and Linda Tininenko, of Longview, Wash., was made on July 11. This contact was by Citizen Band Radio with Carol Lilley of Los Angeles and indicated that the vessel was 60–80 miles off Point Arena, Calif., and in no distress or need of assistance.

The release contained two major factual errors and one omission. The *Triton*'s last radio contact was made not to Carol Lilley in Los Angeles, but to the Coast Guard itself, via the telephone patch set up by N. C. DeWolfe. And the *Triton*'s last position, as radioed by Jim on that fateful morning, was seventy-five miles southwest of Cape Mendocino—not Point Arena, which is thirty miles farther down the California coast.

Most curious of all, the Coast Guard did not mention that Jim had reported on the morning of July 11 that his ship had been in a storm. Perhaps the Coast Guard assumed that the storm was not a factor in the boat's disappearance, since Jim, after all, had said, "We are becalmed." In any case, the families of Jim and Bob and Linda would not learn that there had been a storm until several weeks later. And then they would angrily contend that if they had been given this information on the morning it was received, they would have insisted that a search begin immediately—not a dozen days later. But such hindsight had little value to the *Triton*'s survivors.

A Coast Guard officer telephoned Wilma Fisher and informed her courteously that the official search was over. The government, he said, could no longer afford to keep all those men, planes, helicopters, and ships at sea looking for three people in a sailboat. But rest assured, he continued, everyone would keep an eye peeled while working the ocean on other missions.

"What do you think?" Wilma asked then.

"We are unable to find them," he said. "It means they are . . ."

Wilma hung up. She could fill in the blank. It means they are lost and presumed dead.

EVEN AS WILMA put down the telephone and went to find her Bible, the three who lived within the overturned *Triton* had settled into an almost inviolate daily routine. By now Bob had explained, and all had accepted, the need for an hour-by-hour schedule of activities. Indeed, they were dependent upon it.

At seven a.m. Bob called out wake-up to Linda and Jim. If anyone wanted another hour of rest, that was permitted. But usually they were all anxious to be rid of the loneliness of slumber. This first hour of the morning was for grooming and personal needs. Each washed his face with a hand towel dipped into the salt water. Then hair was combed, teeth were brushed. Linda put on her makeup, then they inspected each other's faces to determine if the eyes remained clear and the skin tone healthy. Jim usually spent the time after grooming in silent prayer and meditation.

Bob filled the remainder of his hour doctoring Linda's sores, which continued to improve with daily applications of penicillin salve, although some still festered angrily.

At precisely eight a.m. the breakfast hour began, and it was just that—a full hour, despite the meagerness of their menus. Linda sipped at the milk shakes that Bob prepared and kept cool in the sea beneath their bed. When she grew weary of the same drink at every meal, Bob alternated a cup of his "chicken cacciatora," which was chicken-bouillon powder mixed with sea-water. "A good cook would put salt in the water anyway," he said encouragingly. Linda preferred the milk shakes.

The men had a few bites of canned vegetables, or half a Vege-Burger, or six peas, sometimes taking ten minutes to savor, chew, and swallow one solitary pea. If one person professed no appetite, the other two would force him to try to eat.

Early in their survival Bob had realized that starving to death would be the easiest thing to do by far. "It's so strange," he whispered to Linda one night, "after a day or two of not eating very much you lose all interest in food. What you'd really like to do is just lie back and sleep."

From nine to ten a.m. came water-distribution hour. Each could draw from the gallon jug an amount ranging from the tiniest of sips up to a full cup. Jim drank half of his portion at this hour, the rest at dinner. Because Linda could sustain only liquids, she normally drank most of her daily cup in the morning and part of Bob's ration later on. Bob usually stretched his intake throughout the day in sips, always announcing them out loud, saving perhaps an eighth of a cup for the middle of the night, when he always awoke, mouth parched and dry.

At ten a.m. discussion hour began, sometimes enduring until past noon. It was not always so. When Bob first introduced this period, the others were confused by it. They wanted to know what the rules were.

"I suppose there are no rules," said Bob. "The point is, we should have a definite time when we must talk to one another about specific topics. It will keep our minds occupied, and it might even be fun."

Only with the discipline of a formal topic could they sustain their interest in conversation and pass the time.

"But what would the subjects be?" Jim asked, for he had never been good at social chitchat.

"Anything!" said Bob a little testily. "People you like, people you don't like, places you've been, politics, your kids." There was no mistaking the dubiousness on Jim's face, but he agreed to try.

At eleven a.m. came an hour of games—Twenty Questions or a mental version of Probe, in which the player who was "it" kept a word in mind while the others tried to identify its letters. At midday, there being no lunch, a free hour was scheduled, during which the three could nap or remain resolutely silent. That became a privilege, silence, for Bob was almost despotic in enforcing the discussion and game periods.

During one free midday hour Bob began fooling with the Boy Scout knife he had retrieved from the submerged cupboard. In the days that passed he became adept, and out of plywood he made a cribbage board and a deck of cards. Realizing that Jim's religion forbade anything related to gambling, Bob eliminated the jack, queen, and king, carving in their place an eleven, a twelve, and a thirteen. This made it a game of numbers. Instead of suits he colored the pieces of wood—one group white with the paint he had been using for his messages, one red with Linda's lipstick, one the black of eyebrow pencil; the fourth remained natural.

From cribbage Bob moved on to a major effort—whittling a pair of dice and a board game he entitled Bump. This consisted of a Monopoly-like set of squares over which markers were moved according to the throw of the dice. The idea was to get to the last square—Rescue.

After midday the afternoon was passed by repeats of the discussion and game periods, with another free hour just before the evening meal. When the sea was calm Jim often pulled on his scuba equipment, attached himself to the *Triton* with a safety rope, and paddled around in the water during this time.

One afternoon toward the end of July, Jim returned to his bed exhausted after his swim, his face drained of color. Bob remarked that swimming claimed too much of his energy.

"Let me worry about that," answered Jim.

FOR A WEEK, until almost the first of August, the Pacific was serene, and the *Triton* floated like a toy boat on a lake. Now the only climatic problem was an oppressive sun which turned the inside of the *Triton* into a steam bath. Toward the end of this week Bob thought he noticed a dullness in Linda's eyes; their hue had changed from vivid brown to the color of worn-out earth. But the dullness went away, and Linda remained cheerful and anxious to participate in their discussions and games.

In fact, one morning she even came up with a topic. "Before we capsized," she began, "I was reading *Anna Karenina*."

Bob nodded, thinking of the hour he had spent searching the waters of their overturned bedroom for the lost book. "That's a good subject. What did you think of the part you read?" He was a brisk moderator.

Linda brightened. "I loved every word of it. And I understand why Anna fell in love with the younger man. She felt imprisoned in the stereotype role of wife. She wanted to assert her individuality. I think she was liberated, in a way."

Linda glanced at Jim, who was listening attentively, but in the manner of a man hearing something for the very first time.

"It surprises me how really modern Tolstoy is," said Linda. "What do you think, Jim? Do you like Tolstoy?"

Bleakly, Jim shook his head. "I haven't read him," he said. "He wrote fiction, didn't he?"

Linda dispatched a discreet can-you-believe-it glance at Bob. Here was a man who had spent a year in Europe studying German, who had graduated from a religious college, and who had served in the administration of both a college and a high school. Yet he was so confined within the boundaries of his faith that even the greatest novelists were forbidden to him.

"I don't read fiction," Jim continued. "It didn't really happen; it isn't the truth. Therefore it is a lie."

Now Bob was roused to make a point. "But there are moral and ethical theories propounded in the great novels that are every bit as interesting and challenging as those in your Bible."

Jim would not have it. "A man could read his Bible every day of his life and never absorb it all," he said. "It's worth all the novels in the world."

"The Bible is a good book, but it's not the only book," pressed Bob. "In fact, I believe that parts of the Bible are fiction."

Stunned by this blasphemy, Jim held up his hands, not wanting to pursue the line any further. "The Bible is the Divine Word and therefore immune to challenge. Case closed."

In the days that followed, Bob tried to steer their discussions away from religion, for such talk always tottered on the edge of exasperation if not anger.

One morning passed with pleasant talk of hobbies. Shyly at first, but warming to his subject, Jim talked at length of his tropical fish. He and Wilma had raised at least twenty thousand and had become so accomplished in breeding and raising rare species that Wilma sold surplus fish to pet stores in Auburn. "We used to tell people that our aquarium was our color TV," Jim said, in a rare attempt at humor.

But this remark made Linda inadvertently resummon Jehovah.

The fish were interesting, she said, but why was Jim opposed to having a television set? Did his religion forbid it? No, came the answer. Then, pressed Linda, were there not at least a few programs of quality, news specials, men walking on the moon, even religious discussions and sermons on Sunday morning?

"Sunday is not a holy day," exclaimed Jim, a little shocked that she would think so. "The Sabbath is on Saturday. Read the Bible and learn that truth. Moreover, television steals time that could be used more fruitfully."

Linda fell silent. Later she told Bob that the idea of families communicating without the hypnotism of a television set appealed to her.

Bob was troubled. On nights when none of them could sleep, or during the free hours, Linda had begun asking Jim questions about his religion. She wanted to know its history and why such a severe moral code was imposed on its membership—what was wrong with a cup of tea?

What if Jim convinces her that all of our problems are because I do not believe in his church anymore? wondered Bob.

ON THE FIRST SATURDAY after Bob introduced his schedule of activities, Jim spent the morning free hour wrapped in his private Sabbath service. Usually Bob and Linda ignored these devotions. But on this day Bob noticed that his wife was praying silently in fellowship with Jim.

When it was time for the discussion hour, Bob introduced Watergate as the subject. Congressional hearings had been stirring the country when they left Tacoma. "What do you think we can learn from Watergate, Jim?"

"I have no thoughts at all about politicians," he said. "They're corrupt, they're worldly, they don't really matter to me. I've never even voted."

"Never?" asked Linda, incredulous. "What *does* matter to you, Jim?"

Jim seemed grateful for the invitation to explain himself.

"My wife," he began. "My children. My family. You. Bob. And, most of all, service to God. I've wanted to be a missionary since I was a little boy. I believe the only thing that matters is to live the kind of life that God will approve of, and I pray that Jesus will raise me into heaven when He comes again."

"And when will that be?" wondered Linda.

"The date is unknown," Jim said. "But the end is near."

The Adventist Church was founded by people who deduced from Biblical dates and prophecies that Jesus was returning to earth in 1844. But when the Second Coming did not materialize, Adventist scholars determined that Jesus has been studying the books of every soul who ever lived on earth. When that task is completed, Jim explained, then Christ will come again, raising the sanctified to heaven, leaving the others to hell. It is not so much fire and brimstone, this hell, but denial of paradise.

"Will only Adventists go to heaven?" asked Linda with unconcealed fascination.

"No," answered Jim. Others could gain admission. But Adventists, he made clear, held priority tickets.

Bob had listened quietly to Jim's sermonizing, but now he felt it necessary to interrupt. He would not tamper with Linda's stirrings, for he considered sacred a person's right to question and think, but he wanted her to have another point of view.

"But don't you think," asked Bob, "that one can be a good Christian without belonging to a formal church?"

"No!" said Jim firmly. A new tension leaped up between the men as they half sat, half lay on their rope beds, shoulders hunched and heads bent to avoid the ceiling. An unreal setting for a duel of souls.

Crouching against the wall to watch the men and hear them out, Linda drew the sheet tighter to her nude body. She could not bear to wear clothes until the sores on her legs healed. Bob turned from Jim to look at his wife, her eyes now deep-set in a face become gaunt. She weighed perhaps ninety pounds, twenty less than on the day they set sail.

This is an impossible position, Bob thought. I must challenge Jim's beliefs, yet I cannot destroy them because of my wife. Linda is concerned for her immortal soul; she is terrified of the unknown; she will accept any hand that is held out to her.

WITH THE SUN at full strength, Bob could not trust his temper. It would be better to delay the confrontation. The grievances he held against Jim might flare up in a midday argument. "This is getting a little heavy," he said. "Let's table the subject. Besides, it's almost noon. Time for games."

"You know I can't play games on the Sabbath," Jim said.

"You wouldn't object to a game based on the Bible, would you, Jim?" said Bob.

"And what would that be?"

"Well, one of us thinks up a Biblical character or situation, and the others ask questions about it. Whoever guesses gets to think up the next one."

Linda brightened. "Okay," she said. "I have one."

"Is it Old Testament or New Testament?" asked Bob.

Linda pursed her lips. "Old."

Jim, suddenly interested, asked, "Before or after the flood?"

Now Linda frowned. "Hmm," she said. "Neither."

Jim laughed. "Is it Noah's ark?"

"I guess it was pretty obvious," Linda said.

"You see," said Bob. "It's fun."

Next, one of them put forth Adam and Eve, which was quickly guessed, and Linda followed with the miracle of loaves and fishes. Thus the afternoon passed, until the sun relaxed and the chamber cooled.

It worked, Bob's game. His Biblical knowledge was stronger than Jim's, even though he had renounced the church. However, if Bob took any pleasure in that fact, it was quickly dispelled.

For that night Linda prayed before she slept. Bob could not hear her prayer, but he could feel her lips moving silently as her body trembled. He wondered if she trembled from illness or from her newfound fear of the Lord.

ON THE MORNING of August 1 Bob carved the date on the calendar beside his bed. Then he listened to the sea. He rarely went outside anymore. He believed that he could best conserve his energy by lying still. Also, it frightened Linda to be left alone.

The winds must be at least fifteen miles an hour today, he estimated, and they were erratic again. Generally, the winds came from the north and west, giving Bob daily hope that the *Triton* would sooner or later run into shore. But if they ever turned and blew steadily from the east, the *Triton* would be pushed deeper and deeper into the Pacific.

"How many days?" asked Linda weakly. She had slept well past the seven a.m. wake-up, but Bob had not disturbed her. She was sleeping more and more.

"Today begins the twenty-second," Bob said, kissing her gently. A bluish cast had come over her, and the blood vessels at her temples threatened to push through the taut skin. She frequently complained that her fingers were cold, and Bob would place her hands under his armpits to keep them warm and rub them to stimulate her flow of blood. Her fingers were like ice.

Picking up the water jug now, he poured Linda a morning swallow. The water supply was going quickly, for she required more and more. At first Bob had sacrificed half of his daily cup to his wife; then he asked Jim if they could increase her ration. Jim agreed immediately. Now Linda was drinking from three to four cups a day. On this morning there were but five gallons left from the thirteen found in the outrigger. Only a pinch or two of powdered milk remained. The eggs were almost gone, too. Linda's milk shakes would be impossible to prepare within the week.

She was failing, Bob knew, and so he worked harder to combat the gloom. At night he would lie awake, trying to hit upon something to make the morning hours less long. He devised a game called Wedding Gifts. Looking out at the empty seascape, Bob would think of a wedding gift he and Linda had received, then challenge her to determine its identity, who gave it to them, and where it had been placed in their house.

Enchanted by the memories, Linda liked this game best of all. She played it for hours, sometimes falling asleep in mid-interrogation, then waking and resuming her questions without knowing she had gone limp in Bob's arms. Over and over she guessed the hand-carved teak fruit bowl, and the tie-dyed wall-hanging from Africa, and the braided rug her parents had given them.

Once, Bob began to talk of the piece of land they owned near Kelso, Washington—three acres of woods on the side of a hill, with a view of the river that threaded below. They would build their dream house there when they returned. It would be of rough-hewn timber with interior walls of stone and wood, and would settle among the trees as a member of the forest, not as an intruder.

When Bob stopped talking for a while, Linda lay in silence.

He permitted her a brief meditation. Then he broke into her thoughts.

"What are you thinking about?"

"I was just arranging the furniture in the house. I have every room all planned."

Realizing that the dream of their house sustained his wife better than any game, Bob pulled off a bracing beam from the *Triton* and began to carve a model of the house. As Linda watched the rooms emerge from the block of wood, her dulling eyes brightened. But Bob knew as he carved, as he held her, that unless rescue came soon, the time left to Linda could be counted in days, if not hours.

Chapter Six

A yellowed-finned tuna weighing perhaps thirty pounds, swam into their chamber the next morning. Seeing the fish, Bob lunged for it, almost rolling off the bed. The tuna flicked its tail and darted easily to freedom.

"I wish we could catch some fish," he muttered, imagining the supply of fresh meat, liquid, and protein for Linda. But all of their fishing equipment had been claimed by the sea.

Suddenly Jim sat up. "The attenna!" he said, and worked his way to the submerged cockpit. In a few minutes he returned, carrying the five-foot radio antenna.

Jim asked for the file, which Bob kept under his mattress and used daily to hone his knife for carving. As Jim began sharpening the point of the antenna, Linda stirred.

"Good morning," said Bob cheerfully. "Jim's promised to catch us some breakfast."

Linda looked at Jim's makeshift harpoon but asked, "Where are we?"

Bob grew worried. "What do you mean? We're still on our vacation cruise."

"I know that," she said, smiling normally. "I mean approximately what part of the ocean?"

Bob's guess, and it was little more than that, would put the *Triton* somewhere off the coast of southern California, perhaps out from Santa Barbara. Linda digested the information.

Meanwhile, Jim had dressed in his scuba suit, taken the harpoon, and dropped into the water beneath his bed. He would try his handmade spear here before using it in the open sea. Several times within the next half hour he emerged, shook his head negatively, and plunged down again.

Suddenly, a dozen feet from their beds, the water began to churn. Jim came up thrashing, trying to lift the bent harpoon above water. Presumably he had hit an enormous fish, which was struggling to expel the antenna from its flesh.

"Stay with him!" Linda cried in encouragement.

The battle lasted another minute. Then the water stopped churning. Jim surfaced, ripping off his mask in disgust. He had lost the harpoon. "I had him good," he said, climbing wearily onto his bed. "But the wire inside the antenna started unraveling. It disintegrated in my hands and the fish yanked it away."

The three sat dejectedly for a long while before Linda broke the spell. "Somewhere out there is a very funny fish," she said, and then all managed to smile at the image of the creature trailing a long antenna wire.

The flurry over the lost fish had worn Linda down, and she lay back on the bed, her body racked with dry coughs. Bob felt it best to cancel the morning talk and games so she could rest, but Linda wanted discussion hour.

"Okay," said Bob. "What'll it be? Wedding Gifts?"

"A new one," said Linda. "It's called People." A simple subject, she explained. The point was for each of them to talk about people whom they had admired and why.

Instantly Bob understood. Linda knew her condition was desperate, and she did not want to die without saying a figurative good-by to those who had enhanced her life.

"That's interesting," said Bob. "You want to start?"

Linda shook her head. No, she wanted Jim to be first.

Still angry at losing the fish, Jim was not in a mood for games. But he recognized that Linda's need must be attended to.

"Okay," he said. "People. Wilma, first of all. She's the most wonderful woman a man could wish for. She works so hard, she never complains, she keeps a good home. She's given me two children, and there'll be another one if—when we get home."

Then he stopped, but Linda prodded him gently to go on.

"At college we were both working in the cafeteria. I got up my courage and asked her out. I fell in love with her and we got married, and I've never regretted a second of our life together."

Abruptly Jim terminated his instant biography. When he spoke again, he fought against sobs which threatened to break. "I—I just wish I could tell her right now," he said haltingly.

Linda reached across and touched his arm. "You are telling her, Jim," she said. "Wilma feels your love this very moment."

How excellent is this woman, thought Bob, as he watched her console the strange man who was his brother-in-law. Here she is, trapped in an upside-down boat, wasting away, hungry, thirsty, gravely ill, and she reaches out to comfort a man distraught because he cannot be with his wife.

Linda turned to her husband, indicating that it was his turn.

Had he yielded to temptation, he would have spent the hour, if not the day, telling Linda of his love for her. But he would save that for the next time Jim went topside, when they were alone in each other's arms. "Let's see," said Bob. "People I admire." Quickly he listed several—a horticulturist and his wife, at whose home he had boarded during college, a teacher who had challenged and inspired him, assorted friends and relatives. Then he paused. "And my dad, of course."

Looking up, Jim appeared surprised. "You told me once that the two of you were not very close."

Bob shook his head. "No, but there was a long time when I didn't understand him. When I was a little kid all I saw was this very hard man, a disciplinarian. He plowed the fields, he stored the hay, he expected me to sit on a tractor without complaint for ten hours a day. He slept a little, he worked a lot, he went to church, he prayed. I guess I felt he was a cold, emotionless man."

Jim could understand. His own father was from the same hard-working, God-fearing mold.

"What made you change your feeling about him?" asked Linda. She knew the answer, but she wanted to hear it again.

"You," answered Bob, gazing at his wife with tenderness. "And Mother Russia."

The story began pouring from him. After he decided to resign formally from the Adventist Church, there ensued several years of coldness between him and his devout family. Only on two or three occasions during those years did he even speak with his parents. And these times had been difficult, filled with their exhortations for him to reconsider. Always Bob refused. Even exile from his family would not change his decision to live outside the Church.

Then, when Bob proposed to Linda, he felt it necessary at least to introduce her to his parents.

"Dad's face just lit up," said Bob, happy in the recollection. "I don't think he had ever seen anything so pretty." Shortly after that Bob had an idea. He and his bride-to-be had decided to go to Europe for their honeymoon. They had thought about including Russia in their itinerary. Would his parents like to join them? Both had been born in Russia, both had left as small children, neither had ever returned. Perhaps on such a trip, Bob thought, the wounds between him and his parents could be healed.

"Well," Bob went on, "much to my surprise, Dad jumped at the chance. In a Volkswagen camper we drove to the Russian border in Finland. Dad was so excited at finally setting foot in Russia again! He was just like a kid going to grandma's farm."

As he reminisced, Bob picked up the scale model of the house and began to carve. Linda moved closer to him.

"Tell Jim about Boguslav," she said.

"Okay. Boguslav." At Kiev, Bob said, they had inquired about making a side trip to the village of Boguslav, where Bob's father had been born. It was possible, said the Intourist guide, but it would require an official escort and a chauffeured car. The price: one hundred dollars.

Outraged at such capitalistic greed, Mr. Tininenko had a better idea. He ushered his clan onto a public bus, and for fifty cents they all rode happily to Boguslav, unescorted.

"When we got there," said Bob, "it was like the homecoming scene of a novel. Hugging, kissing, feasts, vodka toasts. Dad ran all over the village—he must have inspected every inch of it. I remember him exclaiming at a pear tree that he had planted as a child, a tree now fifty years old. It all became a jumble of laughing and crying and singing.

"That was the day I finally understood my father. He's from a culture where tradition is all, where one obeys the will of the elders. All those years when I was trying to be as American as I could, I did not understand my father. Well, I like him now. I'm just sorry I didn't learn about him sooner. We've been great friends ever since."

Bob stopped and drew in his breath before adding another detail. "Linda was the biggest hit of all," he said, looking at his wife. "She learned a little Russian and she flat stole their hearts.

Particularly the dirty old men." Linda laughed, remembering the village elders bringing her flowers.

When it was her turn, Linda said there were so many that she feared she would omit someone important to her. But she would try. Her sister. Her father. A childhood friend named Keith. "And my mother," she said.

Linda spoke emotionally of her mother, how Hisako fell in love with an American she met at a dance in Tokyo in 1946, how they defied parents and authorities to marry, how her father brought his new wife to Pennsylvania because he was afraid to take her home to Montana.

She told of how her mother struggled with English, how she adapted to life in a trailer park, how she kept a Japanese ceremonial gown and obi in a box whose wood she rubbed with scented oil. "My mother went through more than most women can imagine," said Linda, "because she loved a man. I understand that."

By the end of her story Linda was crying, and Bob held her, enraged at his inability to do anything more for her.

At the dinner hour Linda lacked the strength to eat. She had but a few sips of water before she fell asleep.

"A FEW DAYS AGO," said Linda on the morning of August 5, the twenty-sixth day of their existence inside the capsized trimaran, "you were going to tell us whether a person can be saved without belonging to a formal church." As she spoke to Jim her voice was stronger. In the depths of her agony she had found unused resources. She had scrubbed her face with salt water, and then Bob had brushed her hair, worried that she would notice the places where tufts were falling out.

Jim nodded. He had been waiting for the time when he could speak again to Linda of his God and his faith. "I feel," he began softly, "that if a person knows the truth—and the truth is the teachings and precepts of the Church—then that person must live by the Church. And it is almost impossible to do that without attending regularly. Because only there do you find good people, Christian people. We encourage one another. We gain strength from the minister's leadership, from our study of the Bible. These things prepare us for the last days of mankind, which are surely near. And they lead us finally to sanctification."

Bob cut in sharply. "But, Jim, you can do these things without ever setting foot in a church. And life just can't be as narrow as your church wants it to be."

"You're wrong," replied Jim. "My life isn't narrow. My life is rich and full."

Bob shook his head. "I know people who lead exemplary Christian lives," he said, "and they don't belong to a church."

"Perhaps," said Jim. All he needed was the Church, the fellowship, the nearness of Christ. "I am lost without it." Then he stretched out his arms to Linda. "I pray for you."

"Let her alone," Bob said hotly. "Can't you see she needs rest?" He drew his arms around Linda and helped her lie back. She fell asleep immediately, breathing in rattles and gasps. When she awoke she cried out Jim's name. He answered quickly.

"What is sanctification?" she asked.

"Sanctification," he said, "is obedience to God's holy word and law. Sanctification is a life led in pursuit of the truth. Sanctification is faith in Christ and the spirit of humility."

She slept again. But when it was almost dark in the chamber, when only the faintest gold shadows lingered across them, Linda raised herself on her elbows. Suddenly she seemed cheerful.

"Why don't we go and get some fried chicken." She drawled the words in a Southern accent.

Bob was pleased and amused. But then he saw the fixed blankness in her eyes. She stared not at him, but through him, to a private world of her own. She began to strike him, screaming like a distraught child.

Bob accepted the soft blows, weeping as he did. What could a man do when his wife was going insane as she lay beside him?

FOR HOURS Linda raved on, twisting her fingers in her hair. Then near midnight she finally fell asleep. And when she awoke a few hours later, it was as if nothing had happened.

"I was asleep, wasn't I?" she asked. Bob nodded.

"Are you hungry?" he asked. Perhaps if she would eat, he thought, the cells of her brain would be nourished and their deterioration eased. Linda shook her head.

"You haven't got a can of peaches or a watermelon, have you?" she asked, almost merrily. "That's what I was dreaming about."

For the rest of the night Bob dared not sleep, fearful that Linda would stop breathing. But reassuringly her chest rose and fell until dawn, when she stirred restlessly, then awoke and smiled. "Can we take that off?" she said, gesturing to the piece of wood that covered the exit hole. Quickly Bob removed it, and helped her move on the bed so that she could see the morning.

"I'd like some milk shake now," she said.

Bob shook his head in despair. "There isn't any more," he said. He poured her a cup of water and held it to her lips.

Jim had put on his scuba suit and excused himself to go topside. He knew that Bob and Linda needed these hours together.

It was to be the longest morning of Bob's life. He tried to play the games, but for the first time Linda was too weak, too disoriented to join him. "Come on, honey," he said over and over. "I'm thinking of a wedding gift. What is it? Where is it?"

Linda closed her eyes. Bob enveloped her frail body in his arms. "Please, hon, it's the game hour. You can't sleep now. You know our rules. Now come on, I'll give you a hint. It's from Japan. . . ."

Linda opened her eyes. They had no color. "I'm afraid I'm pretty sick, Bob. I can't breathe . . . I can barely talk."

All right, then Bob would talk. Nonstop. He wrapped her in a blanket of memories—the tea cozy they had bought in Leningrad, the antique sideboard they were refinishing, the breakfast of wild blackberries they had eaten on the slope of Mount Rainier.

At midday Linda rallied for a few minutes. Now she wanted to talk. Bob had to place his ear to her lips to hear her fading whispers. Friends in their town were on the brink of divorce. "Tell them it is my last wish that they resolve their problems and stay together. Life isn't meaningful without someone to love. . . ."

"Don't talk about last wishes, Linda. That's silly." Bob picked up the half-finished carving of their dream house and held it before her. "Where do you want the washer and dryer to go?"

"I'm serious, Bob. Unless rescue comes soon, I'll have to go. . . ."

"No!" Bob pressed his head against her breast, but refused to break down in front of her.

"Haven't we had the best marriage?" she said. "I'm so sorry it has to end this way. . . ."

Bob looked at her. Now it was beyond denial. She simply had too few resources left. "I'm sorry, too," he said, his tears falling freely. "I do love you so."

She began to talk of her father, then suddenly she stopped and fought for air.

"I can't breathe," she said, frightened.

Bob threw his head to hers and blew air into her mouth. For half an hour he worked, until her chest began to move, almost imperceptibly. When her eyes opened, they could not focus; they rolled about in their sockets. Then she blacked out again.

His own consciousness beginning to dim, Bob called up to his brother-in-law for help. Quickly Jim dropped through the hole and onto the bed and pressed his lips against Linda's. Bob fell back, trembling.

Then he heard Linda whisper, "Am I sanctified, Jim?"

Jim lifted his lips from hers. "Yes," he said solemnly. "You are sanctified."

Bob could not let Linda die in another man's arms. He pushed Jim away and resumed breathing for her, but she did not speak again. Her face turned from gray to blue, and after a time he said resolutely, "Linda's gone."

It was not Bob who screamed but Jim. He wailed, bemoaning a death he did not understand. Lunging over her lifeless body, he clawed his way up through the hole, across the *Triton*'s surface and fell into the cold water. Splashing, falling, holding his knuckles to his chest, he leaned against the submerged rail and sobbed. The sea rose up against him, crashing waves to mingle with his tears. For half an hour he stayed there, ignoring the waves that pounded him, feeling perhaps for the first time the enormity of his doomed voyage.

Below, Bob sat beside Linda, stroking her cheek. But now he must decide what to do with her. He could wrap Linda in the bedclothes, carry her to the outrigger, to wait for a rescue ship that would take her back to Washington for proper burial. But it was August 6 and the broiling sun would quickly cause decay. Nor could he bear the thought of Linda resting in death but a few feet away from him.

No, the only way was the most obvious. He must drop her into the sea. But what if she floated, her face turning toward him, haunting him forever? He shuddered. He must find a way to weight her body before delivering it to the depths.

And then he remembered the anchor.

Linda's shroud was the sheet—secured by fishing cord—on which she had lain for twenty-six days. Around her Bob tenderly wound the piece of rope that had bound them together the morning the *Triton* capsized. He lifted her, marking the lightness of her body, and carried her up to the daylight. Then he took the anchor—fifteen inches wide, eighteen inches long, with a shaft extending down four feet—and placed it across her chest like a crucifix. He wrapped the anchor chains around her, turn after turn, long past the requirements of mere weight, because it was a way to delay for a few moments what must be done. Finally he dragged the bulky package that contained his dead wife to the edge of the *Triton*. Hovering behind, Jim stood helpless.

"No prayer," said Bob. "You understand? Just think what you want to think."

Standing silently himself, Bob meditated. Then he began to hum, so low that only he could hear, the song "People." It had been Linda's favorite, and she had had it played at their wedding. When he was done, he knelt and placed his hands on the body Jim said to him in solace, "You'll see her again, Bob. When Jesus comes and lifts us to paradise."

Breaking, Bob whirled. "No!" he howled in anger. "This is all there is! There's nothing more!"

Hurriedly, Bob pushed Linda into the sea and watched the choppy waters receive her. Bending over, his face almost touching the sea, he watched until there was nothingness. Linda was a thousand feet beneath him.

He heard Jim begin to sing "Old Hundred," and he joined him. The two men sang the hymn of praise with vigor, their voices ringing out. Why did I sing that? Bob questioned himself when it was silent again. And why did I say Amen?

He could not rise. He seemed frozen as he faced the water. He could join Linda. It would be a relief, an act of love and sacrifice just to lean forward and tumble into her tomb. For the first time the water even felt warm to his touch.

The advantages: he would not have to explain her agony and her death when he returned to shore. He would not have to answer the question, "But why are you alive when your wife is dead?" His wrists were fast becoming as thin as hers. Why drag it out; why continue the belief that rescue would come?

The disadvantages: he had lived before he met Linda, he would live after her. He could keep the memories of their years together. She would not want him to throw himself after her. The idea would outrage her.

As the competing forces pulled at Bob, Jim suddenly cried out, and Bob raised his head. Two cargo ships, smoke billowing from their stacks, were bearing down on them. Less than a mile away, unless their course changed, they would run the *Triton* over.

Chapter Seven

Bob's first reaction was a bitterness, a curse for the timing. Why couldn't the ships have come yesterday, to save Linda? Failing that, at least they could have appeared but two minutes earlier, before he dropped his wife's body irrevocably into the sea.

But Jim stood with arms outstretched, murmuring gratitude to the Lord. For His reasons God had taken Linda, but He had not abandoned the two men.

The ships bore down so purposefully that there seemed to be a planned rendezvous. "Praise God!" he cried. "Thank You, Jesus!"

But the ships suddenly turned. And the *Triton* bobbed unseen between them.

A scream burst from Bob's throat. "Oh, please! See us! We're here!" Ripping one of the orange life jackets from where he had nailed it, Bob waved hysterically. Then he dashed below and found Linda's purse and took it back up to flash her mirror at the ships. At the same time he blew energetically on the police whistle she'd carried. Jim did not move or utter a sound.

When there was nothing more to see, when the frail wisps of smoke had vanished, Jim finally spoke. "They'll be back," he said confidently, "because the Lord sent them."

"They'll be back on their return from Tokyo," said Bob angrily. "By then who knows where we'll be."

"Then the Lord will send another one," said Jim. "There must be a reason why they didn't stop for us."

"They didn't stop because they didn't see us. We only stick up a few inches above the water," snapped Bob. "Tomorrow we're going to put everything we can find on top of this boat."

The two ships, even with the terrible disappointment they caused, gave the men something to think about that otherwise unbearable night. For the first time since July 12—twenty-six nights before—Bob was alone on the narrow bed, the scent of Linda tormenting him. He thought of her last hours, her death, her burial—but the vision of the two ships kept intruding on his mourning, pushing Linda briefly away. One thing was certain, he figured. Because of the ships he would not consider suicide again. He would live as long as there was life within him. The instinct to survive, he reasoned as he grew sleepy, is most powerful.

EARLY THE NEXT morning Bob festooned the *Triton* with anything that would make her more visible to potential rescuers. He nailed more orange curtains around the edges of the boat as gaudy trim. A piece of metal rod from the bow pulpit became a six-foot flagpole, secured with cable, on which to fly a banner of plastic. Finally the galley sink and stainless-steel cooking plates were removed and fastened to the two outriggers; the metal might send forth flashes in the sun.

By midmorning all of the work was done, and the outburst of labor had exhilarated Bob. He had not waited for breakfast before his frenzy of activity, and now he was hungry. "How much food is left?" he asked. "Let's take inventory."

Jim went to where he kept the supplies. He called them out: "Almost three cans of sardines, about half a jar of peanut butter, one pack freeze-dried peas, couple packs of Kool-Aid, one can of root beer, and some caramel chips."

"And the water?" Bob knew well, almost to the drop, the extent of their supply, but he wanted to have the amount spoken.

"Two full jugs. And this one, minus one cup." The missing cup, both men knew, had been Linda's final nourishment.

Bob spoke urgently. "I feel that it is even more important than before to keep up our schedule and conserve our supplies," he said. "We've been taking half a cup of food a day. Let's cut that down to a quarter. And let's try to get by on half a cup of water."

"DO YOU remember the ABCs of prayer?" asked Jim suddenly, waking Bob from the late-morning drowsiness brought on by his work. Pushed instantly into the past, Bob could hear the voices of the preachers and teachers drumming into his ears. "Ask! Believe! Challenge! These are the ABCs of prayer." But he remained silent.

"Don't you remember," persisted Jim, oddly exuberant, "what the ABCs taught us? That wonders, that *miracles* could be worked through the power of Christ?" Like a defiant fist, Jim's words seemed to shoot out and grab Bob, refusing to let him go.

He nodded, almost agreeing. Then he quickly shook his head to clear the thought. He would not give in so easily. "The power of Christ didn't help Linda much, did it?" he accused.

At this, Jim's face lit. "Linda *is* saved! She died believing. She died in the arms of Christ."

"She died in the arms of her husband."

"Listen to me!" Jim commanded. He grabbed the water jug and held it high between them. "I make you this promise. There's enough water in this container to last us five days—according to your rationing. Five days! But if we give our hearts to Christ, if we commit these five days to nothing but Him, then Jesus will send rescue. At the end of the fifth day, when the last drop of this water is gone, then we will be delivered."

Bob shook his head in denial.

But Jim would not lower the jug. He held it with awe, as if it were a sliver of the true Cross. Against his will Bob was drawn to it and the water sparkling within. The moment was more seductive than when he was tempted to join Linda in the sea.

"What do you want me to do?" he asked. He could feel the balance of power between them shifting. His will was draining from him.

"Worship with me!" Jim cried. "Dedicate the next five days to Christ. And at the end of the fifth day, be ready for rescue with me!"

Bob held up his hands. All right, he reasoned, unexplained events *can* happen. What of those cancers that shrink and vanish, and those shriveled legs that suddenly become whole? There are miracles in this world. What harm can Jim's faith do to me for five days?

"Touch it!" commanded Jim. Slowly Bob raised his hand and, almost fearfully, pressed his fingertips to the water jug. Both men were trembling.

Wreathed in ecstasy, Jim began to pray. But now it was a different kind of prayer. No longer was he humbling himself before an invisible, faraway God. Now he was on closer terms with the Lord. "We *ask* for rescue, Lord, because we *believe* in Your power. And we *challenge* You to deliver us from this long ordeal. We will drink this water for five days, and when it is gone we challenge You to deliver us, to lift us with Your grace. Ask! Believe! Challenge! Thank You, Jesus. Amen."

Together the two men held the jug. "Say 'Amen,'" cried Jim.

"Amen," said Bob.
"Again!"
"Amen!" This time, from Bob, a full-blooded shout.

THE FIVE DAYS spun by in an orgy of evangelism. As if setting the stage for the miracle, the sea became smooth, the breeze soft. The men prayed together throughout the day and even at night, when they were too excited to sleep. Over and over they chanted two verses from the book of John, "*And whatsoever ye shall ask in my name, that will I do*," and, "*Ask and ye shall receive*."

Never in their relationship had the brothers-in-law been so close. They played the Bible game with new enthusiasm. There were laughter and good feelings between them.

On the third day, near sundown, Bob went topside to stretch his legs, and what he saw on the horizon made him summon Jim hurriedly. Toward the east, settled across a large portion of the lower part of the sky, was a bank of mustard yellow.

"It's smog!" shouted Bob. "We *must* be near Los Angeles."

On the fourth day, convinced that the winds were sending them so close to the California coast that the *Triton* would surely come within sight of a fishing boat, Bob set about to surprise Jim. He would try to hasten their rescue by starting an attention-getting fire with paint, diesel fuel, and oil.

While Jim napped during the midday free period, Bob slipped quietly topside and poured the fluids onto a pile of rags. He then removed a magnifying lens from the binoculars and held it patiently at an angle through which the sun's rays would pass. Within thirty minutes a wisp of smoke was born. Moments later the rags began to burn. Triumphantly, Bob yelled for Jim.

When Jim saw the black smoke curling from the wadded rags, he burst toward the torch, hands outstretched. "No!" he cried, beginning to weep.

"What's the matter, Jim?" said Bob, dumbfounded.

"You're interfering with God!" he cried. "This is not God's plan!"

And Bob understood. In Jim's mind every action in their preordained five-day drama was being played from a master script.

"I'll put it out!" shouted Bob, dumping the salt water on the rags. But as he did so, a cloud of smoke rose and spread about them. Jim watched the cloud in despair. Then, wordlessly, he descended to his bed and wept for more than an hour.

"I'm sorry," murmured Bob. "I was only trying to help."

Near dinnertime, Jim composed himself and forgave Bob. The Lord would still send rescue tomorrow, he said, for He was a forgiving God. But Bob must never again try to alter His will.

THE FIFTH DAY. Saturday, August 11. Jim's Sabbath. He was up early, before the seven a.m. deadline. When Bob awoke, his brother-in-law was busily combing his hair, brushing his beard. "By tonight," said Jim, his fervor once again at its summit, "we will be at a feast."

After they had prayed and chanted, Bob reached for the jug of water. There was but an inch left, enough for two portions. He unscrewed the cap, poured a swallow and handed it to Jim, who looked at it curiously. Finally he shook his head.

"No," he said, "I want to wait until the end of the Sabbath."

So convinced was Jim that rescue would come by nightfall that Bob was once again caught up in the ecstasy. The hours raced by. Conducting Sabbath services, Jim preached to his audience of one, and Bob listened attentively. During the week he had been ambivalent about his participation in Jim's challenge to God. I have not really returned to the Church, I'm just humoring Jim, he reassured himself. It cannot hurt. Once during the five days Bob had even wondered out loud what would happen if God did *not* send rescue. Jim would not even answer such a skeptical question.

Now, in the final hours of the fifth day, Bob felt no such doubts. His commitment, for the moment, was total. In his lap he even held the souvenirs he would take ashore from their ordeal—the carved house, Linda's purse, the compass, the knives.

Near five p.m., when the winds turned chill, Jim stopped praying. He raised himself through the hole, and Bob followed, ready for the most important moment of his life. Ceremoniously Jim poured from the water jug every last drop into their two cups.

With the solemnity of communion the men drank, Bob sipping slowly, Jim throwing back his head, letting precious drops splash on his beard. When he was done, Jim lowered the cup and smiled. Had the whistle of the rescue boat shattered the silence, Bob would not have been surprised.

Now they waited.

They sat on top of the overturned trimaran and they waited. Until the sun slipped away, ending the Sabbath, they waited.

Finally Bob felt the cold and began to shiver. He went below, saddened. But Jim stayed on top, his lips moving in prayer. Waiting. Waiting for God.

"AUGUST 13, 1973."

When Bob finished carving the thirty-fourth day on his calendar of survival, he went topside to paint the fourth (or was it fifth?—he had lost count) piece of wood to set afloat.

He painted carefully the now familiar legend—the name of the trimaran, the date it capsized, the fact that as of this day there were survivors. What is happening to these? wondered Bob, as he flung the board out and watched it ride the swells until it could be seen no more. Are the others still afloat on the sea? He went below to tell Jim the news of the morning—that he had thrown another board into the sea, that the ocean was calm.

Jim lay curled in a fetal position, facing the wall. He had scarcely moved since the failure of the five-day drama of the water jug two days before. He hadn't expressed his apologies to Bob or shown any emotion at all, and the silence was beginning to get at Bob's nerves. "I can't take this coldness from you much longer," he said now, pouring himself a swallow of water no larger than a teaspoon. It was their next to last jug. "I'm taking a sip of water, Jim."

No answer.

"I'm telling you, Jim, because that's our rule, remember? You hear me, Jim? I don't want you to look at the jug later on today and accuse me of taking an extra sip."

Silence.

"Listen, Jim. I put up with this silence of yours Saturday night and all day yesterday because I knew you were disappointed. But I'm not going to take it another day. I'm sorry God didn't come through for us, but, like you said, He has His own game plan."

Jim stirred.

"After all, Jim, a fellow could say, 'I believe in You, Jesus; therefore I ask You to give me a million dollars, and I challenge You to do it.' That would be pushing Him pretty far. We're going to be rescued, Jim. I believe that. We've *got* to believe that. But we can't put a deadline on it, and we've got to help each other."

Finally Jim turned. His face showed pain and bewilderment. "I really believed we would be rescued," he said.

"But we weren't," Bob said, shocked at Jim's appearance. "And it's not fair to take it out on me. Now pull yourself together. The topic today is how socialist nations are similar to the capitalist society. Or," Bob hurried on, "we could talk about baseball."

Jim just shook his head sadly. Neither baseball nor political structures interested him. "We're going to die," he said.

Bob pretended not to hear. And for the next hour one man spoke of life, the other of death, neither relating to one another. They might have been speaking in different languages.

Finally Bob stopped. This is absurd, he thought. I am the one who should be lying with my face to the wall. I am the one who lost his wife. But if I don't pull Jim out of this, he will die. And I will be left alone. And then I will die. I need Jim. I *must* keep him alive.

"What shall we do then, Jim?" he asked sarcastically. "Just lie back and wait to die? Is that what you're suggesting?"

The silence again.

"Is your life so meaningless that you're giving up?"

Nothing but the song of the waves beneath their beds.

Finally it occurred to Bob to fight with holy fire. "Do you remember the story of Job?" he asked.

"Yes," Jim answered reluctantly. "He suffered a lot."

"Exactly," said Bob. "God decided to see if Job was a true believer. So He caused Job's cattle to run away and his field hands to be killed. He sent a wind to cave in the roof of Job's house and kill his children. And He covered Job's body with boils."

Jim nodded his head. Bob had told the story correctly.

"Wait," said Bob. "That's only act one. Then Job broke down and cursed God. He wanted to die and be rid of all his trouble. But the Lord spoke to Job, from a cloud, I believe—"

"From a whirlwind," corrected Jim.

"From a whirlwind, and he told Job that it had all been a test, for he had been getting too comfortable. And then Job realized that life was pretty good, and he got his faith going again. He lived another hundred and forty years. Had a couple more wives, too."

The allusion worked. Jim was suddenly renewed.

Later that morning, while playing the Bible game, Jim stumped Bob with the character of Jonah.

"Oh yes," said Bob. "Jonah and the whale."

No, that was *not* the Jonah situation he had in mind. Before the whale incident, Jonah had been on a boat and was considered such bad luck to the other passengers that he had to get off in the middle of the voyage.

"Well," said Bob, "if there is a parallel to this story, I'm not going to get off. And I hope you don't, either."

Jim laughed. "I won't jump off," he said. "I promise you."

AFTER THAT the two men agreed not to make moral judgments on each other. It was better to play their game of mental Probe for an hour, then a hand of cribbage; with an afternoon nap, the day was gone. Jim, his depression seemingly concluded, once more spent most of his free hours in the company of his God.

Just before dark one night Bob was distracted by a faint buzzing noise. The tiny sound came closer, and he looked up in astonishment. "Jim," he said, his voice very quiet, "it's a fly."

With mounting excitement the two men watched four flies buzz briefly about their beds, then disappear through the hole.

"That could mean we're close to land," said Bob. "But let's not get our hopes up."

During the next two days Jim spent the daylight hours topside, watching for ships—or for land. The flies did not appear again. Bob stayed below, conserving his energy. But he made a mental note to determine someday how far flies can journey from land.

ON AUGUST 16, for the first time since Linda's death, the waves rose in ten-foot swells and the skies turned gray and ominous. With the pocket compass, and by wetting his finger and sticking it in the air, Bob made an approximate wind reading: it was blowing from the east.

"It's changed direction on us," he told Jim dejectedly. This was the wind that Bob had been dreading. It would blow them away from the coast and carry them deep and westerly into the Pacific.

"If we only had a piece of the boom," Bob went on, "and a part of the sail, I could rig up something. We could at least hold our own."

Jim swallowed his morning sip of water and looked uncomfortable. By now Bob knew that look. Jim was obviously troubled by talk of boom and sail. But as any serious argument might send Jim into the silence again, Bob changed the subject. "It looks like rain," he said. "Maybe we should try and catch some rainwater."

Jim agreed. For an hour the two men worked harmoniously, finding boards, cutting them to size, and nailing them together. Jim was a splendid craftsman. Bob appreciated well his brother-in-law's building the *Triton* with his own hands. And the boat *was* well built. Even in the storm and shock of capsizing, she had held together. He felt the *Triton* was capable of sailing forever upside down.

The men erected their funnel with its wide top sticking out their exit hole, its bottom inside a plastic water jug. But they caught no rain this day; only salty spray trickled into their container.

Annoyed, Bob dipped his cup into the sea beneath their beds and sipped at the salt water. He could tolerate up to two cups a day. The only problem was that the seawater sometimes brought on diarrhea. But since his daily intake of food was so minimal, there was little to evacuate.

The rains appeared on August 19, their fortieth day lost at sea. Jim took the timing as a small omen from above. The parallel of Christ's forty days in the wilderness was unspoken. But the two men watched with fascination as almost a cup of fresh rainwater dribbled into the container. Jim prayed his thanks. Then each man took a swallow and saved the rest. Later that morning, Jim asked if they were going to have their discussion period, as he had a subject to discuss. "I know you're touchy about this," he said very carefully, "but I'm really curious about why you stopped going to church."

Shrewd use of terms, thought Bob. Not why I *quit* the Church, only why I "stopped going."

"It's a very personal thing," answered Bob pleasantly enough. "And it goes back a long while. It wasn't a snap decision."

If he knew the full story, said Jim, then perhaps he could better understand. So Bob told his tale.

He had been born into a devout Adventist family, and his earliest memories were marked by the isolation indigenous to that faith. He had grown up on his father's two-thousand-acre farm in Montana in an area settled by Russian immigrants. Work was long and hard and they prayed that the vegetable crop would be bountiful enough to last until the spring that never seemed to come.

There were eight children in the Tininenko family, and Bob was the third eldest. Toys were not bought but made. Games were practical—who could pile the highest stack of potatoes the fastest.

School, for the most part, was more churchly than scholarly. There the severe tenets of the Adventist faith were taught, and there Bob discovered that life on earth, according to the Church, was but a prelude to the better life on the day that Jesus came again. "When Jesus comes" became the byword of his formative years. On the long days when he plowed the field, sitting on the tractor from dawn until night, he found himself looking up, hoping to be the first to see the bearded man in white robes descend.

"I guess the trouble began when I started asking questions," Bob said. "Other kids would sometimes invite me to go to movies, but my mother wouldn't let me go. And I'd say, 'But why not?' She'd say, 'Because *we* don't go to movies,' and I began wondering why *we* were different from everybody else. Then in Sabbath school I was always pestering the teacher about how a man could rise from the dead, or how a virgin could give birth. Understand, I was a farm kid. I knew how babies were born. And always they would tell me, 'Don't ask those questions. Just believe.'"

When he was fourteen Bob was sent away to an Adventist academy. "The regimentation nearly drove me crazy. Morning worship. Evening worship. Bible study. Friday night services. All-day Saturday services. It was like being in a monastery.

"I had to work to help with the tuition, so I got a job as night fireman, steaming up the boilers. There was this little man about five feet tall who was my boss, and he harassed me constantly. I hated him. Finally I was so tortured by it all that I actually got ulcers. A fourteen-year-old kid with ulcers!"

After his freshman year Bob convinced his family that he should continue his education at home. Jim smiled. They were coming to Bob's famed "hell-raising" year. Wilma had spoken of it.

"I really didn't raise all that much hell," said Bob. "I just got accused of it. For example, there was the time our sophomore class gave its picnic for the junior class. One of my friends borrowed his ma's car—she owned the local bar—and in the back seat was every kind of booze. We found a picnic site right away and spent the rest of the day drinking. By the time we got back to school for the last period we were bombed. I mean, bombed."

Wincing, Bob paused. "Did you ever try booze, Jim?"

"I took a sip of wine once. It tasted terrible."

"Would you drink an ice-cold beer if I gave you one this very minute?"

No hesitation. Jim refused even an imaginary beer.

"When I staggered home that day," Bob continued, "my dad just stood there looking at me, shaking his head as if I were a sinner, forever lost."

Predictably, Bob was ordered back to the academy, where he endured the remainder of his high-school education. And it was during these years that he commenced an intellectual adventure that would consume him for almost a decade.

"I decided to determine for myself if what the Bible taught and what the Adventists taught made sense. I even enjoyed the Bible classes then, because I was studying for a purpose. There would be days when I'd say to myself, 'All right, this makes sense. I believe.' But then something would come up, like the controversy over whether the Sabbath is on Saturday or Sunday. To me, it didn't seem to make any difference whether a person observed Saturday or Sunday as the day of worship."

"But it's God's law," Jim said. "It's basic to our religion."

"*Your* religion," said Bob. "Let me finish. I enrolled in an Adventist college, where I decided to major in theology. Naturally my folks were delighted. They assumed that I was going to become a minister. Well, it was a possibility, but actually I was more interested in exploring religion as deeply as I could. I even studied Greek so I could read the Bible in its original text.

"That study revealed too many contradictions for me to accept blindly the religion of my family. And so by the time I was a senior, I had definitely decided against becoming an Adventist minister. But I was still racked with indecision about whether I could in all honesty even remain a member of the Church. So I took a job teaching at an Adventist college. I stayed there two years, listening to them, talking to them. I even became an elder, and you know that's no easily achieved position. Didn't smoke, didn't drink, didn't dance, didn't cuss, didn't go to the movies. I did absolutely everything they demanded, but it did not work."

"And so you dropped out?"

Bob nodded. "I wrote a formal letter asking that my name be removed from the Church rolls. It was deliberate. I didn't want to just drift away. And I never even got a reply! I didn't have the heart to tell my folks about the letter, but somehow they heard. I know, because our relationship suddenly turned cold. We didn't get back together until Linda appeared in my life."

And this, thought Bob, is the first time I ever put all the pieces together for anyone, even myself. He waited for a response from Jim. Finally, softly, it came. "Do you believe in God?" Jim asked.

The bottom line, thought Bob. I could answer a thousand questions, and he asks the one for which I don't yet have an answer.

"I don't know," he replied simply. "All I can conclude is that I neither believe in God nor disbelieve."

"I feel a little sorry for you," said Jim not unkindly.

"But didn't you *ever* waver?" Bob demanded urgently. "Weren't there ever moments when you asked yourself some of the questions I did?"

"No," said Jim firmly. "I never questioned what was taught to me. I certainly never questioned the existence of God."

Bob dismissed the subject. If he and Jim did not know and respect one another now, they never would.

Chapter Eight

On the day after his long explanation of himself, Bob was awakened from his nap by a shout from above. He quickly shoved his head through the hole.

Five ships were coming directly at them. A fishing fleet. If they did not find the *Triton*, thought Bob, nothing ever would.

The two survivors shouted and leaped and waved the orange life jackets and flashed the mirror and implored and prayed. But the fishing boats did not see the overturned trimaran, even though one ship passed within a few hundred yards.

That night Jim curled in his bunk, wrapped once again in depression. Bob tried to be practical.

"I don't think we can be seen," he said. "And I don't think it does any good for us to do this big yelling number every time a ship passes. It just wears us out. One day a plane or a ship will see us, Jim. That's the only way it's going to happen. There's no use in killing ourselves with exertion."

Jim nodded. But during the long night Bob heard him sob.

LITTLE OF NOTE marked the next ten days, August 21 to the end of the month. Three more ships passed, but they were on the far horizon, and the men did not bother to call to them.

On the morning of September 1, Bob carved the date on his

calendar. Fifty-three days. He fell asleep during the morning free hour, murmuring the astonishing figure to himself.

The next day Jim grew incoherent during the discussion hour and Bob terminated it. Later, during the game period, Jim could not even think of a five-letter word for Bob to guess. He fell asleep, thrashing in his bed. At the evening meal Bob opened the next-to-last can of sardines and handed one to Jim. He shook his head in refusal.

"You've got to eat," said Bob.

"I can't. I don't think I'm going to make it, Bob." His eyes were opaque now, hidden behind a film.

"Of course you are. Eat this terrific sardine."

Jim held the tiny fish to his mouth, then dropped it uneaten onto his chest. "I think I'm going to sleep," he said.

Panic building within him, Bob moved closer to Jim. Did he mean sleep or did he mean die? Bob couldn't bear being left alone on the sea. "Jim, you can't give up now," he pleaded. "You've got everything in the world to live for. What about Wilma? And the new baby? And Costa Rica . . ."

Shaking his head, Jim tried to raise himself from the bed. He fell back. However, he had something he must say.

"I've got to tell you something," said Jim. "I can't . . . *go* . . . without telling you." Bob moved to Jim's bed.

"I drank a can of root beer," Jim blurted out. "I found it that first day when I was swimming around. I was thirsty, and . . . I just drank it. I never thought we'd be here so long."

"That's okay," murmured Bob. "We still have a can left. We're going to drink it in celebration when we get to shore."

"And I took an extra sip of water. And the peanut butter. I ate a little of that, too."

Bob patted Jim's arm as if to say the confession was made and accepted and forgotten, but Jim had more to say. "There *was* a piece of the mast, and the sail, underneath, that day when I first went down in my scuba suit," he said, his words broken and pained. "But . . . but I cut them off. I didn't think we should interfere with the Lord's will."

Had Bob not known the awesome hold of Jim's God, he might have screamed in fury. But he did know, and all he could do now was nod. He didn't ask about the cheese balls and the water-distillation kit. He knew the answers.

THE NEXT morning Jim refused food again. There remained only sardines, freeze-dried peas, peanut butter, and Kool-Aid on the menu. Jim could eat none of them, he said.

"You're committing suicide, you know." Bob's voice was harsh.

Jim did not answer. His eyes remained shut.

Bob felt helpless. Then he had an idea. A long shot. He leaned close to Jim and began to curse him.

"You cowardly bastard!" he yelled. "How dare you give up!" A torrent of obscenity followed, and Jim opened his eyes to stare incredulously. He begged for the curses to stop. But Bob refused. The tempo of his tirade swelled and built to a scream. "God damn you!"

Jim shuddered and flung out his hands. "Please," he cried. "Stop! I'll try! I'll live! Don't curse me again!"

It worked. Proud of his cleverness, Bob was almost smiling.

By his confessions, Jim had prepared himself for death. But Bob's sinful profanity had soiled his state of grace. He could not die now, before Bob died, because there would be no one left to cleanse Bob of his sin. Moreover, Bob had used God's name in vain. Jim could not depart this world with *that* resounding in his ears.

AFTER BOB'S CURSES the two men endured still another two weeks. But Jim was very ill. In the game period he lacked even the energy to move a marker on the board. The final square, the one marked Rescue, seemed more and more unreachable.

Further, Bob insisted that they continue to examine one another's countenance each morning, to note the tone of the skin. Usually Jim muttered, "You look okay." But Bob could not respond in kind. Gray sand was filling the hourglass of Jim's face. His beard was dark and scraggly, his eyes like ashy coals.

On September 4 a butterfly appeared beside their beds, suspended in dazzling orange and black beauty. It darted about for a few seconds, then vanished through a crack, as if a magic spell had been broken. But since the sight of flies and birds before had not meant that they were soon to see land, this newest creature was observed without excitement or hope.

Tuesday, September 11. Bob remarked that it was the two-month anniversary of their life in an upside-down boat. Three days later, at seven a.m. promptly, for he still attempted the semblance of their daily schedule, Bob called Jim. But Jim only stirred restlessly and fell asleep again. Bob left him alone until eight, when he cried his name sharply. When that brought no response, Bob physically raised him from the mattress.

From the can of sardines opened days earlier, Jim picked one and handed it to Bob, who began to eat slowly, trying not to smell the rancid morsel. But Jim regarded his own rotting sardine with hate. He put it back in the can and fell back asleep.

Being Friday, it was water-dispersion day. Under their newest agreement one cup of water had to last each of them for five days. There was only one jug left, with approximately nine cups remaining.

It can be done, Bob assured himself. He had repeated the promise so often that it was possible to believe it now. A swallow now, another at night, a sip of seawater in between. All we need is a drop or two of water and the determination to live.

"Jim," he called out. "You want your water now or later?"

"Now." Jim held out his hand, clawlike, shaking.

Pouring the few drops, watching them hit and barely cover the bottom of the cup, Bob handed the portion to Jim.

"Fill the cup," Jim said.

"That's your whole five days' worth," Bob protested.

"I know."

Bob warned him emphatically one more time. "You know that there won't be any more water for five days."

"I don't care," Jim said impatiently. "Give me the water."

Bob filled the cup and extended it reluctantly. Jim gulped its contents in one incredible swallow. For the first time in days he seemed at peace.

"I'm giving up," he said. "It's too painful to go on. If God wants me to live, I'll live. If not, then I'll die."

Bob racked his numbed mind to find something—anything!—to sustain the life in Jim. True, he thought in the dark part of his soul, if Jim dies there will be more food and water for me. But I will be left alone. And then survival will become impossible. The ghosts of Linda and Jim will torment me until I join them.

He cursed Jim again. No response. Then he pleaded with him to fulfill his obligation for missionary work. Still no answer.

Finally Bob asked quietly, "Are you ready to die?" And after a long time Jim raised himself and held out his hands in supplication. "No," he said. "I have to tell you one more thing."

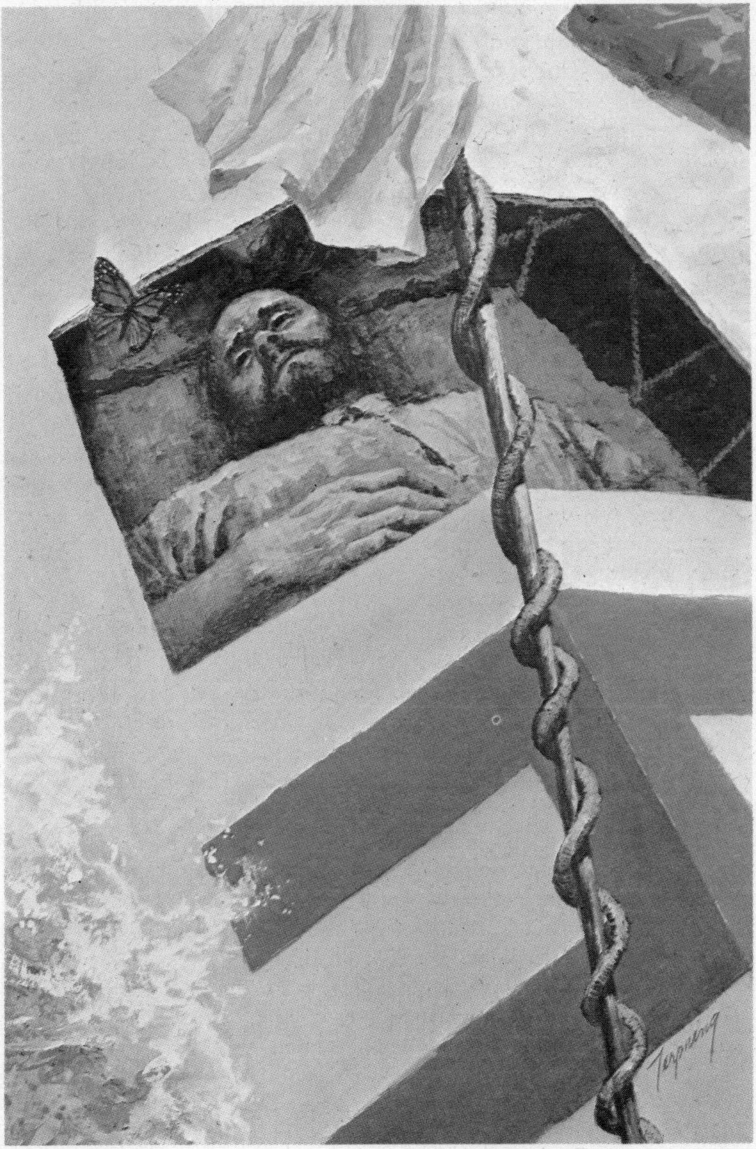

"I'm tired," Bob lied quickly. "Wait until tomorrow." That would drag Jim into another day.

"No, I have to tell you now. Once," he said, as if in a great rush, "when I was in the academy, I broke a specimen slide for the microscope. The teacher asked who had done it, and no one confessed. Then the teacher asked me directly, and I denied breaking it. I never told anyone. I can't die with that lie."

In his fear, Bob almost smiled. Was this a sin worth carrying half a lifetime? "I don't think anybody will hold that against you, Jim," he said gently.

"I had to tell somebody."

"I heard you. If it means anything, I forgive you."

DURING THE NIGHT Bob tried to stay awake, listening intently to Jim's breathing, ready to give him mouth-to-mouth resuscitation should his lungs stop pumping. Watching, Bob thought of another possibility to extend Jim's life.

"Where's your last will and testament, by the way?" he asked Jim the next morning. "I presume you've left everything to Wilma and the kids."

"I never wrote one. I'm only thirty years old."

"I know. But what about your estate?" Bob had his questions rehearsed. He hoped they sounded convincing. He, too, felt weak this morning, but he had to keep Jim alive.

"There isn't any estate. We sold all our furniture . . . and our car . . . before we left. You know that."

Bob nodded. "But you had traveler's checks, didn't you?"

"They were lost . . . when we capsized."

"How much?"

"About a thousand dollars' worth."

"Wilma can get a refund. *If* you leave a will. Just write whatever you want and sign it. I'll make sure that Wilma gets it."

Again Jim fell silent, pondering this newest obstacle. Time passed. The sun beat so cruelly on the *Triton* that Bob imagined they had missed California, sailed beyond Mexico, and drifted somewhere near the equator. Finally he asked, "Have you written the will yet?"

"No."

"I was just thinking. When you do, you should tell Wilma to remarry."

Jim's voice took on a sudden edge. "I couldn't do that."

"The boys need a father."

Shocked, Jim turned so that he could stare at Bob and read his eyes. The two men faced one another, sprawled on their stomachs. "They'll remember me," Jim insisted.

"For a while," said Bob. "But later on, they'll want a father. It's true, Jim. If Wilma makes them live on their memory of you, the boys will grow to hate you."

For a moment Jim grew angry, as if he were going to lash out at Bob. Then he sighed. "What can I write on?"

In Jim's hand, clutched tightly, was his copy of *The Great Controversy*. "Use that," suggested Bob. He found Linda's purse, took out a pen, and tossed it to Jim.

Jim read from the book for a while. Then he began to write on the blank pages at the end. His words were filled with eloquence and love and undiminished faith.

Dearest Wilma, Todd, Bradley, and all the family:

Bob and I are about done. We have hoped and prayed that rescue would come, but twelve ships and several airplanes failed to see us. We are thankful for the time the Lord gave us to put our lives in complete harmony with His will. We look forward to that great resurrection day when we will be brought up incorruptible. It is my earnest prayer to see all of you there. If you study *The Great Controversy*. carefully and put into practice what you learn, we will be together again in the earth made new.

Wilma, I had a thousand dollars in traveler's checks which were lost when we capsized. You should be able to redeem them from the bank in Auburn. $112 must go to tithe. The rest is yours. It is hard for me to say, but please find the boys another daddy soon. They need one at this age. I know that the Lord will bless you in anything you do for Him. Just remain as true to Him as you were to me.

I trust you will forgive me for leaving you. Only the Lord knows the end from the beginning. We must always trust His ways even though we may not understand them. . . .

Linda died on August 6. Since then Bob and I have tried to stretch our lives as far as possible. Lately, down to $\frac{1}{4}$ cup H_2O/day and $\frac{1}{2}$ tsp. food. Just can't go much longer than this. I can hardly hold this pen.

I am deeply grieved not to have had the chance in mission work. I hope you can find someone who will give you this chance. Just make sure you love Jesus each day and die for Him each day and we will soon meet where there will be no separation. Be sure to bring the boys and (?). I'll be looking for you on Resurrection Day.

Love, Hubby & Daddy

When he was done, Jim tore the pages from the book, folded them, and put them in his wallet. Cleansed, almost happy, he closed his eyes and waited for whatever his God had in store.

"I'M THIRSTY," said Jim three long days later. He had not taken a drop of water. Dried blood caked his lips. He could not have weighed more than a hundred and thirty pounds.

"I warned you . . ." Bob moved his head so that he could watch the water jug. Rarely did three minutes pass during the day without Bob examining the water. It was more precious than his blood.

Above them thunder rumbled. Bob would not give Jim any of his water, but perhaps he could trap a little if it rained.

After putting up the rain funnel, Bob fell asleep from the effort. When he awoke, almost a full cup of fresh cool rain had dribbled into the jug. He took a sip and handed the rest to Jim. The dying man looked at it curiously.

"It's rainwater," said Bob. "Drink it. Or save it."

But Jim only stared vacantly at the offering.

Bob pried open his mouth and dropped the water slowly into the dry throat. "Thank you, Jesus," murmured Jim.

That night Jim convulsed, his body torn by spasms.

Awakened, Bob cried, "Jim! Are you all right?"

"Yeah."

In his half sleep something had come to Bob. "I was just thinking, Jim," he began slowly, "what happens when one of us dies? We're both too weak to lift a body through this hole." The grim vision settled over the two men.

"Just cut the ropes," said Jim. When the rope bed was severed, the person lying on that bed would fall into the sea beneath him.

"But *both* beds would fall," said Bob in alarm.

In the midnight quiet Jim's words gnawed at Bob. Now that the idea of cutting the ropes had been spoken, it was possible that Jim, on the brink of delirium, might actually do just that. I may die of starvation and dehydration, said Bob to himself, but I will not die of drowning, not after seventy days in hell.

Somehow he must get Jim's knife away from him. "Jim?" Bob tried to keep his voice casual. "Can I borrow your knife?"

"What for?" grunted Jim in his semi-consciousness.

"I want to carve." Bob gestured to a new carving he had begun on the wall beside him. When finished it would read, TRITON: CAPSIZED JULY 11, 1973. PLEASE NOTIFY THE U.S. COAST GUARD, SAN FRANCISCO OR LOS ANGELES.

"Where's *your* knife?" Jim asked.

"I dropped it in the water this afternoon," Bob lied.

"It's night. You can't see to carve."

"There's a moon, Jim. I can't sleep. Lend me your knife."

"No." The answer, cold and final, chilled Bob.

After more eternal minutes crept by, Bob raised his head and saw Jim's knife gleaming in the moonlight, wedged next to a beam beside Jim's head.

Bob called out softly, "Jim, are you awake?"

A sigh.

Bob counted to a thousand. "Jim?" This time nothing.

Holding his breath, clenching his teeth, Bob inched his hand toward the knife. Finally, cautiously, his hands pressed around the handle. Now! In a frenzy of movement he seized the knife, yanked it from the wedge, flung it safely to his own bed.

Instantly Jim awoke. As if he had seen the theft in his dream, he went for his knife. His eyes, in the light of the moon, were crazed. "Where's my knife?" he demanded, surprisingly strong.

"I borrowed it," said Bob. "I asked you. I want to carve."

Exhausted, Jim fell back asleep.

THE FOOD.

As the morning sun crept into the chamber it occurred to Bob that he had never actually *seen* the food supply. When it had been time for a meal, Jim had always produced the food from the unseen storage place at the foot of his bed.

A new worry ignited within Bob's jagged consciousness. What if Jim dies today and I won't be able to find the food? Or worse, what if he goes into a religious frenzy and drops the food into the sea while I sleep, and tells me it was a command? I must get the food. Now.

"Jim?" Bob shook the sleeping man lightly. "Are you awake? Can I have the food, Jim? All of it?"

With enormous effort Jim raised his head an inch. "What for?"

"You're giving up, aren't you? So give me the food!" Bob almost screamed, startled that his lungs held the power.

"Why? Do you think I'm dying?" Jim asked almost pleasantly.

"Well," said Bob, "you keep telling me you're waiting to die. And I don't know where the food is. If you die, I can't waste my energy searching for it. . . . Please, Jim, give me the food."

"I can't."

Too weary for argument, Bob let the subject drop. He turned in his bed and saw the calendar. He had not marked the date. His hands trembled as he chipped it out—September 19. Then his eyes fell upon the house he had carved for Linda.

Hugging the house to his breast, he wept. This is all I have, he thought. This is the sum of my thirty-five years on earth. At that moment, desperately hungry, so thirsty that his throat seemed lined with leather, he teetered once again on the edge of surrender. How easy it would be to lie back like Jim and wait.

He fell asleep again on the seventy-first morning of life within an eighteen-inch air pocket.

In the late afternoon he awoke in fright. A hand was on his shoulder. Wildly he turned and saw Jim's face bending close to him.

"What is it?" asked Bob frantically, groping for the place where he had hidden the knives. With relief he felt their blades between his mattress and the ropes.

"The food," Jim said. "Here." He pitched the piteous lot onto Bob's bed. One last can of sardines, the jar of peanut butter less than one-quarter full, a pack of cherry Kool-Aid, a packet of freeze-dried peas, and a can of root beer.

Eagerly Bob prepared a meal. He filled his cup with seawater and dropped in five peas. He ate them one at a time, taking a full hour to consume them.

But never did his eyes stray from Jim.

WHEN BOB awoke on the morning of September 20, sun was streaming through the opening in the exit hole. He went through his morning routine—washed his face, took a swallow of water, and tried to do some carving. By noon the chamber was a steam room. And the heat and the gentle rocking of the boat lulled him back to sleep.

At the first sound Bob thought he was dreaming, but when the noise continued, he opened his eyes and spun around in his bed.

He screamed at what he saw. "No, Jim!"

While Bob slept Jim had taken a long piece of the fishing cord and looped it about his own throat. Tying it to the beam behind him, he had lunged forward in his bed, clumsily seeking to push his body off the edge into the water. Now he lay struggling, feet dangling above the water, the cord garroting his neck.

In a blur of motion Bob grabbed his knife and sliced the cord. Then he seized Jim's shoulders and dragged him back to his bed.

Both men were spent. They lay in their beds, limbs jerking involuntarily. Neither spoke of what had happened. He must be totally mad to risk the wrath of his God, thought Bob.

In the middle of the hot, quiet afternoon Jim's sobs broke the silence. "I'm sorry," he said.

"That's all right," answered Bob. "You didn't know what you were doing."

Somehow they endured yet another day and night.

ON THE MORNING of September 21, as they drifted into their seventy-third day lost at sea, Bob felt somehow better. Perhaps yesterday was the bottom, he thought. If Jim died that day, he decided, he would cut the water ration down even further. There were perhaps fifty swallows left. That could be fifty days. Thanksgiving, Bob said to himself. I will be home by Thanksgiving.

ON THIS SAME morning, in Longview, Washington, members of Bob's and Linda's families were gathered to pack up the possessions of the lost couple. Although no hope was held that they would be found, no one could bring himself to the final act of having a court declare them dead. So instead of selling Bob and Linda's white frame cottage they had decided to rent it.

All morning the family members worked at the unhappy task, wrapping Linda's china, silver, her wedding gifts. The tenants had voiced no objection to having the missing owners' possessions stored in the attic. The day before, the college where Bob taught had voted to establish a scholarship fund in his memory. Another teacher had taken over his history classes.

BOB WAS DOZING, but he awoke with a start. He felt vibrations. The *Triton* was shuddering. Breathlessly he waited for the trembling to go away.

Then he heard something else: the whine of a machine.

He was afraid to draw his breath for fear that it was a dream and the dream would shatter. But the sound remained, grew, came closer. Finally there were voices. Other voices.

With his last strength Bob crawled halfway through the hole to look at the outside world. Less than twenty yards away was an enormous yellow lifeboat crowded with sailors waving, snapping photographs, bearing deliverance.

"Jim," he cried, still fearing that it was a hallucination. "People, Jim! I think there are people out here!"

When no response came from Jim, Bob wondered if the supreme irony had transpired. Was Jim dead at the precise moment of rescue? Then Bob felt a hand clutch at his leg. But no strength was left in Jim to witness his rescuers.

Not willing to endure even another few seconds on the *Triton*, but realizing he must have energy, Bob seized the packet of Kool-Aid and crammed the contents into his mouth, hoping the sugar would supply the energy for what he must do.

"We're alive!" he screamed as he pulled himself through the hole and lunged into the sea, not even feeling the cold, heading for the lifeboat which now nuzzled the capsized trimaran.

Two heavily muscled arms reached quickly into the sea and lifted him into the boat. They swaddled him in warm, dry blankets. "Jim's still in there!" Bob gasped.

Two sailors leaped easily onto the overturned hull and descended through the hole to Jim. As they lifted him he wept.

"Thank you, God," he murmured, then, blinking his eyes wildly, he cried out, "We're missionaries!"

Bob started to correct the curious declaration, but as he raised his head he saw before him the most dazzling sight he had ever beheld—a glistening new cargo ship. He sobbed uncontrolledly.

Moments later, as the lifeboat ascended by pulleys to the deck of the great ship, he glanced back at the *Triton*. Already she was but a speck on the sea. For even at less than five hundred yards the trimaran was difficult to locate, her orange jackets and curtains and nailed-down sink and cooking plates somehow blending into the sun and shadows.

Chapter Nine

Two hours before, a young Scottish merchant seaman had gazed routinely out from his watch. He served the *Benalder*, a fifty-eight-thousand-ton British container ship. The huge vessel, almost a thousand feet long, was a few days out from the Panama Canal and hurrying to the Orient via the great circle route.

Something odd broke the monotony of the sea to the sailor's eye. When he lifted his binoculars he saw a capsized boat.

Briskly the seaman strode to the ship's master, who peered down through his glasses. Then he made these notes: "Upturned trimaran, blue and white hull, possible number on side WA 5456. Showing red flag. No signs life."

The *Benalder* was only a few thousand yards away at that moment, and the sea was calm, visibility good. If there were life aboard the pathetic little boat, said the master, surely someone would be out waving a distress signal.

The master decided not to stop and inspect the mysterious sight. But he ordered the news radioed to the U.S. Coast Guard in San Francisco. There the message was relayed to Lieutenant Victor Hipkiss, controller on watch in Honolulu. By a stroke of fortune Lieutenant Hipkiss had been on duty during the fruitless search for the *Triton* two and one-half months before.

Lieutenant Hipkiss was intrigued enough to request the master of the *Benalder* to turn his ship around and dispatch a search party to the trimaran. The lieutenant also told a skeptical colleague that it was unlikely that this could be the *Triton*. The *Benalder*'s position was more than a thousand miles due west of Los Angeles, almost halfway to Hawaii. A trimaran simply could not drift that far without breaking into pieces.

A thousand miles!

But the mystery, said the lieutenant, was too tantalizing not to investigate.

THE TWO MEN were carried on stretchers into the sick bay, and were put to bed. No doctor was on board, but a crew member familiar with routine medical procedure took their life signs.

Meanwhile radio messages hurried back and forth across the Pacific. The nearest port was in Hawaii, but the *Benalder* would have to make a costly detour to get there. It was arranged, therefore, that the ship would take her new passengers to Midway Island, where a U.S. military plane could fly them to Honolulu.

The U.S. Public Health Service in Honolulu cabled the *Benalder* for information about the patients' condition. A report was quickly returned. Both men were in fair condition. Neither had sunburn or skin infection. Jim Fisher had lost a hundred pounds, Bob Tininenko only fifty. Neither was able to stand or walk. Their diet had been chiefly sardines and peanut butter. No known medical problems prior to departure on July 2. One item of concern: while Tininenko's pulse rate was a surprisingly stable 65, Fisher's was erratic and high, from 90 to 110.

"Both men," radioed the *Benalder*'s master, "are extremely weak, especially Fisher, but they are in good shape, considering their extraordinary ordeal."

Within an hour of boarding the *Benalder*, Bob was happily sipping orange juice. Jim could not hold a cup, so he was fed drop by drop with a syringe.

No sooner was Bob done with the first cup of juice than he asked for a second. Then he took a glass of beef broth. Off went another cable to Honolulu: How much liquid could he safely consume? If the kidneys are functioning, came the reply, as much as he wants. On the first day aboard the *Benalder*, Bob drank an astonishing ten gallons of liquid.

Telegrams were sent to the parents of Bob and Jim, and to Jim's wife, Wilma, in Moses Lake, Washington, where she was staying with her husband's parents. For two and one-half months she and her two small sons had drifted on a sea of their own, from relative to relative, not knowing her husband's fate, not willing to accept the verdict of "lost and presumed dead." She had told her children, "We may not see Daddy again." But in her heart there was still a small fire of hope.

For seven hours on this day of rescue the Coast Guard attempted to reach Wilma, but the telephone in her father-in-law's home was out of order. Finally Jim's sister was located and given the news, and she drove from her nearby home, bursting into the house screaming, "They're safe! Wilma, Jim's alive!"

When she heard the news Wilma shut her eyes before the tears filled them, and, like her husband, she thanked God.

The two survivors spent five days on the *Benalder* en route to Midway Island, and on each morning they seemed improved. Bob's was the most remarkable progress. By the fourth day he was sitting up, eating roast beef, and holding the sailors spellbound with his tale of survival.

Jim remained flat on his back, dozing and suffering the nightmares that continued to torment him. He asked for a Bible. And while sleeping, he held it tightly.

The two men rarely spoke to one another. There was no sense of "Look, we've come through." They were men who had journeyed to the outer reaches of human endurance, and perhaps they had shown too much of themselves to each other. Now they wanted to be done with the memories. A new and chilling but not surprising barrier of silence rose between them.

Beyond this a bizarre kind of competition developed, with Jim anxious to regain health as rapidly as Bob. It was as if the duel of their conflicting philosophies had ended in a draw, to be won by the first man who could walk and laugh and return to his full capacities. When Bob walked unsteadily to the toilet, Jim attempted the same. But immediately he fell back, perspiring; he could not stand alone.

On September 26 the officers and crew of the *Benalder* spruced up in gleaming whites to salute the U.S. Coast Guard, which had dispatched a tugboat to fetch the two passengers to Midway. From there they were flown to Honolulu. En route, Bob learned that their destination was Castle Memorial Hospital, a renowned Seventh-Day Adventist institution in Kailua. This was on orders of Jim's family, and Bob felt a wave of annoyance. Was the Church he had rejected going to make a propagandistic miracle out of their delivery?

The hospital had mobile beds ready to rush Jim to intensive care and Bob to a specially equipped room. Now, at last, their families would see them again.

WHEN WILMA entered her husband's hospital room she tried to hide her shock at seeing the shell of a man who waited for her. All the encouraging news she had heard from the press and the Coast Guard—"doing remarkably well, considering," "taking nourishment," "gaining strength"—all these descriptions must have come from another's chart, not that of this bearded man with the ashy eyes who grew weary even as he whispered her name.

She bent and kissed him, and both began to cry. "I told you I was going to lose weight," he said.

She managed a laugh. Then she told him not to use his strength talking to her. They would have the rest of their lives for that.

He would not have silence. "I love you so," he said. "I'm so sorry I ran away."

"But you *didn't* run away," Wilma said. "You were on a mission for God. You were lost."

Somehow Jim had come to believe that he had abandoned his family, and he was happy with her forgiveness. Then he whispered Linda's name. Wilma nodded, indicating she knew.

"It's so sad," said Jim. "But Linda was ready to meet Jesus."

Jim closed his eyes and fell asleep as Wilma held him.

IN BOB'S ROOM the families gathered. He told the story of the seventy-two days to his parents, to Wilma, to his brothers and other sisters. He sent a telegram to Linda's parents, promising to visit them as soon as he could, to tell them of her courage and love.

By coincidence an important international figure in the Seventh-Day Adventist Church was in Honolulu at the time, and Bob's parents joyously brought the news that this great man wished to visit the two who had survived the sea.

"I don't want that," said Bob sharply. "I won't have this turned into some religious circus."

But the parents pleaded. Couldn't the man just drop by and say hello? Bob sighed. It was easier to give permission than to argue. And he realized that nothing he said would dissuade his people from their belief that rescue was by the hand of God.

When the Adventist leader came to his room, Bob turned immediately to the wall and feigned sleep. The leader chatted briefly and warmly with Bob's parents, then went to see Jim.

ON HIS THIRD DAY in the Adventist hospital, Jim suffered kidney failure and was transferred to a Catholic hospital that had better facilities for renal cases—an ironic turn of events, because one of the beliefs of the Adventists is that the Catholic Church perverted God's Sabbath, changing it from Saturday to Sunday.

At the Catholic hospital Jim was put onto a dialysis machine. The next day his lungs congested with pneumonia. Then a blood infection was discovered. His condition was so poor that there was no consideration of a kidney transplant. The family intensified its prayers.

On October 2, Wilma spent much of the morning reading to her husband from the Bible. Passages from the Revelation of St. John comforted him especially. "*I saw the dead,*" she read, "*small and great, stand before God; and the books were opened: and another book was opened, which is the book of life: and the dead were judged out of those things which were written in the books, according to their works. And the sea gave up the dead which were in it; and death and hell delivered up the dead which were in them: and they were judged every man according to their works.*"

Jim took her arm and pulled her close to his lips. "No matter what happens, we must believe in the will of God," he whispered.

Wilma hurried to finish before her voice broke. "*And God himself shall be with them. . . . God shall wipe away all tears from their eyes; and there shall be no more death, neither sorrow, nor crying, neither shall there be any more pain: for the former things are passed away.*"

Jim tried to raise his head. Wilma put her hand to his neck and cradled him. "God heard my prayers, didn't He?"

"Of course, hubby."

"I tried to do the will of God, Wilma. You understand that, don't you?"

She nodded again. Then, seeing the profound weariness moving over her husband, she kissed him and went downstairs, promising to return after he slept. When she came back less than ten minutes later, Jim was dead.

THE DOCTOR who brought the news to Bob wept. But Bob did not. He felt sorrow at the news but not the pain of bereavement. He tried to analyze his feeling, but he did not understand it.

In one sense Bob had won. He had proved that if a man husbanded his energy and used his mental powers resourcefully, then he could pass through the most excruciating of ordeals. Jim had gambled all on his passion for God. And he had lost.

But Bob felt no victory. If he had won, why was his spirit so troubled? Why did he find himself, in fleeting moments, envying Jim, who had slipped serenely to death and its promise of resurrection? He tried to put the thought away. But he knew that after his muscles were rebuilt and his health restored, he would wrestle with God until the last day of his life.

Two weeks later Bob was finally on the plane to Los Angeles, where specialists waited to restore his arms (only four inches around at the biceps) and his legs (less than seven inches at the thigh). He took a seat next to the window. Once, when the clouds broke, he glanced down through the window and saw the Pacific stretching forever below him.

Fascinated, he observed the sea. A Coast Guard officer had told him that one day, perhaps, the *Triton* might wash ashore somewhere. At first Bob was elated at the prediction. In his haste to leave on the morning of their deliverance he had forgotten to take with him the house he had carved for Linda and the calendar and the compass, all of which he had wanted. Nor had he remembered to drink the can of celebratory root beer.

But now he turned his eyes from the sea and changed his mind. He hoped the *Triton* would never touch land. Better that she contain her secrets, better that she stay forever adrift, a prisoner of the sea.

Thomas Thompson

His first meeting with Bob Tininenko, confesses Thomas Thompson, began inauspiciously. His agent wanted him to have lunch with Bob, describing him as a young man who might have a story to tell about a sailing experience. "I agreed, but only reluctantly," he says, "because when I first began my writing career in Houston, Texas, it seemed I wrote hundreds of 'lost at sea' stories. They were for the Monday morning edition of the newspaper, when there was little news, and usually by noon the people at sea would have been found by the Coast Guard and my story would be yanked out of the later editions."

But when Bob Tininenko began to recount the events of his ill-fated voyage, Thompson was immediately spellbound and captured by the project of putting together a book from what Bob told him. "I spent hundreds of hours with Bob," Thompson explains, "both at my home in Los Angeles and at his in Kelso, Washington. We went over every detail, over and over, until the tears would come to his eyes and we would put it aside for a time. I also travelled up and down the West Coast talking to boatbuilders, Coast Guard personnel, weathermen, ham radio operators, and most important of all, to the families of Linda, Bob and Jim.

"I liked Bob Tininenko very much," continues Thompson. "And though at first I was tempted to dislike what I heard of Jim Fisher's zealousness, he was a good man, possessed of some basic qualities which I grudgingly came to admire."

From 1961 until its demise in 1972, Thompson was on the staff of *Life* magazine, and his articles have appeared in most major periodicals. His first book, *Hearts*, about pioneer heart surgeons, was named one of the year's outstanding books by *The New York Times* in 1971, and a later one, *Blood and Money*, the account of a bizarre Texas murder case, was a huge bestseller.

SHARPE'S EAGLE. Original full-length version © by Rifleman Productions Ltd. 1981. British condensed version © The Reader's Digest Association Limited 1980.

MAN, WOMAN AND CHILD. Original full-length version © by Erich Segal 1980. US condensed version © The Reader's Digest Association, Inc. 1980. British condensed version © The Reader's Digest Association Limited 1980.

THE CITADEL, first published by Victor Gollancz Ltd. British condensed version © The Reader's Digest Association Limited 1980.

HELL AND HIGH WATER. Original full-length version © by Thomas Thompson 1975. US condensed version © The Reader's Digest Association, Inc. 1975. British condensed version © The Reader's Digest Association Limited 1980.

PICTURE CREDITS: Page 151: Rifleman Productions Ltd. Page 417: Com Zurich.

BB109